The Magic Crystals

The Cloak of Steel

by

Stephen Hayes

The Cloak of Steel

Book 5 in the Magic Crystals series

Written by Stephen Hayes

Published 2017 by Stephen Hayes, Australia

Formatted by www.eBookIt.com

www.StephenHayesOnline.com

ISBN-13: 978-0-9944590-5-3

Table of Contents

Part 4: The Cloak of Steel

Prologue

Since the beginning of June, television stations in various countries around the world had been airing informational programs about the Hammerheart rule. In each one, Arnold Hammerson (referred to throughout as Lord Hammerson) would be accompanied by his most important underlings in that particular territory and together, they would conduct a large press conference with just about every media outlet of that country, the subject being all the dos-and-don'ts of the new regime. If the country in question primarily spoke a language other than English, Lord Hammerson would place an enchantment upon himself so that although he would speak English, it would be heard to everyone else as whatever language they understood the best.

Each time one of these press conferences was held, that country (so far the United States, Great Britain, France, Germany, Russia, China, Japan, Canada, Mexico, Italy, India, Pakistan, Bangladesh and Indonesia) would cease to be a country but would instead become, by title, a territory of Hammersonia. This political arrangement was only temporary; it would cease to matter when the Hammerhearts had taken control of the entire planet, but so far they had still not made moves toward any countries south of Panama in the Americas, or southwest of Egypt in Africa. Once the Hammerhearts had established their rule everywhere, all political borders would be severed, an action that would surely create cultural chaos if done too quickly, but Lord Hammerson insisted that by the time it happened, the world would be ready for it.

On the night of June 14, 2010, it was Australia's turn to join Hammersonia. The hour-long program aired on all commercial and government television stations and was attended by every news outlet in the country, as well as a few pro-Hammerheart bloggers who would be given the opportunity to spread the word to all their readers using more modern technology. More than one hundred media personnel were there, crammed into the large convention room with their various note-taking devices, and at the head of the room, seated around a large table, were the important men and women who were now running the country including Lord Hammerson, Hank Cornish (currently the Prime Minister, although about to be repositioned), Dermott Hall (the Australian Chief of Police, now entitled the Commissioner of Police, and therefore in charge of all law enforcement in the country as all state police forces had been merged with the federal force) and a number of other ministers who made up what was still being referred to as the Governing Committee of Australia.

Because his main job was to act as the liaison between Lord Hammerson and the local ministers, Hank Cornish had been selected to mediate the press conference (he was hardly the most important person in the room, after all). He stood up, spread his arms and welcomed everyone (press and television audience alike) to the conference, and introduced everyone at the table. Before he opened the floor to any questions, however, he turned the spotlight on Lord Hammerson. He then sat back in his seat while the man in charge of so much of the world stood up to address the country.

"For hundreds of years, humankind has strived for the ideal society," he began. "We have evolved at a steady rate over the centuries, and the rate of evolution in recent decades has accelerated as we use technology to better our quality of life. However, this acceleration comes with several problems. One is that the entire purpose of evolution is to reach a point where we can be comfortable and content with our existence, but what happens when we reach that point? We stop; that's what happens. As a general rule, once we find a system that works for us as individuals, we stop looking to improve upon it. Another problem is that never before have we had any control over our own evolution. You only have to look at how the Internet has changed our lives in the last ten years to know what I mean. I highly doubt anyone who tried to predict where technology would lead us all those years ago would have guessed at how it has turned out. This is not a good thing because it means that the technology itself may slip out of our control and ultimately be quite damaging to our society.

"Now, before you get any ideas, our goal is not to regress technology to achieve the ideal society—we will merely take what has already been done and alter it so that we can control where it takes us. That is essentially what all of this is about, except that we will take it further. Human nature itself would make the ideal society just about impossible, but anything is possible when we have magic at our disposal. You only have to believe it is so and it will be so. All I ask of each and every one of you out there is to have a little faith and open your minds to the idea of change in your lives. Yes, we have a tough road ahead of us, but just think of the ultimate benefits: A perfect world in which crime, poverty and disease will be things of the past.

"And that is essentially all it takes. Don't listen to all the fear-mongering because it will only serve to blind you to the truth of the matter. This can be done, and the more we all push in the same direction, the quicker we can reach our ultimate goal. Just keep your head down, follow the rules as they come in, and you can live a life just as peaceful and prosperous as you could want. Now, it's time to learn a bit more about those rules. Australia will, as of tonight, come under the complete jurisdiction of Hammersonia, but the laws that have been passed in the last two months served to make the transition as smooth as possible, so again, do not fear."

He sat back down and Cornish got back to his feet. "With that settled, it's time to open the floor. If you have a question to ask, raise your hand, and when the spotlight lands on you, you will be allowed to ask away. Make sure you speak nice and clearly so that the microphones pick it up."

He sat back down and hands shot up all over the room—at least, this was the assumption, for the television cameras continued to focus on the head table, not showing the journalists filling the room. Eventually, a man somewhere in the crowd had permission to ask his question.

"Where are the Sorcerers? What moves have been made against them recently?"

Lord Hammerson himself got back to his feet to answer the question. "The Woodwards and Fletchers are, at this stage, in hiding. They are still trying to put up resistance against us but other than a few minor victories here and there, they aren't doing much to disrupt our march toward perfection. We do have a number of plans in place to deal with them, however, and I will now invite Commissioner Hall to tell you a bit about them."

Commissioner Hall got to his feet as the spotlight landed on him. "Well, naturally, I am not going to tell you much about our plans; it would be a poor lookout if I gave the enemy a heads-up. However, rest assured that they will soon be brought into custody, and when they are, they will be stripped of their magic so that it can be put to better use."

"What will happen to them after they have lost their magic?" another journalist asked.

"Well, our initial policy was to either kill them or descend them to whatever the lowest place in the new society will be, but we have since revised that," Hall told the country. "They will now be brought around to our way of thinking and then placed somewhere within our ranks in an advisory capacity. Their knowledge of magic may be useful to us down the track and we would like not to waste that."

"What about the Chopville Quartet? Have they been caught yet?"

"No, I'm sorry to say that they have not," said Hall. "They have sought sanctuary with the Sorcerers, so when we bring them in, the Chopville Quartet will come with them. Unfortunately, given the trouble they have caused, they will probably be put to death or life imprisonment, but this policy may also be reviewed. Hammersonia itself will not have a death penalty, but we're not sure, after the crimes they have committed and the timing of said crimes, if their punishment will fall under Hammersonian law or traditional Hammerheart ruling—that remains to be seen."

"I must say, it speaks volumes about the Sorcerers, that they don't mind harbouring mass-murdering fugitives," Hank Cornish said, and there was a ripple of uncomfortable laughter.

"Next question," Lord Hammerson invited.

"Have any decisions been made regarding the future of the countries which haven't been claimed yet?"

That was the polite way of saying 'invaded'. Lord Hammerson got back to his feet, frowning at the offending journalist. "Maybe so, maybe no. Either way, that does not concern the people of Australia. Next question."

"How will the law be enforced in Australia in the future?"

Commissioner Hall took the spotlight again. "As already stated, Australia now falls under Hammersonian jurisdiction. That includes both law enforcement and the laws themselves. Lord Hammerson makes the laws; the Minister of Law Enforcement—that's Ian Smiter, by the way—passes the laws down to the Commissioner of each territory; the Commissioner —that's me, by the way—is responsible for providing the tools and the people for the job.

"I'll explain a little of how it will work. Every police officer on duty will be armed with a variety of newly created weaponry, all of which is designed for either people control, surveillance or both. If a person is caught committing a crime, they will be brought in for questioning. The questioning will involve using magic to browse the accused's memory for details about what they did before his or her mind is altered to make sure they do not offend again, at which point they will be released. If they were proven innocent by the interrogation, the search for the true culprit will continue. This may sound a bit hit-and-miss but I assure you, it's far more reliable than anything the police have ever had before."

"Wouldn't this be an invasion of privacy?" someone asked.

"If you have nothing to hide, you have nothing to fear from it," Hall said, smiling nastily at the camera. "Next question."

It went on for some time. The questioning moved through healthcare throughout Hammersonia, and the thorny issue of Hammerhearts (those who had been on board since before the revolution) getting preferential treatment. Lord Hammerson stated that those who had been faithful all along were entitled to a few perks, but it didn't mean that those who hadn't would go without—it would be against the overall policy. Eventually, healthcare itself would be free—and compulsory, so that nobody could risk spreading diseases to others. Special liquid medicines, tablets and vaccinations were being invented, all of them with magical enchantments that would regulate a person's health from the inside and keep them healthy against all ailments known at the time. (The Woodwards had since uncovered evidence that such medicines contained subtle influential charms which would make population control very easy for the Hammerhearts when the medicines were compulsory to everyone in the world.)

In the meantime, hospitals all over Hammersonia were being installed with new and better (magical) equipment, and a top-secret research centre was being developed (somewhere) where those who had magic (Arnold Hammerson being the only one at present) could develop more cures as diseases kept popping up. There were bound to be more because the more were eradicated, the weaker the human immune system would probably become as a result. When a cure was distributed, it would be free for anyone to acquire it.

This led to infrastructure the world over, and how much of it was to become infused with magic at some point. It was to be a long, arduous job that would probably take at least a decade to do properly. Those with magic would have the responsibility of performing it while the crews assigned to perform the labour would build those things which did not require magic. This was the second time the phrase 'those with magic' had been mentioned, and the question was naturally followed up.

"Yes, I am the only one at present," Lord Hammerson told them, "although Commissioner Hall here has a bit more up his sleeve than most of my associates. There will be more of us, of course, when my line is continued. My daughter Stella will have her magic back whenever we get hold of the Sorcerers;

she won't be required to work as hard as I am, though, not for another twenty years or so anyway."

"Where is Stella now?" one woman asked.

"She is taking a well-earned break," Hammerson said, smiling pleasantly. "She's been through a lot this year, particularly losing her grandmother so recently, but when she's ready, she'll come back and assume her position."

Another question was asked, this time by a young man who had been cut off by other reporters twice since the topic of infrastructure had come up. "Is there any truth to the rumours that Hammersonia will soon have a base currency that can be controlled and manipulated with magic?" he asked, and then before anyone could respond, he went on. "If so, is it also true that people and businesses can be disqualified from access to the currency if they don't follow the rules?"

Arnold Hammerson had gotten to his feet halfway through the second question and was giving the reporter in question a very level look. When he finished, Lord Hammerson said coldly, "Yet more fearmongering, I can assure you. We are quite happy to continue trading in existing local currencies for the foreseeable future, and will utilise Special Drawing Rights for major transactions. Next question."

The rebuked reporter didn't speak another word during the press conference, and a flurry of activity outside the view of the cameras that was nevertheless picked up by the microphones suggested that he may have been surreptitiously escorted from the room. Two days later, posts began appearing and briefly circulating through various social media websites, written by the young man's family and friends, asking with some desperation if anyone had seen or heard from him since the press conference. Then these posts disappeared as suddenly and mysteriously as the reporter who, so far as anyone knows, was never mentioned again.

The questioning continued into the realm of education. One journalist asked why they didn't just use magic to fill children's heads with knowledge so that schooling wouldn't even be necessary, and Brendon Lawson (in charge of education in the country/territory) stated that doing so would limit a child's ability to develop a personality through experience. Schooling would go on as it always had but any anti-Hammerheart teachings were prohibited. He strongly assured everyone—media and viewers alike—that this was for the purpose of social cohesion, and had nothing to do with government overreach or authoritarianism.

The next issue to be exposed was transportation. Almost all maritime travel was to be outlawed except for military purposes (cruises would probably be permitted down the track) while air travel would be phased out and replaced by teleportation. Teleportation would be cheap, almost instantaneous, and completely painless, and wouldn't require an area the size of a small city like the larger airports in the world currently did. It would also be much kinder to the environment. Rail transportation would still exist but Hammerson projected that eventually, people probably wouldn't want it. Cars, too, would continue to run on the streets, but as new models were developed, they would be infused with magic to make them safer and cleaner to the environment.

This led naturally enough to the environment itself and the issue of climate change. Once again, Lord Hammerson took the spotlight.

"We care greatly about protecting the environment," he said, "which is why we will find magical solutions to the type of things that have been trashing it for the last two hundred years. However, it still means that people will need to be mindful of pollution, and we intend to maintain existing environmental agencies to keep track of climate change around the world. Further regulations may be put in place, and money diverted to locations struggling to progress in an environmentally sustainable way, if the problem becomes worse."

By this time, there remained only about ten minutes before the press conference was to wrap up. Most of this time was filled with questions about how multiculturalism would work in Hammersonia. Anyone could have expected that it would be the most sensitive issue of the program and to make it worse, there were no definitive answers. The general consensus was that language barriers would be broken down by the same sort of magic that had allowed Hammerson to be understood in other countries when he spoke English, but after that, it was everyone for themselves. The police would come down on any issues as they came up but once travel by teleportation became practically unrestricted, all cultures would merge, spread and probably clash until eventually, they found a way to coexist. Lord Hammerson told the world that this would ultimately be a good thing for everyone, and the prospect of greater diversity the world over was something to look forward to.

At last, though, the end of the program rolled around, and Hank Cornish, who had remained very quiet throughout (other than being named Lord Hammerson's personal assistant, since there was no longer a need for a Prime Minister) stood up and took the spotlight.

"We hope this has been both entertaining and instructive for everyone out there," he said, smiling at the camera—it was a nicer smile than the one Hall had given earlier. "If you would like more information, we have set up a website with many useful tools and documents which will cover everything you need to know, and probably a fair bit more. You should also subscribe to our YouTube channel because over the next few months, we will be uploading a series of videos which will demonstrate how you ought to behave in our new society. Thank you, Australia, and good night."

Part 1: And on the Third Night...

Chapter 1: The First Night

It's not every late Sunday evening you would find a fourteen-year-old boy contemplating the meaning of the word 'normal', but that was certainly the case on this particular late Sunday evening for this particular fourteen-year-old boy. Perhaps on a normal Sunday evening, homework wouldn't be so unexpected, particularly if you had an assignment due the following day. In fact, at times over the last couple of years, Peter and I had been in that position plenty of times, and with each other's encouragement, we always got the work done (and usually did pretty well too). James, of course, had never ended up in that position.

But this was no normal Sunday evening for more than one reason. For one thing, it was the start of the winter holidays, and although I couldn't say it was the case in all schools around Victoria, I'd never been given homework in the winter holidays in my life; Easter and spring, sure, but never winter. That, we can counter, with the fact that this unfortunate fourteen-year-old boy had been subjected to the most suffocating form of schooling over the last month he'd ever experienced in his life, and you know he's had just about enough of it when he starts talking about himself in the third person, so I'll cut that out now.

The situation was this: Yes, we were allowed to have school holidays coinciding with the holidays all other schools on the outside were having (that phrase, 'on the outside', had taken on great and significant meaning around the Woodward base in recent weeks). By holidays, it meant that we didn't have to troop into the schooling hall, as it had become, and sit down to lessons every weekday, but it really wasn't a holiday at all when you considered the mountain of homework we had been given in its place. We all knew the real purpose of the homework: It had nothing to do with learning and everything to do with keeping us busy and out of trouble.

None of this would have been normal twelve months ago, but then how could I have known exactly what sort of homework we would have gotten in year nine if we'd been allowed to continue it without all this interference? It was these questions that naturally led me to ponder over the meaning of the word 'normal', because this going around in circles led me to believe that nothing could be called normal, full stop. That didn't make sense though, because if nothing could be called normal, then why was the word 'normal' part of the English dictionary?

Perhaps the more pressing question, at the end of this, should have been why on earth was I doing homework on a Sunday evening at all if I didn't have to submit it the next day? Why not save it for the end of the holidays? Now that would have been normal. There you go, John; question answered. As to why I was doing homework at all, leading me to ponder over philosophical questions that couldn't be answered, was simply the state of mind I'd been carrying for some five weeks now. If you asked me to explain the assignments I was working on, I'd be able to give you every single detail, all the requirements, with all the enthusiasm of a boiled potato.

I had no interest in the work at all; I was only doing it because, as the adults had intended, I had nothing else to do. The alternative at this moment was to descend to the floor below and sit in the lounge room with the rest of us poor imprisoned teenagers. They would have to get through this homework at some stage too, but most of them were slightly more in touch with reality than I was. Of course, none of them (with the possible exception of Marc) were carrying a weight anything like mine. Most of them weren't being hunted like a criminal, referred to in the newspapers all over the country as part of the 'Chopville Quartet' along with Marc, Tommy and Lucien. Most of them didn't have a specific path to follow, a path which they were being denied, and of course, none of them had caused almost the whole world's worth of problems by allowing the most powerful of all the Magic Crystals to fall into the wrong hands.

Some people blamed me for that (not to my face, but I knew what they were thinking) but most of the blame was self-inflicted; I'd been having nightmares about the creators of the Magic Crystals, John Leoard and Mary Sien, condemning me for allowing their precious crystals to cause so much destruction in the world. I knew what was causing the dreams, of course; recognised that they had perhaps little to do with guilt and plenty to do with one of several magical quirks I possessed, but that didn't change the way I felt. All things combined to take away my sense of...well, my sense of pretty much anything.

I would go where I was supposed to go, do what I was expected to do, but sometimes I would ascend the stairs to the third level, where my old bedroom was, and simply stand in front of the door, leaning against the rail, watching it. I put no thought into these disturbing ventures; I simply did it. Several people told me I should stop doing it (they worried about me but I tended to think it disturbed them more than anything else) but I knew I couldn't do it; it wasn't a private place, and yet it drew me. I preferred my own company these days, and I usually got it, because most people around me had become tired of my ways and no longer paid any attention to me. Only Peter and James persisted, and part of me was grateful for them, but not enough to help them out.

I wasn't completely unaware of what was going on around me; I was keeping up with the progress of the war outside and was reasonably knowledgeable of the gossip that floated around within the base, but none of it made any impression on me. I was also aware of the words people were using to describe me—zombie (I'm still alive, wanker), dormant (that was the one Dad and Charlie were going with, and was probably closest to the truth)—but in my mind, I was simply waiting, waiting for the door of my prison to open.

The door burst open with an almighty bang that made me jump out of my skin. I'd been so lost in my musings that I hadn't heard the running footsteps outside the bedroom in which I now slept in the family suite on the first floor. It was

Peter, of course, one of only five people (including myself) who could get this far into the Playman suite with their own key. There was a wild look in his eyes that caught my interest at once. I hadn't seen that much expression in his face since the night six weeks ago when we had faced Arnold Hammerson and the wrath of the Sien-Leoard Crystal.

"You gotta come quick," he said in a rush. "Tommy's been attacked."

"What?" I said, his words sinking in quickly and my heart sinking along with them—that surely had to be a joke. "Attacked by what?"

"By Jessica—she tried to stab him! He's in the hospital!"

I shrugged and got wearily to my feet, leaving my homework where it lay and barely noticing. It was almost eleven o'clock and I was getting rather tired. I decided I would see what was up and then head to bed—the homework would be right where I left it the next morning. I didn't believe Tommy could be in any serious trouble; it was impossible, given the current setup, for any of us 'children' to get so much as a paper cut, even though paper was about the most dangerous weapon we could get our hands on these days. I would simply work out what was going on, determine whether there was any real trouble, determine if there was a prank in the works, then call it a night.

There certainly was a considerable hubbub in the main hall when I followed Peter from the suite a minute later, but I still wasn't particularly interested in the cause of it. That changed when I spotted the splotches of blood on the stairs. I stopped dead where I stood and stared down at the blood, following it slowly with my eyes. It came down from the floors above and continued to the bottom of the stairs. The splotches seemed to be worse up towards the second floor than they were down here.

Now I was paying attention to my surroundings. Turning to Peter, I said, "What did you say happened to Tommy?"

"Jessica attacked him," Peter replied, very slowly and very clearly, and my heart froze.

"No way! Why?"

He didn't answer but instead pulled me out of the way of four men, who hurried up the stairs past us towards the floors above. He didn't let me go but instead dragged me down to the bottom level, where most people seemed to be congregated. It looked as though everyone who had been in the lounge room had been attracted by whatever had happened; they had all run out into the main hall to get a good look at what was going on. The blood splotches, meanwhile, trailed towards the wall where the door to the main corridor used to be before Mr. Woodward had sealed us in. The person to whom the blood had belonged had clearly been carried through it and, if Peter was right, down to the infirmary.

"Oh Christ," I heard Peter say, and I focussed on the crowd around us. Most of them were looking up, and I followed their gaze. What I saw was the final slap in the face required to wake me up completely: Jessica Thomas, the girl who had been like a big sister to me for most of my life, was standing up there, on the third level just outside Tommy's room. She was staring down at the crowd but seemed not to be seeing any of them. Her face was completely stunned. As I watched, the four men who had passed Peter and me on the stairs emerged and approached her where she stood. She saw them no more than she saw us, and when they manhandled her, actually lifting her into the air and proceeding to carry her back toward the stairs, she made no struggle at all.

The scene seemed to be suspended for about half a minute as the quintet made its way down the stairs, but upon emerging into the open again on the bottom level, a small crowd converged. Naturally, Marge was in front, ranting and raging at the men holding the still-stunned Jessica between them. Felicity and James were right behind her and as they approached, Peter and I followed along closely behind. To cap the scene, Brian Fletcher suddenly emerged before the wall which now blocked in the former doorway to the corridor. It was the first time I'd seen an actual Sorcerer (not counting Marc) for over a month.

"Tell them to let her go at once!" Marge shrieked at the Sorcerer as he approached the gathering, advancing on him, and I had to give Mr. Fletcher points for appreciating the gravity of the situation (in other words, he looked scared of this little woman before him).

"We need to determine what actually happened before we act," he told her firmly, making to move around her, but she blocked his path to Jessica. The men holding her had also been brought to a halt, unable to move past Marge to wherever they intended to take her.

"How's Tommy?" Marc asked from just behind me—I hadn't heard him approach the gathering. "Will he be okay?"

"There has been no lasting damage," said Mr. Fletcher. "He'll be fine—in fact he already is fine. He's still a little shaken up though, so we're keeping him in the infirmary for the time being. Again, he'll be allowed to return here once we've determined the cause of this incident. Please bring Jessica into the lounge room so I can interview her," he told the men over Marge's shoulder, and they changed course, cutting between James and Felicity and heading for the lounge room.

"You're interrogating her in the lounge room?" James enquired; his face was very pale. "Isn't that a bit public for something like this?"

"No bloody way known is he doing that," snarled Marge. "Isn't my daughter entitled to a bit of dignity?"

"*Interviewing*," Mr. Fletcher insisted, "and I wish to do it in public in order to put a quick end to any rumours that might circulate about Jessica's stability. That, I think, is showing her great confidence to begin with.

"Please move into the lounge room, everyone," he called over our heads to the surrounding crowd, and they moved for the doors, babbling excitedly.

"Don't mince words with me," said James coldly. "It's an interrogation, and that's insulting my intelligence."

Mr. Fletcher made no response to that but moved around us towards the lounge room. The rest of us scuttled along with him, but just as Peter and I were about to enter the room behind

James and Felicity, a hand fell on each of our shoulders. I hadn't seen where Mum was through the crowd, but I wasn't surprised that she would be nearby in a time like this.

"Up to bed with you two," she said fiercely. "You don't need to see this. Get going, now."

Without a word, Peter and I shrugged away from her and proceeded into the lounge room. I wasn't sure about him, but I had no intention of listening to what my mum had to say nowadays. As she was responsible for the greater part of my recent depression, I had lost a lot of respect for her. Mr. Woodward was responsible for a lot of it too but at least I knew that his reasoning was practical. All Mum cared about was keeping me safe, and that just didn't sit with me while the war raged on all around us.

Jessica had been deposited in a seat at the far end of the room and Mr. Fletcher had used magic, both to keep her still and to keep a space around her clear. People pressed in all around her like a dark shadow and Peter and I had to push and shove to make our way to where she sat, unbound but unable to move around very much. The Thomases had fought to the front of the pack and now Peter and I were able to join them. James and Felicity, both of whom were taller than us, made a space for us to get in front of them, for which I was appreciative.

Mr. Fletcher created a seat for himself and sat upon it, about four feet in front of Jessica. His seat looked considerably less comfortable than the one Jessica sat on, which seemed a strange role-reversal. Jessica didn't remain comfortable for long, though, for the first thing Mr. Fletcher did when he sat down was withdraw a small device from his pocket and point it at her. I recognised it at once as the same thing I had used when interrogating Stella on Mr. Woodward's orders; that had caused her to chuck up and wet herself, such was the effect of it. No wonder he'd avoided directly discussing dignity.

Jessica shuddered as the magic of the thing washed over her. She doubled over and made a horrible gasping sound, trembling all over, beads of sweat appearing on her forehead and running quickly down her face. A disturbed muttering ran through the crowd, as most of them had never seen such magic in their life, and a short distance to my left, Marge screamed at Mr. Fletcher.

"What are you doing to her? Stop that at once!"

Mr. Fletcher obliged, ceasing his continual clicking of the thing and hiding it in his pocket. Jessica now looked up at him, tears in her eyes, but finally they were eyes which appeared to be seeing the people around her. I realised that far from wanting to take away her dignity, all Mr. Fletcher had intended was to bring her out of her stunned state, and it looked like he had succeeded in that at least.

"Can we talk now, Jessica?" he asked calmly.

"Please don't do that to me again," she wept.

Mr. Fletcher smiled and showed her his empty palms. "No more of that, I promise. Would you like to tell me what happened upstairs between you and Tommy? What you remember of it? I've already had a somewhat hysterical version from him but until he calms down, I ought not to take him too seriously. Did you attack him with a bludginator?"

"I didn't," she said in little more than a squeak. "I swear I didn't mean to do anything to him. I'm not a violent person."

And that was true; even through all of this, Jessica was one of the least violent people I knew. She had helped us when it came to a tussle with Moran such a long time ago, but that was the only time I could remember her entering into a physical confrontation at all. The only other time had been the first of the three Chopville High battles, and that had been purely self-defence.

"You were with him in his bedroom, yes?" he persisted. "Were you and he perhaps having an argument at the time? Tommy was unwilling to discuss this part."

You know bloody well what they were doing, I thought sourly. Tommy and Jessica had, in the last few weeks, entered into a relatively steady relationship. I wasn't too surprised (I had vague memories of imagining those two together months ago, before Tommy had told me of his feelings for Natalie). Theirs wasn't the only new relationship to blossom within the confines of the base but it was probably the most advanced, and that didn't surprise me either. I knew Jessica wasn't new to sex, but even if she wasn't the type to give it away cheaply (and I didn't think she was), I knew that Tommy had a somewhat demanding appetite, and since they were still together this long, I could only assume.... Mr. Fletcher probably hadn't known about the relationship (he had bigger things on his mind) but surely a man like him would look at two sixteen-year-olds in a bedroom together, one male and one female, and make a calculated assumption.

"We weren't fighting—we were just talking," she said, looking into his eyes, and he nodded, satisfied. He could read her mind, of course, so whatever they had really been doing, she didn't need to say aloud. I looked at her carefully and, noting that her hair was still neat, decided they probably hadn't been up to too much dodgy.

"Tell me then," he said quietly, but not quietly enough that we couldn't hear him clearly in the otherwise silent lounge room, "can you actually remember attacking him? Is it clear in your memory?"

She shook her head—no hesitation at all. He stared at her for several seconds before nodding, but whatever he'd seen in her mind troubled him. He got to his feet and vanished the seat he'd been sitting on.

"What's the diagnosis, doctor?" a voice rang out from the doorway. I couldn't see the owner of the voice, but I knew who it was all too well: Charlie, Jessica's father. He had been due to return from whatever business on the outside tonight and it looked like he'd turned up just in time to catch the end of the incident.

"Something I don't understand," Mr. Fletcher said heavily, "which is why I must leave this up to the Woodwards. Jessica, as much as I would release you, I'm afraid I can't take any chances where those around you may be in danger. You'll have to be isolated until we understand the cause of this."

Jessica nodded again, and I felt a great sadness swell up inside me. Jessica seemed to have no better idea what was going on than anyone else but she understood that if she could act involuntarily, she could be dangerous to just about anyone. That showed a great level of maturity, in my mind, for her to be able to accept that fact so quickly.

"Isolated where?" Marge snarled at Mr. Fletcher's back.

She couldn't see his face where she stood, but I saw a faint look of surprise on it before grimness took over. "The prison yard, I'm afraid," he said heavily. "We have nowhere better for this sort—"

Both Marge and Jessica screamed at the same time, cutting him off. Marge's words were incoherent but I heard Jessica quite clearly: "No! They'll beat up on me in there! Don't send me there!"

"Can't we just keep her in our family suite?" James asked loudly. "Just make it so she can't come out. At least she'll be looked after in there."

"And what if she attacks you next?" Mr. Fletcher asked him. "Or perhaps you?" he added, looking at Felicity.

"We can defend ourselves," James replied. "Tommy was just caught unawares—that won't happen to us."

Mr. Fletcher stared at him for a few seconds before nodding reluctantly. "I don't like it, but I suppose you're right. Also, I think I may have to assign a body guard for her, in case she loses control again."

He used magic to raise Jessica into the air. She was still bound by some unknown magic, so the sight of her levitating a foot off the chair, still sitting as though in it, was extremely odd. He turned and, Jessica trailing along behind him, began cutting a path through the crowd. They parted like the Red Sea before him, unwilling to touch the floating girl. Marge, James and Felicity followed along behind them, and Charlie joined them as they left the lounge room and headed for the stairs. Peter and I turned and attempted to follow them, and now Marc made to join us, but once again, Mum got in our way.

"You are going to bed, *both* of you," she growled at the pair of us. "Get up there now and not a backward look from either of you. Understand?"

I shook my head. "I'll go after I've had a quick word with Mr. Fletcher."

Mum opened her mouth in a snarl of outrage, and perhaps her next words would have had a lot to do with insolent teenagers, but Dad put a resting hand on her arm. I hadn't even seen him but since he and Charlie went on just about all business assignments together, it made sense that he would have turned up at the same time.

"Let him stay here just till Brian gets back down," he said soothingly. "How do you expect them to sleep tonight after all this has happened? At least Brian can put their minds at ease once he's sorted out Jessica's arrangements."

"They already know she'll be taken care of—they don't need to get involved," she snapped, whirling on him. "It is not their business to worry about Jessica."

"She's like our sister," Peter said quietly, "and besides, Tommy's a wanted criminal, remember?"

"What are you implying?" Dad asked sharply. "Do you think this was an assassination attempt?"

"I'm sorry, was I too subtle?" he said sarcastically.

He certainly was a wanted criminal, I thought, as were I, Marc and Lucien. I thought they might have backed off Tommy since Tankom had died, and it was she who had wanted him dead for reasons of her own, but Hammerson hadn't changed his line. It seemed that there was no obvious reason to back off looking for him, since he was a dangerous criminal and he was in league with the rest of us. That would have been the public line; his own reason was probably that since Tankom had wanted his death, there must have been a good reason for it, so he would continue her work without understanding what that reason was.

"His point is that it could just as easily have been me instead of Tommy," I pointed out. "Tommy just happened to be closest to Jessica at the time."

Dad shook his head. "This is Jessica we're talking about. Jessica's a good girl—she'd never stray to the dark side."

"That's a rather cliché way of putting it," said Peter distastefully.

"You go and get some rest," he said kindly to Mum. "I'll send the boys up after they've spoken to Brian. I'll be up myself too—pretty tired."

She wanted to argue, as always, but she had a hard time getting mad at Dad these days. Whatever faults she had when it came to her children, she understood the danger he put himself in every day as he worked for the Woodwards' cause. Every time he returned safely to base, her relief made her softer than she would be any other time.

She sighed and turned to Peter and me. "Be sure you come straight up to bed when you're done with Mr. Fletcher," she said sternly. "No loitering around, and especially no trying to go into the Thomases' suite. If I get word from Marge tomorrow that either of you were in there, there'll be hell to pay. You understand?"

"Sure thing, Mum," said Peter wearily.

She sighed again and headed for the stairs. The four of us watched her out of sight before Dad turned to Peter and me. "Why do you want to talk to Mr. Fletcher?"

"Just want the final word on Jessica's condition," said Peter, but I shook my head.

"I have something else I want to ask him," I told him.

"And that would be…?" Dad enquired. "Do I take it that you do wish to speak to Jessica tonight?"

I shook my head again. "No, it's Tommy I wanna speak to."

"Me too," said Marc, who had been watching this Playman exchange silently for some time but now felt safe enough to weigh in. "I need to ask him something very important, which I bet it would never occur to Mr. Fletcher to ask."

He met my eyes and I knew we were both thinking the same thing. Dad looked like he wanted to ask what we were up to but decided against it. Instead he said, "there's a good chance he won't let you speak to Tommy this soon. You do realise that, don't you?"

"Yeah, he probably won't," I said, "but it can't hurt to ask."

As the Thomases had been gone for several minutes already, the crowd around us had settled down a little. Some of them had gone off to bed while others had returned to the lounge room to continue whatever discussion they'd been having before all this started, or more likely to continue discussing Jessica's attempt on Tommy's life. Before long, Dad, Marc, Peter and I were the only ones left in the hall, leaning against the wall between the stairs and the lounge room doors where we could wait for Mr. Fletcher to return. It was almost midnight when he did, and he looked very grim indeed.

"How is she now?" Peter asked him at once.

"She'll be fine," he said wearily. "She's being kept in her bedroom—no keys and no weapons. I'm on my way to speak to Mr. Woodward about assigning a body guard for her now. I would prefer it if you boys stayed away from her though, for the time being. Once we work out what's going on, I'm sure you'll be able to see her again. She doesn't look dangerous at all anymore but we have to be sure."

"Brian," said Dad, approaching the Sorcerer, and I was grateful that he was going to back us up—these two were very good friends of old. "Would it be okay for these three to visit with Tommy this evening?"

Mr. Fletcher hesitated, appraising me, Marc and Peter. "I'm not so sure that's a good idea. You did hear me when I said he was shaken up?"

"Yeah, we heard that," said Marc quickly, "but it's important we see him now. It can't wait for morning."

"Why is it so urgent?"

"Because I've got half an idea what might be going on here," said Marc, "and if I'm right, a whole lot worse stuff could happen in the next few hours."

Now that was a masterstroke from Marc. His words were terrifying, because I knew I was onto the same possible theory, and if we were right, nobody in the base was safe. Nevertheless he had taken perfect advantage of the situation; Mr. Fletcher didn't understand what was going on, and if Marc had any ideas, the one who does not know must bow to the one who does. Best of all, Mr. Fletcher recognised the situation for what it was.

"Fine, just you though," he said to Marc, but Marc shook his head.

"John comes too—I need to make sure we're on the same wavelength here."

He sighed. "Okay, just you too. You stay," he said to Peter. "Make sure he does," he added to Dad. "Come on, you two. I'll escort you. I need to speak to Frederic about this, but I'll pass by on the way back, and when I do, you two are coming back with me. Understand?"

"Sure," said Marc. "You might be right about Tommy being a little hysterical, but it probably won't take long to find out what we need to know."

I'd only been in the Chopville hospital enough times to count on one hand, but even I recognised the feelings that came with finally leaving the living quarters and entering the corridor outside. It was not unlike being confined to a hospital bed for a great length of time and then being allowed to tour the ward for the first time in what felt like ages. It was still in the Woodward base but it was so much better than what I'd had to put up with for such a long time. It was an ironic analogy, I thought, as Mr. Fletcher led Marc and me into the Woodward infirmary.

Tommy had been dozing before the three of us entered his room but came to attention quickly. When he recognised Marc and me, he managed a grin.

"I can only give you—maybe—five minutes," Mr. Fletcher told Marc and me. "I don't intend to spend long with Frederic and when I'm done, I'll be coming back this way, so make it quick, whatever you have to do."

"Don't worry, we will," said Marc, and Mr. Fletcher left the three of us alone in the room.

"You managed to get out," Tommy said happily as soon as the door shut behind the Sorcerer. "Blimey—I was so sure they wouldn't let any of you guys come down here."

"He wasn't too keen on it," I said as Marc and I pulled up chairs beside his bed. He had pulled himself into a sitting position but as far as I could see, he looked unharmed. Whatever damage had been done by Jessica's bludginator had been completely repaired.

"Mate," said Marc, reaching forward and patting Tommy on the arm, "glad to see it's all worked out okay, but you're so damn lucky she didn't kill you."

"I know, right?" he said, and then the happiness went quickly out of his face. "She's okay, isn't she? They're not gonna punish her for it?"

"They've isolated her," Marc told him. "They were gonna put her in the prison yard but Mr. Fletcher agreed her own suite would be good enough as long as there's someone to watch her. Er—can you remember it?"

Tommy hesitated, then said, "I think I can, but—it just seems so unreal. That's not like the Jessica I know—she was totally different."

"Yeah, she was," I said heavily, and looked enquiringly at Marc. He and I were probably on the same wavelength, but it was his idea, so I waited for him to ask the question.

"Did...," he said, trying to think how to say whatever was on his mind, "did Jessica...change? Did you actually see her change?"

Tommy hesitated again, but he seemed to understand where Marc was heading and was doing his best to provide the right information. Eventually he said, "Her eyes changed. I mean—they were still her eyes, same colour and everything, but they looked...different. And then she spoke, and it was her voice, but the way she spoke was different. You know what I mean?"

"What did she say?" Marc asked.

"And where was the bludginator?" I added. "Surely she doesn't normally carry things like that around in here."

"It was my bludginator," Tommy said, "and it was in my top bedside drawer. She'd seen it before so she knew it was there. I thought she was getting—er—well I thought she was getting something else out of there, so I didn't think anything of it until she—she lunged at me."

"What did she say before opening the drawer?" Marc asked again.

"She said something like, 'I'd like to try something new tonight, honey', and that's weird enough in itself because she's never called me that before."

Marc and I swapped another look. Our theory was looking more and more likely by the second. Marc took a deep breath and asked the all-important question. "You say that it didn't sound like Jessica? She spoke differently?" When Tommy nodded, he added, "Did she speak with an American accent?"

That took Tommy by surprise, but he considered carefully, smart enough to make the connection. Finally he shook his head. "Australian accent. Not as Aussie as the way Jessica normally speaks, but still Australian. It sounded—kind of— older, if you know what I mean."

Now that was significant indeed. It wasn't quite what Marc and I had been thinking, but it was very close. We swapped another look and once again, I knew we were thinking the same thing. The hair stood up on the back of my neck as we sat there, and I knew the three of us weren't alone in the hospital room. I looked around to the right, towards the door, and sure enough, I saw his face there, hidden in the deepest shadows of the room, no more than a shadow himself, watching us. A blink later, he had vanished; there was nothing in the shadows but more shadows, and anyone who hadn't been through all the crap I had would have dismissed it as imagination, but I knew better.

I looked back at Marc, who was watching me in alarm, eyes wide. He hadn't seen what I'd seen, I knew, but he understood what had just happened, and judging by the terrified look on his dark face, Tommy understood too.

"I'm not gonna live through the night," he whispered into the silence, and neither Marc nor I could think of a single thing to say to the contrary.

Chapter 2: The Anti-Shadow Movement

He had lived through the night though; everyone had in the end, although it had been a long way from restful for all those aware of what was going on. Marc and I had told Mr. Fletcher what we had deduced when he returned and thankfully, he hadn't asked us to prove it, because there really was no proof—none that we could offer anyway. He had escorted us back to the living quarters and promised us that he would take our news to Mr. Woodward before anything else, including following up on Mr. Woodward's orders to check on Jessica. Good move too, because Jessica wasn't the problem anymore. The problem, the biggest problem, was that none of the Fletchers' minds were protected; they had never needed to be protected since the Hammersons had lost their magical powers. Mr. Fletcher was to wake all those Sorcerers who were sleeping so they could conference and decide what could be done about this new threat.

Meanwhile, Marc and I had separated and although he knew he would be completely safe once he was in his room (his mind was protected and nobody else had a key, other than the Sorcerers), I knew I could be vulnerable. Both Peter and I were also protected but Mum, Dad and Hilda, my grandmother on my mother's side, weren't. So as soon as I got back into the Playman suite, I hurried through to the back where the bedrooms were, listening hard for any sounds from anyone else; the doors for my parents' and Hilda's rooms were closed, so they had probably gone to bed. Not wasting any time, I had gone to find Peter, knowing he would be waiting up for me, and told him everything we had found out. He had been horrified but after giving it some thought, decided that it wasn't too surprising. I had then gone back to my own room and once inside, proceeded to block the door with as many large objects as I could find. It wouldn't keep anyone really determined to do harm out, but at least they would wake me up in their attempts to break in. Fortunately there hadn't been any attempts and after a few restless hours, I eventually fell into an uneasy sleep.

The talk at breakfast the following morning had been all about Jessica and naturally, James and Felicity were surrounded by people almost as soon as they entered the dining room. Marge and Charlie too were accosted on a regular basis throughout breakfast by other parents, wanting to know how Jessica was coping. I sat with Marc, Peter, Harry, Simon and Lucien, but nobody came to bother us, believing that the Thomases would have a better idea what was going on, so we were able to quietly bring the twins and Lucien into the circle of truth.

It was as we were leaving the dining room, Peter and I being shepherded by Mum, who wanted us upstairs and working on our homework for the next three hours, that Mr. Woodward entered the living quarters for the first time since he had created the passage to the meeting hall and outdoor area. He was escorting Tommy back into the living quarters and as soon as people saw him, they rushed forward to find out how he was doing. Before anyone could ask any questions, however, Mr. Woodward stepped in front of him and addressed the crowd that was quickly gathering.

"Please, people, you will have your chance to badger Tommy as much as you like later on but before you do, I need to talk to him upstairs. I would also like"—he glanced around the room—"you two," he said to Peter and I, "you," he added to Marc, "and perhaps you too," he called over the heads of pretty much everyone to James, who was standing just outside the doors to the dining room.

"No surprises," I muttered to Peter as we joined Marc and headed for the stairs.

"How's she doing?" Peter asked James when he caught up with us.

"Quiet," he said after a moment's consideration. "I've never seen her so quiet. I mean, I know she's not a loud person, but— I guess she's just devastated."

Mr. Woodward was ahead of us on the stairs, already up at the third level waiting for us. When we reached him, he beckoned us into Tommy's room, where Tommy was already waiting. There was blood on the bed and floor, I saw, and after only a second of surprise, Mr. Woodward vanished it with a wave of his hand.

"Come sit down, boys," he said pleasantly enough, heading for the couches at the back of the room, and the five of us followed. "Did everyone sleep well in the end?"

Nobody answered; nobody needed to; all five of us looked like we'd last got a good night sleep some time in 1992, which was saying something as none of us had been born then.

"Right," he said a few moments later, "well firstly, Marc, John, I'm impressed with you both for coming to such a conclusion so quickly. Brian told me everything you discussed and—and what you saw," he added, a little doubtfully as he glanced at me. "The Fletchers have been dealt with, and I'm thinking that the only long-term solution is to protect everyone in the base the same way, but that is a job which, given how hard we need to work on the outside, isn't likely to get done any time soon."

"What are you talking about?" James asked, looking from me to Marc and back again.

"We'll get to that," said Marc quickly. "Sir, why do you believe us? I'm sure we're right but there's no proof."

"There may be no hard evidence, but I do have something which has led me to believe your theory is correct," he said, and from his pocket, he withdrew a thin piece of paper. He used magic to smooth it out perfectly and then to make it float in front of us so that leaning forward, we were able to read it.

It was the front page of today's issue of the Chopville Daily Telegraph. What I saw there made my heart leap into my mouth. There he was, the same face I had seen the night before in the shadows, only in this picture he was much more solid, much more real than a mere shadow of himself. He was smiling in a knowing way at the camera, a picture which was supposed to project confidence and surety, I felt certain. The headline, stretching across the top of the photograph, read, 'CHOPVILLE QUARTET: POLICE COMMISSIONER HALL ANNOUNCES BREAKTHROUGH'.

"Breakthrough? What? What?" James asked, his voice becoming sharper with every word.

"The article," Mr. Woodward said to the rest of us, gesturing at the floating paper, which folded itself neatly back into his lap, "states that Hall's detectives have uncovered evidence that the Chopville Quartet, as you've been dubbed in the public eye, have sought sanctuary with the Sorcerers." He uttered the word distastefully. "The point is actually stressed further that we are up to absolutely no good by allowing known killers to be joining with us, the purpose being to turn whatever is left of our support base in the public against us."

It certainly would, because the Hammerhearts had done a very good job spreading our supposed notoriety all over the news. The most damning evidence against us had been published while we had been away on Rock Haulter, and we hadn't found out about it until several days after we had returned. How they had taken those particular photos, I had no idea, but there had been three of them and they had been horribly persuasive: One had shown Bernard Moran, standing in the glass doorway of the gym at Chopville High; he'd had no weapons in his hands but he had had a look of concentrated determination on his face. Another had shown Lucien standing against the lighted backdrop of the car park at school in the back door of the gym, and he had been holding a gun. The final photo had been of me; I'd had Hall's enormous gun in both hands and had been carefully steadying it against an oncoming rush of people, none of whom were distinguishable in the picture. It had been done in such a way that I looked about to fire on a group of innocent bystanders. The public seemed to have swallowed the line exactly as the Hammerhearts had meant them to.

"That's bad and everything," said Marc impatiently, "but it doesn't actually prove anything."

"The evidence they claim to have uncovered," Mr. Woodward went on calmly, "isn't detailed in the paper, but states that in order for them to catch you where you are hiding and may be unlikely to emerge except to cause trouble, they will have to attempt to infiltrate our base. Of course, they go into no explanation of how they plan to do that, but I think we can work the rest out for ourselves."

"Can someone please explain to me," said James, his voice low but throbbing with impatience going on anger.

"Your sister did not attack Tommy of her own free will last night," Mr. Woodward told him. "She was possessed, probably for only twenty seconds or so, but Tommy noticed the change just moments before she attacked him. We believe, based on what Tommy could tell us of Jessica's behaviour in that moment, that this man"—he tapped the front page of the Telegraph, still folded in his lap—"was responsible."

"Hall possessed her?" James said, stunned. "How is that possible?"

"As to that, I'm not quite sure," Mr. Woodward sighed, "however as we know he has been using the Villain Crystal for some time now, it stands to reason that he would be one of only two people capable of doing what he did. What none of us are sure about, and will endeavour to find out, is how he was able to get inside the base at all. We're quite certain that all the magic we have set up would prevent him entering physically, but he has made it clear that he does not need to be here in person to do us damage. My belief is that he may have been separated from his body for some time, as you have both done a few times," he said to Marc and me, "and has mastered how to operate both physically and mentally in separate locations. The only way I can think of how he could have entered in spirit was by hitchhiking in someone else's mind, not taking possession but simply squatting and allowing himself to be carried in."

"Do we know that possessing people is all he can do from the outside?" Peter asked.

"We don't, and if he were using the Darkness Crystal rather than the Villain one, I would be almost certain that he could do a lot more," said Mr. Woodward. "Arnold Hammerson, of course, could do plenty more should he turn his attention our way, but we're doing enough damage to his plans and flying under the radar as it is. He is quite happy, for the time being, to let Hall take care of us. That is his job, after all."

"So what you're saying," I said slowly, "is that he could take possession of anyone whose mind isn't protected, and make them attack the rest of us?"

"That is a reasonable conclusion," he said, and sighed. "As I said, the long-term solution would be to protect everyone, but not only would that take a very long time, probably longer than we have, it would give Hall time to think of a new plan of attack. So, we need to discuss a shorter-term plan. Firstly, though, John, I need to know how you saw him last night."

"I have no idea," I said honestly. "He was probably there the whole time but I never noticed anything until Marc and I worked out it was him and not Hammerson behind the attack. I just felt weird, and I looked around at the door, and I saw his spirit there, or his mind, or whatever it was; really just a shadow but I'm sure it was there."

"If it was there, how is it possible that you could have seen it physically?" Mr. Woodward prompted. "The times when you did that, you were sure that you couldn't be seen."

"He couldn't have," Marc spoke up. "Neither Tommy nor I saw anything but we knew the same thing. I only had to see the look on John's face to know we were right."

"He can see ghosts," Peter pointed out. "You reckon that could have had something to do with it?"

"Perhaps," said Mr. Woodward. "Now, firstly, Tommy, I want you to keep what I gave you last night, and I want you to use it on a regular basis, even if there's no evidence that Hall is in the area."

"Gave you what?" I asked Tommy.

"This," Tommy answered, pulling something out of his pocket. We all gasped and covered our eyes, dazzled by the brightness in his hands. "Whoops, sorry," he added sheepishly, putting it away again.

"Why do you have that now?" James asked, squinting at the place where the Light Crystal had disappeared.

"It is designed to chase away this type of evil," Mr. Woodward told us. "It may be designed to counter the Darkness Crystal in particular but it can also counter any type of evil, and that includes the Villain Crystal. I put it over Tommy's bed last night on the off-chance that Hall would send someone else into his room to deal with him in the night; I'm glad to see it worked as it should have."

"Made it pretty hard to sleep, though," said Tommy grumpily.

"Are you saying," said James slowly, watching the Sorcerer, "that you are letting him use the crystal now? I thought we weren't responsible enough to be trusted with magic. Isn't that why we've all been locked up like pigs in a pen for the last six weeks?"

His voice was level but I knew he was speaking all the bitter thoughts I'd been carrying for weeks, and I felt instantly ashamed of myself. I had known that I wasn't the only one who hated the position our parents and the Sorcerers had put us in but I had believed, honestly believed, that none of them were quite as affected as I had been. Yet none of them had sunk completely into themselves as I had done. I felt something rise up inside me—no, two things rise up inside me. One of them was shame but beneath it, pushing upwards, was something much stronger: determination. I'd had enough; I was ready for action again, and I would not be stopped.

"The situation has changed," Mr. Woodward said, and I had to give him points for not looking remotely abashed (adults could be so stubborn). "In any case, I tend to think Tommy ought to have learnt his lesson after last night. Right, Tommy?"

"Probably," he said uneasily, "not that I could get up to anything dodgy with the Light Crystal anyway."

"True, but you can get up to plenty good with it," Mr. Woodward insisted. "Using it when you suspect something may be amiss with anyone around you could make a great difference. Now, secondly, Marc, do you feel you are ready to be responsible too?"

Marc shrugged. "I don't see how I can prove I am."

"You can start by adopting a slightly more gracious attitude," the Sorcerer said, frowning slightly.

"I'll rephrase it then," he said. "You tell me if you think I'm responsible; John too, for that matter, as nobody would have any idea what was really happening if it wasn't for us last night. You'd still be thinking there was something wrong with Jessica."

"What I think he means," said Tommy, digging an elbow into Marc's ribs to make him shut up, "is that he understands how serious the situation is, and will do all that he can to make sure nobody else in the base can be hurt. Isn't that right, Marc?"

Marc glared at him, and he wasn't the only one; Peter and James were glowering too, and I had no idea what my expression looked like, but nobody protested. Tommy's words were snivelling, almost manipulative even, designed to make the most of the situation, but for all that, they weren't untrue.

"I would like you to have the Hero Crystal back," Mr. Woodward told Marc, "because unlike the Light Crystal, it *is* designed to counter the Villain Crystal directly, and would go a long way to making sure Hall can't do any serious damage within the base. Yet I need to be sure that is all you will use it for; what is happening on the outside is being taken care of by the six of us. You only need to concern yourself with what is happening within your living quarters. Can you do that, Marc?"

"I expect so," Marc said reasonably, still glaring, "after all, I don't want anyone in the living quarters to get hurt, and after the way you lot have been treating us lately, there's no reason why I should give a damn about what happens to you."

"Will you knock that off?" hissed Tommy.

"You're happy about this?" Marc snapped at him.

"Of course not; you know how I've felt for weeks, but he's right about one thing: The situation really has changed."

"You may need to think about changing your attitude," Mr. Woodward said coolly to Marc, "but I tend to think that you'll probably feel better about it in a few minutes. Just remember that your business is in the living quarters; you are not to use your crystal to attack Hall physically, only to counter his attacks from in here."

"Isn't that a little reactive?" Peter asked. "I mean to say, the attacks will just keep coming if we don't stop them at their source."

"That's very true, but as Hall is on the outside and has been a target of ours for weeks, it will be *our* responsibility to trap him, not yours."

"That's great to hear," said Marc cheerfully. "I'm already looking forward to you telling me when you've caught him."

Mr. Woodward shrugged and made no direct response to that, but I recognised the look on his face as one my own father had worn on several occasions when Nicole had been particularly stubborn about something or other: It was that look that simply said, 'teenagers—what can you do?'. The Sorcerer put his hands in his pockets, withdrew two crystals, handed them to Marc, then withdrew two more. He didn't stop until Marc was holding all six glowing Sorcerous Crystals in his hands, and they were melting and reforming into the larger Hero Crystal.

"Now, here's the deal," Mr. Woodward said when he had all of our attention. "I think that since Hall still has a day job, he is far more likely to attack at night time. I also think, like last night, he would prefer to target someone who is with only one other. I'm not sure, but I don't think he would want to attack just anyone, though; he would know he may only have so many attempts, and he would want to use those attempts mainly on you three, and Lucien too. However, if he realised that you saw him last night, John, he will probably want to avoid getting too close to you in case you give away his position again."

"Or, he'll want to put John out of action as quickly as possible," said James uneasily. "That's probably what I'd do in his position."

"I'm glad you're not in his position then," I said, just as uneasily, though not entirely for the same reason.

"I'll leave it up to you how you want to deal with him then," Mr. Woodward said, getting to his feet. "One other thing, though, Marc; if anything does happened and you are forced to leap into action, I'd like you to send a telepathic message to one of us for our assistance. We may not get there quickly enough to catch him, but if any damage is done, we can be sure that it is minimised."

"Which of you should he contact," Peter asked, "now that all your minds are protected?"

"Any of us," the Sorcerer said. "That sort of telepathic communication is different from the standard mind-reading which we are all protected against. Since we all have our own magic, we are able to filter certain messages through, without them taking us over. I'm not sure if you have ever done it before, Marc, but I know John has done with both myself and Amelia, so he can tell you whatever you need to know. You five discuss what you think will be the best way to protect the living quarters against what Hall might try next. I have to go and check on Jessica before I head out."

"One thing, sir," said Marc quickly, and Mr. Woodward paused, looking apprehensive. But all Marc said was, "Can I have that paper, please? I wanna read what the article says."

We did as we were told after the Sorcerer had left, discussing the best ways we could protect everyone within the living quarters. It was James who came up with the two best ideas and once we had developed a plan, we all left Tommy's room. Marc separated from us where he would firstly create the magical devices we would use against Hall, before beginning to spread the word of his tactics around the base. The rest of us went down to the Thomases' suite where we just caught Mr. Woodward on his way out. He wasn't pleased to see us, perhaps thinking that we ought to be working harder, but told us that Jessica was fine and would, when she chose, be allowed to leave the family suite.

"She's probably still not herself," James said as Mr. Woodward headed for the stairs, "and honestly I don't blame her. You reckon you'll have it bad, Tommy; imagine the trouble people will be giving her now?"

"Best thing is to just deal with it," I said, remembering how, four months earlier, I had gone through exactly the same thing. "People are gonna talk one way or the other, but the longer you give the rumours to circulate, the more weird they'll be when you finally face them. We should bring her down, sit her in the lounge room and let people see her all day; they won't get to talk to her if we surround her but at least they'll see the object of interest and see that she's not dangerous."

"Object of interest?" James said scornfully. "Can I remind you that you're talking about a living person? My sister, no less?"

"Trust me, I know what I'm talking about," I said reasonably. "Remember what I had to put up with the day after Tulip died? That was hellish after what I'd been through, but people had already got over it after a couple of days. It probably would have lasted a lot longer if I'd hidden myself, and I reckon it would get worse for Jessica if she doesn't just get it out of the way."

"That makes sense, but do you reckon she would understand that?" Peter asked.

"Well, we can try to explain it to her," I said a little doubtfully. "We can put Tommy next to her; that should make it easier for both of you, and make it easier for people to swallow the truth of the matter."

"Once Marc's done, we should be fine," Peter said. "You reckon we'll have a meeting about it this evening?"

"Never mind all that," said Tommy impatiently, looking from Peter and me to James. "Let's just get in there and make sure she's okay. She's probably still beating herself up—she needs to know what really happened to her."

* * *

The meeting in question took place just after lunch that day, rather sooner than any of us had expected. Marc's thoughts were simply that the sooner we did it, the better it would be for everyone. It took place in Marc's room, which didn't surprise me, but the number of people Marc invited to the meeting did. It was the most people I'd seen in a room on the third level the whole time I'd been in the Woodward base—so many that there weren't enough seats in the couched area to accommodate everyone; Marc had to re-arrange the room for the occasion.

Tommy, James, Felicity and I were able to persuade Jessica, after some time, to allow herself to be seen in the public (we sat with her in the lounge room as I had planned, allowing nobody other than the twins to join us; talking casually so that eventually, she felt comfortable enough to be herself again). While that was happening, Marc, Peter and Lucien had been busy, moving quietly around the base, informing certain people who could be trusted that an important meeting would be taking place at two o'clock that afternoon. It had to be done quietly for two reasons: We didn't want everyone in the whole base knowing what was going on, for the more unprotected minds were in on the secret, the more Hall could learn from them. Also, we didn't want the adults to get in the way, as they seemed to enjoy doing these days. It didn't matter that we were acting on Mr. Woodward's instructions; they would see that something was in the offing and would automatically try to interfere, for no reason other than the simple fact that adults always believed they knew what was good for all, better than teenagers ever could.

In the end there were seventeen people in Marc's room that afternoon: he, Lucien, Tommy, Peter, James, Felicity, Jessica (who had agreed to get involved after learning the truth of what had happened to her), Harry, Simon, Katie, Sophie, Erica, Liam, Lena, Darcy, Siobhan and, of course, me. The young army had been bigger than this gathering, but quite a few of its former members were either dead, unable to attend or, in the case of Sebastian, turned traitor.

"Okay, everybody shut up for about five minutes or so," Marc called us all to attention. "I know you all wanna talk to Tommy and Jessica but before you do, let me explain what really happened last night, because I guarantee it's not what you're thinking."

And he launched into the story, starting with everything we had done and seen last night, and finishing with our meeting with Mr. Woodward hours earlier.

"So that's our job now," he said, "to do whatever we have to to stop Hall causing anymore trouble in the base. I've asked all you guys to come because I want you all to help me—it would be better to have as many eyes open as possible. If you're not interested in helping out, you'd better speak up now."

He fell silent and looked around at us all; everybody met his eyes and nobody said a word. After ten seconds or so, he nodded, satisfied.

"So let the Anti-Shadow Movement begin," he announced brightly.

"I suggested the Light Squad," said Tommy dully.

"Which the rest of us agreed was lightweight," Peter added.

"Now here's what I think," Marc went on. "Firstly, I think that we're extremely lucky that Hall was unable to kill Tommy last night; if his plan had worked as I expect he meant it to, Tommy would have been lying dead in his room for perhaps a couple of days before anyone thought to check why he wasn't coming down, and Jessica wouldn't have remembered a thing. Secondly, I think Mr. Woodward is probably right about how Hall is most likely to attack, and I think the only way to prevent it is to have someone with each of us at any time—that is to say, me, Tommy, John and Lucien, since we're the ones he wants to kill."

"Wouldn't it be better not to have someone with you?" Katie asked. "That way there won't be anyone who can hurt you."

"I'm talking about any of you," Marc pointed out, "and for the record, I intend to have all your minds protected before you leave this room, so none of you will have to worry about being possessed yourselves. Trouble is, Mr. Woodward's right about something else too: It will take too long to protect everyone in the base, that's why it's down to all of us to make sure they can't do any damage. I don't think Hall would want to kill just anyone—he only has so many attempts and he would want to make the most of them."

"How do you know he won't do other stuff?" Sophie asked. "Other than just possessing people, I mean?"

"We asked the same question," Marc said, "and the fact is, we just don't know. There are enchantments around the base that should protect us from magic done on the outside, but since Hall is on the inside already, at least in a spiritual form, we just don't know what he could do. I do know that the enchantments aren't that strong going the other way, though, because when the global coup was starting, John and I used our crystals to do magic on the outside, and that worked fine."

"So what's your plan, Marc?" Harry asked.

"Firstly, when we're done here, I'm going to recall all the bludginators, agonators and solid-outliners in the base," Marc said. "I know just about anything can be used as a weapon if a person is determined enough, but those are the main ones we need to worry about. Secondly, I'm going to arm all of you with devices I've created just this morning which we might as well call exorcisers—Hall's close enough to a Demon for that to work. If clicked when pointing at a person who's being possessed like Jessica was last night, they will force Hall to retreat from that person's mind, but I have to admit, I'm not happy with the way that one turned out."

"What's wrong with it?" James asked indignantly.

Marc sighed. "Fact is, no magic I can think of can force Hall to retreat from the base altogether, nor can it knock him unconscious, or anything physical, because of the enchantments I mentioned just before. If Hall wants to avoid trouble, he can jump away from that person as quickly as he likes, and I expect when he does take possession of a person, it would only be for no more than twenty seconds or so, like Mr. Woodward suggested. If he really wants to hang around, he only has to wait a few seconds after we click these things, then he can just repossess that person all over again. Other than knocking the repossessed person unconscious, I can't think of anything else to do."

"What we need to do is find out where Hall is and put him out of action," said Erica. "Why don't we focus on that?"

"Because Mr. Woodward says we're not allowed to," said Marc, and he paused for a moment, allowing his words to sink in, allowing people's reactions to take hold of them before adding, "he says that's the Sorcerers' responsibility, but of course, if they haven't caught him after all this time, I doubt they will any time soon. As per usual, the adults have seriously hamstrung us, but if we try to go against that, he'll just take the crystal back off me, and we'll be in even worse trouble. This is the best we can do."

"You don't know that there's no way to kick him out of the base," said Lena. "That's just guessing."

"Yeah, it is," Marc said heavily, "but unless I can find a way to do it, I have to assume that it can't be done—at least, it's not straightforward. Also, the other thing I created this morning was a signaller, like the ones the Woodwards gave us a while ago, but this will signal to me instead of them. This is if you do catch someone being possessed and you want my help dealing with them. Take one each and pass the rest on."

He began passing a couple of small bags around the circle of couches, one clockwise and the other anticlockwise. The signaller got to me first and I saw that unlike the Woodward signaller, it only had one button, and I didn't have to guess what it did. The exorciser was small and long, about the size of my thumb; it was jet-black with a single bright yellow button. Again, that looked fairly self-explanatory.

"Anything else, Marc?" Simon asked when everyone had one of each device.

"A couple of things," Marc said. "Firstly, you should all know what to look for—it's all well and good being armed against Hall but it won't do any good if you don't recognise him when he's staring you in the face. So, I'm going to try to possess one of you now so you can see what the difference looks like."

"Er, Marc?" said Tommy uneasily, glancing at Jessica, who had gone very pale.

Marc shrugged. "I'm not gonna do anything dodgy. In fact it would probably feel good by comparison to whatever Hall dealt out. Just out of curiosity, Jessica, can you remember feeling anything last night? I know you said you didn't remember doing anything but—"

"Marc, cut that out," Felicity snapped at him.

"It's okay," Jessica said quickly, looking directly at Marc. "I didn't then, but I've had time to think about it since and—well…"

She faltered, noticing how the attention in the room had sharpened perceptibly.

"Go on," Marc prompted.

"Cold," she said quietly. "I can't remember actually doing anything but I remember—coldness."

Marc looked around and his eyes met mine; once again, I knew we were thinking the same thing. Was it because of Hall's nature that it had felt cold? Or was it because of the Villain Crystal? It could have been either, but either way, it meant that the coldness probably wouldn't be there if Marc did it.

"Well, Tommy described how it looked to him," said Marc, "but I think the only way to make you all understand is if you see it for yourselves. Of course, I've never done it before, but I don't imagine it would be too difficult. If you don't wanna watch, Jess, I guess I can knock you out until it's done."

"You might as well just do it to me again," she said flatly.

"Are you sure you wanna go through that again?" Tommy asked quietly.

"He won't make me do anything," she pointed out, "and I won't remember anything. What's the harm?"

"Up to you," said Marc. "Everyone go quiet now and let's see what happens."

Everyone did as they were told. Marc closed his eyes and sank limply back into his seat, his fingers wrapped loosely around the Hero Crystal. Everyone was watching Jessica, and she was sitting still, staring straight ahead, looking apprehensive. Nothing happened for perhaps fifteen seconds, but when it did happen, it was one of the weirdest things I had ever seen. It was exactly as Tommy had described, but there was no trace at all of Hall in Jessica's features. It was still Jessica, her appearance hadn't actually changed, and yet the expression on her face, the look that suddenly came over her eyes, was indicative of Marc.

"Did it work?" she said flatly, and although it was Jessica's voice, it spoke with the exact accent and inflection of Marc's voice, and several people gasped in either amazement or horror, it was hard to tell.

A moment later, Jessica was suddenly herself again, and Marc was opening his eyes and pulling himself straight in his seat. Everyone's eyes flickered from Jessica to Marc and back again, perhaps wondering if they would see any more traces of him in her features. Marc was looking pleased with himself while Jessica looked slightly confused.

"Feel anything?" James asked her.

Jessica shrugged. "Whatever you did wasn't the same as what he did."

"Yeah, but only because I used a *good* crystal," said Marc. "Essentially, it's the same thing, and you can all see how she changed in that moment."

"But I remember it," Jessica pointed out. "I felt you use me."

"Oh," Marc faltered, looking confused. "You remember it? All of it?" When Jessica nodded, he said, "well—Hall must have wiped your consciousness as well. Maybe he'd already thought of it—in fact, he almost certainly did, if he wanted you not to remember what happened. He might have spent days practicing with it before he even got in the base."

"That was weird as," said Harry, a little shakily.

"It'll look worse when Hall does it," Marc said, "so don't get freaked out by it—just point those things at the person and you should be okay. Now, the last thing I'm gonna do is a little test for all of you."

"You do realise that we're supposed to be on school holidays, don't you?" said Katie.

"Not that kind of test," Marc shrugged. "I'm sure you'll all remember what you're supposed to do. This is a test of the mind. If you pass, you're allowed to leave the room. If not, you have to stay until you've passed."

"What are we supposed to do?" asked Sophie.

"You'll know if you succeed," Marc said ominously, and I saw him grip his crystal.

What happened next was very odd indeed. I felt a great wave of magic sweep over all of us, and I imagined that it brought with it a cool gust, although in actual fact I neither saw nor felt anything physical. What I did see, though, was the reactions of many people around me. Their expressions went completely vacant, their eyes dulling as all conscious thought left them. I recognised the domination charm immediately, a charm to which I had become immune months earlier when I had beaten it, shielding my mind from external penetration in the process. Marc, Tommy, Peter, James, Lucien and the twins were the only others who were still entirely themselves; everyone else was completely under, although I saw that two people (Katie and Erica) were twitching slightly, as though there was the tiniest bit of resistance deep down somewhere within their minds.

"Well, there you go," Marc said brightly. "You guys are all fine—you don't need to stay. Looks like I'll have to spend a bit of time with this lot."

"Isn't there a simpler way to protect a person's mind?" Lucien asked. "Or is beating the domination charm the only way?"

"It's the only way I know," Marc said, "because as far as I can tell, the only magic powerful enough to resist it has to come from within the mind, not outside. Each of them has to do it—I can help them with it, but I can't do it for them."

"We'll leave you to it, then," said Peter, getting to his feet. "I guess that went well, but—I dunno about you guys, but I've got a bad feeling about all this. Doesn't seem like we're anywhere near the right track to beating this."

Chapter 3: Dinner Guest

As predicted, the parents were certain we were up to no good. Quite a few of them were hanging around in the main hall near the lounge room, sure that we would eventually appear there. When Peter, James, Tommy, Lucien, the twins and I came down the stairs and into the open, Mum and Marge were quick to converge, and the only reason Harry and Simon's grandmother wasn't right with them was because she couldn't move as quickly.

"Upstairs, you two," Mum said sharply, pointing back from whence we had just come. "Homework beckons and you've still got more than three hours before dinner."

"And you get along too," Marge snapped at James, also pointing at the stairs. "Where are your sisters anyway? A few hours out and they've already disappeared off the face of the Earth."

"Stop panicking already," said Peter wearily. "Felicity and Jessica are just upstairs; they'll be down pretty soon and I'm sure they'll be delighted to see you. If we're gonna be stuck doing homework all afternoon, James is coming with us."

"Hear, hear," I said at once; I had little intention of studying now, but whether we did or didn't, I wanted James to be allowed to hang with us.

Mum hesitated for a moment, glancing from Marge to James and back before saying, "That should be okay. James, you make sure they work."

"Will do, Mrs. Playman," said James wearily, and the three of us backtracked quickly up the stairs, Mum and Marge trailing us like a couple of sheepdogs.

We entered the Playman suite and shut ourselves away in the study, and as per usual every time I stepped into this room, I found myself sorely missing our old home on Lopher Lane. Dad and Charlie had told us a few weeks earlier that Hammerhearts had moved into our old houses and had made themselves quite comfortable there. It was a depressing thought, and it was always brought on by the knowledge that since we had been forced to live in this ridiculously stifling family suite, our resources in just about every area were limited. That was the case whenever we studied together because there was less space in all of our bedrooms, and there was only one computer in each suite; prior to coming here, the Playman and Thomas families had had three computers between them, and that wasn't counting Dad and Charlie's old laptops.

"Are we really gonna study?" James asked miserably. "Because this is one occasion when I doubt I could concentrate myself, let alone force you two to work."

"We don't have to, but we'd better make it look like we are," said Peter, opening his Maths homework while I spread the work I'd been doing the night before on the floor. "I guarantee Mum will be checking on us regularly, probably every half-hour, on the half-hour."

"I would have said every ten minutes myself, but whatever you say," said James dispiritedly.

"You know what I reckon," Peter said, glancing at the door and pausing for a few seconds, listening for footsteps outside. When there weren't any, he said, "now that Marc and Tommy have their crystals back, we have to attack again."

"Marc said why we shouldn't," said James quietly, "but I agree with you. The Sorcerers are too busy looking at the whole thing from a political point of view; they're not focussing on the actual root of the problem, which is Hammerson himself. Unlike the Sorcerers, other than Natalie, we know how to beat him. All we'd have to do is find a way to steal his crystal and then strangle him to death."

"Sounds like a walk in the park," I said dully.

"True, it's way more complicated than that," said James, "but essentially, that's what it comes down to. We've got a lot of other crap going on as well, Hall being only part of that, but we shouldn't lose sight of the big picture, and the big picture is Hammerson, the Sien-Leoard Crystal and the spell he put on himself to protect his life after he lost his magic."

"We'd have to get Marc to agree before anything can happen though," I pointed out.

"I don't see why he wouldn't," said Peter. "He sees the situation the same way we do—we just have to get him to understand that it's not worth letting the adults intimidate us. If worse comes to worst, we can leave the base and go on the run."

"You reckon we should do that?" James asked nervously.

"I don't reckon we should, but I do reckon it's better than letting them control us to the point that we can't do anything to help," said Peter, "and they themselves don't do anything to end the war."

"I tell you what I think we should do," said James, and now he looked at me. "Hammerson's flying pretty high now because as much magic as we've got, he knows with his magic and sheer weight of numbers, he'll always be several steps ahead, but there is one thing he is afraid of. You know what I'm talking about?"

I shrugged. "I thought we determined that it could be wrong."

"It's not wrong," said James shortly. "Look at the facts: Sien and Leoard predicted that Marc would be the Seventh Sorcerer, and so he is. They predicted that you will be the one to defeat the most powerful Sorcerer of all time, and so you will—"

"It said I *can*, not I will," I said fiercely.

"And I don't know about you two," James went on loudly, Peter and I both waving our hands to hush him lest Mum hear, "but I do believe that Hammerson is the most powerful Sorcerer living, which means it must be him. I don't think it could have been Tankom."

"Did you hear what I just said?"

"I did, and the only way you could be prevented from reaching your potential is if Hammerson finds a way to stop you," said James firmly. "John, if you're supposed to be capable of finishing this business, don't you think you should try?"

I hesitated. When James put it that way, I had to agree with him. I was all in favour of weighing up the risks against the benefits and if there was any chance that I could end the war, as Sien and Leoard seemed to be predicting that I could, surely it was worth taking the risk? Even if failure could mean my own death? Additionally, since Hammerson believed I would be a danger to him as long as I lived, he would stop at nothing to kill me. Even though he was using this time to strengthen his own hold on power, I highly doubted he had forgotten about me—Hall's interference in the base was proof of that. So basically, my life was in danger either way, and if some contest between myself and Hammerson was inevitable, which it would be as long as we both lived, I would have to be as best prepared as possible.

"Okay, fine," I said dully, "you got me there. All the same, though, I said I wanted to hear the prophecy for myself and I stand by that. I can't decide to act on it until I know what it says."

"That makes sense," said James. "So, if we can get Marc on side, that's the first thing we'll do."

* * *

We stayed in the study, doing a bit of work but mostly talking disjointedly, for nearly all the afternoon. Mum was impressed that we had done so and had allowed us to come downstairs half an hour before dinner so we would have a chance to socialise in the lounge room. There was indeed a buzz of chatter coming from the lounge room as we emerged into the main hall (I could hear a voice I was sure belonged to Erica), but there were four people standing outside it, along the wall where I had stood on a number of occasions in the past. Marc, Tommy and Lucien were deep in conversation, and a short distance from them, her arms folded and her face irritable, stood Rebecca Fletcher.

"You three," she said, taking a step towards me, Peter and James, "you gotta come with me."

"What have we done this time?" Peter said wearily.

"Apparently an invitation has been extended," Marc told us when he noticed we had come down the stairs, "and the rest of us aren't allowed to take a step after you."

"Don't blame the messenger," said Rebecca irritably. "The invitation is that you three are allowed to have dinner with us this evening, if you wanna come. Your sisters are in there," she said to James, "and Harry and Simon too. You're the only ones who've been invited."

"You mean Marc's not coming?" Peter said, exchanging a look with me. "What's going on? Has Mr. Woodward lost his marbles? I've been predicting it for a while now."

"It's got nothing to do with that," said Rebecca, at last beginning to look amused. "It's Natalie's birthday and she's finally being allowed to see some of you guys."

"Geez, I totally forgot about that," said James in astonishment, but his shock was nothing compared to mine. How on earth could I have completely forgotten about Natalie's birthday? It was a date I had drilled into my memory for five years, and I hadn't given it a single thought in the lead-up.

"Still, no Marc," Peter commented, looking from Marc to Tommy. "No Tommy either?"

"She never requested Tommy," said Rebecca, shooting a nasty look at Tommy, "because I'm fairly sure she doesn't know he's moved on—she's never had time to sit down with me and catch up on the news of the boring. You guys wanna come on now—they'll be starting pretty soon. Where on earth have you been the last hour anyway?"

"Our mothers locked us up," Peter told her as the four of us headed for the wall. Rebecca was the only teenager in the base, besides the two Sorcerers, Natalie and Amelia, who'd been enchanted to be able to pass through the wall, and by each of us taking hold of her arms, we were all able to pass through into the corridor with her. Once we were through, Peter said, "Why is Marc *really* not coming?"

"Because my dad and Mr. Woodward don't want to give Natalie and Amelia a chance to 'collude' with him," she told us. "What does that mean anyway? 'Collude'?"

"In this case, it means he doesn't want the three of them to start planning stuff," said James. "What's Natalie been doing all day then? Just the usual?"

Rebecca shrugged. "My dad took her out to work, but I think it was easier stuff than what they usually do. He wanted her to have a light day for her birthday but he couldn't give her the day off because she would have come to see you guys, and he didn't want that. Amelia's been out all day too and for pretty much the same reason."

"Geez, and we complain about how we've got it," said Peter quietly.

Rebecca shrugged again. "They see a lot more than we do, a lot of bad stuff, and Natalie seems harder every time I see her, but I'm not so sure they've got it worse than us. They can't die, they can avoid any physical pain, and they get to go out and do stuff. They don't get a break but at least they're not locked up."

"Let's just say they're both bad," James said as we turned at the end of the corridor and approached the Fletcher living quarters. I'd been inside the Woodward living quarters plenty of times in the past but this was only the second time I'd entered the Fletcher living quarters; I remembered them to be a mirror image of the Woodwards'. There were no people in the entrance area when Rebecca opened the door and allowed us entry, but there were adult voices coming from the dining room, and younger-sounding voices coming from the lounge room, and it was in that direction Rebecca led us.

There were six people sitting in the Fletcher lounge room when the four of us entered: Felicity and Jessica, sitting closest to the door; Harry and Simon, sitting across from them; and there, to our right and at right angles to the twins, were Natalie and Amelia. All of them looked around as we entered and I saw at once what Rebecca had meant. Both young Sorcerers had undergone a noticeable change since the last time I'd seen them; it was as though the two girls I'd come to know so well had put up thick shields around themselves. They both looked healthy, physically anyway, but emotionally? It was impossible to say, because whatever experiences they'd had, whatever they'd seen and done, they were burying deep.

"John, my boy," said Harry in a deep, vibrant tone, standing up and striding forward with his hand outstretched, "nice to see you in the land of the living. And James, my fine portly sir, it has been just too long. And Peter, my dear lady, may I have the honour of kissing *your* hand?"

"Bite me," said Peter.

Harry beamed and said, "I assure you, Madame, I use only the lightest touch of my lips."

"I'll never understand how Katie and Sophie are able to tolerate sharing a bed with you two," said James, and everyone in the room was able to enjoy the look of astonishment that crossed both twins' faces.

"Ah, James," Simon was able to sigh eventually. "If you are attempting to understand how it feels to share a bed with us, my friend, perhaps my brother ought to be kissing your hand instead."

"Go on," said Rebecca, and she actually grabbed James's hand and thrust it out in front of Harry, who jumped back so quickly that he staggered and almost fell into Simon's lap.

"Ah, it appears that everyone is here," said a voice behind us, and I turned to see Mr. Fletcher watching us from the door to the dining room. "Dinner will be in twenty minutes, you lot. Entertain yourselves in the meantime."

And so we did, the rest of us taking seats and chatting for a while, but I didn't have too much to add to the conversation, and I noticed that Natalie and Amelia, though they spoke when spoken to, didn't seem to have much to say either. I couldn't tell whether they were happy to be surrounded by us or not. If what Rebecca had said was true, they would have wanted to be with us this afternoon, but now that they were, they didn't seem to be enjoying it too much.

That was confusing, but I was almost as confused by my own emotions. I had wanted to be here for weeks, to see both of these two girls again; particularly Natalie, but taking nothing from Amelia. Now that I was, I was having a hard time enjoying it. I would have thought I'd be asking them a lot of questions, telling them about everything that had happened in the last twenty-four hours in our part of the base. What I did feel, though, was an odd peace. I didn't seem to need to be talking to them to enjoy being with them, but at the same time, I wished I could see a bit more expression in their faces. If I could have been alone with either of them, I would surely have tried to break through those shells and reach the girls inside, the girls I'd come to know so well. That made me remember how Natalie had looked at me in the moments before I'd killed Tankom; I had hidden myself in a shell similar to theirs now, though for different reasons, and I imagined she'd wanted to bring the old John back. If that had been correct, I now understood how she had felt.

When Mr. Fletcher re-entered the room and told us all to make our way into the dining room to begin Natalie's birthday dinner, something different but not entirely unrelated sprang to mind, and as everyone began moving from the lounge room, I cut through the group so that I ended up right next to Harry. I gave him an elbow in the ribs to slow him up and as we fell a few paces behind the rest of the group, I said quietly, "What did you mean when you said 'land of the living'?"

"What?" he looked confused for a moment, then slightly chagrined. "Aw man, I was only kidding. You know how it is."

"Yeah, that's you about ninety percent of the time, I know," I said, "but what did you mean by it?"

Harry shrugged. "It's just good to see you looking like you give a damn about something again."

"Thought so," I said, satisfied.

"Is it being back with those two again?" he asked as we began walking again.

"I don't like what's going on in there with Hall and all, but I have to admit, having something going on is better than nothing."

"Something big's coming, isn't it?"

"Yeah, I've got that feeling too."

The dining room had been changed for the occasion, I saw as Harry and I entered. Instead of a rectangular table which could have seated six, which had been present the one and only time I'd been in here, had been replaced by a much larger circular table to accommodate all sixteen of us. I wasn't entirely sure but I thought maybe, just maybe, one of the Sorcerers had made the room seem larger than it had been to make it a more comfortable fit. Other than the table, though, nothing else about the room had changed; I wasn't entirely sure what Natalie had wanted for her birthday celebrations but other than the table, and a fairly large and tasty-looking chocolate cake sitting in the middle of it, there were no other decorations —no other indications that it wasn't just an ordinary dinner.

People were already picking seats around the table when we entered. Harry moved away from me to sit with his brother, who had seated himself beside Rebecca and appeared to be good-naturedly taunting her about something or other. Natalie was on Rebecca's other side, and Jessica and Felicity past her, so that option was unavailable. Amelia was sitting beside Natalie's grandmother, but there were two empty seats on her other side, and I decided to take the one beside her. Score, I thought, though I hardly knew whether Amelia's company would be worth much. The empty seat on my other side was taken a few minutes later by Natalie's mother, which was a little disappointing, but I wasn't about to complain.

"Okay, everyone," said Mr. Fletcher loudly, and all those seated around the table at the time (everyone except Natalie's parents and Lillian Woodward by that stage), "there's nothing formal about this—just a casual sit-down dinner for Natalie's special day, so everyone sit back and enjoy the food—it'll be coming through in a few minutes. Happy birthday, Natalie. Do you wanna make a speech?"

"Do I have to?" she asked, looking a bit scared.

"Just say something," he prompted.

"Er," said Natalie, looking around at all of us, wide-eyed.

"Would you like us to write a speech for you?" Simon asked her, leaning forward and winking at her. "Harry and I can compile something both sincere and inspiring for you."

"That's true, Nat," said Peter. "They dished up a pretty good presentation about Chopville's sewerage a few months ago. If you ever saw that, you'd want them doing a birthday speech for you."

"No, that's okay," said Natalie quickly. "We don't need the whole thing butchered. Er—just—thanks everyone, for coming, and you guys for setting this up for me. I appreciate it, really. That's all I can think to say."

"A few words," said Harry solemnly, "yet just enough to prevent us having a bit of fun with it. Perhaps a wise decision, on the whole, Ms. Natalie."

The conversation descended into a predictable debate concerning who was responsible for punching Harry and Simon after dinner, the adults at the table adding very little to the discussion (unsurprisingly) and again, I had little to say myself. A few minutes later, Natalie's parents began bringing the dinner in (roast lamb—wonder if that was Natalie's choice or her parents'...) and the discussion broke apart as people started eating. A number of smaller conversations began around the table: To my left, Natalie's parents and Lillian Woodward were talking about something or other (not a conversation I was interested in); past them, Peter and the twins were continuing on how Harry and Simon were to be punished when they returned to the living quarters (that was the loudest of the dinner conversations); further around, Rebecca, Natalie, Felicity and Jessica were in quieter conversation; James and Frederic Woodward were in a more serious conversation, but it was too quiet for me to hear what they were saying, and Natalie's grandmother added to it from time to time.

That just left Amelia and me, but for a few minutes, I completely forgot that I had seated myself next to her on the off-chance that we could have a decent conversation about things. Those few minutes were spent eating, trying to listen to what James and Mr. Woodward were talking about, and trying not to listen to Peter and the twins, who were getting sillier by the minute. When it occurred to me to shoot Amelia a sideways glance, I saw that she appeared to be listening to the conversation beside her as well (I assumed) but as before, had very little to say herself. Across the table, Natalie was doing a little better now—still not entirely herself, I thought, but the three girls around her seemed to be forcing her to converse with them. That could only be a good thing for the young Sorcerer, I thought, so I decided that it was up to me to do the same for the other young Sorcerer.

"Don't have nothing to say to them?" I asked her when I'd got her attention (by nudging her in the side), jerking my head sideways in the direction of her father.

"Not if I can help it," she replied. "I thought James was smart—if I'd known he was stupid enough to talk about that stuff tonight, I'd have sat over with them."

I laughed in spite of myself. The statement wasn't funny on its own (in fact I was a little surprised she wasn't sitting with Natalie and the rest of the girls) but it tickled me simply by virtue of the fact that I'd expected a one or two word answer instead.

"He's logical to the end, but that's not always the same thing as common sense," I said, and she laughed too. Doing well so far.

"Is he like this all the time?" she asked, eyebrows slightly raised, and I knew there was more in her question than her words alone indicated. I wished I knew what she was really asking because I couldn't work it out myself.

"If you mean does he often pick the wrong times to get serious, he sometimes is," I said.

"Guess that would be a fair bit lately then," she said in an offhand voice, shrugging slightly, and now I understood.

"Lately, I'm not so sure," I said, and now it was my turn to be offhand. "I haven't been paying a lot of attention to his conversational habits lately."

Her eyebrows flew up, and I knew I'd either said too much or not enough.

"What does that mean?" she asked. "I would have thought you guys would be hanging together a lot now."

"We do—well, sort of," I said. "I dunno if you know much how things are being run in there now—"

"Bugger all—they won't tell me anything. It's all Natalie and I can do not to lock our fathers up for a few hours so we can get down there."

I laughed. "You're missing nothing, believe me. Or at least, you were until last night. It's all school, school, and more school now. I'm sure the others have been talking about the war, keeping up with it on the news, and in a way I was too, but I guess I haven't really been with it."

"What does that mean?" she asked, looking concerned now.

"Er—not now," I said, glancing around the table. Nobody was paying us any attention, but I preferred not to discuss my recent depression in this company. "Maybe I can tell you some other time."

"Oh sure. Maybe they'll let you come back for Christmas dinner," she said scornfully.

"There may be occasion for it sooner than that," I said cagily.

"Do you know something I don't?"

"I may know a few things you don't," I pointed out, "though I'm sure you know a truckload of crap that I don't. I just got a feeling, and quite a few of the others do too."

"Is it something about the Hall business?" she asked.

"You know about that?"

"I know *of* it, but that's about it. My dad and Mr. Fletcher know all you know but they won't tell the rest of us—they don't want us to get involved."

I smiled. "Adults reckon they know so much they don't need to learn anything more. To be honest, I have no idea what's gonna happen; what I do know is—"

I was interrupted at that moment, and I had a split-second where I was irritated by it for no other reason than I'd been having a good conversation with Amelia. It hadn't been personal, and yet it had been easy, much more than I'd expected from her. That shell I'd observed earlier hadn't been lifted entirely but it had been weakened just a little for my benefit. The emotion only lasted a split-second though before confusion overrode it, giving way shortly to panic.

Being the middle of winter in Chopville, the sky had already gone dark outside. The room we were in now had windows that were enchanted to look out over the Jade River, though there was nothing to see through them at the moment. The illumination came from a single light bulb in the ceiling, making it not unlike any other dining room in the country. There were other lights on in the Fletcher living quarters too but at that moment, they all suddenly went out. All the conversations around the table staggered to a halt as everyone looked around in confusion—my night vision was just good enough to see people's heads moving.

"Faulty wire?" Peter said into the silence.

"We don't have electrical wires in this building," said Mr. Woodward, whose voice was extremely grim by contrast. "We don't use electricity."

That was when the panic began to set in as people realised something untoward was going on. It was a silent but palpable panic—everyone around the table could feel it. Along with it came a kind of chill; it felt vaguely familiar, and I didn't like it one bit. On the other side of the table, I heard somebody get to their feet—judging by the relative position, I guessed it was Natalie.

"Get the bloody lights on," Lillian snapped at no one in particular, but a moment later her son obliged. All the lights came on at once and we all blinked in the sudden glare—thankfully it wasn't too bad given the lights hadn't been out too long.

Blinking a few times to clear my vision, I saw that I'd been wrong a moment ago; Rebecca was the person on her feet, not Natalie. She was standing a few feet back from the chair she'd been sitting in and her eyes were fixed on Mr. Woodward.

"They can stop him," she said in the silence, and I felt my insides chill at her words, because they weren't her words at all, nor were they her eyes. Rebecca had gone extremely pale and her extremities appeared to be trembling—it was costing her some effort (or perhaps it wasn't her effort at all) just to remain on her feet. Felicity and Jessica, both of whom recognised this for what it was, screamed and attempted to get out of their seats; they fell right over the back of them and ended up on the floor.

"What's she talking about?" Natalie asked shrilly.

"They know how to stop him," Rebecca went on, but it wasn't Rebecca who was really talking, and most people around the table knew it now. Unfortunately, all the Sorcerers were transfixed by her words and hadn't thought to put their magic to use yet. "Let them out tomorrow, and it will all be over the day after—they know how."

She moved then, and she was no longer having trouble maintaining her footing; apparently the person possessing her had gained complete control now. She leapt sideways and then forward, straight at Peter, who had been the only person alert enough to withdraw his exorciser. To everyone's astonishment, she hit him, once; twice; three times. He yelled and put his hands up to cover himself as she assaulted him.

"The girl is ours," said Harry; he and Simon were quickly on their feet. They flanked Rebecca and between them, were able to hoist her into the air. She screamed and lashed out at them but the two of them were able to manipulate her body into a position where she could barely move.

"You bloody fools—let someone with magic take care of her," snarled Mr. Fletcher, getting to his feet and approaching the group.

It was James who finally ended it, taking aim from across the table and using his exorciser to force Hall to leave Rebecca's body. I was sure it had been Hall, as sure as I had been the night before, because I recognised him in her face, and the way she had spoken; it was severely creepy. Rebecca's body went completely limp in an instant and I saw something dark flit away from her. I knew what it was, even though I'd only seen it in that single instant, and the feelings I'd been having prior to this event began to increase. Hall wasn't done with us yet, and he would continue to up the ante, so to speak, until he drove us out. Rebecca's words were all the proof I needed.

Harry and Simon lowered her gently onto the floor where just about everyone quickly gathered around. Felicity and Jessica were still trembling and clutching each other; Natalie was in tears; Peter was in shock; and Mr. Fletcher was in a rage.

"How dare he do this to my daughter," he snarled. "That man has got plenty coming, I can tell you."

"How could you think to protect the Sorcerers and not do Rebecca?" Peter snapped at him. "If this is anyone's fault, it's yours."

I had to admit Peter was right, but on that score, Mr. Fletcher paid a moment later. As he helped Rebecca into a sitting position, she opened her mouth and expelled her dinner, still warm, all down his front.

"The girl's aim is true!" Simon announced to the room at large. "What an amazing score! A bullseye if ever I saw one."

"Keep that up and I'll remove your vocal cords from your body," Mr. Woodward warned him, and he fell silent at once.

"You gonna be okay, Rebecca?" Amelia asked her. "Did he do any serious damage? Does anyone know?"

"What happened?" Rebecca whimpered, and I glanced quickly at Jessica, who was nodding. Of course Rebecca wouldn't remember.

"You—" Mr. Fletcher choked on his words. He considered a moment, then said, "get to your feet—we have some work to do on you, young lady."

Rebecca wasn't up to standing just yet though, so her father levitated her into the air and began directing her out of the room. As he reached the door, he looked back at his other daughter. "Sorry, Nat, looks like your birthday dinner's been ruined."

He was right, in a way; the vibe of the dinner had been mucked up completely. Lillian Woodward cleaned up the mess Rebecca had left, and the dinner continued, but the casual air was no longer in it. There were no small conversations anymore and only one serious conversation, and of course, it surrounded Hall, the fact that he was still in the base, and what he had hoped to achieve by showing himself to the Sorcerers.

"He obviously knew that his cover had been blown," said James, "which he would have, if what John said about him last night was true. He made the lights go out so that he could get to Rebecca without being detected, and I guess he wants to trick you guys into letting Marc, John, Tommy and Lucien leave the base."

"That's what I thought too," said Mr. Woodward. "Knowing how to destroy Hammerson? There's no secret there: Just take the crystal from him and it'll all be over. Does he really expect us to fall for that?"

Amelia was nodding, but my eyes met James's, and both our eyebrows were raised. We *did* know the secret to finishing Hammerson, but Mr. Woodward didn't, as several others around the table didn't. Neither of us spoke, and I was glad that Peter and Natalie, the only others who knew the truth, followed our lead, but I had to wonder—why shouldn't we tell them? It was probably necessary for the Woodwards to know, and maybe we would be able to tell them eventually, but it couldn't be now. I assumed Natalie would have told them, but it looked as though James had been right on that score. Why hadn't she?

"Let them out tomorrow," Peter mused. "That's what she said, right? I guess it means that whatever he's got planned, he'll do it tomorrow night, or perhaps the day after. He made the lights go out, which answers one of my questions— obviously he can do more than just possessing people. Now, question for you guys." He looked enquiringly at the three Woodwards, Natalie and her grandmother. "What are you gonna do to stop him?"

They all looked at Mr. Woodward for his reaction.

"We'll attempt to set up protection around the edges to keep him out," said Mr. Woodward heavily, "but if he decides to stay in here, as I fear he might, I'm not sure there's much we can do, unless we can find a way to drive him out first. You'll have to assign that task to Marc, I think. In the meantime, tomorrow, the rest of us will attempt to track Hall down. I fear that he may be untraceable but that doesn't mean we can't find him—we'll just have to be a little more crafty."

"So you're shifting the responsibility onto Marc?" James asked sharply. "Are you suggesting that if something goes wrong, it will be his fault?"

"If you don't have anything respectful to contribute," said Lillian, just as sharply, "then you can head back to your living quarters immediately. No one person will be blamed for anything that may or may not go wrong in this war, and we all need to pull together here."

James met her gaze for a few seconds before getting to his feet, glancing around at the rest of us. At once, Harry, Simon, Peter, Felicity, Jessica and I stood up to join him. Natalie and Amelia were looking at us, eyes wide, expressions of frustration on both faces, but I knew their frustration wasn't directed at us.

"Have a great birthday evening, Nat," Peter said to her. "Nice seeing you both again."

The rest of us echoed similar sentiments as we trooped out of the room, through the Fletcher living quarters and back into the corridor outside. Of course, we couldn't get back into our living quarters without a Sorcerer, but right now, none of us cared. I wasn't sure about them, but I knew I was glad to get away from those adults, who could be so goddamned infuriating in their absolute belief that they knew what was good for all.

Chapter 4: The Second Night

There were eight of us sitting in the little box: me, Peter, James, Harry, Simon, Marc, Lucien and Tommy. A group of the boys, as it were, but none of us felt like talking about the sort of stuff guys our age would normally contemplate. Mr. Fletcher had come to let us into the living quarters after about ten minutes waiting outside it, and when asked how Rebecca was doing, he had said she would be fine, and that her mind was now protected. He refused to comment any further, so it was back to the old tricks as far as the Sorcerers were concerned.

Felicity and Jessica had disappeared into the Thomas family suite immediately, while the rest of us had hurried to find Marc (hurried because as soon as Marge knew we were back, she'd quite happily drag James kicking and screaming back to the suite). He had been in his room with Tommy and Lucien, sitting inside what looked like an enormous Transgator, sitting in the middle of the floor. They knew we were outside though because, apparently, one of the walls was transparent on that side, although once on the inside, I was unable to see through it at all. They had allowed us to come in before locking it up tight again the moment we were over the threshold. The inside was roomy indeed, larger by far than it had appeared on the outside. The three of them were sitting on comfortable sofas along one wall, a group of unidentifiable objects on the seat next to Marc.

"I can tell you, it's so great to be able to use magic again," Marc told us as he created more sofas for the rest of us.

"What have you been doing here, Marc?" Peter asked. "And what is this thing anyway?"

"Welcome to the mind box," Tommy proclaimed.

"That is essentially what it is," said Marc, smiling slightly as he took his seat again. "I've been thinking all day about what we can actually do to drive Hall out of the base; those things I gave you guys earlier were the best I could do on my own, but Lucien reminded me of something I should have thought of before, so now I'm working on these"—he indicated the things on the seat beside him—"which we can put to use tomorrow."

"Doesn't really answer my question," said Peter, looking from Marc to Lucien and back.

"We're safe from Hall in here," said Lucien. "Put it that way. He can't get through these walls, no matter what magic he tries. Most importantly though, he can't float through them."

"They employ similar magic to what we used on camp," said Marc, "in the ghost deflectors, I mean, only I've altered the charm slightly so that Hall can't find a way around it. This way, we can plan against him in here and he can't overhear us. As for these things, they will allow us to set up walls all over the base. Not physical walls, though; we'll be able to walk right through them, but as far as Hall in his mind is concerned, they'll cut him off at every turn. If we put enough of them up, I reckon we can shepherd him out of the base."

"I like it," said James enthusiastically, "though I'm sure you understand that you'll have to cover all corners of the base to do that effectively, and the Sorcerers won't like that."

"Yeah, we probably will have to leave the living quarters to do it properly," Marc admitted. "We may even need to leave the base altogether to chase him out, but that's just something the adults will have to cop—it's better for all, after all. I don't think we'll need to cover the whole base though, not if we do the thing properly. Did any of you guys ever play a computer game called Jezzball?"

That was a little off-topic, I thought. Just about everyone's eyebrows went up.

"Until very recently, computer games were little more than an urban legend in our house," said Harry solemnly.

"It's a really old one, I mean," Marc went on quickly, "from the nineties—nothing like what we get on the Xbox or PlayStation. You had two or more balls bouncing around on the screen; they always moved diagonally; they bounced at perfect angles off the sides of the screen; and they never lost momentum. You had to cut them off by drawing lines on the screen so that their room to move became smaller and smaller, and you had to do it so that the ball didn't hit the wall while you were creating it, otherwise you lost. When I played it, I always started by drawing a line straight down the centre of the screen so that the space would be halved immediately. I bring it up now because if we do the same thing to the base, we'll only have to cover as much as half of it—whichever half we can trap Hall in."

"Marc, you're a genius," said Simon fervently.

"Yeah, you've nailed it this time," said James admiringly. "I suppose we'll be able to move the walls around when we do trap him?"

"Yep, that's how we shepherd him out," said Marc, "so it would be good if we can do it up here, where we have a bunch of rooms on the second floor we can use to get him out. Once he is out, we'll have to make sure he can't get back in; I guess that's more up to the Woodwards though."

"He said he would," said Peter, "but who knows with them Sorcerers these days. It's more urgent than ever now——"

He launched into the story of what had taken place in the Fletcher dining room, and the disagreement which had followed it. Marc, Tommy and Lucien had been startled at first but none of them quite alarmed.

"Okay in the long run, though," Tommy said. "Rebecca will be fine, and the adults reacted as any of us could have predicted they would. Not something for us to worry about now though; we've got our own job. It's gonna be difficult, but at least it's doable, and I dunno about you guys, but I feel way better about this one than what we were doing this afternoon."

* * *

Two o'clock in the morning. I was awake, sitting up in bed and sweating on the back of a nightmare which, for the most part, I couldn't remember. The only bit I could remember was at the very end, when I'd had an extremely itchy left elbow. I had gone to scratch it with my right hand, only to find that my left arm was no longer attached to my body. I couldn't scratch my elbow, and yet it itched on like crazy. Crazy dream, I thought, and as I did with all dreams these days, I did my best to analyse all I could remember, just in case it was actually the Enlightener trying to tell me something.

"Ah, nice to see that you're awake, John. Say, did you know you're going to have an itchy elbow today?"

I had to laugh at that, and the sound startled me in the completely silent Playman suite. Predictably, as it always does when you think about itches, my elbow began to itch. I scratched it impatiently and lay back down, thinking that I could just go back to sleep, if the bad dream was all that had woken me up, but as I found a moment later, that hadn't been all of it. I hadn't noticed the soft tapping on my bedroom door at first in my preoccupation, but now it came again, and I heard it clearly.

I froze where I lay, because there was something ominous about that sound. The only other people in the Playman suite were Mum, Dad (who was due to go back out again in the morning), Peter and Hilda, and I couldn't think of a reason why any of them would come wrapper-tap-tapping on my door at this ungodly hour. Nobody else was able to get into the Playman suite because their keys wouldn't work, and most importantly, Hall wasn't able to get in, because Marc had taken the time to protect us, along with the Thomases, Maivises, and a few other rooms before turning in himself.

It's my imagination, I thought, as I lay there, but I didn't think it was, and I strained my ears to hear any other sounds from outside my bedroom door, but none came. The Playman suite was completely silent and deserted other than those who were already sleeping...

The tapping came again, a little more insistently this time, and I sat bolt upright in bed. Maybe it's Mum, I thought, and she just doesn't wanna startle me too much. Or maybe—I gripped my sheets hard as the thought occurred—maybe it's either Natalie or Amelia, as either of them would be capable of getting in here if they could find a way around their fathers. Part of me still believed it was my imagination, but the logical part of me, which had come to accept some extraordinary things, reasoned that if I called to whoever was there and didn't get an answer, I could confirm there was really no one there.

"Whoever's doing that, knock it off and let me sleep," I said aloud, loud enough so that if someone was out there, they would hear my voice, though not necessarily the words I had spoken.

For a moment, there was nothing, and I allowed myself to feel the relief that it really had been my imagination. But then the knocking came again, and this time it wasn't just tapping— now it was actual knuckles on wood, and the sound made me jump.

"Who is it?" I called more loudly now, trying to pack all my irritation into the words. Part of me was still a little freaked by the way the tapping had started, but now annoyance was overtaking it as the predominant emotion. Whoever was out there was gonna cop it for scaring the living daylights out of me.

"It's me, John," a voice called back; a soft call, and yet every word was clear. "Can I come in?"

It was a girl's voice, and certainly not Mum or Hilda. Even Peter, whose voice hadn't broken properly yet, didn't sound that effeminate. My mind returned to Natalie and Amelia, but only perfunctorily, because I didn't think it sounded quite like either of them. Of course, neither of them had called on me in bed at two in the morning before.

"Hello?" the voice said, tapping on the door. "You still with me, John?"

I took a moment before answering, because I couldn't think of a single thing to say. Surely it's every fourteen-year-old boy's dream to be called on by a beautiful girl at any hour of the night so that the two of them could do God only knew what, but now that it seemed to be happening for real, I just couldn't credit it. Yet I didn't want to ruin it just in case it were real, so the only thing I could think to say was, "Who is that?"

"What?" the voice said, and the surprise sounded familiar; I cast my mind around wildly. "It's me, John. Come on, let me in; I haven't seen you for so long and I've missed you so much."

I didn't answer for a moment, because a quick scan of my memory had come up with two possible voices which could match the one I was now hearing through the door, and one of them belonged to a dead person. That just left...but how could it be Stella? All I could say was, "Go away."

A brief silence on the other side of the door and then: "You don't mean that. Come on; I wanna be in there with you and I know you want it too. We can do so much together. Come on..."

The doorknob began to turn. It wouldn't open, of course, because whoever it was wouldn't have a key that could open this door. That thought only lasted a moment before cruel logic set in: Anyone who could get this far in could get the rest of the way in, and sure enough, the knob turned all the way and the door began to open. I was frozen where I sat, and I could never have said whether it was fear or disbelief that held me there— disbelief of the sort that was to say, I couldn't believe I was about to be visited in the middle of the night in bed by Stella. I didn't really think it was Stella though; the voice did sound like hers, more than any other I could think of in fact, but I just couldn't imagine Stella saying things like that, even in a weird situation like this.

It was too dark to see who was there; there were no windows at all in the family suite and no lights were on. Nevertheless I saw the shadow of the door as it moved one way, and then the other as whoever it was closed it. That was when I was able to move, but all I could do was reach for the lamp sitting on my desk. It was just within arm's reach and when the light came on, casting shadows all over the room, it threw just enough light in the direction of the closed door, and the person who stood beside it. It wasn't Stella, but I hadn't been entirely wrong. I had come up with two possible voices which could have matched the one I had been hearing through the door, and one of them had belonged to a dead person...

I yelled in horror and dismay, because I knew immediately what must be going on. I was horrified, but more than anything else, I was angry. There wasn't anything particularly horrific about her body as it were; her skin was much paler than it had been in life, her eyes were empty and her face lacked any expression at all, and there was a large scar on her neck that had never been there when she had been alive—I knew it to be the place where Tankom had stabbed her. Mr. Woodward (or perhaps it had been one of the other Sorcerers) had repaired and preserved her body with magic, along with the other two bodies which had been brought back after that night in Germany ('that night in Germany' was another phrase that had taken on significant meaning in the last month and a half), and their clothes (which they had been buried in) had also been repaired. If not for the pale skin and lack of expression, she could have been alive. She wasn't being possessed (the lack of expression proved that) but reanimated. She was a puppet, and I knew who was pulling the strings.

"You're a monster!" I shouted, not knowing where Hall could be, but sure that if he knew how to control Serena, he could hear me. "Why can't you let the dead rest in peace?"

A little melodramatic, maybe, but what the hell.

In response, Serena pressed a finger to her lips to shush me, and I saw that there were small scars on her hand as well (where the nails impaled her, I thought, and shuddered). "Keep your voice down, or your parents will hear, and we don't need them telling us what we can and can't do."

She raised her arms and moved slightly towards me, her empty eyes fixed on me, inviting me to come to her. One bad dream straight into another, I thought, because that was exactly what this felt like. She moved straight but not smoothly; whatever Hall was doing to her, it didn't change the fact that her body was stiff, and her movements were slightly jerky as a result. My emotions were in a tangle, but mostly I felt pity and sadness for the girl before me, fury at Hall for dragging her back out of the ground where she now belonged, and a small amount of fear: Serena had never had a key to the family suite, and if Hall knew how to get her in here, he could perhaps do more.

More to clear my head than anything else, I scrambled off my bed and moved sideways along its length, away from my desk and towards the wall opposite. If I were quick, I could easily bound for the door and get to it before Serena could move (her stiffness would be my advantage if I moved quickly enough) but the thought to do so didn't occur to me until later. Now that I was moving again, I was able to consider the situation with some logic. If Hall wanted to use Serena to hurt me, it could only be done by physical contact, which meant that I had to avoid touching her, something I had no desire to do anyway. Yet she would continue following me until she did, which meant that I had to put her out of action. I hated the idea of hurting her, after all she'd been through, and telling myself that Serena had gone where she wouldn't feel any of it didn't help.

Meanwhile, Serena had turned slowly so that she was facing me. Her arms were still raised, inviting me to come between them, and now the first expression crossed her face; her eyes remained empty, but her lips curved in a horrible smile.

"Well, I thought you'd wait for me on the bed, but I guess this way works too."

She lowered her arms and backed up so that her legs hit the base of my bed. She fell backwards onto it and began pulling herself (laboriously it looked like) backwards with her arms, her empty eyes fixed on me and the light from my lamp shining brightly on her in a way that didn't look good at all.

I scrambled for the thread of thought I'd been following moments before and after considerable effort, managed to catch it. Hall wouldn't have the consideration to put Serena back where he had found her, which meant that I had to put her back there, but that meant I would have to put her out of action first. I doubted stunning would work, nor would knocking her unconscious, which meant that I had to immobilise her physically. I moved slowly across the room to my desk, where

I opened my top drawer and looked inside, by the light of the lamp on the desk, which illuminated all of its contents.

My heart sank when I saw that my solid-outliner was gone, and I remembered that Marc had vanished all weapons that could be dangerous if Hall, in any form, got hold of them. The only things that were there were the signaller and the exorciser, which wouldn't do any good in this situation. The signaller would though, because if ever I needed Marc's help, it was now. I grabbed it and hammered the button, but the moment I threw it back down, a cold hand touched my shoulder. I knew Serena was close, of course, but I hadn't heard her move towards me in my preoccupation. I turned to look at her, and my stomach twisted in horror. The light made everything all too clear, and that wasn't even the worst of it, though; the worst, the very worst, was her coldness…her paleness…

I let out an involuntary yelp and jumped backward. It was enough to break the physical contact but was made a lot less effective when I lost my balance and tumbled backwards onto the floor. I broke my fall by throwing both hands out behind me, rolled over and scrambled back to my feet, but by the time I was fully upright, Serena was on her feet again, and much closer than I would have liked. Her hands grasped my shoulders (I could feel the coldness even through my pyjama top) and pulled me towards her. Dead or not, there was enough strength in her and for a moment, I couldn't resist, despite all my revulsion.

What I did manage to do was throw one leg out between her legs and sweep it sideways. It did what I meant it to do (knock her off her feet) but it also caused me to lose my balance again, and unfortunately, she was still holding onto me. The result was that we both fell on the floor together. I landed on top of her, which was lucky for me in more ways than one (given that I had no way to break my fall). She should have been hurt, especially as her head smacked hard on the carpeted floor, but of course, Serena would no more feel pain than shame for what was going on here. Having been active for some time now, her body wasn't as stiff as it had been when she had first entered my room, and she was able to use this to her advantage by wrapping her arms around me and twisting her body, using her legs to pull me sideways so that she was able to roll over on top of me. Apparently Hall wasn't trying to hurt me after all—he had decided to scare me to death.

Her face was very close to mine, those empty lifeless eyes directly above my madly rolling ones. Her body was so cold against mine—none of the warmth you would expect to feel if you had a girl lying on top of you. The only good thing was that considering she was dead, she didn't smell at all. I felt her hands release my shoulders for a moment and had a moment to guess that she was about to kiss me, and frantically clamped my jaws shut in preparation. Instead of taking my face, however, her fingers closed around my neck, and now I had no doubt whatsoever of Hall's intentions. Her fingers tightened and above me, her dead lips were curled in a horrible smile.

"Just like old times," she whispered. "I've missed you so much. Now, we can do all sorts of things together, and no one will stop us."

I had no room left in my mind to be disgusted with what was going on—now it was a matter of survival. I took a firm hold of her waist, braced my legs and attempted to heave her off me. It sort of worked—I was able to raise her slightly off me and push her sideways, but her fingers were still around my neck, not loosening in the slightest, and I began noticing the horrible gagging sounds issuing from my throat. My strength was waning, and as I raised my hands to my neck in an attempt to pry her fingers loose, I knew it wouldn't be any good—she was being fed strength from a truly evil source.

That was when someone hammered on the door from the outside and it flew open, and I'd never been so pleased to be disturbed in the middle of the night. It had to be only a matter of time before the racket disturbed the rest of the Playmans. Light flooded through the open doorway from the hallway outside, which had been lit since Serena had been there only a few minutes earlier. It was Peter who was silhouetted in the doorway—I knew it was him even though I couldn't see his face.

"John! You won't believe—" he said, breaking off when he registered the struggle on the floor in front of him. For a few seconds he did nothing but gape before pulling himself together. He bounded in, seized Serena's wrists, muttered "sorry" in a distracted sort of fashion, and twisted. It didn't hurt her at all (how could it have) but it did loosen her grip, which was enough for me to scramble away from her and stagger to my feet, spluttering and coughing.

Without looking back, I hurtled from the room, colliding with the wall opposite and bouncing back, spinning around to look back into the relative darkness of my haunted bedroom. Peter was emerging from it, white as a sheet—almost as pale as the dead girl, who was pulling herself to her feet behind him.

"That wasn't very nice," she said in a voice not at all like the tantalising one she had used earlier; it sounded much closer to the pouty tone she had used at several points throughout our relationship, the one that had indirectly caused me to cheat on her. "We were having fun."

I might have responded, not to Serena but to Hall, who I wished I could throttle as he had just attempted to do to me, but was distracted by another voice further down the hallway in the direction of Peter's bedroom. "Pety," it crooned, and I knew immediately who it had to be, but couldn't stop myself from looking anyway. She was ambling up the hall towards us; her body had also been repaired and preserved, but her head had not been reattached; she was cradling it under one arm as she walked, and the dead eyes were fixed on Peter.

"Oh shit," I said under my breath.

"What's going on?" another voice said, this time from the opposite direction. Mum and Dad had come out of their bedroom and were staring at Peter and me in amazement. They couldn't see Serena, who was now standing a few feet behind Peter but still too far inside my bedroom, and apparently they hadn't noticed Kylie yet either.

"Go back in your room," Peter said without looking at them, moving sideways so that Serena wouldn't touch him as she emerged from my bedroom. "Nothing to see here—just go back in your room."

It was no good, though, because that was when Kylie walked under one of the lights in the roof and became clearly visible to all in the hallway. Mum let out a scream of horror and Dad's mouth fell open. Fortunately, before either of them could do more, Marc arrived on the scene. Better late than never, I supposed, but given that we had disturbed his sleep, he had done pretty well to get here as quickly as he had. He was in his pyjamas and looked only half awake, but the crystal was in his hand, and he would certainly need it.

"They're puppets," I said, staring straight ahead of me at Serena, who was once again holding her arms out to me, inviting me to come between them. "Just cut their strings and they'll fall down."

Marc's eyes widened when he caught sight of Kylie. Who knew what he might have made of the situation if not for what I'd just said, but I was glad that he chose not to waste time asking questions. A moment later, Kylie dropped like a stone, her head hitting the floor and rolling away from the rest of her body. Peter let out a moan of despair as it came to rest facing upward, and I couldn't blame him. Peter was in a new relationship now, but seeing that happen to someone he had cared about (still cared about) would hurt, and I found out for myself a moment later when the same thing happened to Serena. She landed beside Kylie, facing down, which was better, but still terribly painful to watch.

"Holy crap," Dad whispered, staring at the bodies of two girls who had, not so long ago, been part of our group.

"How," Mum said, but couldn't seem to manage any more.

"Don't tell me anything," said Marc wearily, approaching where Peter and I stood above the two girls. "I reckon I can work it out on my own. Stand back—I'll take them back to the cemetery."

"I'm coming with you," said Peter at once.

"Er, you sure you wanna do that?" Marc asked, staring at Kylie's head.

"I have to," Peter replied. There was a hardness in his expression but I knew he was both deeply hurt and enraged by how his late ex-girlfriend had been defiled, and I felt exactly the same. I didn't want to look at Serena—it would be an insult to her memory to see her like this—but I knew I had to see that she wouldn't be disturbed anymore. If Hall were here, I would do him in just as I had done Tankom, only I would make it last longer so that I could enjoy his pain.

"What about you, John?" Marc asked.

"Yeah, I'll come with you," I said shakily.

Marc did the honours, looking grim but determined. A few moments later, Kylie and Serena were both floating several feet off the floor on stretchers. It was exactly what Fewul had done for Tommy when we had been leaving Rock Haulter so long ago. Mum and Dad were still standing outside their bedroom door, staring transfixed at the scene. I expected them to stop us from leaving the suite, and especially from going to the cemetery, but neither of them made any moves to do so. Perhaps they were simply too stunned to register what we were about to do; either way, I felt my respect for them increase slightly. It didn't make up for the misery of the last six weeks, but it was a start.

Through the suite the three of us went, the stretchers following along behind, and out into the hall outside, passing through a silvery sheet of light in the doorway which I assumed was the physical representation of the ghost-deflecting wall Marc had placed around the suite. I looked at the door on the first level for damage but there didn't seem to be any. I returned my mind to the question of what magic Hall had performed tonight. How had he managed to get Kylie and Serena into the family suite? There were several barriers that should have prevented them getting that far, having been buried under the ground being only one of them. Had he dug them up himself, or made them dig themselves out? That question probably didn't matter, but he had managed to get them out of the cemetery and into the living quarters, which should have been impossible—the only way in and out was through a solid wall. Had he teleported them? Had he turned the wall into a door for a minute? Had he enchanted the bodies so that they could go through the wall? Who could say for sure, but whatever he had done, it was very worrying. The Villain Crystal was giving him far too much potential for causing trouble, and I was beginning to think there was very little he wouldn't be able to do, despite all the supposed enchantments that should have been protecting the place.

The confirmation of this came when we reached the cemetery and were able to see for ourselves the damage that had been done. Kylie and Serena's graves, which were side-by-side, were both open and neatly dug out, which supported the theory that he had used magic to open the graves before reanimating the girls. The most insulting and enraging thing was the way he had vandalised their tombstones in the process, but the most worrying thing was that there was a third open grave a short distance away. Who else was up and walking around this evening? Marc repaired the coffins which had been ruined, lowered the girls into them (Peter and I closed our eyes for this part) and lowered them back into the ground, causing dirt to fall in on top of them.

"He's making it more personal every time," said Peter in a low voice. "I swear to God, I wanna kill him."

"We can do it together then," I said in a low voice, wishing very much that we would get a chance to do that.

Marc wasn't listening. Once he had repaired the tombstones, he walked over to the other open grave to look at its tombstone. When he straightened up and turned to face us, his lips were trembling with rage.

"Who is it?" Peter asked. "Jane? Tommy's other body?"

Marc shook his head. "It's Amelia's mother."

Without another word, the three of us hurried from the cemetery and for the Woodward living quarters, sure that was where the third dead person had been sent. I hoped to God that Amelia hadn't been confronted with her dead mother—after all she'd been through, Hall couldn't offer her a greater insult. The last thing I considered was that we wouldn't be welcome in there; it only occurred to me when we arrived and found the state in a total uproar. All three Sorcerers were awake and clustered in the lounge room, while the woman's body, as clean and pale as those of Kylie and Serena had been, was struggling against ropes tied to the far wall. They had clearly been able to subdue her with their own magic but hadn't been able to cut her strings completely.

"What are you three doing here?" Mr. Woodward asked sharply when the three of us stopped in the doorway, observing the scene. His mother and daughter looked around at his words, their eyes widening as they took the three of us in, still in our pyjamas.

"Looking for the third resurrection," said Marc grimly, stepping over the threshold and turning his gaze on the dead woman opposite him. Immediately, she went completely limp against the ropes that bound her.

"How did you do that?" Lillian asked. "We tried everything to still her but nothing worked."

But that wasn't what concerned Mr. Woodward. "The third resurrection?" he said sharply. "Who else has been disturbed?"

"Serena and Kylie," said Marc, approaching the body of Mr. Woodward's late wife. "They called on John and Peter in the night, gave them a hell of a fright."

"I want you to do me a favour," Peter said, addressing the three Sorcerers, who looked at him warily. Or at least, two of them did—Amelia sat herself down quickly on a couch and covered her face with her hands.

"What would that be?" Mr. Woodward asked.

"When you catch Hall," said Peter, "don't kill him. Just bring him in here, so that John and I can strangle him to death."

Chapter 5: Escape Plan

For the second night in a row, sleep was a long time coming. At least this time I'd got a few good hours in before all the crap went down but it didn't make me feel much better about things. I lay in bed, listening to the silence around me as four o'clock came and went. I kept imagining sounds around me, slight phantom breezes and muffled footsteps, but they were all in my head. It looked as though Hall had retired for the night, which made sense given that he still had a day job on the outside.

Gradually, as the minutes ticked by, I began thinking less about Hall and more about Serena. The fury and fear I felt towards my former English teacher, had been feeling since at least the basement episode in February, had intensified yet again after what he had done to Serena tonight (the fear stemmed from the knowledge that he was becoming increasingly more dangerous every time he revealed himself). As those emotions had intensified, now I found that my feelings for Serena had also. It was hard to nail exactly what they were, though. What I kept returning to was the way she had collapsed when Marc had severed the link between her and Hall; somehow, that had been so much worse than what Hall had done to her. Those thoughts led me back to the way she had been killed, the way Tankom had so brutally taken her life. I felt the anger at Tankom flare inside me again, but only for a moment—it was an old anger now, and I had already had my revenge.

No; what I was feeling right now wasn't complicated at all. I had grieved for Serena for the first couple of weeks after her death, before the depression had taken hold of me. From then on I'd spent too much time feeling sorry for myself to spare too much thought for Serena. Now it came back to me, stronger than it had been before, and it was regret I was feeling, regret and sorrow. Immediately after her death, it had been the fact that I had been unable to make things right between us that had haunted me. Now, I simply regretted the whole nasty string of bad treatment I had put her through. I could make all the excuses in the world about how my own thoughts and feelings were so confusing; that between her, Natalie and Amelia, I couldn't decide which way to turn at any given moment; but none of that excused the fact that I had treated her so cruelly while we had been together.

If she were still alive today, we almost certainly would have split up long before now, and probably wouldn't be too friendly with each other either (something that would be very bad given how much she knew about my business, but that was way beside the point). I'd never decided how I would handle breaking up with her, whether or not I would have told her the whole truth, part of the truth, or just said the feelings were gone and offered no more explanation than that. Never having broken up with a girl before, I had no idea what would have been the best way to do it. However I would have done it, I could never have made up for everything I had done to her in that time, and that was what was coming back to me now.

What I wanted more than anything else at that moment was to tell her how sorry I was; if it were possible to do that, it would be the most genuine thing I would ever say to her, and I actually caught myself whispering the word 'sorry' several times before forcing my mouth closed. Nobody, not even Smiley, could have said if Serena would ever forgive me; if she would ever know how sorry I was; if she did, how much bad feelings she could retain from life; those were things those of us still living would never be allowed to know. Now, it was just something I had to live with, and in that moment, the only sane thing I could hold on to was that I should always remember these feelings, because they might just prevent me doing such stupid things in the future. I couldn't share the moment with anyone though, because despite what Hall had done tonight, Serena, along with Nicole, Kylie and so many others I had known recently, had gone where no apology would ever reach them.

Sleep eventually came to me, and by the time I rose in the morning, I had missed breakfast. I scrambled hastily into some clothes and hurried from the suite, thankful that it appeared to be empty, and down into the hall below, looking around to see where everyone was. The lounge room was full and buzzing with chatter, the gym and games room were also in use, and the library was just as it always was. The dining room was practically empty though, but for a small number of people cleaning up the end result of a good breakfast.

There were no people loitering in the hall where I was either, so it looked as though I would have to go and find them. I wasn't exactly sure who I was looking for (any of the boys who'd been in the box the previous night probably would have done) but I just felt like I needed to be with someone, to find out what was going on and what would be going on, and get going with our plan to get Hall out of the base. First stop was the lounge room, and there were indeed plenty of familiar faces in there, including a few who'd been in Marc's room the previous afternoon (Felicity, Jessica, Katie, Sophie and Erica) but no one I was looking for.

"You weren't at breakfast, were you?" Jessica asked me just as I was about to backtrack out of the room.

"Nah, slept in. I don't suppose you know where Tommy is, do you?"

"He was with Marc at breakfast," she said, "and they wanted to know where you and Peter were, but I have no idea where they went since then."

"Peter wasn't there either?"

She shrugged. "Didn't see him."

I shrugged in reply and left the lounge room, thinking I would knock on Marc's door and see if I got an answer, but before I got to the stairs, all my questions answered themselves at once. The first glance upward revealed Peter, standing on the level above me just outside our suite, the door of which stood open. He was dressed, but the state of his hair suggested he'd only just woken up. At the same moment, I saw when I returned my gaze to the stairs, Marc and Tommy had appeared in front of the wall that should have been a door out to the corridor outside, and they were followed by a depressed-looking Mr. Woodward.

"Hey you," said Tommy, "you missed breakfast but you've timed this one nicely. You gonna come upstairs with us?"

"Hadn't made any other plans," I said, following in their wake and waving to Peter that he should join us; he did so as we reached the first landing and continued up to the third.

Apparently this meeting had already been in the planning stages because Lucien, James and the twins were already waiting on the third floor in front of Marc's bedroom door. Marc let the lot of us in and as we had done the night before, we congregated inside the box, which was still sitting in the middle of the bedroom floor.

"So how's everyone doing?" Marc asked everyone, not expecting much of an answer. "For the record, you two," he said to Peter and me, "I've already filled the others in on what happened last night, so we don't need to go over that again. This is about what we're gonna be doing today."

"You're absolutely sure that you have closed any loopholes through which Hall may eavesdrop on this discussion?" Mr. Woodward asked him.

"Certain of it," said Marc. "If John could see him, then he must be bound by the same enchantments that hold ghosts. This stuff worked against the ghosts on Rock Haulter, so I'm sure it'll do the job here. I've even made it specifically to work against Hall, so I can't think what could go wrong with it. I just thought it would be better to talk about stuff in here; I'm sure Hall knows about it after last night, after I put it around the Playman suite, since he apparently couldn't get in there without sending a physical form in instead, but I'd rather he not see too much of it, if he's watching now."

"I suspect he's not, but you're right not to take the chance," Mr. Woodward said, and sighed. "You boys will forgive me if I'm not quite at my most efficient this morning."

"Sure thing," I said wearily. "Pete and I probably won't be either."

In fact, I thought he would be doing much worse than us, since he had been married for approximately twenty years before his wife had been taken from him; that was certainly more to hang your hat on than less than three months worth of dating. Amelia, if she was still in the base, would probably be doing even worse again, and I asked after her before Marc could get back into any more business.

"She's very distressed after last night," he said. "I thought it best not to send her out today. As far as I know, she's still sleeping. She'll be okay eventually; she's a strong girl but I think she needs this time to recover. I hope very much that we are able to find Hall soon; for us, it's almost as personal with him as it is with Arnold Hammerson."

"And in the meantime," said Marc, "we have a job to do in here. I've been thinking a lot about how we're going to do it and I'm trying to think of any way Hall could find to get around it. Firstly, I need to know if we'll be allowed to make use of the entire base tonight, when we attempt to put this plan into action, because I'm sure that we'll need the whole base."

"You said last night that you would divvy it up," Simon reminded him.

"I will, but the fact is, I have no idea which part we're likely to trap him in," Marc said, looking at the Sorcerer.

"I don't think that will be a problem," said Mr. Woodward. "I'll let the other Sorcerers know by telepathy what to expect in that regard. Incidentally, Marc, these walls you plan on constructing, will they cover the ceiling and floor as well?"

"Absolutely," said Marc, looking shocked. "We're dealing with a mind here; no regular floor is gonna get in his way. If we're gonna trap him, it'll have to cover all three dimensions. Here's the other thing, though: I need to know what's around the base. That is, I need to know where Hall will go if he crosses the outermost boundary and ends up on the outside. Where will he end up if he does that?"

"The base is located in a secure locker within our house in Chopville," said Mr. Woodward, "but I'm not entirely sure he will be able to reach it due to the enchantments that should have kept him out in the first place."

"That's what I thought," said Marc, "but the fact is we just can't be sure whether it'll work or not. If there's any way he can slip out and back in again, it will muck up the whole coordination. That's why, if it's okay with you, I'd like to go out of the base and put a protective wall around it from the outside. It wouldn't be practical to do it on the inside because there would be too many real walls getting in the way."

Mr. Woodward said nothing to this for a few moments. After giving it considerable thought, he said, "How do you intend to force him from the base if there's a wall around the outside of it?"

"As long as it's there, we can't get him out completely," Marc admitted, "but we can at least trap him in one corner, nothing he can do about it. Then once he's there, we can get rid of it on the outside, and he'll be out in a flash. Then to top it off, I'm also gonna put another charm around the outside of the base, exactly the same as what I put in the exorcisers, so that he can't hitchhike his way in again. I reckon we'll cover all angles if we do it in that order."

Again Mr. Woodward thought it over for a few moments before sighing. "Well, since I have no better ideas myself, I'll go along with this one. You'll need me to accompany you on the outside though; the magic around the outside of the base is quite extensive, as you can imagine. A shield for ourselves mightn't be a bad idea either; I don't expect an attack in our house today, as there haven't been any for weeks, but you can never be too careful."

So that was what the two of them did, leaving the rest of us sitting in the mind-proofed box waiting for them to return.

"While we're waiting," said James, watching nervously through the supposedly transparent wall which I still couldn't see through, "I've had an idea that I wanna float with you guys about what we do after tonight; after we've got Hall out, or not, if it doesn't work. John, Peter and I have already talked about it a bit, but I've had a further idea since then."

"Is this the one about the prophecy?" Peter asked.

"It's the one about taking matters into our own hands," James said. "You do realise that as long as we're sitting here, no moves to stop the war are being made? Nothing will change, the way things are going."

"I think it's reasonable to assume that the Woodwards are doing their best," Lucien pointed out. "How much are you expecting them to achieve, given how much they're working against?"

James shrugged indifferently. "I'm sure Mr. Woodward's got some master plan he intends to unleash sometime in the next seventeen years, but in the meantime all he's doing is cutting Hammerson off wherever he can, making life as difficult as possible. He hasn't actually made any moves to stop him."

"So James's big idea is to head on out of here, hide ourselves from everyone, including the Sorcerers, and work on taking him down," said Peter, grinning at James. "Isn't that the crux of it?"

"Actually, the idea to go on the run was yours, Pete," James pointed out, "but it may be the only option we have in the long run. This place is nowhere near as secure as we've deluded ourselves into believing; you all realise this, surely. Hall is doing a fair amount of damage as it is; if Hammerson ever decided to pay a visit, we'd be in a world of trouble. Not only is his crystal more powerful, but he is more experienced with magic than Hall—more experienced by fifty years, no less."

"Okay," said Lucien slowly. "I agree with your point about our safety here, but you can't do much without a plan of your own. All you have to go on is the prophecy, and that in itself is nowhere near sure enough."

"Hear, hear," I said, raising my hand; Peter slapped it.

"Actually, we have a little more than that," said James, looking at Lucien now, "something we know about that not even the Woodwards do—unless Natalie's told them, but based on something Mr. Woodward said last night after the Rebecca incident, I don't think she has."

"Have you not told them about the prophecy?" Lucien enquired.

"Never got a chance to," Peter said, "although I suppose it's John's choice to do that, not any of ours."

"Okay, I think we've been polite for long enough," Simon said loudly, "and that's definitely not something that comes naturally, you understand. Would someone mind filling us in?"

"And he's not talking about our heads, for a change," Harry pointed out. "What's this prophecy you guys are going on about?"

Everyone looked at me for my response. I considered for only a moment before nodding at James; Harry and Simon were both protected, and I trusted them not to blab about something this serious. So James launched into the story of all I had learned about myself on Rock Haulter: How my ability to see ghosts had allowed me to travel back in time in my mind and see things inside the Main Hall fourteen years earlier; where that ability to see ghosts had come from; the Enlightener, the cause of many a bizarre dream; the prophecy, foretelling the only ordinary person who would be capable of defeating the most powerful Sorcerer who ever lived; the fiasco that had followed as Arnold Hammerson attempted to prevent the prophecy from coming true; how his actions had caused the mind link between Stella and me, and how I had been adopted by the Playmans for my safety. It took a long time to get through it but to his credit, James didn't miss a beat. Harry and Simon had been stunned into silence, something that didn't happen very often, though predictably, it didn't last long.

"So you're a Moran?" Harry asked, looking at me now. "Wow, no wonder you're screwed."

"That's what Marc said when he found out," I said, laughing slightly. "Have we cleared that up? If so, get back to what you were saying before, James, but I don't see how it changes anything."

"One thing first," Lucien cut in. "John, why wouldn't you tell the Woodwards about the prophecy? Has it occurred to you that they may be able to help you fulfil it?"

I shook my head. "I never got a chance to, but even if I did, I don't think I would tell them. Mr. Woodward already knows a fair bit but he hasn't helped me at all; why would he help me with this? He'd probably just say that as long as I'm safe, Hammerson can't do anything about it either."

Lucien considered this for a moment before nodding. "You're probably right about that. It's an adult thing, I've noticed. Well actually, it's more a parent thing, but even with the prophecy on your side, John, it won't help you if you actually have to fight him, especially if he's got magic."

"Then, John fights him after we've stripped him of his magic," James said, "and we arm John with that same magic beforehand. You know it's not that difficult to do—"

"On the contrary, I'm sure Hammerson is protecting the Sien-Leoard Crystal with immensely powerful magic," Lucien said. "He is very skilled and will know how to prevent anyone taking it from him while he's using it, and he would set magic around it while he sleeps. I suppose Marc would be the only person capable of slipping under his guard, but even then it would be extremely risky. Unfortunately, as well as he's done so far, Marc is not a normal Sorcerer, and even with the Hero Crystal, he is perfectly mortal."

"All that's true," said James, "and we will have to plan for that very carefully once we're all out. Of course, this is assuming Marc agrees to it; I'm sure he would, but I guess we have to run it by him first. I also think Natalie and Amelia should be allowed to come along, if they choose. I would understand if they want to stay with their families and fight the way they have been doing, but I got the impression last night that they're frustrated with the way things are going."

"Taking them would make life very difficult for their families," Lucien pointed out. "Six are struggling; how would four be better?"

"Because the two we take away would be doing more useful things," said James.

"What was your idea, James?" Peter asked loudly.

"My idea was that we leave as soon as we can," James told us. "We gather up as many people who want to come as we can and then skedaddle. I'm not against taking any well-meaning adults along but I'm thinking we would have a less complicated time of it if it's only teenagers. Lucien's close enough to an adult to count, I suppose."

"Are you charging me with the responsibility to make sure you kids don't do dodgy things after the lights go out?" Lucien asked, grinning. "Seriously, though, I agree with everything there, except leaving without any notice. Don't you think your parents will panic somewhat if they wake up tomorrow morning and your beds are empty?"

"They will," said James heavily, "especially my mother. We'll have options once we're out and safely protected. We can send a note back, or we can call, or send an email, or even telepathy, if Amelia and Natalie agree to come along."

Lucien sighed. "That'll have to do. As far as protection goes, I think I have enough ideas about how we can achieve that. What worries me is getting out there and then sitting around with absolutely no idea how to proceed. I hope you have ideas for that, James, because I certainly don't."

"We start by doing what John wanted to do before we all got locked up," said James, "find out about the Enlightener, and get the full wording of the prophecy so we know exactly what it says. After that, we'll have to start making plans to track down Hammerson and see what protection he's surrounding himself with. Once we know, we'll be better equipped to move against him."

"What about us then?" Tommy asked. When everyone looked at him, he shrugged and went on, "What we do to get the ball rolling? Remember, we still have to try to get Hall out of here. Even if we're leaving, we can't let him stay here."

Everyone looked at Lucien, who shrugged. "We can coordinate more easily when Marc gets back. I'm fairly sure he'll want a few of us to help him set up the walls, but the rest of us should quietly spread the word, like we did yesterday. As for Natalie and Amelia, we'll get to them later this evening when we know they're both in the base. I suppose Marc will have to find a way of contacting them without their fathers being aware of it."

* * *

Lucien's prediction was pretty much spot-on. Marc returned to us after about twenty minutes, alone, and told us that he and Mr. Woodward had come up with a new idea for dealing with Hall.

"The protective wall around the outside is up," he had said, "but we've decided to just leave it there. If we trap Hall in a corner somewhere and he can't move, his only option will be to recall his minds-eye to his body. That may or may not work, but either way, it doesn't matter, because he won't be able to do anymore damage."

We had told him of everything we had discussed in his absence, and to our delight, he agreed with everything we had said. Marc thought it would probably be appropriate to bring along, not just those who had sat in his bedroom the previous afternoon, but everyone who had accompanied us to the Hammerheart base that night in Germany. Peter, James and the twins were tasked with quietly spreading the word around the base, floating the idea with all those who could be trusted to keep the secret and compiling a list of all those who were interested in coming along. We would discuss a plan for rounding them up when the time came later.

In the meantime, Marc, Lucien, Tommy and I sat back in the mind box and began planning how best to set up walls around the Woodward base. Marc used the Hero Crystal to create a model of the layout of the base, which he set down on the floor in front of us so that we could examine it. It would have been simple if the shape had been symmetrical, but it wasn't. Much of it was flat, though certain places stuck up higher than others, while others jutted downwards. Of course, our living quarters, which was some nine storeys high on the inside, rose much higher than the rest of the base.

"Okay, so cutting it in half isn't gonna work," said Marc resignedly. "That's fine. What we can do instead is block off sections of it. I'm thinking we put one along here for a start."

He indicated the wall—the real wall—that separated the living quarters from the rest of the base, the one that had been like a jail door in recent weeks.

"If we can keep him out of the living quarters while we work on him, he won't get a chance to hurt any innocents in retaliation," Marc went on.

"What if he turns out to be in the living quarters all along?" Lucien asked.

"We'll have to divide it into sections," said Marc. "That should be easy. It'll be harder to direct him in there with a lot more people around, but nothing we can do about it if he does turn out to be in there. I also wanna put a wall here." He indicated the spot which linked the living quarters to the meeting hall and outdoor field magically created for our benefit. "I don't know what'll happen if he goes into one of those areas that's shrunken compared to the rest of the base and I'd rather not find out. That also means putting walls around the sides of the prison yard, on the outside of that box you created, John. We ought to cover this wall here"—he indicated the usual entrance point—"just in case, and of course, we have to block off the Woodward and Fletcher living quarters, because we don't know what they've got in there he could take advantage of. As for the rest of the base, I'm thinking we just line our walls along the real walls."

"Floors and ceiling too?" Tommy enquired.

"Er," Marc faltered, considering. "In the living quarters, yes, but the rest of the base looks to be single storey by comparison; I don't think it'll matter too much. He won't be able to go through the floor or roof in most of these places because of the walls we put on the outside."

"If you think the exit is worth doing, what about the second floor rooms?" I asked.

"Yep, we block as much of that off as possible too," said Marc. "Course, that could be pointless, what with the walls on the outside, like I just said, but you can never be too safe."

"One last thing to consider, Marc," said Lucien quietly. "Once the walls are up, what's your next move? How do you determine where you have trapped him? How do you determine if he is active or not?"

"I've thought about that," said Marc. "I don't think there is any way to know for certain. I'll send my own mind out and see if I can see him, but I'm not too hopeful that will work. If it doesn't, I'll see if the crystal can't tell me directly where he is and what he's doing. If it can't, I'll consider going outside and calling Fewul. I'm thinking it might be a good idea to do that anyway but only when I know it's safe to."

"Okay," said Lucien, checking his watch. "It's gonna be lunchtime really soon, so I suggest we all grab something to eat and then set to work around half past one this afternoon. Is that okay with everyone else?"

It was, so we left the mind box and descended to the bottom floor to see what was happening in the lounge room. We had barely glimpsed the people within when, most unluckily, Mum caught sight of me. She had been on the first floor landing, watching people moving in and out of the lounge room below, clearly on the lookout to see where I was. When she called out to me, I waved cheerily at her before following Marc, Tommy and Lucien into the lounge room. It wasn't enough to stop her, of course; she appeared in the doorway a minute later, so that all those seated in the lounge room (about a dozen people, including Katie, Sophie, Erica, Lena and Siobhan) all got to enjoy the spectacle to follow.

"Where have you been all morning?" she snarled at me. "I have been looking for you everywhere, and I'm betting you haven't got any work done, have you?"

"I've been working very hard," I said wearily, "and before you get on your high horse, lunch starts in fifteen minutes, so I'm not getting started on anything now."

"Rubbish. You can go upstairs right now and get cracking. There's no reason why you need to have lunch in fifteen minutes; I can bring something up for you later."

"Yeah, I don't think I'm gonna be doing that."

There was a brief silence in which Mum swelled ominously, and I distinctly heard Katie mutter to Sophie, "Mumzilla."

"You are *not*," Mum finally breathed in a low, cold voice that was far worse than her shouts, "going to sit around down here, wasting time and causing trouble, while there are much more productive things that you could—"

"Productive, my foot," I said dismissively. "That homework is even more useless than the crap we were getting in real school. Where are James and Peter? Did you send them up there too?"

"I found them twenty minutes ago," she huffed. "They thought they could avoid me, but they could not and neither can you. Now get going, young man, before I have to really come down on you."

They were empty words, I knew, and didn't bother me in the slightest. I had enough room in my mind to be mildly embarrassed to have this episode displayed so publically, but I could sense that far from being entertained, most of the people around me looked sympathetic and slightly frustrated. What worried me far more was that if Peter and James really had been sent upstairs, where they would now be seething like no one's business, that cut the hunting party in half, but it could be even worse than that.

"What about Harry and Simon?" I asked her. "I suppose their grandparents have sent them upstairs to study too?"

"How is it any of our business what the Maivises do!" she screamed at me, and several people flinched. "What matters to me is what you're doing, and more importantly, what you're *not* doing! If you don't get up right now, I will drag you up."

"Have they?" I asked, looking over at Katie and Sophie now, and they both nodded.

I looked back at Mum, my mind now made up. "Mr. Woodward gave us a job to do this afternoon, and Peter and James are involved. If you don't let them come down to help, you'll be putting the whole base at risk of attack. You saw what happened last night; do you want even worse stuff to happen, all for the sake of doing some pointless homework?"

I felt slightly stunned. That was a great speech, even by my standards. The idea had been there but I'd never expected the delivery to be so effective. I glanced sideways at Marc, who winked at me. He had a hand in his pocket, around the crystal which lay there, and I understood what had enabled me. Mum, meanwhile, had gone very pale.

"Frederic Woodward would never entrust protective duties to Peter and James, or you, for that matter," she finally managed to snap at me. "You boys can do what you like, as far as I'm concerned," she said to Marc, Tommy and Lucien, "but you, John, are not getting involved. If Frederic has a problem with that, I'll deal with him myself. Now, unless you want things to get much worse for you—"

"That's the third time you've said that," I said wearily, putting my head back in my seat and closing my eyes. "I said I'm not going anywhere and you're not scaring me into doing so."

Another silence followed and I was forced to open my eyes to see the reaction. Mum's face was red with rage, a not-unfamiliar sight, and her eyes were blazing. I shook my head wearily.

"Not…going," I repeated firmly, meeting her eyes and staring her down.

Six months ago, I wouldn't have been capable of meeting Mum's eyes in a situation like this, but I had changed since then. Mum now saw the change and she took a step backward, disconcerted.

"Is that so?" she said coldly. "Fine, young man. You make this bed, you lie in it, but you haven't heard the last of this."

"I bet I haven't," I muttered to myself as she turned on her heel and stormed away, probably heading for the stairs. I supposed she was heading back to where James and Peter were imprisoned and would probably take it out on them. I felt sorry for that, but not for what I had done; I was sick and tired of being told by my mother what to do.

"Nicely played, John," said Tommy, leaning around Marc and patting me on the back. "We shall make this day, June the 29th, 'stand up to your crazy mothers day'."

Everyone in the room laughed and a few began clapping and cheering. Under cover of the hubbub, I leaned into Marc and Tommy and whispered, "They couldn't have spread the word; we'll have to do it."

They both nodded agreement. I looked carefully around the room, taking note of everyone present: Katie, Sophie, Erica, Siobhan, Lena, Liam and Darcy were all okay. As for the others: Rebecca Fletcher, Candice Young, Jason Pont (Lisa's younger brother), George Tuck (Lena's younger brother) and his girlfriend Belinda, Robyn Lloyd (a fellow year nine student who had been here since the battle of Chopville High), Dean Abbodi and his sister Joanne, and Della Rockson (the late David Rockson's older sister). Most of them I didn't know all that well, any better than I had known Tulip prior to the first Chopville High battle in fact, but I thought that they could probably all be trusted.

"You gonna bring 'em all in?" Tommy asked Marc and me.

"Might as well," said Marc, getting to his feet. "You three get started while I stand guard outside."

"One of you two had better do it," Lucien hissed at Tommy and me. "Some of these people still don't quite trust me after the business a couple of months ago."

"They don't really trust me either," I pointed out, "after I lost the crystal. Tommy, looks like you're up."

"You guys suck," Tommy muttered, but he was grinning.

Most of the group had once again descended into several smaller conversations, but when Tommy called them to attention, they went quiet immediately. It seemed that many of them had sensed that something was going on. I was pleased by this.

"Can I have a show of hands, you guys," Tommy said, looking around the room, meeting all of their eyes, but not talking very loudly (quite a few people leaned forward in their seats to hear him better). "How many of you want this war to end?"

A few people raised their hands at once but most merely looked their confusion, and Liam said, "You're making us feel like we're back at school, mate."

"Just go along with me here, guys," Tommy said, "I'm getting to something. So hands up, who wants the war to end?"

Everyone put their hands up this time, and Lucien and I followed, for the sake of it. I looked around at them all again and saw that most of them were looking curious and excited.

"Good," said Tommy. "Now, keep your hands up if you want to be involved in making the war end."

They all kept their hands up, and Darcy said, "That's what we agreed to when we first came here, you know. If I'd known I'd be locked up like this, I probably would have rejected the offer."

"Okay," said Tommy. "Well, if you're all interested in helping us out, we've got a plan. It's not much yet, but it's more direct than what the Sorcerers have been doing. The only thing is, we'll be leaving the base to do it, and we're not taking any adults with us. None of them are allowed to know about it because they'll try to stop us from leaving. What happened a minute ago is proof of that. So, if you're not interested in keeping the secret and coming along with us, speak up now."

Nobody spoke. Nobody moved. All eyes were on Tommy, and Lucien and me, as we were sitting closest to him. Tommy allowed the silence to spiral for several moments before sighing.

"Good to know," said Tommy. "Now, Mr. Woodward's given us a job to do this afternoon that's not related, but later tonight, we plan on sneaking out while they can't stop us. We don't know exactly when it will be, or how we'll let you all know, but you should be ready for it any time. Remember, it's a secret, to be kept from anyone and everyone."

"Who else is coming?" asked Sophie.

"We three," Tommy said, "Marc, Peter, James, Harry and Simon. That's it for now, but there are others we'll catch up with later. They were supposed to do this before their crazy parents locked them up."

"What about the Sorcerers?" asked Erica. "Do they know about this?"

"No, and they won't know until we're gone and they can't stop us," said Tommy. "Natalie and Amelia may wanna come along, though, so we'll put the offer to them when we know they're in the base later tonight, but the rest of them? No, they can't know. So, is everyone up for this?"

Everyone was. The excitement in the room was palpable now.

"It'll be dangerous, won't it?" asked Lena.

"No more dangerous than going to their base in Germany was," Lucien told her.

"Won't we be living rough?" Katie asked. "Where will we sleep?"

"We'll have magic," I pointed out. "We'll be fine as far as that stuff goes."

"True, that," said Tommy. "So, those of you who have parents living in have to be really careful, but I suggest you all pack as much of your stuff as you can later this afternoon, because there won't be any notice before we have to leave."

Chapter 6: Ghostly Walls

It was an uncomfortable sort of afternoon. After we ate our lunch, Marc, Tommy, Lucien and I set to work on what, for security reasons, Marc had begun referring to as 'Operation Jezzball'. Lucien, Tommy and I were tasked with going around the rest of the base, separately, and following all the real walls and laying them over with ghostly walls. Marc assisted us in this by creating three magical keys, identical to those which the Woodwards used around the base, that could open any doors. He himself was to stay back in the living quarters, as it was the most open area, and use the Hero Crystal to access the higher rungs of the place so that he could create a grid of walls all over it.

"I know this is sort of cheating," he told us as he created a six-foot slab of wood for himself to stand on as he floated around the room, "but I don't think the Woodwards would mind too much if you used those keys. You're doing it for the right reason, after all."

"Don't you feel sort of exposed, doing this?" Tommy asked nervously. "I mean, once we get started, it'll be obvious what we're doing. We have no idea how much of this Hall is about to see; how much will be done when he decides to jump into action."

"That's all true," Lucien admitted, "but on the positive side, at least we'll know where he is if he decides to exercise his right of reply. That'll make the job much easier."

"You three go get started," Marc told us.

"One thing first," I said, nodding in the direction of the stairs.

"Oh right," he said, thinking hard. "Okay, here's what we'll do, and I hope you guys will forgive me for doing all the organising here. Tommy, you block off everything to the left of the door out of here, except the meeting hall; just block it off altogether, no need to go inside it. Lucien, you go the other way, in the direction of the Woodward and Fletcher living quarters, but don't worry about doing them; just focus on everything in between. John, you go find Peter and James and rescue them from your mother so they can get on with spreading the word, and if they can get Harry and Simon out too, all the better. Then you go block off your prison yard, and then do the Woodward and Fletcher living quarters. If you see Amelia and Natalie there, without their parents around, tell them what's going on. When you're all done out there, just wait outside for me to let you back in; I'll check every half-hour or so. Everyone got all that?"

We all nodded and set off, Tommy and Lucien for the wall to the corridor outside, Marc right behind them with his wall creating device out, and me for the stairs. As I ascended to the first floor, I took a moment to examine the devices for the first time. The key Marc had given me was identical to the one I'd once had to my third floor room, except of course, this one could open many more doors than that one had been able to. As for the wall-creating device, that had only one button and two toggle switches. The button, of course, would create the wall, and one of the switches had a letter on either side; 'H' to the left, and 'V' to the right. Horizontal and vertical walls, I supposed; that made sense, but I would have a better understanding of how it worked when I began using it. As for the other toggle switch, that had the letter 'C' to one side and the letter 'A' to the other; it was currently set to 'C'. I racked my brain but couldn't think what that could be for.

I walked right through one of those shiny ghostly walls in the doorway of the Playman family suite, but most unluckily, the wall, which was only slightly transparent, made it impossible for me to see clearly what was on the other side. I wasn't surprised to find Mum in there, sitting at the table, reading a book and looking extremely miffed, but I wasn't all too happy about it either. She glared when she saw me.

"If you haven't changed your mind about actually doing as you're told for a change, why have you come in here?" she asked coldly.

"Woodward business," I told her, holding up the devices I held in my hands so that she could see them clearly. "Marc may come in here later too, I don't know. Anyway, I need to get James and Peter to help me with something."

"Peter and James," she said even more coldly, "are on school business, as you should be. If you need their help with anything, young man, it would be how to listen to your mother."

I shook my head wearily and walked right past her. It cost a pang to do this, but the situation was far too great for me to be standing across the table from Mum, arguing the point about nothing. Perhaps she would be more forgiving after we had all left the base? Somehow, I doubted it. All the same, I was very glad that she decided not to follow me down the hallway to the study to listen; something I would have expected her to do any other time. She would probably be waiting to stop the three of us from leaving, I supposed, but I would deal with that later.

Peter and James were on the study floor when I knocked and opened the door, books spread out before them both and by the look of it, no work done whatsoever. I wasn't surprised to see that they looked pretty miffed too, but their faces brightened when they saw me.

"Oh no," Peter said in a tone of mock despair, "you have been captured and imprisoned too."

"Are you responsible for putting your mother in such a crappy mood?" James asked. "'Cause if you are, you owe us big-time, buddy."

I shrugged. "Yeah, put it on the tab. Anyway, I've come to get you two out of here, something you shouldn't have needed me to do, but we really need to get going with this thing. You'll be pleased to know we've already done some of your job for you, but there are a bunch we still haven't caught up with."

"Like whom?" James asked.

"Like your sisters, for two," I told him. "I have no idea where they are; maybe your mum locked them up too. Also, Harry and Simon's sisters; maybe they're locked up too."

"Who have you told?" Peter asked, getting slowly to his feet and cracking his joints.

"Katie, Sophie, Erica," I listed off, "Liam, Siobhan, Lena, Darcy, Rebecca and a bunch of others who were in the lounge room when we went down. They all agreed to come along."

"Okay," said James slowly, also getting to his feet. "Yeah, I can think of a few we still have to catch up with. What about the Sorcerers then? Natalie and Amelia?"

"Haven't seen them yet," I told them. "Don't worry about them for the time being; once I'm done here, I have to go down to their living quarters and put up a few walls. If I see them there, without their parents around, I'm supposed to tell them what's happening. I expect I'll find Amelia, if she's still too upset to go out, but Natalie probably won't get back for a few hours yet, so I'll have to deal with her later."

"Great," said Peter. "So, let's get to it then."

"Watch out for the parents," I hissed as the three of us left the study and proceeded down the hallway. "I imagine quite a few of them aren't in very good moods."

Mine certainly wasn't. Mum glared at the three of us as we approached, but James said quickly, "We've done ninety minutes without a break; we're due, Mrs. Playman. You can understand how the mind gets a little strained after a lot of work, can't you?"

"Do you have any intention of doing any more work this afternoon?" she asked Peter, ignoring James.

Peter shrugged. "Guess so. I only plan on doing what John needs us for and then getting something to eat. I suppose once that's done, I can do a little more."

"Are you an undertaker?" James asked. "Because I think you've just booked your own funeral."

Mum stared at him for several seconds before nodding. "Fine, but you had better, mister, or you'll be doing eight hours straight tomorrow. Understand?"

"Capisce," Peter agreed.

With much relief, the three of us left the family suite. The first thing I noticed was the increased brightness in the hall outside, and it only took a moment to identify its source. The far wall in front of us, as well as the one to our right (the corridor wall) had been completely covered by shiny ghost walls. They were completely smooth and stretched all the way from floor to ceiling, and all the way from one side of the hall to the other. They were so bright that I had to squint in order to look at them. Beside me, Peter and James didn't notice a thing.

"What's up with you?" Peter asked me.

"Those walls are so bright," I muttered, choosing to look at the floor instead.

"What?" Peter asked, glancing at James in confusion.

"Ghost walls?" James asked me, and when I nodded, he grinned. "Well, you can see them. Good for you."

"You can't?" I said, looking up at him, before understanding properly what was going on. "No, you couldn't, because you can't see ghosts. Lucky you; they're very bright."

"But you can sort of see through them too, can't you?" Peter asked me.

"Yeah, but not a lot," I admitted. "I mean, they're only covering walls so far, and they're a fair way away. They look more solid from this distance."

While we had been talking, Marc had erected another wall, this time to our far left, along the wall at the very end of the hall, not far from the resident gym. It added to the brightness in the place. Knowing that he would be putting up more and more of them before too long, I knew I had to get out of here quickly.

"You two get to it," I told Peter and James, nodding down toward the rest of the family suites.

I hurried away from them, down the stairs and towards the wall to the corridor, but stopped short when I realised that as great as this key was, it couldn't get me through this wall anymore than I could get through with my bare hands. I therefore squinted around the hall for Marc, and saw that he was beginning to isolate the gym from the rest of the living quarters. I took off at a run and reached him in about twenty seconds.

"What's up with you?" he asked me in surprise.

"Need a hand getting out," I told him, "but I think we've got another problem as well."

"What? What's happened?"

"These walls are really bright," I explained. "I'm the only one who can see them, and they're really bright for me. I'm not sure I'll be able to cope too well once you've put them all up and the place is glowing with them."

"Oh," he said, stopping short and considering the issue. "Never thought of something like that. I tell you what, you just worry about what you've gotta do for now; we'll try to work out something about this later."

We continued to the wall, where he assisted me through to the other side. The corridor was empty (Tommy and Lucien had obviously moved off into rooms on the side) but I could see that they had been here not too long ago. This place was even brighter than the living quarters had been, because not only did the silver walls cover both walls of the corridor, all the way to both ends, but they were much closer together than the ones in the living quarters had been. It was positively dazzling. I thought back to the ghosts I'd seen in the past, Hal and Pol Maivis, and my mother, and couldn't remember any of them glowing this brightly. Was it because the ambiance of the chambers in which we had been on Rock Haulter had been so different from this? Or was it because these walls were, apparently, a more solid ghostly substance than they had been? That last one didn't entirely make sense, and at the same time it did. I didn't know; all I did know was that I didn't like what was confronting me this afternoon and evening. The sooner we got out of the base, the happier I would be.

Well, first things first, I thought.

"We need to get through here," I said, indicating the wall directly opposite us, "but you need to make it so that we bypass the enchantment I put there that's supposed to take us into the prison yard. We only wanna go through to the other side of this wall."

"Sure thing," said Marc, moving forward and putting his free hand on the wall. As it made contact with the silvery wall that coated the far more solid one beneath, his hand glowed slightly, making him look almost ghostly himself.

I grabbed onto his arm and we went through the wall. It worked as I'd hoped it would. What we found on the other side was greatly relieving; the prison block was much darker than the corridor had been, with no silvery walls in sight. The corridor was lit, as all parts of the base were, but it had the feel of a place that hadn't been used for quite some time. It was silent as the grave and the cells, which all stood open to my left, were all empty. The box containing the prison yard was stuck to the ceiling in the corner above the doorway where I had put it. As I looked at it, I thought that the best way to deal with it would be to separate it from the walls around it, then coat it with ghost-proof walls before re-attaching it. I explained this plan to Marc, and he nodded in agreement.

"That's much the same as what I did on the outside with Mr. Woodward," he told me. "That'll make sure he can't go through any walls to get around the enchantment. Are you sure it won't break any enchantments if I separate it?"

"Fairly sure, but just to be certain, maybe you should ask the crystal not to break any enchantments on it when you separate it."

"Always the simplest way to get stuff done."

The box detached itself and floated down so that it hovered a few feet in front of me. I raised the wall-creating device in my right hand, checked to make sure it was set to vertical, pointed it at the box, and pushed the button. A bright jet of light shot from the thing, but the moment it hit the box, the jet itself vanished. White stuff spread over the side which had been hit, much as thicky prison spread over anything it got hold of, but unlike thicky prison, this stuff was more silvery, slightly transparent and, most importantly, stopped when it reached the sides of the box. Thicky prison would have wrapped the entire box but these devices only did one side at a time.

Marc rotated the prison yard for me so that I was able to cover the other three sides. I then switched to horizontal and shot at the box from below; this time, it spread across the bottom of the box, so that now the floor was ghost-proofed too. Marc lowered the box so that I could do the same for the top of the box before raising it back into the air and re-attaching it to the ceiling where it had been before we had come.

"A job well done," he said, taking hold of my arm and marching me back through the wall and into the dazzling corridor outside. "I'll get back to doing the living quarters; you get going down to the Woodwards' and Fletchers', and remember what I said earlier: When you're done, just come back here and wait for me. I'll check every now-and-then."

"Righto," I said, and after patting each other on the shoulders, we set off in different directions; him through the other wall, me down the corridor towards the Sorcerers' living quarters.

It didn't take long before the brightness of the place was too much for me to handle. I squinted my eyes almost shut and used the wall to my left to feel my way along the corridor, moving more slowly than I would have under normal circumstances. I started every time my hand went over something different from the bare wall, whether it be a doorframe, a picture frame or a vent. Eventually, though, I reached the end of the corridor where once again I was afforded some relief by the relative dimness. The corridor here ended in a T-shape with the Woodwards living on the left and the Fletchers on the right.

It was clear that Lucien had obeyed orders not to come down this far because the long side of the T, as well as both short sides, was not coated with ghost-proofed walls. I therefore withdrew the device, which I had pocketed while walking, switched it to vertical, and shot at all three walls as well as the two doors at either end of the T. I also, reluctantly, coated the ceiling and floor of the corridor; I had no idea how far it would spread, but I figured the only person who would be hurt by this extra precaution would be me, because it would make the whole place even brighter. On that score, I was only too correct.

I decided to start with the Woodwards, as I would be more likely to find a Sorcerer in there, and better explaining myself to one of them as opposed to Natalie's mother, who probably wouldn't have a clue what was going on. I pocketed the wall-creating device, withdrew the key and using my free hand, felt my way almost blindly down toward the door to the Woodward living quarters. Finding it, I fumbled the key into the slot, felt it click, quickly withdrew it and pulled the door open. It was bliss to be able to get inside and shut the thing behind me, cutting off that almost unbearable glare, even though I knew the relief would be short-lived; after all, my job was to effectively make this place as uncomfortable for myself as possible.

Once I had allowed myself to enjoy the relief for several seconds, I became aware that there was someone nearby; I could hear noises in a not-too-distant room. I looked around and became aware that the noises were coming from Mr. Woodward's study. Good, I thought, because there was only one person likely to be in there. The door itself was closed, though, so he probably hadn't heard me come in. I therefore went to it and knocked.

"Come in," I heard his weary voice call from the other side.

"Just me," I said, sticking my head inside. He was sitting at his desk, a lot of paperwork spread before him and a laptop computer sitting behind all that. He looked busy, exhausted and, something else all at the same time...sad? I thought so.

"Ah yes, hello, John," he said, looking up at me. "What can I do for you?"

What a change, I thought. No asking what I was doing here? How I had got out of the living quarters, or how I could be so daring as to disobey the wishes of my parents. A second relief in less than a minute.

"Nothing right now," I said, showing him the key Marc had created. "That's how I got in, by the way; Marc created them for me, Tommy and Lucien so we could set up walls around the base. I'm doing the ones in here and the Fletcher living quarters. Is that okay?"

"No worries," he replied. "I suppose you'll only need to trail around the outside, but you just do as much as you need to."

I took a moment to look around the study, then back into the corridor. Once I was sure there was no one around but us two, I said, "Is Amelia anywhere? Or have you sent her back out?"

"She's probably in her bedroom," he said. "You can go see her if you like, but I can't predict what state she'll be in. We haven't seen much of each other today. If she's doing better, maybe she can help you; she knows this place, after all."

"That's not such a bad idea," I said hopefully, not sure whether Amelia really would be up to that, but hopeful all the same. "I'll get to it then; shouldn't be more than ten minutes, hopefully."

I began by spraying all the walls of the study, plus the ceiling and floor, plus the back of the door, before closing it behind me. What I hadn't predicted was that the silvery substance was also spreading over the floor out here, clearly having gone under the door. The same didn't hold true for the ceiling though, and that was a relief. I therefore cast my eyes upwards as I began spraying all the walls and doors around me, covering the hallway, lounge room, kitchen and dining room before moving on to the hallway where I knew the bedrooms were.

Amelia's bedroom door was shut but the one opposite it, which belonged to her grandmother, was open. I therefore covered the inside of that, as well as the walls along both sides of the corridor, before moving on. Most of the doors in the hallway were shut, apart from the next one down belonging to Mr. Woodward. I also covered his room, and the laundry, which was the next one down. At the very end was the bathroom and toilet; I knocked on both doors, not wanting to open the door to the possibility of finding someone doing something in there, but fortunately they were both empty. I covered them both before moving back down the corridor to Amelia's room and knocking on her door, slightly nervous about seeing her again but comforted by the knowledge that I had been in this room on a few occasions before.

"Yeah?" I heard her call from the other side of it. How did she sound, I wondered? She wasn't crying, I thought, for which I was greatly relieved. She almost sounded sleepy, and I had to wonder if I had woken her up.

I took a deep breath, opened the door about halfway and looked in. "Hey, it's me," I said. "Can I come in?"

She was sitting cross-legged on her bed, leaning back against her headboard, listening to music on a small radio beside her bed and apparently doing something strange with her magic. Bright little lights appeared to be circling her head, dipping and diving and spiralling. It was mesmerising for a second, but a moment after she broke her concentration to look at me, they disappeared. She wasn't crying, I could confirm, but unfortunately that shell I had observed the previous night was still there. If anything, it was even tougher now than it had been before. She clearly was distraught, and was dealing with it the way she had become most familiar with over the last month.

"Hey," she said, clearly surprised to see me. "What are you doing here? This makes three times in twenty-four hours; has someone lost their mind?"

I needed only a moment to decide not to respond to that remark. Instead I said, "Your dad knows I'm here; it's sort of on his orders, actually. Can I come in?"

"Sure," she said flatly.

I pushed the door open the rest of the way, entered, shut it behind me, and shot a ghostly wall at it. The floor was done in here just like everywhere else , so I covered the four walls and the wardrobe door instead. The place became as dazzlingly bright as everywhere else, but I was amazed at the effect it had on Amelia. She didn't see it any more than Peter and James had, but it seemed to make her glow with amazing brilliance. Add to that the fact that her long, blonde hair was rather messier than it would be had she maintained herself as she normally would... there was only one thing for it; she looked like an angel.

"Er, what are you doing?" she asked dully, staring at the device in my hand as I approached her wardrobe.

"Protecting the joint," I said, stopping short of the door. "Er, is it okay if I check in here for a moment?"

"The wardrobe?" she said, raising her eyebrows. "I never dreamt you'd be asking to see what's in my wardrobe."

"Not being creepy, I swear," I said, feeling my face flush.

"I believe you," she said, and I saw her grin for the first time. A promising sight, I thought, my own spirits lifting slightly. "So you wanna explain exactly what's going on?"

"All part of a plan to get Hall out of the base," I told her. "He can go through walls as it is, so we're coating all the walls around the base with a substance he won't be able to go through. Once we've got him cornered, Marc's gonna shepherd him out."

"Wow," she said, looking impressed. "That's not a bad plan. Whose idea was that?"

"Mostly Lucien's, but we all chipped in, really," I told her. "So, can I put this stuff in your wardrobe? Just in case he tries to get in your room through there?"

"I don't imagine he could do much in there, unless he wants to take possession of one of my bras or something," she said, "but sure, do what you gotta do."

That last remark made me rather self-conscious indeed, but as it turned out, there were no bras in sight when I opened the door. I covered the walls inside, plus the top, bottom and front of the shelf on top, before stepping back out and shutting the door behind me, relieved to get that part of the episode over with. Of course, I'd done the same in the other bedrooms, but as their occupants hadn't been there to see it, it hadn't been nearly as awkward. Amelia had been watching me the whole time, smiling slightly, though as I looked back at her, I could tell that she was still holding her emotions back. She still hadn't returned to the Amelia I had come to care for so much a couple of months ago.

"That it?" she asked me.

"For the wardrobe, yeah," I said, approaching the bed and sitting down on the end of it, a good few feet away from her; I would only close that distance if she indicated it was okay to do so. "Listen, can I talk to you about something?"

She didn't answer for several seconds, during which time her lips trembled as she fought to keep her emotions in check. Finally she managed to say, in an admirably steady voice, "What on earth happened last night anyway?"

My stomach dropped; that hadn't been what I'd wanted to talk about, and once again my vision was haunted by the memory of Serena dropping to the floor in front of me as Marc removed Hall's influence over her body. Now that she had mentioned it, however, I knew I had no choice but to get through this before getting to what I needed to tell her.

"Hall," I said flatly. "He knew he had no way to get to us just by possessing people, so he dug them up and reanimated their bodies. He wasn't trying to hurt anyone"—I didn't mention the strangling part—"it was just his way of torturing us."

"He's so mean," she said, raising her knees and locking her arms around them. "He's so mean. I wish he would just quit. It's bad enough with Hammerson out there, and all the killing and torturing and blackmailing and raping—"

She stopped dead, her face going very pale. This was getting worse and worse.

"Hey, don't do that," I said quickly, abandoning my decision of less than a minute ago and scooting up the bed so that I could be beside her. She was now rocking back and forth on the bed, her eyes wide and horrified as she clearly recalled what horror she had been through at the hands of Ather Hignat and Ugine Wilwog.

"We see so much out there," she said, rocking faster now, her voice little more than a squeak. "I dunno how much you know about what happens out there, but it's horrible—just horrible. And now this—this—"

"Stop thinking about it," I said firmly, taking her hands and prising them away from her knees. She allowed me to do this, but it certainly required some effort on my part.

Amelia shook her head and went on, her voice getting progressively higher and faster all the time. "Do you know they've started taking people's kids away from them to keep them in line? It's all blackmail, and in fact they have no intention of giving them back; they're indoctrinating them all, turning them into Hammerhearts. If they go back to their parents, they'll be more like spies than anything else. Some of them get hurt really badly, others get—get taken advantage of by creepy—"

My stomach was falling further with every word she said. I wasn't surprised by any of it (this was war, after all) but I was alarmed by how much of it she (and the other Sorcerers, presumably) had been exposed to. I was still holding her wrists in my hands but that appeared to have had no impact at all. I therefore did the only thing I could think of; I let them go and put my arms around her instead, pulling her towards me so that she could lean on me. It broke off her dialogue, which was good, but she was still trembling worse than ever.

"Stop it," I said firmly, almost harshly. "Stop saying stuff like that, Amelia. You're making it worse for yourself."

That was partially true; if anything, she was making it worse for me, making it more difficult to keep my mind on what I needed to tell her. I knew it would be much better for her to let all of this out somehow, but now wasn't the time. Perhaps tomorrow, just twenty-four hours from now...

"We try to save them," she squeaked, and now she was on the verge of tears, "we try to save them, but for every one we save, they kill two more. For every child we take back to their parents, they abduct a woman and—and—"

I squeezed her hard, almost painfully, and this time it did the trick. She went quiet and began sobbing against me, and although it wasn't comfortable by any stretch of the imagination, it was better than the horrors she was putting me through. I knew all this stuff must be happening out there, far more than what the almost entirely Hammerheart-controlled media was reporting, but to hear it like this was just horrible. I reminded myself that Natalie would have seen all this too, that she would be holding all this in too. In the relative silence, I had a moment, before I spoke again, to register that the little radio beside Amelia's bed was playing Lady Gaga's 'Bad Romance'; totally inappropriate for the moment.

"Listen to me, Amelia," I told her quietly, holding her tightly, wishing I could enjoy the closeness of this situation, as I would have done a couple of months ago. "All that stuff may be happening, but it may be possible to stop a lot of it, and there's no reason why you ever need to see it again. Does that sound good?"

The trembling didn't stop entirely but it did lessen enough that she was able to pull back slightly so that she could see my face. There were tears in her eyes but seeing them there made me feel a touch of relief; the shell was beginning to crack, and there were traces of the old Amelia poking through. "What are you talking about?" she choked.

"I mean we've got a plan," I told her. "Not your father's plan; this one's strictly ours, and none of the adults know about it. It's thin, but unlike the stuff you've been forced to do, it goes right to the root of the problem. You don't have to help us with it if you don't want; if you wanna stay with your family then that's fine, but we would love to have you and Natalie come along for it."

"What plan?" she asked. "How can you have a plan?"

I shook my head. "Won't say too much just yet, but you'll know if you come along. We're leaving here sometime tonight, basically the Young Army—or what's left of it. We're gonna hide ourselves and go after Hammerson directly."

She also shook her head. "If you do that, my dad will just track you down and bring you back. He'll have to because your parents would make him."

"He won't be able to find us," I said firmly. "He gave Marc the Hero Crystal back so that he could help protect the base from Hall; Marc will make sure we're all properly hidden.

Lucien's got ideas about how he can do that, and if you wanna come along, you can help too."

"But they'll be so worried——"

"Yeah, but once we're gone, they'll have no choice but to accept it," I told her. "We can make a phone call or send an email or something to let them know, once it's too late to stop us, but we can't give them a chance. You know what they're like…"

She nodded and rested her head on my shoulder, sighing. "If you know what you can do, I'm up for it. I'm sick of things going the way they have been; we're doing our best and making no difference at all. This thing will just go on for years and by the time we get anywhere, it'll be too late to turn it all around. I think it may already be too late in some parts of the world."

"Good," I said, feeling as though a weight had come off my shoulders. "We may leave sometime later today but we don't know exactly when, so you'd better make sure you're ready to go at any moment."

"How long has this plan been in the works?"

"Since about five hours ago. Peter suggested it yesterday but now it's taking proper shape, particularly after what happened last night, both at dinner and in the night. This place just isn't safe anymore."

"Does Natalie know about it yet?"

"No. She's been out all day—I think, anyway—so we haven't had a chance to tell her."

"I can tell her now, if you like," Amelia said, and I felt my own eyes widen.

"You mean telepathically?" I asked, and when I felt her shrug, went on, "But what if she's with her father and he gets some of it?"

"He wouldn't; I've been doing this for years," she said, leaning back so that I could once again see her face. There were still tears in her eyes, but now she wiped them away. "She just has to keep it to herself and not tell anyone that I've contacted her."

"If she does before she gets the message, tell her to tell whoever she's with that we're busy protecting the place against Hall, and that was why you called."

"Good idea."

We both went quiet for several moments. I watched Amelia as she closed her eyes and went still, concentrating on the communication she was making. I examined her while she couldn't see me, and felt pleased with what I was seeing. With or without the glow of the ghostly walls around the room, she still looked very good, even after she'd been crying and hadn't done her hair or anything. What was more pleasing to me was that I was able to appreciate that, after having several weeks of appreciating nothing about girls at all, after having that part of me knocked out in the wake of losing Serena so suddenly. In that time, I'd gone from being quite popular with several girls to being entirely unwanted, at least to those around me. Whether Natalie or Amelia were still interested, I knew not. Lena had been interested at first, as I had known well and good, but after I had retreated into myself, she had turned her attention to Marc instead, and they had since begun dating. Perhaps if this continued, I may be able to move on from Serena properly very soon, as Peter had done from Kylie in the last few weeks by entering tentatively into a relationship with Siobhan (although last night may have been a setback for him). The question for me was whether it would be with Natalie or Amelia....

It took another half-hour after that meeting with Amelia to finish the job. After she had communicated the message to Natalie, who had agreed emphatically with the idea (Amelia's words), the two of us set off around those parts of the Woodward living quarters that I hadn't yet covered, me coating them with ghostly walls as I went. I had seen some of these parts before, during my mental rummaging in Sebastian's mind as I uncovered all his misdeeds, but this was the first time I'd seen them firsthand, and I saw many that he himself hadn't seen. Amelia may not have ever used these hiding places before, but she sure knew about them.

Amelia also accompanied me over to the Fletcher living quarters, which were a mirror image of the Woodward living quarters, but without all the special hiding places. Having her with me here was a good thing because Natalie's mother, who might have tried to stop me if I'd been on my own, instead allowed us straight in to do pretty much whatever we needed. We didn't talk much during this time, and when we did talk it was always about what I was doing, about the job at hand, but I couldn't deny to myself that I felt glad to have her by my side, and not just because she was assisting me in finding my way around. The more of these walls I erected, the more they seemed to dazzle me.

She assisted me back to my living quarters, where we found Lucien waiting for us, leaning against the enchanted door to the prison yard and staring at the wall opposite him, the one he needed to go through.

"It went okay for you then?" I asked him.

"Yeah, no trouble," he said, smiling slightly. "I don't think I missed any spots; at least, I hope I didn't. How are you, Amelia?"

"I'm okay," she said, shrugging. "I can help you guys through here, if you like, but I won't stay; I haven't had a shower today and I feel like I need one. I might catch up with you when I'm done with that, if I'm allowed to—or if I'm not," she added, smiling slightly.

"Do I take it from that, that you're in with us?" Lucien asked.

"In every way," she said, holding out her hands to us. "Come on, then."

The three of us went through the wall into the living quarters, where I found I was unable to see a thing. It looked as though every single surface in the place was now blindingly bright, but it was more than that. Not only were the surfaces coated, but there seemed to be more ghostly walls throughout the hall itself, stretching from floor to ceiling several metres apart, with yet more walls stretching across at intervals of a few metres. Marc had apparently taken it into his head to turn the whole hall into a three dimensional grid, further isolating any spot where Hall could be trapped. I looked at the wall creating device in my hand and took note of the other toggle switch, the one that was set to C; now I thought I understood what would happen if I switched it to A.

Perhaps it was a good thing over all—it could only help Marc—but it certainly didn't help me. I'd had enough trouble seeing before, but now I couldn't see a thing. Just about everything around me, other than Lucien and Amelia, had become almost completely invisible. Each wall was transparent, but when you put so many of them together, they eventually added up to a substance that was almost opaque. Worst of all, though, it was so bright that I had to quickly close my eyes to stop them from practically falling out.

"Too bright for you?" Amelia asked me.

"Way too bright; I can't see a thing through it all."

"I'll help you out," said Lucien, grabbing onto one of my elbows. "We'll go in the lounge room; maybe there'll be fewer walls in there."

"I'll hopefully be back with you in less than an hour," Amelia told us, and she turned and disappeared through the wall back into the corridor.

Lucien marched me (practically dragged me) forward into the hall. I kept my eyes shut the whole time but it was a scary feeling indeed, and on several occasions I found myself pulling back, wanting to slow him down. Eventually, though, I heard the noises around us change as walls (solid walls) closed in around me. I opened my eyes and saw that we had entered the lounge room, which was still very bright, but only as bright as the corridor and the Woodward and Fletcher living quarters had been. The walls were all coated, but there were no ghostly walls hanging in the air across the room to obstruct my vision any further. Many of the same people who'd been in the lounge room before lunch were still there now, and there were several more with them, including all three Thomases, Peter and all four Maivis twins. Marc was absent, but that was okay; he was probably still busy putting up walls throughout all the bedrooms.

"Good day to you, blind Freddy," said Harry, beaming at me. "How be you today, good sir?"

I shrugged wearily. "I'm seeing bright lights and listening to a lunatic. How do you reckon I'm doing?"

"Did you get it done?" Peter asked as Lucien and I took seats on a free couch.

"It's done," I told them. "At least, our part is. Tommy still hadn't got back when Amelia let us through, and it looks like Marc's not done either. Have you guys seen him?"

"Yeah, but not in here," said James. "He's been zipping around, and perhaps if you were with him, you could tell us he was working hard, but of course, we can't see the result of it."

I shrugged. "Consider yourselves better off. Have you done your part of it?"

"Spoken to everyone worth speaking to," Simon said solemnly. "They all say hurray, hurrah."

"Except Natalie and Amelia," said James. "Have you?"

"They're both in," I told them. "Natalie wasn't here but Amelia told her telepathically and she's all for it. So, I guess we just wait till Marc and Tommy get back in here, then we see what we can do."

"That sounds like the best way to do it," Lucien agreed. "It would be a good idea if all the Sorcerers are in, though, so perhaps Marc should contact Mr. Woodward and ask him to come here and call for the others to return. Once they're all here, he can probably use the crystal to identify where Hall is in the base. Once we know, we can begin working against him. It's"—he checked his watch—"almost three o'clock now, so we've only got a couple of hours before he'll knock off work. Hopefully they don't take too long, because if he's ready before we are, it won't be a good thing for us."

Chapter 7: Deathtrap

The following hour was very nerve-racking indeed. Amelia joined us about forty-five minutes into it, joined by an exhausted Tommy, who sat down beside us and began complaining immediately about how he'd had to wait for half an hour for Marc to turn up, only to get Amelia instead. She, meanwhile, had been accosted by the many teenagers who hadn't seen her in over a month and wanted to know how she was and what was going on on the outside. She held up fairly well under the torrent of questioning, although I caught her eye on a few occasions and knew that she would have been much happier not having to speak about such things again. Other than that, we just sat around talking and waiting.

Finally, at around four o'clock in the afternoon, Marc joined us. He too was exhausted, but pleased with the work he'd done.

"I've probably done more than I needed to," he told us, sinking into the seat beside Tommy, "but that can only be a good thing for us. I didn't go into the bedrooms, but I coated all along the outsides of them, so if he is in any of them, he won't be able to get out. More importantly though, if he's on the outside of them, where I expect him to be, he won't be able to get in and possess anyone in them. You do realise that is the one thing that will thwart our whole plan, if he does that? We have to make sure we trap him somewhere where he won't have anyone to possess, that way he won't have any physical form to break through the ghost walls."

"I think we'd better get to work," Lucien told us, checking his watch again. "I can't tell you how jumpy I'm getting just sitting here, knowing something's coming and having no idea when or what it'll be."

"Now you know how we felt when you made us sit beneath that trapdoor, remember?" Peter told him, and Lucien smiled weakly.

"Ah, that was such a long time ago," he said, shaking his head sadly. "Amelia, can you contact your father and let him know that we're getting started in here? Also ask him to send for the other Sorcerers; hopefully they won't be too busy to join us, because we don't know how dangerous this is going to be. Marc, I'm not sure if you'll be able to do this, but give it a go anyway. See if you can get the crystal to tell you what part of the base Hall's mind is currently in. I know it won't show you if he's untraceable, but even if he's not, it might still give you an indication."

"I'll try," he said, taking the crystal from his pocket and examining it carefully. Beside me, Amelia had once again sunk into the concentration of telepathy.

"You raise an interesting question, Lucien," said James interestedly. "When a person does become untraceable, does the enchantment bind their body, their mind or both?"

Lucien considered the question before shrugging. "As to that, I have no idea. Body, yes, I'm fairly sure it does, since when Marc has used his minds-eye, he hasn't been able to identify an untraceable person even while he's been looking at them. As for the mind, though, that might be a different thing. When the mind separates from the body, does it leave any trace at all? I suppose it must, since John was able to see Hall's face in the shadows the other night, but then what does that mean for Marc? So many questions and unfortunately I have no idea about any of them."

"Don't beat yourself up over it, Lucien," James told him. "I was just wondering, that's all. Mr. Woodward said last night that they may still be able to track Hall down, even if he is untraceable, by being craftier than usual. Perhaps Marc can get the crystal to do the same; he's been using magic long enough to do that, I reckon."

"Okay, he's calling them back," Amelia told us. "According to him, they've had a very light day out there because apparently hardly any of the important Hammerhearts have turned up to work. Cornish is the only one who they could find, and even he's kept a low profile today. Hammerson himself has done nothing of note, and Hall reported in sick, so all sources they could find told."

"Yeah, right," said Peter, his eyes widening in alarm. "He might have slept in a little late, after what he did last night, but he's not sick. If anything, he's busy preparing to do something nasty to us tonight. God, if he hasn't been at work all day, he might have been watching us the whole time."

As soon as the words were out, I knew they had to be true; or if not, close to the truth. There had to be a reason why Hall, Hammerson and so many other important Hammerhearts had chosen to hide themselves today. What could that be? There was only one possible reason in my mind: Hall was preparing a massive assault on the Woodward base, and he would have assistance this time; people waiting on the outside to deal with everyone who fled from the place. This wasn't going to be good, but then Marc spoke, and his words added confusion to the sudden mix of fear.

"He's not here."

"What?" said several people.

"Not in the base," Marc repeated, looking around at us all, his eyes wide. "According to the crystal, he has returned to his body."

"So where is he now then?" Harry asked.

Marc shook his head. "The crystal couldn't tell me, because he's untraceable, but it could tell me that there were no ghosts in the base, nor were there any living bodiless minds in the base. I was very direct on that and got negatives both times."

"But if there are walls all over the base," said Amelia, "how could he have left? How could he have returned to his body?"

"We weren't entirely sure if he'd be able to do that," Marc admitted, "but I'm not surprised that he can. He wouldn't have needed to direct it; he only needed to yank the string that connected his mind to his body. It would have pulled him straight back in, bypassing all the walls in between. Again, I don't know for sure, but since he's not here, and that I do know for sure, I have to assume—"

His words were cut off by a dull thud from somewhere above and to our right. It wasn't loud, but it sounded heavy, and the walls and floor shook slightly with the impact.

"What the hell was that?" said Peter, jumping to his feet. All around, others had done the same, eyes wide and horrified.

Seconds later, another thud, this time much closer and louder. The walls shook and somewhere in the distance, a crash resounded. This was followed by the clear sound of screaming from several floors above.

"Go check," I muttered to Amelia, and she dashed out into the main hall to get a better look at what was going on.

Next came shouting from the hall outside. I recognised Mr. Woodward's voice, along with Amelia's; they weren't in any danger, but I could still hear distant screaming, and the Sorcerers sounded panicked. In the time it took Amelia to return, three more thuds shook the room, one of which was very close. Something very bad was going on.

"There are bombs in here!" she shouted. "My God, there are bombs in——"

Another bomb went off in the distance, and now the place was beginning to collapse. Crashing sounds were coming more and more frequently as ceilings of bedrooms collapsed inwards and the weight on floors above increased. It hadn't reached the floor above this one yet, but there couldn't be much time.

"Everybody into the hall!" Amelia shouted at all the terrified teenagers, and none of us dared disobey. I grabbed onto Lucien's elbow as he took off, hurtling out into the blinding brightness.

People around me began screaming as they caught sight of whatever was happening above. I looked upward but couldn't distinguish anything but more brightness.

"What's going on?" I asked impatiently.

"We're under attack," Lucien said grimly. "How on earth did Hall manage to smuggle bombs in——"

"There are people up there!" a girl nearby shouted, but I couldn't see who it was.

Everyone around me looked further up, and judging by the gasps and exclamations around me, I knew it wasn't good. Yes, there were people up there, trapped and running out of ways to get down, but it sounded like there were more people further up, people who weren't trying to get down…people who shouldn't have been in the base at all….

"Marc, where the hell are you?" I shouted into the brightness. "Get rid of these bloody walls; they're serving no purpose now."

Marc appeared by my side a moment later. His face was panic-stricken.

"There are Hammerhearts in here," he said. "Hall's managed to get them in here; no wonder they had a light day. We have to go. Never mind shepherding Hall now; the whole place has been breached."

"But everybody's scattered, and I haven't even packed my—"

More screams sounded around us, and this time, people began pushing and shoving to get out of the way. Both Marc and Lucien looked up, and both swore in horror.

"What's going on!" I bellowed. "For God's sake, Marc, get rid of these bloody walls!"

Marc put his hand to his crystal, and a moment later, all the silvery ghost walls vanished with a dizzying pop. I blinked a couple of times, but it took several seconds for my eyes to adjust to the lack of brightness. As they did, I began to see all the horror unfolding around us.

The towering structure of bedrooms, which had always looked so neat and impressive, now seemed to be winking down at us. There were twitches here and there as rooms were collapsing, the weight of floors above weakening the structure of the next floor. So far, all the damage had been done on and above the fifth floor, but it wouldn't be long before the structure became so weak that the whole thing came down. Even as we stood there, more explosions could be heard, some further inside the structure, others in rooms we could see.

Every time a bomb went off, the building shook and part of it collapsed.

People were running all over the structure like little ants, many of them in fits of panic as they either tried to find a way down or tried to get to their bedrooms to save some of their possessions; a very bad idea, but nothing we could do about it now. There were people lined up along the top floor, though; they were wearing Hammerheart uniforms and none of them were masked. Clearly they had a plan for how to get down safely. I scanned the faces and saw that Hall wasn't among them, nor was Cornish, but Tom Hignat was there, as was (my heart sank at the sight of him) Arnold Hammerson himself. Whether or not this was Hall's plan or Hammerson's was something we would never know; nevertheless they were clearly going to flush us out now. There were maybe two dozen of them up there, but I was prepared to bet there would be many more waiting outside the base, ready to catch us when we fled.

But all that wasn't the scariest thing going on around us. There was something else in the room with us, a great blob of a thing that was zooming around in the air several storeys over our heads. It took on no exact shape, but it had eyes, and they were mean with intent. It was big, big enough to swallow any one of us whole, and as I found out a moment later, that was indeed its purpose. A year-eleven girl was hurrying along the fourth floor landing toward the stairs; as I watched, the thing swooped low over her head and inhaled. It made no physical contact with her, and yet her feet flew into the air as its intake sucked her upwards. It zoomed upward as it sucked her into the opening that resembled its mouth. A moment later, she had disappeared, and the thing was zooming out over our heads again, looking for its next victim.

The only good thing was that all six Sorcerers were now on the scene. Hammerson's presence had been registered and Mr. Woodward and Mr. Fletcher were engaging him in combat, even with all those floors between them. Alice Fletcher, Natalie's grandmother, was trying to organise and protect those milling in the hall, children and adults alike, while Lillian Woodward had gone up to the first, second, third and fourth floors to make sure there was nobody trapped in any of the rooms there. Under cover of all this, Marc, Lucien and I hurried to where Natalie and Amelia were attempting to assist people in the hall.

"We have to go," Marc told them, "now. We don't have any time to spare."

"How can we get out with all of this?" Amelia asked frantically.

"You two go ahead," Lucien told them. "One of you be ready to help people through the exit, but make sure only those coming with us get through. One of you also has to make sure there's nobody out there waiting for us, and to protect anyone who goes out. We'll meet up in the Stretch. Marc, you have to round everybody up who's coming with us, and try to do it discreetly."

"I haven't got any of my stuff ready," I told them.

"Neither have I," said Lucien, "but do you think that matters—"

"It could, if the Hammerhearts are able to search the place," Amelia pointed out. She clicked her fingers a couple of times, and a couple of doors above us burst open. To my amazement, everything I had intended to take with me came zooming out of my family suite and fell to the floor beside me, what little possessions Lucien had also dropping to the floor before us.

"I need help though," Marc told us. "How can I keep track of everyone—"

"I'll stay back with you," I told him and the others. "You three go, now. Marc, can you do what Amelia just did? 'Cause a lot of people are gonna need help—"

"I reckon I can."

Lucien and the two Sorcerers had already taken off, one of them hovering my stuff along with them, for which I was grateful. I looked around to see what was happening; the crowd in the hall was swelling now as more and more people joined it, shepherded into the pack by Natalie's grandmother. Tommy was on the edge of the pack, but when we beckoned to him, he shook his head.

"She's put a shield around us," he told us. "Don't come near me 'cause it's designed to take in anyone who comes close enough."

Marc dealt with that by simply popping Tommy out of it. Tommy looked nervously back over his shoulder.

"It's still there," Marc assured him. "She won't know what happened. You gotta go now, through there."

Marc looked over at the wall separating the living quarters from the corridor, and a moment later, an opening appeared in it, revealing the corridor for the first time in many weeks.

"You sure that's safe?" Tommy asked. "What if—"

His words were cut off as another bomb exploded, but this one was closer and louder than any so far. It was on the third floor, and it caused a massive chain reaction resulting in several rooms collapsing on the floor above. Several more fell through from the fifth floor, and then about a dozen walls fell inward on the sixth. The works were really coming down now. Meanwhile, the Hammerhearts on top of the structure had stunners out and were attempting to freeze anyone trying to flee from the monster, which was still zooming around over our heads. I knew not whether it had caught any more victims since I'd last watched it.

"Just go," Marc said to Tommy, brandishing the crystal. A moment later, a bag that Tommy had already packed came zooming down towards him, almost knocking him off his feet. "Just go, and be careful."

He picked up the bag and ran for the opening, leaving Marc and me alone. I racked my brains, knowing my task was to keep track of everyone who'd been sent out and everyone who hadn't been found yet. Marc and I circled halfway around the crowd in the hall, not wanting to get too close to Mr. Woodward and Mr. Fletcher, who were standing in a very dangerous position. I also had to be mindful that if Hammerson saw me, which he probably already had, he might take it into his head to make an attempt on my life. We couldn't afford to take long doing this.

Fortunately, most of the people we needed to find had been in the lounge room when the disaster had struck, and were now stuck in Alice Fletcher's shield. Marc worked his way around the pack while I went right into it, allowing the shield to take me so that I could locate all those within it and bring them to the edge so that Marc could release them. While he waited, he was to cause all those possessions which each of them was taking to zoom from their bedrooms before they could collapse. I dragged Peter to the edge first, followed by the three Thomases, each of us pushing and shoving rather nastily to get through. I located Katie and Sophie along the way and dragged them along with me. On my next voyage in, I located the four Maivises, and was able to retrieve Liam and Robyn on my way back to the edge of the shield.

Unfortunately, on my third trip inward, I ran into Mum, who flung an arm around me and began crying on my shoulder.

"Oh thank God you're okay!" she moaned. "Oh thank God, but I don't know where Peter is—"

"He's fine," I told her, hurriedly separating myself from her grasp. "I saw him earlier; he's fine. I'll be back in a minute."

I wouldn't, of course, and it cost a pang to have to lie, but I knew the truth couldn't be uttered at a moment like this. I delved back into the crowd, locating a frantic Erica, and managing to lead her, Siobhan, Lena and Darcy back to the edge of the shield, where Marc was once again waiting. I was pleased to see that all those I had previously let out were now nowhere to be seen.

"How many left?" Marc asked me.

"Not sure; a few. Just hang in there, mate."

It was becoming more and more difficult to locate those teenagers I wished to find because more and more of the crowd were adults, and their bigger bodies masked the smaller ones I was looking for. Fortunately, Rebecca Fletcher was able to locate me instead, and not long after I was able to lead her, Candice Young and Jason Pont back to Marc. On my next trip in, I found Dean and his sister, George and his girlfriend, and David Rockson's sister. Once I'd managed to lead all of them back to the edge, I had to stop and think to make sure I hadn't missed anyone. I thought I must have found most of them by now, but I had to be sure.... All the Playmans, Thomases, Maivises, Fletchers, Morans, Tommy, Katie, Sophie, Erica, Siobhan, Lena, Liam, Darcy, Candice, Jason, George, Belinda, Della, Robyn, Dean, Joanne—yep, that's everyone.

I came back to the edge where Marc was waiting and nodded. "All done; let me out."

He obliged and a moment later, we were standing together on the free side—the unprotected side.

"You got all your stuff?" I asked him.

"Not yet; guess I'd better do that."

Screams sounded around us. People had been screaming in terror the whole time but these were much louder and more alarmed than before. I found out why a moment later when a shadow passed over my head and the quality of the air around me changed. A great vacuum suddenly opened over my head and I felt myself sucked irresistibly upwards. It wasn't an entirely unfamiliar experience (it was very much like the tentacle that had guarded the Sien-Leoard Crystal on Rock Haulter) but that didn't make it any less uncomfortable. Then next thing I knew was suffocating wetness as a cold, slimy mouth closed around me. It covered my whole body in a matter of moments and it was pressing very tightly on all sides. I couldn't move and I couldn't breathe, and I knew only a moment of resignation as I realised the game was up, that it was about to crush me and digest me, as it had done to at least one person already.

But it didn't happen. The moment seemed to be prolonged, and prolonged some more. It went on forever, and all I could do was sit/stand/lie here, unable to move, unable to breathe. It would kill me anyway just from asphyxiation, I knew, and I thought I would much rather it simply crush my scull and put me out of my misery. This was a miserable way to go, miserable indeed....

Then, when I thought I must surely be about to black out, I felt a great whoosh as the thing gobbed me out. I fell a short distance onto a hard surface that was uneven, sharp and seemed fragile under me. I forced myself up onto my hands and knees, looking dazedly around me. It took a long time, perhaps several minutes to deduce that I had absolutely no idea where I was. The place was dim, the light coming from a source I couldn't identify. It could have been a cave, such was the jagged shape of the walls, ceiling and floor, except that those surfaces seemed to be made of wood, brick and plaster rather than rock. There was no sign of the monster that had brought me here, but I knew I couldn't have gone far, because I could still hear the thunder around me, now sounding much louder than it had before. I could still hear screaming too, panic, people running and shouting, but that was a very distant thing.

It was only when I was finally on my feet that laughter interrupted my contemplation, and the sound of it caused everything to clunk into place in my mind. I hadn't been brought to some secret monster chamber, as I had originally thought. No, this was within the rubble of the bedrooms, right in the middle of the bomb-ridden death-trap that had recently been like a prison. Oh how some things never changed. The difference here was that this place, which should have already collapsed inward on itself, was being held up by magic, and the person responsible for performing that magic was standing about ten feet away, on the far side of this deathly room, laughing nastily at me.

"So many times you have escaped me, boy," Hammerson hissed, "but let's see you get out of this one. Go on, boy; amuse me."

Oh boy, what a mess I'd landed myself in this time. The floor was shifting beneath me and it was all I could do to keep my balance. He, meanwhile, was standing on a support beam of some sort and was having no trouble at all.

"What are you gonna do?" I asked as insolently as I could, while in all honesty I was pretty much packing myself. The simple fact was this: Nothing Hammerson could do to me would be pleasant. He wouldn't just kill me and get it over with, because for whatever reason, he couldn't; he had once tried and it hadn't worked. So what would he do? Torture me until my body simply quit, no doubt; that would work, and even if it didn't, I would be wishing it did.

"What am I going to do?" Hammerson repeated, smiling nastily at me. "Well, we can start by…"

The uneven, unsteady floor beneath my feet jolted alarmingly. Both my feet flew out sideways and I felt as though I may have snapped a couple of muscles in my inner thighs. That wasn't all, though; a sharp piece of wood came jutting up between my legs from whatever had been below the floor. It would have impaled me in the worst of ways (and indeed it did leave my groin protesting loudly at its invasion) had I not thrown my weight back at the last moment. It was more like an uppercut than anything else. I landed hard on my back on the shifting floor, and for a moment I worried the sudden movement would cause it to collapse, but if it had been about to, Hammerson had other ideas. It didn't settle down entirely, but it remained intact so far. He, through all of this, was laughing happily.

"You can't kill me," I reminded him, scrambling around to face him, my legs and groin screaming in protest. "You've tried once, remember? How did that turn out for you?"

"Oh, I'm not going to kill you, boy," he sneered.

Just as I had suspected, and was not pleased to have confirmed.

"Oh really?" I scoffed, wanting to see how long I could keep him talking, wanting to give anyone on the outside as much time as possible to rescue me. "Does that mean I'll live to tell everyone how pathetic you are? Can't even finish off a kid with no weapons and no power, while you're supposed to be the most powerful of all?"

Hammerson wasn't fazed in the slightest; he merely laughed again. "Wrong again, boy. I'm not going to kill you, but even if I can't do it with my own magic, I can certainly arrange your death for you."

"It's still you're doing, though," I pointed out. "So what are you gonna do?"

"*I'm* not going to kill you," he said for the third time, "but the room is." He roared with laughter. "Get out of this one, boy. There's no help for you this time. All your friends think you were swallowed by the big bad monster; they're not coming to help you. You're on your own, boy, and your time is up!"

A second later, he had vanished. He didn't teleport, I knew, perhaps was unable to teleport due to the enchantments around the Woodward base, but I had tracked his movements, quick as they had been. It was as though his body had mutated, forming into something that could have resembled a tapeworm, something skinny and flexible enough to worm its way through the wreckage without getting squashed. A moment later, he shot up through a crack in the makeshift ceiling and was gone from the room, leaving me in one hell of a nightmare.

I looked all around me hopelessly, for what I had no idea. Any gap I could crawl through…any space I could occupy that might hold up better than the rest should it collapse…a steady place to stand…it was all hopeless. There was nothing I could do to survive this one. I had no idea how deep within the wreckage I was, but even if I were reasonably close to the top, I would still be trapped beneath several tons of brickwork, plaster, wood and God knew what else if it came down. I wouldn't stand a chance, unless…

I stopped moving and listened to the rumbling around me. It covered just about every other sound as more and more rooms around me collapsed, more and more air pockets like this filled in, and all the while explosions continued to rock the building. How many bombs had they put in here? Had to be at least a hundred, by the sound of it. Through all of that, though, I could still hear, very dimly and distantly, the sounds on the outside: screaming, shouting, crying, panic. Who knew what the Hammerhearts were doing by now, whether they were even still there or if Hammerson was already engineering an escape for them all. It hardly mattered; what mattered was trying to make those out there aware that I was in here.

"I'm in here!" I bellowed, staggering and stumbling across the room to where I thought the sounds were loudest. "I'm in *here!*"

I made the mistake then, the dreadful mistake indeed, of leaning against the wall on that side of the room so that my mouth would be as close to a gap in the works as I could get it. Something above my head snapped and came down; a long slab of wood. It missed me but the effect it had on the structure was monumental. I ducked as another part of the wall came down, narrowly missing me, released by the beam that had snapped moments earlier. At the same time, the floor beneath my feet gave way, causing both me and a whole lot of debris to tumble about two metres into another air pocket below.

I came down painfully on my knees, but barely had a moment to register where I was. I was in complete darkness now and my ears were ringing with the sound of the collapsing building. Something very hard and heavy hit my back: an enormous stone pillar, judging by the feel of it. It would have crushed me but at the same time, two more large beams were released. They fell down above me, and the three came together, resting against each other and their weight temporarily supporting the rest of the structure.

I was trapped in a small space beneath them with barely any room to move. I had been forced into a sort of hunch, my legs trapped (but not squashed) beneath part of the pillar behind me. All I was able to do was hoist myself up on my elbows, as far as it took for my head to hit the stone above me. I quit then and just lay there, exhausted and now hurting in several places. If I tried too hard to move, I would be nothing but strawberry jam, and at the same time I could barely move anyway. All I could do was wait, for what, I had no idea. Perhaps I would simply run out of oxygen…that wouldn't be so bad; only minutes earlier, I'd thought I was indeed meeting that end.

The situation changed when I felt something strong surround me, pushing the beams away slightly and giving me a touch more room. I raised my head in surprise and promptly smacked it on the stone above for the second time. I swore loudly in frustration, but the hopeless feeling had vanished, because I recognised what was happening to me. Someone knew I was here: Someone had put a protective shield around me...no way could I be squashed now. I still couldn't go anywhere, but now I only had to wait for whoever was coming to get me.

Of course, I wasn't surprised to learn that Marc was behind the shield. It took perhaps five minutes for him to get to me, in a bubble of his own, pushing rubble aside to get to me. He was exhausted but not unhappy with his evening's work.

"Sorry, man," he said as he reached me, forcing the beams away and allowing me enough space to get unsteadily to my feet. The chain reaction of this was quite massive, the sound of the collapsing building deafening as bits and pieces tumbled all around us, but none of them affected us. A moment later, my shield was gone and I was alongside him in his bubble.

"You knew where I was?" I panted, just about ready to collapse myself now, my legs still aching furiously.

"Sure I did, but we'll talk about that later; we gotta get out of here while we still can. Hang on, we're going down."

It was hard to describe exactly what was happening now. Marc and I weren't standing on the unsteady wreckage as I had been when I'd been alone; we were in a bubble of some sort. The bubble took on the properties of the shield which had protected me, but it also allowed Marc and me to float in its centre, so that we didn't have to make any physical contact with the rubble at all. Now, Marc sent the bubble straight down; all the wreckage around us parted as the bubble came and attempted to collapse on top of us all the while, but it never came close.

A minute later, we had reached the very bottom of the rubble. I knew we had because I recognised the floor, the bottom of the base, the floor of the hall outside upon which the building had been set. Marc stared at the crystal for a moment before turning and guiding us in a certain direction.

"Don't say a word," he told me. "I'm making us invisible; I'm gonna see if we can get out of the base undetected."

"Won't they see when the thing opens up?"

"Yeah, but with a bit of luck, they won't be paying close attention. Let's see how it goes."

On we went until another minute later, we emerged into the light of the main hall, coming out where the stairs had been, and which had since buckled in the destruction. There were a lot of people milling around nearby, outside where the lounge room had once been, and the two elderly Sorcerers were still protecting them from the monster that had taken me to Hammerson, which was still zooming around the place, perhaps still in hope of some dinner. Mr. Woodward and Mr. Fletcher were in the air, once again battling with Hammerson. He had surrounded himself with loyal Hammerhearts and was perhaps contemplating a way to get them all out of the base safely, now that he had achieved what he'd wanted.... Or maybe he wouldn't stop there. Maybe he would work his way around to the Woodward living quarters and empty them of everything they possessed, thereby defeating them as thoroughly as he could without actually taking their magic.

That was all speculation, of course, and none of it mattered. What mattered was that we were out, that nobody appeared to have noticed, and that the opening to the corridor outside was still an opening. I did take a moment to look over my shoulder at what had once been so spectacular, and was astonished by what it had been reduced to. Not a single floor was intact now, and not a single room was recognisable; they had done a very good job destroying it.

Once we were out in the corridor, Marc made us visible again and removed the bubble so that we could run for the exit. Well, he ran; I hobbled along, my legs, groin, shoulders and just about everywhere else still paining me. Amelia was waiting, white-faced, at the end. She held out her hand for Marc when he reached her and wordlessly led him through. I was still ten feet away when she ducked back and hurried to meet me.

"What happened to you? You look awful——"

"Never mind; just let me through the wall."

She didn't listen. Instead she screwed up her face, and miraculously, all the pains were gone in an instant. I straightened up, still a little gingerly, but that was only in my head now. Without giving me a moment to thank her, Amelia grabbed my arm and practically dragged me to the exit, where we hurried through into the study. Even after all the horror I'd just been through, I had a moment to register that this was the first time I'd been out of the base since that night in Germany.

The second thing I noticed, as soon as we left the study, was the bodies. There were unconscious bodies all over the Woodwards' house, and many more littering the lawn outside. They had even fallen unconscious on the path into the stretch, and on the Morelle Street bridge across the Jade River. I had to assume they had been waiting for us after all, quite a lot of them, and Natalie (perhaps with Amelia's help) had dealt with them quite efficiently.

Without a word, Amelia and I took off, hurrying after Marc, who was someway ahead on the path, heading for where all the others were waiting for us, hidden deep in the trees off the path. We were running westward across the park so that the whole time it took us to reach the cover of the trees, we were running with the glare of a Chopville sunset right in our eyes.

My watch said it was just after six o'clock when we finally reached the rest of the group, who were standing in several huddles, talking nervously amongst each other.

"Is that everyone?" Lucien asked us, and when we both nodded, he went on, "Good. Now listen, people, we don't have much time. It might be the Sorcerers who come looking for us, or it might be the Hammerhearts. Either way, we need to get ourselves protected and hidden immediately."

Chapter 8: On Our Own

Lucien organised the group of thirty (yeah, there were thirty of us in the end) into a large huddle, with Amelia, Natalie and Marc on the outside so that any magic they performed would encase the whole group. Natalie walked first around the group, casting her invisibility veil, which hid us from all on the outside but not from each other. Amelia walked right behind her, erecting a one-way soundproof barrier around us, which meant we would be able to hear people on the outside, but they wouldn't be able to hear us. Like the invisibility veil, the magic only surrounded the group as a whole and didn't apply to each person. Finally, Marc walked behind the two girls as they encircled the group, and his untraceable spell (which he had never performed before but was confident would work) applied to the whole group in just the same way.

"Now that that's done," Lucien said, "we have to find somewhere safe and set up a base for ourselves."

"I don't see why we would need to go anywhere," Marc said. "We just set up a base in here and make it mobile. After all the spells we did on the thing we used to get to Rock Haulter, we should be able to stay hidden."

"I'll take your word for that, but the fact is there's just not a lot of room in here," said Lucien. "Also, I don't know about you guys, but I'd feel much better being out of Chopville tonight. We don't know what we left behind back there but we have to assume they might come looking for us in here. Even with all the spells we performed, if they walk into one of us, the game will be up. I suggest we get in a line and move north into the farmlands out that way. We shouldn't need to go more than a kilometre from the town."

"South is closer from where we are," Peter pointed out.

"It is, but the cemetery's that way," Lucien said, shuddering. "Call me a coward but I don't wanna be walking around in there tonight. Now, feel free to disagree with me, but I suggest we get in a line and move slowly. If anyone goes past us, we step off the path and stay still until they've passed; they may not see or hear us, but if one of us kicks a stone, that could be enough to make them suspicious. Everyone get into two lines; Amelia, you lead the way, and Natalie, you bring up the rear. Marc, you stay in the middle, and all three of you stay on the lookout."

It took some time to get organised, particularly as it was so dark where we were under the cover of the trees in the park, but eventually we were in two lines. Or, most of the group was in two lines; Amelia was on her own at the front and Natalie on her own in the rear. I was at the front, right behind Amelia in fact, with Lucien beside me.

"Everyone be listening hard," Lucien called to all of us. "One thing we can afford to do is shout, so if I shout something at you, pay attention. Now, let's go, and remember, slowly. I'm as tired and scared as the rest of you but hurrying in this situation wouldn't do any good. So, let's go."

And on we went, snaking back through the trees to the clearing where, months earlier, many of us had played in the river, jumping from the bridges and having a good old time. It was winter now, of course, and that had only ever been a summer activity, but how I would have liked to be able to do that again. Now, I had to wonder if I would ever get that chance again. Only fourteen years old and I was already looking back on what should have been my teenage years like an old codger; what a sad thought.

"Wo, hold up," Lucien called at the top of his voice, bringing the group to a stop about ten feet from the footpath which led through the park, from the entrance gate at Main Street to the entrance gate near the Woodward's house at the other end. We all staggered to a halt, many people looking around to see what had caught Lucien's eye, but I didn't need to look far.

Hammerhearts were converging on the Woodwards' house. Many were already there, having accessed it via Morelle Street (they were in the process of dragging those laid low by the Sorcerers out of the house) but many more were hurrying across the path from Main Street. A long line of them ran right past us as we stood there. Fortunately none of them took it into their heads to consider that there were invisible people around them. Lucien watched the park entrance, which was fortunately lighter than the opposite direction due to the setting sun, waiting for the flow of Hammerhearts to ease.

"That's all of them," he said after about five minutes. "Come on, let's go."

We kept moving, stepping onto the path and slowly snaking along it towards Main Street. We had almost reached the gate and the closed canteen that had once belonged to Grillion when two sounds reached us clearly, carried to us from the other side of the park on the perfectly still air. The first sounded like a great whoosh of air, and the second, far clearer and louder, was a triumphant cheer from the Hammerhearts. We all looked over our shoulders, and although it was darker in that direction, the Woodwards' house could still be seen, thanks to the flames that were quickly consuming it.

"Keep moving," Lucien said not unkindly, taking Amelia by the shoulder and turning her firmly away from the destruction behind. She allowed this, but her face had gone very pale.

"You gonna be okay?" I asked, increasing my stride slightly so that I could talk to her as we went through the gate and turned right, due north.

She nodded. "I'm not surprised. The house itself means nothing to me; they've wrecked it loads of times. It's just—it feels different this time."

"Because you're not going back," I said, understanding her point. "Pretty soon we'll be walking past my old street, and you reckon that won't hurt, but we'll be okay…somehow."

"I can't believe how much damage they've done to our home," she said, unable to stop herself looking up the river toward her flaming home as we crossed the bridge.

"Not now," said Lucien firmly. "I know it hurts but we'll have time to think about all we've lost later. We may have plenty of time, depending on how fast we choose to move, but for now, let's just keep walking."

Things became easier for us once we reached the northern bank of the river. The sounds and sights of the Hammerhearts faded as houses closed in on either side of Main Street. There were lights on in most of them, and televisions playing in many front rooms, but it would have been easy to forget that we were in a war zone if not for the knowledge of what we had left behind. Compared to the south side (which had been relatively bustling with the Hammerheart attack), the town central (which had been lit up like a birthday cake) and, although we hadn't seen it, the on-ground Hammerheart base set up in our old school grounds, where we were now was practically sleeping.

By the time we reached Bater Road and Rosewood Street, the two most northern roads in town, the sun had set and the light in the west was fading rapidly. It took all the warmth from the air, not that there had been much, leaving us all feeling very chilly indeed. There was still no wind but compared to what we had become used to, we were certainly braving the elements tonight. Once we snaked our way across Bater Road and past the house on the corner, we were following Main Street out of town and into the farmlands between the town and the Goulburn Valley Highway. I had been out here many times before, but this was maybe the second or third time I'd ever done it on foot. Dad and Charlie had lived out here when they had been kids, before their fathers had sold their farms so that they could go and fight in the war against the Hammersons. Those farms, and others like them, were probably still out here, and I supposed it would be in one of those paddocks where we would be spending the night.

"We need a spot with plenty of space," Lucien told Amelia, as though he had been reading my mind. "It won't matter once we get in some sort of base, but until then, we need somewhere to settle down."

"I don't really know my way around out here," Amelia admitted, coming to a stop. The rest of the line stuttered to a halt behind her.

"You can't use your magic to find a place?" Lucien enquired.

Amelia shrugged in the darkness. Now that we had left the light (what little there was) of the town behind by a few hundred metres, I could see little more than her outline, even though she was standing within arm's reach. Nothing happened for about a minute after that; we all just stood, waiting for Amelia, half the group having no understanding of what was going on up here—I could hear them complaining about it further down the line. Finally, Amelia raised her head again.

"If we go a little further down the road, then turn right and cut through a field and slip through an electric fence, we'll be in a paddock. It's empty at the moment so we'll be fine there."

"What's your plan for getting over the fence?" Lucien asked.

"Er," Amelia faltered, shrugging. "Magic?"

"Why don't you just teleport us in there?" I asked her.

She shrugged again. "Have you ever done this many people spaced over this kind of distance?"

"We'll get everyone to gather in a group, like we did in the park," said Lucien. "There are no cars coming now, and if we do it quickly, we can be out of here before any decide to come along here."

So that was what we did. Lucien went up the line and told everyone what was going on, directing them like a conductor into an organised pack in the middle of Main Street. Once everyone was gathered, Amelia walked around the outside of the group, as she had done when performing the soundproof barrier, performing another binding spell this time. Once it was done, she teleported us over a very short distance into the paddock she had located before. It was the first time I had teleported since returning after that night in Germany, and like coming out of the base, it felt good to be back in familiar territory.

"Okay, everyone listen up," Lucien called, stepping out of the pack and addressing us like we were the class and he was our teacher. "You're all free to relax a little while Amelia,

Natalie and Marc work on setting up a proper base. I know it's not ideal but hopefully it won't take too long. All I advise is that you stay in this area; don't leave the paddock, and be ready to return to us once the base is ready. The first things we'll be doing once we're in is having some dinner and getting in touch with the adults to find out what happened. Everyone got all that? Any questions?"

There was a general murmuring of assent. No questions were raised, but I did hear a few people commenting on Lucien's leadership abilities, wondering why he was the one giving orders instead of the Sorcerers. I didn't have a problem with it because so far, he was doing the job as well as any of us could have. Lucien stepped aside with Marc and the two Sorcerers and the four of them began talking urgently. That just left the rest of us standing around looking at each other, but after a while the group broke up into several smaller groups. I simply stood where I was for a while, watching the Sorcerers, until in the darkness, they seemed to vanish. I squinted at the place where they had gone, but all I could see was some rectangular object on the ground. It took me a moment to understand that they had shrunk themselves so that they could work out the interior of the base, just as I had done when creating the prison yard.

With nothing left to see, I began looking around for someone to sit with. Some way away, I could see Peter, James, Harry, Simon and Tommy sitting together, each of them with his arm around his girlfriend (Siobhan, Erica, Katie, Sophie and Jessica respectively). A few weeks ago, such a sight wouldn't have bothered me, but now it came accompanied with a sharp stab of jealousy. I would have to sit with them because I couldn't see anyone else I wanted to be with, but I had to wonder, as I moved over to them, if I was now the only person in the group who didn't have a partner. I supposed I couldn't be, but it sure felt like it.

"Is this how you imagined it would be when we left?" Peter asked when I sat down on his right. "I'm still waiting for the five-star hotel to pop up."

I forced a laugh. "It'll be more like how we imagined when they're done creating the base. I hope they think of everything we'll need."

"If they don't, we can just modify as we go," said James, who had turned to listen. "I'm sure they'll be wanting your input, John."

"Why me?" I asked, disconcerted.

"Sure they will," Erica chipped in. "You did a lot of this sort of stuff when you had magic; they'll want you to tell them if they missed anything."

I shrugged. "Marc's done a lot of this too. Come to think of it, all three of them have, so they won't need my help."

That turned out to be incorrect, though. I'd been sitting there for about ten minutes, feeling sorry for myself, when Marc appeared out of the darkness and plonked himself down on my free side.

"You guys doing all right here?" he asked brightly.

"Yeah, but my bum's getting soaked here," Peter told him. "I don't suppose you could make us a nice, comfortable mat to sit on?"

Marc laughed. "I dunno about that, but I'm sure I can make a nice heater for you to stand in front of once you get inside. Would that be okay?"

"Beggars can't be choosy," said Peter, laughing. "Besides, a wet arse is the least of our worries just at the moment."

"Very true," Marc agreed. "John, can you come and help us out with a few things?"

"Er," I said, trying to ignore Peter and James, who were sniggering triumphantly, "I guess so. Why do you need my help?"

"We may not," said Marc, as the two of us got up, "but since you've done a lot of this stuff before, you might be able to help us think of everything."

Déjà vu all over again, I thought.

"I can try, but isn't that what Lucien's trying to do?"

"He is, but he wasn't with us when we did a lot of this stuff before. Me and the girls are trying to cover all corners but it's tricky. Hold onto your hat…"

We had reached the little box on the ground and now I felt the familiar sensation of the ground expanding below my feet as he and I shrunk to a tiny size relative to the base. When the sensation stopped and Marc led me through the opening in the side of the box into the interior, which was presently illuminated by magic, I saw that it had to be at least the size of the prison yard. The vastness of it took me completely by surprise.

"Is this really necessary?" I asked him as we approached the spot where Lucien, Natalie and Amelia stood waiting.

"Well, there are a lot of us," Marc pointed out, "and we don't know how long we'll be restricted to this spot."

"How much stuff are you wanting to put in here?" I asked.

"That's what we've been talking about," said Lucien as we joined him and the girls. "For a start, there need to be at least thirty bedrooms, and they can't be too small either; we want to be comfortable. I would even recommend a few extra as we don't know if we might pick people up along the way."

"Oh sure, and while we're at it, why don't we make a little prison downstairs as well," I added mockingly. "We can call it the Sorcerers' dungeon."

"That's actually not such a bad idea," Lucien agreed, taking me by surprise. "We don't know how many Hammerhearts we'll have to take out of action, and I don't know about you, but I'll sleep easier at night if we don't have to kill them. That means locking them up. We can worry about that later, though."

"So where are you going to start?" I asked. "When I did the prison yard, the first thing I did before doing any magic was work out the design of the building. Shouldn't you think about that?"

"How about we line the bedrooms up along the back of the base?" Amelia suggested. "We can make a corridor with five on either side, and have that on three floors. There should be enough space down there for that."

"Yeah, that's good," Marc agreed. "We can put staircases at either end, like John did in the prison yard. Come to think of it, we can probably do a fourth floor, to account for extra bedrooms."

"Hang on," said Natalie, who looked troubled. "I don't know about you guys, but this is making the place feel like a prison. People aren't gonna like that, you know."

That brought us all to a halt. Finally, Lucien said, "I guess it will be. It won't be safe for anyone to be walking around in the open, but—"

"If we're taking safety into account," Marc interrupted, "then that also means we have to cut off communication to the outside world, except for when we're dealing with Hammerson. It's not gonna be much different from what we just left behind."

"There will be one big difference," Lucien said. "We'll be doing something more constructive which, in the long run, will mean we won't have to be locked up. The rest of the group can understand that because we'll let them help out. That's what they wanted; that's why they came along."

"That's true," I agreed, "but you're right about something else too: We'll have to appease them by making the place as comfortable as possible. I reckon we should do what I did in the prison yard, that was make the ceiling reflect outside; filter in some of the atmosphere but don't let it rain. Can you do that?"

"I can try," Marc said, gripping his crystal and going still. There was a few seconds of nothing before it worked; I knew it had because the ceiling lightened very slightly. Not much, but it was clear that it was revealing sky, rather than a solid roof.

"Good," said Lucien. "So, I suppose the middle part where we are now can be an outdoor area. That means we put all the functional areas around the edges."

We all set to work. Marc began the entrance to the base, setting up the protection that would stop people getting in and only allow people to leave the base when they had permission to do so. It was necessary because we just didn't know what any of these teenagers could do in a moment of madness. He also took care of the controls to the base, those which made it open and close, and those which moved it around in the air. He was also to set up an enchantment that would allow us to return to normal size when we left the base, but that was likely to be tricky. I thought he might leave that one until last. Lucien supervised him during all this.

Meanwhile, I went to the back of the base with Amelia and began supervising her as she began creating the bedrooms, leaving Natalie to take care of the outdoor area, which would be the easiest. We measured the area and deduced that each bedroom could be as big as those that had been on the third floor in the Woodward base, including the bathroom and wardrobe. I told her it was necessary for each bedroom to have a bathroom because having one for thirty people would be disastrous. Half the bedrooms faced the yard, so they had normal windows, while those on the other side had magical windows which would reflect their opposite counterparts. The design worked perfectly, except that there was some space between the rooms and the stairs on each of the four levels. After some deliberation, Amelia decided to fill that space with a lift at either end of the corridor.

"Is that really necessary?" I asked her, thinking of what had happened the last time I had been in a lift—of who had died there.

"Probably not, but it fills the space," she said, shrugging. "Besides, some days, some people might be too tired to climb the stairs."

"Yeah, maybe the ones on the top floor," I said, "like...oh yeah, nobody."

"Wanker," she smirked. "Okay, come help me out with a dining room. I suppose we put that on this side, and maybe the lounge room on the other side."

"Yeah, but put a corridor along the side too, so that we don't have to walk through the dining room to get to whatever comes after it. Also, a door from the yard near the stairs wouldn't be a bad idea."

In the end, the main building in the base took on the shape of an upside-down U. The bedrooms stretched across the top of the base, the dining room and games room on the left-hand side, and a large lounge room and a small gym on the right. Only the library wasn't represented from the base we had left behind. The other building, at the bottom of the base that Marc and Lucien had worked on, wasn't connected to the main building. That was the control room and could be entered only by Marc, Amelia, Natalie and anyone to whom they had given permission. Such permission could be granted programmatically through electronic cards, similar to those from the Woodward base, which would also be necessary to access our bedrooms. What Natalie had done in the yard was quite impressive. There was a covered swimming pool, along with a nice garden and several park benches.

"Perhaps an indoor pool wouldn't be a bad idea either," Lucien mused, staring at it in the darkness, "as it's winter now and that thing will be freezing."

"We can work on that later," said Marc. "Right now, you two need to start working on a prison," he said to Natalie and Amelia. "I reckon it should be accessed in the control room so that nobody else can get in, and the door should be locked to all except us three with magic."

"Eliminating the possibility of anyone in here doing a Sebastian?" I enquired.

"I don't think anyone here would, but you can never be too safe," he replied.

"We'll get started on it," Amelia said, taking Natalie by the arm and leading her away from the rest of us.

"Now, I need you two to help me here," Marc said, entering the control room and allowing us to come through with him. "The controls are all set up, but I'm not sure how to control the process of entering and leaving the base."

"I've been thinking about that," I told him. "It needs to be much the same as the level two rooms back in the Woodward base. There should be no way to get out unless you set a door down somewhere, and that door needs to be our size on this side and real size on the other, so that when we go through it, we'll become normal size when we step out into the world. Does that make sense?"

"It does, sort of," Marc said nervously, "but what about getting back in? We need to make sure only people we want to come through are able to."

"And that includes new people we bring in," Lucien added.

"Make it invisible to everyone except those who left the base through it," I suggested. "You need to put a button here to put the door down and lift it up, though."

"Oh, right."

Marc worked on the button and then pondered over the door for a bit. He then left through it and created the door on the other side, the door that wouldn't always be there. Once it popped into being, Marc was staring through it at Lucien and me, and he was grinning.

"One of you step outside," Marc said, "and tell me if you can see the door. Also, one of you get over here," he called to those in the paddock whom we couldn't see, "and give me a hand here."

Marc stepped back through the door while Lucien stepped to the outside, and he was momentarily joined by Darcy.

"Where'd he go?" Darcy asked, raising his eyebrows. "You're not Marc, are you?"

"No," said Lucien. "Can you see anything there?"

"Sure, I can see Liam pulling ridiculous faces. What's your point?"

"Question answered," Lucien told Marc and me. "So, how do we get him in?"

"He can walk straight through it," Marc said. "He doesn't need to see it. Incidentally, can you hear us, Darcy?"

I knew he couldn't because he was still looking at Lucien, showing no sign that he could hear a word we were saying. After a moment, he said, "Er, who are you talking to?"

"Allow me to show you," said Lucien and, taking Darcy by the arm, he marched him right through the door into the control room. Darcy did a double-take and almost toppled over when the room suddenly materialised around him.

"Holy crap," he said, his mouth open wide. "Is this it? Is this where we're staying?"

"Not in here, exactly," Marc told him. "You can go on through there and have a look around, but don't disturb the girls; they're still working."

Still goggling, Darcy stepped into the yard, leaving Marc, Lucien and I staring at each other.

"Looks like it's all good," Lucien said. "Shall we see how the girls are doing?"

But as it turned out, the girls were already finished. They came into the control room a moment later, Amelia holding a certain rectangular box in her hand. There was a door floating along in mid-air behind them. Without a word, Amelia shot the box into the top corner of the room while Natalie sent the door flying through the air. It attached itself to the far wall.

"That was quick," Marc observed.

"Yeah, we just duplicated the one John created," said Amelia, stepping up to the door and trying to open it, but it wouldn't open. She was satisfied.

"You have to use magic to open it," Natalie told him, "so that should make it perfectly safe. Have you done all the spells in here?"

"Yeah, this room's set," Marc said. "Is the dining room ready to be used?" When Amelia nodded, he said, "Good. I suppose we start bringing them in then."

So that was what we did, stepping back through the door into the chilly paddock where all the others had been waiting for over an hour now. The temperature had dropped even more now, and even worse, a breeze had picked up. It now felt like it had to be not too far above zero degrees Celsius.

"Before we do anything," I said, touching Lucien's arm as he was about to call out to the rest of the group, "should we put a few spells around the base itself?"

"Oh yes, we should," Amelia said quickly. "All the same ones. It needs to be invisible, soundproof and untraceable."

"And something else too," I said, and when they looked at me, I shrugged and withdrew something from my pocket.

I had still been carrying the device that I had used to create ghost walls in the Woodward base, an exercise that had turned out to be entirely pointless, as had everything we had tried to deal with Hall. I now pointed it at the box on the ground and began shooting each of its sides, as well as the top and bottom.

"Good thinking," Marc said. "We'll work on the rest of those spells while you two start helping people get through the door."

"Sure," said Lucien. "Okay everyone," he bellowed, his voice bouncing all over the paddock. It should have disturbed people for miles (exaggeration maybe) but in fact nobody other than those in the paddock would hear. At the sound of it, they all fell silent immediately. "Everyone gather around here. The base is almost set and you can start entering it, but you'll need our help to get through because the entrance is hidden. Could everyone gather around here, please, so we can do a head count. How many are already in there?" he added more quietly to me.

"Only Darcy, but if you're including us as well, then six."

People began gathering around and Lucien and I began assisting each of them through the door and sending them onward into the yard. It was a long exercise because we could only do one at a time, but eventually we were able to count twenty-four heads as they each passed through. Once they were all through, Marc, Natalie and Amelia joined us in the control room.

"And now, we hide ourselves," Marc announced, shutting the door firmly behind him.

He then stepped up to the controls and pushed the button to hide the door. A little red light which had previously been shining above the button went out immediately. I now took a closer look at the controls. They were very basic indeed: Three levers, one to move the base along each of the three dimensions, and a wheel to turn it around. There was also a little LCD screen which presently showed, magically illuminated (though there had been no light outside) the paddock we had just left.

"Do they know what to do in there?" Natalie asked, looking through the door into the yard.

We went through and saw that it was almost deserted. Everyone had hurried to the back to explore the building. I was glad to see it; they were certainly more enthusiastic than the Hammerhearts had been when I had loaded them into their prison yard.

"They'll converge on the dining room in a minute," Lucien said. "We might as well go get something to eat."

"Now that we have a moment to think," I said to Marc as the five of us began walking, "would you like to tell me how you knew I hadn't been killed back there?"

"What?" said both Natalie and Amelia, stopping dead in their tracks.

"Oh yeah," said Marc, shrugging. "I just thought that Hammerson would have wanted to sort you out himself. I assumed that monster, whatever the hell it was, would have had orders not to hurt you. I thought maybe it was just taking you to him, so I watched it, and it went straight to him. Then they both disappeared into the wreckage of the place, so I sent my mind in after them. I couldn't do anything to help you until I was sure Hammerson had left, otherwise he would have made it more difficult to help."

"What are you talking about?" Natalie snapped. "What happened? When was this?"

"Back in the base," I told her, Amelia and Lucien, who were looking impatient for an explanation. "I had a bit of a standoff with Hammerson. He got me under the wreckage and intended for me to get crushed in there."

"Oh my God," Natalie moaned, and I saw, with some satisfaction, that she looked like she wanted to hug me. I had to tell myself I'd only imagined it.

"That must have been pretty scary," said Lucien shakily as we reached the building and slipped through the door closest to the dining room.

"More resigning than anything else," I admitted, "but I can't tell you how relieving it was to get that shield around me."

"No wonder you were so hurt," said Amelia. "I just assumed you'd worked so hard to find everyone."

There were about ten people in the dining room already, and more came in as we went up to the conveyer belt and began ordering our dinner. Under my guidance, for she had never performed a spell like this herself, Amelia had managed to duplicate most of the qualities of the Woodward dining room. The only one that hadn't been taken care of was the cleaning aspect, but unless we took it in turns to do it manually, we would probably have to set up spells to automatically keep the whole base from becoming dirty, assuming such spells could be performed. We could worry about that later; right now it was time to get some food.

"Okay, folks," Lucien called to everyone who was present. "The time right now is"—he checked his watch—"almost nine o'clock. I know many of you are tired; so am I, but we still need to find out what happened back at the base, and let the adults know we're okay. We'll have dinner now and meet up in the lounge room on the other side of the building at ten o'clock. I want everyone to be there, so please, don't be tempted to just go off to bed."

"Not that you can," Amelia added, "since you need a key to get into the bedrooms, and we haven't created the keys yet."

"That was clever," Tommy muttered.

Chapter 9: Forward Progress

The meeting at ten o'clock ended up happening about fifteen minutes earlier, as everyone had finished eating and was just sitting around talking by then. Most people weren't very tired at all, as it turned out, although I was certainly in the minority there, probably because I'd had a much busier day than a lot of them. Only Marc, Peter, Lucien, Natalie and Amelia were flagging as badly as me. When I sat down on a couch in the lounge room, I almost sank right back into it and might have fallen asleep had not Rebecca, who'd sat down next to me, dug an elbow into my ribs.

"Can't be doing that just yet," she told me, winking.

"You wanna bet?" I said exhaustedly.

The couches in this lounge room, like those in the one we had left behind, were large, soft, comfortable and arranged in a large ring around the room, excepting the gap in the doorway from the corridor outside. There was easily enough room for all thirty of us to take seats.

"Okay, everyone," Lucien said, calling the group to order. He and Marc had seated themselves on either side of the two Sorcerers so that the four of them would be the centre of attention. "We've talked about this bit and this is how it's gonna go. First, Amelia is going to make telepathic contact with her father to let him know we're okay and to determine where he is. If he is available to chat, we'll try to set up a video link from here to wherever he is now, so that we can find out what's happened to the base, and to let him and the rest of the adults know we're not coming back."

"When do we start attacking the Hammerhearts?" asked Liam.

Lucien smiled slightly. "We *don't* attack the Hammerhearts," he said patiently. "To answer your question as directly as I can, a few of us who know what we're gonna do will have a private meeting tomorrow about what we're going to do first. Once we've worked it out, we'll have a larger meeting to let the rest of you know as much as we can, and work out how you can help."

There was an excited muttering around the group. I wondered how excited they would be if a few of them were to be killed on this little mission, then I chastised myself for thinking along those lines. If that happened, it happened, but I didn't have to go predicting it.

"So, Amelia, you ready?" Lucien asked.

"Okay," she said. She looked nervous, and I couldn't blame her: The adults were likely to be extremely pissed off that we'd upped and left without a word.

She lapsed into the communication, as I'd seen her do twice already that day, and the group went silent and still as they watched. Some thirty seconds passed with nothing whatsoever, but I knew Amelia had made successful contact judging by the expressions that flickered across her face. I couldn't identify them but whatever was going on, it wasn't to her comfort.

"Okay," she said slowly, almost in a monotone. "He's okay and safe, and we can try to set up a link so we can see him."

"Have they got the Hammerhearts out of the base?" Marc asked.

"They're not in the base," Amelia replied, getting to her feet. "They're out in a desert somewhere."

"What the hell?"

"I don't know, but we're about to find out. Everyone might as well gather behind me so that you can all see."

We all scrambled off the couches and took seats on the floor instead, crowding in around Amelia as she created a large screen against midair in front of her. I supposed it would serve as both camera and display. Amelia didn't speak for several seconds as she engaged again in telepathy. Eventually, she cast some sort of spell at the screen, and immediately, it revealed Mr. Woodward, Mr. Fletcher, and several other adults, who had crowded in around a similar screen wherever they were.

"You really are all there," Mr. Fletcher said; he looked both mightily relieved and ready to spank a few butts. The expression was very similar to the ones Mum and Marge had once worn when we had returned safely from fighting Moran so long ago.

"We're all here, and all safe," Amelia replied in a steely tone that said, all too clearly, that she wasn't going to tolerate being treated like a child today. "Where are you?"

"We're hiding out in the Tanami Desert, as I told you before," said Mr. Woodward fiercely. "Our exact location is irrelevant at this point. Now, where exactly are you?"

"We're still in Chopville," said Lucien. "Or at least, the Chopville district, but we're very well hidden. Mr. Woodward, why are you hiding?"

"As I'm sure you're well aware, our base has been breached," said the Sorcerer, frowning at us all. "It is no longer safe for any of us there. We were able to retrieve all our belongings before leaving, but we had no choice but to destroy what we left behind, so that the Hammerhearts wouldn't have a chance to investigate and learn our secrets."

"So you're gonna be hiding in a desert now?" Peter asked, horrified.

"No. We'll set up a new base, as it sounds like you have done," he said, frowning even more deeply. "Now, are you going to tell me what game you're playing at?"

"In a minute," said Amelia. "Dad, what happened back there? How did they get in?"

Mr. Woodward surveyed the screen for several seconds before responding. "We didn't get much of a chance to investigate the rubble we left behind. What we are certain of, however, is that Hammerson couldn't have done it himself. I'm almost certain they entered through one of the second-floor rooms, and they can only be opened from the inside, no matter how powerful the person trying to get in may be. That can only mean that Hall was responsible for letting them in. As for the bombs, I can only assume they were busy hiding them all day, and on that score, I think Hammerson himself must have been responsible; only his magic could have allowed them to do so much damage without any of us being aware until it was too late."

"How long have you lot been planning to run out on us?" Mr. Fletcher asked fiercely.

"Since this morning," Peter admitted. "Sorry, it was my idea, but we had to do it. You guys can keep doing what you're doing, while we focus on ending the war."

"What are you talking about?" Mr. Woodward asked sharply. "If you have useful information that you haven't made us aware of, now would be a good time to speak up."

"Dad," Amelia said warningly, "aren't you always the one who says we shouldn't keep all our eggs in the one basket?"

Mr. Woodward looked for a moment like he was going to shout, but he quickly composed himself. "Very well, but if you do have useful information, young lady, I trust you'll know how to best use it. Keeping secrets when such secrets could make a big difference is extremely irresponsible."

"Sure thing, Dad," said Amelia in a bored voice. "Who have you got there with you?"

"Almost our entire army," Mr. Woodward told us. "We brought everyone over from the base whom we could find and teleported everyone who's part of our charge who was out on duty. We're missing thirty-five people; is that your number?"

"No," Amelia said, her face falling. "We have only thirty."

"Some people did get killed back there," Marc said. "I definitely saw one girl get swallowed by that monster thing. What the hell was that anyway?"

Mr. Woodward sighed. "The Hammersons created a number of creatures like that, all with different functions but all with the purpose of doing their bidding. That was one of those, although I've never seen that particular specimen before. I suspect you're right about the five missing, too; I'm going to need to know who you all are so that I can deduce who we've lost."

We went around the group, each person saying their name while Mr. Fletcher wrote them all down and compared them to a list of those they had already deduced were missing. Mr. Woodward sighed when he identified the five who were missing.

"We'll have to let their families know," he said. "Incidentally, many of your parents are here with us now, and quite a few of them would like nothing more than to come in here and see you all. Are you game?"

"Do we have a choice?" Amelia asked.

"I'm afraid I have no control over you anymore," he said, resigned. "You could tear this connection down right now and I could do nothing to stop you, but many of your parents are very worried about you. I think it would be cruel of you not to allow them to see you, as now none of us know when you'll be able to see them again."

Amelia sighed. "Okay, but maybe it'd be best to do one family at a time. If there's gonna be telling off, the rest of us don't need to hear it."

"Unless it's John's mother," said Tommy, "'cause we all saw that earlier."

"Bugger off," I muttered. "You reckon I enjoyed that?"

"What parents have you got there?" Amelia asked.

"All of them who were in the base," Mr. Woodward replied.

Amelia shrugged. "Guess I should have known that. Okay, everyone," she said, turning to address the group at large. "We'll all go out in the corridor and send one person in at a time, or families at a time. Er, maybe you should start," she said to Natalie, "since your dad's already here."

We all got up and trooped out of the room, leaving Natalie and Rebecca sitting in front of the massive display screen. The trouble was, the corridor hadn't been designed for a gathering of this sort. We all had to line up along both walls while we waited. In the interim, Amelia sat down on the floor and began creating electronic keys for the bedrooms.

"Guys, these keys can access a bedroom, and all the public areas in the base," Amelia announced. "I suppose the doors will be open most of the time, but if they're not, you can use these keys to open them. Now, everyone catch!"

All the keys went flying into the air, each of them soaring directly into the hands of each person in the corridor. Those which were supposed to belong to the Fletchers hit the closed lounge-room door and fell limply to the floor. I looked at my key and saw that I had room 1L3; floor one, room three on the left. I looked suspiciously at Amelia as she gathered up the Fletchers' keys: Had she just done that in such a way that we would each be sleeping where she wanted us to be sleeping? I had to wonder how close my room would be to hers...how close we would be to those who had been in the Smiley hunt. ... I would have a better idea once I saw where everyone else was sleeping.

"Don't go yet, though," Amelia said quickly, "unless you know for sure that your parents aren't in there. I suggest you all stay anyway, though."

A few minutes later, Natalie and Rebecca came out of the lounge room.

"Playmans and Thomases next," Natalie called as Amelia gave them their keys.

"Oh goody," said Jessica as she, Felicity, Peter, James and I moved away from the wall and walked down to the open door.

Through the screen to wherever the adults were, Mum, Marge, Dad, Charlie, Hilda and Violet were all getting into position at the same time the five of us approached the screen and began crouching down in front of it. Sitting would have been more comfortable, but for myself, I didn't want this to last any longer than it had to. The expressions on the faces of the adults weren't at all comforting: Mum and Marge were predictably angry, upset and worried, all balled up into one very familiar package; the grannies were also angry and worried but the emotions didn't look as strong in their faces; but it was the looks on Dad and Charlie's faces that hurt the most. About a year ago, during a soccer match, one of the twins had attempted a long kick to get past a couple of opposition players; the kick had come off, but it had cannoned into my stomach with the force of a—well, with the force of a cannon, because I hadn't been able to turn my body in time. I wasn't hurt, but the winded feeling I'd had for some twenty seconds was very similar to how I felt as I observed the disappointment on Dad and Charlie's faces.

"You do realise this is the last time we'll believe anything you kids tell us," Mum said, calmly for the time being. "Mr. Woodward's orders indeed——"

"Mr. Woodward did give us orders," James said calmly, "and we spent most of the afternoon following those orders. We told you that, we just didn't tell you about this part."

"Not lying, just not telling the whole truth," Jessica added.

"Whose idea was this?" Marge asked. "I'm sure one of you is behind it, or that Marc character. Why would you do such a thing? What makes you think you'll be better off on your own?"

"Anything's better than what we left behind," James said reasonably. "If we'd been in our rooms doing homework this afternoon, we probably would have been killed by the roof caving in. I would have thought you'd realise how pointless all that homework is in the scheme of things in the wake of what happened today."

"The homework itself isn't the point," Charlie told him. "Your lives are what matters here. The Woodwards have plenty of experience in developing safe places to hide; why wouldn't you trust in them to do the same for where we are now?"

"Er, perhaps they're not as reliable after what happened earlier?" Felicity suggested.

"No, that's not it," Peter said quickly, before any of the adults could respond. "Look, the only reason we're out here now is so that we can actually do something to help, instead of being locked up like a bunch of animals who really don't have any useful function."

Dad sighed. "Haven't we had this conversation before? John, Peter, haven't you had enough dangerous experiences to teach you that this is not a fight for children?"

"Jessica's the same age you were when you went to war," I pointed out, "and the rest of us aren't much younger. Besides, you said it yourself: We have had a lot of dangerous experiences, and we know how dangerous this war is."

"And you've seen a lot of your friends go as a result," Mum flared up, "including your own sister. Why are you so determined to join them?"

"What we're so determined to do," said Peter, his voice shaking slightly, "is make it so that none of us have to worry about joining that list. We're quite happy for Mr. Woodward and his army to keep doing what they have been, and in the meantime we're gonna work on some of the stuff Smiley told us so that we can end this war once and for all."

"If you know a secret to taking down the Hammerhearts, why wouldn't you tell Mr. Woodward?" Dad asked.

"He's got enough on his plate as it is," James said. "And besides, if Hammerson finds out that the Woodwards know, he'll find new ways to prevent it from happening. If nothing changes as far as he's concerned, we can catch him blindsided."

Mum and Marge didn't look at all happy about this, nor did the grannies, but Dad and Charlie looked thoughtful.

"It's only a matter of time before they realise Natalie and Amelia aren't out in the open with the rest of us," Dad said slowly. "I suppose we could put out a story that we don't want them to fight anymore."

"How safe are you where you are now?" Marge asked.

"Very," said James. "We're invisible and untraceable, and have a sound proof barrier around us. There's no magic Hammerson or Hall could use to track us down directly; they'll have to be very clever. If they do happen to find us, we'll be ready for them."

"How so?"

"We've got three people with magic," said Peter, "and I assume the rest of us will be armed pretty soon. Marc might even call Fewul, which will give us fair warning."

The adults still didn't look happy, nor did they have a great understanding of just how protected we were. Finally, Charlie said, "I suppose there's nothing we can say that will change your minds about doing this."

It wasn't a question, but the sadness in his voice was worth another soccer ball to the guts.

"If you'd let us do this over a month ago, we probably wouldn't have had to run out on you," said Jessica firmly. I turned away from the screen for the first time to look at the others; they had been kicked the same as me, but thankfully they were all keeping their faces as blank and emotionless as possible.

"I can't believe you're actually gonna do this," Mum said, beginning to tear up.

Peter shook his head. "Stop worrying about us. We're gonna be fine. Believe me, we're well hidden, and we'll be taking all possible precautions before we attempt anything."

"Nice try, mate," said Dad, smiling slightly. "It's just about impossible for parents not to worry. All I'd ask is that you keep in regular contact with us here. I'm sure Freddy will want regular updates on what you're doing, and remember, if there's anything at all we can do to help, you only have to ask."

"Duly noted, but I don't think we'll be saying too much about what we're doing or where we are," said Felicity reasonably. "I mean, we don't know if the Hammerhearts can see all this, or if they find a way to bug your base or something."

"The fact that you thought of that possibility puts my mind at ease a little," said Charlie wearily, getting to his feet. "In any case, we're glad you're okay, but I guess there's nothing else we can do here but hash over old ground. You might as well send the Maivises in; their grandparents look ready to blow a gasket."

"Thanks for being understanding," said Peter as the five of us also got to our feet, with pins and needles in my case.

We trooped out of the room to find the corridor absolutely packed. The same people were still waiting (in fact, a few had departed since we'd entered) but it seemed more full due to the bags and suitcases littering the floor.

"Wow, which ones are ours?" said Peter, almost tripping over a bag at his feet.

"You guys are next," James called to the twins, "and your sisters. Where are they?"

"Oh, this will be like an episode of..." said Harry, before realising he couldn't think of any television program that could compare to what was about to happen.

"'Days of the Maivises' lives'," Peter suggested as Harry and Simon bunny-hopped through the maze of bags towards the lounge room doors, followed by Misty and Michelle.

"Here," said Amelia, handing a small bag to me. "You're stuff's in here. I've been hanging on to it. The rest of you will have to find the ones with your names on."

"Thanks," I said to her, moving around behind Peter and Jessica and moving carefully up the corridor toward the bedrooms.

I reached the lift at one end of the corridor and stopped, checking my key again to see which room I was in. Floor one, room three on the left, according to the key. That was fine, but was it the left from this end of the corridor or left from the other end, which would be right from this end? I looked to my left, down the corridor where five doors stood on either side. A few of them were already open, light streaming into the corridor through their doorways, and I moved along to see who was in them. The first on the right was open, and a quick look inside revealed Rebecca, who was presently unloading her bag. The sign on the door proclaimed that room was 1R1, which answered my previous question. A quick look in the other open doors revealed that Marc was in 1L4, Lucien in 1L5, and Natalie in 1R5. I backtracked to my own door, slid the key into the slot, heard it click and pulled it open. There I spent the following few minutes unpacking my few possessions and loading them into the drawers.

Once I was done, I realise that I no longer had anything to do. My watch told me it was just after half past ten in the evening, and a wave of exhaustion crashed over me as I looked at my bed, easily the most comfortable-looking bed I would have the pleasure of sleeping in since I had been evicted from my third floor room in the old base. Before I could act on my desire to go to bed, however, a knock sounded on my open door, startling me.

"Sorry," said Marc, smirking at me. "Don't even think about sleeping yet. I want to too, believe me, but we have a meeting scheduled at eleven o'clock."

"Another one?" I said wearily. "Who's coming?"

"You, me," he listed off, "Lucien, Amelia, Natalie, Peter, James and Tommy. We're meeting up in the control room, or whatever it's gonna be called."

"No twins?" I said, surprised. "Felicity or Jessica?"

"Well, Amelia told me that was what was happening before I came up here," he said, shrugging. "She probably didn't think to invite anyone else. I can see her sense though; it'll be a lot easier to plan stuff if there's not too many of us. We can bring the rest of the group into the plan tomorrow."

"I guess so," I said, though I wasn't enthusiastic; it had been a very long day, preceded by a very long night. "I've got nothing to do in the meantime so I guess I'll just have to—"

"Do something that won't cause you to fall asleep," he finished the sentence, though differently from how I would have. "Let's go have a look around, see where the others are sleeping."

It wasn't a bad idea, I thought, remembering my suspicion from earlier. I found that two more rooms on the first floor had been opened since I'd entered my own room; Felicity was in the room next to Rebecca, and Lena was in the room next to Natalie; directly across from Marc, I realised. Did Amelia know about those two now being in a relationship? Possibly, though I couldn't see how, especially as both their minds were protected now. Perhaps she'd done some sort of spell that would automatically put each person nearest to those whose rooms they would most like to enter in the dead of night. I wondered who would be in the room next to mine, across from Felicity…and who would be in the room directly across from me…Natalie was already very near, of course….

We took the lift up to the second and third floors to see what was going on up there, joined for the first half of the rise by Dean and Joanne Abbodi, who had apparently just finished talking to their parents. Apart from those two, the only other people on the second floor so far were Lena's brother George, and Misty and Michelle. The third floor was easily the most interesting; Simon, Harry, James and Peter were all lined up along the left side, in that order, and given that Siobhan was directly opposite Peter, and Jessica was opposite the one empty room on the boys' side, I didn't have to wonder too hard who would be in the other four rooms. Amelia, you little rascal.

That was pretty much where the fun ended for me, though, because following our exploration, Marc went back down to the bottom level to spend some time with Lena before the meeting. That was not a scene I felt comfortable being witness to, given my own history with Lena, so I just hung around in the corridor near the lift, watching as Liam and Darcy took two of the three remaining rooms on the bottom level, while others took the lift or climbed the stairs to the upper levels. The door opposite mine remained closed and I began to suspect that would be Amelia's room.

Finally, about ten minutes before eleven o'clock, the lift doors opened to reveal Peter and James.

"Wow, you look bored," James observed. "We're heading on down there if you wanna join us."

"The sooner we get this over, the happier I'll be," I said as Peter pushed open the door and we stepped out into the dark yard.

"Me too," said Peter. "I would have preferred to do this in the morning; I need some recovery time."

I nodded, knowing what he meant, but James seemed confused. "What do you mean, recovery time? I could do with a good night's sleep, sure, but there doesn't seem to be much to recover from for us. Everyone we know is alive, nobody was injured, and it's not like we had any special attachments to that Woodward base."

Peter shook his head. "I know, but James, they destroyed it. The whole thing doesn't even exist anymore."

"So? We got all our stuff out."

"James, Kylie and Serena were still in there. Do you think it would have occurred to the Woodwards to get them out?"

"Oh, is that what it's about?" James asked, stopping halfway across the yard, and Peter and I stopped with him. "Pete, you know it really doesn't matter? It's only their bodies, not their souls. In fact, maybe it's better; at least they can't get up and walk around in the night anymore."

"Is that meant to be a joke?" Peter asked coldly.

"No, it's serious," said James earnestly. "Look, if their bodies don't exist anymore, it just means that they can't be abused. It doesn't change our memories of them or the legacy they left behind."

Peter shook his head and resumed walking. "I know you're right, but it still hurts to think about it."

"On a different subject, you know we can't get into the control room until one of the Sorcerers catches up with us," I told the two of them, "unless Amelia programmed our keys to work in there as well."

"Didn't know that," said James. "Oh well, it's not too long; Amelia might take a while yet, but Marc and Natalie should be along pretty soon."

In fact, Natalie turned up only a few minutes after us, and Lucien wasn't far behind her. Marc and Tommy took a little longer, and by the time Amelia arrived, we were running fifteen minutes late. Everyone was tired now and it took some effort to get the ball rolling.

"Sorry," Amelia said regretfully, closing the door behind her. The rest of us had been provided with seats, crammed into the control room, which really wasn't suitable for a meeting like this; it would have made more sense to use one of the bedrooms. "My dad didn't want to let me go; I had to hang up on him, effectively."

"Well now that we're all here, we might as well get going," Lucien said, straightening up in his seat. "It's pretty late and everyone's tired. I guess the point of this meeting is to work out what our first order of business is?"

"I think it's pretty straightforward," said Marc. "We were talking about it earlier. Find out about the Enlightener and the prophecy, then move against Hammerson and Hall; get their crystals off them, corner and kill Hammerson. After that, I guess the recovery is mostly a social and political issue, so we'll leave that to the adults."

"That will definitely be the hardest bit," said Natalie. "Believe me, we can't just knock off the Hammerhearts and expect things to just go back to the way they were. I have no idea what the cleanup was like after the last war but I'm sure it was extensive. This will be even worse since the Hammerhearts have actually installed their own laws in a lot of places."

"That's not our issue," said Lucien firmly. "It may become our issue later, but for the time being, we have to focus on one thing at a time. I think Marc's right; Hammerson is our priority, but to get to him, we need to learn about the prophecy first. Once we know what it says, we can form a plan to deal with him."

I shook my head. "That'll be my decision. Believe me, if the prophecy is even a tiny bit ambiguous, I won't be taking responsibility for it."

"Really, John?" said Lucien, raising his eyebrows. "Are you saying that you're not prepared to take a risk that could result in the end of the war?"

"Sure, if it's a reasonable risk," I said. "I'm not taking him on if I've got no chance. What good will I be when I'm dead?"

"That's eloquently put," said James, smirking slightly. "We have to believe the tests the Hammerhearts did that found you were connected with that prophecy are accurate, and we also have to assume the prophecy is correct. I'm basing that on the fact that Marc is the Seventh Sorcerer, and the Hammerhearts worked it out, and they were right on that score."

"Well, we have one thing on our side," said Marc. "We know how to kill him. You only have to do the same thing to him as what you did to Tankom——"

"You say it like it was a stroll in the park," I said distastefully.

"Yeah, it can be," James said firmly. "John, I still have the thing you used to kill her. It'll be easier a second time around because we can form a plan to corner Hammerson and get him when he has no way to defend himself. Once he's rested of the crystal, he'll be a piece of cake. The challenge will be locating him and spying on him to work out said plan, but we can certainly do it."

"Let's not get carried away," Lucien interrupted. "I agree with your ideas, James, but that'll be a job for after we've seen the prophecy and learned of the Enlightener."

"How is the Enlightener relevant to Hammerson?" Tommy asked. "Or is the whole game plan here to centre all our work around John and his wacky abilities?"

"I'm curious about it," I said quickly, before anyone else could interject. "It probably doesn't matter, but given that it was detected the same way as the prophecy, maybe I can use it in some way. That's what I'd like to find out, but it's very much a side plot to the prophecy."

"But we don't know that it isn't important," said Natalie. "Also, it's possible that information about the two things will be in the same place. That's why we were talking about those CDs we got from the magic display last time."

"Let's focus on that for the time being, then," said Lucien. "Let's brainstorm; where could those CDs be now?"

"In the base that the Woodwards destroyed?" suggested Peter sourly.

"Get over it, Pete," said James, not unkindly. "I would suggest Lisa's house, or where the Ponts used to live, although I doubt any of their stuff will be there now."

"Does anyone know what happened to Lisa's things when she died?" Marc asked. "What did her family do with them?"

"I don't imagine they would have got rid of them," said Natalie. "I suppose we can get back in touch with her father. It's possible that some of her things will be in the new

Woodward base; one of us might actually have to stop into their lair to get it."

"Yeah right, and have the parents not let said person come back?"

"Let's sit on that for the time being," said Lucien firmly. "Next time we contact the adults, we can ask Mr. Pont that very question. In the meantime, tomorrow, we can go have a look at their old house, see what's happened to it. Are there any other possible places those CDs could be?"

"Felicity and Jessica don't have them," said James. "I already asked them. Nicole could have had them, but somehow I doubt it; she wouldn't have focussed too much on schoolwork in those last few weeks of her life. I'm thinking Lisa almost certainly had them; the question is, did she bring them to the base on that night before she died, or did she leave them at her own place? Or perhaps she left them in her locker at school. It's gonna be quite a challenge to work out what she did."

"Could you use the crystal to determine where they are?" Peter asked Marc.

"I could try," he said doubtfully. "On that, do you guys think I should call Fewul to help us out?"

"I think so," said Lucien, "if you're sure it's safe to do so. If you have to leave the base, one of us can come out with you. We should be safe if we stay in a place like where we are now. One other thing we need to do, while I think of it, is move the base into the air."

"Why? We're invisible and untraceable."

"And if we get stepped on?"

"The base is strong enough to withstand things like that," said Amelia.

Lucien shook his head. "That's not the point. If a person suddenly steps on it, they're gonna wonder what happened. It's best if we're off the ground. I'd recommend twenty feet in the air."

"I'll do it," said Marc, getting up and approaching the controls.

"Does anyone else have anything to add?" Lucien asked.

"Yeah," said Natalie. "Nobody's mentioned Stella, but we agreed last time that we ought to bring her into safety."

"Yes, we probably should," Lucien said, thinking, "so that her father can't use her open mind against us. She's untraceable, though, so locating her will be even more difficult than finding Hall or Hammerson, especially if she doesn't interact with anyone."

"Have you heard anything about her?" Peter asked Natalie and Amelia.

"Not a lot," said Amelia, "only that she hasn't been found by her father, and apparently he's really unhappy about it."

"What can you tell us about her, John?" Tommy asked, as I had been waiting for someone to. "You seen her lately?"

"Yeah, about a week ago," I said, a little anxiously, knowing I would be pressed to tell them all I knew. It wasn't a story I liked to think about too much.

"What was she doing?" Marc asked. "Where was she?"

"I'm not sure exactly where she was, except that she's still on her own and still in the wild," I said. "I think she's really toughened up, living off the land and stealing to survive and all that."

"That all you know?" Peter asked. "She hasn't given anything away in her thoughts?"

"Only bits and pieces of what she's been up to," I said. "I don't know for sure but I think she's gone north of here over the last couple of weeks; she could be in New South Wales by now. I only knew I didn't recognise her surroundings."

"She stayed in the area before that?" said James sharply.

I shrugged. "Guess she felt more comfortable staying where she knew where stuff was. She definitely went east about as far as Euroa, then came back this way. She never wanted to go far because she didn't know if she could survive in a place she didn't know."

"What made her change her mind?" asked Marc.

"Why didn't she use the Hammerheart Highway?" Amelia asked.

"Maybe it's too unsafe now, or maybe she couldn't get in," I said, beginning to feel assaulted by the barrage of questions. "As for why she changed her mind, she had a run-in with a Hammerheart that caused her to run for it."

"What happened?" asked Natalie. "Is she okay?"

I groaned inwardly. Of course, I'd said too much, and now I had no way of getting out of telling the story. I sighed. "You guys remember how Lester Hammerson had looked in that memory where he was about to die? How old and weak he was?"

Everyone except Lucien and Amelia, who hadn't been present when we had viewed Smiley's memories, nodded.

"Well, apparently Hammerson's been remembering it too," I said. "He's got a plan regards that, and it involves Stella. He sent 3K17—you remember her—to find Stella and bring her in so that he could get on with it. I have no idea how she managed to find Stella but somehow she did. She told her the plan but before she could subdue her, Stella—well, she had to hurt her so that she could get away. She's still alive, though, 3K17; it was probably no worse than a broken finger or something."

"Did you actually see all this?" James asked sharply.

"No, I just entered her mind when she was thinking about it."

"What was this big plan of Hammerson's?" Peter asked.

"Oh, I reckon I can guess," said Marc darkly. "He wants Stella to have a baby, right?"

"Right in one," I said heavily. "It basically goes like this: He wants his family to have all six crystal chips, which means six generations have to be living at the same time. The only way he can prevent the oldest generation getting like his grandfather was in the end is if they all reproduce at a very young age—say, Stella's age. He wants Stella to spend the next sixteen or seventeen years being a mother until her child is old enough to reproduce, then once she's a grandmother in her early or mid thirties, she'll be allowed to rule."

"That is seriously messed up," said Peter shakily.

"How does Stella feel about all that?" Tommy asked.

"You need to ask?" I retorted wearily. "She wants nothing to do with it, partly because she doesn't want to have to have sex with Hignat, and partly because she doesn't want to rule—"

"What!" several people yelped, and I forgot, a moment too late, that I'd forgotten to mention that last bit.

"*Hignat!*" Peter cried out. "Yikes, I don't blame her."

"Ather Hignat, right?" James enquired.

I sighed again. "Yeah. Apparently he was chosen to be the father of the next generation's Sorcerer. Sebastian wanted to be the one, but apparently he's got too much traitor blood in him, and Hammerson doesn't want that passed to the next generation. Stella got all of this out of 3K17. Hignat got all the credit for the breakout and delivering the crystal, even though Sebastian was actually the one who handed it over. Hammerson's really happy with him."

"We'd heard that too," said Amelia. "We've heard he's given Hignat a lot of rewards for that, but I had no idea he's provided him with…"

She broke off, going pale, and I didn't need to hear what she'd been about to say. Unfortunately, Tommy also knew what she'd been about to say, and unlike most of the rest of us, he didn't know about what Hignat and Wilwog had done to her months earlier. "I imagine it's more than just sex," he said. "Hammerson may have provided Hignat with loads of young ladies by now, for all we know, but Stella's worth a lot more than that, in Hammerson's eyes anyway."

"Okay, so we need to find Stella before her father can," said Lucien quickly. "We'll have to be clever to do it, but I'm sure it's possible."

"Yeah, I think so," said Marc. "I found her that night in Germany because I saw a spot that hadn't been filled, so we can probably do the same thing to find her again."

"Great," said Lucien. "Now, before we turn in for the night, we need to discuss how we're going to deal with the rest of our little army. What information are we going to give them and how are we going to organise them so that they can all do their bit to help us…."

The following ten minutes were spent discussing the agenda for the meeting that would take place the following day.

Part 2: Hunting

Chapter 10: Tracing

Another night, another nightmare. I knew almost immediately that this was indeed the Enlightener, because by the end of the dream, I was sitting up in bed, wide awake and suddenly in possession of a horrible piece of knowledge and understanding I would have been much happier without. In the dream, I was standing before Amelia and Stella on the Moran front lawn as Marc threw three of the Sorcerous Crystals to each of them.

"I'm not going to kill you, but even if I can't do it with my own magic, I can certainly arrange your death for you," said Stella, but it was the voice of her father rather than her own that issued from her mouth.

She and Amelia caught three crystals each and began juggling them around, changing each of their properties so that the six crystal chips would correspond to themselves, their fathers and their grandmothers, thereby removing Moran's magical power.

"And once I have killed you both, I will be whole again, and you will be nothing, just as you should have been from the moment that plane went down," said Amelia in the voice of the deceased Tankom as she juggled her crystals around, changing the properties of each of them, unaware that one of the crystal chips was damaged, oblivious to the knowledge that the damaged crystal chip may not necessarily be returning to the Sorcerer responsible for the damage…

That was when I woke up, and unfortunately, I remembered every detail of the dream, along with the knowledge it contained. It was a dreadful truth that explained a question I had spent plenty of time pondering for several months. At the time, Stella and I had agreed that a possible reason why Hammerson had been unable to kill me was the connection that existed between us; in other words, we could only die together as long as the connection bound us together. That would have been nice because it would have made it much more difficult for Hammerson to kill us.

It had always been too good to be true, and the time had come for me to acknowledge that. I cast my mind back to the period of less than two weeks during which Hammerson had had the magic given to him by Stella. Had he attempted to kill anyone else in that time? If not, then he wouldn't have realised that the problem lay in his own impaired magic, rather than any special ability of mine. Yes, I suddenly realised; he had killed the big, bulky bloke who had been in that fateful room along with the two of us when he'd attempted to kill me, so that blew that theory out of the air....

Or did it? What if that man had only been temporarily knocked out, as I had been, and before he had come around properly, Hammerson had summoned that horrible monster that had killed Tulip. What if that guard had been alive, and had died exactly the way Tulip had? If that had happened, it would have made no difference to Hammerson. If he hadn't attempted to kill anyone else in that time, how could he have known the truth?

Of course, Tankom may have had a better idea of what was going on. She had offered to kill me herself when Hammerson had been unable to do it, perhaps because she knew that she now could. She had offered instead of telling her son the truth, which meant that she had probably never confided in Hammerson about her own limited abilities. If that were true, she must have survived thirteen years without being sprung, never needing to kill anyone by magic, though perhaps she'd found ways around that. It wasn't too hard to imagine; she could have used magic to slit a person's throat, instead of killing them outright; it would have taken longer, but the end result would have been the same.

So what did all this mean for me? Unfortunately, it meant that I was nowhere near as safe as I thought I had been. The only piece of good fortune was that to this day, Hammerson didn't know the truth. If he had, he would have killed me in that air pocket in the wreckage of the Woodward base; I wouldn't have been given even the slightest chance. He must have been extremely thick not to have realised that with the power of the Sien-Leoard Crystal, any limitations he'd had before would no longer apply. Then again, he may have still been thinking that I was the extraordinary one, that it was through some abnormality (or misplaced spell) that I was able to stay alive through his killing curses.

Meanwhile, one of the Fletchers was still operating with an impaired crystal chip. At least, I had to assume they were; Tommy was now normal, with the death of his German body, but that had been by way of suicide rather than having the actual spell undone. I had to assume that it still applied, and that the crystal chip was still damaged as a result. The Fletchers, never having had magic before, would never have known the difference. None of them would have attempted to kill, I felt sure, so unless they had attempted some other deep, dark magic, they may never have uncovered the truth.

And what did all that matter to me? Nothing at all; what mattered to me was that I now had to watch my step, as I should have done all along. It took a long time (perhaps twenty minutes) to reach this conclusion. I lay back down in the darkness, thinking. It shouldn't make much of a difference, but as unpleasant as it was to know this, it may be useful knowledge to have. It applied to both me and Stella, as she may still be thinking she was also protected from her father's death curses, but for Hammerson himself? It may occur to him to kill me with the Sien-Leoard Crystal, or else order Hall to use the Villain Crystal, but in the meantime he still didn't know the truth, and that was fine with me. I had to be thankful that as evil as the Hammersons were, they were still good enough about doing us a huge favour by not confiding their secrets in each other. If Hammerson and Tankom had been more open and honest with each other, about both Tommy and me, they probably could have finished us both off, well before we could have a chance to get back at them. It was all a bit of history, which, thanks to a bit of good luck, would never play out.

I went back to sleep after that and, thankfully, slept through until just after seven o'clock. I was by no means completely rested but I did nevertheless feel a little fresher than I had twenty-four hours earlier. I was dressed and showered half an hour later, but this was where the conundrum presented itself. We had never exactly discussed a standard time for meals, nor had anyone thought about how we would make announcements to an army of thirty, never knowing where they all were at any given time. It was understandable, after the stress we'd been under the night before (particularly Natalie, who'd been out all day, and Amelia, who'd just lost the home she'd had all her life), but it was something we would have to deal with at some stage today.

Consequently, when I left my bedroom, the base was very quiet. I sensed rather than heard that there were some people who were already awake, probably showering as I had just done, but all the other bedrooms on the first floor were shut and, I assumed, their occupants not risen for the day. I headed to the end of the corridor, turned left, walked past the door into the yard (which was now dimly lit under an overcast sky) and entered the dining room. To my slight surprise, there were already a few people having breakfast: Dean and George closest to the door, and Harry and Simon on the other side of the room.

"John, you're one of the authorities around here, right?" Dean asked me. "What's the deal for dishes around here?"

"At the moment, there is none," I said flatly. "That's something I'll have to cover with one of the Sorcerers when they get out of bed."

"So what do we do in the meantime?"

"Leave them on the tables for all I care; we'll clean up later."

"So this is what it's like to live without parents," said George, and he and Dean laughed. I left them to it, got my own breakfast from the conveyer belt and sat down to eat with the terrible twins.

"You're up all nice and sprightly in the morning," Harry observed, waving his spoon at me.

"I wouldn't say sprightly," I said, beginning to eat. "Still a little tired, would consider having a nap later today if I can get away with it."

"Late night, hey?" said Simon, grinning at his brother. "Now what were you doing last night that would cause you to feel tuckered out so early in the day?"

"Did you do it by yourself or did you have someone with nice hands help you out?" Harry added.

I started at that and most unfortunately, the twins took that for assent.

"Well, well, well, this is excellent news," said Simon, leaning around the table and patting me on the shoulder. "Good work there, you old dog; knew it wouldn't take you long."

"You're a nut," I said wearily, "and keep your voice down in case any girls come in and think you're talking about—about—"

"You're worried they'll falsely assume that we're talking about you doing nasty things?" Harry enquired. "Well, you need not fear, my boy, because if they do happen to make that assumption, they'll be correct."

"I had a disturbing dream last night," I told them, "that's what disturbed my sleep. It had nothing to do with nasty stuff."

"Oh really? Who was in this disturbing dream of yours?" Simon asked, grinning broadly.

"Er, that doesn't matter," I said, stopping myself from saying Amelia and Stella just in time; they would have jumped on that. Unfortunately, they took my lack of an answer to mean exactly that.

"Be that as it may, my boy, we are pleased that you are up before so many of our comrades," said Harry, straightening up in his seat and surveying me. "Perhaps it was your ears burning that caused you to leap out of bed when you probably could have done with an extra hour?"

"No," I said, taking a moment to understand his meaning. "Oh, wait, have you guys been talking about me?"

"Now, now, who's looking a wee bit self-conscious," said Simon, winking at me. "We couldn't help noticing the interesting sleeping arrangements Amelia fixed for us, and it occurred to us that in an earlier time, you would have been up with us on the third floor."

"All the third floor rooms are taken," I pointed out.

"He's also a wee bit slow this morning," Harry said quietly to his brother, as though I couldn't hear him, though he spoiled the effect by winking at me. "Do tell me, my dear lad, do you really think Tommy and Jessica belong in the same class as the three of us? Peter and James, sure, but Tommy? I would have had him pinned for the room beside Marc, and yet for reasons we can't even begin to contemplate, you got that room. Now why is that?"

"What are you getting at?" I said, staring at both of them. "If this is some private joke, I want in."

"Of course you do, young man, and isn't that the whole point?" said Simon, attempting to fix a sympathetic expression on his face, but once again ruining it by virtue of his trembling lips as he forced himself not to laugh. "So we were discussing said problem, and it occurred to us that a possible reason for you being shunted down to the bottom of the barrel, if you'll pardon my terminology, is because there's no one to put in the room opposite you."

I groaned, understanding where they were going. "I don't see how that matters, does it?"

"Now, now, bear with us here," said Harry, watching me closely. The twins leaned forward and I followed their lead so that the three of us could talk more quietly. "Today is June the 30th, and you, dear boy, have been single for more than six weeks."

"You think I'm not aware of that?"

"There is no need for it, young John; we know perfectly well that there is at least one young lady who would be quite happy to—well, never mind sleeping opposite—just cross the corridor so that you have a fun way to deprive yourself of sleep."

"Guys, this is kind of a sore spot," I said, having had about enough of their fooling around. In times gone by, if Serena were still here, I would be up on the third floor, and so would she, but those days were gone and I couldn't appreciate the twins bringing it up.

"That's exactly what we thought," said Simon, and to my relief, now he did look serious. "Maybe you should take a closer look at Peter and the relationship he's managed to conjure up with Siobhan. He lost his girlfriend and she lost her whole life, and they seem to work quite well together."

"You know it took a few weeks for them to start dating after Kylie died?" I pointed out. When they both nodded, I said, "That's because he needed time to appreciate other girls again."

"Are you telling us that you're going through the same healing period?" Harry said. "You know, if it's taken you this long, maybe what you need to help you move on is a good, supportive girlfriend who will be there to—well, not make you forget, but be able to live without being followed by the pain of what's happened and what can't be undone."

"There's a difference," I said. "I never started healing until the night before last, until I had to face Serena again. Before then I was too depressed to make any forward movement in anything. I think I can start now, but I don't think I can date anyone yet."

"Are you perhaps worried that if you do, you won't be able to appreciate a girl to the level you would like to?" Simon asked.

I thought about that and decided that he was probably right.

"Well, never fear, my boy," said Harry more loudly, leaning back and indicating that Simon and I could do the same; the serious part of the conversation was over for the time being. As clownish as the twins often were, I appreciated that they could be quite mature and insightful when they wanted to.

"Indeed, you must never fear, because the Maivises are here," Simon proclaimed. "We are here to help you, dear boy."

"Okay, now you're making me nervous," I said warily.

"Now, that wasn't the point," said Harry, swapping a look with his brother. "Just leave everything to us, Mr. Playman; we will see to it that you will have more interesting things keeping you awake during the night than a few dodgy dreams."

"You?" I said, startled. "What can you do?"

"What can't we do?" Simon asked, raising his eyebrows. "You need not worry about it; just leave everything to us, dear boy."

"Has anyone told you two you're nuts?"

"No need. We look down every morning and see that we have two nuts," said Harry, and all three of us burst out laughing. I still had no idea what they were really talking about, or even if they were being serious, but nevertheless they had once again managed to cheer me up.

It was an odd sort of morning. Everyone got up at different times and had breakfast at different times and there was no organisation about anything. Amelia was able to sort a few of our problems out mid-morning, when Peter and I cornered her and explained the various issues that had so far come up. She installed an enormous dish washer that would use magic to clean the dishes as opposed to detergent; a general cleaning system which would keep public areas like the dining room, lounge room, the corridors and the yard from getting dirty or dusty; and a public address system which could be used to alert everyone in the base, wherever they may be, to an impending meeting (it operated out of the control room). We also put signs up on the lounge room door, the dining room door, the yard doors and the lift doors, stating that meal times would be the same here as they had been in the old base (six to nine o'clock in the morning for breakfast, half past twelve to half past one in the afternoon for lunch, and half past six to half past seven in the evening for dinner).

It wasn't until around two in the afternoon that we were finally able to round up everyone for a meeting, which again took place in the lounge room. It took a long time to get going, though, because Lucien, who was chairing the meeting, wanted to do some housekeeping first. Questions and suggestions came thick and fast, and unfortunately, many of them had to do with things like television, phones and, of course, internet access.

"Believe me, I'd love to be able to get a few computers working with the Internet in here," Marc said earnestly. "I miss doing that stuff too, but we have to put safety ahead of everything else. We heard that Hammerson's developed a computer virus that is capable of spreading from computer to monitor, from monitor to the eyes of the person using the computer, and from the eyes to the breath, so that it can travel on the air."

"There are two viruses like that," Amelia said. "One is supposed to kill those it infects after a certain amount of time, while the other is more like a bug, meaning that the Hammerhearts can spy through the mind of that person, and even take control of them if they choose. That was initially the reason why my father disconnected the Internet; he didn't want that to get into the walls of the base. I'd be quite happy to set up computers with internet access if I could be sure that we could fight a virus like that, but we just don't know if that'll be possible, especially if Hammerson keeps making new ones that'll just get more and more powerful."

"There's another reason too," said Lucien. "While I'm sure you are all trustworthy, the fact is if any of you access your Facebook, Twitter, or any other accounts, even your email, the Hammerhearts will know. Many of those servers are in the US and the Hammerhearts have control there. It stands to reason they would have their fingers dirty in the social networking scene; it would certainly be beneficial for them. If they can use those accounts to track us down, or deduce anything about what we're doing, it could put us at a disadvantage."

"Can't you just block those sites?" suggested Katie. "You know, that way we can still keep up with news and stuff, but we can't accidentally give anything away."

Amelia shook her head. "It comes back to the virus; we just don't know how it spreads. We can't take any chances with it."

"I do agree with one thing, though," said Natalie. "We do need to keep up with the news. We'll be doing plenty of spying on the Hammerhearts but it might also be useful to know what's being published by the media, what propaganda they're spreading and how the public are responding to it. I'm thinking maybe we can set up some sort of news feed that's completely separate from the Internet. It can just use magic to lift articles out of the Chopville Daily Telegraph and other newspapers around the world. As for the public's response, well—"

"There's really no way to do that, other than spying," said Amelia. "The fact is, people can get in a lot of trouble if they post anti-Hammerheart sentiments on the net and they get caught out. We saw some really nasty consequences of that in the early days. Nowadays, most people know better, so there's no way to use those outlets to get a true reflection on what's going on."

"Question on that," said James. "How important is it to know what the public are doing? Unless they're planning a mass revolt, which would be the stupidest thing they could possibly do, how is anything else relevant to us?"

There was a silence as everyone pondered his question. Finally, Lucien said, "You're right; it doesn't really matter to us. It's the Hammerhearts' movements that are more important. I think the best way to do that, other than our own spying, is this news feed that Natalie suggested, but also TV and radio access. I don't suppose Hammerson's made a virus regarding TV and radio?"

"Don't know," said Amelia, "but he could think of it. Do you think he would target analog or digital?"

"I suppose he could do both if he thinks of it," said Lucien.

"Is there any way you could create a TV and radio that doesn't allow anything other than the program to get through?" asked Erica. "And everything else will be filtered out?"

"Possibly," said Amelia. "It would be much easier to do that for traditional media than it would be for the Internet. In that case, we'll have to stick to analog, but we'll only make them available here in the lounge room; that way we have control over everything that comes into the base."

"Okay, we'll get on that after the meeting," said Lucien. "Does anyone else have any issues to raise?"

"Our phones," said Robyn. "When can we use them?"

"You can't," said Marc flatly. "Cellular transmissions are too easy to monitor; they'll track us down too easily. We'll use magical links to keep in touch with our parents—well, not mine—but anything other than that is out, I'm afraid."

A few people didn't look happy about that, but nobody objected. Sophie said, "When are we gonna speak to the adults again?"

We all looked to Lucien for the response, but it was Amelia who answered. "I'll contact my father telepathically tonight and see what's up. Some of it I'll just pass on to the rest of you myself, but as for when we'll actually speak to them again, it depends what they're doing and if they need to see us again. If any of you are desperate to communicate something at some point, let me know and I'll ask my father if it's okay to set up a link."

"Anything else?" Lucien asked, and when nobody answered for about ten seconds, he nodded, satisfied. "In that case, we'll get down to business. Now, as some of you know, a few of us had a meeting last night to discuss what our first orders of business would be. There are too simultaneous things we want to get done before we begin moving against the Hammerhearts. One is to locate Stella and bring her into hiding with the rest of us; we have our own reasons for wanting her away from the Hammerhearts, and her knowledge of her father could be useful for us. The other thing we need to do is track down some information that we intend to use against Hammerson. It's very important and quite specific as to how we can defeat him. Now, what we've decided to do is split the group into two groups of fifteen, where each group will focus on one of these tasks. Are there any questions so far?"

Several people called out in unison, and Lucien had to raise his hands. "Please, hands up so we can keep some order about this. Sorry to play like we're back at school," he added, grinning slightly.

Silence fell and several hands shot in the air. Lucien pointed first at Liam, who said, "How come you want to get Stella here before the Hammerhearts get her?"

"Two reasons," said Lucien. "Firstly, she knows things which, if they found out, would be bad for us. Unfortunately, her mind is unprotected, so Hammerson could get pretty much anything he wanted out of her. Secondly, her father has his own plan for Stella. If he gets hold of her, the first thing he'll do is put a spell on her so that she can't object to what he wants from her. We don't want to give him that chance."

He next pointed at either Misty or Michelle (I couldn't tell them apart) who said, "How can you be sure she's trustworthy? What if she's like Sebastian, only pretending to be on our side?"

"Or what if she's infected with one of those computer viruses?" her twin added before Lucien could respond.

"We're almost certain she's not like Sebastian," said Amelia.

"*Completely* certain," Natalie corrected, looking sideways at Amelia. "Stella's done a lot of very good things for our side while she's been on the run, including stealing the Darkness Crystal from her father back in April. Also, I had a good look at her mind the last time I saw her, and I'm sure she's genuine. You can't fake thoughts like the ones she was thinking."

"And as for the virus," said Lucien, "we will obviously use magic to locate her, and when we do, we can—for lack of a better word—quarantine her before letting her inside the base. Anymore questions?"

A few more hands shot into the air. Lucien indicated Felicity this time, who said, "What information are we supposed to be looking for that's gonna help us?"

"That's a stupid question," said Rebecca. "If they knew, why would they need to look for it?"

A few people shot nasty looks at Rebecca. Before an argument could break out, Lucien swiftly intervened. "That's a good question, and on the whole, we would rather not say for the time being. We don't know exactly what the information is, Rebecca is right about that, but we do know what it's got to do with. You are all aware, I think, that a number of us went to Rock Haulter shortly before I myself returned to the Woodwards; it was there that we were pointed in the right direction."

"So how do we go about finding this information?" Darcy asked.

"I'll ignore the fact that you didn't put your hand up," said Lucien, looking at Darcy as if he were a misbehaving student in a classroom (though nothing like the way Hall would have gone about it). "The information we need was collected by Natalie and Lisa during the magic display at school at the start of the year. I'm sure you'll all remember what happened on that day. We don't know where the information has since gone, though. We think it may have been in Lisa's possession when she died but if it was, it could have gone anywhere since then. Any more questions?"

Two hands went into the air. Lucien indicated Jessica first, who said, "Nat, didn't you get that information off the computers?" When Natalie nodded, she added, "why don't we look for those computers then? They're probably still at the school."

"May I remind you what the school has become since the last time we were there?" said Peter. "That gym in particular has a pretty shady recent history."

"And it's full of Hammerhearts," said Lucien heavily. "Plus, we don't know if that computer is still there, if the information is still on it, or if it's on a CD-ROM somewhere, or where said CD-ROM may be now. There are too many variables."

"No more than what we started with, by the sound of it," said Jessica, and sighed. "It was just a suggestion."

"Any more questions?" Lucien asked.

Only one more hand went up, and my stomach lurched with anticipation when I realised Lisa's brother Jason had something to contribute. Could he know anything that might help us? When Lucien pointed to him, he said, "Mum and Dad gave me her laptop when she died. There was a lot of her stuff on there already; I didn't wanna keep it, since I'd planned to use it for school, but I didn't wanna delete it either; that felt disrespectful. I burnt it to a DVD and kept it. It'll be in my room upstairs if you wanna check it out. It mightn't have anything useful on it, but she did have a lot of homework stuff, and there was stuff about magic in there."

"There would have been, since we were studying the history of magic back then," said Natalie. "It's not exactly what we want—she probably didn't copy every single document from those discs—but it might help us out. Thanks for that, Jason."

"Anymore questions?" Lucien asked. This time, nobody moved, and he nodded, satisfied. "Right, what we're going to do now is divide the group into two groups of fifteen. Once we're in our groups, we'll separate so that we can begin planning what we're each going to do. We've organised you in terms of which assignment we think each of you will be more valuable to. Marc?"

Marc handed him the piece of paper we had worked on the night before and he glanced down at it. "Group A will focus on locating Stella. That group will be led by Marc and Natalie, and will include Candice, Darcy, Harry, John, Katie, Lena, Liam, Peter, Rebecca, Robyn, Simon, Siobhan and Sophie. Group B will focus on tracking down that missing information of Lisa's. Amelia and I will lead that group and it will include Belinda, Dean, Della, Erica, Felicity, George, James, Jason, Jessica, Joanne, Michelle, Misty and Tommy. Is everyone clear on where they're supposed to be?"

There was a general mutter of assent, and Lucien nodded again. "Good. In that case, one group can stay here, and the other group—er—any ideas, you two?"

"The other group can have the afternoon off," said Amelia. "Not trying to get out of working, but you guys can get started, while Jason shows me what stuff of Lisa's he's got. I'll let you guys know later on if it's useful at all."

And with that, group B got up and trooped out of the lounge room. Those of us who were left gathered closer around Marc and Natalie so that we didn't have to talk across the whole room.

"Operation Stella-grab," Simon proclaimed. "So, what's our first order of business, people?"

"Well, the thing we have to bear in mind is that Stella's untraceable," said Marc. "For those of you who don't know, it's a spell that hides her from magical tracing. I can't use my crystal, Natalie can't use her magic, nor can any other magic simply pinpoint her location. That doesn't mean we can't find her; it just means we have to find other ways to do it."

"What have you got in mind?" asked Lena.

"First order of business is to call Fewul," said Marc. "It won't be able to track her down either, but with that extra bit of magic, not only can we protect ourselves better, we can come up with other tricks that might help us along the way. I'll put the base down somewhere safe between now and dinner so I can step out and do that."

"What form is it gonna take?" asked Peter. "We never discussed that last night. We can't make it Lucien again; that'd be weird for him, I reckon."

"Make it one of us," said Harry, indicating himself and Simon, "that'll make us triplets."

Everyone in the room burst out laughing, and Katie slapped her boyfriend. "It's hard enough as it is. I don't wanna accidentally take the Beast of Magic to bed one night."

"Why not? He's bound to be better in the sack than Harry," Peter said, and the room exploded once again with laughter.

"You know what, I think we'll actually do that," said Marc, grinning broadly. "It might be confusing for some, but I reckon the big giveaway is that one triplet will be way smarter than the other two."

"Hey, you can't help bad luck, right?" Simon called over the renewed laughter.

"I suggest we make Fewul walk around with no clothes on," said Darcy. "If Harry and Simon wanna confuse people, they'll have to follow his lead."

There was yet another roar of laughter. A few people looked slightly concerned that Marc might actually follow that advice, and the twins looked appropriately abashed, but fortunately that was where it ended.

"I won't do that, but I guess I will make him wear something distinctive," said Marc. "With that settled, we need to work out how we're gonna begin looking for Stella. I'm open to suggestions here."

"Can't John do that?" asked Siobhan.

I shook my head. "I can try, but if she's not thinking about where she is, it won't do any good. Er," I faltered, noticing that several people looked mightily confused, not having been told about my connection with Stella, "take my word for it and don't ask questions."

"Let us know when you see her again," Marc told me, "but since we don't know when or if that'll happen anytime soon, we have to plan without that knowledge. So, any ideas?"

"Do we know anything about where she is now?" asked Rebecca.

"Only that she's on the run and in the open," said Marc, "unless John can tell us more, can you?"

"North," I reminded him, "and I think she's following a highway, but she was staying out of sight of it so I'm not sure which one."

"If we can work out where she's going, we can head her off," said Liam. "Maybe we can trace her movements back from Chopville and work it out that way?"

"Possibly, but she's been untraceable for months, so she mightn't show up in any magic we do to uncover her route over the last few weeks," said Marc.

"That's just guessing, though," Lena pointed out.

"True," said Marc heavily. "Anything's worth a try."

"Does this untraceable deal make her invisible as well?" asked Sophie.

"No, but she might have made herself invisible in addition to being untraceable," said Natalie, "if she got hold of one of our invisibility toggles. She's stolen from Hammerhearts before, and it stands to reason that they would have them now; Sebastian would have supplied them with them while he was spying."

"But if she is invisible, we can deal with that," said Marc. "Ghost goggles can see invisible people, so I guess we'll have to wear them when we're looking for her."

"In that case, why not just scour the landscape for her?" asked Katie.

"If you mean manually, that would take an age to cover all the places she could have gone," said Marc. "She may have started moving north, but she could have gone south since then, or she could have stolen a car and gone just about anywhere. We have to think of all these possibilities."

"Not necessarily," said Peter, and his eyes were alight with an idea. "Marc, you remember that night in Germany, and the Hammerhearts were able to pinpoint our position in the maze? Remember what we suspected could be behind it?"

"We weren't untraceable," Marc said, but he looked interested.

"It doesn't matter," said Peter. "Look, I understand if we can't move the base out of Chopville; Amelia's group will probably wanna stay close so they can work on getting those discs. What we can do is create some sort of device that can scour the landscape for moving objects, and present visuals to us. It won't look for people because obviously if we set it up like that, it won't find anyone who's untraceable."

"If she's invisible——"

"I can enchant it so that it can see ghosts," said Marc, and now he looked excited too. "That's not guaranteed to work but it's definitely worth a try. Good one, Pete; I'll start working on that today. In fact, maybe Fewul can let me know if it will or won't work, and how to make it better. Okay, I reckon we're getting somewhere now."

Chapter 11: The First Step

By half past three, the meeting had concluded, with only Marc to continue working on our plans into the evening. This left three hours before dinner, during which time the lounge room took plenty of occupants, as there really wasn't much else for anyone to do. I hung around long enough to register that about half the group stayed in the lounge room, while plenty of others (Peter, James and the twins among them) retired to their bedrooms with their respective girlfriends. I suspected what they could be doing in there but of course, wouldn't take it as a given. Marc, Amelia and Lisa's younger brother Jason were the only ones unaccounted for, but I supposed they were continuing with the plans we'd laid out during the meeting.

This left me with nothing to do and no one with whom I was particularly interested in keeping company for three hours. Of course, Natalie hadn't been doing anything in that time, but not until later on would I even realise I'd missed an opportunity to talk to her—about what, who could have known. Instead I retired to my own bedroom, alone, and caught up on a bit of sleep for the next few hours. Yeah, not an interesting way to spend the afternoon, and it left me feeling even more tired come dinner time than I had been beforehand, and would probably keep me up late into the night into the bargain. So, all in all, not a very smart move, but what can I say? I was bored, and unlike before, I didn't have any homework to do....

By the time I left my bedroom, dinner had already been going for fifteen minutes and the dining room was packed and well in motion. I got my dinner before bothering to look around for a place to sit, but what I found wasn't to my liking. The tables in this room all seated four, and Peter, James, Siobhan and Erica were on one table together; Harry, Simon, Katie and Sophie on another. Tommy was sitting with Felicity and Jessica, and there was an empty seat near them, but I didn't want to be near a happy couple if I could avoid it, even if it was only Jessica. Meanwhile, Natalie, Amelia and Lena were on yet another table, and there was another empty seat beside them. Not great, I thought, with Lena being there, and the awkwardness that could ensue if we were close together, but that still seemed like the best option available, until Marc and Fewul entered the room.

To say this caused a bit of a reaction would be a colossal understatement. Fewul had taken on the exact form of either Harry or Simon; it didn't matter which, since they were identical, but he (and I use the pronoun loosely) had done it in such a way that even I, who was very familiar with the twins and their subtle differences, couldn't determine which one he was impersonating. However, there was no way anyone could have mistaken him for either Harry or Simon; all the Beast of Magic needed was a helmet and he could easily have passed for a pink Power Ranger.

The general reactions were whistling, cheering, laughing, clapping, and several people whipping out their camera phones to take full advantage of the moment. Harry and Simon, ever the performers, jumped to their feet and hurried to embrace the Beast of Magic, as though he really were a third of their breed.

"Ladies and gentleman," Harry announced to the room at large, stepping to one side of Fewul, and with Simon on the other, they each flung an arm around his shoulders, "may I introduce our long lost brother, Hugh."

"Hugh?" several people said questioningly.

"Indeed, Hugh," Simon said, bowing. "His middle name is Jorgan."

There was an explosion of laughter which could have rattled the window in its frame. Several people actually slapped their tables. Marc, who had bore all this patiently, now shooed the twins away so that he could take the seat I'd been considering taking. The first thing he did when he had seated himself was lean towards Lena and give her a kiss on the cheek. It didn't affect me at all, but it certainly affected Amelia, who clearly hadn't known until then that those two were an item. Her eyes widened in surprise and what could have been irritation before she quickly cast them toward the ceiling. That was pretty low class of Marc to knowingly do that right in front of his ex, but perhaps he just hadn't thought of that in time. Who could say? I wondered briefly if Natalie had gone through the same motions with Tommy and Jessica yet? Upon looking back at their table and registering that she had seated herself with her back to Tommy, I assumed she must have deduced their coupling by now.

Meanwhile, Fewul, perhaps on silent or telepathic instructions from Marc, was coming towards me, though not as though I were the object of his interest. Of course, he was getting Marc's dinner for him, and I stepped aside, resuming my search for a table. In a corner, out of the way of most of the others and hard to spot at first, sat Lucien, Liam and Darcy. No happy couple among those three; there were three guys, one of whom had lost his girlfriend the same way I'd lost Serena, another of whom had had his happy relationship screwed up by an influential charm that had caused him to simply cut off communication with the girl he'd been seeing (I'd heard this story in the weeks since he'd returned). Then there was Liam, who'd always been something of a misery-guts ever since Daniel had died. Yep, that was definitely my table.

Even so, dinner still went slowly. The four of us didn't have much to say to each other, and given my position at the table, it was too easy to see all those I would normally have sat with. I only ended up eating about half of my dinner, partly because the nap had left me without an appetite and partly because I wanted nothing more than to get out of the dining room and— and do what? I had no idea. As I started later than everyone else, a lot of people were finishing around the same time as me. As Amelia was one of them, she began calling over the throng to the people heading for the door.

"Everyone clear out of the lounge room this evening," she called. "We're doing some magical testing in there and we don't know how long it will take, or if it'll be dangerous to anyone else."

"What's that all about?" I asked Lucien.

He shrugged. "I understand it has something to do with their plan to monitor the media. I guess they'll be trying to find the best way of doing it and they want it cleared in case a virus does somehow get in."

"Great," I said, dropping my eyes. "Suppose people will stay in their rooms for the night." Not a happy thought.

"Well, if you do that, just bear in mind we've got another meeting at ten o'clock tonight. This time, it's in Amelia's room."

"Another meeting?" I asked, looking up at him. "What's happened now?"

"That's what we'll find out," he said. "We wanna know how you guys went, and we all wanna know if Amelia's looked at the stuff Lisa's brother gave her. Then of course, there's what they're about to do tonight. There's a bit to talk about."

I shrugged. "Ten o'clock, righto. Any reason why it couldn't be right now?"

"They have business to take care of and they don't know how long it might take," he said, looking at me now as though I were rather slow, and I guess I was tonight.

"Sure, sure," I said, and walked away.

People were moving in all different directions now and I decided to watch them, hanging just inside the dining room. Natalie, Amelia and Marc headed for the lounge room, Amelia determinedly not looking at him and the three of them being followed by a very striking Beast of Magic. Felicity and Jessica got talking, and they were joined before too long by Lena; they went upstairs in one of the lifts. Peter, James, Harry and Simon were once again with their girlfriends, and given that they were all taking the stairs, I didn't need to wonder what they were doing, despite the fact that they had almost certainly spent plenty of time doing such things that afternoon. I had room to wonder, now that there were no adults around, if those guys (and girls) were enjoying themselves in a responsible manner.

Not far from where I stood, Lucien, Liam and Darcy were chatting about passing the time by playing cards, and they were joined before too long by Tommy, who clearly had nothing to do while Jessica had chosen to hang out with girls instead of him. Good of him, I thought, but although I could probably have joined them as well, I really didn't feel like it, and I couldn't quite put my finger on why. There were still people hanging around, now breaking off into smaller groups (Misty and Michelle walked past me in the next minute, and George and Belinda weren't far behind them, both pairs heading up the stairs). So, while I hoped no one was looking, I quickly and quietly stepped around the corner, opened the door a crack and slipped out into the dark yard, shutting the door softly behind me.

This isn't a very healthy state of mind, I thought as I moved stealthily away from the lights and into the darkness. It was very dark in the yard, being after seven in the evening in the middle of winter, though not impossible to see where I was going. It was certainly no worse than it had been the previous night when I had crossed it with James and Peter. I headed down one of the paths, past the pool Natalie had created, before turning right and moving into some bushes off the side of the path. I had no idea exactly what I was doing or why, but I felt better almost immediately the moment I left the path and was no longer in the open. I moved in a little further, then stopped and sank to the leafy ground, raising my knees and wrapping my arms around them. It was pretty chilly out here, and the way the base was enchanted meant that the atmosphere on the outside filtered in through the roof (not counting rain). At least the bushes protected me from the breeze, but ultimately I found the whole situation refreshing more than anything else.

There, in the silence and completely alone, I was free to examine what was going on in my head that would cause me to come out here in the first place. Of course, part of it was to do with the fact that there really wasn't much to do in here, what with only a gym and games room for recreation—oh yeah, and the lounge room, which would be very useful when those I considered my friends weren't too busy with their partners to remember that I even existed....

Okay, that hit a little closer to the truth. It had to be, because even without the lack of activities to occupy me (would I have preferred to do homework now?), the new arrangement should have quickly diminished the depression I'd been carrying for weeks already. Most of that had been caused by the imprisonment, the trapped feeling, the feeling that I was being denied a path I needed to follow. That no longer applied, because the whole point of all of this was so that I could do what Smiley had suggested I do, so that I could do what I needed to do in order to (hopefully) find a way to end this war and get back to—well, life would never be normal again, could never be the way it had been, and that was depressing, but surely it wasn't too much to ask that we be allowed to walk around in the open without fear of being struck down by Hammerhearts.

No, this depression was different to what I'd been going through before. I would have preferred the old depression, because it had enabled me to put up with what was going on around me without it affecting me. I had been aware of what was going on in the Woodward base; I hadn't been oblivious to it, but I hadn't cared about it. Now, I was no longer oblivious, and I couldn't deny the truth of my own feelings: I was lonely.

It wouldn't have bothered me so much if any of my friends would hang out, as we had always done for years, instead of disappearing into their rooms to satisfy themselves and their girlfriends, as we had all been dreaming about doing for a few years now. If that were true, though, why hadn't I gone to play cards with Lucien, Tommy, Darcy and Liam? That was a little more complicated, and in the time I sat there in the dark, I couldn't quite put my finger on why I'd made that decision.

But I was a forward person in the sense that I felt happiest when I had a path to follow. I liked to know where I was going and I didn't want to stay stationary for long. If I could get stuff done, I would feel satisfied. That was what had been wrong with me before, so I had to apply it to my current situation. There was no reason why I should return to a sad, mopey state of mind. What could I do to turn this thing around?

For a start, John, you can stop worrying about what your friends are doing. Do you think they'll appreciate you lamenting that they're not paying attention to you anymore? Of course not; if you were them, how would you like it? That had never been a problem for me, of course, because the whole time I'd been with Serena, James and the twins had been with Erica, Katie and Sophie. Peter had lost Kylie, and Marc had lost Amelia, but as hurt as they had been, they didn't let it consume them to this degree.

That was part of it, and now that I came to accept it, I understood that I'd made a silly mistake before coming out here. I didn't catch what card game the boys were playing, but I should have joined them. It probably would have been fun; we could have had a few laughs, maybe put some music on and had a few drinks (such things were possible in those rooms, as they had been in the ones in the old base, although Amelia had enchanted them to go very sparingly on the alcohol). It didn't matter that there wouldn't have been any girls with us; in fact, given that we were all single and probably lonely (not counting Tommy), it would have made us all feel better, for the time being, not to have to see any girls.

And speaking of girls: I suspended my train of thought as quiet voices reached my ears. I was very glad I had left the path, instead of sitting on one of the park benches out there, because there were people walking up the path. There couldn't be many, but they weren't too far away and they were heading in this direction. I turned my body toward the path and carefully and quietly parted the bushes just wide enough for me to see a small section of the path. I didn't have to wait long for them to walk past me: Two girls, both of them small in stature, talking quietly; I heard their voices but not their words. I couldn't be completely sure but I thought it was probably Rebecca and Candice, out for a night-time stroll together for reasons best known to themselves.

As they left, I turned my attention to the final part of the equation. I had been single for quite a while (well, six weeks is quite a while for a fourteen-year-old boy who's had his first taste of dating), and although I certainly hadn't forgotten Serena, it was time to acknowledge that Harry and Simon had been right in their taunting way. It was time to move on, and I could do that by finding myself another girlfriend. Perhaps it wasn't strictly necessary, but I couldn't deny that in the current environment, having one would probably help me. As I had been tempted to jump up and run back to the building to find the boys a minute earlier, now I considered the two girls who had just walked past me, thereby putting the idea in my head.

They were both friendly enough, although I knew Rebecca to be pretty loose-moraled, even by my not-so-admirable standards. For a thirteen-year-old (or had she turned fourteen yet, I didn't know), she'd had her share of experience with guys. I hadn't seen her hanging out with any in the Woodward base (Tommy was the last one I knew for sure she'd been with) but it was impossible to forget what I'd learnt about her when I'd entered her mind months earlier. Then of course, she was Natalie's sister, not to be considered for even a moment simply based on that fact alone. As for Candice, other than having a history of being a Hammerheart, I knew nothing about her dating preferences.

It was fun to explore those two, but at the end of it all, there was only one person I wanted to be with, and fortunately for me, she was still single. Whether or not she was still interested in me, I didn't know. What I did know is that unlike Amelia, she hadn't had much of a chance to vent about everything she'd seen since the Sorcerers had been cut off from the rest of us. She was coping pretty well considering (both girls weren't quite normal yet but the shells weren't as thick as they'd been two nights earlier) but did all this mean she would want to date again? How long would it be before she wanted to date again, after what Tommy had done to her? Then, of course, there was Amelia, but it was time to accept another cold hard truth: I would never be happy with myself and any decisions I made regarding girls if I kept worrying about both Natalie and Amelia. I had to choose between them, and as much as I cared about Amelia, it was Natalie I wanted more than anyone else, as it always had been.

I lost track of time after that as I sat there in the bushes, no longer contemplating my solemn state but simply fantasizing about being with Natalie, as I had been doing for a long time; imagining how it would be to be beside her again, as I had been on the top of Rock Haulter, enjoying her company in an entirely innocent fashion—among other things. I wondered if the other guys who currently had girlfriends felt as strongly about them as I did for Natalie? It was possible, but somehow, I doubted it, and I had to keep reminding myself that I was probably over-estimating my own feelings simply based on the fact that I'd had them for so long, and none of them had been interested in any of those girls until six months ago at the earliest.

Eventually, deciding that I'd finally gotten too cold to be comfortable, wishing more than ever that I had a certain sixteen-year-and-two-day-old girl to cuddle up with, I stood up and made my way back to the building. When I reached the light, streaming from the lit corridor before one of the lifts through the door I had used to come out here, I saw by my watch that it was already nearly nine o'clock. Still an hour before the meeting, but perhaps rather than go to my room and continue my lonely contemplation, I would walk around and see what was what.

At first I didn't find anyone; both the dining room and the games room were completely empty, which was a slight surprise, though it didn't take long to remind myself that many of them were probably still in their bedrooms, not in a position to open their doors. There was one open bedroom door on the first floor, the room that belonged to Rebecca, and as I walked past, I registered that she and Candice were in there, sitting on the bed and talking quietly. They both waved at me as I passed and I raised my hand in response without breaking stride. I also registered that two of the bedrooms on that level, though shut, weren't empty; voices could be heard from inside Felicity's room, and I remembered that she'd been with Jessica and Lena.

I thought they'd gone upstairs, but apparently something had happened to make them prefer being down here. There were also voices coming from Darcy's room, male voices, and I thought I knew who would be in there too. I decided that if I found nothing to do in the hour before the meeting, I would knock on their door and see what was up.

This almost turned out to be the case; there were no open doors on the second or third floors. In fact the third floor was quiet and dark, as though everyone in the rooms was sleeping (yeah right, perhaps they were just taking a break). I got a bit of a surprise when I came back downstairs and approached the lounge room. I'd intended to walk straight past it on my way to the gym, not that I wanted to work out just now but perhaps there could be someone in there with whom I could spend the remainder of my time before the meeting. I never found out if anyone was in there, though, because Natalie was standing just outside the lounge room door, leaning against the wall opposite and staring glumly at it.

"Hey," I said when there were only a few metres between us, giving her a start—apparently she'd been lost in whatever thoughts and hadn't heard me coming. "What are you doing out here? Aren't you supposed to be in with them?"

"I screwed up," she said, trying to smile, but it was a feeble thing; something was definitely troubling her. "What are you doing here if you know you can't go in there?"

"Just having a look around," I said, stopping and leaning against the wall beside her, not knowing how long I would get with her but wanting to make the most of what I had. This was the most proactive I'd felt in quite a while, although I certainly had no intention of making my thoughts clear this soon. "There's really not a lot going on; everyone's hiding in their rooms and I'm pretty bored."

"Oh," she said slowly, surveying me; it made me self-conscious, but I found I didn't mind so much. "I guess we do need to come up with more things for people to do in the off-time."

"Yeah, maybe," I said, thinking that this particular train of thought could lead us to the certain activities many of our friends were undoubtedly partaking in at this very moment, and wanting to change the subject. "So, what happened in there that you came out here and didn't bother leaving?"

She shrugged. "Well, we got a lot of stuff done quite easily at first. Fewul made us a device that'll let us know when a new magical virus comes out so we can protect ourselves against it before it spreads, and we've got TV and newspaper feeds all ready to go. We were trying to work out a possible internet solution when it all went to hell."

"What does that mean?" I asked anxiously.

"A virus got in," she said, shivering slightly. "I had to get rid of it because Marc and Amelia had their hands full monitoring the magic. Only I missed it, and it almost killed Marc. It *would* have killed him if Fewul hadn't stepped in and nullified the magic."

"Oh," I said, thinking I possibly understood what her problem was. "You can't blame yourself for that; anyone would panic under that sort of pressure."

"I didn't panic, I'm just lousy with magic," she said hopelessly.

"No you're not," I said at once. "I've seen you do great magic."

"Really?" she said doubtfully. "I dunno how you figure that; even you were better than me when you had magic."

"I dunno how you figure that," I retorted, not enjoying this turn of the conversation, wishing I hadn't caused it, but wanting to reassure her all the same. "All the time we were on Rock Haulter, you did great magic there, and you created the invisibility veil. Even Mr. Woodward said that was impressive."

"I'm sure he was just flattering," she said flatly. "I mean, come on, it was two simple spells combined and given a fancy name. What's so impressive about that?"

I shrugged, unsure how to continue this line without it degenerating into a pointless argument. Instead I said, "How long have you felt this way?"

She gave me a look then. It was a speculative thing, and I could have been misreading it, but it looked like the first tiny piece of confirmation that she was at least a little bit interested in me. I hoped I was right in thinking so. "Most of the time I've had it," she said, looking away at me and back at the lounge room door. "I thought it would be pretty cool at first, but it's been nothing but trouble. If this business is over anytime soon, someone else can have it."

"You'd give it up?"

"Yeah, I'm sick of it. I don't need magic. The only people who think they need it are the ones who want power. That's what this whole war is about, you know?"

"Whoever has the crystals has the power," I said quietly. "Yeah, that's become pretty clear to me too."

"I don't need it," she said quietly. "I dunno if that makes me simple or whatever, but I'd be quite happy without it. Let someone else carry the responsibility."

"'With great power comes great responsibility,'" I said, unable to stop myself speaking the quote that had instantly sprung to mind at her words.

She managed another weak smile. "It certainly does now. I've got no issue with being generally responsible, but not on such a grand scale, and at the same time my father thinks it does me the world of good to try to protect me from having to do too much; he doesn't want me to have to do the worst of it."

"Okay," I said slowly, not entirely sure what point she was trying to make. "I think he knows you are responsible, though; he wouldn't have let Mr. Woodward give you magic to start with if he didn't think you were up to it, and he'd be one who'd know, after being involved in the first war."

"You'd think so, but he changed after that night in Germany," she said. "He was pretty mad that I went out but he was even madder at Hammerson for what he did to me. He's been trying to give me easy jobs ever since. I've still seen some nasty stuff but nothing compared to the rest of them."

"Isn't that a good thing?"

Natalie sighed. "Easy jobs," she repeated. "They know I'm not as good as the rest of them."

"Ah," I said, hoping that this time, I understood what her problem was. "You know, you really should be in there with the rest of them."

"What? Why?" she asked, looking at me sharply.

"So that you can learn and get better," I said. "I still don't reckon you've got much of a problem but it'd make you feel better about yourself to be helping out, instead of being out here, waiting for them to get it done."

She shook her head. "You're probably right, but it wasn't my decision to leave. Amelia said we couldn't take any more chances. Marc was all for letting me stay, like he hardly knew how close he came to carking it, but she snapped at him."

"Oh great," I sighed. The last thing we needed was a rift between Marc and Amelia, but after the episode at dinner, I could hardly be surprised. It was still disappointing that she would take it out on Natalie though. "Well, beside tonight, you know what you probably need?"

"Heaps of stuff, but what have you got in mind?" she asked, giving me another speculative look. It was impossible not to be self-conscious under that gaze, because I was sure she was thinking of very different things she could need from what I had in mind. I would remember that, but for the time being, I wanted to stay on topic.

"You remember what we saw Tankom doing to Stella in Smiley's memories?" I asked her.

"You mean teaching her how to fight with magic?"

"Exactly. If it's really a problem for you, maybe one of them in there can help you out. I'm sure they'd prefer to put in a bit of time for that than to keep sending you out of the room."

"I hope you're right about that," she said darkly.

Why wouldn't they? I thought. Natalie's tone sounded doubtful but I couldn't think why. Amelia's power was the same as Natalie's (unless she had the dodgy chip) and I couldn't think why she wouldn't be good enough about helping Natalie out. Her magical experience far outweighed anyone else's (not counting Fewul). I wondered if this was all in Natalie's mind, all her own self-doubt, or if there was actually something else going on here that I didn't know about. I could understand why Amelia would be feeling pretty pissed at Marc, but why Natalie? I decided to see if I could find out.

"Well, if you reckon they may not," I said slowly, "why stay out here waiting for them?"

"'Cause Marc said they might still need…" she said, then stopped, staring hard at the lounge room door, as though she could see through it (and maybe she could for all I knew).

"He's right, they might," I said, "but what do you think?"

"I think," she said, checking her watch (I checked mine too but there was still forty-five minutes before the meeting), "I think they can get stuffed."

I laughed. "That's putting it more eloquently than I would have."

"But I've got nothing to do between now and then," she said, "unless you reckon I should practise magic between now and the meeting."

"Join the club," I muttered. "I thought I heard Jessica and Felicity in her room earlier; maybe you could hang out with them."

Not that I wanted her to; I wanted her to hang out with me, but I had to at least offer the option. I was pleased when she shook her head. "I'd rather not, not right now."

"Okay," I said slowly, taken aback. If it had been Amelia, I would understand, not wanting to be around Lena, but Natalie? Oh but of course, Jessica was with Tommy now. Those two had been friends for a long time; maybe Natalie would consider it some form of treachery for Jessica to be dating Tommy after her own unpleasant experiences with him. That wasn't something I wanted her to spell out (maybe some other time, but not tonight).

Before I could think of anything else to say, any way to continue getting some insight into what was going on in Natalie's mind, a few more people entered the corridor from the bedrooms: Harry, Simon, Katie and Sophie.

"Good evening, Ms. Natalie," Simon boomed down the corridor as he and the others approached, "and you too, John, of course."

"Glad to see I'm still an afterthought," I said, unsure how to feel about this interruption. I settled on anxiety almost immediately when I saw the twins swap a knowing look. All three of us were remembering our conversation of breakfast that morning.

"Now what are you two doing here?" Harry asked, stopping just short of the lounge room door and scrutinising the pair of us. "Standing around in an otherwise empty corridor having a nice, leisurely chat?"

"Actually, I was going to ask you the same thing," I retorted, while Natalie shifted uncomfortably beside me, not helping my cause one bit. "What are you all doing here? I went up to the third floor a little earlier to see what was up and I assumed that you were all very busy to even notice my presence."

"You were up there?" Katie asked, her eyes widening in horror.

"Absolutely," I said, grinning broadly. "I only opened each door for a few seconds, just long enough to deduce that my assistance wouldn't be needed—not tonight, anyway. Now Harry, Simon, the fact that you are down here before Peter and James is rather surprising. Care to explain?"

Natalie burst out laughing and provided me with the first genuine smile of the evening. Seeing it lifted my spirits enormously. "See, that's how you taunt. I think you two are losing your edge a bit."

"I'm not sure which part of that to address first," said Harry, swapping a look with his brother. "Simon, we have been officially schooled."

This time we all burst out laughing.

"So seriously, what are you guys doing down here?" I asked them.

"Well, passing over the finer points which I'm sure you two innocent specimens would be happier not knowing," said Simon, "we wanted to see if the lounge room was available yet, and of course, to see how our dear brother in there is doing."

"You didn't really open the door, did you?" Katie asked, her eyes still wide.

I burst out laughing again. "Come on, now, after all the time you've spent with these two, you should recognise banter when you hear it. Besides, I don't think my key's supposed to work for other people's bedrooms."

"I'm not sure how much longer they'll be in there," Natalie told Harry and Simon. "The TV and newspaper feed are done but getting safe internet access is proving to be a challenge."

"May I return to my question of earlier?" said Simon, once again glancing from Natalie to me and back again. "What are you two doing, just hanging around in an empty corridor together?"

"Because John was bored and I got kicked out," said Natalie at once, "and don't ask any questions about that 'cause I don't wanna talk about it."

"We can respect that," said Harry, grinning at Simon. "So tell me, you two, what did you think of our dear brother's rather unconventional outfit?"

"Very daring," said Natalie, covering her grin with a hand.

"I imagine those pants would be pretty snug about the old sperm firm," I pointed out. "Hopefully, we won't have to see that."

We all laughed, and the twins beamed. "I expect your right, John."

"Although, come to think of it," I said thoughtfully, grinning at the twins, "I reckon Katie and Sophie might be interested in getting a look. It would be interesting to see a Maivis with a *big* penis for a change."

Katie and Sophie both blushed madly at that, but everyone else laughed.

"Two from two, John," said Simon, clapping me on the back. "We'll have to make sure Marc has fitted him with a little extra equipment, I think—besides the magic, I mean."

"Don't forget brains," said Natalie.

"I didn't think Fewul had a brain," said Sophie. "Isn't its intelligence based on magic?"

"That's still a lot of extra equipment," I pointed out.

"What about you then, Natalie?" Harry asked, grinning wickedly at her. "I imagine you'll be interested to see old Hugh and his middle stump, right?"

"Not really," she said cautiously, "I don't care for cricket."

"You don't need to care about cricket to care about a good, solid pole," said Harry, winking. "Would it interest you more if we took said pole and persuaded Marc to attach it to a body that would be more your speed? Innocent you may be, but I'm sure you won't quite know where to look."

I didn't miss the brief glance he shot at me as he spoke, and now I fully understood exactly how the twins intended to help me get a girlfriend. The thought made me very nervous because one could never know just how far they would go, or if they would unwittingly make it more difficult for me.

"Do I have to answer that?" Natalie asked, flattening herself against the wall behind her, as though she wished she could sink into it (which she probably could if she tried).

"Of course not," Simon cried ecstatically. "Your lack of an answer is all the confirmation we need."

"You guys," she said, shaking her head.

"Don't worry, Nat," said Harry, dropping his voice so that we would know he was being serious. "We know you would prefer it if it was a real person we spoke of, rather than the Beast of Magic."

"Give it a rest, you two," I said quietly, still smiling but a little nervously now. Beside me, Natalie was twisting her hands together as she tried to think what to say to that.

"Aw," the twins moaned in unison.

"Well, we won't taunt Natalie if you say so, John," simpered Harry, shooting yet another glance between us.

Fortunately, at that moment, the lounge room door opened and Marc stepped out into the corridor.

"We were wondering what all the noise was," he said, looking at Harry and Simon. "Why am I not surprised to find you two behind it?"

"You know what they say about people who assume, dear Marc," said Simon.

"True, but the only other people around here who are anywhere near as loud as you are your sisters, and your voices sounded too deep to be them."

"I dunno," I said lightly. "I've always suspected Misty and Michelle have more testosterone in their bodies than those two."

"That wouldn't surprise me," muttered Sophie, and she and Katie grinned at each other.

"Anyway, Natalie, can you come back in?" Marc said, looking at her. "We're almost done but we need another person."

"Really? And you couldn't get Fewul to split into two Maivises?"

"If he does, we can call the second counterpart Hugh Jass," said Harry.

"Two brothers called Hugh?" Katie said doubtfully.

"If it's good for Rob and Bob, it's good for anyone," said Simon.

"Come on, Nat," said Marc, more quietly now. "We want you to help."

Natalie sighed. "Fine, whatever. All the better if you're nearly done."

She entered the lounge room and Marc shut the door behind them, leaving me with Harry, Simon, Katie and Sophie, and feeling better than I had all evening. It wasn't just the humour that did it. Most of it was the smile Natalie had given me when I had 'officially schooled' the twins, but it was also the knowledge that, for the first time, I was in control of my destiny when it came to girls. Even counting the twins and their good-natured interference, I felt I had taken the first step on a path that would hopefully lead me straight to Natalie.

Chapter 12: The Bigger Picture

In what little time remained before the meeting, I hung around in the corridor near the bedrooms with Harry and Simon, Katie and Sophie having gone upstairs to take refreshing showers. We were gradually joined by Lucien and Tommy first, then Peter and James about five minutes before the meeting was due to start.

"I have an announcement," Peter said to everyone in the bottom floor corridor. "James has officially lost his marbles."

"You say it like it's breaking news," Simon observed.

"That's a pity, James," said Harry, watching him with a sympathetic expression on his face. "I think Erica was counting on you and your marbles to work well for her in the future."

"You two could do us a favour by buggering off," James said to the twins, who began to laugh.

"We won't stay around for your top-secret meeting, dear James," said Simon, "but I'm sure you'll forgive us for being concerned about the well-being of your marbles. Do tell us, Peter, what went wrong up there?"

"I was referring to his mind," said Peter, grinning slightly. "He was thinking some strange stuff up there that he's actually serious about talking about in the meeting. You know what the response is gonna be, don't you?"

"Don't jump to conclusions, Pete," said James. "It's not nice to think about but it is a very serious issue."

Marc, Amelia, Natalie and Fewul entered the corridor a short time later.

"Is everyone ready to get started?" Marc asked us all.

"What's the agenda?" asked Tommy.

"We'll discuss that when we get in there," said Amelia, jerking her head in the direction of her bedroom, stepping around the group without looking at anyone so that she could access her closed bedroom door.

"Amelia's so diplomatic," said James, grinning at the twins now. "Allow me to put her words more directly: You two need to bugger off now."

The twins threw their hands in the air and cheered in unison.

"You tell it like it is, dear Jamesy," Simon cried jubilantly. "We wouldn't dream of crossing you, good sir. Perhaps a good use of our time at this point would be to see if Katie and Sophie are done in the showers? If not, perhaps we can assist them."

"Just out of curiosity," said Peter before the twins could depart, "you don't *really* swap girlfriends, do you?"

The twins laughed. "Come on, Pete; do you think they would ever forgive us if they found out?" Harry asked.

"We've got a good thing going here," said Simon, looking more serious than he had all night. "We don't wanna ruin it, as much for each other as for ourselves. We shall be off now. You can speak of serious disturbing things, while we ourselves do unspeakable things. Ciao, folks."

"I think I forgot, over the last few weeks, how crazy those two are," said Natalie, watching their backs as they took the stairs.

"Everyone in now," Amelia called from inside her room. "We've got a lot to get through and I dunno how long it's gonna take."

Like the bedroom's we'd once had in the old Woodward base, these rooms had an area encircled by couches at the rear that was suitable for meetings such as these. The nine of us gathered in Amelia's room and, once the door was shut and locked, took seats on the couches. Perhaps due to my nap earlier in the afternoon, I was feeling more alert than I had in quite a while, and I noticed a few things in the seconds before we got underway.

Amelia was sitting in the seat closest to the door; Lucien sat on one side of her, but on the seat on her other side sat a small laptop computer; I recognised it as the one Marc had created for Lisa on that fateful morning we had faced Moran as a Sorcerer. Her eyes were fixed on the ceiling, and the reason for this was fairly obvious: Marc and Natalie were sitting almost directly opposite her, and she clearly didn't want to look at either of them. I had to wonder what was going on in her head now to cause her to react in such a way. Was all this because of seeing Marc with Lena? I made a mental note to track Amelia down sometime over the next couple of days to find out. Marc was watching Amelia unsurely, apparently unaware of what was really going on with her. Natalie seemed more aware of the situation, for she was taking a similar approach, looking anywhere but at either Amelia or Tommy. I could have groaned inwardly, because given that we were now on our own, social issues within the core of the group were the last thing we needed.

"So, what order are we going to do this in?" Lucien asked. "Should we start by covering this afternoon?"

There was a brief silence, during which all three Sorcerers seemed to wait for someone else to speak. Finally, James obliged. "Yeah, let's do that. We need to know if there's anything on that computer, and what you guys did this afternoon. Then, we need to know what you guys were doing in the lounge room before. Also, I've got something I wanna address, but we can leave that till last."

"You're not serious," said Peter incredulously.

"That sounds like a good way to go," said Lucien approvingly. "Have you had a chance to look at what Jason gave you?" he asked Amelia.

"I did look at the DVD," she said, reaching for the computer and pulling it onto her lap. "There was a lot of school stuff in there, including what she'd done on her history of magic project, which was way better than mine——"

"You're joking," said Tommy. "You? A Sorcerer?"

"She was a much better student than me," said Amelia, shrugging, "although I'm sure I would have done well enough if we'd had time. That's irrelevant though. What is important is that I couldn't find any documents on there that were directly from the magic display. I also looked through the research she'd done herself and the notes she'd taken, but there were no prophecies and no mention of the Enlightener in any of them."

"Oh great," said Natalie. "So we're at square one as far as that research goes?"

"More or less," said Amelia, shrugging again. "There's nothing we can use to track that information down, but there is something I wanna show you guys. Lisa kept a diary, which is pretty normal, and most of it not worth our reading now since most of it was either about school stuff or other trivial things that aren't our business. The thing is, she kept writing in it in the two weeks between her two deaths, and those entries were much more interesting."

"Did she remember something about being in the in-between?" Peter asked.

Amelia considered this question before slowly shaking her head. "She couldn't remember so much; it was more a case of remembering it gradually, as though it were happening parallel with her real life. It's kind of hard to explain, that's why I want you guys to see it for yourselves. It's pretty scary because her last entry was written about six or seven hours before the gym business, and she knew she was almost out of time—she could sense death coming for her again."

A horrified silence followed this as we all tried to digest the enormity of what she had just said, of how Lisa must have been feeling that morning. I found myself remembering back to the gym, to how Lisa had taken the enormous risk of attacking the Hammerhearts around her, knowing that her chances of succeeding and escaping were just about impossible, not knowing that a person with magic was ready to help her, and all for the safety of the students around her. This, two weeks after she had sacrificed her life so that we could take possession of the Sien-Leoard Crystal, highlighted how incredibly brave Lisa had been, and how that bravery had gone almost entirely unappreciated for such a long time.

"She must have meant for us to know this," said Natalie in a hushed voice, "but she didn't wanna have to talk about it while she was alive—we would have hounded her with questions."

"I don't think we can assume she meant for us to read her diary," said Marc.

"Well, why don't we decide that after you guys have read it," Amelia suggested, a hard edge in her voice.

"How many entries do we need to read?" Lucien asked.

"There are six," she said. "I saved them in a separate document."

"In that case, we'll come back to them," said Lucien. "Now, how did you guys go this afternoon? Marc? Natalie?"

"Well, we've got a bit of an idea," said Marc. "What I've done, or what Fewul mostly did 'cause I wasn't sure I could get it right, was set up a structure a bit like the second floor rooms back in the base we left behind."

"You mean it can separate from the rest of the base and put you down somewhere else?" I asked.

"More or less," said Marc, "except there's only one, and it's in the control room. We can use that to get Stella back here without needing to do any teleporting ourselves, or to take the base away from Chopville, 'cause we thought you guys would wanna stay here so that you could look for those discs."

"Good thinking," said Lucien, nodding. "We certainly will need to stay in the area for the time being. So, what measures did you come up with to track Stella down?"

"Basically, motion sensors," said Marc. "It's not ideal, but we can't set up anything that'll track people down, because someone who's untraceable will be immune to it. I used magic to create it, but it basically uses technology rather than magic to operate, which means that the magic around Stella won't apply to it. What it does is detects anything that moves and displays it to us on a screen in the control panel. If we wanna follow something in particular, we can get it to lock onto that device, and according to Fewul, that will work just as well on untraceable humans if we can locate them. The only magic it uses is to see ghosts, because that's the only way I know will display invisible people, just in case she is invisible."

"That's a fair bet," said Lucien. "She could have stolen devices from Hammerhearts, and she would need to be invisible to avoid being recognised by Hammerhearts, particularly in light of what happened the last time one managed to find her. That's well done, Marc. It's up to you how you coordinate the situation but my advice to you will be to get your group of fifteen to alternate the use of this device so that you can monitor it around the clock, and whoever is using it at the moment we find Stella can lock onto her until you yourself can attend to her."

"That's a pretty good idea," said Marc. "We'll show everyone how to use it tomorrow then."

"Very good," said Lucien. "Does anyone have any questions about that?" When nobody answered after several seconds, Lucien nodded. "Okay, in that case, we'll move onto tonight's business. How did it end up going in there?"

"Pretty well in the end," said Marc, chancing a questioning glance at Amelia which the latter ignored. "We have a way of knowing when new magical viruses are created so that we can protect ourselves against them in advance, and we have a special TV and newspaper feed that will allow us to keep up with what's going on out there safely. Those things are really easy to use and I'm sure anyone who's gone in the lounge room will already be testing them. We've also found a way to use the Internet, which is gonna make a lot of people happy, but I still think we should block most interactive websites, just in case someone accidentally gives something away."

"I agree with that," said Lucien heavily, "and they won't like that, but you're right—it could happen accidentally. What solution have you come up with to keep viruses out?"

"A magical anti-virus," said Marc. "What it does is sends everything that comes into the base through a sort of test environment, which is a magic-proof box I've stored away in the control room. Every bit of code, every page, app, script— pretty much everything that comes in will be debugged in there to make sure it won't have any effects on people or machines. If it's okay, it'll be let through to the computer; if not, an error message will be sent through instead and the packets of data will be destroyed, all inside the box."

"You sure that's safe?" James asked.

"Fewul reckons it is," he said, inclining his head to the Beast of Magic, "and I made my enquiries very specific. I reckon we'll be okay."

"What web browsing are people likely to do if they can't access any interactive sites?" Tommy asked. "Maybe I'm just not nerdy enough, but I think the Internet would be pretty boring if you couldn't use it to communicate."

"It would be very restrictive," said Lucien. "I'm not sure what's the best way to handle this—"

"Here's an idea," said Peter suddenly. "If you can make magic to determine what code is dangerous, maybe you can make magic to determine what content is safe to let out. I suppose it would have to include any text relating to who we are, where we are, what we're doing, etc."

"And audio, video and images would be out altogether," said Lucien, nodding approvingly. "That's not a bad idea. Do you think any of you three could do that?"

When neither Amelia nor Natalie gave any response, Marc said, "I'm not sure I could, but maybe I can get Fewul on that tomorrow. So we say no Internet access until we've set that up too?"

"Question," said James. "All these monitoring measures, Marc, how much are they going to slow the Internet down?"

"They do slow it down a bit," Marc admitted, "but that's no different from any antivirus; they all slow computers down to some degree. I have to say, what we've got here is about the same speed, maybe a little faster, than what we had at home."

"That's because we've set it up to use the latest technology," said Natalie, "and no disrespect to Chopville, but they're not exactly leading the way in technological advancements these days."

"True, but at least they're past dial-up," said Lucien, "and that doesn't even matter to us anymore. Our days of using Chopville's facilities may be behind us for a while. So, is that all there is to report from tonight?"

"I think so," said Marc uneasily, glancing again at Amelia.

"Yeah, that's it," she said, choosing to look at Lucien instead of Marc.

"In that case, it's time to open the floor, so to speak," said Lucien, smiling slightly.

"Your turn, crazy person," Peter said to James. "Go on, tell them what you were telling me in the lift earlier."

"All right," said James, seeming to brace himself. "I'm not sure if this will go over too well, but I think we seriously need to consider a much bigger picture than we have been doing so far. I've been thinking long and hard about something Mr. Woodward and Mr. Fletcher said some months ago, and also about what you said last night, Natalie."

"You'd better not be about to blame me for something," she said warily, and I wasn't sure if she was joking or not.

James shook his head. "When this began, one of your fathers adopted a very simple philosophy regarding the Hammersons: Cut off the snake's head and the snake dies. At the time, I thought they were probably right. After all, the Hammerhearts would have no focal point without Arnold Hammerson, but I've had time to think since then and I think they were mistaken."

"Hear, hear," said Tommy, nodding. "We've abducted the Hammersons on two separate occasions and it didn't stop them from continuing business as usual."

"That's true, but it would have if Sebastian hadn't let them out," said Amelia reasonably. "They would have tried to keep fighting but they wouldn't have been able to coordinate properly."

"That sounds even worse," said James, shuddering. "Just imagine what would happen if the Hammerhearts were let loose with all those magical devices they have—"

An uneasy silence followed this as we all contemplated what he had said. Yes, there was a lot of unpleasantness in the world as it was—a lot of fighting, torturing and other unspeakable business—but we had to consider it a good thing that it was, to some degree, under control. Sure, it was the wrong sort of control, but control it still was. If that control were to let go, it would be every man for himself, and many of those Hammerhearts would fight for their own power; and unfortunately, they would already have a fair amount of power on their side.

"You see the problem?" James said impressively. "Now, I'm sure the Woodwards would understand as well as anyone how important it is to restore control once Hammerson is taken out of the equation, but my worry is that they will be as incapable of restoring that control as they were preventing the Hammersons taking it in the first place. I don't know what the Hammerhearts' numbers are now, but I expect they would be in the hundreds of thousands, perhaps the millions by now. That's a lot of people doing their own thing in all corners of the world. How can six people take control of that? How can the Beast of Magic, even, take control of that?"

"Fewul can do anything," said Amelia, but James shook his head.

"What would you instruct Fewul to do in that situation, Marc?"

"Er," said Marc, looking nervously around the group, "vanish every Hammerheart device on the planet?"

"Then they'll use non-magical devices," said James. "Remember all those military weapons they stole prior to the coup? Think of this: Hammersonia has already swallowed such places as the United States, Great Britain, China, Japan, Russia, India, and loads of others, many of which already had very strong defence forces. If the Hammerhearts had their way, they would become attack forces."

"Nuclear war," said Tommy in a hushed voice, and James nodded.

"Way to put the fear of God in them," Peter muttered.

"I'm not spinning anything here, Pete; I'm simply telling it the way it is," said James. "It's stuff we don't wanna think about but we have to consider it as a very real possibility. It would be very unwise of us to take Hammerson out of the equation without first weakening his army."

"James, that'll take an eternity," Natalie snapped. "Everything we do to weaken him now, he'll just strengthen himself and his hold by double."

"That's true," said James. "It's like Smiley said: The situation has fallen this way and we have to deal with it the way it is."

"James, if you're saying what I think you're saying," said Lucien slowly, "we have to make Hammerson undo the damage himself before we can take control. How do you intend to do that?"

"Influential charm?" suggested Marc.

"That's essentially what we have to do," said James, "but an influential charm wouldn't work; they would just rebel against him if they found out we'd hoodwinked him, and the result of that would be much the same as killing him outright."

"You're very good at spotting problems," I said, finally deciding to chip in—I'd had enough of this unpleasant discussion. "If you have a solution, you might as well tell us now."

"The solution, the *only* possible solution," said James, "is to do what the Woodwards were able to do last time. They found a way to get the Hammersons to back down. It was a ruse, but it worked."

"If it had worked properly, we wouldn't be in this situation now," Natalie pointed out.

"What are you guys talking about?" Amelia asked. "Do you know something I don't about the last war?"

"Er, yeah," said Peter warily. "Smiley told us what really happened in 1981 to end it. They killed about ten thousand Hammerhearts—well, they didn't do it, but they made the Hammersons believe they had, and that they would do the rest if they didn't back down."

"Natalie makes a good point, though," said James reasonably. "They did back down, but they didn't abide by that treaty at all in the end. They kept all their structures in place, fully intending to have another go at it when they were once again strong enough."

"So what's your solution to *that*, then?" I asked, feeling my stomach beginning to sink. The fact that we were on this subject at all was not a good thing.

"The solution is you, John," said James, surprising me completely—I'd been expecting him to continue on the Honnie line of thinking. "The solution is that Hammerson must be killed, but only after he has been weakened to the point where he would rather surrender or go down swinging."

I bit my lip, not wanting to respond to that in any way. I was getting sick of that bloody prophecy.

"All that can't be done until we see the prophecy," Marc said, "which means that what you're talking about has no relevance to us right now."

"Actually it does," said James, "because the thing I've been pondering over is how exactly we can weaken his army without giving him a chance to retaliate. The fact that he has bogglers and such a wide recruiting area means that we have to launch such an attack that will knock all his support beams out from under him all at the one time. That is why I believe that our only option is to do what the Woodwards did to end the last war."

"So we have to kill ten thousand people?" said Amelia distastefully. "Well, you can do that if you like, James, but I'll sit that one out."

"Killing is a part of war," James went on relentlessly, "and it will probably be impossible to get through this without a few people dying—"

"That's true," said Peter, clearly unable to hold himself back any longer, "but what he's not telling you is that it's probably gonna be a few of us who have to die to make it happen."

Marc's mouth fell open. "Are you suggesting that you should hand me, Lucien and Tommy over so that Hammerson can kill us? Then he'll back off? You really *have* lost your mind."

A babble of angry talk broke out but James was quick to break it up, raising his voice so that we all heard him clearly.

"That is not what I was going to say. Honestly, do you really think Hammerson would accept that as a negotiation? The whole reason he wants you guys out of the way is so he has nothing to stop him from ruling. No, that was not my plan, and I'll thank *you*, Peter, to stop making this more difficult than it already is."

"So why would Peter say a few of us may have to die to make it happen?" Tommy asked. "We all know that might happen anyway, but it sounds like you're talking about sacrifices."

"What I meant," said James, ignoring Tommy's question for the time being, "is that we may have to kill Hammerhearts along the way, or allow them to be killed in the line of fire; that's something we probably won't be able to help. However, I don't think we'll have to kill nearly as many as the Woodwards did in 1981, not if we can take complete control of them all instead."

"Oh, hang on a moment," said Marc, and I saw the light of understanding in his eyes—he looked seriously disturbed. "Are you saying that we need to do what you were suggesting to Smiley? You think we should try to get a Honnie to help us?"

"Of course he's not," said Tommy at once. "That would be suicidal—Smiley said so himself—"

But he broke off as he too seemed to understand something. The moment held for about two seconds before he rounded on James. "That *is* what you're saying, isn't it? You think we should go into their world and ask one of them to come back and help us?"

"Told you he'd lost his mind," muttered Peter.

"James," said Marc slowly, "Smiley told us about those creatures, and we saw a couple for ourselves. They don't do anything for anyone unless it is for some benefit to their society; not to them as individuals, but to them as a society. They have no sense of self, remember?"

"What are you guys talking about?" Amelia asked again, looking from Tommy, to James, to Peter and back again.

"*Who* are you talking about?" Lucien clarified.

"Oh damn," Marc muttered. "This is all stuff Smiley went over with us, and we saw it in one of his memories too. This is gonna take a while to explain."

"Honnies," said James, "are creatures from another dimension. They're a similar shape to humans, but the two we saw were quite tall and very attractive. They're incredibly physically strong, and they have a lot of mind power, which they can use to read our minds and take possession of us. It's the possession part I'm counting on here: If we can get one to help us out, it can take control of the entire army, stop them from doing anything stupid, while we ourselves can attend to Hammerson."

"Creatures from another dimension?" Lucien repeated, looking incredulous.

"Smiley can access a fourth dimension," Peter told him. "That's how he knows about them, and how he was able to go back in time and see those memories. What James is suggesting has nothing to do with time travel; it's a case of stepping into their world and attempting to persuade one to come back with us."

"I told you, Honnies don't do stuff like that," snapped Marc. "They regard humans the same way we regard cows—"

"Some people worship cows," Amelia pointed out.

"Great, we'll know we're doing well if we can find a couple of Hindu Honnies," snapped Marc. "They make themselves stronger by absorbing our minds, which is more or less killing us, and then they feast on our bodies for good measure. That's the only benefit we have to their society. If we go into their world, we'll be like walking hotdogs."

"That's why it's an incredible risk," James agreed, "but the fact is, Smiley went into their world, and lived to tell the tale. That is proof that it can be done, even if it requires a lot of luck."

"It may be worth the risk," said Lucien slowly, "because you're right about the danger we're in if we can't control their army."

"And what's our bargaining tool?" Peter asked. "What can we offer them in exchange for helping us? The Honnie that helped the Woodwards in 1981 required ten thousand people to satisfy him, and even then he just did his own thing in the end. Even if we can bring a Honnie back here, he'll do much more deadly stuff than take possession of some Hammerhearts."

"Can't we just explain our situation to them?" Amelia asked. "If they can read minds, they'll know we're being sincere—"

"They'll also know we're using them for our own ends," Tommy pointed out. "Humans don't enjoy being used, so why would they?"

"Because they're not human," James replied. "I agree with Amelia, sort of. Explaining the situation won't gain their sympathy, of that I'm fairly sure, but like humans, it stands to reason that every Honnie has a degree of individuality about him or her. That Smiley could have a reasonable discussion with one of them seems to prove that. Some won't agree, but we may be lucky enough to find one that is up to the challenge. I honestly believe that compared to what could happen otherwise, we have to try."

"Well, let's take a vote on it," said Lucien. "Those in favour of trying to get help from a Honnie, raise your hands."

James, Lucien, Amelia and, to my surprise, Natalie all raised their hands. Marc, Tommy, Peter and I remained motionless, and the Beast of Magic, perhaps following Marc's lead, also didn't move. Lucien looked around the circle for a moment before saying, with a wry smile, "Looks like we need a tiebreaker."

"How come you're up for it?" Marc asked Natalie. "You saw how deadly those things are."

"Yeah, but that doesn't mean we can't protect ourselves," she said. "We have a key advantage over both Smiley and the Woodwards: We know what they're capable of doing to us. If we arm ourselves properly, find ways to protect our minds against their kind of power, there's no reason why we should be killed in their world. That doesn't mean we'll automatically find one to come back with us, but the longer we stay alive over there, the more Honnies we'll have a chance to check out."

"She makes a good point," said Amelia, a little grudgingly. "We have to assume that if our magic is strong enough to get us into their world, it will be strong enough to deal with them as they are."

"You have no idea how hard that's gonna be, though," said Marc, glancing at Fewul. "Even if we can find a way to protect our minds, what about our bodies? Remember how that Honnie stripped the flesh off those people just by using his tongue? That's the sort of physical strength we're up against here."

"That sounds a little ominous," said Lucien, master of the understatement, "although I think there'll be ways to deal with that as well. What I think we should do, and feel free to disagree with me here, is table this idea for the time being. We'll return to it in a couple of days after we've all had a chance to think about it. I strongly advise you all not to mention this to anyone else in the base: They'll have no understanding of Honnies so we can't really trust in their opinions on the matter. Everyone should think seriously about how we can make this work, even if you're against it on principle, because like I said before, it may be worth the risk."

"Thanks," said James, looking relieved as he sank back into his seat. "I didn't expect everyone to be happy about it, but it has to be considered."

"Is there anything else we need to go over tonight?" Lucien asked, and when nobody answered for several seconds, he nodded. "In that case, let's have a look at Lisa's diary, and then we'll call it a night."

"I think what I'll do is project the computer screen onto the window there," said Amelia, sliding the catch on the laptop, lifting the lid and turning it on. She was indicating the wall directly opposite her, which was fine for where I was sitting, but it would require Marc, Natalie and Tommy to change positions, perhaps to sit on the floor to get a good view. This was the wall at the back of the bedroom which, unlike my room, had a magical window rather than a real one.

Amelia typed on the computer, loading the document in question, before performing a spell which caused the wall to suddenly fill with words, and the outlines of the application around those words. I saw that the first entry was dated February 13, two days after we had retrieved the Sien-Leoard Crystal from Rock Haulter. It was quite short, but the next entry, from February 17, stretched beyond the bottom of the screen.

"Can everybody see it?" Lucien asked, and when we all nodded (Marc, Tommy and Natalie had indeed moved to the floor by now), he nodded. "I guess we all just indicate when we've read it all so that Amelia can press page-down?"

"That works for me," said Amelia, sitting back in her seat and closing her eyes. I looked quickly at her in that moment before she opened them again and registered that she looked both tired and miserable.

The room fell silent then as we all began reading some of Lisa's last contributions to the world.

Saturday, February 13, 2010, 8:17 AM

Dear diary, I know I said I would write in you the moment we returned from Rock Haulter but I was so tired last night. Strange, because I slept a bit on the boat, but I guess that's just how it works.

Once again I won't write everything we did on camp, for the same reasons I told you on Monday, but this morning was very boring and makes me think the school is really not making the most of their rights to use the island. Come on, quiz writing? Rock climbing? Swimming? Horse riding? Those are things we can do just about any time—

maybe not in Chopville, but we wouldn't need to go far. They still have a few years left of their contract, so maybe I'll write them a memo.

Got a strange feeling in light of what happened to me. I remember being a ghost but not what came between the switching, both times. Whatever it is, I think I will remember, because there's something beginning to play out behind my eyes. Can't tell what it is yet and not sure I want to write about it, but if I tell anyone, you will be first, dear diary.

Today's a homework day. Might call Nat and see if she's up for a bit of boning.

Valentine's Day tomorrow...where's my Valentine? ☹

Words of wisdom: Part of being smart is knowing when to keep your mouth shut, but part of being smarter is knowing when to share what you know...

Wednesday, February 17, 2010, 10:18 PM

Dear diary, can you tell me why I feel like my legacy will be determined by what I do in the next week or so? A day of school and studying with the girls this afternoon and I don't feel right about it. Why is that, I wonder?

Looks like we are going to the party. Had the meeting last night, which I won't talk about, but it's actually happening. Should be interesting if we take the right precautions.

Speaking of interesting, just spent over an hour on the phone with Nat. Looks like she's finally getting her stuff together. Great to know. She knows we've got her back.

Update on what I mentioned on Saturday. Something really is playing out behind my eyes. I'm getting really worried about it. It's scary, it's dangerous, and the worst of it, it's already halfway through. I have something to learn at the end of it, a great secret, and I don't know if I'll be able to handle the knowledge, which is incredible coming from someone who has always sought knowledge.

What do I know so far? Well, there is a cave, and there's a woman in the cave. I don't know who the woman is but she is strong, cunning and ancient. She's also evil personified, and she's looking at me. She knew I was coming, and she knew I wouldn't be staying long, but she leers when she says that, like she knows something I don't. If only I had stayed there longer—if only I'd distracted her from telling me what I fear she already has.

I'll write everything I find out from this, dear diary, but when the climax hits, and I know it will hit hard, I'm afraid I won't be able to tell you about it. I doubt I'll be in a fit state to tell anyone about it. I'm still debating if I should tell the others, but I really don't want to scare them; they're already scared enough of the Hammersons as it is. They don't say so, but I can tell some of them are understanding the danger we're in.

As to that, will speak of any further updates on the party and what surrounds it tomorrow.

Words of wisdom: Curiosity killed the cat. Stay curious, stay alive.

Sunday, February 21, 2010, 12:21 AM

Dear diary, I just got home from the party but not tired enough to sleep. Perhaps I should have stayed later? The place was beginning to clear out and I would have been conspicuous, and I didn't want to be where many of the others were going.

The good news is that no danger came of tonight. I noted everyone alive when I left, except for those few who left before me. The bad news was the social side of it. I got to dance with Daniel but I don't think he enjoyed it as much as me. Need to know what he was thinking about it all. Marc left Nicole for Amelia and Nicole left not long after that; will call her in the morning. Saw Natalie kissing Tommy (did not see that coming); must call her in the morning too. A drink or two and she very quickly forgot our conversation of the other night.

But all that is petty. Makes a person feel lonely to think about, while I'm sitting in this dark, silent room, writing by lamplight. I'm getting very scared of what's going on behind the scenes, dear diary, and I'm not talking about the

Hammersons, who clearly have plenty going on of their own. No, what's in my head is bad enough, except that it's not in my head at all: It's well beyond just my head. It's well beyond life itself.

I've learned something about what I'm seeing. It came to me in my dreams last night, as I returned to that dank old cave, in greater clarity than ever this time. The woman is Mary Sien, as I suspected all along, and she is trapped there for eternity. She is the same now as she was when she died more than 2,000 years ago; she has not changed, and I know the reason for that too. There is no time in the cave. I could have stayed there forever and I would not have changed. I could have stayed there for days, years, decades, and I could have returned to my life as it is now, at any point. There is no time in the cave. Why didn't I stay long, I wonder? Was it because I knew I was coming back and just wanted to return to my friends? Or was it just to get away from Sien?

If I dream of the cave again, I'll write more, but that is all that has played out so far. More will come, because Sien is still looking at me, and she is talking to me. I wish she would stop. Where is Leoard? Isn't he the better of the two original Sorcerers?

Words of wisdom: If you're a sensible girl, get your own damn drinks!

Sunday, February 21, 2010, 8:15 PM

Dear diary, the worst has happened; someone did get hurt last night. I was so wrong. We never should have gone. I don't know the full story but from what I gathered from Nicole's phone call, they may have done it away from the premises, which means it must have been quite close to here. Oh Daniel, why oh why did you have to look so much like Marc?

I feel like I'm in way over my head here, but I can't tell if it's because of the Hammersons or because of something else. There is a meeting later tonight to discuss what we'll do, and I'm sure everyone will have questions for Stella (assuming she turns up). I hope it's okay, whatever it is, because I think I'm finally starting to realise how much danger we're all in. I feel like an ant under a magnifying glass; it's hovering right over my head, and pretty soon, the sun is going to come out.

Words of wisdom: I don't feel very wise at the moment.

Wednesday, February 24, 2011, 12:09 AM

Dear diary, don't criticize me for writing in you when I should be sleeping, but it's been such an eventful two days. That magnifying glass I was talking about, it's still over my head, I can feel it, but I think there were others under it as well. The Hammersons caught and trapped a number of us, and I don't want to think what hell they went through while they were locked up, but we have them all back with us now, and the only permanent damage that may have been done was psychological. We were very lucky.

Through all this, dear diary, I'm more concerned with what's going on in that cave, because it's almost over. I can feel it. It's like I'm in a tunnel, but I can see the light at the end of it, and it's bright—too bright—and soon I will be immersed in it. What I have learnt since the last time I wrote about it is that this cave is the very essence of magic. It may or may not exist now, but it definitely existed at one point in history, and the crystals themselves were created here.

I still don't fully understand why I'm here though, why Mary Sien is here with me, and what will happen when I leave, but I do have a suspicion. If I get a chance to speak to William Playman and Carl Thomas, I may be able to confirm what worries me most. If I'm right, Lord help us. Lord? If I'm right, I should be saying Lady, not Lord, and the lady in question is leering at me. I can't even think of words strong enough to convey how scared I am right now.

Words of wisdom: Don't make any sacrifice without understanding what is to be elsewhere gained. I wish I'd known this before I jumped into that death hole; hope that the others understand the cost of acquiring that crystal, and that they use and protect it accordingly.

Thursday, February 25, 2011, 4:57 AM

Dear diary, I know it's early but I've been up for three hours already, and I think my sleeping days are probably over. I don't think I have much time, so I need to write all I know now while I have the chance. I am on the verge of learning something all-important about magic, something that the Sorcerers are incapable of knowing, but I fear that I won't get a chance to write about it. If I do, I will find a way to convey it in some way, even if it's not here, but I fear that the knowledge itself may render me incapable.

I have been sitting here in my room in the Woodward base, leaning against the wall behind my bed for hours now, just watching things play out behind my eyes. Firstly, I was right about at least one thing: William and Carl are just as much victims of this as I am. They have been in the cave with me all along; I just never noticed them in my preoccupation with Sien. Secondly, I was also right in my belief that I will be trapped forever, but I was wrong about it being here in the cave. I'll be able to return here if I choose, I've got that much out of Sien, but pretty soon, I'll have to walk out into the light and learn whatever it is that is awaiting me. When I do, that magnifying glass will be over my head, and the sun will shine through.

I'm as practical as the next person, so I'm trying to think of any way I can possibly convey this knowledge to people who won't be trapped by it as I almost certainly will be. I'm sure it is possible for anyone who isn't seeing all this as I am, and if the knowledge is known, it will be the ultimate answer. The Woodwards, and soon the Fletchers, have plans for the Hammersons, but with all the magic they've already performed to protect themselves, I fear there are very few things that can truly stop them. Indeed nothing will if they never give up on getting all the crystals back, and even if we can kill the Hammersons, there are so many with their ideologies. No, there is only one permanent solution, and I want those who'll have the power to enact it to know it.

I can only think of two things that could possibly work. One is for the Sorcerers to locate this cave, because I'm sure it was once a real place, and may still be real. If it's not, the site must be found. The other solution is to come to me, wherever I will be, so that I can share the knowledge with them. I fear that the only way to do this will be to go through what I went through, and if that's the only way, it probably won't work—probably.

If I get a chance to write more before I run out of time, I will do so, and share anything I can learn, however small.

Words of wisdom: Accept death as a part of life.

But anything Lisa may have learned, she never got a chance to write, for her meeting with Candice Young took place less than eight hours after her last written words. We all stared at her last diary entry for several minutes before, silently, Amelia closed the document and turned off the computer.

Chapter 13: Extraction

Both groups were to work early the next morning. Lucien and Amelia took their group into the lounge room this time to discuss their next course of action, while our group proceeded to the control room to have a look at what Marc and Fewul had done the previous afternoon.

"Speaking of Fewul, where is he?" said Peter, staring around as he and I approached the control room. The group were coming across the yard in dribs and drabs; Marc wasn't too far ahead of us, but the Beast of Magic was nowhere to be seen, and let's face it, he would be just about impossible to miss.

"He might already be in there," I suggested. "It's not like he needs to sleep, so perhaps Marc had him using the thing in there all night."

"That would be useful, except I don't think that's it," said Peter, "because I saw him at breakfast."

"Maybe he got peckish and needed a break?" I suggested, smirking.

"We don't really need him this morning," Marc told us when Peter put the question to him a few minutes later. "I figure the other group may need a little more help since they haven't really got a plan yet, so I've ordered him to take orders from Lucien just for this morning."

"You feel safe enough giving up control over him?" Liam enquired, raising his eyebrows. "What if Lucien orders him to forget that you're his master?"

Marc laughed. "This is Lucien we're talking about—a non-cursed Lucien," he amended. "Besides, any orders I give have veto power over any of Lucien's. I already checked that this morning, just in case I need to call him back."

"Smart move," muttered Liam, causing Peter to scowl at him.

The control room had hardly been big enough for eight people. Now there were fifteen of us trying to cram into it, and the strain clearly showed on many faces. We didn't even bother with seats this time; everyone just stood around the walls, where we all had a clear view of Marc, who stood alone by the controls. A new panel had been added to them, along with a new door which Katie and Sophie were presently leaning against.

"The plan we came up with in our private meeting last night was that we would all take it in turns to use this device," Marc told us. "There are enough of us that we should be able to cover it around the clock. A bit of maths: Can anyone work out how long each of us would need to watch over a twenty-four hour period?"

It took several seconds for Katie to come up with ninety-six minutes. Marc considered for a moment before nodding. "Yeah, that sounds about right. So, each of us will work this thing for ninety-six minutes at a time. We'll do up a roster when we're done here. I know none of you will be particularly interested in working at all hours of the night, but this is something that needs to be done around the clock, especially since we don't know what times of the day Stella is most likely to travel."

"I would guess she'd do most of her moving under cover of darkness," said Peter.

"I'd assume that too, but that's only if she has somewhere safe to rest up in the day," said Marc. "I guess the good thing about this, though, is that if we do ninety-six-minute intervals, we'll each get the same time every day, so we'll all settle into the necessary sleeping patterns before too long."

"What happens if someone doesn't turn up for their shift?" asked Liam.

"I can only say don't miss your shift," Marc said, frowning. "I'm sure none of you will want to, since you all agreed to help. I guess if something unexpected does happen, the person just leaves the scanner where it is until the next person shows up. If you do miss your shift altogether, don't bother turning up later for another one; just wait till the same time the next day. That's the best course of action I can think of."

"Wouldn't it be better for the person who's waiting to be relieved to just continue until the next person shows up?" Siobhan asked.

"If the person in question wants to do that, that's fine," said Marc, "but if it's in the middle of the night and the person is dead tired, there's no point hanging around and doing a half-arsed job. Anyway, what I'm gonna do now is show you all how to use it. Can everyone see from where you are?"

When everyone nodded, Marc turned to the newest controls and pointed out a display screen. At the moment it was showing a whole load of blazing red dots, each flickering around very slightly against what was probably a black background (and indeed the blackness showed through in the larger gaps in the dots). It was mesmerising to watch, but I couldn't work out what it was all supposed to mean.

"Each of these dots indicates something that is currently moving in the area," Marc told us. "If you wanna see what it is, you have to move the blue dot to it and press the V button, like this."

He began pressing some arrow keys below the screen, and suddenly a bright blue dot appeared in amongst the mass of red dots. He moved it so that it was in amongst the most heavily populated area of red dots and then pressed the V button. Immediately, the screen changed; now it appeared to be following the progress of a shopping basket that was swinging from the arm of an elderly woman as she walked down a sidewalk. I recognised the location too; she was in the Chopville town central.

"You see what it did there?" Marc asked us. "It picked up on the basket rather than the woman herself. That's the drawback, but if I set it to focus only on people, it probably wouldn't be able to find Stella."

"Couldn't you set it to find moving objects of a certain size?" asked Sophie. "I mean, we know Stella is larger than a shopping basket."

"Normally she would be, but we don't know if she hasn't found a way to shrink herself," Marc said wearily. "If not for that, it would be a good idea."

"That looks like a tedious process," said Natalie. "Are you sure that's the best we can do?"

"Unfortunately, yes," sighed Marc. "Trust me, I went over this with Fewul. This is as specific as we can get without eliminating Stella from its radar. What we do know, according to John, is that Stella went north, so my suggestion is to move north. When you view it in dot mode (he pushed the V button so that the screen switched back to that view of all those red dots), up is north, down is south, etc. It's not difficult to move it in the direction you want. It probably will be boring and tedious, though, at least until we get a clearer idea of where she might be."

"It does look easy, though," said Darcy. "Is that all there is to it?"

"Yeah," said Marc. "One other thing though; focus on looking for Stella when it's your turn. You'll probably see a lot of interesting stuff on here, but if it's not Stella, just pass it over, however tempting it might be to keep watching it."

"You're taking away our fun," sighed Simon. "Oh woe is us, we shall never understand how it feels to be that poor old spider who got gobbled up by his honey during their love making."

"That's pretty much all there is to say," Marc went on, "so I guess we do a roster, the first shift beginning at—let's say half past nine, since we're almost there now. I'll go first, and Nat, you go second."

"Convenient that you two get the good shifts," said Katie scornfully.

"Actually, I wanted the two of us to work on something else in the afternoon," Marc said, "that's why I wanted to keep our schedules clear. I really need to write these down, I think."

A moment later, he was holding a piece of paper out of nowhere, and also out of nowhere, there were already words printed on it. He read them out to us, and I was pleased that I had the shift between 12:42 PM and 2:18 PM, between Natalie and Liam. It meant I would miss most of lunch, but other than that, it was a pretty good draw for me. Peter and Siobhan ended up with the two shifts between 5:30 PM and 8:42 PM (no dinner together for them, unless they ate it in here) and most amusingly, the twins and their girlfriends got all the night hours (between 11:54 PM and 6:18 AM). Perhaps that was payback for Katie's cheek.

"Other than that, I guess you're all free to do what you want the rest of the time," Marc told us. "Just don't neglect your duties here. Oh, except you, John, you have one more job."

"Yeah, I know, let you know if I see her."

"Actually, I was gonna say do a lot of sleeping," said Marc, smiling slightly. "If you've got nothing else to do at any time, lie down and take a kip. Who knows, you could get lucky."

"I would have thought John would be more interested in getting lucky while he's awake," said Harry loudly, and there was a smattering of laughter.

"Douchebag," I muttered.

"What was it you wanted me for later?" Natalie asked nervously.

"Oh, just to help me with what we were talking about last night," Marc said. "You know, the content screener for the net."

"You sure you want me to help after what happened last night?" she persisted.

"Sure I do," he said earnestly. "I'm not entirely sure Amelia will wanna help, and I certainly can't do it alone."

"You can't get Fewul to help?" she asked.

"Just help him out, Nat," said Peter, looking surprised. "You're a Sorcerer; pull your weight a little."

Natalie shrugged. "Sure, but he's probably safer if I don't; I nearly got him killed last night."

"Nearly ain't good enough, Nat," said Harry, winking at her. "You gotta help him out today so that you can finish the job properly."

"Seriously, I nearly got him killed," Natalie shot back. "Maybe I can do simple magic, but when it comes to the dangerous stuff, you'll all be a lot better off if I stay out of the way."

"Spare us, Natalie," said Rebecca disdainfully, and to everyone's astonishment, she picked up the empty chair that sat a couple of feet in front of her and hurled it across the room at her sister. Those nearest to Natalie leapt out of the way, and she too ducked, but not before sending the chair, with a cracking sound, back at her sister. Rebecca had to throw her arms out in front of her to stop it smashing her face. I was one of the closest people to Natalie who hadn't jumped out of the way, and through all of it, I'd been unable to take my eyes off her. I had rarely seen her look so beautiful as she did in the moment she responded with reflexes she didn't even know she had.

"What the hell was that for?" she shouted.

"Proving my point," said Rebecca, panting slightly as she set the chair back on the floor in front of the control panel. "You only think you're no good, but you didn't have any trouble with that, now did you?"

"That's different—"

"Actually, it's not," said Marc firmly, looking hard at Natalie now. "That may not have been magical, what Rebecca did, but what you did certainly was. You acted instinctively and in my short experience, that's all you really need. There's no reason you can't have my back while I'm flirting with danger this afternoon."

Natalie bit her lip, and I knew it was his wording that was bringing her around. Finally she said, grudgingly, "Okay, but don't expect too much of me."

"If she's not up to scratch, Marc, you can always throw a chair at her," Harry suggested, beaming at Natalie.

"I would have suggested throwing a person at her," said Simon, his eyes on me, "because then she would need to act with his well-being in mind as well."

"I think we'll wrap this one up now, shall we?" Marc said loudly, stepping into the middle of the room. "It's almost half past nine; time for my shift to begin. You all remember when you're due in here, but otherwise, you're free to do whatever you like for the rest of the day. Just give me a chance to modify your keys so that you can get in here before you go."

I had no idea what those plans would be for me though; it wouldn't be sleep, since I would have to be alert in three hours' time. Everyone left in a rush after that and I found myself walking quite close to Natalie on the way back to the main building. Whether anything interesting might have come of that, I never found out, for Peter joined us halfway across the yard.

"I've just had an idea, you guys," he told us.

"Regarding what?" Natalie asked warily.

"Finding Stella," he said, his gaze shifting to me, and I didn't like what I saw there. "I just wanted to float it with you guys before letting the rest of the group know about it, 'cause you'll have the best idea if it's possible."

"What's your idea?" I asked.

"Did you say you saw the confrontation Stella had with that Hammerheart about Hignat?"

I shook my head. "I didn't see it; I only entered her mind when she was thinking about it."

"I don't suppose you saw in her mind where it happened— the exact location?"

"Er—" I faltered, trying to think, "no, not the exact location. I think it was in this area though—near Chopville, I mean."

"I was thinking, if we can get a handle on where it happened, you can go back and see it, like you did in the Main Hall on Rock Haulter."

"What good would that do?" I asked. "I already have a pretty good idea of how it happened."

"Yeah, but you'll see where Stella went afterwards, right?"

"I wouldn't be able to follow her, if that's what you're suggesting. Even if she didn't make herself invisible, I can't move my body while I'm doing that thing—I just come straight back to the present when I try."

But his words made me wonder. It was true that I couldn't move my body, but could I move my mind along any of the first three dimensions in addition to the fourth? I had to consider that it was a possibility, based on what happened the very first time my mind had left my body. On that occasion, I had reached out a steadying hand, only to have it sink right into a box beside me—a very solid box.

"Pretty flaky idea," Natalie said, looking disappointed.

Peter shrugged. "I still reckon there's something in it, John, even if it's not the same as Smiley, what you can do. If we can find a way to work out the exact location of that meeting, perhaps you can test your abilities some more."

"How do we find that location?" Natalie asked. "Stella was just as untraceable back then as she is now."

"She may be, but I'm not so sure that 3K17 is," I said. "Also, if we can find her now, we can probably read her mind to work out where it happened. It might even be useful to know how she managed to find Stella in the first place."

"Great," said Natalie, "so the plan now is to go out and capture 3K17?"

A short silence followed this. Capturing that particular Hammerheart may not have been Peter's original idea, but now that it had been voiced, all three of us knew it was definitely the way to go, and I couldn't believe it had taken this long to realise it. She had managed to find Stella even while Stella was untraceable—that would be very useful knowledge to have.

"Don't get your hopes up about her being able to help us much, though," Natalie warned us as we reached the building. "I mean, if she knew a secret, all the Hammerhearts would know it by now."

"Sure," said Peter, "that's why we should stick to my plan for the time being. So, what are you two gonna do for the morning?"

"I dunno, but I don't wanna sleep," I said, "not since I'll have to be on duty in a few hours."

"If you guys aren't doing anything, you can keep me company," said Natalie, stepping into the otherwise empty corridor and looking around gloomily. "I've got nothing to do, and I don't really wanna think about what Marc wants me for later."

"In that case, why don't we go find 3K17 now?" Peter asked us.

"You don't think we should check it with the rest of the group first?" I asked, startled at the idea of jumping into action so quickly.

"Don't see why," said Peter. "We don't need to get ourselves in any danger, so they don't need to know until we're ready to tell them. Only Marc will have to know, since he has to let us out."

"What's the plan for finding her?" Natalie asked. "I'm not sure I know how to track people like that."

"I can probably help you with that," I said. "There's no reason why you couldn't do it as long as she's not untraceable. I guess I'm up for it if you two are."

Natalie considered for a few moments before something, I couldn't tell what, snapped inside her and she said, "okay—let's do it."

So the three of us went back from whence we had come, giving Marc somewhat of a surprise.

"I've already got this thing up near Shepparton," he told us, "and I tell you, there are a lot of things moving around in Shepparton this morning. What are you guys doing back here?"

"We've got an idea," said Peter. "It's kind of complicated, but basically, we need to go out and capture 3K17—you know the one?"

"I remember her," he said warily. "Why do you want her?"

"Well, she found Stella," Natalie pointed out, "so she might know something we don't. Even if she doesn't, there might be some other use we can find for her."

"Do you have a plan to find her?" Marc said, sitting up straighter in his seat and abandoning the tracking device for the time being.

"I've got a bit of an idea," said Natalie. "I'm not sure if I'll be able to pull it off, but I guess I have to try, or I'll have more chairs thrown at me."

"Very true," said Marc, lazing back in his seat and grinning at her. "I might help you with it sometime, assuming I can do whatever it is you're thinking of, but only after you've had a good go for yourselves. Do you just want me to let you out here in the paddock?"

"That should be fine," said Peter. "Natalie can just do whatever magic we need her to when we get out there."

"You're not helping," she snapped at him.

"Okay," said Marc, leaning forward and hitting a button on the control panel. The door through which we had entered the night before last swung open to reveal the paddock, now much better lit than it had been the last time I had set foot in it. "I'm sure I don't need to tell you all to be careful, though. Do you have any magical weapons?"

Peter shook his head. "You took all our weapons so that Hall couldn't get hold of them, remember?"

"Yeah," said Marc. "Guess I'll have to remedy that at some stage, but not right now. Nat, you just make sure nothing happens to them if anyone dangerous should come walking your way."

"We'll be fine," she said pointedly, stalking through the door without looking at any of us. Swapping amused grins, Peter and I followed.

The weather in the paddock was identical to what we had endured while crossing the yard, and yet in some way I couldn't quite put my finger on, it felt fresher. Perhaps it was nothing more than being in the open air, as opposed to closed air enchanted to feel like open air, which meant it was entirely in the mind. I looked back after a couple of steps and saw that the door to the base stood open against nothing, the interior of the control room visible through it.

"What happens if you shut the door?" I called to Marc.

"You won't be able to get back in until I open it again," Marc said, "but since you left through it, it'll remember you, so you'll be able to find it again. Don't worry though; I don't mind keeping it open for a little while."

"What about a long while?" Peter asked.

"In that case, you can sort yourselves out," said Marc. "In fact, Natalie can just contact me telepathically when you guys are ready to come back in. How does that sound?"

"That should work," said Natalie. "At least that's something I know I can do."

A moment later, the door swung shut and vanished, leaving the three of us alone in the paddock. There were cattle on the far side but the area around us was deserted. Good, I thought.

"So how are we gonna do this?" Peter asked.

"We should start by trying to trace her," I said, trying to think what I would do if I had the crystal, so that I could guide Natalie, who was standing there as though she were completely lost. "If we can, then I guess we try to get her on her own so we can teleport her here; that'll depend on where she is and who's around her. If we can't trace her, I guess we just look around the area. We have an advantage here because we know she's probably still in the Chopville district."

"Can you do that?" Peter asked Natalie.

"I can try," Natalie said doubtfully, "but all the magic I've done before, I've had complete control over. This sounds like I have to command my magic to do something on its own; I'm not sure I can do that."

"That's exactly what it is," I said, remembering how I'd had to command the crystal to do these things, and I mentioned this to the others. "Since you don't have a physical object to command, you'll probably have to command yourself."

"And how do I do that?"

"Separate your mind's-eye from your body," I told her, "then you'll be able to direct it to pretty much wherever you like. You can do it manually or you can get it to take you to a certain location. Go on, try it; it's easier than you think."

"Okay," she said nervously, and she went still, hugging herself as a sudden breeze kicked up around us. I knew when it worked for the look of astonishment and disorientation that crossed Natalie's face.

"Oh yeah, I forgot to tell you to close your eyes," I said hurriedly, "your *physical* eyes, that is."

She obliged, and her expression changed to something that might have been more comfortable. "I think I'm doing this right," she said, raising her hand experimentally. "I can see us from the sky."

"Can you see yourself move?" Peter asked, intrigued.

"I can," she said, surprise and delight evident in her voice. "You're right—I can go anywhere with this."

"See if you can get it to take you straight to 3K17," I told her. "You probably don't even need to remember what she looks like if you can just remember her identity. Have you ever actually met her before?"

"I think I saw her in the staff room at school," she said vaguely. "I mostly remember hearing her when we captured her that time, how she gave it back to Hammerson."

"Focus on that, then," I said, grinning as I too remembered that occasion, then feeling the grin fade as I recalled that it had been less than twenty-four hours after Lisa's final death.

"And if it doesn't work?"

"Then she's untraceable, so we'll work on something else."

"Or I'm just no good at it—"

"If you can't do it, it doesn't matter whether you're the problem or not," said Peter, doing well to maintain patience. "Just give it a go."

Natalie chose not to argue the point, which was definitely a good thing. She went still again, her eyes still closed, and did whatever it is she was doing. All Peter and I could do was stand in the freezing paddock (if it were above ten degrees Celsius, I would go and join those cows over there) and watch her doing her thing. I wished there was some way we could follow her without breaking her concentration. I knew there had to be something going on, judging by her flickering expression, but whether it was good or bad was something I couldn't gauge. Finally, after a good minute of nothing, she spoke.

"I've found her."

"You have?" Peter said excitedly. "Where is she?"

"In the school," Natalie said vaguely. "Er—I mean our old school, the one that's a Hammerheart base now."

"Couldn't be better," said Peter, punching the air in triumph. "We know that place like the back of our hands; I could probably sleep walk in it if I ever fell asleep there. Come to think of it, I'm surprised I didn't walk right out of last year's history classes."

But I wasn't quite so optimistic. "What's she doing there?" I asked Natalie. "How many people are there around her?"

"Quite a few," she said. "She's working on a computer in one of those open-plan offices that the teachers used to use. There are about (she paused for a moment) eight other people in there, and they're all Hammerhearts. I don't recognise any of them, but I'm almost certain they'll all be armed."

"They will be," I said heavily. "So, we need to find a way to get her out of there discreetly. Any ideas?"

"Wait for her to need to go to the bathroom?" Peter suggested, then added, "Assuming we don't freeze before she needs to do that."

"Natalie, do you remember how you got 2L11 to separate from his mates when we were getting the Darkness Crystal?" I asked her, beginning to grin again.

"Sure, we gave him apocalyptic diarrhoea."

"That's a good name for it," snorted Peter.

"Can you do that to 3K17?" I asked her.

"I guess, although I'd never wish that upon any woman."

"This is not really the time to think of things like that," Peter pointed out.

"Then when she goes to the toilet," I went on, not wanting to be distracted, "what's the plan for getting her out of there and into this paddock? Do you think you can manage long-distance teleportation?"

"It's a pretty short distance compared to some of the stuff I've done," she said, "but won't she put up a fight?"

"Knock her out first, then," I said. "Knock her out, then teleport her quickly, before she can fall all the way to the floor. If you can't do it perfectly then don't worry about it; it'll be fine as long as nobody hears. They can think whatever they like after she's gone."

"Okay," said Natalie, and she began concentrating on something neither Peter nor I could see, but could imagine quite well. "I've planted it in her; I've made it the same as what Amelia did to 2L11, so it should work the same. It'll take a few minutes to really get going, though."

"Beggars can't be choosy," Peter muttered.

"What are we gonna do with her when we bring her in?" I asked. "She's gonna be the only person in that prison yard; I kinda feel sorry for her."

"Can we put the influential charm on her?" Peter asked. "Make her useful to us, then we won't need to lock her up."

"I don't wanna do that," Natalie said, still vague as she continued to watch 3K17, "because you just can't be sure if she'll be entirely trustworthy. If she's already boggled then I guess we can sort her out, but otherwise, I guess she'll have to go in the prison yard after all. With a bit of luck, she won't be alone for long."

"Sure, Hignat and Wilwog are on my list," said Peter enthusiastically. "Hall and Sebastian are right up there too. There's something thrilling about the idea of having them all locked up where they can do nothing except bow to us. Oh, and by the way, I'm not a bad person."

He and I both laughed and high-fived each other, after which the three of us fell silent as we waited for 3K17, three kilometres to the south of our current position, to succumb to Natalie's apocalyptic diarrhoea. In the few minutes that followed, I was able to marvel at the knowledge that I'd probably never had such a good opportunity to appreciate Natalie at such close range without her having any chance of catching me. Peter saw it, of course, and I could tell by his amused expression that he understood what I was thinking, but that hardly mattered. Being able to watch her so uninhibited, even for only a few minutes, made standing in the cold so much more bearable. Finally, after this had lasted for a few minutes, Natalie sniggered.

"Is it happening yet?" Peter asked.

"Not quite," she said, her voice still far away. "It's just that they've got a lot of security around there, checkpoints and such. She justified leaving her station to her superior by saying that he really didn't want her to drop what she was carrying in the office."

Peter and I both burst out laughing. "I wouldn't blame him," said Peter. "I bet he got right out of her way after that."

"Somehow, when it comes to things like that, human instincts take precedence over orders," said Natalie, and we laughed again.

"So is she in the bathroom yet?" I asked.

"Almost," said Natalie, "but I think we'd better let her do her thing first before knocking her out."

"You mean because we don't want her bringing that stuff along with her," said Peter, nodding. "Yeah, good idea."

We went silent for another couple of minutes, during which Peter and I prepared ourselves for just about anything, not knowing if or when 3K17 would appear, what sort of state she would be in, or if we would be required to jump into some sort of action. Finally, Natalie spoke again, and the steel I heard in her voice gave me some comfort; she had temporarily forgotten her misgivings about magic.

"Okay, she's got it all out of her system, but she's too weak to move, and the bathroom's empty except for her. I'm bringing her in now."

"Knock her out first," I reminded her.

But Natalie didn't need reminding, it seemed. A few seconds later, the woman I remembered so clearly from several occasions, all of which I would be happy to forget, appeared on the grass before us. She had appeared in a position that indicated she had previously been sitting and leaning back, as though against the wall behind the toilet, and as a result, collapsed onto the ground in a heap. Peter and I swapped embarrassed looks when we registered that her pants were still down. Natalie, who still hadn't opened her eyes, didn't seem to realise the undignified position in which she had left her victim.

"Is she here?" she asked, and when Peter and I confirmed 3K17's arrival, Natalie nodded. "Good. In that case, how do I rejoin my body? Do I just close my mind's-eye and open my real eyes?"

"Er—just give the string a yank," I said, not paying attention to what I was saying as, deciding someone had to do it, I crouched down beside the unconscious woman and began setting her to rights. Peter, seeing what I was doing, hurried to help.

"What do you mean?" Natalie asked, sounding nervous all over again.

"I mean, just imagine your body reeling in your mind. That'll make them rejoin automatically. That's how Hall managed to get out of the base through all the protection we put around it before the shit hit the fan."

"Okay," she said, and went still again. It took her about half a minute to get it right, and by the time she opened her eyes, now entirely herself again, Peter and I were straightening up over 3K17, who now looked considerably more peaceful on the ground than she had with her pants down.

"Good, she's okay," Natalie said, and the slight smile on her face told me that she knew exactly what Peter and I had just done. "I guess I'll let Marc know we're ready to come back in."

"Good idea," said Peter. "I think I'll need a good half an hour to defrost after this."

"I seem to remember being exposed to worse than this on certain school days in the past," I pointed out.

"Yeah, but we had a toilet block to block the worst of it; they didn't send us out in remote paddocks."

"Incidentally, how long will she be unconscious for?" I asked Natalie.

"Isn't it twenty-four hours if you don't specify a timeframe?" she asked.

"Yeah, it is," I said, and breathed a sigh of relief. "That'll give us time to work on her without resistance. Also, could you tell if her mind was protected?"

"I didn't try to read her mind."

"Could you see it, though?" I persisted. "Did her head look kind of ghostly?"

"Er—maybe," she said, looking like she was beginning to understand something. "I thought I was just imagining that. How do you know that's what it looks like when someone's mind is unprotected?"

"The first time I did what you did," I said, "was in the Woodward base when she was there, and I saw her. In fact, I think she was the first unprotected mind I ever saw—her and Stella, anyway."

"So does that mean you can read her mind?" Peter asked. "If so, that'll be a better way to get what we want without having to actually question her."

That was when the doorway to the base suddenly appeared where it had been when we stepped into the paddock.

"How'd it go?" Marc called from his seat in front of the controls.

"The fact that we're here so soon and uninjured should be all the answer you need," Peter said as he and I moved through the door and into the relative warmth. Natalie brought up the rear behind us, levitating the unconscious Hammerheart behind her.

"Yep, that's her," said Marc, grinning. "Prison yard, I suppose?"

"Someone needs to make time to browse her memories in the next twenty-four hours," said Peter.

"I guess you'll have to do that, Nat, since you know what you're looking for," said Marc. "I'd suggest doing it straight after dinner; I don't think you'll have anything else to do then."

"You're making my plans for me?" Natalie asked, narrowing her eyes at him.

"Just call me your social secretary," he said, grinning a little sheepishly.

Chapter 14: Blow by Blow

The time following our capture of 3K17 passed fairly quickly for me. I spent a couple of hours with Peter and the twins, hanging out in the otherwise deserted games room, playing cards and having plenty of laughs. We then had a slightly early lunch so that by the time I was done, I had a few minutes to get to the control room for my shift. Natalie informed me, when I relieved her, that the tracer was well north of our current position, somewhere near the New South Wales border, in a small town whose name neither of us knew.

Once I started my shift, the time slowed down drastically. All I had to do was flit around, watching the moving objects (everything from trucks passing through to insects flying by) and never knowing if I was heading in the right direction or not. Not knowing, I decided my best course of action was to move northeast, but only a short distance. I brought the tracer to rest shortly before the end of my shift in a small town just over the New South Wales border, wondering if Stella had been this way, if she was heading this way, or if she had gone off in a different direction altogether.

With these thoughts fresh in my mind after Liam took over the post at around a quarter past two, I decided to go and attempt sleep for the next few hours, even though I really wasn't feeling very tired. Alone in my room, I changed out of my clothes and back into my pyjamas and, hoping nobody would knock on my door and see me like this (the questions), slipped into bed and tried to make myself as comfortable as possible. It worked, in a way, but not quite how I had intended; instead of drifting off, I found my mind wandering.

At first, I thought about Stella, what she might be doing at this very moment, assuming she wasn't sleeping. In a way, I almost hoped she was, and that she was listening to my thoughts; if so, she would know we were looking for her, and would find a way to make herself known to us. I also found myself wondering how she would be around us, after how it had been back in February, and all the crap that had gone down since her exile. I still missed her and hoped that when I saw her again, we could return to the state our friendship, if that was all it had been, had been before I'd been forced to practically torture her on Mr. Woodward's orders. If what Natalie had once told me of Stella's thoughts was true, she wanted it as much as I did.

These thoughts led me, naturally, to think about Natalie, who at this moment would be with Marc, finalising a system by which our little army would be able to access the Internet safely. After having missed her so much right up until just three days ago (really, only three days?), I was now being allowed to spend quite a lot of time with her. Based on the interaction between the two of us the previous evening, though I could have been reading the signs wrong, she was still interested in me, as I had never lost interest in her. If not, I had to hope that she would still have a spot in her heart for me, because I felt sure that soon, very soon perhaps, I would get my chance to be with her. I wasn't exactly sure how I would go about doing it, but I felt safe in assuming we were heading in the right direction. Perhaps the answer at this point was to simply find excuses to hang out with her more and more and see what happened....

This was when I finally drifted off to sleep, and this was where I began dreaming. The dream involved being stuck in the cold, in the dark, and knowing there was something dangerous all around me, knowing it could move extremely quickly, knowing I could never outrun it if I tried. The more I tried to get away from it, the more I was unable to move until eventually, I collapsed to the ground in a heap, my legs no longer operable. My final moment was to attempt to scratch an irritating itch on my left elbow, only to find that I no longer had a left arm, and therefore had no way of scratching that persistent itch.

I got back out of bed at around half past five, hoping that unlike the day before, I would have enough time before dinner to regain some appetite. I took the time to take a quick, refreshing shower, even though I'd already had one that morning, and then went out to see what else was happening around the base. At least half the people in the base turned out to be in the lounge room, where Marc and Lucien were demonstrating the use of a brand new computer system that had been installed. Everyone present seemed to be very happy with the way it worked, that they would have access to most areas of the Internet, and would only be restricted if they were unknowingly bordering on dangerous territory. James wasn't here, but Peter was, and it was him whom I sat beside.

"Where have you been all afternoon?" he asked.

"Sleeping," I said quietly, "hoped I could make it happen, but it didn't work out this time."

"Maybe it can't happen if you're both sleeping at the same time?"

"I've thought of that, and I guess it couldn't, but still, we don't know when she sleeps. Where's James?"

"Upstairs with Erica, I think," he said, shrugging. "I'm starting to wonder when people around here will start getting sick of each other."

"Are you sick of Siobhan?"

"No, she's just busy with her shift. I'll join her there for dinner but for the time being, I'll stay around here."

I took another look around the room, trying to note who was there. I was a little unnerved to realise that neither of the Sorcerers were present. When I made this enquiry of Peter, he shrugged.

"Natalie left about two hours ago; I don't know where she went. Once she and Marc were done making that thing"—he nodded at the computer—"she just wanted to get out of here. As for Amelia, she's been out of sight all afternoon, as far as I know. Do you reckon she could have left the base?"

"If so, she didn't do it before half past two," I said. "Why would she have done so anyway?"

"Maybe her group came up with something to find those discs and she's out there checking it out?"

"Could be. If so, she should be back in time for dinner, you'd think."

In fact, dinner came around only a quarter of an hour later. I chose to sit with Marc this time, wanting a run-down of how it had gone that afternoon. It became awkward when Lena sat down with us a few minutes into the conversation but that was something I just had to rise above.

"We're having another meeting tonight to discuss it," he said, "and to follow up on what the two groups did today, but basically, it does everything it's supposed to do. It'll let us know when there are new viruses, it won't let any come in, and it'll prevent any potentially dangerous information leaking out. It does slow the net down a fair bit, more than I'd like, but I reckon most of them would be happy enough to cop that if it's the only way."

"So how many computers are there?" I asked. "And is the lounge room really the right place to keep them?"

"I'm not entirely sure," he said. "The more we have, the slower the net is probably gonna get—or maybe I'm wrong about that. I'm not sure how much our screening devices can handle at one time. I don't see a problem with them being in the lounge room if those using them use them for the right reasons—you know, for keeping up with news and stuff. If anyone has something to hide, that can't be good for us."

"What if they're only interested in hiding pornography?"

"Then they should share it with all of us," said Lucien, who'd just joined us and only caught the last part of our conversation; we all laughed.

I kept my eyes out for Natalie and Amelia throughout dinner, but was disappointed as neither of them turned up for a long time. Amelia finally arrived at around seven o'clock, by which time plenty of people were beginning to finish up. She was alone, and although I didn't know it for sure, didn't look like someone who had achieved anything good that day. She looked simultaneously miserable and sleepy; I thought maybe she had spent the afternoon the same way I had, though for very different reasons. What was going on with Amelia these days, and what (if anything) could I do about it? I watched as she got her dinner from the conveyer belt and sat down to eat with Jessica, Tommy and Felicity, but she didn't look in our direction.

After dinner, I had a little trouble working out who to hang out with. Peter was on shift up until around a quarter to nine, and the twins were probably sleeping early in preparation for their shifts throughout the night. To cap matters, I still had no idea where Natalie was, and was beginning to worry about her. Marc had disappeared with Lena, probably to engage in things I could still remember doing with her on that one regrettable but memorable occasion, but I wished I could ask him if Natalie had screwed up that afternoon, or if anything had happened that could cause her to want to hide herself from the rest of us. In the end, I just sat in the lounge room with the majority of the group, listening to the conversation and occasionally getting involved; with Harry and Simon not present, it was their sisters who dominated the conversation, proving that it ran in the blood.

At around nine o'clock, not having seen Peter and assuming that he and Siobhan had taken the time they had before the meeting to enjoy each other's company intimately in a room that actually had a bed, I got up and left the room, intending to return in a few minutes but feeling like I needed a drink of water. I wasn't tired, per say (I had no reason to be after having slept half the afternoon) but I seemed to be flagging nevertheless. Also, just quietly, I wanted to give myself a glimpse of the rest of the base, to see if I could find either of the Sorcerers. Neither Natalie nor Amelia were anywhere around, but on my way out of the dining room, I met Darcy outside one of the lifts. He seemed to be on his way in there to get some food, because by the sound of it, he, Liam and Lucien were hanging out again.

"You sure you don't wanna join us?" he asked. "We're having way more fun than that lot in the lounge room—just us guys, you know."

"Sounds tempting," I conceded, "but I was hoping to catch Peter after his shift."

I was actually hoping to catch a couple of people of the opposite gender, but Darcy didn't need to know that.

"Oh, right," he said, glancing around our little part of the hallway, then back over his shoulder. "Well, feel free to join us any time before your little meeting later. I kinda wanted to ask you about something but I guess it can wait till tomorrow."

"Ask me about what?"

He shook his head. "Dunno how long it'll take, and they'll miss me. Catch ya."

That roused my curiosity, but before I could enquire any further, Darcy slipped past me and into the dining room. So, after that, I had no choice but to return to the lounge room, where after all that, I had no interest in being. All I had to do was the same as what I'd been doing all evening, feeling as though I were wasting my time when I could have been doing —well, what could I have been doing instead? At this stage, nothing productive. If only I still had the Sien-Leoard Crystal; I could be useful if I had that bit of power. As it was, I had to rely on those around me with power to get stuff done.

At around ten o'clock, I decided I'd had enough, and even though the meeting wasn't due to start for half an hour, I headed back to my bedroom to wait. In the bottom floor corridor, I checked out the scene. Tonight's meeting was due to be in Marc's bedroom, the door of which was closed. I briefly imagined him and Lena in there, then shook my head hard to rid it of these thoughts, and I would be lying to myself if I didn't admit that it was out of jealousy. Part of it was him being with a girl I'd previously been with (however briefly), another part was her sheer attractiveness, and none of it was because I wanted to be back with her (not seriously, though, that was a different story), but most of it was because he had a girlfriend and I didn't.

Almost every other door in the corridor was also closed. Liam and Lucien were both in Darcy's room, from which I could hear laughter and music. Lena was in Marc's room, or perhaps he was in hers; the doors were closed and I couldn't hear sounds coming from either, but considering where the meeting was going to be, I hoped they were in her room. It wouldn't have been a nice thought if someone discovered stains on his sheets, or a smell of something suspicious in the air. As for Natalie and Amelia, both their doors were shut, sounds coming from neither, and I wondered if they were in there, if they remembered there was a meeting tonight—if they even knew.

The only door that was open on the bottom level was the room belonging to Rebecca, and I'd been in the corridor for about five minutes, trying to decide what to do, when she emerged from it and shut the door behind her.

"What are you doing here?" she asked, coming to a surprised halt when she spotted me lurking in the corridor, as it would have looked to her.

"Just hanging around," I said, feeling a little better that I now had some company, if only briefly. "What are you up to?"

"My shift in a few minutes," she said, shrugging. "I know this is the best idea you guys could come up with but honestly, from what I've heard, everyone who's tried it reckons it's a waste of time."

"It does feel that way," I agreed, "but it's the best we've got for the time being. It may get better soon."

"Why do you say that?"

"Just take my word for it," I said, not wanting to go into my connection with Stella, or what we had done earlier that morning.

Rebecca poked her tongue at me in response. "Your word is gospel."

"I've been waiting for someone to figure that out," I teased.

"Yay!" she cried, throwing her hands in the air, and then turned and headed for the door to the yard.

About a minute after she had left, Peter arrived, wearing the look of someone who is thoroughly relaxed and contented with the world. I knew that would change once we got down to some serious business, but once again, it was hard not to feel jealous of what he had been enjoying upstairs all this time. The feelings didn't last too long though, because about another minute later, Natalie finally rejoined the world, entering the corridor from the door through which her sister had left.

"Where have you been all day?" Peter asked her, glancing sideways at me.

"Out, for a bit," she said, looking down at an unfamiliar device in her hands. It was almost certainly a magical object, about the same shape and size as a summoner—devices the Hammerhearts used to recall dead people as ghosts. "Mostly though, I've been with our new prisoner."

"Browsing her memories?" I asked, and when she nodded, added, "learn anything useful?"

"Nothing about where Stella could be now," she said, "because obviously her memories stopped when Stella knocked her out, but other than that, I learned quite a lot. We could be in serious trouble."

"You mean more than we're already in?"

"Has it not occurred to you that since 3K17 found Stella, even while she was untraceable, they could know a secret to tracking down any untraceable people? Namely, us?"

"Oh crap," moaned Peter.

"The only good thing we've got on our side for the time being is our size," Natalie said, "and I can only assume that's the reason why they still haven't found Stella—she's found a way to shrink herself. That won't last forever, though, so we're going to have to be prepared for some sort of attack, or attempted attack, very soon."

"You're scaring me, Nat," said Peter shakily.

"I'm scaring myself," she said, grinning slightly.

"What is that thing anyway?" I asked her.

"What 3K17 used to find Stella," she said, looking down at it. "I'm not sure if it'll work in here, and even if it does, it only works over a fairly short radius. Once I found out where it was and how it was protected, I went out to steal it. No trouble there," she added, seeing the looks on our faces.

That was when more people started arriving; James emerged from the lift, and he was followed in short order by Tommy; both of them were wearing expressions similar to the one Peter had carried when he had first joined me. In the same moment, Amelia finally emerged from her bedroom, looking similar to how she had at dinner, but ready to talk all the same. It was a relief to see her again.

"Nice," said Peter, checking his watch. "We've still got a few minutes before we're due to start, but since it's only the Morans we're waiting on—"

"Aren't we having it in Marc's room though?" Tommy asked, stopping at his friend's door and knocking on it. "Oi, you in there, Marc? We're about to get started."

"He's probably in *Lena's* room," said Amelia distastefully. "He's usually good about turning up on time, though, so we might as well go in there and get comfortable."

She had been using her magic to unlock Marc's door as she spoke, but was brought up abruptly when it opened and we saw what was going on in there. Natalie let out a gasp of horror; Tommy groaned; and Amelia hurriedly leapt backward, bringing the door with her so that it banged shut again.

"What the hell?" Peter asked sharply, not having been in a position to view the worst of it.

"They were—they were—" Amelia was gasping for breath, arms wrapped around herself, eyes wide with horror.

"I can't believe that just happened," Natalie moaned, dropping the magical tracer to the floor with a clang and collapsing against the nearest wall, her eyes closed.

Peter groaned. "Oh no. What were they doing?"

"Really, Peter? You need a blow by blow description?" Tommy retorted.

Amelia, meanwhile, seemed to be on the verge of a nervous breakdown, such was her horror; just one more thing on top of a pile of horrors she had endured. I stepped up to Natalie and took hold of her shoulder, causing her eyes to snap open in alarm.

"I think you'd better knock her out," I said, nodding at Amelia, who was trembling so badly that she wouldn't be able to stand much longer. Natalie obliged immediately, and I was a little horrified to see the satisfaction, however slight, on her face as Amelia's legs gave way and she dropped like a stone, sprawling in the middle of the group clustered around Marc's door.

"So," said James into the shocked silence that followed, "is the meeting still on?"

Nobody knew; nobody wanted to take charge. Fortunately, we were saved by Lucien, who emerged from Darcy's room at that point, but stopped dead when he saw Amelia on the floor and the rest of us standing over her.

"What happened?" he asked sharply. "Is she okay?"

"We'll find out when it's safe to wake her up," said Peter shakily.

"I think your brother won't be joining us tonight," said Tommy, glancing sideways at the closed door, behind which Marc was now doing who knew what. Would he have the courage to come out here and confront us after what we had just seen? Would Lena?

"Why's that?" Lucien asked, hurrying to join us. "Did he do this to her?"

"He made it necessary to do that to her," said Tommy, nodding at Natalie. "She was the one who actually knocked her out, and if the rest of you don't mind, I think I need a drink after seeing that."

"Hang on," I said, my eyes darting from one face to another, trying to think of any way to prevent this scene slipping out of control. The only way I could think to do that was to get everyone out of the corridor, particularly before anyone else turned up and started asking questions. I could already see Darcy and Liam poking their heads around the corner, watching the episode with concern. "Let's all come in my room instead; we can have the meeting in there, since Marc's room's already been double booked."

"John!" snapped Peter. "Seriously, that's too much, even for me."

"Sorry," I said, a little sheepishly, then added, "thank God the twins didn't see that. Let's all agree not to let them find out about it."

"Just out of curiosity," James asked as they all followed me one door down to my room, "did anyone see if Fewul was in there with them?"

"I'd prefer not to imagine that little threesome myself," said Peter, shuddering.

"Wow, seriously?" Lucien asked, his eyes widening. "You saw Marc and Lena together?"

"It was sort of an accident," I told him. "Tommy knocked on his door first and when he didn't answer, Amelia assumed he was in Lena's room and said we should go in and wait for him, since we're supposed to be meeting in there. Only, turns out he and Lena were in there after all."

"So, it's Amelia's fault?" he said, looking around at Amelia, whom Natalie had levitated onto my bed—now I had that to think about when I lay down there in a few hours—maybe Amelia would still be in here in a few hours—okay, John, stop getting carried away.

"It's not her fault," snapped Tommy. "She didn't ask for that to happen."

Lucien gave him a very level look. "She opened his door without his permission; you can't tell me that's not an invasion of privacy."

"Let's be reasonable here," said James. "Marc knew the meeting was in his room. He has to be responsible for the fact that he wasn't ready by the appointed time, and by the sound of it, he wasn't almost done either."

"That may be true, but otherwise, he wasn't doing anything that most of you haven't been doing this evening," Lucien pointed out. "So before you go being critical of him, you should look at what you could have done to prevent that from happening. Also, try to imagine someone doing that to you. How would you feel facing the rest of us after that?"

"Thanks for the sermon, Reverend Moran," said Tommy, scowling, "and for the record, that's why I said we shouldn't expect him to join us tonight."

Lucien also scowled as he looked back at Amelia. "You know, part of me thinks she actually wanted that to happen, almost like she's looking for an excuse to fight with him."

"That's really unfair," said Peter indignantly. "Seriously, we can't go saying stuff like that. If we start fighting, how are we supposed to get anywhere in this war? Hammerson would probably laugh at us if he saw this now."

Nobody answered for several seconds. I looked around at them all; Lucien and Tommy were scowling at each other, while Peter and James were looking on nervously. Natalie, for whatever reason, was watching me, and I only realised then that she'd been waiting for some kind of reaction from me, whether to the sex, or to the fact that it had been Lena in there. I decided that this wasn't the time to get any deeper into what had just happened.

"Look, we can probably get by with the six of us tonight," I said. "We can catch Marc and Amelia up later—separately, I mean."

"Why can't we bring Amelia around now?" Peter asked.

"Because then we'll have to spend the evening settling her down," I said, glancing at him, and then back at Natalie. "You can sort her out when we're done here, can't you?"

"Do I have to?" she asked doubtfully. "I'm not sure she'll listen to me."

"I think I'm safe in assuming you're the one she'll listen to, John," said James.

"Damn it," I muttered; I'd been hoping to catch up with Marc after this meeting, to make sure that he slipped straight back into the fold with as little embarrassment as possible. As for Lena, who knew what would be the best thing to do. "Okay, fine, but in the meantime, let's get started. I can say that other than the regular watches from the control room, which you all probably know about by now, there's really nothing to report from our group. What did your group get up to?"

"Hang on, what about 3K17?" Peter asked.

"We'll get to that," I said, staring at Lucien. "Go on."

"Well, our first order was for Amelia to contact her father and ask to interact with Lisa's father," Lucien told us. "If she could, she'd tell us how that went. I have no idea if she got around to doing that but as there's been nothing else going on all day, I have to assume she did. What we decided was that if it's possible to trace Lisa's belongings through her father, we would ask him to check for any discs and if any existed, we would try to come up with a safe way to transport them here. If not, we would give up looking for the discs at all."

"Really? That soon?" Peter asked incredulously.

"The discs aren't really important in the scheme of things," Lucien reminded us. "It's the information on the discs that matters, and Natalie and Lisa copied that information from some sort of encyclopaedia of magic. It stands to reason that the information may be available from other sources, even if they are few and far between. If we can't find Lisa's discs, we'll look into tracing the source of the information that was on them."

"That sounds like a plan," I said. "I hope you're wrong about that information being freely available, though. The less the Hammerhearts know, the happier I'll be."

"John, I think Hammerson already knows all there is to know about you," James pointed out. "He certainly knows more about the prophecy, the Enlightener, and the fact that you can see ghosts. He could even know about your connection with Stella from reading her mind, so there's not much else he could know that would hurt him, other than knowing how much we know, of course."

"I do know of one other thing," I told them, James's words reminding me of my dream of two nights earlier. "What you guys don't know—what very few people know—is that the reason Tankom hunted Tommy was actually because her failed attempt to kill him damaged her own magic."

"How the hell do you know that?" Peter asked, his eyes widening.

"And how long have you known?" Tommy added. "Blimey, that would've been kinda useful to know."

"That part I found out from Stella," I said. "I only remembered it when I was locked in that basement cell, contemplating killing her. In light of everything else that happened that night, I guess I forgot to mention it. In any case, that's why she wanted to undo it, so that she could repair her magic, because of course, she intended to get it back. More importantly for us now, though, is that Hammerson never knew about Tankom's magic being damaged. Lucky for us, those two kept secrets from each other."

"Is her magic damaged now?" Natalie asked. "If it is, I guess my grandmother would have it now."

I shook my head. "This is the important bit. You remember when we were locked up in the Hammerheart base back in February, and Hammerson tried to kill me that night?"

They all nodded expectantly.

"When he couldn't, Tankom offered to do it for him, but he said that it had to be him. She would have known, of course, but it only occurred to me the other night, thanks to a dodgy dream, that he had her damaged magic. Amelia and Stella never paid attention to who they were giving their crystal chips to when they took them from Moran that time. So Hammerson had the damaged magic and that was the reason why he couldn't kill me. All this time, Stella and I thought that it was something about me—something odd that was protecting me from him. Hammerson believed that himself, otherwise he would have used the Sien-Leoard Crystal to kill me the other night back in the base. The good thing for me is that he still hasn't worked out the truth, and hopefully, he won't."

"Holy crap," Peter breathed. "So—so that's how close you came to being killed the other night?"

"Oh my God," Natalie whispered, her eyes shining, and for a moment, I thought she might actually cry.

"So yeah, there are definitely things I'd prefer he not know," I summarised, "though admittedly, there wouldn't be anything about that on those discs. Other than us, and possibly Stella, there's no one else alive who knows the truth."

"Yet another reason why we need to hurry up and get hold of Stella," said Peter. "On that note, should we tell them what we did this morning?"

"Might as well," I shrugged. "Go on; it was your idea."

"Well," said Peter, taking a deep breath as everyone's attention turned his way, "I just thought that if John saw the exchange between Stella and 3K17, he could get an idea of where she might have gone by tracing her visually from her last known location. You know, he would go back and see it all the same way he saw the stuff in the Main Hall on Rock Haulter."

"That's not a bad idea," said Lucien, "but it would depend on knowing exactly where that encounter took place. How would we learn that?"

"From 3K17, of course," said Peter, "since she is traceable and her mind is unprotected. More importantly, the fact that she was able to find Stella at all is something we ought to know about. So, earlier this morning, John, Natalie and I went out and captured her."

"Just like that?" James said incredulously. "You didn't discuss it with anyone?"

"It was really more of a spur-of-the-moment type thing," said Peter, shrugging. "We told Marc about it, since he was on duty, but we didn't explain the whole point of it. Natalie just traced her and then got her on her own so that we could teleport her to us without any of the Hammerhearts being aware of it."

"So you didn't make any contact with any Hammerhearts other than 3K17 herself?" Lucien asked.

"We didn't even make contact with her," Peter said. "Nat knocked her out before teleporting and we never bothered to bring her around."

"So where is she now?" Tommy asked.

"In the prison yard," Natalie said. "We couldn't think of anywhere else to put her. I've spent most of the day going through her mind, and quite apart from learning about who she is, found out that she's been a Hammerheart for ten years, and her reasons for joining were entirely self-motivated, so there was no influential charm going on with her."

"What were her reasons for joining?" James asked curiously.

"She was getting nowhere in her life," Natalie shrugged. "She was in her mid-twenties and had nothing to show for it. She joined up in the hope of seducing Hammerson so that she could get a share of his power, even if it was only over his army, which was really nothing much back then. It was all she felt she needed to set herself up in life. It didn't take her long to work out that seducing Hammerson wasn't exactly possible, but by then, she'd come to realise that their way of doing things was probably the right way after all, so she never looked back."

"How old is she?" I asked.

"She's thirty-five now. Why do you ask?"

"Just thinking," I said, quickly crunching the numbers in my head. "If she'd turned up a few years earlier, she could have been Stella's mother, and Hammerson would never have needed to kill that poor American woman. I mean, he must have known 3K17 liked him; he could read her mind all this time, he'd never bothered to protect it, and he always kept her fairly close to him."

"Maybe so, but he never gave her the power she sought," James pointed out. "He could have ordered her anywhere and she would have had to go, but instead he kept her here in Chopville, under his thumb but always a level-three-ranked Hammerheart; never enough power to have any influence. Also, for the record, if she had been Stella's mother, Hammerson probably would have killed her anyway; she would have had leverage over him, and she would have bugged him for either affection or security for the rest of her life. He wouldn't have put up with her for long."

"Geez, you know a lot about it," said Peter, a little disturbed.

"Just thinking through it, Pete," said James, shrugging. "So, did you learn anything about how she found Stella?"

"Or anything else useful about the Hammerhearts?" Lucien added.

"She used that," Natalie said, pointing to the large magical device which she had placed on the spare seat beside her. "It's a device that sort of reverse-engineers the process of making something untraceable."

"It can make something traceable again?" Lucien asked sharply.

"No, it just knows what to look for," Natalie corrected. "Do you guys remember, back in the Hammerheart base in Germany, when Marc thought he found Stella sleeping in one of the upstairs beds?"

"Yeah," said James slowly. "He said that since she was untraceable, the bed she slept in would become untraceable too; it became invisible, so that corner of the room appeared empty."

"That's how it would have looked to him," said Natalie, "because he was viewing it visually. The visual representation of something being untraceable is that it simply becomes invisible, but there's actually more to it than that."

"Isn't visually the only way to view something?" Peter asked. "Or am I missing something here?"

"A few screws from the top panel?" James suggested, and Peter elbowed him hard.

"It's hard to describe," said Natalie, whose face was screwed up in concentration. "Picture this: You draw a picture of a landscape, but then you want to blot out the sun. I guess using white-out would be good enough to make it invisible, but it would still be there behind the white-out, wouldn't it? But if you got a pair of scissors and cut through the paper so that there was a hole where the sun used to be, that would mean it was no longer there. Being untraceable is basically the magical equivalent of that, except of course, it only applies to magical methods of tracing; we all know that behind that, the object still exists."

"Wow, that is a deep one," said Peter slowly.

"Yeah, but only half as complicated as the stuff Smiley came out with," said Tommy reasonably. "So are you telling us that that thing"—he nodded at the tracing device—"detects these—these holes in reality, for lack of a better description?"

"That's exactly what it does," said Natalie, "but it's limited. It works on a size over distance ratio; that is, the smaller something is, or the further away it is, the harder it is to detect. I'm not sure what its exact limitations are but if she had come into our paddock with this device, she wouldn't have found our base unless she stood right on top of it."

"So we're still safe from it," sighed Lucien, clearly relieved.

Natalie shook her head. "They're working on bigger and better models. It's only a matter of time before Hammerson comes up with something so sophisticated, it can pinpoint the exact locations of every untraceable person and object in the world, no matter their size. I don't think he could make it provide visuals, but he wouldn't need to; he could just teleport to each location and flush the person or thing out himself. We're going to need to think long and hard in the time we still have before he does this about how we can throw him off our scent."

"That is a problem," said Lucien, looking a little scared. "I suggest everyone put some thought into that over the next twenty-four hours. I take it from that, that 3K17 couldn't locate Stella any further because she got too far away?"

"I assume so," said Natalie, "plus she could have shrunk herself. I never saw that myself, and in fact I don't think Stella ever knew how 3K17 found her, but she must have become more scared for her safety after that."

"She was," I said, "that's why she chose to keep moving further away. So, now that we know this, we have a direct way to trace the untraceable. We need to find a way to plug this sort of magic into the tracer Marc already created; that'll cut down on our tracing work in a big way."

"I suppose Marc had better do that then," said Lucien, "once he's informed of this meeting. Perhaps he can get Fewul onto it tomorrow. Incidentally, I don't suppose you have any new leads for us, John?"

I shook my head. "Slept this afternoon, and will try to sleep a bit more tonight, if I can, but so far nothing."

"You can only keep trying," he said, nodding. "So, I guess that's it for tonight?"

"What about 3K17?" James asked. "We can't just leave her all alone in that prison yard. It'd be bad enough with other prisoners, but all alone?"

"Do you have a better idea?" Tommy asked.

"No. Sadly, I don't," he sighed.

"I don't know what's the best way to hold her," said Lucien, "except that since she was never under an influential charm, she must be kept locked up. We can use her mind to learn more about what the Hammerhearts are doing. In fact, it mightn't be such a bad idea to release her, but find a way to keep tabs on her mind, similar to what the Hammerhearts are doing with their viruses."

"Wouldn't they kill her if they found out?" James asked.

Lucien sighed. "You're probably right, and we can't have that; she'll be no use to us dead. Also, whatever she may be as a person, from my experience of her, she's actually a relatively good one by Hammerheart standards; a lot more humane than some of them."

"Good that you say that," said Natalie, looking amused. "I see what you were trying to do, though; she'll only know what they've been doing up to this point, and only some of it, but that's still pretty good—a lot better than we had before. She'll come around tomorrow morning just before my shift, so I might meet her, give her a bite to eat and explain that she's now a prisoner of war. Not the first time for her, I suppose."

"Don't forget to take her watch if she's wearing one," Lucien reminded her. "Actually, you should probably take everything she's got, and I mean everything, including clothes. You can manufacture some for her. I just think we have no idea how she may be bugged; if they can somehow monitor or trace her from afar, or communicate with her in any way. When I was a Hammerheart, the watch was the only method they had, but they may have developed more methods since then."

"Thanks, I'll do that too," said Natalie, grinning at him. "You wanna keep me company while I do?"

Lucien shrugged. "I'm not sure I can offer any more advice than I just did. Why do you ask?"

"Well, one other thing I got out of her mind is that over the last few months, she'd spent a lot of time fantasising about being alone with you, Lucien."

We all laughed, and even Lucien managed to crack a grin. "Not sure I needed to know that, but if you're suggesting I stand around and watch you undressing her, I think I'll pass."

"Really, Lucien?" Peter teased. "You know they say women in their thirties have great sex drives? You could probably enjoy her company a fair bit while she's here."

Lucien shrugged, doing remarkably well to maintain his composure. "I've heard that about women in their thirties too. Whether it's true or not, I don't know, but I'll still pass."

"Shame," sighed Peter. "That would certainly make her lonely stay in that prison yard a little easier to bear. Now if she were one of those less humane Hammerhearts you spoke of, Lucien, I would say she didn't deserve it, and after all, you are a single seventeen-year-old guy. You know they say guys around your age are at their most sexually active as well? You two would be a match made in heaven."

"You're trying to tempt me, aren't you?" Lucien asked, raising his eyebrows.

"I think he is," laughed Tommy. "Is it working, Lucien?"

Lucien shook his head. "Unfortunately for all concerned, I'm not quite so desperate. Now, if we've settled that, is there anything else we need to discuss before calling this meeting to a close?"

"I have two items," James said, and when Lucien nodded, he went on. "Firstly, I'd like to call a vote. All those in favour of Lucien entertaining our prisoner, raise your hands."

"*Serious* items," Lucien said flatly as everyone around him raised their hands before we all broke into laughter.

"Great," James called. "With that settled, the second item was about our proposed Honnie solution from last night."

"*Your* solution," Peter muttered.

"I just wanted to know if anyone's given it any more thought," James persisted.

"I have," said Natalie quietly.

"So have I," Lucien agreed, "but I think it might be best not to discuss that one tonight. Wait till Marc and Amelia are back with us and we can get a few extra opinions. I would suggest, though, that those of you who haven't given it any thought, seriously consider it, for the reasons we discussed last night. Very well; anything else?"

There was nothing else, and with that settled, we agreed that Lucien and Amelia's group would once again use the lounge room at nine o'clock the next morning, while our group wouldn't be required to meet up until after our tracing device had been modified to include the magic from the tracing device Natalie had brought in. Then tomorrow night, we would all meet up again, in a location to be determined sometime the following day.

Chapter 15: Hitchhiking

As the others began filing out of the room, I firstly took 3K17's tracing device and placed it on my bedside drawers with the intention of handing it over to Marc the next time I saw him. Then, before she could leave, I caught Natalie in the doorway.

"Hang back for a minute," I told her, leading her out of the doorway so that Peter could leave, casting a curious look at the two of us as he did so. After he had gone, though I hadn't specified what my intentions were, Natalie reached out and quietly shut my door.

"What's on your mind?" she asked me, looking curious and somewhat anticipatory. I realised then that if I played my cards correctly in the next few minutes, I could probably have her tonight, but sadly, that couldn't happen while Amelia was lying unconscious on my bed. Still, I allowed myself a moment of fun.

"You," I told her, jerking my head in the direction of my bed.

"What!" she yelped, her eyes widening in surprise, interpreting that exactly as I'd intended, but clearly caught off guard that I would be so forward.

The expression on her face when she saw Amelia there, and realised what I was actually talking about, was comical: simultaneously relieved, disappointed and resentful. She swore under her breath. "Okay, fine. What do you need me to do?"

"Just bring her around," I told her reasonably, moving towards my bed and sitting down beside Amelia, "since you know I can't do it myself. You don't need to talk to her if you don't want to."

"Really? You don't wanna just let her sleep through the night and deal with it in the morning?"

I considered this for a moment before shaking my head. "It won't be any less unpleasant, no matter how long we hold it off for. It might be a good thing if she has time to calm herself down before she sees Marc around the base in the morning."

"Or maybe that'll give her time to work herself up into a frenzy over it."

"You really think she would do that?"

"Honestly, I don't know with her anymore."

I shrugged. "Let's just get it over with; I hate the idea of having this thing hanging over all our heads. The quicker we sort it out, the less people will need to know about it."

Natalie sighed, giving me a regretful look as she waved her hand at Amelia, who slowly returned to consciousness. I waited patiently enough for her to open her eyes and take in her surroundings.

"Where am I?" she said a little thickly, her eyes finding me. "John, what's going on? What room is this?"

"It's my room, and there's nothing going on," I told her. "You were just unconscious for a while, but you're okay now."

"What am I doing here?" she asked, pulling herself slowly into a sitting position, using my shoulder for support; I carefully didn't look at Natalie through this. Perhaps I should have pushed her back down to the bed, not knowing if she would be dizzy, but she seemed to be coping okay.

"Er," I said, unsure exactly how best to proceed, "we just brought you in here 'cause we had the meeting in here, but it's over now so don't worry about it."

"Oh—the meeting," she said slowly, looking around the room in some confusion, her eyebrows raising when she caught sight of Natalie, now leaning against the wall near the door and watching impassively. "We were…"

She broke off, and I could see that she was starting to put it all together: The meeting, the meeting that was supposed to happen in Marc's bedroom, Marc's bedroom. Her eyes widened in alarm, horror, dismay, or something similar.

"Aw geez, did that really happen?" she said wildly.

"It happened," I said flatly. "None of us have seen him since."

Amelia seemed to struggle with herself for several seconds, during which I quickly looked around at Natalie to make sure she was ready for anything, not knowing whether Amelia would cry, rage, or (hopefully) take it in her stride. Natalie was still watching, but not as though she had any intention of helping. Finally, Amelia let out a gusty sigh.

"Is he still going to help us or is he gonna spend all his time between her legs?" she said bitterly.

"He'll help," I said, fairly sure I was right. "He mightn't be able to look at us for a few days, but he knows how serious this thing is."

"I can't believe he was doing that," she said to no one in particular, staring towards the foot of my bed.

I shrugged. "It's not that surprising. He wasn't doing anything we didn't know he was doing, and like Lucien said, a lot of other people in the base are doing that stuff too."

It was an extremely awkward moment as Amelia looked around at me, and I felt Natalie's eyes on my back too. It might have been my imagination, but I thought all three of us were thinking the same thing. It had never been spoken of directly between any of us but I knew that both of them were aware of my own experience with Lena. Now was definitely not the time to bring that up; this thing was complicated enough as it was.

"Maybe people just need to put their priorities in order around here," Amelia said grudgingly. "He knew we were having the meeting then; we were only early by a couple of minutes, and from what I saw, he didn't look like he was nearly done."

"You can't blame him for doing that, though," said Natalie unexpectedly. "I would have preferred not to see it either, but I'm sure if you were in that position, you'd wanna finish it too."

Amelia glared at her. "Are you inferring I'm jealous?"

"No," said Natalie, who looked more amused than cautious, and I found myself wishing she would leave (she was not helping the situation). "I was only implying it."

"And what's that supposed to mean?"

"Seriously, are you saying he wasn't doing anything with her that he wasn't doing to you a few months ago?"

"Oh my God!" Amelia snapped, and she would have been on her feet had I not quickly grabbed her by the shoulder.

"Don't start fighting. Come on," I said hurriedly, looking from one to the other. Amelia looked ready to breathe fire, while Natalie looked simultaneously wary and vindictively satisfied. "Amelia, are you gonna be okay with all this? Are you gonna be able to look at Marc tomorrow without wanting to hit him?"

Amelia continued to stare at Natalie for several seconds before looking back at me. Something seemed to soften in her expression when she did, and I had a nasty revelation about what could actually be going on here. "I guess so," she said, sounding like all the fight had whooshed out of her, "but I'd prefer not to have to be around him."

"You're going to have to," I said, "at least for the important meetings. He'll be just as awkward as you, though, so I think he has a little more to worry about there."

"Fine," she said, "if I have to."

She got up off the bed, stretching. She was good to look at when she did that, but it would have been better if she'd looked happier. "If the meeting's done, I might as well go to bed. Someone can catch me up in the morning."

"Sure," I said, relieved that I'd gotten through this episode without any further fireworks. I'd been worried for a moment there that the two Sorcerers would put their magic into action against each other. What could I do then? Me, of course, being the most vulnerable person in the room. Amelia passed Natalie as she headed for the door; neither girl looked at each other, and my suspicions with regard to their behaviour grew.

"Well there you go, problem solved," said Natalie, the moment the door shut.

But I wasn't going to let her off that lightly. "Did you really have to say that to her?" I asked reproachfully.

"Oh come on, we all know that's what's really going on here," she snapped, looking at me in a speculative way that made me uncomfortable. "She only started doing this as soon as she saw Marc and Lena were together, although I doubt she's interested in getting him back now."

"She'll get over it," I said, hoping I was right.

I got up off my bed, stretching and feeling like I wouldn't mind a bit more sleep despite having slept half the afternoon, but I knew I couldn't rest yet. There was a piece of business that I wanted to take care of tonight, if possible. I gestured to the tracing device I had left on my bedside drawers.

"You mind if I hang onto this for now?"

"Sure," Natalie replied, "not like I'm gonna use it."

"Cheers," I said, moving slowly across the room to my wardrobe, as though I were about to get ready for bed, but in fact I was really buying a bit of time. I had no intention of getting back into my pyjamas just yet, but I needed Natalie to be safely in her bedroom before I put any further plans into action—that would avoid unnecessary questions on her part. "You might as well go get some sleep," I told her, not looking around as I opened the wardrobe door.

"Yeah," she said, stretching as she moved away from the wall, and I resisted the urge to look around at her. "See you in the morning."

"Night," I said vaguely as I heard her opening my bedroom door, but to my confusion, after several seconds, she didn't close it.

After several more seconds, I looked over my shoulder. Natalie had left, but she'd left my door open for some reason. For a moment, I wondered if she'd made herself invisible, but then I heard a door open further down the corridor, and knew she had just entered her bedroom. I resumed my contemplation of the interior of my wardrobe, listening to the silence outside, waiting for Natalie to disappear into her bedroom, thinking of the episode that had just taken place.

At first, I might have thought that Amelia's ill feelings towards Marc and Natalie had to be related to magic, given that that was the common denominator between the three of them, but Natalie was right in pointing out that all this only began when Marc had kissed Lena in front of her. Was Amelia jealous of Lena, wishing she had what Lena had? I didn't think so, but did she wish she had what both of them had? Yes, that sounded more like it. Amelia was lonely, and after all she and Natalie had seen and done prior to coming here, it was no wonder. As for why those two didn't get on, I didn't want to think it, but I had to consider that it was because they both wanted the same thing. Girls seemed to be more perceptive when it came to who was interested in whom, and I knew that at various points this year, they had both been interested in me. It wasn't nice to think of myself in those terms, but even worse was the knowledge that I could only return the feelings for one of them, and it wasn't Amelia. I wanted to do something for her, though; I just wished I knew what.

I pushed these thoughts away when I finally heard Natalie's bedroom door shut further down the corridor, and silence fell. I briefly wondered if she'd kept our doors open in the hope that I might follow her into her room, but didn't dwell on it for long; that seemed more like a fantasy of mine than a reality of hers. The time was a quarter to twelve and it seemed that most people had turned in for the night. I wasn't about to, though, not yet. I had one order of business remaining, but whether I would be able to complete it depended on whether or not Marc was still up and about. It had been awkward enough dealing with Amelia, but I knew that if we were to put this nasty business behind us quickly, it had to be done tonight, before he could sleep on it.

I went to my open door and looked out into the corridor. It was all dark and silent and every door other than mine was shut. Listening to the silence made me feel as though Marc would probably be asleep like the rest of them, but I had to give it a go. At least I wouldn't be able to barge in as Amelia had, I thought as I picked up the tracing device and carried it down the corridor to Marc's door. I shifted it under one arm so that I could knock on his door with the free hand, again expecting nothing.

"Who's that?" I heard Marc's voice call from the other side, though only just loud enough for me to hear. It didn't sound sleepy, which was what I'd hoped, but other than that, I couldn't get a gauge on how he was feeling.

"It's John," I called back in much the same way lest Natalie hear. "Can I speak to you?"

Wrong words, I thought bitterly, as I immediately played them back in my mind. Saying it like that made it sound like I was going to reprimand him, which wasn't my intention at all, but fortunately, Marc didn't take it as such. I heard him call back, "Hang on," before making me wait for some twenty seconds, during which I reflected that it took some guts to open the door this soon, particularly to a guy who'd been with the girl with whom he'd just been caught.

"What's up?" he asked, opening the door just wide enough so that I could see him, but not much of the room behind him.

"Just wanted to make sure you're okay," I told him, "and to show you this."

"What is that?" he asked, looking at the tracing device. "Looks a bit like one of those things they used to call ghosts back—except without the tap."

"It's what 3K17 used to find Stella," I said. "Can I come in so I can explain it? And is Fewul around anywhere?"

Marc sighed, and I had a good look at his face in the instant before he raised his eyes back to my face. He looked simultaneously curious and resigned. The curiosity was probably for the tracer, but what about the resignation? Was that about having a long conversation with me, or was it about what he was facing regarding what happened earlier?

"I guess so," he said, stepping back and letting me in. "Fewul is here, by the way, but invisible. That's what I make him do when he's not needed."

"Okay," I said, entering after him and slipping the door quietly shut. It was only when I turned back to the room that I noticed that Marc wasn't alone in here: Lena was sitting cross-legged on his bed. Thank God both of them are dressed this time, I thought, doing my best to keep a straight face. Her eyes were downcast and she appeared more sulky than anything else, and I wondered how they had spent the time since their unexpected interruption.

"So what is this thing?" he asked me.

"Well," I said, looking sideways at Lena and choosing not to comment directly, "Natalie was reading her mind all evening and she went out to get this. It traces things that are untraceable by reverse-engineering the process of making something untraceable. So, it knows what to look for that replaces untraceable things. This won't actually find Stella, though, because she's too far away. That's why we want you to hook its brand of magic into the tracing device we already have."

"That sounds kinda difficult."

"Yeah, I know, that's why I asked after Fewul—he can do it for you, or at least make it easier for you to do it."

Marc sighed and reached for the device. I handed it to him, slightly amused at how its weight seemed to catch him off-guard. He put it down on his bedside drawers with a clang, exactly as I had done, before straightening up and yawning.

"Anything else happen in there that I missed?" he asked, looking sideways at Lena; she didn't respond to the glance.

"Er—don't think so," I said, trying to think back to the meeting. "We didn't get any updates on Lucien's group because Amelia didn't join us."

"Why not?" he asked, more sarcastically than anything else.

"Because Natalie knocked her out—she went a little nuts."

"Serves her right," Lena muttered, and both Marc and I looked at her. Once again, she didn't respond, and my curiosity was roused. What exactly was going on here? When Marc had looked at her, his glance had seemed angry, but the anger seemed to be mostly directed at her.

"Serves her right?" I repeated mildly, not wanting to get involved but unable to resist.

"She shouldn't have opened the door," Lena snapped, finally looking up; her eyes were burning as she looked between Marc and me.

Marc shook his head. "The meeting was supposed to be in here."

"How is this my fault?" Lena snapped at him, and now I understood what must be going on here. It wasn't entirely Lena's fault, I thought, but one had to admit that it was hard not to think about having sex with her when one was alone with her. I'd worked that out for myself on the few times I'd been alone with her, as she'd certainly wanted me to think about having sex with her on those occasions, so I could understand how it would be so easy for Marc to forget about all else around her. It still seemed a bit unfair to blame her for it, though.

"You don't get it, do you?" he snapped right back at her. "You've turned me into a bloody sex maniac. I would never have missed a meeting before getting with you. I was with Amelia for more than two months and we only had sex maybe five times, but now I want it every night."

"You think this is a good time to bring up your ex?" Lena snapped, and now she was on the verge of tears.

Marc shrugged, looking tense and angry, but not as though he were about to shout at her. In the momentary silence, I listened hard for noises from any of the surrounding rooms, but didn't hear anything.

"At least she never distracted me," he said grudgingly, "even if she was a bit distracted herself. You, though; how am I supposed to keep my mind on important things when you're around?"

"Well please, forgive me for being me," Lena said sarcastically, jumping to her feet and whipping her hair out of her face. "Maybe you just need to learn to think with your large head instead of your little one. Oh, and by the way"—she rounded on her heel as she reached the door, and I thought she was surely about to tell him she'd been faking it all along—"he was way better than you!"

Damn, I thought, as the door swung shut behind her. That was definitely not the ideal way to end such a discussion, for lack of a better word. Marc and I both stared at the door for several seconds before looking back at each other.

"Sorry you had to see that," he said wearily, sinking down onto his bed.

"That was a little unfair, wasn't it?" I asked, not sure if I wanted to get into this discussion with him now, but knowing that if I didn't, it would almost surely be the end of his relationship with her. Quite apart from wanting him to be happy, I knew that Lena being on the market again could complicate things even more for me.

He sighed. "Maybe, but it's true."

"Remember what happened the last time you told the truth?" I pointed out.

He sighed again. "Yeah, sure. I guess I'll have some cleaning up to do in the morning, unless she wants nothing more to do with me. Geez, we sure know how to make things more complicated for ourselves around here, don't we?"

"This is what it's like to live without parents," I said, and we both laughed. "So, if you don't mind me asking, how much of it really is her?"

He considered before answering. "I'm not so sure. You know as hot as she is, she looks quiet and demure from a distance; but once you really get with her, she's like a—a—nymphomaniac."

"Yeah, that sounds about right," I agreed. When one looked at Lena, one was almost forced to imagine what she would be like in bed, but Lena herself didn't normally behave like she was thinking about sex; but all that changed when you got her alone.

"I guess it's mostly me," he admitted, "but honestly, you know as well as I do how hard she is to resist, and all because she never appears to want it so much—she makes me want her instead."

"Maybe that's a good thing," I said. "That's not how she treated me, and it made life very difficult."

"That might be the case again very soon," he said, looking more serious now. "I don't wanna break up with her. She's a really good person once you get past all this stuff—quiet, smart, trustworthy—but I need to find a way to keep her at arm's length while we're still in danger."

"Good luck with that," I said, deciding I'd had enough of this and making for the door. "I'll do my best to stay away from her in the time being. See you in the morning."

"See ya."

I left his room, grateful that the corridor was still deserted (part of me had expected Lena to be waiting for me) and returned to my room. I undressed and slipped back into my pyjamas, not expecting to get much sleep but willing to try for it all the same. I got into bed and lay down, thinking about all that had transpired this evening. I wanted Marc to get back with Lena and find a way to resolve their differences; I wanted Amelia to find someone who could take away her loneliness so that she would be less hostile towards Marc and Natalie; and most of all, I wanted Natalie to be mine. That was all true, but a certain part of my body wanted none of that to happen. A certain part of my body wanted Marc and Lena to break up, so that she would be available once again, and she would come after the person she supposed had been 'way better' than Marc. A certain part of my body wanted Amelia to be back on my bed, only conscious this time, and under the covers to boot. A certain part of my body wanted Natalie along with all of that. I cursed that certain part of my body, thinking that it had to be held accountable for a lot of the group's current problems—or rather, that certain part of the male body in general.

It was with these thoughts that I drifted off into a light sleep, not having been too tired, and it was this, perhaps, that finally led me into Stella's thoughts for the first time in more than a week. The dream didn't last long, but it had been packed with useful information. When I woke up from it, I wrote as much of it down as I could remember before the dream could fade from my mind. Then, more awake in the dead of night some three hours before breakfast would be due to start, I sat in my bed and, by lamplight, reread what I had written, analysing it.

The first thing to note was that Stella didn't think there was any chance that the Woodwards, or anyone affiliated with them, would be coming to save her. By reading local newspapers of the towns she had passed through on her travels, she had learnt about the attack the Hammerhearts had launched on the Woodward base. The reports stated that they had driven the Sorcerers out of their hiding place, that most of the Chopville Quartet had regrettably escaped, but that one member (notably me, she knew) had probably been killed in the attack, although they had been unable to recover his body in the wreckage. The thought that I, John Playman as it were, was probably dead, had filled Stella with despair and a solemn resignation. She had decided now that there was to be no safe life for her anymore unless she moved away, as far as she could go. She would head for a remote location, change her identity, and begin her new life as a simpleton.

Her reasoning was simple enough: The Hammerhearts' laws may spread to all corners of Australia, and soon the world, but their influence would take a lot longer to spread. It was thick in the Chopville vicinity, of course, and even thicker in the more populated areas of the country. That was why it had become necessary to move north, as she had been doing on foot for some time now, but Dubbo (her current location) was not nearly far enough. That was why she had snuck into an empty house a week ago and used their Internet and printer to provide herself with a map, and a plan.

When I entered her mind, Stella had been awkwardly positioned between several large boxes in the dark, silent cargo hold of a semi-trailer. The truck wasn't going anywhere now but it would be tomorrow, and by casually chatting to the driver the previous evening, she knew where it would be going. She had hitchhiked all the way from Perth to Adelaide in this fashion once before (that had been when the entire southeastern corner of the country's Hammerheart bases were cut off from the rest of the network, thanks to Moran and Lucien), so she knew what she was doing.

She had no intention of going all the way to Brisbane, where this truck was headed, though. Her course was laid out on the map before her, which she was conveniently studying by torchlight when I entered her mind. She would find a way to get out of the truck in or around Goondiwindi, preferably when the driver chose to refuel, but if she had to get out a little earlier, it would be no disaster. From there, she needed to find a way to get to a town called Miles, where her next free ride would pass through. How she would do this was something she hadn't quite worked out yet. If a truck came along that was heading in that direction, all the better, but if she had to steal a vehicle to accomplish it, she had the tools necessary to do the job.

Doing this made her acutely uncomfortable, though: Firstly because she had never driven a car in her life, but more importantly because of the trouble that could arise if she were pulled over by the cops—those men and women who answered directly to Commissioner Hall—and the strong possibility that Hall would order them to bring her in where, once her father got hold of her, she would be subjected to the influential charm.

From Miles, she would hitchhike on board a truck heading for Darwin, but once again, she would disembark long before the final destination. Exactly where she would disembark, though, she hadn't yet decided, though it would be no further northwest than Cloncurry. It would be a matter of picking out a small town (no more than a few thousand people) that was fairly well isolated in outback Queensland, somewhere where she would be noticed and draw curiosity at first, but where she could eventually blend in and, hopefully, count on new friends and a new community to keep her cover. And if it didn't work out—well, she could just move onto the next small town.

The whole journey was a long one—perhaps as much as two thousand kilometres, and perhaps even more, according to the map, but she hoped it would be worthwhile. She was prepared as it was possible to be; she had a bag like the one the Maivis twins had used on Rock Haulter that would duplicate her food so that she would never need to go hungry. The best thing was that all the food she'd put in their so far had been fresh when she'd placed it, which meant that it would always be fresh in the bag. She was also heavily armed, although only with devices that weren't visible on the outside; she had stolen plenty of things before she had left her father, plus a few extra goodies from other Hammerhearts along the way, including several new creations that hadn't existed when she'd had magic. She could only assume her father had been busy since he had obtained the Sien-Leoard Crystal. Finally, she had a small but secure tent which, although cramped and far from luxurious, was strong enough to protect her from people, animals, bad weather and, most importantly, magical attacks.

Stella had been thinking that she ought to sleep at night because she would need to be alert while the truck was driving so that she didn't miss her stop when I woke up. Exactly how Stella intended to keep a close eye on where she was from the inside of a cargo hold on a semi-trailer was something I could only speculate about; there were certainly no windows to speak of, and judging by her stealth, I assumed she had no intention of asking the driver to let her out. I looked back at my notes and memorised the locations: Goondiwindi, Miles, Cloncurry. Now that I knew that, I had my own plan for her. Stella would never get as far as Cloncurry; in one of those towns, we would be waiting for her.

I didn't get any more sleep during the night, which didn't surprise me, but was still regrettable given that I no longer needed to see Stella. I sat in my room for a while, pondering what I had written and how we might go about approaching Stella once we found her. After I got bored with this, I left my room and patrolled the corridors for no reason, but being on my feet helped clear my mind. There was certainly a lot to think about, both relating to the war and the social situation within the base. Out of my room, though, I quickly became cold, and was turning to go back to my bedroom when one of the outside doors opened right beside me and Simon appeared. Both of us got a nasty shock.

"Jesus, John," he breathed, slipping in and shutting the door behind him, though not in time to stop a cold draught following. "What on earth are you doing up at this ungodly hour?"

"I was told to sleep in the afternoon yesterday," I said, "so I'm not tired anymore. What are you doing up?"

"Fulfilling my duty as guardian of the control room," he said proudly, "for all of ninety-six minutes anyway. Sophie just relieved me."

"Doesn't Sophie relieve you on a daily basis?" I taunted, and he managed to smirk.

"Maybe so, but not usually at this hour; not that I'm complaining, though."

"You may be interested to know something," I said, considering how much of the shambles of the night before he ought to know. Deciding nothing was best for the time being, and seeing that he was waiting, I told him, "I saw Stella a couple of hours ago. She's in the back of a truck in Dubbo."

"Right now?" he said, his eyes gleaming in the darkness.

"Yeah, but she won't be there much longer; she's on her way to outback Queensland somewhere."

"You got all this tonight?" he said, turning back to the door. "We've gotta tell Sophie—get the tracer up to Dubbo before she can get going. Are you saying she's hitched a ride in a truck?"

"Yeah, but don't bother getting her tonight. She plans to get off in Goondiwindi on the Queensland border. She was looking at a map," I added, seeing the surprised look on Simon's face. "Our best bet is to wait for her there. I was gonna tell Marc in the morning. He's gonna make some other changes as well."

"What other changes?"

"It doesn't matter; just know that with a bit of luck, you've just completed your one and only shift."

"So what's your plan to get her? Wait in Goondiwindi and then what?"

"Trace her," I said. "We've sort of worked out how, and then I'm not sure what we'll do."

Simon shrugged. "I'd suggest just getting one of the Sorcerers to knock her out so she can't attack. Then when she wakes up in here, she'll see that we're all right."

"That might actually be the best way," I said, impressed. "Now, if you don't mind, I'm freezing and feeling in need of a warm shower."

"Don't think I'll join you for that," Simon laughed. "You enjoy yourself now."

"Will do, Mr. Maivis."

* * *

Breakfast that morning was an interesting affair. I sat with Lucien, Tommy and Jessica, no longer bothered by sitting near a couple (good to note that I had quickly pulled myself out of my depression before it could get a strong hold on me), and in a position where I could see much of what was going on around the rest of the hall. Not too far to my left, Amelia had initially sat alone, but Natalie joined her halfway through the meal and appeared to be trying to reconcile with her. I couldn't hear their conversation, but judging by their expressions, they seemed to be prepared to forgive each other for the time being; that was a relief. Not too far to my right, a similar thing happened with Marc and Lena. She had sat alone; he joined her a short way into breakfast, and in this case, I could hear some of their conversation.

"Hey, can we talk?" was Marc's way of opening proceedings.

"Are you ready to apologise?" Lena asked rather waspishly.

"Yes," he sighed, "but it's a little more than that. Can I sit with you?"

She must have consented, but I tuned the discussion out by turning to Tommy and Lucien and informing them of what I had seen during the night. It didn't matter that Jessica was there; she listened with interest, knowing that since we were talking about Stella, it wasn't really her business.

"This is excellent, John," said Lucien, his eyes gleaming just as Simon's had. "We have to be prepared for the possibility that she won't be able to get out of the truck in Goondiwindi, but that shouldn't be a problem. Now that we have internet access, perhaps a good use of your time this morning would be to look at a few maps—not just of Queensland and New South Wales, but also of the typical truck routes between Melbourne and Brisbane, and Brisbane and Darwin. Maybe get a few people from your group onto that this morning."

"You won't mind them being in the lounge room at the same time as your group?" I asked.

"Shouldn't make a difference, as long as they're quiet," said Lucien fairly. "In fact, John, maybe it wouldn't be such a bad idea for you to join our group this morning too."

"Why do you say that?" I said, surprised.

"Well, we still don't know what Amelia's got to say," he said, "but that's beside the point. Your group's mission is almost over. Once Marc has sorted out the tracer, you've made Stella's plan clear to the rest of your group, and you've sorted out your own response plan, there won't be anything else to do until Stella gets out of the truck. You might as well help us out instead—it's for you that we're tracking that stuff down, after all."

"Fair enough," I said, "but in that case, you'll have to hold off starting until maybe ten o'clock, so that we've got time to sort everything out."

Chapter 16: Documents

By ten o'clock, everything was indeed sorted out. I got hold of Marc, Natalie and Peter immediately after breakfast and told them everything I had told Tommy and Lucien, including the ideas Lucien had laid out. They were most impressed, and in the hour between nine and ten, the four of us set to work on finalising the plans to catch Stella. Firstly, Marc had placed the tracing device beside the one he had created two days earlier and instructed Fewul to modify his tracer so that it would use the same magic as the one Natalie had brought in. When this had been achieved with remarkable ease, the display screen turned completely black.

"I suppose that means there are no untraceable objects within range?" Marc enquired of the Beast of Magic, which nodded its confirmation. "Good. So, what's the plan now?"

"Is there any way to lock onto an object and follow its movements?" Peter asked, watching the empty display screen. This seemed to be easier than looking at Marc, apparently; none of us had mentioned the episode of the night before, but apparently Peter found it a little difficult to look straight at Marc this morning. Natalie, to her credit, was handling the situation very well.

"Not automatically," said Marc, "but I suppose once you find something and show it, the screen will follow it until you return to this view.

"Where is it now? North or south of Dubbo?" he asked Robyn, whose shift was still going and who had remained behind to complete it. When she merely shook her head, he sighed. "Okay, never mind. Maps of New South Wales and Queensland are in order, but I'm thinking that even if Stella hasn't been through here today, the best bet is still to head North. Robyn, you might as well head off; my shift is about to start anyway."

"Okay," she said, and was out the door in a matter of seconds.

"So what's the plan?" Natalie asked.

"Seems simple enough," said Marc. "The shifts will continue as normal until someone finds Stella. They continue again until she gets out of the truck, and when she does, we pounce. Whoever is on duty at the time should notify us immediately when this happens, because I think we'll need magic to help us get her—she's apt to put up a fight before she works out who we are. She would need to be that cautious just to have survived for this long. In the meantime, John, you go help the other group, and I guess you two go find us some useful maps of the area. Don't forget your shift starts just after eleven, Nat."

"How do we let the rest of the group know what's going on?" Peter asked.

"Tell each of them when they come in for their shifts," Marc said. "I think you're after Natalie, John, so you tell whoever comes after you what the plan is, and tell them to pass it along to the next person, and so on. I think the good thing is that if any of them do find Stella, they'll have the sense to keep track of her, even if they don't have the sense to let us know."

We left him to it after that, the three of us heading back to the lounge room and getting stuck into the first real use of the Internet since it had been safely installed. It turned out to be about as fast as what we were used to in Chopville, even with all the safety precautions we had set up, which only showed how much we had been missing out on in Chopville all these years. We were there earlier than the other group so I watched Peter and Natalie for a little while before Lucien and Amelia turned up, the rest of their group filtering in over the next ten minutes.

"Don't mind our visitors," Lucien told the group as they cast curious looks at Peter and Natalie. "They're doing research for the other group and won't be getting involved. As for John, he'll be joining us with our mission."

"For the time being," I assured them.

"So, let's get straight down to business," Lucien said, clapping his hands and looking across at Amelia. "How'd it go with your dad yesterday?"

"Well, I couldn't get a meeting set up with Lisa's father," she said, "but I asked him to pass on a message for me, and I checked back with him before breakfast this morning. He says that Lisa's father does have some things of Lisa's, including a lot of CDs. He made it sound like they were all music but he's willing to check more closely for us."

"Is this your dad or Mr. Pont?" Lucien prompted.

"My dad," Amelia said, "although I suppose Lisa's father could do it as well. It doesn't really matter; I didn't tell him what we needed the discs for, only that they contained a lot of research for a project on magic Lisa had been doing before she died. I'm not sure when they'll have time to do it, though, or how they'll transfer the discs to us if they find them."

"Okay," said Lucien slowly, seeming to feel his way. "So where does that leave us? What can we do in the meantime?"

"Look for the information somewhere else?" suggested Tommy.

"If it's possible to arrange it," said James, and everyone turned to him immediately (apparently his input had become extremely valuable in these meetings), "I would suggest a couple of us go into their base and look through Lisa's belongings ourselves."

"What if they don't let us leave?" asked Tommy. "I wouldn't put that past a few certain parents, such as yours, James."

"There may be a way around that," said Lucien. "James, I like your idea, but doing it will require the Woodwards to let us in. Fewul could probably infiltrate their base but I don't want to weaken their defences when we don't have to—it might make it easier for Hammerson to do the same thing. Tommy, I think you should be one to go, because your parents are unlikely to stand in the way, and because you should recognise the discs on sight, having had possession of them for a while. I think Amelia should accompany you, and I also think, if Marc will consent to it, Fewul should go with you. That ought to make them think twice about holding you hostage there. Amelia, are you okay with this?"

"I think so," she said, "although I'm not sure how they can let us in when they're in a desert in the Northern Territory. I suppose we'll have to teleport to them but we'll need to find a way to reveal ourselves to them without risking being discovered by the Hammerhearts."

"Between you and Fewul, I don't think any Hammerhearts should give you any trouble," said Lucien. "Do you think your father would be okay if you contacted him now? Or is he likely to be too busy?"

"He probably is busy," she said, "but as far as telepathy goes, he'll converse with me whenever he can just 'cause he's so relieved to hear from me every time. Do you want me to try now?"

"If you would," said Lucien, smiling reassuringly at her.

The room went almost completely silent then but for the quiet discussion between Peter and Natalie that didn't quite carry across to my ears. Everyone was watching Amelia as her face changed subtly while she conversed with her father. After a couple of minutes, her eyes cleared and she looked back around at Lucien.

"One o'clock," she said. "Me, Tommy and Fewul go out there just before one. We'll need to lift all our enchantments off ourselves, though, so that they can find us easily."

"Will that affect the rest of us?" James asked.

"Don't see why it would," said Amelia, "if we do it so that it only lifts off the two of us and stays in place for everyone else."

"How will you get back in then?" asked Dean.

"That depends," said Lucien. "Who's on duty in the control room then?"

"If you get back before two, I will be," I told them. "I can let you back in but I can't put any enchantments around you."

"So when we come back in," said Tommy slowly, "the base will look empty to us, even though you guys will be all around us; we won't be able to see or hear you."

"That's how it would go," said Lucien. "I suppose Fewul can fix that? Or come to think of it, Marc or Natalie could probably do it too."

So that turned out to be the plan. Immediately after that meeting, I went back down to the control room with Natalie and Peter to tell Marc what was going on and to request the services of the Beast of Magic. On the way, I told them both what was going on. Even though they'd been in the room, they hadn't been paying close attention to our discussion.

"I don't mind fixing them up when they come back," Natalie told me. "My shift finishes just into lunch, so I'll just come back to the control room after I've had something to eat."

"Okay," I said, thinking that for a while, she and I would be alone in there together...nice.

Marc, however, was wary when I told him this plan. I didn't have to wonder why: He had been good enough about relinquishing control of the Beast of Magic to his brother, but would he do the same for Amelia, given their current relationship?

"I suppose I can do that," he said, looking at the display screen and frowning, "but I'll instruct Fewul to only make that apply while they're out of the base—that should be fine. How'd you go with the maps?"

"Pretty good," said Peter, who was also watching the screen, "but not as good as you, by the look of it. Good job, mate."

I quickly looked at the display screen too, and was delightfully surprised to see that in the short time we had been away, Marc had locked onto our target. The inside of the truck was still dark but Stella was visible; she appeared to be half dozing, half looking through something that resembled a tiny telescope.

"What is that thing?" Natalie asked.

"I don't know," Marc said. "I'd be guessing, but I think it might be something she can use to determine her location, but there's no way to know. I wouldn't even know the truck was moving unless I switched back to the other display, but it doesn't really matter; we'll see when she gets out. Can I see your maps?"

"Sure," said Peter, handing two pieces of paper over, "although it doesn't really matter anymore. See, there's Dubbo, and Goondiwindi is here, and Miles is further north by about 220 kilometres."

"Well wherever she manages to get out, this thing will be right there with her," said Marc. "We can set a door down wherever that may be so that we can bring her in, no probs."

* * *

The rest of the morning passed in similar fashion to the previous morning, as far as I was concerned. While Marc continued his monitoring of Stella, and Natalie went into the prison yard to see 3K17, who would have woken with a start at some point, Peter and I went back to the main building where we found the twins in the game's room once again. The only difference this time was that James joined us. I had a slightly early lunch, as I had done the previous day, before heading back to the control room to relieve Natalie of her post.

"There's been all of nothing to watch," she said, "but I think it must be getting close now. She looks more alert now than she did a couple of hours ago."

It was true; Stella seemed not to be dozing at all anymore. She was facing the front of the truck and looking through that telescope likeness again, as though it were somehow showing her what was ahead of the truck. For all I knew, that was exactly what it was doing.

"Okay," I said, sitting down before the screen and settling in. "You'd better get moving if you wanna be back here by one o'clock to see them out."

"Do I need to see them out?" she asked. "Surely Amelia can let herself out."

"Of the base, maybe," I said, "but I dunno if she can lift the veil off herself, or the other enchantments."

"Okay," she said, "but for the record"—she looked back as she reached the door—"I think we should just make Fewul do that."

Assuming Fewul was even coming, I thought, but didn't say. The Beast of Magic did turn up though, at exactly ten minutes to one o'clock, as though Marc had ordered him to be on the spot whenever Amelia and Tommy were ready to go. A few minutes later, the two of them turned up, and Natalie was right behind them. Good timing, I thought, or good thinking—whichever it had been.

"So what exactly is he doing?" I asked them, nodding at Fewul.

"Guarding us," said Amelia, "and doing any complicated magic if I can't."

"Marc's ordered him to obey Amelia," Tommy told me, "but it only applies until they're back in the base."

"Okay," I said, having known this already. "So I guess you just get out there and teleport? Do you know where you're going?"

"Yeah, Dad gave me a landmark to focus on. We'll try to be back within the hour, but no promises there. If we're not, you don't have to stay," she told me, and then turned to Natalie. "But you do."

"I know," said Natalie coolly.

I pushed the button on the control panel to open the door and watched as the three of them left before closing it up again.

"I guess you watch that screen," I told Natalie, indicating the one that showed Amelia, Tommy and Fewul in the paddock, "while I watch Stella."

"Sounds like a plan," she said, magically creating a second seat so that she didn't have to stand around for the duration.

"How'd it go with 3K17 earlier?" I asked her.

She grimaced. "The moment she realised she was trapped, she just went all quiet. It was like talking to a wall."

"Yeah, she did that to Mr. Woodward too," I said, remembering the occasion. "What did you say to her?"

"Just explained what we'd done," she said. "I think she was a little relieved that she wasn't really sick or anything. I didn't tell her why, though; she doesn't need to know about the whole tracing thing. I also told her that she had the option of cooperating with us and providing information, or we would get it out of her mind. She knows enough about magic to take me seriously, but she still didn't say anything."

"Maybe we should send Lucien in there after all," I said, and we both laughed.

A silence fell after that. Perhaps I should have made the most of that time; perhaps I should have engaged Natalie in conversation about personal matters; perhaps I should have tried to gain her trust in such matters, but at that moment, I didn't feel up to it. With horrible timing, I felt tiredness beginning to creep up on me. I sat back in my seat and watched Stella, but it was impossible to stop my eyes shooting sideways to where Natalie was watching the now-empty paddock. On several occasions when I did this, I caught her looking at me in exactly the same way. So, although we didn't talk, we seemed to say quite a lot to each other. In fact, after nearly half an hour of this, I felt I had progressed further along the path to being with Natalie than I ever had before. The only trouble was, I had no idea what the next step would be.

My mind was drawn away from this when three figures suddenly appeared in the paddock. Natalie sprang to attention immediately.

"That's them," she said, reaching out and pressing the button to open the door. "Er, will they see the door or will we have to drag them in?"

"Probably the latter," I said, imagining how lost they must feel out there—well, not Fewul, but the other two. "I'd suggest doing the enchantments out there, if you're up to it."

"Okay," she sighed, getting up and heading out into the paddock, stopping beside Amelia and tapping her on the shoulder. Amelia jumped and looked around wildly before realising it must be one of us.

I stood up and moved in front of the doorway to get a better view of what Natalie was doing. Apparently she had spent time thinking about how she would do it because she seemed to know what she was doing. She was holding three lights in her cupped hands, and as I watched, she raised them over her head and began performing the motion I recognised as her invisibility veil. If those lights were anything to go by, she was performing the untraceable spell and the soundproof barrier in the same way. It only took a couple of seconds, but when she was done, I saw Tommy and Amelia relax visibly.

"I can see the doorway," Tommy said, and he skirted around the two girls to charge through it. Amelia, Natalie and Fewul followed, and once they were all in, I shut the door behind them.

"You did that well," I said to Natalie.

She shrugged. "I practised on 3K17 earlier; I figure there's no harm in her being under the same protection now, and I needed to do that to interact with her."

"So how'd you go?" I asked Tommy and Amelia.

"*Booya!*" Tommy cried, brandishing two CDs from his pocket for our inspection. "Piece of cake."

"Really?" I said, surprised. "You didn't take very long."

"That's because it was so easy," said Amelia, who looked elated. "Lisa's dad wasn't in but my dad took us to where he kept all of Lisa's things—the ones he was able to recover anyway. There were a bunch of CDs there, mostly music, but there were also these two."

"The discs look the same as the ones I remember," Tommy said, looking at them, "and have a look at what Lisa put on the covers."

He held them out for our inspection. One of them said, 'Magic Display—Lisa', while the other said, 'Magic Display—Natalie'.

"What if they're different discs in those covers?" Natalie asked.

"That's what I thought too, but Fewul says they're the original discs," said Amelia. "I know—it feels too good to be true—but in this case, it really is."

"Well, I guess the next step is to check them," I said.

"You can't," Natalie told me, and when I raised my eyebrows at her, "you've still got forty-five minutes left on your shift."

"Oh right," I said. "Well, I hope you guys don't mind waiting for me? It's just that this stuff concerns me most of all, so I wanna be one of the first to see it."

"That's not a problem," Amelia said. "When will you be done here?"

"When Liam turns up, and that's supposed to be at 2:18."

"Very precise, aren't you?" said Tommy, amused.

"Only way to split twenty-four hours into fifteen people," I said, grinning, but the grin was mostly outward. It was hard not to be a little pleased with the progress we had made; we now had the discs, and very soon, we would also have Stella. What was holding me back from being entirely cheerful was that on those discs was information that concerned me greatly—information that had altered my life since I had been a year old. Very soon, I would learn that information, and I couldn't expect it to be any more charming than everything I had learnt on my last visit to Rock Haulter.

I continued the rest of my watch on Stella alone, where nothing whatsoever happened. This was a little surprising; the driver hadn't stopped for lunch at all, and he had been on the move since at least ten o'clock that morning. At least, I thought he had been; perhaps he had actually started a little later than that. Given how dark it was, it was never possible to tell when the truck was moving. All I knew was that Stella hadn't moved, and of course, she would know if the truck stopped. It would need to pull over soon, if not for food then certainly to fill up its tanks, and when that happened, Stella would be out of there.

It would happen soon, but it didn't happen during my shift. Liam turned up bang on time and was thrilled when I showed him how much progress had been made during the morning. I explained that he only needed to watch the screen, and to come running for the Sorcerers when Stella left the truck. He nodded his understanding, leaving me free to head back to the main building to find Tommy, Natalie and Amelia.

After some searching, I located one of them—Amelia—in the lounge room, which was packed with most of the base and very noisy indeed.

"Do you have the discs?" I asked her.

"No, Tommy's still got them," she said, getting up. "Come on, everyone's in Natalie's room. We were waiting for you before we looked at them."

"Natalie has a computer in there?" I enquired as I followed her from the lounge room.

"No, we're just gonna use the laptop," she said. "I should have given it back to Jason by now, I suppose, but once this is done, we definitely won't need it anymore."

"Okay," I said, suppressing a yawn with difficulty. Amelia looked sideways at me, and I shrugged. "I was asked to sleep yesterday afternoon, in case I saw Stella. I've screwed up my sleeping patterns a bit."

"Well, what better way to fix them up than to have people like us preventing you from resting," she said wickedly as we arrived at Natalie's room. Amelia made a point of knocking and waiting for it to be opened from the other side before we could enter.

"And we are whole once again," Peter announced brightly.

Indeed we were; the whole group were present this time: Peter, James, Marc, Tommy, Lucien, Natalie, and now Amelia and I. They were sitting in the couched area at the back of the room, as we had done in my room last night and in Amelia's the night before. Also like that night, the laptop was occupying one of the seats.

"This could be a very important moment for all of us," Lucien said as we sat down on either side of the computer, "but especially for you, John. Are you ready for it?"

"I'm not sure," I said honestly, "but waiting it out won't make me any more ready than I am now. How are we gonna do this?"

"I'll use the computer," Natalie told us, "since I made one of those discs, and it'll be projected up on the wall, like it was last time. I suppose you all get where you can see it."

Marc and Peter, who had been on either side of Natalie, moved to sit on the floor in front of us so that all of us were facing Natalie, and more importantly, the bare wall behind her. Ironically, Marc ended up sitting right in front of Amelia; he could have leaned back against her legs, but fortunately for everyone in the room, he chose not to play with that kind of fire. Amelia made a point of looking high over his head at the wall as Natalie performed the necessary magic to project its screen up for the rest of us to see.

"Can you look for the Enlightener first?" I asked hopefully.

"Er, I guess so," said Natalie, loading the list of files and folders on the disc, "but if we find the prophecy first, we might as well read it."

I shrugged, not entirely happy with that but understanding the logic in it. My thoughts were that once I read the prophecy, I probably wouldn't want to be around the others for a while; I would need to speculate privately on it before talking it over with the others. They would have their own views, of course, but in the end, their opinions of my destiny didn't matter—I would do what I wanted where that was concerned. I looked up at the screen and saw that it was indeed one of the discs from the magic display; apparently it had already been checked before Amelia and I had turned up. We watched as Natalie browsed slowly down the list of documents, checking the root directories before moving on to the sub directories.

"How exactly would the Enlightener be categorised anyway?" James asked.

"My only suggestion at this point would be to look for anything to do with innate magical abilities," said Lucien. "I'm not sure if the Enlightener falls in that category, but I don't think it's inherent like seeing ghosts is."

"They could be in the same category," said Peter, "even if one is inherited and one isn't. If it's not, though, how did John end up with it?"

"That's one of the things we're trying to find out," I said.

"A lot of spells in this area," said Tommy, reading the screen. "This stuff looks interesting. We should keep these discs handy."

"Which disc is this, anyway?" Amelia asked. "Is this yours, Natalie, or Lisa's?"

"It's mine," said Natalie. "Why you ask?"

"Well can anyone remember what disc that other prophecy was on?" she asked. "I'd bet the one we're looking for is probably in the same file."

"I bet you're right," said James, "but I can't remember which disc that was on."

"Not this one, I think," said Tommy. "See those folders there? Stuff about the last war, stuff about the history of magic through the Middle Ages...I think this is the one that had a lot of information about Fewul and the Seventh Sorcerer, but if I remember correctly, the prophecy was on the other disc. We should probably give this one a good look-through anyway, though."

"Yeah, especially as you sound like you're guessing," said Peter.

We continued the search for ten minutes, looking through the file names but not bothering to open any files because none of them looked as though they would have any useful information. That didn't necessarily mean they didn't, but in order to determine that, we would need to perform a far more exhaustive search. I knew the others didn't want to do that unless they had to, and I concurred.

Finally, I became convinced that the information we were after was on Lisa's disc, and the conviction came from what I remembered of Lisa's last few weeks with us. She had known quite a lot about people who were born with special magical abilities. When questions had been raised about Sorcerous Seers, she had been almost as knowledgeable as Daniel, who had possessed that particular quirk. Then, one afternoon about a week before her final death, James and I had overheard her talking to Nicole, Jessica, Felicity and Natalie about another such quirk which I couldn't remember anymore. She had known far more than any of the others, and that may have been because she had found those particular documents. I didn't suggest it, though, because the girls had never known we had been eavesdropping that day.

Eventually, the search of the first disc ended with nothing at all.

"Switch them over," said Lucien, "but I agree with Tommy; there's a lot of interesting reading there for another day."

Natalie ejected the first disc, slipped it back into its cover and inserted the second disc into the drive. Once it was closed and we had given it enough time to start spinning, another list of files and folders appeared on the screen. The two files we were looking for appeared on the screen almost immediately; Ancient Prophecies was fairly close to the top, one of the first files in fact under the directories; and Innate Magic was towards the bottom of the screen.

"Check the innate one first," I told Natalie.

"You know that still mightn't be it," Peter said as Natalie moved the arrow down to the file in question and double-clicked it.

"Can't hurt to check, right?"

The document loaded, providing us with an extensive contents page. Visual defects were covered, as were many other things, many of which had little asterisks next to them; I wondered what the meaning of those was, but there was no note. Sorcerous Seers were there, as were people who could see ghosts (the name given to such people was 'imprinterals')' and there it was, towards the bottom of the screen, the Enlightener. Natalie clicked a spot just below the text, then performed a search of the next occurrence of the word 'Enlightener', and the search took her straight to the heading of the section. Unfortunately, it was very brief, but what we needed to know was there. Like we had two nights earlier, we all silently read the words on the screen.

A person possessed of the Enlightener is gifted with knowledge from an external source. The knowledge may pertain to events in the past or future, or else is intended to aid the enlightened in a present event. The knowledge is usually presented to the enlightened in the form of prophetic dreams, although there have been claims of it also presenting itself in wakeful moments if the brain has been affected by alcohol. Enlightening dreams are often recurring and supposedly become clearer with each occurrence. The Enlightener will continue to provide the required knowledge until the enlightened understands its significance, or the knowledge itself is rendered irrelevant by recent events.

For a person to be gifted with the Enlightener, he or she must also be an imprinteral. It is believed, although no source has ever been able to confirm, that the Enlightener itself may be rooted in the same magic that enables some people to return to life in the form of ghosts. The two abilities go hand-in-hand, but being an imprinteral is not enough. The person in question must also be of a certain mind-type. The Enlightener only hands itself to a man or woman if that man or woman is capable of taking its messages and using them to his or her advantage. As with many innate magical abilities, the decision of who qualifies and who doesn't is made well outside the bounds of human perception.

That was all there was. I finished reading the words, feeling a small piece of understanding clunk into place in my mind. Yes, I supposed I did qualify for the Enlightener under those rules; I could see ghosts, and the first time I could remember seeing the Enlightener, I'd understood its meaning very quickly. As for where the knowledge came from, the external source that provided me with these weird dreams, I thought I knew the answer to that. The document didn't spell it out, perhaps because there was no one alive who knew the answer, but it would have read very differently if Rafael Smiley had written it. It also would have been different if it had been Lisa's words because more than the fourth dimension, my mind kept turning back to that cave she had written about. There was no way to know for sure, but I suspected that cave to be the external source I kept connecting with. If that were the case, I dearly hoped it kept its distance.

"You okay with that, John?" Peter asked.

"Reckon so," I said, deciding not to mention my cave theory. "The most important thing out of all of that is that I'm supposed to be able to work it all out when it happens; at least, either that or it won't matter anymore. The only challenge for me will be getting used to it so that I recognise when it's happening and not just a normal dream."

"You can tell the difference?" Marc prompted.

"Not for sure, but it's happened a few times lately that I've suspected. The other night when I found out why Hammerson couldn't kill me—that was definitely the Enlightener. There have been a couple of other ones as well; they both ended with me trying to scratch my elbow, only to find that I was missing my arm."

"Maybe that's you taking a walk in my shoes," said Natalie, flexing the arm which, not so long ago, Hammerson had blasted right off her shoulder, "although I don't remember itching; it was too quick for that."

I shrugged. "Hopefully it doesn't mean I'm going the same way. Maybe it's a little more subtle than that—hopefully."

A brief silence followed before James cleared his throat. "So, should we move onto the prophecy?"

My heart skipped a beat at his words, but I nodded bravely. "Go on."

Natalie closed that document and opened the Ancient Prophecies file. It loaded quickly, leaving us to stare at the first prophecy, which was something about a tall man walking down a long flight of stairs.

"So what exactly are we looking for here?" Tommy asked.

"A prophecy about the most powerful Sorcerer ever," I said, trying to think back to exactly what Moran and Cornish had said that fateful day. "The whole point is that I don't know the exact wording, that's why I need to see it."

"Search for the word 'powerful'," Lucien suggested. "If that doesn't work, maybe try the word 'defeat', and if that fails, maybe we'll just have to read them until we find a likely prophecy."

"What if we can't find it?" Marc asked. "What if it's not even in this file?"

"Unfortunately, that may be possible," said Lucien. "Lisa said she got these prophecies because they might be a useful reference point in her assignment, but she never said if she copied all the prophecies she found. We don't even know if they were all there that day. I tend to think that it probably is in there, though. From what I understand, Arnold Hammerson is a big believer in Sien and Leoard's prophecies; that's why he was so quick to jump into action in response to this one. It seems to me that if Hammerson knew it so well, it must have been as freely available as the one about the Seventh Sorcerer."

While he had been speaking, Natalie had been searching. The first occurrence of the word 'powerful' was in a prophecy referring to the great, sightless stone (that would have been the invisible Sien-Leoard Crystal, of course) but the second occurrence was something different. I knew almost immediately that it was the right one; the giveaway was the word 'tyrant' on the last line.

"Let's read this one," I said in a voice that seemed to have lost all its strength.

> *To defy this man is to kiss Lady Luck,*
> *but to defeat him requires these actions*
> *three: to remove his cloak, to still his*
> *heart, to chase him from the soul on*
> *which he feeds.*
>
> *The master of death is the master of*
> *life, to that this man is eternally bound,*
> *but only one can initiate the three*
> *momentous steps, for the tyrant to fall*
> *irrevocably to the ground.*

Chapter 17: Gotcha

As predicted, once I'd read the prophecy, I wanted some time alone to mull it over. My initial reaction was that it mightn't be so bad: It said 'initiate', not kill; that could possibly mean that I wouldn't necessarily have to be the one to do the deed if I triggered a sequence of events that would lead to Hammerson's death. Whether or not it was Hammerson to whom the prophecy referred seemed a moot question to me: Who else could it possibly refer to? It was the 'three steps' part that troubled me most though—what on earth could that mean?

When I told the others that we could discuss the matter that evening when we met up as usual, they seemed to understand where I was coming from. I was sure they would have plenty of their own theories about its meaning but I still believed that in the end, it was my opinion that mattered most. Natalie withdrew the disc, shut down the computer, and said she would give it back to Jason. The rest of us decided to split up and do our own thing for the rest of the afternoon. There was still time before dinner, so I thought I might catch up on a bit of sleep.

This plan changed when we left Amelia's room and got a feel for what was happening in the rest of the base. When we emerged from the room, there was a shout from either end of the corridor, making us all jump. I looked both ways and observed Felicity hurrying toward us from the lounge room end, and Darcy coming at us from the dining room end. Their expressions weren't so much panicked, but there was a definite feel of urgency in the air.

"There you are," Felicity said, stopping just short of the startled group. "We've been waiting—nobody knew where you were."

Even as she spoke, more people began pouring into the corridor, alerted by the shout that our location had been discovered.

"What's going on?" Marc asked, looking around at everyone.

"Liam was looking for you guys a little earlier," Darcy told us, and my heart leapt. "He told us all to tell you to go to the control room as soon as possible."

"Did he say what for?" Amelia asked.

"No, only that it was really important you go right away."

I looked around at the others, particularly Marc, Natalie and Peter. It appeared that the time had come. Woe is me; my sleep would have to wait a little longer.

"Let's roll," said Marc determinedly.

We all took off out the door and across the courtyard, all eight of us. Amelia, James, Tommy and Lucien may not be quite up with the Stella hunt but they seemed to understand that the moment had come. When we got to the control room, we found Liam in the seat in front of the controls, lazing back in the chair and watching the display screen monitoring Stella's progress. He looked around at us when we entered, and the relief in his face was unmistakable.

"Thank God," he said, getting out of the seat and indicating the display screen. "She's out of the truck, like you wanted. I was worried she might go somewhere else but she seems to be taking cover for the time being."

"Taking cover?" Marc repeated, approaching the screen and looking at it. "This just shows her sitting in bushes and eating an apple. I think she's made herself invisible too."

"Is that what that was?" said Liam. "I was wondering why she looked like a ghost."

"Where is she?" Natalie asked. "What town?"

Liam shrugged. "I dunno. I only watched her get out of the truck; she actually cut a small hole in the back doors with a bludginator, but she seemed to know when it had stopped because she didn't get hurt. Then she just took off up the street and into this park. Dunno what town it is—don't suppose it matters."

"No, it doesn't," said Marc, looking around at the rest of us. "If she's been stuck in that truck all day and last night, she must be hungry, and probably tired too. This is our best chance to grab her, and if she's invisible, even better—no one will see it happen."

"So what's the plan?" Peter asked.

Marc considered the problem for a few moments before speaking. "I suppose the best thing to do is just go out there and grab her. She's armed for sure, but if I knock her out before she has a chance to do anything, there won't be a problem. She won't see or hear me—"

"Not necessarily true, Marc," said James soberly. "If she's that thickly in bushes, she may not hear you, but if she hears the bushes moving—"

Marc swore. "Damn, you're right. Okay, in that case, it won't be possible to get to her without moving a few bushes. Maybe you two should come out with me, so that if she does jump to attention before we can deal with her, we can minimise any damage."

"Is that all we've got?" said Amelia nervously.

"I'm only guessing here, but I think it's quite likely that Stella's only weapons would be of the magical variety," said Lucien. "Perhaps if you set up a shield around the three of us that only repels magic, and won't have any physical effect on the things around you, you can get close to her without her being able to hurt you."

"That's a good idea," said Marc, nodding and taking hold of the Hero Crystal. There were a few moments of nothing before the magic seemed to be performed. It wasn't the kind that pushed the three of them together, but when the two girls began feeling the air around them, it indicated that they felt something. Marc nodded again, satisfied.

"Okay," he said, pressing the button on the control panel to open the door—not the one that opened onto the paddock in which the base was still located, but the other one, which opened onto wherever the tracer was located. Looking through the open door, it was impossible to see Stella at all. This was because she was invisible, of course, but it made it impossible to know how much distance stood between her and the door.

"How's this for a change of plan?" said Tommy suddenly, pointing at the display screen. "Why not just knock her out now—don't even step out until she's unconscious. You'll see if it works on the screen."

Everyone looked quickly at Marc, who shrugged. "Can't hurt to try."

He gripped the crystal and stared, not at the screen, but at the open door, perhaps thinking that it would direct his magic a little better. When nothing happened for several seconds, he switched to the screen. Almost immediately, Stella simply collapsed into the grass where she had been sitting, her half-eaten apple rolling away from an outstretched hand.

We all stared in wonder at the screen for several seconds before Peter spoke. "Poor Stella. After all her care and precautions, she goes down in one hit."

"Can't blame her," said Lucien fairly. "What we did was pretty much a king-hit; just lucky for her it's for a good reason, and it won't hurt her."

"So what now?" Natalie asked.

"Send Fewul out there first," Marc said, indicating the Beast of Magic, who had followed us down from the building —followed Marc, I should say. "He can undo her enchantments, put her under ours, and make sure she's not carrying any computer viruses or tracing things the Hammerhearts can use against us."

"Do you really think she would be?" Liam asked. "I mean, wouldn't the Hammerhearts have caught her by now if they could trace her?"

"You'd think so, but we can't take the chance," said Marc. "So Fewul, do all of what I just said, then bring her in here."

"Yes, Master," Fewul said in the voice of the identical twins, though with much less inflection.

The Beast walked past us and through the door into the bushes where Stella lay motionless. A moment later, he appeared on the display screen, and yet another moment later, he was right beside Stella, casting spells around her. As we watched, she became perfectly visible again (not transparent, as she appeared on the display screen); the same thing happened to the bag beside her. Around twenty seconds of nothing followed this, as Fewul continued to perform spells, the results of which weren't visible, either on the screen or through the open door. Finally, he levitated her into the air, and with her floating limply along beside him, returned to the control room. The moment he and Stella were both through, Marc pressed the button to close the door.

"And that's that," grinned Tommy.

"Is she safe?" I asked, staring at Stella. It was the first time I'd been so close to her in a very long time—the first time I'd actually been able to look at her for a very long time. Not counting the incident when she had her face covered, this was the first time I'd been face to face with her since I had practically disowned her in her old bedroom in the Chopville Hammerheart base. It was a slightly surreal feeling, and a bit of an emotional one too. I'd missed her for so long, and now, finally, she was back with us again.

Marc looked enquiringly at Fewul, who nodded. "She is safe. She is under the umbrella of our invisible, soundproof and untraceable spells. The spells she was using to protect herself before have been neutralised, and she was not carrying any viruses."

"And she's unconscious," Marc added. "She won't come around for twenty-four hours, but I suppose we bring her around before then."

"Of course we do," said Peter, "and could you please put her on a stretcher or something? I hate watching her dangle like that."

Marc obliged, creating the stretcher from thin air and, taking control of Stella from Fewul, lowering her onto it. He then looked around at the rest of us. "What now?"

It was Amelia who spoke. "Let's take her up to one of our bedrooms and lay her down. She might be calmer if she wakes up on a bed. We'll need to feed her and give her a chance to shower as well, but that can come later."

"And we should take her weapons from her too," Lucien added as we began filing out of the control room. "I don't think she'll mind once she knows what's happening, and she won't get a chance to attack before she sees who we are."

"One thing first," said Marc, doubling back as James, who was last in line, shut the door behind him. Marc approached the closed door and used the Hero Crystal to perform some sort of spell on the doorhandle.

"What was that?" James asked.

"Just resetting the lock," he said. "We agreed in the beginning that only me and the Sorcerers could get in there, and only with our own magic. I had to change that so we could monitor the controls but now that we've got Stella, I can change it back."

After he'd put a sign on the door stating that screen-watching duties were cancelled, we trooped back up to the building where just about everyone was waiting for us in the corridor, anxious to know what was going on. They all came to attention when we entered through the door near the dining room, and started when they caught sight of Stella, whose stretcher was floating alongside Marc as he walked.

"Oh my God," said Jessica, her mouth slightly open as we passed.

"People, please," Lucien called over everyone's heads. Those nearest jumped back, slightly startled, but I knew that he was only raising his voice so that everyone, particularly those furthest, could hear him. "Yes, we have her, but we would appreciate it if you didn't all gawp at her. She's gonna have a hard enough time getting comfortable in this environment as it is. Just go about your business as usual, please."

They muttered, a little annoyed, but no one raised any objections. Natalie and Lucien's bedrooms were nearest, and after quick consideration, it was Natalie's room into which we took Stella. When we closed the door, only Marc, Lucien, Natalie, Amelia, Peter, James, Tommy and I kept Stella company—oh, and Fewul, of course. Marc levitated Stella off the stretcher and onto the bed. There, we all crowded around and looked down at her. She definitely needed a shower; she was dirty, and she smelled bad. It was clear that her clothes too hadn't been washed in a very long time. For all that, though, she looked good. However she had been living, she had done well to keep healthy; she had always been in good shape, but now she was fitter than she had been when I'd known her months earlier.

Amelia, who was closest to Stella's waistline, leaned over her and began feeling her waist to see what was hidden there. Rather than keeping her arms in her pockets, Stella had them attached to a belt around her waist. Amelia unbuckled it, slid it off and raised it for us to have a look. There were a lot of devices there, including some I recognised (agonator, bludginator, solid-outliner, stunner and invisibility toggle) along with several others that were completely unfamiliar. Lucien smiled at the sight of them.

"We should keep them safe," he said, taking the belt from Amelia and setting it down on Natalie's bedside table. "We'll need her to tell us what they do, but we should duplicate them as well. It's high time we armed our army."

"Agreed," said Amelia. "So, should we wake her up now?"

"Yes, but let's step back from the bed a bit," said Lucien, indicating the rest of us. "You stay close to her, Amelia. She could react any way to the rest of us, but if she sees you, she'll know she's safe."

"How am I any better than the rest of you?"

"You're a Woodward," said Lucien simply. "She knows that."

"Okay," Amelia sighed as the rest of us moved back a step. I hadn't initially understood Lucien's thinking until then, but now I knew that it was so that we would look less threatening to Stella, lying there on the bed.

Nothing happened for a few seconds as Amelia prepared herself, during which the rest of us watched Stella, glancing sideways at each other a few times. When she did raise her hand and Stella quickly came to life, she did so in a way that surprised everyone. I'd expected her to be defensive but I hadn't expected such a stark contrast to the way Amelia had come around on my bed the night before. It was as though she had known that, at some point, she might suddenly vanish from wherever she had been before and wake up in a totally unfamiliar place. She had probably been expecting it ever since 3K17 had tracked her down, and knowing that she could do nothing to prevent it if it happened, she could at least be ready to fight.

It took her only a second to be on her knees, having already discovered that she had been disarmed. She probably would have taken a swing at Amelia had Amelia not used her magic to push her gently but firmly back down on the bed. Stella struggled for a few moments but Amelia didn't let up.

"Stella, calm down, it's me," she said, trying to sound harmless but unable to prevent some of her alarm coming through.

Stella stared at Amelia for several seconds, still struggling, before seeming to recognise her. Her eyes widened in surprise and what I thought was probably hope.

"Amelia?" she said disbelievingly.

"Yeah," Amelia said shortly. She looked for a moment like she was going to say more, but instead lapsed into silence.

Stella was no longer struggling. She sat up again, and this time, Amelia allowed her to. Stella took her in for several more seconds before seeming to believe what she was seeing. She then turned her attention to the rest of us. Her eyes widened when she saw Lucien, and even more so when she saw me; her face lit up in that moment, and I pretended not to notice the undisguised happiness there. I'd forgotten, until then, just how bright her eyes were—they were dazzling. The moment broke when she noticed Fewul; not knowing it was the Beast of Magic, her mouth fell open in what was probably disbelieving horror.

"Where am I?" she finally asked. "What's going on? How did you find me?"

"Er," said Amelia, looking around at the rest of us, "a little help?"

"You're in our base," said Natalie, "not the Woodwards'."

"Oh," said Stella blankly, "'cause, I thought you guys were caught."

I exchanged confused looks with Peter and James, but Marc understood. "They got in, but we got out. We split from the parents 'cause they weren't letting us do anything—we probably would've come for you six weeks ago otherwise."

"What are you going to do with me?" she asked, and the moment the words left her mouth, I knew this was the test—it was as much a challenge as an enquiry.

"Put a roof over your head for a start," Tommy said lightly.

"We figure that as long as you're out there, the possibility exists that the Hammerhearts could catch you," said Lucien calmly. "If it's a choice between having you with us or having you with them, we would prefer the former. We know you don't want to be a party to your father's antics, and we also figure that you could be useful to our side—if you want to be, that is."

Stella levelled her gaze at Lucien and said coolly, "Is that what *you* want?"

Once again, I had no idea what she was getting at, but Lucien understood immediately. As usual, he maintained his calm demeanour as he replied. "It's what we all want, because we all want the same thing. My presence in this room with these people should be proof that I'm back on the right side."

"Oh right," Marc said quickly. "We've got devices that can undo influential charms, and we got Lucien with one."

"Seriously?" she said, her eyes widening. "I thought that was impossible. They're not supposed to leave any traces of their magic."

As Amelia started to explain how it worked, I relaxed inside. Stella still looked stunned, and more than a bit relieved, but she no longer looked sceptical. She kept looking around at us (particularly me) as though checking we would still be there, as though we might just disappear and she might wake up from some wonderful dream to find herself back in the truck.

"So what are we gonna do now?" Peter asked when Amelia had finished talking. When we all looked at him, he shrugged. "Well, do you wanna see the base we've made, Stella?"

"How big is it?" she asked warily.

"Pretty small, but there are about two dozen people out there who are working with us," said Natalie. "You know they'll be gawping at you at first."

"Like they did four months ago?" Stella said, shrugging. "If it's okay, I think I need to sleep before I do anything else—and wash up, I think. Where exactly are we?"

"Natalie's room," said Amelia, "but you'll be up on the top floor 'cause that's where the free rooms are. Right now, though, you guys can go take a hike; me and Natalie can sort Stella out."

We all looked quickly at Lucien, as though he were the only one with the authority to contradict Amelia. He didn't, though. "That's a good idea. If it's okay, Stella, I'll just take this belt of yours."

Stella nodded. "I'll be happy if I never see it again."

"Sadly, I don't think you can relax that much," he said, picking it up and opening the door for the rest of us to proceed him. Peter, James, Tommy and Marc did so, and I wasn't far behind them, stopping only to scoop up Jason's laptop computer on the way out.

Back in the corridor, we were once again greeted by just about everyone in the base. They'd all been hanging around waiting for news.

"Do I need to repeat my speech from earlier?" Lucien said loudly.

"How's she doing?" Jessica asked. "Is she okay?"

"When are we gonna be able to see her?" asked Felicity.

"After she's had a shower and a long sleep," he said, "and possibly a good meal. We'll have a private meeting with her first, to determine her state of mind, and after that, we'll show her around and you can all talk to her. Remember, if she doesn't want to answer your questions, don't push it."

"Speaking of private meetings," said James, "I think maybe we should have a quick one now."

"But Natalie and Amelia——"

"We'll catch them up later. We need to discuss our next course of action. The sooner, the better."

"Shouldn't we learn as much as we can from Stella first?"

"I'm not so sure anything Stella can tell us will influence our next move."

"What does that mean?"

"It means we should step into one of our rooms and sit down."

"I think it's my turn," said Lucien, smiling slightly as he led the way. "Come on, James, but we're not making any decisions until at least tonight. The girls should be able to have their say too."

We followed Lucien into his room, me reluctantly bringing up the rear and not at all enthusiastic about this turn of events. I hadn't forgotten that I had sleep to catch up on, and I certainly hadn't forgotten the private contemplation I needed to have. Unfortunately, it looked as though James hadn't forgotten it either. I waited until the door was shut before rounding on him.

"We are not talking about that prophecy now. I told you, I wanted time to think about it, and so far I've had none."

"If you say so," he said calmly. "I actually wanted to talk about the Honnie solution, because I still feel that that is what we need to focus on now."

"Oh James," Peter moaned, slapping a hand to his forehead.

"Let's all sit down," Lucien said, indicating the couches. "I've been thinking about that too, and I think the time has come to discuss it in more detail. I've spent some time thinking about ways we can make sure we'll be able to get in and out of their world with as little risk as possible; I honestly believe it can be done."

"This is coming from a bloke who never saw a Honnie in action," Marc muttered.

"I saw just as much as the rest of you," James pointed out. "What ideas have you had, Lucien?"

"Well Marc, you and Natalie will be able to perform spells specifically designed to work against Honnies," Lucien told him, "because you two have seen them and are aware of their substance. Is this not true?"

"Maybe, but we won't know if they work until we get over there," Marc said, "and if we stuff up, we'll be cooked."

Lucien shook his head. "It was Tankom's misdirected magic that opened the door for Smiley to access their world, which means that their existence does not sit outside the scope of our magic. By 'our', I mean the magic that we possess as a group. I think that Fewul would be able to let us know if our protection would work in their world."

"What spells have you got in mind?" Tommy asked doubtfully.

"Well, the most important things are to protect our minds and bodies," said Lucien. "Defence will be so much more important than weapons, since we won't want to look like we're threatening them. I was thinking that we could attach helmets to our heads, which would put up a shield around our minds that the Honnies won't be able to break through. If they attempt to take possession of our minds, they won't be able to access or manipulate our thoughts. As for our bodies, we need some sort of spell that wouldn't necessarily make us stronger, because that would make the Honnies more suspicious if they tried to test us. We need something that could prevent our bodies from being hurt, without actually making them stronger."

Marc stared at him, his mouth slightly open in confusion. James seemed to understand where he was coming from, but he looked dubious. "That sounds awfully complicated, but I suppose it can be illustrated easily enough. If a brick wall were to collapse on top of us, we wouldn't be hurt at all, but we wouldn't be able to lift the rubble off ourselves. Is that what you're thinking?"

Lucien nodded. "I think any more would look too dodgy, and any less would be too dangerous."

"The Honnies may still take that to mean we're dangerous," said James. "The other problem is the helmet thing. If we don't let them access our minds at all, we'll be cutting off our only means of communicating with them. They have their own language, but mind-to-mind is the only thing that would work between them and us."

Lucien frowned. "Way to burst the bubble, James. You're right, unfortunately. Is there any way we can provide just enough protection for them to make suggestions to our minds, but not enough to actually influence our thoughts?"

"Is there a difference?" asked Tommy.

Marc considered the question carefully. "The line between them is very fine. It would have to be designed specifically so that they can only plant questions in our minds, but not ideas. It would need to present our minds to them like an index, where they can control our thoughts just enough to look things up, make enquiries, but not enough to give us ideas, to influence our way of thinking."

"And especially not enough to take possession of us or dissolve our minds," Peter added.

"Does that sound possible?" Lucien asked Marc.

"I can try," he said, "but you're right—I would need to ask Fewul if it works. If he tells me that he doesn't know if it will work or not, the plan is off. Agreed?"

"Yes, agreed," said Lucien, and sighed. "I hope it doesn't come to that, because what James said the other night is far too true. We would have a lot of trouble controlling such a large situation, even if Hammerson is out of the way."

"So what's the plan for the time being?" Peter asked.

"Well, let's do an informal vote," said Lucien. "All those in favour of what we've discussed so far?"

He and James put their hands up immediately, and Marc wasn't too far behind them. Peter, Tommy and I swapped nervous looks before hesitantly raising our hands as well. It sounded very risky indeed, but it also sounded barely possible. What was more, no matter what plan we went with from here, there would be a lot of risk involved. The alternative would be to start spying on Hammerson and the protection around him, something we would have to do eventually regardless, and we would be kidding ourselves to think there wouldn't be much risk there.

"Okay, good," Lucien said approvingly. "We won't actually put anything into practice until tomorrow, and that's only after bringing the girls up to speed. If I remember correctly, they were both in favour of the Honnie plan on Wednesday, so they shouldn't provide any resistance. Now, the other thing we need to discuss at some point is who should go on this dangerous mission. It would be extremely foolish to send the whole group, or even half the group. I'm thinking a small brigade should be responsible for that while the majority of our little army remain here, sussing out the Hammerhearts' structure."

"I think we should take a vote on who should go," James suggested. "I think perhaps five or six would be enough, and they should be anyone who is willing to put themselves in that situation. I also think they should be pure in the mind, because it's their thoughts that will need to be convincing. They'll need to be good at communicating our dire situation to the Honnies, and they'll need to be completely understanding of the way Honnies work."

"That's a lot to remember," said Tommy. "Should someone write it down?"

"We can describe the plan to everyone when we've worked it out in its entirety," said Lucien. "However, I don't think we can send just anyone to do this. Marc, you'll need to stay behind so that we have Fewul available. I should probably stay behind so that I can coordinate our movements here, and I suppose John should stay behind too."

"I wasn't interested in going anyway," I pointed out, "but why do you say that?"

"Because of the prophecy," said Lucien, and I glared at him.

"I thought we agreed not to discuss that."

"Sorry, but you asked the question," he said, shrugging.

"I disagree," said James nervously, glancing sideways at me. "I know you don't wanna discuss it now, John, but it does play a part in deciding what your course will be."

"I know that, that's why I want time to think about it."

James shrugged and looked back at Lucien. "I don't think it means John can't go, because the prophecy didn't actually say he had to be the one to kill Hammerson. It said he was the only one who could initiate a sequence of events that would lead to Hammerson's downfall; that could mean he is the one who can bring a Honnie through to help us."

"Aw geez," I moaned, horrified at this turn of the discussion. "Whether or not I go will be entirely my decision, and it won't be based solely on the prophecy."

"That's reasonable," said Lucien fairly, "but as it is, I do agree with James, John. I think you should bear it in mind, but nobody will make you go if you honestly make something different of the prophecy. Back to what I was saying before, I think that one of you two should probably go"—he looked to Peter and Tommy—"or one of the others who met Smiley. I just think that kind of firsthand knowledge could be invaluable in the heat of the moment. And, of course, either Natalie or Amelia will need to be there, to perform the magic to let you return here, and for a bit of extra security should the worst happen. I guess we clear that with them later."

"One of us two," said Peter incredulously. "Well, I'm not keen on it, but I guess I'll decide when we know how the protection will be."

"Ditto," Tommy nodded.

"Nobody will be going if the protection isn't as foolproof as we can possibly make it," Marc said firmly. "I don't care how difficult it may be later: Taking risks is one thing; casting six people out to what will be almost certain death is quite another."

* * *

Following the meeting, I went straight to my room and got into bed, as I'd been planning to do for a couple of hours now.

My intention had been to contemplate the prophecy, something that had to be done before the meeting that night, but before I could even get started on it, I slipped into a light sleep. I dreamt, and it may or may not have been the Enlightener, but whatever I dreamt of, I had no memory of when I awoke. Far from feeling rested, I now felt even more weary than I had prior to going to sleep, just as I had two nights earlier.

When I checked the time, I found that I'd missed the commencement of dinner by fifteen minutes. I got a move on then, even though I hardly had an appetite and had no intention of eating much. Of course, dinner was well underway when I entered the dining room. I looked around, scanning the room for a good place to sit. I'd hoped for but not really expected to see Stella here—we were well overdue for a reunion—but I was unsurprised to find her absent, probably sleeping. Peter, James, Siobhan and Erica were once again sharing a table, as were the twins and their girlfriends. Marc and Lena were sharing their table with Tommy and Jessica, while Natalie and Amelia (who I was pleased to note were sharing a table) were sitting with Felicity. I could have gone there, and was even tempted to, but something about being with both of them at the same time made me a little nervous. Instead, once I had decided what to eat and collected a very small amount from the conveyer belt, I sat with Lucien, Liam and Darcy.

"Had a good sleep, John?" Liam asked, winking.

"How'd you know I was sleeping?"

"You've got sleepy eyes," he said, "and you're hair's all over the place."

I shrugged and began to eat.

"You gonna tell us what's up from here now that both groups are done?" Darcy asked. "We've been hounding this bloke but he won't let nothing slip."

"Doesn't that mean he is letting stuff slip?" I grinned. "Double negative."

"I can't tell you the plan from here because we haven't worked out exactly what it is," Lucien said firmly, sounding like he'd said this a dozen times already. "Yeah, we've got ideas, but I'm not about to spark any rumours until we're ready to call a mass meeting like we had on Wednesday."

"How's Stella?" I asked Lucien. "Have you heard what's going on with her?"

"I asked," he said. "The girls created new clothes for her, let her shower and organised a room on the top floor for her. She's probably gonna get lonely up there, so I wouldn't be surprised if a few people move up there to keep her company, but in the meantime, she doesn't really care. I get the impression she's really nervous about facing the public, but she's extremely relieved to be back with us and relatively safe."

"Is she sleeping now?"

"Yeah, or perhaps lying awake. Either way, I'm sure she doesn't wanna be down here in plain view—not yet anyway."

"Well, the longer she puts it off, the harder it'll be when she gets around to it," I said, remembering how I'd said the same thing about Jessica just four days ago—really, only four days?

Liam and Darcy continued to probe Lucien and me about what the immediate future held for our little army, but neither of us were about to tell them about the Honnies. Eventually they subsided and began talking of more trivial things, such as what they would spend the evening doing. The meeting was scheduled for half past ten this evening, and for the first time, we would be heading to the third floor for it—it was Tommy's turn to host. Of course, we could have gone back to Marc's room again, but nobody had to point out that mightn't be such a wise move so soon after the mishap of the night before. With that in mind, I decided that I would take a short amount of time to myself, during which I would contemplate the prophecy, but if I ran out of things to think about, I would join the three boys who currently shared my table; they were once again planning on playing cards, listening to music, eating chips and drinking Coke. As I could have (perhaps should have) joined them two nights earlier, I was already looking forward to it.

At the conclusion of dinner, which came rather quickly given that I'd arrived so late, I put my surprisingly empty plate back on the conveyer belt and was on the point of leaving the room when Darcy waylaid me.

"Hey man, need to talk to you about something," he said, and I recalled our impromptu meeting just outside this very room the night before. "You got a moment?"

"Sure," I said, a little apprehensively, but unable to think why. I couldn't think of anything Darcy could have to say to me that would cause me angst.

We left the dining room together in the midst of a crowd of people heading either for their bedrooms, the lounge room, or in the case of a few, out into the yard for an evening stroll. Darcy and I followed these few through the nearby door into the relative darkness and chill of the courtyard, but rather than heading down the length of the building as they did, we went across the yard so that by the time we reached the lounge room window, there was no one else within earshot.

"So what's up?" I finally asked. All the time we'd been walking, Darcy had been mulling over something, probably working out what he was going to say, and anything that required that much thought was worth being curious about.

"Well," he took a deep breath, "something's up with you guys, isn't it?"

"Sure," I said a little sarcastically, because even he had to know I wouldn't know what the hell he was talking about.

He shrugged, seeming to know what I had just implied. "Lucien won't say, but people are talking. Seems to a few that there's a bit of dissension in the top ranks around here."

"Er—what makes you think that?" I said, understanding why this was such a touchy issue now. How much did he know?

He stopped walking and leaned back against the wall behind him. Where we were, it was quiet, dark and very cold.

"Well, mainly the Sorcerers," he said fairly, "all three of them. We don't see them together very often, and when they are, it looks pretty tense. Marc looks more and more frustrated every time I see him, Amelia looks miserable and Natalie doesn't have any confidence in her magic, judging by the chair thing yesterday. You can't tell me there isn't something going on there, but like I said, Lucien won't talk about it."

"I don't know what I can tell you either," I said, wanting to be truthful but unable to think how best to proceed. "You're right about Natalie, but it's complicated why she's feeling like that. She and Amelia are both holding a lot back, 'cause you've gotta remember what they were going through before all this happened; they were out in the thick of the war every day and they saw a lot of crap. Amelia saw some horrible stuff that she tried to tell me about earlier in the week and—well, I guess it's catching up with her. As for Marc, I…"

I broke off then because, unless there was something I didn't know about, there was only one reason why Marc could possibly be frustrated, and it had nothing to do with his magic. It seemed that Darcy didn't care so much about the answer, though, because he chose to focus on what I'd just said instead.

"How come no one's trying to help those two more? If what you're saying is right, they need all the help they can get, and we need them to be at their best."

"Again, I don't know what to tell you," I said to him, wondering why he cared so much. "From what I can tell, Natalie's coping fairly well with it all, and the more we get her to do, the better she's feeling about herself. As for Amelia, we're all prepared to help her, but that's only if she's up for it."

"She's not?" he asked, raising his eyebrows almost imperceptibly in the darkness. "You're not telling me she's one of those depressive, wallowing, self-pitying types, are you?"

"Well it sounds a lot worse when you say it like that," I said, unable to stop a small smile. "No, I don't think she's that bad, but she's been through a lot that anyone would struggle with. The fact that she's still with us and still helping us as much as she can says a lot about her strength of character, even if she is flagging."

"Is there anything the rest of us can do to help her?" he asked, and I felt myself relax a touch. As he had back in the lounge room earlier in the week, Darcy was demonstrating his willingness to help us. Unfortunately, I couldn't think of much he could do to help Amelia…or could I? A curious idea came to mind then, and I examined his expression more closely. It was very guarded, but very interested too. Still, he couldn't do anything unless Amelia were willing to be helped by someone like Darcy, but maybe, just maybe, I could find a way to set this up the right way.

"You probably couldn't do much for the Sorcerers," I said, choosing my words carefully. "We're managing that the best we can, but feelings run pretty high in a few areas. Amelia's only just found out about Marc being with Lena in the last few days; she's probably a little lonely, but not like she wants him back. If anything, she's looking for reasons to hate him, that's how we had that mishap last night."

"What mishap?"

"Er—doesn't matter, but it may have made things even worse for Amelia."

"You make it sound like all she needs is for someone to give her a good root," he said, and a few seconds of silence followed this before we both burst out laughing.

"She needs more than that," I said, feeling as though I were slowly tearing something away from myself, "but that would probably make her forget about Marc, at least for a little while."

"You said she didn't want him back?"

"I'm fairly sure she doesn't. It was her decision to break up with him in the first place."

"You don't think she regrets it?"

"Possibly," I said fairly, "but only because maybe being single didn't quite work out the way she'd wanted it to."

"She thought she'd be free, instead she ended up being lonely?"

"Something like that."

I wasn't about to tell him that while I'd been with Serena and he'd been with Jane (prior to the night they were both taken from us), Amelia and I had been very close—too close. I could still feel part of myself being torn away, and like the gap in your mouth left by the removal of a tooth, it was leaving a hole behind where it had been. It was painful, but I knew it had to be done. It was best for my hopes with Natalie, and if it worked out the way I hoped it would, it would be best for Amelia too.

Chapter 18: Responsibility

After having spent several minutes out in the cold, I was more than relieved to get back in the warmth of the base. While Darcy went to find Liam and Lucien, who turned out to be in Liam's room this time, I went back to my own room and, for the second time that day, decided to take a refreshing shower. This two-showers-in-one-day thing was turning to a habit, but in a place that had an endless supply of water, I didn't see anything wrong with it. It was for the sake of freshness after all; it had nothing to do with vanity.

While I stood in there, enjoying the warmth of the water on my body, I turned my mind back to the conversation I'd had with Darcy. It may come to nothing—either he or Amelia may not take the bait—but I had to think I'd done the right thing for once. What I felt now was the same as how I felt about Lena, only this was stronger. In that case, while I'd never seriously wanted to be with Lena beyond a few dirty fantasies, it nevertheless cost a pang to know that someone who had wanted me had now moved on. This time, it was someone I still wanted, in a way, but knew I could never have.

No, that wasn't quite true. I could have had Amelia by now if I'd really put my back into it. In fact, the more I thought about it, the more I believed that Amelia still wanted me too. I had no proof of this, of course—I hadn't once caught her watching me discreetly since leaving the Woodwards'—but what I did have was the fact that her discord with Natalie came about at the exact same time as her discord with Marc. If that was related to him and Lena, how could I know the former wasn't related to me and Natalie? Of course, Amelia would have known about Natalie's feelings for me, and it stood to reason that she knew how I felt as well. I wasn't so egotistical that I could convince myself that all this was centred around me, but it stood to reason, and if it were true, it also stood to reason that I could cheer Amelia up considerably by hooking up with her.

That would only be a quick fix, though, and it wouldn't fix all the problems. Additionally, it would leave me with a whole bunch of other problems, including the one I'd struggled with when I'd been dating Serena: I still wanted Natalie, and however I felt about Amelia, Natalie would always be number one. Part of me would always have a spot for Amelia, because it was impossible to pretend these feelings had never existed. Considering all we'd been through, how much we had shared and how comfortable we were with each other, Amelia would be an ideal partner if Natalie weren't in the picture.

There was only one thing for it, and I knew this would be a big test of my maturity. Maybe someday I would get a chance to be with Amelia, but for the time being, I had to let her go. I could still feel that tearing sensation, but I knew that this self-inflicted pain was the sort that would make me stronger once I came through it. I could never redeem myself for my bad behaviour while I'd been with Serena, but perhaps I could atone for it now. I could make myself a better person by making the right choice now. I wanted Natalie, and she seemed to want me too. It was like Graham, the old man from the Woodward base with the alcohol issues once said: They would move on, find other people and be happy. I couldn't be responsible for Amelia's well-being forever: She had to take control of her life, and with a bit of luck, she and Darcy could fill the voids in each other's lives.

That was all well and good, and I felt happy with myself for finally coming to the decision to let that one go and hope, but in the meantime, I indulged myself somewhat. Amelia was perhaps not as beautiful as Natalie in the way only I seemed to notice, but she was still very pretty—still very attractive. She was also a very nice, fairly quiet and extremely trustworthy person. I also happened to know, through an experience I didn't dare tell anyone about, that she was an awesome kisser. Through another experience that not even Amelia knew of, for she hadn't seen me that night, I'd also seen her completely naked—not a moment I would forget anytime soon.

Afterwards, as I was getting dressed again, I was now ready to turn my attention, at last, to that dreaded prophecy. Although James and Lucien had forced me to think about it earlier, now was the time to consider it more thoroughly, without any outside pressure.

The first few lines of the prophecy made it fairly clear that it was referring to Arnold Hammerson. It said 'he' a number of times, which probably meant it was Hammerson and not Tankom (although given how long ago it had probably been written, the masculine pronoun may not have meant very much, but I decided not to give that too much thought). Great influence? Immense power? That was certainly Hammerson; he had always been the most powerful Sorcerer, and now he had more magic than anyone in the world (apart from Fewul) and of course, he had changed the entire global landscape. 'He is the greatest, the mightiest, the most powerful of all, with wingspan wider than the world he will own.' The first part of that seemed to back up what I already knew, but what about the last bit? So far, the Hammerhearts only controlled four continents (including those which had been overthrown but not claimed as territories of Hammersonia, and the man in question clearly had an ego the size of the Pacific Ocean to come up with a name like that), and even in those continents, there was still plenty of resistance. The fourth line in the prophecy suggested that things were going to get a whole lot worse before they got better. If that were true, Hammerson hadn't yet reached the peak of his power, and he wouldn't be toppled until that time came.

Line five of the prophecy was fairly self-explanatory (I'd certainly gotten lucky on pretty much every occasion I'd faced Hammerson) but it implied that one would need a lot more than luck in order to defeat him. 'To remove his cloak, to still his heart, to chase him from the soul on which he feeds.' Those were the 'three steps' the prophecy said one would need to play out in order to defeat him, but what exactly did that mean? What was this so-called Cloak of Steel? Why was stilling his heart only the second step? On what soul would he feed after his death, and what did that even mean?

It was the second last line of the prophecy that was most important though, because that was the line that drew me into the fray. That was the line that, from the moment I'd gone to Rock Haulter for the first time as an infant, had altered my whole life. It said that only one could initiate the three momentous steps, and according to whatever test had been done by the Hammerhearts, I was that one. That didn't mean I had to be the one to carry out all three steps, but I had to do something that would set them in motion; I had to do something that no one else could, or would, do.

I had to believe it was true for the same reason that James believed it: Sien and Leoard had been right about Marc being the Seventh Sorcerer, and so had the Hammerhearts when they'd worked it out. On that basis, Sien, Leoard and Arnold Hammerson also had to be right about this. The trouble was, it didn't seem to mean anything, as far as I could tell. If I only knew what those three steps meant, I could perhaps do more to help the situation. As it was, all I could do was keep doing what I'd always been doing and hope that, when the time came, I would know what to do. Although I hadn't come up with any solutions here, I knew what my line would be for the time being: I would not take any stupid risks; I would not do anything that I wouldn't have done before hearing of the prophecy; I would, for now, pretend I'd never read it. The only exception to that would be to tell the others what I'd decided.

And what I'd decided right now was that I'd had enough contemplation for the time being. With around two hours still to spare before the meeting, I decided to have a look around the base to see what was what. I hadn't forgotten the boys, but I would only hang out with them if Peter, James, Marc, Tommy and the twins were all too busy with their girlfriends to think about poor old John—and if I didn't happen to find Amelia, Natalie or even Stella (I hadn't forgotten about her either).

When I left my room, I found that every door in the first floor corridor was shut. I could hear music coming from Liam's room, indicating the boys were still in there, but there didn't seem to be noise from any of the other rooms. I didn't dare go knocking on any doors, particularly those of Marc and Lena, so I instead went up to the upper levels. The silence on the third floor indicated that most of my friends probably were busy with their girlfriends (or somewhere else in the base), and the silence on the fourth floor indicated that Stella was probably still asleep—there wasn't even an indication of which room she was in.

Giving up, I went back downstairs to see who was in the lounge room. Sure enough, Harry, Simon, Katie, Sophie, James, Erica, Tommy, Jessica, Marc and Lena were all missing in action, but to my surprise, Peter wasn't. Even more pleasing, both Natalie and Amelia were also in the lounge room, though they weren't sitting together; Natalie appeared to be in quiet conversation with Felicity, while Amelia was talking to Misty and Michelle. She looked composed, but not altogether happy. Once noting that Siobhan wasn't present, and more than a little curious, I went to sit with my brother.

"Where have you been?" he asked me.

"My room," I said, "doing a bit of thinking. I didn't expect to see you out here. Don't you usually spend this time with Siobhan?"

"We usually do," he said, shrugging, "but we spent time this afternoon today. Nothing wrong with changing it up a bit, but we don't need to overdo it."

I nodded my understanding, thinking of Serena. There had been a few weeks during that relationship when it seemed that no amount of time I spent with her was enough for her, and although I still cared about her, she was becoming more frustrating than anything else. Did that make her clingy, I wondered? That wasn't something I'd seriously thought about, but I had to consider it now. What about Siobhan, then? Was she also clingy in that way? Had she hung around Peter so much that he now needed a bit of time away from her? If that were true, where was she now? Unsure what else to say, I decided to ask him.

"Her room, I think," he said, shrugging. "She hasn't really made friends with a lot of people around here. I wish she would; I can't be the only one she talks to."

"I thought she and Erica got on pretty well."

"I suppose so, but I think Erica's a little too busy for her."

"Are you two all right?" I asked him, watching him closely, and I knew I was onto something just by the way he started.

"I guess we're okay," he said, glancing around to make sure no one was listening—no one was.

"And that means what exactly?"

"Well we didn't fight or anything," he said, a little defensively, "but when I tried to explain it to her, what I just told you, she took it to mean that I'm already sick of her, no matter how many times I said I just wanted to prevent that from happening. That's the thing with girls: Their emotions have a way of overwhelming their logic."

"Don't let a girl hear you say that," I said, grinning slightly, but as my mind flicked back to Serena, I found it hard to disagree. "So what are you gonna do about it?"

"Not sure yet," he said morosely. "You got any tips?"

"Yeah, nip it in the bud."

"By which you mean?"

"Don't let the problem fester or you'll end up like me and Serena did."

"Damn," he muttered. "Well I don't want that, but I'm thinking that we don't have much of a future together anyway."

"What makes you say that?" I asked, surprised. "It's a hick-up, sure, but no reason to throw the towel in."

He sighed. "If that were all, I'd agree with you, but..."

He trailed off, and I remained silent, watching him and waiting to see if he would continue. Eventually, he did.

"Earlier today, we were talking about the future," he said quietly, glancing around again for eavesdroppers, "you know, how it might be when the war ended—all hypothetical stuff. It probably means nothing, 'cause the war may not end for years, so it was more of a fantasy thing, I guess."

"Okay," I said slowly, unsure where this was going.

"I said I would probably leave Chopville," he said, "assuming I'm old enough to get away from Mum and Dad by then. I don't think I could ever live in Chopville again after all this—it's sad to think it but it's also true."

"Hear, hear," I said, understanding completely.

"And she said she would like to go back to England and live there," he went on, and sighed. "I totally understand why she would; that's where she calls home, and she was ripped away from everything she knew and she's had little other than misery in Australia. Trouble is, I don't wanna live in England— I don't think I could live anywhere other than Australia, and nowhere bigger than somewhere like Wodonga."

"Okay," I said again, wondering if that was all he was worried about.

"So what's the point?" he concluded. "If we don't wanna live in the same place, how can we be together?"

"You said yourself—it's all hypothetical."

"It is now, but what about when the time comes?"

"Well if it comes anytime soon, I guess you deal with it then," I said. "The way technology is these days, I suppose you could keep seeing each other from opposite sides of the planet."

I didn't think that would work, though. Even if Peter and Siobhan were capable of maintaining that sort of relationship, what would be the point of it if they didn't eventually intend to be together permanently? If they didn't have to let go of each other, why on earth should they? Peter's snort of derision demonstrated his agreement with this philosophy.

"So what do you wanna do then?" I asked, a little nervously.

"I guess I will just let it go and see how it ends up," he said. "You're right about one thing: We've probably got plenty of time to think about it. Perhaps by then, things will have changed. In the meantime, I guess I just have to make her understand that we do need time apart sometimes so we don't get sick of each other. Any advice on how to do that?"

"Help her find something else to interest her," I suggested, "something she can occupy herself with while you're occupying yourself with other stuff. Other than that, I got nothing."

"It'd be great if she just came down here and talked to people," he said gloomily. "I know she's a social person—she's told me plenty of stories about her and her friends from England—but she doesn't seem to be trying too hard around here."

"I thought she did," I said, thinking of how she had been those first couple of weeks after she'd arrived at the Woodward base. "She was certainly more interested in fitting in than Underwood had been."

"She stopped trying when we started going out," he said. "At least, I think that's when it happened—it might have been a coincidence."

He didn't think it was, though, and neither did I. It sounded like from the time she had broken up with Underwood, however long it had taken her to switch her interest to Peter, she had only really been interested in getting him; she had never been seriously interested in much else. What did that say about Siobhan? The most important thing in her life was having a boyfriend? That could explain why she'd been attracted to Underwood, I supposed, although that was jumping to pretty drastic conclusions.

"Well, maybe she would try harder if you're not around," I suggested, getting up and indicating that he should do the same. "Come on, I've got an idea of something we can do."

It was only when I was turning to leave the room that I swept it with my gaze, having focussed on Peter the entire time I'd been sitting down. Nothing had really changed, but on the other side of the room, Natalie's eyes met mine; apparently she'd been watching Peter and me and on this occasion, she had no issue with being caught. She smiled glowingly at me before turning her attention back to Felicity, and it took some concentration not to skip right out of the lounge room.

"Wow, that's the biggest hint she's ever thrown you," Peter said as we headed down the corridor towards the bedrooms.

"Tell me about it," I said, stunned. "How long was she watching me?"

"Most of the time you were in there."

"How'd you know that? Why didn't you say anything?"

"Just wanted to see how long it would take you to notice," he said. "So what's going on with you two? Looks like it's a little more than nothing."

"Yeah, it's a little more than nothing, but a little less than something."

"Doesn't look like it needs to be less than something anymore," he said. "Got any ideas on how to take it to the next level?"

"I'm not even sure what the next level is," I admitted, "but I'm becoming fairly sure I can. When I asked her to stay back last night to sort Amelia out, she seemed pretty annoyed."

Peter whistled. "Looks like you're on the verge of achieving your hearts' desire. So, what are we doing out here anyway?"

I'd stopped a minute ago at the end of the first floor corridor to finish my conversation with Peter; now I resumed walking. "There are some guys we can hang out with while Siobhan fixes up her social life."

"That's great, except she doesn't know what we're doing."

"You can tell her the next time you see her."

Lucien, Liam and Darcy were more than happy for us to join them, but I was a little dismayed by Peter's reaction. He didn't say anything, but I got the impression that he considered hanging out with Liam and Darcy as what one did when one had been rejected and exhausted all other options—in other words, a last resort. By half past ten, however, he had come around to my way of thinking. We had far more fun with the boys than we would have had in the lounge room—or at least, we had more fun than we would have had if Natalie hadn't smiled at me on the way out.

That smile had been just as bright as the one she'd given me two nights earlier, and a lot more suggestive. I spent most of the time in Liam's room thinking about that smile, and thinking a lot about the girl who'd given it to me. I knew she wouldn't have followed me, regardless of where I had gone (Natalie didn't seem to be the chasing type), but what I didn't know was what reaction she'd hoped for. I couldn't believe she'd wanted me to come and sit with her and Felicity—there were far too many people around for me to pursue her in there, even if she did intend on telling Felicity all that transpired between us. The best I could do was that she'd hoped for exactly the reaction she'd got. Like the game Lena had played such a long time ago, her actions were now designed to make me think about her as much as possible (as if such a thing were necessary, given how I already felt about her). The difference here was that it would work for Natalie as it hadn't for Lena for that very same reason.

At half past ten, Lucien, Peter and I said goodnight to Liam and Darcy and headed up to the third floor to where tonight's meeting would be held. When we got there, we found the corridor full of people. Marc, Natalie, Amelia, James and Tommy were already present, as were Jessica, Erica, Harry, Simon, Katie and Sophie.

"Here they are," said Tommy, waving us over. "Thank God you guys are here; now we have an excuse to tell these two to go away."

"Hey, it's not our fault you're tramping around our territory, good sir," said Simon pompously.

"Come on," said Tommy gruffly, opening his bedroom door and standing back so that we could enter. "The sooner we get started, the less likely I'll be to punch those two."

"Why? What did they do?" Peter asked.

"Seems that our dark stranger here has a few security issues regarding his, shall we say, prodigious manhood," said Harry, and several people laughed.

"You just go," Jessica told him. "Leave me to deal with them."

Harry and Simon both whistled. "James, your sister is beginning to scare us," said Harry. "I think I may need you to come and protect us from her."

"I don't think I will," said James, grinning at Jessica.

"Or perhaps, old chap, he's concerned that Erica wouldn't let him get in the way of a feisty feline such as Jessica," Simon suggested.

"You take one, I'll take the other," Erica told Jessica.

"And the rest of us will leave you to it," said Marc. "Come on, we've got a lot to get through."

Peter and I followed him into Tommy's room, and Lucien, Natalie, Amelia and James were right behind us. Once the door was closed and we were all seated, Peter said to Tommy, "Were those two really giving you a hard time?"

Tommy shrugged. "They were just being their normal silly selves, but seriously, someday, someone's gonna knock their lights out if they don't work out how to gauge a situation."

"They're very public," said Amelia. "They don't seem to mind how much people know about what they get up to, and they're quite happy to air other people's dirty laundry too."

"Well, if it's all good for you, Tommy, I'd prefer we just as soon get started," said Lucien, and when Tommy shrugged again, he nodded, satisfied. "First things first. Amelia, have you contacted your father since this afternoon?"

"No, I haven't. Should I?"

"Up to you," he said. "He knows about the discs, but he doesn't know if we got what we wanted or not. He also doesn't know about us finding Stella. Do you think he should know about those things?"

"I don't see why not," she said, "about Stella anyway. I don't think he needs to know what we found this afternoon—I assumed we were going to keep that as quiet as possible."

"I'd prefer we do it that way," I said quietly.

"What about our next plans?" James asked. "Should he know about those?"

"*We* don't even know about them yet," Amelia retorted.

"I don't think he should," Marc said quickly, "because James, remember, Mr. Woodward doesn't know about Honnies. Telling him about that now would only confuse him. If he wants to know what we're doing, we'll have to feed him some line or other."

"Wait a minute," said Amelia sharply. "Are we actually doing that now? We're going to find a Honnie? For sure?"

"Well that depends," said Lucien. "Are you two in favour of trying? Bearing in mind that we have ideas about how we can enter their world with as little risk as possible?"

"Well sure, if you can be sure," said Amelia, and Natalie nodded in agreement.

"In that case, Amelia, my suggestion to you will be to hold off communication with your father until we know for sure what we're doing," Lucien said, "and then we can decide how much he ought to know. He should definitely know about Stella being with us now. I'm sure he'll tell you to keep a close eye on her, in case she can't be trusted, but I think we can all agree that even if Stella wanted to betray us, she wouldn't be capable of it while inside this base."

"Are you sure about that?" James said cautiously.

"Well, the worst she could try would be to listen in on this conversation," said Lucien, "and so what if she did? She can't very well pass information on to the Hammerhearts, not even through the Internet because of the security systems we've set up; and she couldn't get into the control room, even if she wanted to."

"She could try to steal my crystal," said Marc nervously.

"And if she did," said Lucien, smiling at him, "she would find that as long as you have Fewul, she will be unable to do anything with those crystals. No, I'm quite sure that Stella is completely harmless. The only suggestion I have is that she not be allowed in the control room unless she's accompanied by someone with magic. Other than that, there shouldn't be a problem. While we're on the subject of Stella, does anyone think we should invite her in for this meeting so we can probe her for information and get explanations of the weapons she had with her?"

"Only if she's awake," said Peter. "If she's not, let her sleep; we can probe her some other time."

"Agreed," said James. "We've got enough to discuss tonight as it is."

"Can one of you check if she's awake?" Lucien asked the Sorcerers.

"Isn't she untraceable?" said Natalie nervously.

Lucien shook his head. "Fewul removed the protective enchantments she'd had on herself—she's only protected by the same ones we are now. You'll be able to see her."

Amelia did the honours, but as it turned out, Stella was still fast asleep—had been for about five hours already, I thought, so she must have been very tired. She would probably wake up in the middle of the night and have nothing to do, but other than letting her walk around the rest of the base, there wasn't much we could do about that.

"In that case, let's move forward," said Lucien. "Yes, we were discussing some protective methods we could use for when we enter the Honnies' world this afternoon. We also talked about who would be best for the job; we came up with quite a list."

"One of you two," Peter told the girls. "Which of you is game?"

"What?" said Amelia, startled. "Why one of us?"

"Well, a bit of impromptu magic may be very useful over there," Lucien pointed out. "I would rather not send Marc because I want him and Fewul to remain here, but I think only one of you will be necessary. Let me give you a snapshot of what we worked out. A small party should go—maybe five or six. One of you two needs to be one of them, and me, Marc, John, James and Stella should all remain behind. At least one of the party, preferably more than one, should have seen Smiley's memories of the Honnie, because that kind of information could also be invaluable."

"I guess that means you," Amelia told Natalie.

"I guess it does," she said, more nervous than ever.

"I was thinking earlier too," Peter said suddenly. "If you can be sure the protection will be okay, I don't mind going."

"Does that mean I have my marbles back?" James asked him, grinning.

"I said only if the protection is good."

"If the protection will be fine, I don't mind going either," Tommy added.

"Nobody will be going if the protection is any less than fine," said Marc loudly.

"Okay," said Lucien, looking from Peter to Tommy and back. "If both of you are willing, that would be very good. What about you, Natalie?"

My heart stopped for what felt like a long time. Natalie, go into the Honnie world? That was not something I wanted to happen. She couldn't be killed there, of course, but other than that, they could ruin her completely; if they drained her mind, she would be just as gone as anyone else. If I let her go and I remained behind, I would have an unknown amount of time to wonder how she was going. It would be torture.

"I don't know," she said, twisting her hands together. "I'll wanna see how the protection goes before making any decisions."

"And what about you, Amelia?" Lucien asked, turning his attention to her. "You know that one of you will have to go; it'll be necessary just so that you can get back."

"True," she said slowly, "although I really don't know enough about this dimension thing to have a hope of opening a doorway from their world to this one."

"That may not be necessary," said James. "The Honnie that came here could go between the worlds on his own without any magic, so if we find one to help us, they can bring us back that way. Now, Lucien, I know you said before that John couldn't go, but I have a differing view on that."

"Yes, you told us that earlier," said Lucien thoughtfully. "What do you think, John?"

"Well, I thought about it," I said slowly, "and—well—I don't really wanna be the one to go, but what I decided is that because I don't understand the three steps thing the prophecy was talking about, I have to hope that I can start them without meaning to. In other words, I'm not going to pay any attention to the prophecy anymore; I'm just gonna keep doing what I have been. As far as going, I'm in the same position as Peter and Tommy: I'm not keen on it, like I said, but I'll decide after I've seen the protection."

"Don't think I'm trying to sell you into trouble here, John," said James, and his expression was sympathetic, "but I really think you do need to go. You mentioned the three steps a moment ago; I think I know what they are."

"You do?" I said, surprised. "I couldn't work any of it out. What's that thing about feeding on a soul?"

"That could be the Hammerhearts, because it was the last step," he said, shrugging. "Don't take any of this as fact because I'm only speculating here. It said the first step was to remove the Cloak of Steel; I think that is referring to the enchantment he put on himself that means we can only kill him with our bare hands, like you did to Tankom. We get under that, step one. We kill him, step two. We dismantle the army he left behind, the army that will try to continue his ideals, step three. John, if I'm right, you need to be the one who gets the ball rolling, and that may mean you're the only one who can convince a Honnie to help us."

"That makes it sound like killing him outright won't work," said Peter slowly. "We would actually have to remove that enchantment in order to do it. Hammerson designed that thing so that no magic, not even the Sien-Leoard Crystal, could do it."

"What are you talking about?" Amelia asked warily.

"Oh," said James, his face falling. "Did you not know about that, Amelia?"

"If you tell me, I will."

And so James told her and Lucien, who was also looking curious, about that final piece of magic Arnold Hammerson and Hank Cornish were protected by. Both of them were suitably horrified.

"In that case, a Honnie would be even more useful," said Lucien shakily. "He can make Hammerson come to him, and then snap his neck in a twist—nowhere near as bloody as the way Tankom went out."

"Look, you may be right, Pete," said James, "or you may not be—who can really say. These prophecies are fairly cryptic but I don't think we have to take them literally. That's why we need to be flexible about this, but there is one thing that we should take literally, and that's John's involvement. John, if there's any chance that you're the only one who could succeed in bringing a Honnie back, don't you think it's your responsibility to do so? For the greater good?"

"And what if I get killed over there?" I replied. "Remember, the prophecy also said that I *can*, not that I *will*."

"I guess that means it will be the number one job of either Natalie or Amelia to make sure that no Honnie can do a number on you while you're over there," said Peter, grinning at me. "Your safety will be the number one priority. You must feel proud."

"And your safety will be the bottom priority if you keep talking like that," I muttered. "And you"—I rounded on James—"you seem determined that I should go."

"We also said that it'll ultimately be your own decision," James pointed out, "but remember our conversation on Monday? You said you couldn't decide to act on the prophecy until you heard what it said. Well now you have, and as far as I can see, nothing has really changed."

I glared at him. I could have happily throttled James Thomas at that moment, because deep down, I knew that he was right. If there was any chance I could end the war, I had to try. By extension, if there was any chance I could initiate a sequence of events that would lead to the end of the war, I had to try. By further extension, if bringing a Honnie back was the trigger needed to set those three steps in motion, didn't that make it my duty to see that it happened? Of course, if there was only a chance of it being true, there was also a chance of it being false, but that also came back to what I'd decided back in the Woodward base on Monday: If the risk was reasonable, as this one hatefully was, it was worth taking.

"Fine," I snapped. "If we can get the protection to work and this thing goes ahead, I guess I'm going. Lord help me, I'm actually doing it."

"Okay," said Lucien, clapping his hands and smiling. "In that case, we've already got four ready to go, and I guess we'll find another one or two later. We'll discuss this with the rest of the base once we've decided if we're going and when. What I would suggest, and feel free to disagree with me here, is that we draw this meeting to a close early tonight, and get stuck into business tomorrow morning. I would suggest that the eight of us clear the lounge room out after breakfast and start designing the protection in there. It shouldn't take more than a few hours to work out if it can be done or not. If yes, we can hold a mass meeting in the afternoon; if not, we can wait till the evening for another private meeting, during which someone will need to talk to Stella. Perhaps she'll have some useful advice on how to proceed. Whether the Honnie thing goes ahead or not, plans will have to continue back here, plans that will involve a lot of spying on Hammerson, and that's something Stella could help us with greatly. All those in favour, raise your hands."

Eight hands rose into the air immediately, spelling the end of another day. Though I had slept in the afternoon, I was sleepy enough to go straight down to my room after the meeting, get into bed and almost instantly drop off to sleep.

Chapter 19: A Question of Protection

For reasons I couldn't even fathom, given that I'd slept that afternoon, my sleep that night was utterly dreamless—a rare treat as far as I was concerned. I woke up around half past five on that Saturday morning, feeling more refreshed than I had at any point since leaving the Woodward base. I got up, had a shower, got dressed and then left my room for an early breakfast—I also felt more hungry than I had in a while. The rest of the base was dark and silent, of course, and the dining room was completely deserted. Some people regularly had early breakfasts, but even they wouldn't turn up for at least fifteen or twenty more minutes.

I got some cereal from the conveyer belt and sat at the table closest to the door and began to eat, watching the entrance. Today, we would know if we were going on the Honnie trip or not. If so, Peter, Tommy and I would be in for the adventure of a lifetime. If so, either Natalie or Amelia would be right along with us. When I hadn't been going, I was aghast at the thought that Natalie would put herself in such a dangerous position, but now that I was, I wasn't sure how I should feel. On one hand, she would be safer if she remained behind, but on the other hand, she and I would be apart for who knew how long—perhaps long enough for her to give me up as a lost cause and move onto someone else. If she and I both went, who knew what could happen between us in the midst of danger.

I had been there for maybe fifteen minutes when I heard distant footsteps in one of the corridors—light footsteps, coming from the direction of my bedroom, or at least that particular corridor. I stopped eating and listened for a few seconds, wondering if my very thoughts of Natalie had somehow roused her and caused her to come out for an early breakfast. Of course, the last time I'd thought along those lines, it had turned out to be a dead girl knocking on my bedroom door. Like last time, it wasn't Natalie, or even Amelia, but unlike last time, it wasn't Serena either.

Stella, wearing unfamiliar clothing that the Sorcerers must have created for her the previous day, came stealthily into the dining room, and my heart skipped a beat at the sight of her. The light was still fairly dim, but it was just sufficient enough for me to judge that she still looked good. She didn't seem to understand how the system worked in here, though, because she didn't head for the conveyer belt right away, but looked around the room for some sign of what she needed to do. It was several seconds before she looked in my direction, and when she saw me here, watching her, she did an amusing double-take that almost caused her to lose her balance.

"Oh my God!"

"You get your food over there," I said, grinning slightly at the reaction I'd caused and pointing towards the conveyer belt.

Stella ignored where I was pointing and hurried straight to my table, sliding into the seat beside me and attempting to give me a hug, a difficult feat as the seats were at right angles. The resultant twisting of my body almost caused me to knock my breakfast off the table with my elbow.

"I've missed you," she moaned, pulling back so that she could look at my face, and my God but her eyes were bright.

"Missed you too," I said truthfully, smiling a little awkwardly. I wasn't sure what reaction I'd expected from her, but it hadn't been anything like this.

"I thought—I thought you were dead. They were all saying that you'd been killed."

"I nearly was," I said, pulling my breakfast back towards me, "but I guess your dad didn't finish the job properly."

"So what exactly is this place?" she asked me. "What have you guys been doing all this time? It's been so long since I've known anything about what you guys have been doing."

That wasn't entirely true, I thought. Stella had been keeping up with a good bit of our progress over the last four months by way of looking into my mind when she slept; it had been enough for her to know about my date with Serena, during which she had slipped me the Darkness Crystal, and of course, she'd known about our mission to get Jacob Underwood's Life

Assistant. It would only have been enough to provide a snapshot of what was really going on, though; she would get a much fuller idea of things while she was here. There would be plenty of time for telling stories, but now wasn't it. Additionally, the possibility existed that I would only get a day with her before my indefinite leave to an alternate dimension.

"We're here because Mr. Woodward and our parents wouldn't let us do anything for ourselves," I said. "We would have left even if our old base hadn't been destroyed."

Stella sighed and relaxed back into her seat. The relief on her face was absolute; I knew why, of course, but I couldn't even begin to understand how strong her emotions must be, given all she had gone through since that second last night of February. She continued to watch me as I ate my breakfast, as though she thought I might disappear if she took her eyes off me. Such scrutiny made me feel distinctly awkward before too long. I knew she liked me, of course, and was perhaps more comfortable with me than anyone else in the base (she certainly had been before), but now I came to think of it, I really didn't know exactly how she felt about me. Natalie had said once that Stella's thoughts indicated that she thought of herself as 'my girl', whatever that meant. Was she perhaps hoping to get even closer to me now that we were together? I liked her, of course, but I couldn't allow her to stand between me and Natalie any more than I could allow Amelia. And just when I'd thought I was finally getting things under control...

"You know, if you're hungry, you can get some food up there," I told her, for the second time pointing at the conveyer belt. "Just tell it what you want if it's not already up there."

She shrugged. "I think I'm okay for now."

She looked like she wanted to say more, about what I didn't know, but at that moment, Harry and Simon entered the room. Both of them were looking a little bit sleepy but I knew that wouldn't take anything from their general enthusiasm; they were definitely morning people, not to mention afternoon people, evening people, midnight people—pretty much anytime-of-day people. As they walked past us, heading for the conveyer belt, Stella shifted awkwardly.

"Maybe I'd better go," she said, but before she could get too far out of her seat, I reached out and pushed her gently but firmly back into it.

"You're gonna stay," I told her.

"Why? Are you showcasing me or something?"

"No, I'm giving people a chance to get used to you being around," I told her, "and giving you a chance to get used to being around people again. Get it out of the way now so that it won't be so awkward later."

She sighed. "If you say so."

I found myself wondering how literally she meant that, but before I could contemplate any further, the twins joined us at our table.

"It's so sweet to see you two together again," Harry observed as he pulled out a chair. I stuck my middle finger up at him while Stella, clearly uncomfortable with this turn of the conversation, shifted in her chair.

"Indeed, old chap," Simon added. "It's been a long time coming."

"Do you two ever power down?" I asked them.

"Only at school, and even then it was iffy," said Harry, and they both laughed.

"Seriously, though, it's good to see you back on the winning team," Simon said, patting Stella on the shoulder— she looked even more uncomfortable with this.

"Which of you two was in my room yesterday?" she asked them.

Harry and Simon raised their eyebrows at each other in some confusion. "Were you?" Harry asked his twin.

"Not that I recall," Simon mused. "Is it possible that you were dreaming about us in your room, Stella? Believe me, it wouldn't be the first time a girl has done that."

"No, I mean when I first woke up in here. You were dressed like a…"

She struggled to find the right descriptive word, but it wasn't necessary. All three of us knew what she was talking about and we all burst out laughing.

"You have met our dear brother, Hugh Jorgan," Harry announced. "What did you think of him?"

"I didn't even know you had a brother," she said, missing the joke completely. "Sisters, sure, but not a brother."

Harry and Simon positively roared with laughter, making Stella more alarmed than anything else.

"That was Fewul," I told her. "Marc's got him looking like those two."

"Oh," she said, her alarm solidifying into something almost like fear.

"And speaking of huge organs," I said, directing my attention back to the twins, "what on earth were you two giving Tommy such a hard time for last night? You know he's one who might just fight back."

Harry sighed. "There's no reason for Tommy to be offended. We were simply making light of the perception that dark men are often well-endowed, and how lucky Jessica must feel."

"Isn't that a bit racist?" I enquired.

"There's a difference between racism and observation," Simon pointed out, "and besides, he should take it as a compliment."

"Some people are more sensitive about that stuff than others," I told them, "and most people are more sensitive about it than you two. I hope you don't have to learn that the hard way."

"Hey, we can take as good as we give," said Harry. "He'll chill sooner or later, and his retaliations will hit us right where it pleasures, if you get my drift."

"I hope you don't mean literally," I said, and the three of us laughed.

More people began entering slowly over the next hour, and the flood increased rapidly after seven o'clock. Many of them took Stella in with curiosity, which was only to be expected, but fortunately they didn't come up and ask her questions, or even stare at her all through breakfast—I was thankful for that. A few also noticed that I was sitting with her; Peter, James and Marc all nodded approvingly at me as they passed. Natalie and Amelia both glanced our way, looking reproachful, but not willing to join our table (Harry and Simon had departed when their girlfriends had turned up).

One of the first things Amelia did when she got up that morning, before coming into breakfast even, was attach signs to the doors of the dining room, lounge room, the yard and the elevators. All of them said the same thing: The lounge room would be out-of-bounds between breakfast and lunch, and a meeting would take place in there at three o'clock which everyone in the base would be required to attend. I was surprised by this: I thought the plan had been to call a meeting only if we were definitely going, but perhaps Amelia wanted to let the whole base brainstorm ideas for how to proceed if not.

Stella hung around me all through breakfast and even followed me around when I left it. She knew her way around the base, having explored it before coming into breakfast, but she'd still been very interested to learn the location of my bedroom—a thought I didn't find at all comforting. I managed to shake her off only just after nine o'clock when it was time to enter the lounge room and begin our preparations. Stella had wanted to see what was going on, despite knowing nothing about Honnies, but the core group of Lucien, Marc, Tommy, Peter, James, Natalie and Amelia unanimously rejected the plea. Fortunately, Felicity and Jessica had been in the vicinity, and offered to let Stella hang out with them that morning.

"So how are we going to do this?" James asked when the eight of us, plus Fewul, were alone in the lounge room, and the doors were shut and locked.

The process turned out to be very similar to the way the three Sorcerers and Lucien had planned out the base, and like that instance, they asked me to assist. The difference this time was that Peter, James and Tommy also assisted, and every suggestion that was thrown up had to be verified by Fewul.

Marc ended up creating simple helmets which would automatically mould themselves to our heads when we put them on, so that there would be no way that a Honnie could get in under them. When we wanted to take them off, we had to think our way out, and the thought had to come from within our own head, not outside—that was an extra protective mechanism just in case a Honnie managed to break through enough to get us to let him in the rest of the way. As planned the day before, the helmet wouldn't block Honnies off completely; it would allow them to enter our minds just far enough to communicate, but not far enough to influence.

"The trouble is, even communication can be influential if you don't recognize the thoughts in your head as not your own," Fewul told Marc. "The sensation of dealing with a Honnie may take some getting used to, but since there is no way for me to replicate their talents, as they do not use my brand of magic, you will need to be on your game from the moment you enter their world. You must know when external thoughts are being placed in your head."

"That's okay, I can remember how it felt when Smiley was talking to that Honnie," said Peter. "I think we'll be okay."

"Will they definitely work?" Marc asked the beast.

"You have designed them to be powerful enough to protect you from the Honnies that you saw," Fewul told him. "You can do no more, as they are the only Honnies you can reference. As one of them was a collector, who are generally the most powerful Honnies of all, you should be protected from most Honnies. If you happen to encounter a Honnie stronger than that, I cannot predict how the helmets will react."

Marc looked dismayed as he glanced at Lucien. Lucien shrugged. "It's not completely foolproof, but it's almost foolproof. The decision's yours, Marc; should we continue?"

"We always knew there would be risk," James told us. "Personally, I'm not surprised by this turn of events. I think it would be very unlucky for those who go through to find a Honnie strong enough to do that too quickly."

Marc sighed. "I'm not thrilled, but James is right: No matter what we do, there will be risk involved. I guess the decision has to be made by those who'll be taking that risk."

Peter and Tommy both nodded at once, and I followed their lead. Natalie and Amelia glanced at each other, still unsure which of them would be coming along, but they both nodded too.

"Good," said Lucien. "In that case, let's move onto the physical side of the protection. We need a spell that will bind the magic of the helmets to our entire bodies, as well as our minds. Can you do that, Marc?"

He struggled with it for a few minutes but eventually, with Fewul's assistance, he managed to cast a spell that would protect our bodies as well as our minds by way of the helmets. As planned, it wouldn't actually make us stronger, but would simply make it impossible for any harm to come to our bodies while we were wearing the helmets, which now that I was wearing mine, turned out to be comfortable enough, despite being metallic, but rather heavier than I'd expected. Unlike the mind protection, however, this one could be tested, and to do so, Marc created a brick wall in the middle of the lounge room, stretching half of its length and almost all the way to the ceiling.

"How did I end up with this job?" Peter asked furiously as Marc positioned him next to the wall on one side, while the rest of us stood back against the far wall with a clear view of him imprinted against the brick backdrop.

"Don't worry, you'll be fine," Marc told him, "and if not, you won't be not fine for long."

There was a brief rumbling before the newly created brick wall tumbled forward in a cascade of loose brickwork, showering down on the hapless Peter, who went down beneath it with a yell. By the time it was down, Peter was buried beneath a mountain of debris, but he wasn't so badly hurt that he couldn't struggle somewhat.

"You doing okay there, Pete?" James called to him.

"Too heavy," he shouted, his voice muffled.

Amelia did the honours, vanishing all the bricks with a wave of her hand. Peter was revealed, in a crouched position on the floor, but completely unhurt—he didn't even need a hand up.

"Any pain?" Marc asked. "Anything at all that could translate into danger if the Honnies got hold of you?"

Peter raised his arms, flexed them, bent his knees, tested all the joints in his body, and finally shook his head. "I'm not hurt at all. I felt them hitting me, but they didn't hurt, and as you can see, I'm not even bleeding."

"Was the helmet damaged when the bricks hit it?" James asked Marc, but it was Fewul who answered.

"The helmets protect themselves in the same way that they protect your bodies."

"Okay," said Lucien, "in that case, you should be sufficiently protected physically. Is there anything else we need to take care of? Any more necessary protection?"

Nobody could think of anything else that we could do to prepare for our trip into the Honnies' world. We had already decided that other than food and some camping gear, we wouldn't take anything else with us, anything that the Honnies would take for weapons; we did not want them to think we were threatening them. There was, however, one more thing that needed to be tested, the most important thing of all. The eight of us, plus Fewul, left the lounge room, left the building, and headed across the yard to the control room. We could have done this in the base, but it was Lucien's belief that since we would be normal-sized when we went through the gateway, we ought to be normal-sized when we tested it.

Once we were all through the control room and out in the empty paddock again, the door set against nothing behind us, Lucien said, "which of you wants to go first?"

"I think I should," said Marc. "I know I'm not going, but it occurred to me that the Sorcerer who goes through shouldn't be the one to cast the gateway, just in case it disappears once she's on the other side, or something similar."

"In that case, she just has to be the last to go," said James.

"Let me have a go anyway," said Marc, squeezing the Hero Crystal. "I'm fairly sure I'll be able to do it."

And he could, as it turned out. The hole in reality that opened before us was quite different from what I could remember from Smiley's memories; on that occasion, the Honnie had simply moved from one to the other in a way that didn't allow us to see any of the world beyond, but this was different. It was a clear, circular hole stretching from the ground to about ten feet into the air, a hole which we could easily fall into if we stepped too far forward. What we saw beyond looked fairly plain; there were trees here and there, but not enough for it to be a forest. Where there weren't trees, there were bushes, shrubs, and a few bare patches of thick, green grass. There was a sound, carrying through the gateway to our ears: water, and a lot of it. I wondered if we were close to a river.

"There's a bit of a drop, by the look of it," said Tommy nervously, moving as close to the gateway as he dared and staring downward. "Looks like we'll have to jump maybe three or four metres when we go through."

"We won't be jumping into the Honnies' unfriendly answer to the Jade River, will we?" Peter asked nervously.

"No; there's grass directly below it," said Tommy, "but I hear you—there's water around there somewhere; a strong current, by the sound of it."

"Close it up, Marc," said Lucien, "in case a Honnie comes along."

Marc obliged, and then it was Natalie's turn to repeat the process. It took her longer than it had Marc, and the gateway she conjured was smaller and less distinct, but it was definitely there. Lucien ordered her to close it up and try again, and on her second attempt, she created a hole just as big and deep as the one Marc had. Once she'd closed it up again, it was Amelia's turn, and she too succeeded in opening the gateway, but she confided in us a moment later that she could only make it work when she ordered her magic to copy what Marc and

Natalie had done, and that she had no confidence in her own ability to do it.

"That might still be enough, though," said Tommy bracingly as we re-entered the control room and Peter pressed the button to close the door behind us, sealing us in the base once again. "You can just think back to this moment and make it copy what you just did."

"It's not impossible," Lucien agreed. "At least, it's not if you don't think it is, Amelia. So, which of you two is most willing to take part in this?"

"I don't mind doing it," said Natalie, and I didn't miss the satisfied glance she threw in my direction. I had to admit, I still wasn't altogether happy about Natalie being involved, but it was better now that I knew I wouldn't have to wait for her, never knowing if she would return.

"I'll do it if I have to," said Amelia reluctantly, "but I reckon Natalie looks like she'll be better for the job."

* * *

The mass meeting began bang on three o'clock. Nobody was late, many of them having hung around in the lounge room since lunchtime, all the better to get a good position. Everyone knew we had achieved our first two tasks, both in only three days. The feeling of accomplishment was palpable, and so was the anticipation: They wanted to know where we would go from here. Along the back wall sat a single couch, and Lucien sat in the middle of it as the centre of attention; Marc and Tommy sat on his left, Natalie and Amelia on his right. Peter, James and I sat off to the side along with Stella, and not too far from the twins, and Fewul was probably somewhere, but Marc had ordered him to make himself invisible for the occasion.

"Okay, let's get straight down to business," said Lucien. "We've got a lot to get through and only three and a half hours to do it."

"We're seriously gonna be here for three hours?" said Felicity incredulously.

"Give or take," said Lucien, smiling slightly. "Firstly, if you didn't already know, we have completed both of the tasks we were doing during the week. Stella is now with us, as you can see, and the information my group had been seeking has been found, and it is with that information that we have decided what our next order of business will be—or at least, the next order of business for around half a dozen of you. Before we get to that, though, I think it necessary to go over a few other things first, since we haven't had a chance to demonstrate them to the whole group until now, and I don't think anyone has bothered to experiment—a wise decision on the whole."

He was referring to the news feed and internet access that the Sorcerers had provided earlier in the week. He explained how the protection worked, demonstrated both for the group, and then a discussion ensued regarding how the systems would be distributed. In the end, it was decided that the news feed would only be available in the lounge room, and anyone wishing to use it simply had to wait in line if it was already being occupied. As for the computers, the idea of a wireless network was raised, but Lucien stamped on it immediately, claiming that it could possibly be exploited from the outside. Nobody was happy about the idea of there being only one computer for the whole base to share, but Amelia was unhappy with the idea of everyone having one in their bedrooms. In the end, it was decided that Marc would create a computer room on the second floor, directly above the lounge room, and it would contain at least a dozen computers, all hooked up to the same protection as the one in here (that one would be moved upstairs too).

"With that settled, it's time we told you about our next order of business," said Lucien, "and I am going to enlist the assistance of James to help me explain it, since it was originally his idea. Go on, James; tell us all why you came up with this plan."

"I don't remember agreeing to this," he said doubtfully.

"It's very dangerous," Lucien said, "and many won't like it, unless they understand why it is so necessary. You were able to convince Tommy, John and Peter to be directly involved, and they shot it down originally, so I think you'll be able to do this now. Go on."

James still looked unhappy, but when he began to talk, explaining what he had told us three nights earlier in Amelia's bedroom, it was as though he was transferring his unhappiness to everyone else. By the end, he looked far more comfortable, while everyone else in the room looked horrified and dismayed.

"That's why we had to come up with a solution that would not only take Hammerson down, but take down his entire structure at the same time," said James. "Now, we may have a lot of magic on our side, but not even Fewul could perform an influential charm on every single Hammerheart in the world at the same time, and let's face it, that's the only way we could possibly prevent anarchy post Hammerson's death. The Woodwards and Fletchers will be more concerned with attempting to restore political calm, which will be a big job in itself; I think we can safely assume that many countries around the world will have changed permanently, even if the Hammerhearts are overthrown. I considered the Light Crystal as a possible solution to this problem—Tommy gave it to me to hang onto earlier—but I just don't trust that it could handle this scale of evil: Good generally doesn't remove free will without the human element of evil. In short, the only way we could use our own power to end this thing would be to blow up the world, and I'm not a huge fan of that idea.

"So, what I eventually settled on is something that only a handful of people in the world know about. We are going to end the war the same way the Woodwards ended it in 1981, but we are going to do it consciously. For them, the solution simply dropped into their laps and they were able to capitalise on it, even if their original plan didn't quite work out. We can't count on that happening for us, but unlike the Woodwards, we understand far better what actually happened back then. We are going to actively seek that solution and attempt to use it again, and we will do so with far more assurance given that we are prepared for it, and don't look at me like that," he added coldly to his girlfriend.

Erica and Lena both looked stunned and horrified as they stared at James. They knew about Honnies, having been with us on Rock Haulter when Smiley had explained about the fourth dimension, and they had made the connection between what they'd learnt then and what James was saying now. Siobhan, who had also been there those few days, was looking confused—she hadn't picked up on James's meaning yet. Everyone else looked more intrigued than anything, and none more so than Stella. She'd grimaced several times as James had spoken so casually of her father's death, but she knew better than to interrupt him. Now, it seemed that she knew nothing about what had happened in 1981, and she was keen to learn.

"Yes, that's correct," said Lucien. "Now, I'm not the best one to explain what actually happened, so which of you wants to do the honours? How about you, Marc?"

"Sure," he said, and cleared his throat. "A lot of you know that some of us went back to Rock Haulter a couple of months ago. The reason for that was so that we could talk to a man with a certain magical ability. He was there in 1981 when it all went down, he saw it with his own eyes, and with his experiences since then, he came to understand more about it than the Woodwards, Hammersons or anyone else did."

With some staggering, stumbling and doubling back, Marc began to explain about the fourth dimension and the next world along it. Unsurprisingly, many people didn't know whether to take him seriously or not. He did his best to explain about the Honnies, how they ran their civilisation and how dangerous they were to humans, but by this stage many people were smirking in amusement. It was only when he directed his speech back to the Honnie that had helped the Woodwards that they began to understand that he wasn't just making it all up; they began looking wary, horrified and, in the cases of those who'd jumped ahead to what we would have to do, terrified.

"So that's how it went down back then," Marc concluded, "but if we can help it, we won't have to kill so many this time. We understand more about Honnies than they did back then, which gives us a better chance of negotiating with them—we're not kidding ourselves into thinking that will be easy, though. We think that if we can persuade a Honnie to help us take out Hammerson and take control of the most important parts of his army, we have the best possible chance of stalling this thing without blowing the whole works sky-high."

"So that's the plan," Lucien went on, "to go into the Honnies' world, with certain protection which we developed this morning, and look for a Honnie who would be willing to help us. The protection will allow us to communicate with the Honnies, but not let them take control of us. It will also protect our bodies from any physical harm without leading the Honnies to believe that we are a threat to them. Tommy, Peter, John and Natalie are all going on this mission, but it would be good if we had one or two more to complete the party. In the full understanding of how dangerous it could be, in the full understanding that you will be as protected as possible, do we have any volunteers?"

I didn't expect there to be any this quickly. I was sure that they would want to ask more questions about the Honnies, about the danger, about the protection, about the process we would be going through. But to my surprise, five people raised their hands immediately. One of them was Erica, but James, a stony expression on his face, took her wrist and lowered it firmly back into her lap. She gave him a withering look but didn't resist. The same thing happened on the other side of the room with Jessica; Felicity refused to let her go, and James nodded his approval of this. That left just three people, and one of them was Stella, but Lucien shook his head at her.

"We need you here," he told her. "While I'm sure you'd like to do your bit, you will be far more useful to us back here. You understand why, don't you?"

Stella nodded and lowered her hand, looking imploringly at me. I wasn't sure why she expected me to be able to change

Lucien's mind, but as it turned out, she was far more dismayed that after having missed my company for so long, she would have to say goodbye the very next day. I only found this out later that evening when she approached me and tried to persuade me not to go. I was touched that she cared so much but I couldn't tell her what she wanted to hear. For better or worse, I was in.

There were now only two people volunteering to go: Rebecca Fletcher and Candice Young. Natalie was staring hard at her sister, opening and closing her mouth as she tried to come up with some reason why Rebecca couldn't go, but after all, wouldn't it make her a hypocrite to say that she couldn't? Lucien looked calmly at the two girls, who were sitting together, and smiled.

"So, you two," he said, "what makes you want to put yourselves in such danger?"

"Aren't we in danger whatever we do?" Rebecca retorted.

"True, but this is especially dangerous," said Lucien.

"I have to do this," said Candice quietly, not elaborating, but I didn't need her to. I didn't know Candice's true personality very well, having had very little to do with her other than one chat with her when she'd been a Hammerheart, and the conversation during which I'd removed the influential charms from her mind, but I understood clearly why she needed to do this. She had done very well not to go to pieces in light of the crimes she had committed as a Hammerheart, most particularly murdering Lisa, but she could never have forgiven herself for them either. It would be very difficult for her to redeem herself now, but if it were at all possible, taking on this job would be the way to do it. And if worse came to worst, if necessary, perhaps she could atone for taking Lisa's life. She may have meant to do just that on that night in Germany, but her role in those events had been minor by comparison.

"If you're both going, I'm definitely coming," said Rebecca firmly.

"I'd be a lot happier if you didn't," said Natalie, looking stricken, but seeming to know that she could do nothing to sway her sister.

"I'm not staying behind and waiting for you to maybe never come back," Rebecca retorted, speaking the thoughts I'd been entertaining the night before.

"So what exactly is the plan, then?" Jessica asked, her eyes on Tommy; they were glistening with tears that would probably flow later on when it was just the two of them.

"The six of you will leave tomorrow afternoon, just after lunch," Lucien said, "giving you just under twenty-four hours to mentally prepare yourselves for the challenge. The six of you ought to have a private meeting between now and then so you can prepare yourselves practically. As for the rest of us, we will have a private meeting tonight—me, Marc, Amelia, James, and I think you should also join us, Stella. Once we've worked out what we do next, we'll call another meeting like this one; it may be tomorrow, or the day after. I can tell you now that we will probably be doing a lot of spying before we jump back into action with any sort of plan."

Part 3: Mission Improbable

Chapter 20: On the Other Side

We were all ready to go. Two o'clock the next afternoon found me, Tommy, Peter, Rebecca, Natalie and Candice in the yard outside the control room, each of us wearing our protective helmets which we had aptly labelled as 'thinking caps'; me, Peter and Tommy all wearing bags of goodies over our backs; and all of us being seen off by the rest of the base. The six of us had had a meeting the night before, as suggested, and one of the ideas had been to create three bags, one identical to Stella's and two identical to those which the Hammerhearts called their extender-cases. The first contained plenty of food and drinks, a mixture of the healthy and not-so-healthy (Peter's idea for keeping us up-beat), all of which would duplicate whenever we removed them from the bag. The second bag, the one I was carrying as it were, contained camping gear: tents, sleeping bags and the like. Its contents would not duplicate when taken from the bag, but the bag was enchanted so that it felt like I was carrying barely anything at all. The last bag was the same as the second, only with six compartments within it, each containing a few changes of clothing for each of us.

The rest of the previous day and this morning were spent with everyone else in the base. If I were honest with myself, part of me felt there was a very strong chance that I may never see them again, and I wanted to leave them with good memories of me. I got a feeling that the other five were taking a similar approach. It was very difficult to do this without getting emotional but fortunately, Harry and Simon were able to make the whole thing seem a little less heavy. It was only Amelia and Stella who really managed to catch me off-guard; Stella had pleaded with me the previous evening after dinner not to go, and I got a very similar show from Amelia earlier this morning. Both of them knew nothing could be changed, and Amelia understood why I had to do it, but it didn't stop her from crying out that she would miss me like crazy. To cap the morning, Lena approached me just before noon and, after separating me from the rest of the group, told me that she would give me a treat when I returned from the Honnies' world, because I was so brave. I didn't need to guess what that treat would be and I didn't intend to take it, but I understood why she was offering it; it was her way of giving me more incentive to come back, because she wasn't entirely sure that I would either.

Immediately after lunch, before we were to set off, we had all gathered in the lounge room and, as per Natalie's suggestion, taken a group photo. The thirty-one of us lined up in three rows of ten, ten and eleven, with the people in the front row sitting on seats and those tallest in the back. Those of us who were leaving sat in the middle of the front row along with Katie, Sophie, Erica and Jason; smiling at Fewul, who had been tasked with operating the camera. It felt very much like the class photos the school had made us take every year except that this was so much more significant. Once it was done, the photo was magically developed and duplicated so that every person in the base had one. I intended to hang onto mine and look at it every night I spent in the Honnie world, assuming I could.

At last, though, the time had finally come to say goodbye, and now there really was an outpouring of emotions from all corners. The six of us all did our best to put a brave face on, but by the time we had turned our backs on them and entered the control room, the two Fletcher girls had tears streaming down their faces. I was feeling a little better, though, because somehow, being on the move felt better than standing still. Even though I knew there was almost certainly danger up ahead, and I was heading straight towards it, it still felt better than sitting around, waiting for the moment when I could head towards it. After all the dangerous situations I'd been in, particularly after the ones I had knowingly walked into, I wasn't surprised by this.

"Is everyone okay?" Marc asked us; he and Fewul were going to see us through the gateway.

"I think we will be," said Tommy, shrugging his shoulders and attempting a smile. "I'll feel better when we're on the other side and we know how it feels. Should we get on with it then?"

Nobody protested to that idea, so Marc opened the door and the eight of us stepped out into the paddock once again. This time, however, Marc ordered Fewul to release us from the magical enchantments that surrounded the base and those within it. None of us knew if they would carry through to the Honnies' world, but we didn't want to take the chance. By the time we were all out and exposed (at least, all but Fewul were exposed), we could no longer see the door that was our only way back to relative safety. That was when the full gravity of the situation hit me: We had just passed V1, the point of no return.

Marc began working the same magic he had performed the day before. Within seconds, a hole in reality began opening in the same spot as yesterday, and about half a minute later, it was large enough for us to safely step through—or more like jump through, because as Tommy had observed the day before, there was a drop between this world and that one.

"You holding up okay, Marc?" Peter asked nervously.

"No trouble," Marc said. "I don't have to work to keep it open, but I guess I don't wanna keep it there any longer than necessary. You guys all ready?"

"I'll go first," said Tommy. "I'll call back to you guys if there's anything bad in there, and if there is, or if something happens to me, don't you guys follow—just close the thing up immediately. You got me?"

"Sure thing, bro," said Marc. "I said all along, we're only taking smart risks here. So, at your discretion."

Tommy approached the gateway, took a deep breath, and jumped through. We heard him thud to the ground on the other side, but given the drop, we couldn't see him anymore.

"You okay?" Peter called to him.

"Yeah," he called back. "It's a bit of a drop, but the ground isn't too hard, so you should be okay. Just give me a chance to get out of the way before you follow."

I sighed in relief. I hadn't noticed until then that I'd been holding my breath the whole time. I decided that I would be next to go through; I approached the gateway, put an arm out to stop Rebecca, who'd intended to be next, and as Tommy had, took a deep breath before plunging. Tommy hadn't been lying; it was a considerable drop, but he'd also been right about the ground being soft. We'd landed squarely in one of those small patches of grass, and as I straightened up, I saw that the river we could hear was very close by, just on the other side of the gateway. It was much wider than the Jade River, and the current running much faster; it didn't look safe at all, and I took a few tentative steps away from it, only stopping when I tripped over Tommy's feet.

The two of us gasped in horror when we got a good look at each other, because our appearances had somehow changed. He still looked like Tommy, of course, but something about him was missing. He looked far less attractive than he had in our world, and judging by the look he was giving me, the effect was not exclusive. A moment later, Peter landed in our midst, and I saw that he now looked rather ghastly; he had always had fairly pale skin, but the quality of the air in this world, or whatever was causing this bazaar twist, made him look almost —there was no other word for it—dead.

"Wow, you look awful, John," he observed.

"That makes three of us," I said flatly.

"What the hell is this?" Tommy asked slowly.

"I don't know, but I'll be interested to see how the girls look when they come through," said Peter, and a moment later, as Rebecca joined us, we saw that it was not exclusive to males. Rebecca still looked like herself, and it was possible to recognise those traits which would have been attractive in our world, but somehow, the effect they normally caused had been stripped away. She gasped when she got a good look at the three of us, and began tearing up when she realised that we were giving her the same expression.

A minute later, Candice and Natalie had also joined us, and once they had got over the initial shock of how this place made us all look, we all gathered together and stared up at the gateway, through which we could see Marc, staring down at us.

"Can you feel anything happening in your heads?" he called to us.

"Nothing that shouldn't be there," Peter called back, "although let's face it, there's usually not that much in my head to begin with."

"Oh no," Natalie moaned, raising her hands and looking frantic. "Oh no—oh no—oh no—"

"Yep, sadly, it's true," sighed Peter.

"What's wrong?" I asked, the expression on her face making me rather fearful.

"Guys, my magic doesn't work anymore," she said, frantically snapping her fingers, waving her hands, anything that would normally get some sort of magical reaction. "Marc, I can't use my magic here. Ask Fewul if he knows anything about this."

Marc disappeared from the gateway for a minute or so, and when he returned, he looked grim. "According to Fewul, it's because your Sorcerous Crystal is on this side, and your chip is on that side. He said there was no way of predicting that would happen because no Sorcerer has ever done what you're doing. What do you want me to do? Do you wanna go on, or should I try to lift you all back through?"

"I think we'd better come back," Tommy called. "I'm not saying we give up on this; I just think we should get Lucien's opinion on what to do next, but we can't leave this thing open while you go and ask him."

"Okay," he said. "Get in a line and I'll help you up."

That part of the plan didn't quite work out, though, because Marc's magic didn't seem to work any better on this side than Natalie's had. After several seconds of trying, he finally let out a dismayed cry. "It won't work! I can only perform it here, but it can't reach you there."

There were several seconds of silence before Natalie said, "so what should we do then? Is there any way to get up?"

There wasn't, of course. Tommy was the tallest out of the six of us, and the bottom of the gateway was about twice his height from the ground, and it was placed against thin air. There was no way of getting to it. There was only one thing we could do.

"We have to go on," I told them, loud enough so that Marc could hear. "I know we don't have a way of getting back now, but if we find a Honnie to help us, they can get back the same way that other Honnie did in 1981. It's our only option now."

Marc's mouth was open in horror. "That means you have no chance of returning unless you can get a Honnie to help. Oh my God, I did not expect this. This means—this means—"

"Our chances of coming back have dropped rather a lot," said Peter, "but on the bright side, our chances of succeeding here are still the same. We still have protection, even without Natalie's magic. I think John's right; we have to go on."

"Okay," said Marc. "I'm not happy about it, but I see your point—there's nothing we can do about it. Geez, the others will be happy about this. I guess—er—"

"See ya later," I called back to him. "Close the gateway now before you lose your nerve."

Marc waved once to us before doing as I suggested, knowing it was best. A moment later, it was gone, and the six of us stood alone in an alien world, just looking at each other. I observed that the two Fletcher girls, who had always looked alike (excepting the beauty I saw in Natalie that Rebecca didn't seem to share), now looked almost identical—only the two inches difference in their heights gave away which was which.

"So, what now?" Candice asked into the silence.

"I guess we have to find some Honnies," said Rebecca. "Isn't that the plan, to walk into danger?"

"Smiley said they have cities," said Natalie. "He said they have buildings, skyscrapers and things. A good Honnie may be anywhere but we're more likely to have a choice if we find a large group of them."

"How's this," I suggested, and pointed at the river. "Rivers often lead to civilisation, so why don't we follow this one and see where we end up?"

The others agreed, perhaps because no one could think of any better ideas. For the sake of safety, we ducked back into the bushes and followed the river by sound rather than sight. It was slower going, perhaps, but ultimately safer if it meant we wouldn't fall in.

"Keep an eye out for animals, while you're at it," Natalie told us as we pressed on. "I'm less worried about them than the Honnies, but you never know what they've got over here."

We did as she suggested, but didn't see anything for a very long time. We saw the sun occasionally through the bushes, which suggested that it was in time with our own watches. I supposed that this must mean that the gateway had opened up to this exact same point on this planet at the exact same time. If so, we would have been walking west; again, the sun ahead of us confirmed that idea. It would also have meant that we were walking along the bank of the Jade River, probably well out of Chopville by now. Of course, the paddock we'd left had been more than a kilometre north of the Jade River in our world, but on the other hand, this river was much wider. We were walking downstream, which would have been true of the Jade River if we'd walked West from Chopville. It all seemed to fit together in my mind—different dimension, different world, but in many ways it was still the same planet.

It took hours, and we were all beginning to get rather peckish, but around five o'clock by our watches, the bushes suddenly opened up to reveal a track—not a dirt track, or even a beaten-down track. This was a road, a solid, concrete road. I knew I shouldn't have been surprised by it, after all, Smiley said they were capable of building, but it nevertheless caught me off-guard. The sight of it seemed to impress upon us, not likeness, but unlikeness, as though we were only now beginning to fully comprehend how different Honnies were from humans. The road was solid, but narrow, designed for foot travel, not heavy vehicles. To our right, it crossed the river by way of a narrow but sturdy-looking bridge; again, only for foot travel. I began to wonder what sort of transport Honnies used; did they just walk everywhere?

"I suppose we could stay here," suggested Peter, looking along the road. "You'd think someone would come along eventually."

"We can't count on that," said Natalie. "It still feels like we're in the middle of nowhere. This track though, it probably leads to somewhere in both directions. Which way do you reckon we should go?"

North or south, I thought, looking over the bridge and off at the continuation of the road on the other side. As the river was so wide, I could only just make out the opposite bank in the fading light.

"Left," said Tommy. "In our world, Melbourne would be roughly in that direction."

"We'd have to walk for days to get that far," groaned Candice.

"I agree with Tommy," Natalie said smartly. "See up there?" She pointed along the river; further down, it curved more Southwest, exactly like the Jade River did at various points along its length. "That probably means it's heading for a coast, or some other body of water. Do you reckon we're more likely to find a city near the coast, or further inland?"

We got the gist but we were working far too much on assumptions for anything to be reliable in my mind. I supposed it was the only way to go, though, since we had nothing else whatsoever to work with.

So it was left that we went. The bush we past was quite unremarkable, just as much as that which we'd been passing all afternoon so far. As the minutes ticked by, I began thinking more and more about the food in the bag on Tommy's back, and as my legs began aching from all the walking we'd been doing, I thought longingly of the sleeping bags in the bag on my own back. I didn't dare suggest we stop, though; I was hoping someone else would do it. I supposed we would just keep going till the sun set, then we would have to look for a place to set up camp before then. Through all this, something even more annoying was taking place: My head under my thinking cap had begun to itch. I didn't dare remove the cap to scratch it, but the itch was persistent. It was the sort of itch that only went away if you stopped thinking about it, but that proved to be impossible. It was a vicious circle.

There were drains to either side of the road on which we walked. They were lids that looked like jail doors, at periodic distances of maybe twenty or thirty feet on alternating sides of the path. I supposed they were to keep water off the path if it rained heavily, though thankfully it didn't look like doing that so far. That was one good thing about the current situation: At least the weather was behaving itself for us. It was clearly winter, but it wasn't too chilly; it wasn't too windy, and it wasn't raining.

It was around six o'clock by my watch, not long before I was ready to suggest we call it a day, when Tommy stopped us and pointed into the distance ahead. There, at least a kilometre away, was the first sign of life we'd seen since coming through the gateway other than ourselves. After a quick debate, we decided we might as well see if they were good or bad. I was against this, thinking that if they were bad, I would be too exhausted to run from them at this late hour—not that that would be possible, given how fast they moved. We continued walking, but it took more than ten minutes before we could really see the figures up ahead, positioned just to the left of the road, close to one of the drains.

There were three of them, two facing the road and the other facing away. The two facing us were both males; they were big, muscular, and stupid, judging by the expressions on their faces, and to cap this image, they were both wearing what looked a bit like jumpsuits. The other figure, the one not facing the road, was a female. She was smaller than the two males with long, black hair and dark skin, though not as dark as Tommy's. She was wearing something that looked a bit like a brown robe, much the same as the Honnies we had seen in Smiley's memories. She may have been shorter than her boyfriends but she was still pretty tall by our standards—around Tommy's height, perhaps even more.

The two male Honnies spotted us first but they didn't react to us at all. The girl must have known we were there but it wasn't until we were almost upon them that she turned to face us. The sight of her face was worth a kick in the guts: She was very pretty, much prettier than us humans were capable of being in this world, but even so, she wasn't stunning in the same way that the Honnie who'd helped the Woodwards had been. If anything, she was like the Honnie Smiley had met in 2000; she even shimmered around the edges in the same way that he had, something which those other two (whatever they were) didn't do. I knew I couldn't judge her age based on how she looked but I thought if I could, she would have to be around our age; she certainly looked young. She glanced quickly from one face to the next before, for reasons best known to herself, picking Tommy to address. Perhaps it was simply because he was the tallest, or looked the oldest.

The Honnie spoke then, and the sound made me jump. It was the first time I'd ever heard a Honnie speak, for the two I'd seen in Smiley's memories had satisfied themselves with communicating mentally. The sound was low, throaty, and would probably be impossible for a human to emulate exactly. This one clearly expected Tommy to understand what she was saying, but when he merely shrugged and spread his hands, she looked more closely at him, her eyes lingering on his thinking cap. They began communicating mentally; I knew they were because Tommy's expression changed; he understood what she was saying.

"What's the deal?" Peter asked nervously.

"She wants to know who our owner is," Tommy said flatly, as though it were costing him all of his effort just to speak coherently. I couldn't blame him; if the Honnie was occupying his thoughts with her own questions, it would be difficult to answer someone else's.

"Owner?" Rebecca repeated.

"They treat humans like possessions," Natalie said, "Smiley told us."

"We don't have an owner," said Peter. "What are we supposed to tell her?"

It didn't matter, though, because the Honnie seemed to have picked that information out of Tommy's head. What came next was terrifying to watch: The Honnie screwed up her face in concentration, and in the same instant, Tommy collapsed to the ground, seemingly at random. He cried out in pain, and the rest of us gathered around him, alarmed, terrified that the Honnie had somehow broken through his protection.

"Tommy! Tommy!"

"No!" Tommy shouted. "You cannot control me! Don't even try!"

This took all of us by surprise, but nobody more so than the Honnie herself; she had clearly not expected this resistance. She took a step back from us, looking scared and confused, and Tommy staggered back to his feet, trembling with the reaction.

"What was that?" Peter asked.

"Hurt," he muttered. "A lot of pain in my head. She tried to take my mind in her own, I think, like Smiley said they could, only she couldn't get through the protection. My God, if we have to do that with every Honnie we meet, this is gonna be a painful adventure."

He took a step towards the girl, hands out, palms raised, as though he were proclaiming his peacefulness. The girl continued to stare at him for several seconds before, without warning, she simply turned her back on us. She called something in her language, directing her voice to the nearby drain. I had no idea what words she had used, but even in that language, I understood the tone completely: She was calling to someone for assistance, someone who had some sort of authority over her, almost certainly a more powerful Honnie.

"Should we stay?" Candice hissed.

"I don't think we have a choice," Natalie muttered. "Remember, they're stronger than us; they'll just pin us down if they want us to stay."

The more powerful Honnie in question began to emerge then from, of all places, the inside of the nearby drain. This certainly was a surprise; Smiley had said they had buildings, but he had never intimated that they were sewer dwellers. This new Honnie was also a female, and of the same size, stature and shimmer (for whatever reason) as the girl who had called her. She was older, though (in her late twenties or early thirties, if I were to judge her appearance against human years) and her skin was rather lighter than the younger Honnie's, almost the same colour as my own. Her attire was also the same as the younger Honnie's. She replaced the cover on the drain, appraised us briefly, then turned her attention to the younger Honnie.

They began to speak, and as they did, I took notice of the likenesses in their features. It wasn't inconceivable to think that this new Honnie was the younger Honnie's mother, because even though their skin wasn't the same colour, many of their facial features indicated some sort of relationship. Even the two males, who were still standing by, watching the proceedings, seemed to share some of their features. Had we stumbled over some sort of rural family? I had just marvelled over this possibility when the two Honnies wrapped up their conversation and turned their attention back to the humans who had stood patiently by.

What came next was such an enormous shock that I almost dared wonder if this was really happening: Was I perhaps dreaming of what could happen the next day, as I lay in my bed back in our base in our own world? Smiley had told us that the Honnies had their own language but in nothing he'd imparted could I recall there being anything about Honnies knowing how to speak English. Yet that was exactly what the new arrival did now, and like her fellow, she addressed Tommy.

"Who is your aba?" she asked him, her speech easy to understand despite a thick accent that sounded like any wild mixture of European accents rolled into one.

The six of us just looked at each other in confusion. What was an aba, if that was even how it was supposed to be said.

She had spoken the unfamiliar word in a way that sounded as though it would be spelt A-B-A, but it could just as easily have been A-R-B-A, or perhaps there could have been an H in there somewhere—who could say. Whatever it was, it had to be a word from her language thrown into ours because there was no English equivalent.

"What's an aba?" Peter finally asked.

The two female Honnies exchanged a look I couldn't place before the older one spoke again. "Who is holding you? Who are you with?"

I still didn't quite understand what she was trying to say, but Tommy got the gist of it. In response, he jabbed a finger at the younger Honnie. "I told her we're not with anyone. We're on our own, but now that we've found you, I guess I'm sort of glad. How come you speak English?"

"Pardon?" the Honnie asked, raising her eyebrows. Her face became a little mesmerising to look at when she did that, and I quickly switched my gaze back to Tommy. We hadn't even been here six hours and we were already facing our first major test.

"Why do you speak our language?" Tommy persisted.

The Honnie seemed to understand this time, but for whatever reason, she chose not to answer. Instead she said, "Are you lost? Who were you with before?"

"No one," said Natalie, beginning to look frightened. "We're not from here—we came from a different place."

"Who brought you here?" the Honnie asked, turning her attention to Natalie instead.

"Our friend Marc," she said, taking half a step backward, away from the Honnies. "We came to look for some Honnies like you because we need—need help."

The Honnie's eyes widened in alarm at this. "You say that humans can come here on their own now?"

"No, only us," said Peter. "We have more power than most humans, though probably not as much as you," he added flatteringly.

"When did you come here?"

"A few hours ago," said Peter. "Er, do you know hours?"

"You came today?"

"Yes."

"You came on your own?"

"Yes."

The two Honnies looked at each other again, and even though they weren't human, I recognised the looks on both faces. It was a predatory look, and it chilled me to the bone. Here we have six free humans, free and unclaimed, fresh out of the human world with all their tasty knowledge to feed the mind and flesh and blood to feed the body. As far as these Honnies were concerned, they'd just found a couple of discarded hundred dollar bills on the side of the road, all for the taking. Suddenly, I dearly wished we had run for it when we'd had the chance.

"We came for a reason," I said hurriedly. "Most humans don't even know about Honnies, but we do, and we want to talk to you about something very important."

"No human business is important," said the Honnie dismissively.

"Okay, then can we talk to you about something that's *not* important?" Rebecca asked, her temper getting the better of her. I would have given just about anything to take those words back.

The response came from the younger Honnie this time, and it was utter gibberish to my ears. The older Honnie listened before nodding, a gesture so human that I felt a stab of homesick, and a certainty that I would never see it again. She turned her attention to Tommy, and without warning, took possession of him. The result was far more spectacular than when the younger Honnie had attempted it; Tommy yelled and collapsed, and with a terrifying crack, his thinking cap shattered all around his head. The pieces that were left, all 792 of them approximately, fell to the ground around him. Tommy's head appeared to be undamaged but I got a look at his face in that instant, and knew that for Tommy, the game was up.

"*Run!*" Peter shouted, jumping to the only logical, albeit heartless, conclusion. He never got a chance to follow his own advice though, for a moment later, his own thinking cap went the same way as Tommy's.

The three girls and I were a little quicker, but not by much —not by much at all. I skirted around the two grounded boys, intending to sprint up the path back the way we had come. I just had time to see Natalie and Rebecca, already in a full sprint ahead of me, being seized by the shoulders by the younger female Honnie; she had moved so quickly that it had seemed as though she'd been beside her older fellow in one instant, and further up the path a split second later. The Fletcher girls were unhurt, of course, but they were no match for the Honnie, who dragged them effortlessly back to the group.

I never saw it, though, because a moment after they were seized, my head exploded. The pain hit my skull on all sides before burrowing in. In the next split-second, it was the worst headache that had ever been experienced by anyone in the history of forever. It could have been all the combined pain of the agonator, concentrated exclusively on one part of the body but with no less intensity. I never felt the thinking cap shatter (I was beyond feeling external things such as that by then) but what I did feel was something flexible wrap itself tightly around my head. At least, that was what it felt like, but I knew exactly what it was. Smiley had explained about how the Honnies used their minds, about the way they were like bubbles, and that they could contain other minds within their own. That was exactly the thing the thinking caps had been meant to protect us from, but apparently, this particular Honnie was much stronger than we had anticipated. The only good thing about this was that I no longer felt the pain; along with the bubble came an odd coolness, a sensation I welcomed in comparison, although I still had enough of my own thoughts to wonder if the Honnie was doing that deliberately. If so, she could make the pain return whenever she liked.

I was on the ground, but now I slowly raised myself into a sitting position. Candice was nearest to me on the path. She had tripped in her haste to escape the Honnies and hadn't got much further than that before she had been seized. Behind me, Peter and Tommy were also sitting on the road, looking stunned and horrified. Natalie and Rebecca were both missing their thinking caps too but they hadn't quite come to their senses yet. The four Honnies were watching us; the two males looked stupidly surprised, but the females looked even more shocked; they had no more expected that to happen than we had.

"We're in big trouble now," Peter moaned, rubbing his temples. "Oh God, we are absolutely screwed, every last hole of us."

"That's a charming way of putting it," Candice muttered thickly.

"What did you do?" the Honnie who could speak English asked sharply.

"I think it was your doing, not ours," Peter retorted.

"Guys," said Tommy, and to my surprise, he looked positively gleeful, "guys, we've hit the jackpot."

"Do you have any idea what just happened to us?" I asked him, wondering if the Honnies had already messed his mind up.

"She is perfect," he hissed at us. "Not only can she speak English, but she's obviously super strong. She's exactly what we've been looking for. My God, the first Honnie we find and she's perfect."

"She also said human business isn't important," Candice said flatly.

We slowly got to our feet, looking around at the mess we'd left on the road. There was no blood, not that I could see anyway, but there were sure a lot of fragments of metal littered around the place. My thoughts still seemed to be my own, but I knew that not only could that Honnie hear every one of them, she could wipe them all in a stroke. All six of us were now completely at her mercy; all our protection, the mental and the physical, had been stripped from us. We still had our bags, but that was now the full extent of our magic. Nothing we'd done could have prepared us for this. Why on earth had we gone along with this suicidal mission?

"Did you really have to do that?" Natalie asked the Honnies indignantly.

"I am sorry," the Honnie said, not sounding sorry at all. "What were those things on your heads?"

"They were supposed to keep you out," said Peter gruffly.

"They nearly worked," she said indifferently, while over her shoulder, the younger Honnie watched on with interest. That predatory look was still there, and it was clear that she expected at least one of us to be her dinner. Thankfully it was the other Honnie who now owned us and not her, although I wasn't about to be thanking anyone just yet.

"Now, why are you here?" the Honnie asked us, as though continuing our discussion from earlier.

"Er," Tommy, who was once again spokesperson, faltered; how much ought we to tell her? I supposed it hardly mattered, since she could go into our heads and get it all for herself if she really cared, but still.... "We need one of you to come back to our world," he finally said, deciding that boldness was the best way forward, "as a sort of favour, you understand. There's a situation there that one of your kind could help us with."

"Go to your world?" the Honnie repeated, raising her eyebrows. Her expression told us plainly that she had no taste for that idea.

"Yeah," Natalie took over. "Doesn't really matter who it is as long as they're prepared to help us, and they wouldn't need to stay long either. Do you know of anyone who would be interested in helping? Also, do you know anyone who could open a gateway back to our world for us?"

"No, and no," the Honnie said, with an indifferent shrug.

"You won't help us?" Tommy persisted.

"How could I help you?" the Honnie enquired.

"Would you come back with us?" he asked.

"No," she said simply—no disputing that.

"Oh," Tommy faltered again, and then went on, "well do you know anyone who might?"

"No."

"Jesus Christ," muttered Peter, looking very disheartened.

"Are you religious?" the Honnie enquired, surprising us all.

"Er, no," muttered Peter again, looking abashed. "That's just slang, the way I said it."

"Oh," said the Honnie, considering. "Your language is strange."

"Hang on, let's backtrack a bit here," said Candice. "We know they can open gateways to our world. Do you know where your kind do that? Is it anywhere around here where we can get to?"

The Honnie answered with a single word in her language which sounded to me like 'Lagalia' or something similar enough anyway, and then she went on in English, "It is the capital of this land. We get new humans from places like that."

"Which way is it?" Candice asked.

The Honnie pointed back the way we had come, and I could have groaned aloud—at least five kilometres of walking, and we'd have to do it all again tomorrow.

"That's where we need to go, then," Candice told us. "We can get help when we get there—I hope. Thanks for your help, and for just about murdering the lot of us."

"Wait," the Honnie said, "you cannot leave us now."

"Why not?"

But I knew what was coming, and sure enough...

"You are mine now," she said. "You stay with us."

"But...but..."

We were all protesting now, but the Honnie wasn't hearing any of it. She waved a disregarding hand at us all. "Humans must stay with their abas until they are ready to be processed. That is how it works here."

"What's an aba?" Peter asked lamely. "That word you keep using that we've never heard before."

She repeated the word, and when Peter nodded she said, "It means the Honnie who owns you. That is me now, so you humans cannot just leave us."

"We're screwed," Peter muttered again.

"Is that slang again?" the Honnie enquired.

"Er, yes," said Peter, staring at her in disbelief.

"Oh," she said, and for the first time, she smiled. It wasn't a predatory look now, but a charming look. I felt sure that it was designed to make humans like us feel disarmed and trusting. If so, it would have easily worked on me, had I not known better what Honnies were about. "I just thought you couldn't possibly be...'screwed'." She hesitated slightly before pronouncing the word herself. "You speak a lot of slang, then?" she asked Peter.

"Yeah," he said, still staring at her; he was clearly gobsmacked, and I couldn't blame him.

The younger Honnie interrupted proceedings by saying something loudly in Honnie language. The older Honnie nodded again and gestured us all off the path toward two large shadows in the gloom. The sky had darkened considerably now, and the air was getting very cool indeed. I stared at the two shadows; they were the two male Honnies I had almost forgotten about in my preoccupation with what had just happened to us. The older female Honnie spoke something to both of them, and then added something else to the young girl. The three of them obediently made for the drain and began filing into it, the girl first.

"Come and sit with me," the Honnie told the six of us. "I want to know more about you. We can do introductions and things. My name is May, by the way."

May...she didn't pronounce it exactly like the month sounded, but it was close enough. I wondered if that was her actual name or just an English equivalent...then I decided that in the scheme of things, it didn't make a single bit of difference.

We reluctantly followed the Honnie off the road, past the drain to a small clearing just beyond it. Bushes loomed up all around us, but we were able to sit down on the soft grass in a small circle without being disturbed. May sat down beside me, and I felt my nerve-endings tingle. The idea that I could just reach out and touch an alien creature was somehow a turn-on. I knew it was all sorts of wrong, but I couldn't deny that Honnies were attractive. These two, May and the younger girl, were no exception. I tried very hard to force the feelings away; this Honnie was uncompromising, compassionless and no doubt very dangerous, and yet I was still attracted to her. I should have known better....

The other Honnies soon returned. The two bulky males set to work constructing what looked like a tent around us—some sort of cover anyway. The girl had brought small morsels of food out and was placing small bundles of it before each of us.

"What's this stuff?" Peter asked, picking some of it up in his fingers.

"Gradi," May replied, a word that must have been from their language. "It is good for humans, makes them prime."

"Prime for what, exactly?" he asked, glaring past me at May.

"Just eat it," she snapped. "Stop complaining."

"We have our own food, you know," Tommy told her, indicating the bag he was still wearing. I had forgotten about my own bag in the midst of everything that had gone down. "Can't we just eat that?"

"Is it good food? Does it make you good?"

"We wouldn't have brought it if it didn't."

"You eat gradi first," May told us. "You eat that, and if you are still hungry, you eat your own food later."

I picked some of it up as well. It was difficult to see it, but it felt like sticks of some sort of raw vegetable. I tried one of them, and although it certainly wasn't as good as the food served up on the conveyer belt in the dining room I already missed like an old friend, it was definitely better than some of the vegetables I'd eaten in my time, and so I got stuck into the rest of it. I wondered vaguely if May was making me like it, making me think that it tasted good when it wouldn't otherwise, and then I decided I didn't care. Who really cared if she was invading if she was doing me a favour by doing so. I looked sideways at her to see if she'd picked up on any of these thoughts in my head, but her face was expressionless in the growing darkness.

"Do humans always survive on this sort of stuff here?" Rebecca asked.

"This is always part of the human diet," said May. "Do not worry, you can have something warm when we have a fire set up, but always gradi comes first for humans."

That filled me with relief. A fire—that would be wonderful right now, to have some sort of warmth; I was beginning to shiver.

"While we wait, though," May went on, "I want to know more about you."

Chapter 21: Around the Campfire

The palaver went on well into the night, until my watch said it was after ten o'clock back at home—and here, seeing as they seemed to be on the same time. Before we got into any discussion about ourselves, however, May introduced the other three Honnies. As we talked, the two bulky boys finished their work on what looked like our sleeping quarters—it turned out to be two tents, one on either side of us. It looked like we wouldn't need our own tents but at least the sleeping bags would still come in handy. They then set to work building a small fire in the middle of the circle.

"This is Ingi," May said, gesturing to the girl. "She is my daughter."

"Daughter?" Peter repeated, looking from her to May and back. "But—but—"

I could understand his confusion. Ingi did look a lot like May, as I had noticed earlier, but if she was her daughter, why was her skin so much darker? It was Tommy who voiced the question Peter had been unable to put to words.

"Her father," May replied, as though this were obvious. "He took Penal and I took Ingi; she is my duty."

"Penal?"

"My other daughter."

"Geez, if you were a chick at home and you were named after that particular organ, you'd be racing to have your name changed," Tommy muttered, and he, Peter and Rebecca all began to snigger.

"What happened?" Natalie asked. "It didn't work out with you two or something?"

"Oi, Nat, that's a bit much," said Rebecca reprovingly. "What I wanna know is why did you split your two daughters up? Surely they would have wanted to stay together, or were they too young to know?"

I shook my head, hoping May took that to mean I didn't care if she chose not to answer. May, however, was completely confused by the turn the conversation had taken.

"Penal is his and Ingi is mine," she repeated. "I could have taken Penal instead but it did not really make a difference; they were very young."

"You couldn't have taken both?" Candice asked. "I guess that's not fair on the father if he wanted at least one of them, but in our world, the children often stay together."

"Is that not a bit inefficient?" May asked.

"Not really, if the parent can handle it," said Candice.

May shook her head. "Maybe, but here, every Honnie has two full-breed children. One is the mother's duty and one is the father's duty."

"I guess that's fair," said Rebecca, "but do you see Penal very often?"

May raised her eyebrows, something I noticed she did rather a lot, as though she found us to be a bunch of very odd creatures. "Of course not; she is not my duty."

"But she's your daughter."

"So?" May enquired calmly.

"Forget it," said Natalie flatly. "Come on, guys, it's just their way; maybe they never allow themselves to get too attached to their children. Go back to that other bit you said, May. What did you mean, full-breed children?"

"Every Honnie has to have two," May said. "Some can have more only if they have great enough mind size."

"Is there such a thing as partial-breed children?" Peter asked, his tone joking.

"Half-breed, yes," May corrected. "They are not allowed to breed so no, we don't have other fractions, and we can have as many of them as we can handle."

"Half Honnie, half—what?" Candice asked.

"Human," said May. "These two"—she gestured to the two male Honnies—"are my sons—half-breeds. That one is Dan, and that one is Gob."

"Dan's all right, but Gob?" Tommy whispered. "Wow, he would have been teased something chronic in primary school."

"And their father?"

"Humans."

"Yeah, but where is he?" asked Natalie.

"They had different fathers, and they served their purpose. I used them to strengthen Ingi and me."

"TMI," muttered Peter, looking away from the two full-breed Honnies.

I agreed; that was more than I wanted to know, especially while we were eating. I didn't want to imagine those two tucking into human meat while we were here.

"Enough about us," said May. "You will learn while you are here. I want to know about you humans. Why did you come here?"

"We told you before," said Natalie. "We need one of your kind to do us a favour."

"I remember that. You want a Honnie to go to your world. Why?"

"Well, see, there's this war," said Tommy, picking his words carefully. "Some evil people have taken over the world, and the only way we can regain power is by altering their minds. There's a lot of people to take down, that's why we need your help."

His words sounded feeble by the end, and I knew exactly why. The look on May's face couldn't have been more reproving.

"Is that not a bit—" said May, trying to think of the right word to finish the sentence, and then just giving up. "Surely, if these humans you speak of are powerful enough to take over your world, they must deserve to be allowed to control it?"

"Are you serious?" Peter gaped at her. "Okay, I know you don't know what these people are like, but trust me, they don't have the best interests of the world at heart."

"What are their interests?" May asked blandly.

We all looked at each other. It was Tommy who spoke. "They just wanna put themselves on top, make everyone in the world worship them. See, we have something in our world called magic. These people used to have it, and they believed that it made them the greatest people in the world. We have it now but they intend to get it back off us somehow."

"Then what is your problem?" May asked, still bland as ever. "If you have something they want, they must not have complete control."

"It's what they're prepared to do," said Peter. "They'd just as soon have the six of us, plus all those around us, killed just so they can get what they want."

"Then surely, you only need to protect yourselves," said May, "make sure they cannot kill you, and that will be enough."

Tommy shook his head. "You make it sound so much simpler than it really is. Look, you Honnies have a highly organised world here, as far as I understand. Is that right?"

"Yes, it is," said May. "We all work to a single plan and nobody breaks those rules. We do not even have a word for 'war' in our language; such things are never even thought of."

"Yeah, sure," said Tommy, "and I suppose if one could take over, they wouldn't go changing any of the rules. That makes sense, but what if—and this is hypothetical, you understand—what if someone else took over, someone who had never followed the usual rules here. Let's just say, for the sake of argument, humans took over your world and began turning Honnies into their slaves, so that you couldn't follow your usual rules. Let's just say that humans had the power to keep Honnies in check and not be affected by their mind tricks. Let's just say that many Honnies, innocent Honnies, were killed just for the sake of it. How does that sound to you?"

"Humans could never do that," she said dismissively.

"I know that," said Tommy. "I know humans could never pull that off. Fine, let's imagine a third breed of being exists, one more powerful than either Honnies or humans. What would you feel if that breed came into your world, rounded up every Honnie, human and half-breed and brought them into servitude?"

He had done it. He had finally found a way to break that annoying passivity May had kept all this time. She went very pale indeed and closed her eyes tight for a moment. Some of her thoughts must have been picked up by Ingi, for she made a low, guttural sound in her throat, a sound that sounded terrifying in its menace. The six of us cringed away from her, but one look from May put Ingi back in her place.

"We do not speak of that," May hissed, glaring at Tommy. She then shook her head and seemed to force herself back into that state of passivity before she spoke again. "Did you say," she said to Tommy, "that innocent humans are dying in your world too?"

"Yeah, many of them have and many more will," said Rebecca, "but backtrack a bit, May. Why did you react like that a moment ago?"

May blanched again and shook her head. "Do not talk of those things."

"Fine," said Peter. "Shut up about that, you guys. So what do you think, May? What Tommy just described is more or less what has happened in our world. We're the resistance against this evil force, trying to protect everyone else from whatever mad plans they're trying to do. We used to have a system as well, not like yours but one of our own. These people have turned it all upside-down so much so that people like us have been turned into outcasts. It's way too far over our heads now to change it, which is why we need your help."

"You want one of our kind to come back to your world and find a way to take down this group of humans you speak of so that you can work to get your world back to the way it was. Is that what you are saying?"

"Exactly," said Tommy, looking relieved.

"You need to tell me something else, though."

"What's that?"

"Why should a Honnie agree to do this for you?" she asked. "What you say sounds dangerous, even for one of our kind. Not just that, but any Honnie who agrees to this would have to take a lot of time out of his or her life to go back with you. What makes you think any Honnie would be interested in doing that for you?"

"When you say it like that, nothing," said Natalie, "not unless Honnies can feel a bit of goodness in their heart and help the little guy out a bit."

"Did you not describe this as a favour?" May asked Natalie. "Honnies do not do favours, not for each other and especially not for humans. We only do our duty to our kind; we have no interest in what transpires in your world."

"What about trades?" Tommy asked. "Surely Honnies have some sort of system of trade; it's just about impossible to run an efficient society without it."

"Trade is unnecessary when everyone does what is expected of him or her without looking for payment," May told him. "It is only necessary for you humans because you never do anything for anyone without something in it for yourself. Any Honnie who has ever had a human knows this well. We only ever trade in lives."

"But surely, if we could find some way to make it worth your while," said Peter, "surely you should at least consider it."

"No," said May flatly. "There is nothing you can offer to Honnies that would make it worth my while. I cannot go with you anyway; I have business here. I will be more free when these three"—she gestured to Ingi, Dan and Gob—"are no longer my duty, but I do not know when that will be. There is something else as well that you should know now: The only Honnies allowed to enter your world at all are those qualified to be collectors, and I am not qualified to do that."

"Damn it," muttered Peter.

"Okay, fine," said Tommy, "but May, would you be interested in trying to help us once these three are 'no longer your duty'?"

"I just told you, I cannot go to your world."

"Why couldn't you become a collector so that you can come back with us?" Candice asked.

"You are asking me to change my whole life for you," she said, "for humans. It is laughable to me. How would you make it worth the effort?"

"Well what sort of repayment would you…" Natalie asked, and then the answer came on its own. "Guys, I think the only way to make her happy will be if she's allowed to eat one of us."

Everyone around the circle cringed at the idea, but May looked unimpressed. "That is going to happen anyway. I will not waste humans; it is normally so difficult to get them, and I have six for nothing. Any other Honnie would have used you already, so consider yourselves lucky, and it still does not answer my original question. You can offer nothing that would make it worth the effort."

"We're in trouble," Tommy muttered.

"Only one, though, not all of us," said Peter. "If it's only one of us who has to die, then maybe we can give that some thought. I guess—I guess I could make the sacrifice if it came to that."

"To hell you will," I snapped at him. I couldn't bear the idea of any one of us sacrificing our lives, but not my brother, not so soon on the heels of losing Nicole.

"Come on guys, let's be realistic," he said fiercely. "What are the chances of us getting out of this if I don't? Remember how Lisa gave up not just her life, but her soul, just so that we could get the Sien-Leoard Crystal? Imagine where we'd be if she hadn't done that for us?"

"He's got a point," said Natalie, who had gone very pale indeed in the firelight. "May, we could possibly agree to that condition—possibly. Would you give us time to think about it?"

"Perhaps," she said, "but in the meantime, I will continue as though you humans will not be going back to your world."

"Continue with what?" Peter asked bitterly.

"Making you prime," she said, "so that we can get the most out of you."

"I don't wanna know what that involves," muttered Tommy darkly.

"Wait, May," said Natalie hurriedly. "Surely we can agree to something on this. How much time are you going to give us?"

"I do not know yet," said May. "However long it takes, perhaps. You humans are really quite lucky though; many Honnies would just take you as you are. Not only that, but Ingi is in the final stages of her development, and what we are doing is a round trip which, by the time we return to Malia where we live, she will be ready to graduate. We pass through Lagalia in our travels, so if we can agree to something before then, I may consider helping you, but I doubt that will happen."

"Wow, we really are lucky, then," said Peter.

"But you still think you may not be allowed to help us?" Natalie persisted.

"I think so," she said. "I could only become qualified if I overpower one of their collectors. Even if I can do that, though, I probably would not be allowed to take you back with me; they would take you humans and distribute you like all the other humans they bring through."

"Something else I don't wanna think about," muttered Peter darkly.

"Thanks, May," said Natalie. "Trust me, we are counting our blessings, even if you haven't actually given us much encouragement."

"Okay," said May, looking at Ingi, and then around at the rest of us. "I want you humans to eat everything you have in front of you, and then you will go to sleep in there." She pointed at the tent behind us, and then at the one in front. "The four of us will sleep in there," she gestured back towards the drain.

"You sleep in a drain?" Peter asked, raising his eyebrows.

"Oh yes, it is very comfortable," she said, "but not for humans. You sleep out here."

"Do you hear us complaining?" he asked.

"Most of what you have said tonight has been complaining. We will wake you up in the morning when it is time to eat again, and then we will be walking for the morning. I am sorry about that, but I did not know I would have humans with me, so I could not be prepared for you. I will stop in Pralia tomorrow to get what we need for you."

"If you say so," said Tommy, shrugging.

"Do not go walking tonight," said May. "I could hold you all down but I really don't like doing that. I only control when I have to, but please do not make it necessary for me to control you."

"Again, we appreciate it," said Tommy.

There was silence for a while after that as the ten of us got stuck into our food. For us humans, when the gradi had been consumed, Tommy opened his bag and began passing around sausages on sticks, which we each held close to the fire to cook them. It was Candice who ended up breaking the silence.

"May, you keep talking about how Ingi is going to graduate soon. What about those two? What happens with them?"

"You mean Dan and Gob?" asked May. "They will be ready to graduate soon too, but it is less important, since they are only half-breeds."

"They have a lower place in society?"

"Yes, but still a very important place. That is why there is no limit to how many half-breed children we are allowed to have; there is always a use for them. If any of them turn out to be useless, they are demoted to the level of humans."

"And what about Ingi?" asked Rebecca.

"We have not yet found her great strength," said May, sounding a little disappointed by the admission. "She may need to work her way up with assistant positions for a while until she has found a proper speciality."

"Speciality?"

"Yes, every Honnie has to have one."

"Sounds a bit like what we call a career," said Natalie, "except we can change during our lives."

"We can too, but we usually choose not to," said May. "Once a Honnie has found their great strength, they normally stay with it for all their lives."

"What's your—er—speciality, then?" Peter asked.

"Educating," said May, "putting knowledge in the heads of under-qualified Honnies."

"A teacher," laughed Peter. "Wow, no wonder I was starting to feel like I was back at school."

"Shut up, Peter," snapped Natalie.

"Is that why you have Ingi?" Candice asked. "You're filling her head with knowledge?"

"No," said May, looking shocked. "Ingi is my daughter. Every Honnie is responsible for one child, in addition to their speciality. I do put knowledge in her head too, but not as part of my work."

"Okay," said Candice, shrugging. "I guess you must be very smart then; that was your great strength?"

"Yes," said May. "I absorb all I can from every person I meet, no matter their breed, and remember all of it. It is the reason why I can speak your language, and some other human languages from your world."

"For which we are very grateful," muttered Peter, "although according to Smiley, you could have communicated with us mentally if you couldn't speak our language."

"That is true, but it would have frightened you if you are not used to it," said May. "You humans are very different from any other I have heard of, because you seem to know about us. I will still use you but until then, I will not take away your independence. What is Smiley?"

"A person…a *human*," Natalie amended. "He was the one who first told us about Honnies. He met one thirty years ago when he came to our world to collect humans. That Honnie left with a lot of humans but because he was helping the Woodwards, Smiley wasn't one of them."

"That is why you came, then?" May asked. "You believed that because it worked once, it may work again?"

"It's a reasonable assumption, isn't it?" Peter asked.

"Maybe, although it might cost you your life," said May, not a hint of remorse in her voice.

"Never mind that," said Tommy quickly. "May, what about Dan and Gob? Do they have a great strength too?"

"They are half-breeds," said May simply. "Half-breeds go into construction. They build the world we live in. You can see the size of them; it is what half-breeds are made for."

"I see," he said, looking away from the Honnies and back to his dinner.

Another silence followed this, during which we all finished the last of our food. May was still sitting on my right, and as I ate, I thought of what she had said before about not liking to control people. If that were true, it meant we would still have a small amount of freedom, although I also knew that she'd make us come back to her if we tried to do a runner. She was staring into the fire as she ate, not looking around at any of us, but my eyes kept returning to her every few seconds. That strange attraction was still there, and I still wondered if May had, or would, pick up on it. I tried to speak her name inside my own head, to make myself think of her in as much detail as I could, wondering if doing so would get her attention. If she had noticed anything at all, she pretended not to. I felt slightly disappointed by that, knowing full well that I ought to be grateful; I had no idea if it would make a difference if May knew what was going on inside my head, but I doubted her reaction would be a good one if she did. No doubt having human interest would disgust her.

On May's other side, Ingi was eating her dinner (slivers of some sort of meat they had cooked on the fire) just as inattentively as her mother. Past her, Dan and Gob were looking, if possible, even more absent than the two female Honnies. I wondered if half-breed Honnies only had a fraction of a Honnie's regular intelligence, and supposed it must be so if they were regarded as only fit enough to go into construction. All they would need is to be able to communicate, which would depend on whoever was supervising them, and the ability to follow orders which, based on the way they had set up our tents and built our fire, these two definitely had.

Dinner ended soon enough and we were ordered into our tents, the three girls in one, and Peter, Tommy and me in the other. The six of us took what I thought of as night clothes (not pyjamas but something that would be comfortable to sleep in) from the bag Peter had been carrying and separated to change in our own tents. I followed the other two into our tent, having a look around as best I could as I did. There were three mats and three blankets, and that was it. Camping, that's what this was like, payback for the camping we hadn't done on Rock Haulter. They didn't look very comfortable and I could tell by their faces that the others agreed. Once we had changed, we left the tent to retrieve the sleeping bags from my bag, which had been set down with the other two bags between the two tents.

"Wonder if they'll let us wash ourselves," Tommy muttered. "Do you reckon humans would be tastier if they're clean or dirty?"

"Probably dirty," Peter replied. "At least, smelly dirty; they wouldn't want to be eating actual dirt off us, and blimey, this is a great topic to be discussing after dark."

I didn't say anything. I certainly shared their feelings, but didn't see a point complaining about it. After all, the way things were looking, we might never get back to that life, the life we had always known, the life we had always taken for granted. I placed my sleeping bag down on top of the mat closest to the entrance of the tent and settled into it, listening to what was happening outside. Listening, and thinking—thinking about May. I now had time to wonder if, at some point, she had used the love beam on me. Smiley hadn't said very much about that, how it would feel for a human to be affected by it. In fact, he hadn't said anything about it; we'd only found out about it from his memories later. I thought I probably hadn't been, though; my imagination portrayed that as a much greater obsession than what I was going through. All I could think was that humans were probably supposed to be attracted to Honnies, so that Honnies would have an easier time rounding us up, as if they needed any more advantages. As for May, what could I say? I tried to chastise myself for feeling the way I did, reminding myself that not ten feet away lay another girl, one I wanted much more deeply than I could ever want a Honnie. It was true, but it didn't change the way I felt.

I tried again, as I had at dinner, to get May's attention by calling her name inside my head, not believing that it would do any good though. What did I have to do? I tried to imagine it the way Smiley had described it: May's mind, an enormous bubble, with all of our minds, tiny little bubbles, floating around within it. What did that mean? I supposed for one thing, it meant that Ingi, whose mind would also be inside May's for the sake of protection, would be able to swallow any of our minds from the inside, assuming her mind was big enough; and probably it was, for one of us at least. For another thing, it meant that if I wanted to get May's attention, I would have to make my thoughts penetrate her mind instead of floating around inside my own bubble. To do that, I would have to, somehow, project my thoughts outward; open my mind and the bubble it represented so that my thoughts spilled out of it.

I didn't know if I could even do such a thing. The idea was certainly a scary one, and no doubt with consequences I couldn't guess at. How did I know that my thoughts would only reach May? What if Ingi, Dan, Gob or, heaven forbid, one of the others picked up on them? It didn't make sense that they should, but that didn't mean they wouldn't. I supposed it was a risk I would have to take…why, though? That was the question I simply couldn't answer, even to myself. Why did I have to try? Why did I have to get May's attention at all? Common sense told me it would be much safer not to, to just stay in the background, as I had managed to do for most of the evening. Why draw attention to myself? There was only one reason: Because I wanted May's attention. A sick, demented part of me actually wanted her attention. There was no particular reason why I wanted it. What would I want to say to her if I had her attention? All I knew was that I wanted her to notice me in some way unique from all the others. There was a practical reason, of course, and it wasn't until much later that I would consider it, but for the time being, I could only conclude that it was that sick, attracted and uncontrollable part of me.

"What are we gonna do about this, guys?" Tommy asked quietly. "Nobody at home will know what's happened to us if we don't return. They're depending on us and it looks like we're gonna let them down."

"What are we gonna do?" Peter repeated the question. "There's only one thing we can do; keep trying to reason with these—these things. If we fail, then I guess we won't live to see the result back at home."

"Wonderful optimism, Pete."

"It's the truth, though. You saw the look on Marc's face back there; he knows the chances of us getting back now are barely there, and he would have communicated that to the others. Geez, I wish I'd said a better goodbye to Siobhan."

"You didn't say goodbye to your girlfriend? Wow, I couldn't spend long enough with Jessica."

"I did, but she thought I was only going so that I could get away from her. Damn women."

Again, I didn't participate in their discussion. I agreed with Peter, of course, but my mind was far from worrying about what was happening at home, far from even the reason why we had come here in the first place. My mind made up, a decision what I wanted to do, I pictured May's mind again, a large bubble, with my mind, a much smaller bubble, inside it. I thought hard, thought the words, 'come and see me, May, come and see me', and imagined them as little streams of bubbles issuing from my mind, the bubble representing which had been punctured slightly to allow the thoughts to escape and float loosely inside May's mind. Nothing happened right away, so I kept imagining the same thing again and again, trying to amplify the thoughts as I did, trying to send them in the direction I knew the drain to be, as though I thought May would pick them up that way.

I got nothing for a long time, and more than once was on the verge of giving up and allowing sleep to take me, for I could feel sleepiness creeping up on me. The hours of walking I'd done earlier in the day were also coming back to me, my legs remembering the aching as though it were only yesterday, to use an old cliché (it was today, remember?) and I knew they would be bloody stiff when I woke up in the morning. Eventually, however, I felt something that seemed to me to mean that at least one of the Honnies was aware of what I was doing. An external thought crept into my head, similar to those the Sien-Leoard Crystal had given me but different in one crucial way. If I had not been both familiar with external thoughts and knowledgeable of the mental abilities of the Honnies, I would have easily mistaken it as one of my own. Nevertheless, the power it had over me was such that I reacted to it as though it were one of my own.

Very quietly so as not to wake the other two, who seemed to have fallen asleep, I slid out of my sleeping bag and rolled sideways off my mat toward the flap of the tent. I crawled carefully out of it and straightened up, looking around. The moon had come out and, though not full, was bright enough to illuminate most of the scene around me. For what it was worth, the moon and stars here looked exactly the same as they had at home; if anything, they were even clearer. The campsite had been completely cleared up, and the dark mass across from me was surely the tent in which Candice, Natalie and Rebecca were sleeping. I didn't stay there but walked quietly back towards the path, careful not to rustle any bushes as I passed them. I couldn't recall the exact position of the drain, but knew it to be fairly close to where I was. Not that it mattered, for as the bushes opened up around me and the moon shone through again, showing me the path stretching into the distance in either direction, one of the Honnies intercepted me.

"You have a very interesting mind," May told me, sounding amused; in the moonlight, she looked almost gaunt.

"You were reading my mind then?" I asked, unsure what answer I wanted to hear more.

"Reading?" May asked, raising her eyebrows in a gesture that was becoming characteristic. "Well perhaps, in the same way that you might read a sign if someone slams your face into it."

"Good analogy," I muttered, slightly amused in spite of myself. "It certainly worked then?"

"Obviously it worked. Are you not a normal human?"

"I've just had a lot of not-so-normal experiences."

"What else can you do?"

"Nothing, I don't think," I admitted. She didn't need to know about the inter-dimensional perception or the crazy dreams. "I expect any human can do it if they understand well enough how the whole mind thing goes."

"How did you learn so much?" she asked. "Is this all because of this Smiley human you mentioned?"

"Yeah, pretty much," I said. "He was a very talented person; he could travel between our world and this one at his own leisure, open a gateway whenever he felt like it. He only came here once and got trapped, but whoever the Honnie was who kept him told him a lot of how it works."

"Why did you not bring him with you?" she asked. "It would have greatly improved your chances of returning to your world if you did."

"I don't think he could take other people with him," I said, not bothering to mention that he was probably dead by now.

"Oh, I see," she said, taking half a step closer to me. We were about two feet apart, and I had to look up slightly to see her face. She did look very pretty in the moonlight, even if she did look slightly gaunt, and I felt particularly uncomfortable thinking it, wondering if my thoughts were still filtering out of my mind and into hers.

"What did you want me for anyway?" she asked me suddenly. "If you are going to try to reason with me, you are wasting your time. Humans just do not understand our perspective, especially those from your world."

I shrugged awkwardly. Now that I was here, I couldn't even remember why I'd wanted to see her. My desperate thoughts of wanting her attention seemed rather feeble. "I guess I just wanted to see if it worked; maybe it might be useful to know."

"Perhaps it might," she said, and sighed. "I really hope you humans are not going to be too much trouble for me. It was definitely not what I expected to find, coming out this way."

"Well at least you can find a use for us if we are too much trouble," I said rather sarcastically, knowing May would take me perfectly seriously. "You know, I'm curious. What exactly were you expecting to find out this way?"

"Nothing at all," she said simply. "Perhaps other groups like mine but nothing more than that. It is just to give Ingi the life experience she needs to be able to graduate."

"What happens to her when she graduates?" I asked, thinking I could probably guess the answer.

"She earns rights: the right to do duty to her speciality, as soon as she can discover it; the right to breed; the right to obtain humans. Basically, the right to be an adult. No Honnie can have these things unless they have graduated, even if they grow old."

"Okay," I said, thinking that our world needed something like that to deal with the large number of idiots we bred. "So Ingi is almost ready to graduate then? What will you do when she does?"

"I have to let her go; I have no right to keep her anymore. We may still see each other, perhaps even work together, but I cannot be her aba anymore, not unless she wants me to."

"You mean you can't keep her inside your mind?"

"No. That will be a good thing for me, though, because her mind is getting very big now, and difficult for me to keep hold of. Very soon I will need to increase my own mind power or I would not be able to hold her anymore."

"How would you—oh," I groaned. "Is that where we come in?"

"Maybe. One of you humans will be enough to both give me what I need to hold her until she's ready to graduate, and give her enough to protect her after she has graduated. Educated humans always provide more strength than the ones we breed."

"Do you have any—any—preferences?" I asked, barely able to get the word out.

"Do I want any of you humans in particular? Is that what you mean?"

"Yeah."

"I do not know. Neither me nor Ingi have tasted any of you yet."

My mouth went very dry at that last word. "Tasted?"

"Yes, but I do not think it matters very much; any of you will be fine; all of you will be better. Perhaps you will be the best, though, since I already know how strong your mind is."

That was all I needed. My knees almost gave way, and I had to grab May by the shoulder to prevent myself going down. She barely flinched but allowed me to use her to straighten myself up again. There it was, the first physical contact between myself and the Honnie, and it felt both extraordinary and utterly plain at the same time. That contact had brought us much closer now, so that I had to crane my neck to look up at her, and I couldn't see much of her face as she was looking down at me.

"Can you realistically think of any scenario where you might agree to help us?" I asked, a little desperately. "Anything at all?"

"No," she said flatly. "I am happy with my life. I do not seek any more than I have. You want me to throw it all away for a different life, and in return, I get to come back home to nothing at all. You tell me if I can think of a reason to help you."

She expected me to have no comeback, but I did, because she had touched on something very personal. "Yes, because sometimes, you have to put the bigger picture ahead of your own happiness. When the war began, my father and his father gave up everything they had, and when they were allowed to come home, one of them was dead and the other had nowhere to go. It took him almost ten years to get his life back on track, but he knew that was how it would be before he left, and he still went to do what he could. He did it so that countless other people could be happy, even if he couldn't. Just imagine the difference you could make to hundreds of millions of people if you helped, how happy you could make them."

"And that is supposed to help us?"

I sighed. "That's the difference, is it? Honnies only care about the little circle of world directly around them, no concern for the greater good?"

"Many humans are like that too," she pointed out. "At least, that is what I have heard, and Honnies do care about the greater good, but only for our own kind."

There was no point arguing about it with her; it would do no good. If anything, it would put her off-side and only make it harder for all of us. She had her Honnie logic and unless I could find a way to understand it, I wouldn't have much chance of finding a way of convincing her that it would be worth it. Whatever she said, I honestly believed that a Honnie who was capable of stepping this far from the norm just by not devouring all six of us already could be capable of understanding our perspective, if we could find the right way to explain it to her.

I thought for a moment of turning and heading back to the tent, but no sooner had the thought occurred to me that I felt, once again, that feeling of obsession grip me. It was just May and I here, just the two of us; all around me, there was nothing but silence and darkness. The other five were probably asleep, and the other three Honnies were clearly down the drain doing who knew what. I knew I ought to feel tired, but I didn't, not one bit. All I wanted to do was stay with May, what we did didn't matter to me. Oh, John, you poor dude.

"What are you thinking?" she asked me suddenly. "Are you wanting to go and get some sleep? You will need it; we will be doing a lot of walking tomorrow morning."

"I know that, but I don't really wanna just yet," I said, surprised that she had even bothered to ask when she had the ability to work it out for herself. "I'm not tired, and I'll keep the others awake if I go back."

"So what are you going to do then?" she asked. "I do not want you wandering off."

I shrugged. "Anything in particular you want me to do? I suppose you could just make me do whatever."

She shook her head slowly, considering. Then, taking me by surprise, she put a hand on one of my shoulders. Her touch was gentle enough, but very firm. "Will you let me do something?"

"Are you saying I have a choice?"

"I like it to be your choice."

"Okay, what do you wanna do?" I asked, nervous and excited in equal measure.

"May I taste you?"

"Taste——" my throat went dry once again, but she still had me by the shoulder and prevented me from so much as wobbling. "You—taste—not eat, though?"

"Not eat, just taste."

I stared up at her shadowy face. The sensible part of me knew full-well that, since the choice was mine, I should decline it immediately. There could be nothing safe about having a Honnie taste me, but the greater part of me thought otherwise. Maybe it was dangerous, maybe not. The fact was I wanted to try it, or let her try it. I wanted to get close to her, and surely there could be nothing closer than this; well, maybe a few things, but this was much more than I had expected. It was looking into her face that made my mind up in the end.

"All right then, do your worst."

"It will not hurt you, I promise."

"I'll be the judge of that. Just do what you have to do."

What happened over the next ten seconds or so was one of the weirdest things I'd felt in a long time. It was definitely not nice, definitely not pleasant, definitely not comfortable, and yet it was very arousing and most definitely enjoyable in both the physical closeness and intimacy of the act. May put her hands under both my shoulders and lifted me up so that my toes came an inch off the ground and our faces were on a level—she didn't have to strain in the slightest to manage it. I had several thoughts in quick succession; she would lick my face like a dog, or perhaps she would prick my skin with that sharp tongue I'd seen on the Honnie in Smiley's memories; I hadn't seen her tongue at all while she had been talking so couldn't verify if it was as sharp as his had been. When she pressed my whole body against hers so that our faces were almost touching, I thought she would lick my lips as a lover would, or perhaps actually kiss me. I felt sure of that a moment later when our lips met, but what came next was something I couldn't possibly have anticipated; I felt her tongue slide into my mouth, too quickly for me to notice its shape; it slid right over my tongue and down my throat.

I gagged and spluttered and struggled for a moment, but May wasn't having any of that; she tightened one arm around my back and used her other hand to hold the back of my head still. I tried desperately to relax, hoping that maybe it would make the sensation easier to handle, and in a way, it worked. My throat still felt extremely clogged up and breathing was impossible, but as long as I didn't think too much about what was happening in that part of my body, I could appreciate the position I was in. There was much more enjoyment to be had in thinking about how close I was to May, how closely she was holding me against her. I raised my arms, which up to that point had been stiffly by my sides, and put them around May's shoulders, pulling myself even closer against her. She made a soft noise in her throat as I felt her respond by tightening her own hold on me. Apparently, Honnies were not quite immune to intimacy as I had originally thought.

Somehow, the whole ordeal had turned into something much more meaningful than mere tasting, as it had been to begin with for May at least, but it had to end. I hadn't been able to breathe at all since May's tongue had clogged my throat and now I was feeling the effects of that in my head. I loosened my hold and she followed suit a moment later. I felt her tongue retract, first from my throat and then sliding back out of my mouth and back into her own. I could see her face now; even by the moonlight I could tell that not only had she enjoyed it more than she had expected, but she had apparently felt that brief moment of intimacy just as I had. It could have been my imagination telling me that, but I didn't think so.

"That was," she began, then apparently unsure how to finish she merely shook her head.

"What you wanted?" I enquired, still a little breathless, and wanting my feet back on the ground; she still hadn't let go of me completely.

"I—I suppose so," she said, shrugging. "You do taste very nice."

"Cheers," I said, a little sarcastically. "Okay, after that, I reckon I am ready for bed now."

"I think I am too, after that," she agreed, setting me back on my feet at last.

I needed a moment to steady myself, but once that feeling past, I said good night to May and headed back to the tent. I was stunned by what had just happened. I'd definitely achieved what I'd wanted that night; I'd definitely got her attention in a big way, taken her as much by surprise as I had myself.

It was as I lay there that I came to realise how much I had achieved already that night, and how important it could possibly be. Firstly, May knew of me, and in her mind, I would now be set slightly apart from the others because of what I'd done that night. Secondly, she was not immune to desire; it may not be quite the same as human desire, but if it was there, it provided a small amount of leverage. That could be more dangerous than anything else if May decided it had to be removed, but I would worry about that later. Thirdly, and most importantly, I was now in a better position to bargain with her than any of the others. If this Honnie was the trigger required to initiate the three momentous steps, I was the one who had to pull that trigger.

Chapter 22: Through the Wire

Sleep took me very quickly that night, once I had exhausted my circling thoughts, and when it did, I dreamt of my third floor room back in the now-defunct Woodward base. It was sad to return to it, because now that I had only memories of that room, I had to acknowledge how attached to it I had once been. That had been my first port of call after I had escaped from the Hammersons' basement after that harrowing ordeal, during which we had all been tortured and Amelia had been raped. It had been on that bed where I had lost my virginity to Tulip, just two days before her death, and it had been on that bed that Serena and I had had most of our good times; even that sinful act with Lena had happened in there. In the sad times I'd had while using that room, like the day I'd learnt of my mother's identity, it had been that room where I had gone for comfort.

It was perhaps odd that I would be brought back to that room now, but then perhaps it wasn't. I'd been dealing with homesickness for most of the time I'd spent in the Honnie world (most of eight hours or however long it had been), knowing that I may never see it again, and of course, I would never see that room again even if we did manage to return. Why wouldn't my life be flashing before my eyes now...? In the dream, I wasn't alone in the room. I was accompanied by the girls I had at some point been attracted to; Natalie, Tulip, Serena, Lena, Amelia, Stella, and back to Natalie again, the only one deserving of coming around twice.

I was woken by a cool breeze striking my face from directly above, although in my sleep-addled brain I didn't make that realisation right away. I didn't have time to wonder how that was possible, how the wind could blow directly downward like that; how, even if it could, it could reach me in my third-floor room, nor did I have time to consider the idea that someone above me was causing that sensation somehow. It was two sudden pressures, one around my legs just below my waist and the other around my shoulders, tight around my neck, that brought me quickly to full wakefulness and drew all my attention. Once I was fully awake, I knew exactly what was happening: Someone had picked me up, was holding me across their body and moving quickly in long, leaping bounds.

Horror rose inside me; no human was capable of this. I tried to struggle but the arms around me were too tight. I kicked out with my legs but my feet only made contact with bushes. I opened my mouth but only got as far as a croak before a small but incredibly strong hand slid under my jaw and jammed it firmly shut. My arms were trapped by my sides, leaving me with no method of defence whatsoever. Nevertheless I struggled fruitlessly, using every ounce of strength I had, knowing it was hopeless but unable to help myself. May, Ingi and the two half-breeds must have been asleep; some Honnie had wandered by, sensed some humans in the area and decided to help himself. The desperation of the situation made it all too clear.

It only lasted perhaps twenty seconds, mind you a very long twenty seconds for me. It ended very quickly when the Honnie leapt into a horizontal dive, dropping me to the ground and coming down someway in front of me. I came down painfully but fortunately in a position where I could roll along for a few feet before scrambling back to my feet, ready for just about anything and knowing that I could do nothing to defend myself. I had been dropped in a fairly small clearing that allowed a small amount of moonlight to reach the ground. I looked around me, trying to register as much as I could in the very limited time I knew I had. It was way too dark to see if there was anything I could use as a weapon, or anywhere I could hide—not that that would work, I knew full well.

Too late to even try, though. The Honnie was back on his feet; he leapt at me in a horrifying bound, and it was a considerable miracle that no contact was made. I dived sideways, sprawling on the dirty ground, and the Honnie soared right over the top of me. I scrambled quickly to my feet, but the Honnie had recovered even more quickly, and in the instant before he dived, I saw him clearly in the moonlight. No, I saw *her* clearly in the moonlight. I had been wrong; it hadn't been a passing Honnie at all, but a resident Honnie, waiting patiently for the best moment to claim her prize. Whether or not May could be convinced to help us would be a moot point, if she couldn't stop her daughter from devouring us.

Ingi came at me again. I sprawled sideways, hoping she'd jump right over me again, but no such luck. She landed right on top of me, her small hands pinning both my shoulders down, smacking the back of my head hard on the ground. Stars popped in front of my eyes and I struggled pointlessly to push her off. I could feel her knees digging painfully into my thighs, feel her strong fingers gripping my shoulders as though to break them, feel her hot breath on my face. She raised my shoulders sharply off the ground, then just as sharply through them down again, causing my head to hit the ground a second time.

I wasn't sure if I blanked out for a moment but the next thing I knew, I was off the ground. Ingi had apparently raised herself off me and got herself into a standing position before pulling me up with her. She was the same height as May which meant that she could just lift me right off the ground without me towering over her. In the moonlight, I saw her face again, more clearly this time; her expression contained neither anger nor dislike, but merely concentration, determination and a terrifying hunger. I opened my mouth, forgetting in my panic that she couldn't understand a word I said anyway, but before I could even make a sound, she jerked me forward so that my jaw smashed into her shoulder, shutting it for good. The explosion of pain in my face could only mean that it was broken.

Even with the pain, though, I continued to struggle with her, trying to kick her and push myself away from her, anything to possibly unbalance her. For maybe a fraction of a moment, I thought it had worked, for as she made to grip my right shoulder again, I was able to evade her hand. The result of this was no doubt far worse than whatever she had been about to do to me. She jerked my other shoulder very roughly (I felt another crack in it and thought it might be dislocated) and, gripping my left shoulder tightly, wrapped her other arm around my waist and wrenched.

My world exploded with white-hot pain as I clearly felt all the nerves and veins around my shoulder snap. Everything below my left elbow seemed to be on fire; I attempted to move my fingers on that hand and got no response. The pain was so intense that I didn't even notice that Ingi had let me go until I hit the ground again, but as I fell on my back, the moonlight granted me a good look of what she was doing, and what she had done to me.

To my complete and utter horror, Ingi was holding something long and dripping in her hand. As I watched, she ran it over her lips, using her tongue to strip it down—her extraordinarily sharp tongue, which I now saw for the first time. Three strips later there was nothing left of my arm but bones and a few fragments of flesh, which she wasted no time in cleaning up, apparently believing I was debilitated beyond escape—a correct assumption. So, the Enlightener was right, I thought dazedly. Who woulda thunk it.

The pain was too huge for my brain to fully register it, and so my mind did the only thing it could: I retreated into myself and waited for it to be over. Ingi had destroyed my arm very efficiently; it would be a matter of seconds before she would be back to finish the job, assuming blood loss didn't finish it first. I had landed on my back, but my head had rolled sideways slightly, away from the fatal injury. The moonlight revealed the dirty ground that would be the last thing I saw, and I marvelled at a small rock inches from my nose. It looks a bit like a nipple, I thought dazedly.

Ingi did not return. Just in the moment I thought she must surely come at me, I heard her shriek in—in what? Anger? Dismay? I thought the second one seemed more likely. A series of other sounds followed this; something dropping to the ground, something that seemed to clatter; a rustling sound that, I thought, was Ingi sitting down on the path a few feet away from me; more footsteps, and that was when I realised what must be happening. Was I saved? Did this actually mean that I would live after tonight? I honestly had no idea, yet I couldn't stop my hopes from raising in spite of myself, even while most of my body was begging to be put out of its misery.

Something wrapped around me and lifted me off the ground. I let out a yell for a moment before a quiet coolness spread through my body. It wasn't quite fainting—I knew what that felt like—but this was something completely new to me. Or, almost completely new: The only time I'd felt it prior to now had been immediately after my thinking cap had exploded, only this was much more thorough. I very vaguely felt a great wind striking my face and knew that I was on the move again, that I was being carried away, back towards the campsite or further away from it. A thought entered my head, and the moment it did, I understood what must have happened: Ingi's attempt to dispose of me had been thwarted at the last moment by May, and it was she who was carrying me to safety —or at least attempting to, if I could hold out that long. All this in a moment before I really did faint.

* * *

Apparently, I was extremely lucky to have lived at all. When I came around after who knew how long, I was in such a world of blurs that I might as well have been drunk. In fact I later supposed I was heavily drugged but at that point, the only thought I was capable of mustering up was that I liked floating. I drifted off again and the second time I came around, things were a little clearer to me. I became aware that I was lying down on a fairly hard bed in a place that I had never been before. I was also aware that I couldn't move a muscle.

The third period of consciousness was still clearer. I was able to make sense of the sounds and sights around me now. I was obviously in a hospital—it looked so similar to a hospital from my own world that I quite forgot where I was for a moment. Their technology was certainly right up there with ours, perhaps because they learnt all they needed from the humans they brought through before destroying them. There were other beds around me and people in them, but the ones who could talk were speaking Honnie language. It was this that made me remember exactly where I was, and a moment later, how I got there. The memory brought on a blast of pain that I hadn't felt at all until then, as though it was entirely caused by my mind rather than the physical injury.

My entire left arm below the shoulder was on fire, the shock of the injury having well and truly passed in the time I had been unconscious; I opened my mouth to scream, found that I couldn't, and that made me remember what else Ingi had done to me. I screamed anyway, a closed mouth scream that barely made a sound and sounded extremely pathetic to my own ears. Fortunately, someone did hear, however; I saw a female Honnie pass close beside me and press a button on a drip which, following the lines, I saw was connected to my right hand. It must have been a damn strong drug, whatever it was, because the pain dimmed within ten seconds or so, taking most of my perception with it. I drifted off again.

That sleep was a short one. I wasn't sure how I knew that but somehow I did. When I woke up again, it was because a Honnie, who seemed to be a nurse or doctor, was pulling the infusion out of my arm. I protested; wasn't it a little premature for that? She looked at me witheringly for a moment and I realised that not only did she not speak English, but I couldn't communicate with her by the mind either. That would only work with May, since she was the one holding me. I had forgotten about May until then; she had brought me here, to this hospital, wherever it was. I should have been grateful to her, but somehow I wasn't. It was hard to disregard the fact that May had allowed Ingi even the slightest chance to attack me. Furthermore, she hadn't stayed with me or made any appearance since the accident.

All these were bitter thoughts but above all of them, I knew that reaching out to her now was the only way I could return to my friends. I remembered what I had done the last time I had sent a thought to May and attempted to do it again, ignoring the Honnie beside me; she didn't seem to give two hoots whether I was paying attention to her or not. *Where are you?* I thought these words as hard as I could, sending them out into the bubble of May's mind, not waiting for a response but continuing to send, again and again. Whatever May was doing, wherever she was, if she still had me in her mind and if this was working, she couldn't possibly ignore the force of these words.

Yet there was no response. No external thoughts forced their way into my mind, and I stopped after a while, feeling pretty dispirited. I just lay there, staring up at the ceiling and barely seeing it, wondering what on earth was going to happen to me. Would they recover me only so that they could send me out somewhere to be eaten? If so, I would have much preferred Ingi to have just finished me off completely; at least then she could have matured more quickly and increased the chances of May being able to help the others. These thoughts were pretty extreme, I knew, and not all hope was gone yet, but being stuck in a situation like this one where nothing at all is for certain can turn the mind in a very negative direction.

The nurse, if that was what she was, had just freed my right hand and now she tapped me on the shoulder to get my attention. I turned my head slowly towards her, noticing that it felt heavier than usual. I wished I could feel it with my hand, or look at myself in a mirror, or gain some idea of exactly what condition I was in, but I couldn't think of any way to ask this Honnie for help. She said something to me in that rapid, throaty language they spoke, then looked enquiringly at me. Seriously, did she think I would understand her? I considered shaking my head, decided it would take too long, and tried to speak. There was a lot of wire around my jaws, I noticed as I tried to open them, but I was able to open my mouth at least a fraction and say, using mostly my tongue, "I can't talk."

Thankfully those words didn't require much movement of the jaw, although it still sounded pretty weird. The Honnie stared at me in some confusion for several seconds before seeming to understand something. Without another word, she turned and walked away. Well that was nice, I thought; someone should teach these aliens the art of waving. I turned my head slowly back to the ceiling and turned my attention back to my missing left arm. The pain was no longer there. Instead, I felt various lines of itches all up and down the arm that I knew I could never scratch. That would be the challenge as far as the arm went; getting used to the idea that it wasn't there anymore. I could still feel the ghost of it though, which only seemed to make it feel worse.

"Ah, nice to see that you're awake, John. Say, did you know you're going to have an itchy elbow today?"

Curse my memory, damn it to hell. Last time I'd thought those words, I'd actually dared to laugh, but I was a long way from laughing this time. Worst of all, right on bloody cue, my missing elbow began to itch, and I could do nothing whatsoever about it.

A few minutes later, I was approached by another Honnie, a male one this time. It was the first time I had seen a full-blooded male Honnie since Smiley's memories and I was struck once again by their incredible height. This one was about seven feet, give or take, and very slim, though probably a lot stronger than a human of the same height covered in muscle. The doctor, I thought hopefully, not sure what there was to be hopeful about. How would he be any better than the nurse, who I noticed right then had fallen in behind the doctor? That question was answered when he drew up a chair beside the bed, allowing the nurse to step past him and resume the position she had occupied minutes earlier.

It turned out that he was better by virtue of the fact that I was now contained inside his mind instead of May's. When he was sure he had my complete attention, he began transmitting thoughts to me, slowly and steadily, as though he had done this with many humans before and had determined the best way to do it so that the humans understood every bit of it. This was indeed a hospital, a fairly small one, I gathered, and this particular area was designated for humans only. He then informed me of my injuries, which I'd already worked out anyway: A missing left arm, which couldn't be recovered; and a broken jaw, which would mostly heal on its own, although it was wired into position at the moment and those wires would need to be removed at a later date, assuming my 'aba' gave a damn.

I formed the enquiry about May in my mind, hoping he would understand what I was asking him. When his response came, I learnt that it was standard procedure for humans to be taken by the doctor in charge of their recovery when they were hurt. May, who had brought me in here a full two days earlier, I learnt to my horror, would take me back when I was ready to leave. My next question was when that would happen, and he informed me that it would be either today or tomorrow, a realisation that positively horrified me; if this were our world, I'd need at least a week to be well enough to leave, and plenty more recovery time after that. Sadly, it turned out that since humans often found themselves hospitalised in this world, they were never allowed to occupy these beds for too long.

I went to sleep after that, something I hadn't decided to do but had just done anyway. When I woke, I figured that the doctor had simply forced it upon me, perhaps sensing that I was different from the rest of the humans he'd dealt with, and not wanting to have to answer any more pressing questions. I had no idea how much time had passed since then, and I had a moment to wonder where the others were, if they even knew what had happened, if they were going on without me, or if Ingi had found a way to separate another of them in the dead of night. The doctor who had almost certainly put me to sleep was back at my bedside, and after assessing my condition by way of my thoughts, spoke something to that Honnie nurse who was once again right behind him. In response, she approached my bed and began winding something at the foot of it.

I'd been feeling marginally better before then but that changed quickly when I felt the bed beginning to tilt me into a sitting position. I tried to cry out in protest, but all that came out of my mouth was a muffled noise, and the bolt of pain that jolted through my face shut me up very quickly. I wanted to scream with the agony of it, but I knew I had to hold it in; if I started, I may not be able to stop. As it was, however, my face was far more painful than my missing arm. I could still feel a ghost of it there, and felt sure that I could bend my fingers if I really wanted to, even though I could see that there was definitely no arm there.

The pain was gone by the time I had been moved into a sitting position, and I knew that the doctor was responsible for that too. Now that I was in something like my right mind again, I was able to have a better look around the room. It was a long ward with at least twenty beds, lined up along the walls. There were humans in all of them but they couldn't have been more different from me: They were all dressed like Honnies; they were all older than me, ranging from their twenties to their fifties or sixties; all of them could speak Honnie language; all of them were very fat; and all of them were behaving like children. This realisation put everything about this world into perspective: These people were bred and raised in this world, and their only purposes were to breed half-breeds and to be consumed by the better race. The Honnies cared greatly about fattening them up but apparently not enough about strengthening their minds; it must have seemed easier to them to get smart humans from our world.

The doctor had been watching me while I had concerned myself with these thoughts, but now he quite literally took my mind off them and directed it to the things the nurse was now holding in her hands. In one hand she held a bottle of water, and I began to salivate at the sight of it, although I had no idea how I would be expected to drink it. In her other hand she held three sticks of gradi, and how I was expected to eat that was even more of a mystery. She placed them on a table at the foot of my bed, and then wheeled the table around so that it stretched sideways across the bed, placing the food directly in front of me.

How I was expected to consume the food and water became clear enough when the nurse Honnie firstly produced a straw (smart, I thought), and I almost felt good about this procedure until she began crushing the gradi into powder in her hands and sprinkling it into the water. Sure enough, when she fed the straw carefully through the wires and into my mouth, it tasted bloody awful. The water would have been good on its own, and the gradi, whatever it actually was, had been edible enough, but together, it just didn't work. Still, I drank it all up, an exercise that turned out not to be too painful, and once it was gone, I discovered that I wanted more. It must have been a long time since I'd eaten or drank anything, unless they'd fed me through the infusion. It had been even longer since I'd been to the toilet, but I would worry about that later.

I was not put back to sleep that day, which was a shame because it became extremely boring, sitting in that bed with absolutely nothing to do. The nurse and doctor were gone, although I knew I could call to the latter in the same way I'd called to May if I needed anything; he hadn't believed me when I'd tried to tell him that, and so far, I'd had no occasion to demonstrate it. I thought I might soon, though, if I wanted to lie down. All I had to do in that time was sit and think, wonder, and fear what was to come for me and the others.

The meal I'd been given earlier that day had been lunch, and when dinner came around, it turned out to be exactly the same thing in exactly the same quantity, and delivered by exactly the same Honnie. It wasn't until about an hour after this (a bloody long hour) that the doctor came back to my bedside and sat down to communicate once again. The first thing he told me, by way of my thoughts, was that I would be leaving early the next morning. After a good night of sleep, I should be well enough to walk, at least for short periods. The second thing he told me was that the Honnie who had brought me in was here in the hospital, and would I like to see her? Naturally I did, but more importantly, I wanted to see the other humans she was possessing. He told me that humans were not allowed to visit in here, but as far as he knew, there were five of them travelling with her.

That filled me with enormous relief and I marvelled over that knowledge during the time he went to fetch her. I could have said plenty against May, and even more against Ingi for putting me here, but the fact that Peter, Natalie and the others were still alive and still travelling was enough to make me rub my face with my right hand, carefully avoiding the wires around my jaw. A few minutes later, or so it felt (my watch had been on my left wrist when Ingi had attacked, so I didn't have it anymore), the doctor returned, and he was leading May who, though she was a fair bit taller than me, only came up to the doctor's shoulder.

They both sat down in chairs beside my bed, the doctor taking the one he'd been sitting in before and drawing one up from another bed to accommodate May. I had no idea what the protocol would be here, since May could talk to me, but I couldn't talk to her, and she could no longer access my mind. After several seconds of nothing from any of us, May finally said, "You have slowed us up quite a bit."

I was stung by that. Her tone made it sound like she was merely stating a fact, but the wording suggested that this was somehow my fault. Forgetting that my jaws were wired, I said, "She attacked 'e!" (She attacked me!)

The T sound didn't really come out properly, but May seemed to understand what I'd said. "She only did what she is taught to do. She is supposed to hunt, and you were the easiest human to reach."

Because I'd slept closest to the entrance of the tent, of course. I asked her, "Are da uddash okay?" (Are the others okay?)

This time, May didn't understand what I'd said, but fortunately, the doctor did, and he repeated my words in his own language for her. "Yes, they are okay. They are very worried and very angry, but they are not hurt."

"Sho Ingi 'on't hurt deh?" (So Ingi won't hurt them?)

"I will not let her," May said, after the doctor had translated again. "She was only able to because I was asleep, but I have made her not want to hurt you anymore. She will now only attack you if I say she can."

"Good," I said, feeling angry, and glad that the word came out clearly this time. I wanted to rant and rage at her for allowing Ingi to get away with it in the first place. I wanted to swear like I'd never sworn in my life. I wanted to demand that she at least punish her daughter for this, but I knew it wouldn't do any good, because Honnies didn't see this as such a big deal. It was with some effort I reminded myself that May had brought me in here, when she could have easily let me die. It would have been much easier to just give me up as a lost job and allow Ingi to get all there was to get from me. Now that I thought of it, why hadn't she? Even to me, that logic made more sense. The two Honnies watched me silently as I struggled with these thoughts, trying to work out which way to jump. Finally, I asked, "'y did 'ou sha'e 'e?" (Why did you save me?)

"You are asking why I brought you here?" May said after the doctor had translated, and when I nodded, very slowly if you don't mind, she said, "Because I wanted to. Do you really need me to tell you why?"

Now that she put it like that, I didn't need her to spell it out at all. She'd saved me, not because she was concerned about one of her humans going to feed her daughter, or because she was worried about the cooperation of the others post my demise. She'd done it because of what had taken place between the two of us that night, of how it made her feel. I now came to understand, as though she'd placed the thought in my mind herself, that she was more confused by me than anything else. I wished I could ask her more about her feelings, but that just wouldn't work while talking was this difficult, and while there was a doctor standing by. In the end, all I could think to say was, "'hanksh." (Thanks.)

"He tells me that you will live," she said, "at least, from these injuries. You are very lucky because you nearly died on the way here. This is Pralia and it was closest to our camp. We have had time to get supplies while you have been in here, so we are now prepared to take you humans with us. You will not have to walk much."

"Great," I muttered sourly.

The doctor spoke something to her in their language then, and they both stood up. "I have to go," she said, "I will see you tomorrow morning."

There was no goodbye, of course; the two of them simply turned and walked away. I leaned back against my pillow, and this time I really did swear, not too loudly but fairly clearly. I was pleased with the sound, and I contented myself with repeating the vulgar word a few more times before quitting. Sometime later, the nurse returned, perhaps on some instruction from the doctor, or perhaps she'd simply seen me sitting here, and thought I might like to lie down. She was right, and once my bed had been lowered into its proper position, I dropped straight off to sleep.

* * *

I was woken the next morning by an unfamiliar female Honnie tapping my forehead. I felt tired and stiff, after having slept dreamlessly for who knew how many hours (felt like at least ten) and I wondered how I could be expected to get up and walk out of the hospital in the next few hours. The Honnie who had woken me put my bed back into a sitting position like yesterday and then fed me breakfast, which turned out to be exactly the same as dinner the night before, only this time I was allowed to consume more of it. It still tasted revolting, but I accepted it gratefully.

Once that was done, I felt a little better—still stiff but more alert. My face only hurt a little bit now—it felt more numb than anything else. As for my arm, I could still feel the ghost of it, but that would only be annoying from now on. I took a deep breath as I sat there and, for the first time, looked at what remained of my left shoulder. It actually wasn't too bad; Ingi certainly hadn't put any effort into doing a clean job, but apparently the doctor had. I was still wearing the same clothes I'd been wearing that night—the sleeve had been torn away with my arm, but someone had stitched it shut since then. I could see the shape of what lay beneath it, however, and had to assume they had found a way to close the wound up as well.

The nurse (if that was what she was) had left me, but now the doctor returned to my bedside—the same one who'd helped me the day before. He didn't sit down this time, but once he had my full attention, he began communicating with me again. I didn't like the thoughts that were entering my mind this time, and I attempted to protest against them. He wouldn't hear a word of it, though, and he informed me, in no uncertain terms, that he would make me comply if I didn't do so of my own free will. I had no reason to doubt him.

I pushed my sheets back off myself with my right hand, looking down at my legs for the first time since coming here— nothing interesting to see there. That was the easy bit, and swivelling my body around to face the side of the bed turned out not to be too bad either. Pulling myself up to the side of the bed was far more difficult, because my natural instinct was to use both hands. The moment I attempted to work my left arm, I began feeling it far more than I had before, and far more painfully too. I tried to grit my teeth against the pain, only achieving more pain in my face as well as my arm. I let out a low groan as despair filled me, but it was quickly removed by the doctor, who was still standing by only a few feet in front of me but making no effort whatsoever to help me. Bloody Honnies, I thought savagely.

Slowly, I pushed myself with my right arm toward the side of the bed, attempting to heave with my legs as well as my remaining arm. I felt heavier than usual, and I had a moment to wonder if that was because I'd been weakened, or if I'd actually put on weight since entering this world. If gradi was supposed to make humans prime, and prime seemed to mean extremely fat, didn't that make sense? I supposed I would find out when I got a look at the others. In any case, this movement was enough to put my bare feet firmly on the cold floor. Now came the hard part: I had to stand up, and once again, I couldn't count on the doctor to help me. He had told me himself that not only would he not help me get up, he would not catch me if I fell. I had to be able to get all the way out of this hospital, to where May would be waiting, completely independently; that's how they would know I was good to go.

After sitting on the side of that bed for perhaps twenty seconds, I decided that the best way to do this would be to do it as quickly as possible. I took a deep breath, almost gritted my teeth before remembering what a bad idea that was, shifted all my weight onto my feet and pushed. I had got out of a chair without using my arms plenty of times—it wasn't too difficult to do—and thankfully, this didn't seem to be too bad either. What caught me off-guard the moment I was on my feet was the way my balance had shifted; where it had been standard before, now I felt myself pulled slightly towards the right—the weight of my remaining arm, I felt sure. The only way I could compensate was by leaning very slightly the other way; it made me feel as though I could topple over at any moment, but I knew that if I didn't do it, I could very well topple over the other way.

The doctor gave me perhaps five minutes to get used to the sensation of being back on my feet before informing me, by way of a sharp thought that felt like a needle right through the skull, that it was time to go. He took a few steps away from me and then paused, waiting for me to follow. I took another deep breath and very carefully lifted my left foot. I had to put it down very quickly because the moment I had shifted my balance, I had almost fallen over. Walking normally seemed to be a bit beyond me just now, but it turned out, after some experimentation, that I could do a kind of shuffle, where my feet only left the floor for moments at a time. It was slow going, but the more I did it, the better I got at it. If I were wearing socks, I thought, I could do this much more easily. I made a mental note to wear socks to bed from now on.

The doctor led me up the ward, through a door at the end, around a corner and down a long corridor, lined on either side with doors. There were a few more wards, it seemed, and they were all reserved for Honnies rather than humans. The rest were either offices or operating rooms, I saw through the few that had windows and the few whose doors were open. There was a closed door at the end of the corridor, too, and it was through this door that the doctor led me.

The room beyond was a stairwell, and I groaned when I realised the stairs were the only way out of this place—down would be pretty bad, but up would be even worse. Fortunately, we went down; it was very slow going, and I had to hold tightly to the rail with my right hand all the way down, but eventually we got down the first flight, around the corner and down another flight before arriving at the bottom. By the time I had both feet back on even ground, I was absolutely exhausted. I could see, through a window right beside me, that we were at ground level now, but the journey wasn't over yet.

Down another corridor we went, or at least, halfway down before we turned right and went down another hallway. It might have been my imagination, or perhaps wishful thinking, but I sensed that we had almost reached the exit—this area just felt more like a visitors' centre than a ward. This turned out to be true, for the door at the end of the hallway was open, and I could see a waiting room beyond it. By now, I was actually leaning on the wall to my right as I moved, cramping my right arm a bit and hardly caring. I was so damned exhausted—it felt like I'd been struggling for hours, and it very well could have been an hour by now for all I knew.

At last, though, the doctor emerged into the waiting room and began speaking to someone there in Honnie language. By the time I caught up with him, I was surrounded by my friends.

Chapter 23: Lowly

The city we were in, Pralia (that's what it sounded like anyway), seemed to be fairly small—bigger than Chopville, but probably not by much. It was difficult to be sure, though, because I only saw those buildings which I passed on the way to the place where May, her family and her 'possessions' were staying. I could only gather that since the hospital seemed to be in the city centre, and there was nothing particularly grand about it, it was a small place.

The Honnies had a strange method of travelling, I learned. Once the doctor had transferred me back to May (this was an extremely odd sensation indeed; I felt the two minds link momentarily as I was pushed from one to the other), we left the hospital by way of some sort of cart. I say cart because it didn't have a roof; it was simply a board on wheels with four seats attached. Tommy and Peter helped me get to it because none of the Honnies offered. By the time I was strapped into one of the seats, I was totally exhausted, and had no room in my mind to goggle at how the Honnies made this system work.

With only four seats, Candice and Rebecca were forced to strap themselves into Tommy and Peter's laps respectively, but the Honnies didn't even get on board. It was the two half-breeds, Dan and Gob, who were strapped to the front like horses, but they didn't tug the cart along behind them; they practically flew with it, sprinting in long, bounding steps as Ingi had the night she had abducted me. She and May were on either side of us, keeping pace with the half-breeds with no trouble at all. The cart mostly kept its wheels on the ground, but there were enough bumps along the way for the experience to be terrifying. The only two good things were that firstly, the seatbelts (thank God they had them) were tight enough that there was no danger of any of us being dislodged, and secondly, that neither my face nor the place where my arm had been were hit along the way, so I didn't hurt any more than I had to.

Our destination was the equivalent of a caravan park on the very outskirts of the city, right off the road on which we had probably been caught. It was really just a large plain with about thirty or forty cabins scattered throughout, and they weren't very big either. From the outside, most of them appeared empty, though there were Honnies moving around in a few of them. We came to a stop outside one of them; Ingi and the two half-breeds went straight in, no care for the rest of us, while May stood by, watching as we humans got down from the cart.

As they had at the hospital, Peter and Tommy helped me get into the cabin, the three girls around us, looking ready to help out should it be necessary. The interior consisted of practically nothing; five doors, two off either side and one at the end, and nothing whatsoever in the main room, which was barely big enough to accommodate the ten of us. Only the door directly ahead of us was open; it looked like some sort of food storage.

And speaking of food: It looked like it was time to eat. The two half-breeds went into the storage room and returned with plenty of gradi to go around, plus a few things for the Honnies. I was more tired than hungry, but my stomach was fairly empty and although I wasn't all too enthusiastic about the choice of food, I still wanted to eat it. It had been an exhausting morning, and judging by the position of the sun in the sky (the day was cloudless and, incidentally, looked just like the sky at home), it was just about lunchtime.

After we had all eaten (or drank in my case; May crushed mine and served it in water, as they had at the hospital), we humans were sent into one of the rooms off the side of the main room—the second on the left. There had been very little talk all morning, but there didn't need to be discussion of what was to take place; May simply told us mentally what we were to do. I was able to enquire as to why we were being sent into that room, but I got no response, and the others weren't asking. Either they knew or May was preventing them from questioning her. Either way, it gave the six of us some time together away from the Honnies.

"I dunno about you guys but I'm already sick to death of this lot," said Rebecca the moment the door was closed. "Shall we have something a little more substantial?"

"Hear, hear," said Candice quickly.

The room was about the size of each of our bedrooms back in the base we had created and contained nothing but an open cupboard of what looked like the same mats and blankets we had slept under the other night. Five of these were laid out around the room, indicating that they had slept in here the previous night (no separating of the guys from the girls here). The three bags we had brought from our world were propped against the far wall, and it was to one of these that Rebecca now headed, but I didn't have the energy to follow. I probably could have got over there, perhaps without leaning on one of the walls, but I was simply too tired. I leaned against the wall close to the door and carefully lowered myself to the floor.

Tommy and Candice had followed Rebecca to the bags and were now retrieving some of the food we had brought with us (cheese and bread rolls were the order of the day, by the look of it) but Natalie and Peter stayed with me, sitting down on either side of me; something I found very comforting. The others, seeing what was up, soon gathered around us and began dividing the food.

"How are we gonna do this?" Peter asked, looking at the rolls in his hands and then glancing sideways at my messed-up face.

I very slowly shook my head. "Don't 'orry a'out it." (Don't worry about it.)

Most of that had come out fairly clearly. It was only the sounds that required closing of the lips, such as the B and the W, that were impossible to sound out properly. The T was doable if I took it slowly, which was about all I could do now. I hoped it would get easier over the coming days because communicating with my friends was gonna be a bitch like this.

"You sure you don't want something else to eat?" Tommy asked. "I tell ya, this Honnie food they keep giving us is rubbish."

I shook my head. "You know dey're 'aking you 'at, right?" (You know they're making you fat, right?)

"Er," said Tommy, looking confused, "aching?"

"No, he means they're trying to fatten us up," said Rebecca. "Haven't I been telling you guys?"

"Is that what you said, John?" Peter asked, and I nodded slowly.

"How do you know that?" Candice asked.

"Shaw hu'amsh in dere," I told them. "Dey 'ere all 'eally 'at." (Saw humans in there; they were all really fat.)

"Did we ever doubt that?" said Natalie darkly as Peter swore under his breath. "I mean, come on, Smiley wrote it all out for us. They treat humans like cows, and how do we treat cows? We raise them for slaughter. The more they fatten us up, the more meat they can get out of us."

"We also milk them," said Candice nervously.

"I guess human's minds would be the equivalent there," said Tommy.

"I don't think that necessarily means May will slaughter us the same way, though," said Natalie, and both Tommy and Peter snorted at these words. "No, seriously, I know they could have done it by now, but the fact that they haven't seems to mean they're curious about us."

"Do you really believe that?" said Rebecca scornfully.

Natalie shrugged. "No, but I haven't given up hope yet."

"'Ay ish," I told them, and they all looked at me in confusion. "She could ha'e let 'e die," I went on, my jaw beginning to throb now. (May is. She could have let me die.)

"You're right-handed, right?" Tommy asked me, and when I nodded, he said, "did we pack a pen and pad by any chance?"

"Not that I'm aware of," said Natalie, looking enquiringly at Peter, who shrugged. "I'll go have a look."

"What are you trying to say, John?" Peter asked.

"Ingi," I said firmly, glad that the sound came out clearly, and pleased by the way all their faces darkened at the mention of her name. "'Ay sha'ed 'e 'om her." (May saved me from her.)

"She did," said Candice, the only one who'd understood me completely. She was staring at the place where my left arm should have been, looking thoughtful.

"I think we're out of luck," Natalie said from the opposite wall. "I didn't expect any different; no contingency plan we thought of included us needing to communicate in writing, and of course, I can't do magic here."

"Maybe the Honnies will have something we can use," said Peter doubtfully. "Are you sure you don't want anything to eat, John? What about a drink? Maybe some clean water for a change?"

Now that did sound tempting, but the thought of water made me think of something else. After I had nodded, I said, "dey ne'er let 'e go to de toilet." (They never let me go to the toilet.)

"Aw geez," Tommy moaned.

"Have some water first," Peter said, "then I guess we take you out."

"Out?" I repeated incredulously.

"They don't have toilets in this place," Natalie told me, pushing a bottle of water into my hand and sitting back down beside me. "They don't seem to mind squatting, and we have to do the same."

"'Ill dey let ush out?" I asked. (Will they let us out?)

"Sure they will," said Peter. "In fact, they don't even ask questions. Well, May doesn't, and she's the only one who can. She'll know if we try to escape and she'll just make us come back if we try, so other than that, we're pretty much free to wander around a bit."

"They don't like it when we do, though," Rebecca added, "in case other Honnies take it into their heads to attack us."

"Know how dat 'eels," I said darkly. (Know how that feels.)

I took a few sips of the water. It was so soothing that it almost made my head spin.

"You know, there's absolutely no humility in these Honnies," Tommy told me. "May's kept Ingi in check since but she doesn't even blame her. Ingi doesn't even realise she's done the wrong thing, as far as I can tell. She certainly has no issue looking at us, no matter how much we drill holes in her face."

"Different breed of being," said Natalie in a low voice. "They just do whatever it is that they do and don't give a damn about how we feel about it all."

* * *

I slept on and off throughout that afternoon; as tired as I was, having the others stuck in the same room with me, none of them tired, made it impossible to sleep soundly. Peter and Tommy had helped me out of the cabin and across to a row of shrubs separating the cabins from the road where I was able to relieve myself, something that felt exceptionally grand. Never in my life had I so thoroughly enjoyed having a crap, and never mind the aching jaw, the ghost arm that still itched dully or the brambles that poked my exposed buttocks. Ingi, Dan and Gob had all been just outside the cabin when we had left, not far from the cart that had brought us here, but none of them tried to stop us as we made our way laboriously past them. May must have known what we were doing, for she didn't stop us either; in fact, she didn't even seem to be in the area.

We all had dinner together that evening when the sun was going down, just as we'd had lunch that day. The only difference was the conversation that took place around the circle. Natalie had stayed fairly close to my side for most of the afternoon—since I'd returned from the shrubs, in fact—and she had been quick to sit herself beside me come mealtime. She took every chance she got to help me with my food, making me feel like she was my mother and I was nothing more than a sick little boy. If I'd been in a better physical state, I probably would have enjoyed it more, and needed it a whole lot less. Right now I just appreciated for the simplest thing it was: help that I needed.

Where Peter had sat by me over lunch, however, it was May who took that position this time, appearing ready to assist me if I needed it but satisfied that Natalie was doing the job. The way she kept looking at me was making me a little nervous because I was sure she was remembering how it had felt to have her tongue down my throat (something that wouldn't happen again any time soon with all this crap around my mouth). That wasn't great, but the looks I kept getting from Ingi were a whole lot worse. She looked very similar to how she had as she stripped my arm of all its flesh; there was no emotion in her, or if there was, it wasn't spared for me. I was nothing more than a prize she had been denied and still wanted. I hoped to hell that May kept a very tight hold on her mind.

There was talk over dinner that night, and it went very similarly to the discussion we'd had with May on the first night of our stay in this alien world. I didn't participate in it but I was interested and not a little dismayed by how much the Honnies didn't seem to care about our problems. We all knew how different they were from us but their almost-human appearance made it easy to forget just how different. All living creatures had feelings of some kind, I believed, some more primitive than others. Given how intelligent Honnies were, as intelligent as humans in fact, why was it so difficult for them to be empathetic? There was no resolution that night, but May still maintained that our only chance to get back home would be when we reached Lagalia, the largest city in this land. If we were still with her when we got back to Malia, where Ingi would graduate and become an adult, we would be the guests of honour at the feast that would follow.

The six of us slept together (not literally) in the room set aside for humans, while the two half-breeds took the one opposite us, and May and Ingi had a room each to themselves. The following morning, after a breakfast that consisted of the same food as dinner the night before, not to mention lunch, breakfast, and pretty much every meal we'd had in this world, we set out again. The day was a little cooler than the prior had been, and that made the cart ride all the more unpleasant. The Honnies moved fairly fast, providing us with a pretty good view of what lay on either side of the road as we went, but the wind that struck our exposed faces was bloody awful. I dealt with the pressure by turning my face to my right and watching May as she bounded along beside us.

It turned out that the Honnies only travelled in the morning; the afternoon seemed to be reserved for whatever it was that Honnies did together in that time. All I knew was that it involved Ingi standing with the two half-breeds, and I suspected there was mind-to-mind stuff going on between them, but none of us had asked and May hadn't bothered to tell us. That day, we came to a stop beside another one of those drains by the side of the road about half an hour beyond another city, whose outskirts we passed by (it looked similar to Pralia) and after yet another meal of gradi, May told us we could set up a tent to entertain ourselves for the afternoon.

The rest of that day was spent playing cards in said tent. I was surprised that we even had a deck of cards but it seemed that Peter barely went anywhere without one. I mused that if he were that intent on gaming, he would probably develop a gambling problem in five or ten years. The three girls, none of whom were particularly enthusiastic about the game, got involved because they had nothing better to do, but as I'd learnt in my own way, the camaraderie was infectious. I would have felt better if we were using this time to attend to our mission, that of persuading a Honnie to come back to our world and help us against the Hammerhearts, but as Natalie rightly stated, interrupting their own system wouldn't do us any favours.

Through all this, I felt better than I had at any point since Ingi had attacked me. My arm was still causing me issues in terms of getting used to it not being there, but I was quickly adjusting to the balance issue, and I was also able to move around a little more freely, and for longer than I had before. My jaw was still a problem; there was nothing I could do to make talking easier, but as it turned out, I was able to do it for longer each time before my jaw began to ache. I began to think that it may just be possible for me to survive this; as long as no more Honnies tried to do me in, I would be okay.

Something a little surprising happened that night. We ate dinner around the campfire as we had on the first night, and once again a discussion ensued, a discussion that turned out to be fairly pointless. Afterwards, however, when it was almost time for bed, instead of sending us into our tent to sleep, or setting up another tent to separate the guys and the girls, as they had the first time, May ordered Dan and Gob to take our tent down.

"Are we braving the elements tonight?" Tommy asked anxiously, and I shared his feelings; the elements in the sky were looking rather ominous for the first time since we'd arrived in this world. In fact, there could be a full-on storm this evening.

"No," said May curtly. "I don't want you humans on ground tonight; you will come down with us."

"In the drain?" said Peter incredulously. "We won't have to troop through Honnie sewerage, will we?"

"Won't the drain get flooded if it rains?" Natalie asked, pointing up at the clouds almost directly overhead.

"No, and no," said May firmly. "You will be much better in the ground tonight."

"You know what that means in our world?" said Rebecca, and then answered her own question. "It means you're gonna kill someone tonight."

May was not amused. "No killing tonight. You will be safer in the ground with us this time."

"Can we say Dracula's coffin, anyone?" Tommy muttered darkly.

"What does that mean?" May asked. Tommy shrugged and made no response but May must have picked the meaning out of his head because she didn't pursue the subject.

May had been telling the truth about the interior of the drain we were forced to climb into. We had to climb down a slightly slippery ladder a short distance to some sort of underground room, an operation that was impossible for me (May had to jump down with me in her arms). There was some sort of sluice running with drain water but the ladder took us past it to an area that was protected by the water by a fairly high wall. It wouldn't handle a full-on flood, but a storm?

Probably. The problem wasn't so much the water, or the noise, or even the dank air of the place (although that certainly wasn't great); it was the space. There was barely enough for the ten of us to stand together, let alone sleep.

"I hope you all like imitating scarecrows," Peter called over the noise of the rushing water as we stood fairly close together in considerable but not quite complete darkness (there didn't seem to be any electricity down here).

"Hey, I've always wanted to go to sleep standing up," said Tommy. "After all, isn't that what cows do? And are we not cows?"

"I thought that was horses," said Candice vaguely.

"You will not sleep on your feet," May told us. "There are panels on the floor that have holes in them; we sleep in there, but there are only four, so two of you will have to sleep here."

"Dibs," Peter said at once, quickest to understand what May hadn't said.

"You sure you wanna sleep up here with all this noise?" Tommy asked. "What if you get sprayed with water like you're on a boat?"

"I'd rather that than sleep in a tiny hole with a Honnie," said Peter. "That really *would* be like Dracula's coffin."

"What?" Tommy cried out, staring wildly from May to Ingi and back again.

"Let me show you," May said. "Everyone move over here by the wall."

Everyone obeyed, of course (it was impossible to disobey someone who had complete control of your mind). May moved to the front of the pack and indicated a slit in the floor. The panel wasn't quite in the floor, but rather at a thirty-degree angle to the floor, leading up to the wall. There were two of them over where May stood and I supposed there must be two more on either side of us, but there were too many people around me, human and Honnie, for me to see them. When May opened one of them, we saw that the space beneath was about the same size as a king-size bed and just deep enough to sit in without hitting one's head, which was pretty good, but would still make it difficult not to get pretty close to the Honnie we each had to share with. I felt a thrill of terror when I realised someone would have to sleep right beside Ingi and knew, somehow, that it would be me; the job would be completed tonight, out of sight of the others.

"You sleep in this one," May told Natalie—it was not a suggestion.

"Who am I sleeping with?" she asked nervously, looking indiscreetly around at me. It was a nice thought but I doubted very much that May would allow it (she would know exactly what was happening between Natalie and me), and sure enough...

"Dan," said May, indicating one of the half-breeds. Natalie blanched at the sight of him.

"Will we fit in there?" she asked.

"Yes, you will," May replied, moving aside and approaching the other panel on that side of the room.

"Hang on," Natalie protested, but she didn't get any further. Dan, on some sort of mental order from May, put a massive arm around Natalie, turning her so that her face pressed into his large chest, making it impossible for her to speak. He didn't crush her, or break her jaw as Ingi probably would have, but instead lifted her easily and carried her to the hole in the floor. She struggled all the way but she was no match for his strength. He stepped down into the hole and, still cradling Natalie against his chest, ducked down as he pulled the panel shut on top of them both. He had been firm with her, but he had also been gentle, so I wasn't too worried that he would hurt her in the night. What did worry me was that he might be indecent with her, and I tried to mentally send the question to May, but again, she ignored it.

"Why Natalie?" Candice asked sharply. "In our world, in a situation like this, it would probably have been Tommy who slept with him."

"Yeah, 'cause I would have totally enjoyed that," he said darkly.

"Would you prefer to sleep with Ingi?" Candice retorted, and Tommy shifted his feet nervously.

"Boys do not sleep with each other here," said May firmly, looking almost horrified by the thought. "You," she said to Candice, "will sleep in this one with Gob."

"Guess they don't have homo Honnies," Peter muttered.

Candice was certainly not enthusiastic about sleeping with the half-breed, but he dealt with her the same way his brother had dealt with Natalie. Little more than twenty seconds later, there were only six of us left on the floor.

"John," said Peter quickly, moving up beside me, "you reckon the best course of action now would be for us to share one?"

"'Erha'sh," I said. (Perhaps.) But I knew it wouldn't be allowed.

"Boys do not sleep with each other here," said Tommy, doing his best to mimic May's accent.

"You can share with Ingi," May said to Tommy; he stepped back from the Honnies so quickly that he hit the protective wall behind us. I wondered if he was considering that jumping over it into the rushing water would be safer than what was about to happen.

"Why me?" he asked, his voice croaky as he stared at Ingi. For her part, Ingi simply looked back at Tommy with an almost curious expression; it didn't look nearly as threatening as the one she seemed to have reserved for me.

"She prefers you," said May simply.

Now that was a very scary thought. Tommy backed right up against the wall now, looking terrified. "When you say 'prefers'," he said, "does that mean John was a little too sour for her taste?"

"I do not understand your meaning," said May curtly, "but there is no danger here. Ingi understands this. All you are doing is sleeping."

"As I lay me down to sleep," Tommy muttered, looking a long way from amused.

May had grown tired of talking about these matters with her pet humans. Perhaps on yet another mental instruction, Ingi approached our little gathering (we scuttled out of her way) and opened another panel in the floor, this one just to my right. Its interior looked exactly the same as the other two, though only about three quarters of the size, but I now had a clearer view of it; it looked comfortable enough, if you could get past the knowledge of sleeping beside a blood-thirsty killing machine. Ingi jumped down and turned back to face us, waiting for Tommy to join her. He was standing furthest from the open panel, behind Peter and me in fact, and almost ready to jump in the one remaining panel which must have belonged to May.

"Looks like I'm sharing with Mummy," Peter muttered. "Surely she won't make you get in one of those holes, John."

"Actually, I am going to keep an eye on him," May said, surprising everyone except me (now that Tommy was sharing with Ingi, I knew what must be going on here), "in case he needs anything in the night. Are you coming or not?" she added to Tommy, now looking annoyed.

"If you want me in there, you'll have to drag me," said Tommy stubbornly.

As if a Honnie would even bother. A moment later, Tommy's expression changed completely to one of resignation. Without a word, he pushed past Peter and I and jumped down into the hole beside Ingi. She ducked, pulling him down with her as she pulled the panel shut on top of them. In the moment of relative silence that followed, May uttered something in her own language which was probably their equivalent of some sort of swearword.

"That's your effective way of dealing with disobedient humans," said Peter, now grinning slightly at Rebecca. "Looks like we're sharing the floor."

"We got the good deal," she said, grinning back at him.

"You two," May said to Peter and Rebecca, opening a fifth panel I hadn't seen until now—it was against the far wall and contained the same mats and blankets we were now becoming familiar with. "You use these right here, and whatever you have in your bags. Do not try to run away because I can make you come back; I think you know this."

"Wouldn't dream of it, captain," said Peter, straightening his posture and tipping her a mocking salute.

"Pardon?" said May blankly.

"Never mind," Peter muttered. "Geez, jokes are like aeroplanes around here; they go right over your head."

"We do not have airplanes in this world," May replied, once again missing Peter's meaning. "Silly human contraptions; we do not need them."

"Afraid of heights, are we?" Rebecca asked, a little antagonistically.

"We do not need them," May repeated curtly, approaching us and shepherding Peter and Rebecca back the way she had come. "Come," she added to me as she reached the hole in the floor she and I would be sharing. She opened it and stepped in, turning to wait for me just as Ingi had waited for Tommy. I had no intention of putting up a struggle (I was too tired, and nevertheless knew it was entirely pointless) but I did want to say something to Peter to stop him from worrying about me. In the end, though, all I could think to do was wave once at them before approaching the hole. It was really too deep for me to step down, and of course, May didn't offer me any assistance, so I just had to jump. I probably would have lost my balance on landing if I hadn't toppled into May; she caught me and helped me down, so I supposed it was possible to get help from Honnies if you literally threw yourself at them.

"Are you hurting?" May asked me quietly once she had closed the panel on top of us.

"No, 'hanksh," I said wearily. (No, thanks.)

Now that we were closed in, there really wasn't much room to move around after all. It would be claustrophobic enough if there were only one of us, but two people, one of them quite tall.... May seemed fairly comfortable with the situation though; in fact, a little too comfortable. There were a number of panels around the walls, I now realised, and May began fishing something out of one of them. I almost groaned when I saw, through the almost complete darkness, that it was a clean robe. None of us had seen any of the Honnies change their clothes but I supposed they had to at some stage because through all the wild they went through, they never seemed to be too dirty. Now I understood how the system worked: They took new clothes from each stopping place, leaving their own clothes behind for the next Honnies to pass by—I supposed they must wash them at some point. As the females all seemed to be roughly the same height and all the males seemed to be roughly half a foot to a foot taller, and given the looseness of their clothing, and the fact that they all seemed to wear the same boring robes, their system would work.

This was odd enough, but unfortunately for me, it meant that I had to watch May change from her current robe to this new one. It would have been worse if there were more light, but light or no light, there was barely room to swing a grasshopper in here, so I would be very close to the action. And, worst of all, I might have to change mine too. Peter and Tommy had helped me out of my ruined clothes the previous day; I hadn't changed them since then because of the physical exertion it required. I would have liked to be able to change them now (I was feeling a little dirty, and I could smell myself, but that was another issue) but I didn't want to have to change them in front of May.

All I could do over the following minute was close my eyes and back against the wall behind me, leaving May as much space as she required. It would have been easy to just watch her (she mustn't have minded if she'd dragged me down here before doing it); in fact, watching her might even have been enjoyable (she looked like she had a pretty good body, though their robes didn't give away much of their body shape), but any judgements I made on her body would be totally transparent. It felt easiest to just close my eyes and forgo the whole awkward situation. I only knew it was safe to open my eyes again when May tapped me on the forehead.

"You humans are so squeamish," she said, and I realised that she'd been listening to my entire mental struggle.

The new robe was on, I saw, and the old one must have been in the little compartment the new one had come from. She was watching me closely, seeming to be waiting for something, but I was completely lost. All I could think to say was, "Shorry." (Sorry.)

"Get under," she told me, manoeuvring her body so that she could slide under the blankets. "Do you need help?"

I shook my head, wanting to do this for myself, but as it turned out, I really did need help. One arm didn't seem to be enough to drag myself, in a sitting position, to the pillow where I would be allowed to sleep—unless May had other ideas. She seemed to realise this at the same time I had, for she put an arm around my waist and hauled me up beside her. The contact was much closer than the reasonable part of me would have liked, but it was impossible to forget the other time we had been this close—how that had felt. I had a feeling that as I remembered it, so May did too. I also had a feeling that May had remembered it much sooner than that, and part of me suspected that perhaps the main reason why we lowly humans were allowed down here this time was so that she had an excuse to be close to me again. I had to force myself not to think that way (my opinion of myself had to be lowered), but it was difficult to shake the feeling altogether. And of course, May knew exactly how I felt.

"Do you need help to lie down?" she asked, knowing the answer was probably yes, but I shook my head. This was something I felt sure I could do on my own, and I turned out to be right. Shortly after, I was lying on my back in a bed that was surprisingly more comfortable than I had expected. Of course, this kind of comfort was supposed to be reserved for Honnies, but these lucky humans were being treated. That could be significant; once again, May was showing signs that her opinion of us wasn't quite the same as other Honnies.

May lay herself down beside me, on my left side as it were, which eliminated the possibility of me touching her (as if I would), but where I lay on my back, she chose to lie on her side, watching me through the darkness. I didn't realise this at first (I was just lying on my back, feeling sleep creep up on me as I stared at the black top of the hole we were in). I only became aware of her when she touched me again, but this was no tap on the forehead; she had reached out and put an arm, the one she wasn't lying on, across my body. It was almost as if we were lovers and she wished to hold me while I slept, but that was a thought I didn't want to examine any more closely. I allowed her to do this because she took care not to hurt me, and because it actually felt kind of nice to be close to another person, even if that person wasn't human.

I thought of Natalie, snuggled up there in a tiny hole not much larger than this with a male rather larger than May. I thought of how much I wanted her to be mine, of all the months and years I'd spent longing for her, culminating in the last few days before we had stepped into this world. I thought of how frustrated I'd been with my love life before coming here; Natalie, Amelia; even Lena, who would always be sexy enough to be desirable, however I felt about her as a person. With all that in mind, it felt good to be close to someone, even if that someone wasn't human; even if that someone was quite capable of killing me at any given moment as I lay here, because she was showing no signs of wanting to do that anytime soon.

I turned my head slightly so that it faced May; I was now conscious of her body close to mine, of her head almost touching the shoulder that had been a proper shoulder days ago. She was comfortable with this too, perhaps even more so since she had initiated it, but she also seemed not to want to talk. I followed her lead, feeling the sleep ready to take me, but I did listen for any external thoughts pushing their way into my mind, just in case May did have something to say to me. When none came, I finally dropped off into the deepest sleep I'd had since leaving the hospital, but the one thought I managed to acknowledge before it came: Don't do anything to stuff this up; being close to May can only be a good thing for your chances of getting back home.

Chapter 24: Love Child

One thing I came to learn very quickly was how monotonous life was for Honnies—not that they seemed to mind. Days went by and nothing ever seemed to change for them. They were creatures of habit and had no understanding of how humans generally liked to switch things up. We travelled along the same road for what seemed like an age before May, either on a whim or some preset route, turned us left at an intersection onto a different road which was just as dull as the previous one. It was impossible to judge direction accurately in this world; all we had to go on was the sun and its position in the sky at dawn and dusk. We had been travelling mostly north or northeast before, but now we seemed to be heading dead west. Given the distance we must have covered, I judged that if we were in our own world, we must be somewhere close to the three-way borders of New South Wales, Queensland and South Australia, but who could say for sure. All I knew for sure was that Lagalia must be the largest city in their version of Australia and it must have been somewhere in the middle of the country.

For me, things were beginning to pick up a little. I had a little more energy every day and after a few weeks, I felt almost myself again. The lack of a left arm was still a nuisance but even that was starting to feel familiar. Even more annoying were the wires holding my teeth together and more than once I had considered trying to take them out, but May had turned my thoughts elsewhere on the occasions they had strayed in that direction. When I had plucked up the courage to ask her about them, she said they could be removed when we reached Lagalia. I had no idea how long they were supposed to stay on, if the doctor in Pralia had told her they must remain in place for a certain length of time, or if May just wished to have them out at that time for her own reasons.

Natalie was the only person able to keep track of time in this strange world, and the rest of us were getting into a habit of asking her the date just about every day. We had left on July

4, and twenty-three days had passed since then, making today July 27. A lot would have happened in that time back at home. I often wondered how the others were going, if they had put any plans against Hammerson into action yet, and most of all, if they still believed we would be coming back.

How would it be if we returned home only to find that it was all over? They had found a way to beat Hammerson already and any help we could bring wouldn't be needed. If May agreed to come, she would be mightily pissed off by that. Or, worse, what if we got back to find that the Woodwards and Fletchers had been stripped of their magic, and everyone we'd left behind was now dead? This was a thought that invariably caused me to shudder whenever it occurred, and I had to quickly cast around for something else to think about.

One such thing I thought about rather a lot, during those darkest times when it seemed like we may never get back to our own world, was that moment when we had stood together, looking up at Marc through the hole in dimensions. I had tortured myself as, more and more, I thought of more things we could have done differently then—things that might have saved all our lives. It didn't matter that Natalie couldn't use her magic, or Marc's magic couldn't touch us here, because all Marc would have needed to do was create a ladder on his side and feed it through the hole; we could have climbed it, gone back through the hole, and none of this would be happening.

But as much as I tortured myself with these thoughts, they were utterly useless to us now. All we had to do in the meantime was sit back in the Honnies' strange cart and be pulled all over the countryside. We passed through cities like Pralia, towns like Chopville (at least, Honnie versions of said towns) and once, a much larger city called Herhalia. When we stopped in towns or cities, we stayed in cabins like the one in Pralia, and here, we six humans always shared a room together. When we were between settlements, however, we always slept in those drains, and the sleeping arrangements were always the same as they had been that first night. I was no longer as worried by this as I had been before: May had turned out to be harmless in the night, as had the other Honnies. All six of us had remained in one piece and even Tommy now believed sharing holes in the ground with them wasn't quite akin to Dracula's coffin.

We also became more familiar with their system in the three weeks since our arrival. The two half-breeds were practically the slaves of the family, it seemed, for whenever we stayed in the drains, they would invariably spend the afternoon cleaning them up, washing all the sheets and robes before the rest of us would settle down to sleep that night. They didn't bother when we stayed in the cabins, though; perhaps there were other Honnies around who made sure everything was clean before we arrived. I still had no idea what the Honnies themselves did except that it was something mental, and I really didn't care anyway.

As talking became a little easier for me (the tension in my teeth was loosening and my jaw becoming less painful by the day), I began using these nights to attempt to get inside May's head; not the same way she was in mine, but just to make her realise that perhaps her way of thinking wasn't much different from ours. The fact that we were all still alive and healthy (well, mostly) suggested that she wasn't as bad as most Honnies; still very different, but maybe not as different. I wasn't really getting anywhere with persuading her to come back to help us, but I had a feeling something was going on here, something that neither of us had complete control over. She was still very curious about me and more importantly, she still liked to get close to me on these nights when we 'slept' together. She hadn't tried to stick her tongue in my mouth again, but that may only have been because it was just about impossible to do so. I was able to keep my attraction at arm's-length by thinking of Natalie, someone else who liked to take any opportunity to get close to me these days, but I didn't push it away completely: It may yet be useful.

During the afternoons when the Honnies became absorbed in their own business, we humans were becoming more and more free to do what we liked. Sometimes we just sat together and played card games, or other games we thought of along the way (this was always the case when we were staying in cabins), but sometimes, if we were on the road, we were allowed to venture a short distance from the drain in which we slept and have a bit of a look around the countryside. On one of these occasions, it had begun to rain while we were still roughly half a mile away, but instead of heading back, we all changed into our underwear and ran around in an open paddock, allowing it to soak us. Even the three girls didn't mind being exposed in this way, perhaps because there was little to desire in them in this light. We had all adjusted somewhat to the way this world made humans appear visually, but we weren't immune to it either.

It was on July 28 when one of these ventures from camp went horribly wrong. Natalie and Rebecca had remained behind, both napping in the beds in the drain (May had allowed this) but Peter, Tommy, Candice and I, restless, had wandered a short distance to the south of the road. We weren't too far from another city (we could easily have made it there today), but for her own reasons, May had chosen to stay out here. In fact, we'd slept in drains the last nine nights in a row, even though we had passed through a few towns in that time. I had a feeling May was doing this deliberately, looking for more excuses to get close to me, but once again, I tried my best not to believe that.

As a result of our close proximity to a city, Honnies came and went on the road fairly regularly. We stayed away from them on general principle (not that we could have communicated with them anyway), but it was even more important for us because according to May, we would be regarded as free prizes by virtue of the fact that we were still wearing our own clothing. If we were to adopt Honnie attire, we would be recognised as belonging to another Honnie, and we would be safe from other Honnies. None of us wanted to do this, though, risk or no risk. As it turned out, however, the situation we landed ourselves in on this day wouldn't have gone any differently if we'd all been buck naked.

"I have to ask you something, Peter," said Candice as the four of us pushed through some thick bushes, Peter and Tommy breaking trail for Candice and me, "because Rebecca doesn't say much anymore."

"What would that be?" Peter asked, his tone suggesting he knew what was coming. I thought I knew what must be on her mind too; she was about to voice thoughts that had occurred to all of us, thoughts that were a little discomforting for at least three reasons I could think of.

"Is something going on with you two?" she asked, her tone light.

"You bet," said Tommy, making his voice a little more squeaky so that he sounded remarkably like Peter; Peter aimed a kick at him.

"Me and Rebecca?" Peter clarified. "Come on, do you think so?"

"Yeah," said Candice, totally unabashed. "Is there?"

"Be honest now," Tommy chided.

Peter sighed, defeated. "Look, it's probably not what you think."

"I bet it is what I think," said Tommy, grinning at him.

"You slee' 'ith her?" I asked him. (You sleep with her?)

"Well technically, yes," Tommy grinned. "I mean, there's not a lot of space where those two have to lie."

"Look, we've had a lot of time to talk lately," said Peter. "You know, just the two of us I mean, and we've sort of—you know—got close."

"Because you needed the comfort in each other in this strange, dangerous time," said Tommy, nodding. "Because part of you isn't entirely sure you'll get to see your real girlfriend again. Because it was just the two of you, sleeping together on a cold, hard floor. Is that the crux of it?"

"Yeah, but if I know Siobhan like I think I do, she probably won't wait for me," said Peter, and sighed again. "There's plenty to like about Rebecca, you know, and you're right; we do sort of need each other's comfort now."

"She's pretty good, huh," said Tommy, grinning at him, and we all understood the subtext.

Peter shrugged. "Do we have to talk about that?"

"No, we don't," said Candice firmly.

"She's right," said Tommy, grinning broadly. "Your lack of a response pretty much answered all my questions. Anyway, I know how you feel; I miss Jessica like no one's business, but is it so bad that I seek any comfort I can get while I can? I don't care what Natalie says; I'm not convinced we'll all get back, and none of us want to die alone."

"I hope you're not coming onto me," said Candice nervously.

Tommy laughed. "Maybe you're the only one here I haven't been with, but no; you got nothing to worry about."

"Who are you getting close to, Tonny?" I asked. It was easier to say Tonny than Tommy; they practically sounded the same anyway.

At my words, Tommy shrugged, looking awkward. "Judge not lest ye be judged, right?"

"We'll make up our own minds on that," said Candice bitterly.

"Ingi," Tommy said, surprising us all, and horrifying me a fair bit. I remembered my own strange relationship with May, but Tommy and Ingi? That was way more weird.

"Seriously?" said Peter incredulously. "I know you two sleep together a fair bit now, but how does the conversation go?"

"Has she taken you in her mind?" Candice asked.

"She can't do that," said Peter quickly. "We're all in May's mind."

"Yeah, and so is Ingi," said Candice. "As far as she's concerned, May's mind is like the open. She can take any of us if she's strong enough, and if May lets her."

With a thrill of horror, I realised that she was right, but Tommy shrugged, unconcerned. "Now that you say it like that, she probably could, but I don't think she has. For one thing, I'm getting the same things from May that all you guys are; that wouldn't be the case if Ingi had me. For another thing, we really don't communicate—we really don't have to."

"So what do you do?" Peter asked. "Do you cuddle up or something?"

"Well, it sort of started like that," said Tommy, shrugging but not looking embarrassed at all. "See, thing is, she changes her clothes before she sleeps, and I've seen her naked. Trust me, if you saw a Honnie naked, you'd wanna do her too. She didn't really care at first but the more I get close to her, she's sort of responding to me now. Whatever Honnies may be, they don't seem to be immune to closeness."

"So in this world, people and cows are more closely related," said Peter.

"'E knew dat," I pointed out. "S'iley said dey 'ate hu'ans." (We knew that; Smiley said they mate humans.)

"They eat humans?" said Candice confused.

"Mate," Peter corrected. "Yeah, they do. Do you reckon Ingi wants to make a half-breed with you, Tommy?"

Tommy shrugged again. "Well, we haven't had sex yet, and I dunno—maybe she wouldn't be allowed to until she's graduated. That might be a good thing for me, actually; it'll keep me alive a little longer if they think I can be useful. John, you should think about doing the same with May."

"I think May's got enough kids as it is," said Candice nervously. "How many half-breeds does she need?"

I shook my head. "I trying to talk to her a'out our 'orld." (I'm trying to talk to her about our world.)

"Good luck with that," said Peter darkly.

We had been moving slowly the whole time we'd been walking but now, without warning, Tommy and Peter pushed some bushes aside to reveal a large clearing. We appeared to have reached the back of some settlement (I could see a small cabin in the distance) but directly in front of us, the clearing was full of people. To the left stood five people, two Honnies and three half-breeds (they were unmistakable, even though the distance between us and them was at least two hundred feet). Before them and off to our right slightly stood a large pack of big, fat, stupid humans, all clad in Honnie robes and all as still as statues. My blood froze at the sight of them and I saw by his face that Peter also understood the imminent danger we were in.

"Geez," breathed Tommy, backing up a little so that he wouldn't be visible to those in the clearing. "Those people, my God."

"Let's get out of here before we join them," Peter hissed, also beginning to back up.

We weren't quick enough, though. Whether or not the Honnies down there ever saw us, I had no idea—in fact I would never know. All I knew for sure was that even though our minds were protected from them by May, we ourselves were still susceptible to their other powers. The two Honnies down there were both male, and at that moment, one of them turned to the humans and did something that was evidently supposed to bring them under his control. I tracked its progress through the crowd, not because it was visible, but because of the way it affected the humans as it passed over them. Or at least, some of the humans were affected—the female humans were affected.

It was too quick for us to get out of the way in time. Whether or not it could track us through the bushes, I had no idea, but I would later learn that it had been too late from the moment we had laid eyes on the Honnie who had cast the net. I felt it strike the four of us in the bushes, just as we were on the point of turning and running. It created a momentary feeling of dazedness before clearing, leaving me in one piece—I was one of the lucky ones. Tommy and Peter, the most exposed, had also been lucky, but Candice certainly wasn't. She went rigid where she stood, so much so that she almost toppled over in the grass, but she regained her balance quickly enough to prevent herself going down.

I thought I knew what was going on almost immediately, even though I'd never seen it or been told what it would look like. Bravely, stupidly, I dived at Candice, grabbing one of her wrists as I went down and dragging her down on top of me. I managed to roll as I fell so that I wouldn't damage my jaw any further, but I landed right on my left side, the side that had once had an arm to assist it. A bolt of pain shot down the ghost of my arm, pain that was entirely imaginary but nevertheless caused me to cry out. Candice came down beside me but she was much quicker to recover. I kept a tight hold on her wrist, knowing full-well that it was too late, knowing that she would now be far stronger than me, even if I had too arms. The fact that she was a petite young girl wouldn't stop her from dragging me out into that clearing if it was the only way for her to get out there.

"Hel'!" I shouted up at Tommy and Peter, both of whom stood stock-still, staring down at the pair of us on the ground, faces shocked.

Peter was quickest to understand my meaning. "Tommy, that was that love beam thing!"

"Holy crap!"

Both of them dived down to join us and a few moments later, they were on either side of Candice, holding her in place. She struggled for all she was worth and it took all of their combined effort just to hold her down. I wanted to help them but the only thing I could think of doing was to sit on her chest; my one arm was thoroughly exhausted after the effort it had already put in. Even so, it still wasn't enough. Candice was well beyond the point of reason; she was able to pull herself to her feet, dragging both of the boys up with her, making desperate sobbing noises all the while.

She twisted her body sharply to one side, bringing a knee up between Tommy's legs; he went down immediately, wheezing in pain. Peter threw an arm around her waist in a desperate attempt to hold her back but he wasn't strong enough; she twisted her body back the other way, throwing him easily to the ground. Then, she was off like a cork shot out of a champaign bottle, but in the moment before she burst into the clearing, I saw the expression on her face, and knew it would haunt me till my dying day. Candice was gone—there was nothing left of the girl who had once been a good friend of Rebecca's.

Peter, Tommy and I were all still on the ground. It took some effort for the three of us to get up (in fact, I needed their help to get back on my feet). Slowly, we crept to the edge of the bushes and carefully looked out into the clearing. The Honnie who had cast the love beam had been completely stunned by Candice, who was now hanging off him, her desire to be close to him insatiable. The other Honnie who was with him was watching on with an expression that looked almost worried. He, at least, understood that the beam had picked up a human for whom it hadn't been meant, and he seemed to be thinking of the possible consequences. There was nothing anyone could do to undo the damage; not even the Honnie responsible could fix the problem now, but the fact remained that it was a respected Honnie convention for them not to do that to a human who didn't belong to them.

Sure enough, May was very quick on the scene. Whether she had been paying close attention to us or she simply detected when Candice's brain changed, I didn't know. She burst through the bushes just to our left, passing us without a word or look and tearing down into the clearing to where the two Honnies, three half-breeds and Candice were congregated. Both Honnies started and drew together as she approached them. There was shouting going on now—at least, May was shouting; her voice carried to us on the still air, even though we couldn't understand a word she was saying. The responsible Honnie (or more like irresponsible Honnie), still with Candice hanging off him, took a step back from her, now looking scared and defiant. I had no idea how the dialogue must be, but I could imagine his position: He hadn't meant to do anything to Candice, but she'd been there, and it had been May's loose checking that allowed her to be there. Therefore, it was May's fault, not his.

May made a grab for Candice, perhaps intending to take her back against her will. I felt sorry for Candice, and even more sorry for Rebecca, who would soon hear about this, but I hoped May did bring her back. If a human had to be sacrificed to make May happy, it might as well be a human who was already ruined. That was a terrible thought but it was also a practical thought. Whether Candice had ever considered making the ultimate sacrifice for us, I didn't know, but somehow, I felt that she may have. This would surely atone for what she had done to Lisa, even if nothing else could have. Or at least, it would have been, if May had been able to take her, but the Honnie to whom Candice was now bound had different ideas.

What followed was absolutely terrible to watch. It had been bad enough seeing it in Smiley's memories but this was in person; in the present; in the flesh—literally. The girl who had once been Candice Young disappeared as the Honnie's tongue did its work, as clean and quick as Ingi had stripped down my left arm. In fact, this was even cleaner, because the sum total of drops of blood that hit the grass may have come to about seven or eight. Seconds later, all that remained was a skeleton surrounded by shreds of what had been her clothing. How quickly a person could go from being a healthy curious teenager, wondering if Tommy was coming onto her, to being completely and utterly dead.

That should have been the end of it, but apparently not. Whether for revenge, or because he had gone against more than one respected Honnie convention, May seemed to feel that she could return the favour. Just as he kicked Candice's remains out of his way, May reached out and took him by the shoulders. Her grip was strong enough to hold him in place; perhaps because he was caught by surprise, but I suspected that grip would still be strong enough to break a couple of collarbones if it fell upon human shoulders. He was considerably taller than her—she only came up to his shoulders, as she had the doctor in Pralia—but that made what she did next all the easier.

Her tongue, pointy and lethal, shot out of her open mouth, ripping through his robe and piercing his chest—piercing his heart. Blood didn't just fly—it streamed from him in every direction, and I kid you not, it was purple. May was splattered with it but it didn't hold her back. If anything, she pressed her face close to his chest and pierced even deeper into him. His howl of agony had travelled to us just as her scream of anger had, but it didn't last very long. It quickly became little more than a gurgle, and a minute later, it became nothing at all. The Honnie fell to the ground beside the girl who had ultimately cost him his life.

May turned to face the other Honnie, the one who had stood by through all of this and made no move to intervene. They exchanged words, but there was no shouting, and after about a minute, he turned his attention instead to the three half-breeds and the rest of the humans down there, all of whom had watched the incident with barely any reaction. They all went even more still as he took possession of them but none of us had any desire to watch it. May had turned and was bounding away to the east, away from us and into bushes to our left, but we could all feel her thoughts crashing upon us: We were to return to the drain, no more wandering around, and of course, there was no question of disobeying her.

* * *

They didn't yet know what had happened back at the campsite, but it was clear, when we arrived, that something in the air had changed. The half-breeds were nowhere to be seen, but Ingi was waiting by the side of the road near the cart, looking very apprehensive. When she saw us, she hurried forward, jabbering away in her language and apparently forgetting that we couldn't understand it. It was Tommy she was looking at when she spoke, and Peter and I looked sharply at him to see if he understood, if perhaps she was communicating mentally with him, but he looked completely lost.

"I'll be happy to answer your questions when you learn how to ask them in English," he said, spreading his hands in front of him.

"Where is everyone?" Peter asked, staring around. "Don't the half-breeds usually hang out here as well? And May, how come she's not waiting for us?"

"Cleaning uh, 'erha's," I muttered, (cleaning up, perhaps,) remembering how messed-up she had looked after the murder of that disrespectful Honnie—that Candice-killing Honnie. The shock of what had happened was still heavy on all three of us but I knew that, at some point, it would wear off and we would be able to grieve for Candice—at least as much as it were possible to do that for someone who, herself, was a murderer. It would happen though because the Candice we'd known over the last couple of months was not the same girl who had stood with a gun back in the Chopville High gym.

At the sound of our voices, Natalie and Rebecca began clambering out of the drain. They knew something big had happened, but the expressions on their faces told me that they didn't yet know what. I was sorry for that.

"What's going on?" Natalie asked quickly. "Where have you all been? Where did May go? She just ran for it without a word."

"And where's Candice?" Rebecca asked, nervously scrutinising the three of us. "Is she with May?"

I shook my head, looking at the other two. I couldn't tell them; I wasn't even sure I could have told them if my mouth had been in full working order.

"May killed a bloke," said Peter heavily. "I suppose she'll be back here pretty soon—she got a lot of blood on her."

"What bloke?" asked Natalie. "Why?"

Tommy and Peter looked helplessly at each other, knowing one of them had to tell them. It was Peter who took the initiative, but I could tell that he wished, very much, that he hadn't. Both girls knew as much about the love beam as we had prior to seeing it, so it didn't take them long to understand that once it had washed over us, there was no hope for Candice. When Rebecca managed to ask where Candice was now, Peter sighed and told them that the Honnie who'd done it had killed her before May could stop him, and so she had killed him in retaliation.

The retelling of the story was enough to dull the shock, and now I felt the despair take me. Seeing a life taken so quickly and cleanly was enough to make one realise how cheap it was in the eyes of others. Candice had been just like the rest of us, and now she was just a bag of bones. What would happen to her? Would she be left in that clearing with that Honnie and all those other humans? Would May go back for her and dispose of her herself? And underneath it all, the mantra: One down, five to go.

I turned and walked away from the others, heading just past the drain and stopping just short of the bushes on that side of the road. Peter, all his energy spent on what he'd just put himself through, collapsed against the cart, trying to keep his emotions in check. Rebecca, her emotions well and truly shot, went straight to him and held onto him, confirming what Peter had told us less than an hour earlier. Tommy stood alone on the road, staring blankly in the direction of the city we would pass through the following day. The sight of him like that in the afternoon sun would have been worthy of a front cover of some stupid romance novel, I thought, but there was nothing romantic about this scene. Ingi had watched him for a couple of minutes before going to him and taking him by the shoulder; he started at her touch but relaxed when he saw that she didn't intend to hurt him. Perhaps there was a bit of good in her after all, I thought bitterly. Natalie, having watched all this, now came to me and leaned on my good side, sobbing. I put an arm around her, liking the closeness, but hating the situation that had brought it about.

How long we stood like that, the six of us, the five humans and one Honnie, I didn't know. Several Honnies passed us by on the road, swerving around Tommy and Ingi as they were in the way but never slowing down. Dan and Gob returned at some point; they did nothing to break up the scene but they certainly looked confused by the sight of Ingi standing with Tommy. It was only when May finally returned that we all came back to our senses. I had been right: Whether May had spent all this time cleaning herself up, I didn't know, but she was certainly clean now, her hair and robe damp and her skin seeming to glisten. She looked very grim indeed, and to my relief, she was not carrying Candice's remains.

She ordered us all, including her children, off the road and to a clear spot where we could set up camp for another evening dinner of gradi. She didn't say that, of course; in fact she didn't say any of it. The command came mentally and we all obeyed it without question, but I had enough of my own rationale to feel scared. This immediate return to Honnie convention could be a huge step backwards for our mission over here. If there were any chance May could spare us, or even help us, it had now become extremely slim.

"You know what happened?" May said to Natalie and Rebecca, and when they both nodded, tears in their eyes, May frowned. "You humans should not have gone so far from camp. Humans do not do that in this world. You must understand that you are not at home anymore. You must do things our way, or things like this can happen."

"It didn't have to go like that though," said Tommy in a strangled voice.

"Why would any Honnie do that without making sure there are no other humans in the area?" Peter asked. "What if we'd been there with you? How would you have stopped it."

"I would not have been there with you," she said flatly. "Honnies can feel the minds of other Honnies in the area; he would have sensed me if I was close because I was stronger than him. This is why we keep distances from each other, and this is why humans do not go wandering."

"'Hy did he kill her?" (Why did he kill her?) I asked. I thought I knew the answer but wanting to be sure.

"Isn't that kind of obvious?" said Tommy bitterly.

"Because I wanted to take her," said May. "She was mine and I should have been allowed to take her. She could have been very useful to Ingi and me but he considered that it was my fault for letting her come that close to him, and she was to be his reward."

"But he had all those humans already," said Peter, shuddering. "Were they all his humans?"

"They were trading," said May. "He was allowing his friend to take ownership of two of his sons, and receiving those humans as his repayment. His partner took everything when he died."

"You mean when you killed him," said Tommy boldly; not accusingly, just merely telling it like it was.

May stared at him for a moment, gauging his mood from his mind before responding. "Yes, I did. He did me great disrespect. Things like that are so rare in our world, so I do not think he expected me to retaliate."

"So where is she now?" Rebecca asked in a small voice.

"He had a bin," said May remorselessly. "Most Honnies have them for disposing of what is left of humans."

"Rest in peace, Candy," Rebecca muttered, beginning to cry again.

"None of you will wander away from us anymore," said May firmly. "I was stupid to let you go in the first place. Normally, humans are not even given the choice, so now it looks like I will have to take your choice away too. I hope you understand how foolish you were."

"I think you've got the message across," said Peter flatly.

"Can I ask a question?" said Natalie nervously. And when May looked at her without raising an objection, "What would you have done with Candice if that Honnie had let you take her?"

"I am not sure," said May thoughtfully. "Probably I would have given her to Ingi; it would lead her to graduate much sooner."

"You wouldn't have even considered letting her live?" said Peter harshly.

"For what purpose?" May asked, genuinely surprised. "She was ruined. I still had her mind but as a person, there was nothing left of her. Only her body remained useful."

"'E knew dat," (We knew that,) I told Peter, who looked ready to argue the case further. He shrugged, looking disgusted, but didn't continue that topic.

"Can I raise another pertinent question, then?" Natalie asked. When May looked back at her, she said, "What does this mean for us?"

The atmosphere around the circle changed immediately. Where before it had been a mixture of grief, sorrow and distaste, now everyone's posture straightened rigidly. Every face looked wary, and Ingi and the two half-breeds weren't immune to the tension; the boys exchanged a puzzled, alarmed look while Ingi let out a soft growling noise. Only May looked relatively calm; she seemed to be giving the question great consideration.

"I do not think it means anything different for you," she finally said. "The only difference I see is that before, I had six humans; now I only have five. To me, that is a loss."

"It shouldn't be," said Tommy boldly, "because in case you've forgotten, finding us was a bonus in the first place. Five may be less than six, but it's a fair bit more than zero."

"Geez, Tommy," said Peter, covering his face in disgust.

"Don't look at me like that; that's how Honnies think."

"That is correct," May agreed, "but what I said is also correct. I still want Ingi to have at least one of your minds when she graduates, because she is presently not strong enough to be an adult Honnie. She would be vulnerable."

"You couldn't trade something to get a human in return?" Tommy enquired.

"All I have to trade is Gob and Dan," said May, "and why should I trade them when I already have humans? That is a foolish waste of resources."

"So if she gets one of our minds," said Rebecca slowly, "what does that mean for the rest of us?"

"I will decide that when the time comes," said May firmly. "You are all intelligent, so you may be extremely valuable to me later. It is only if I wish to take advantage of that. If not, I think Ingi could use all of you."

"And what about us?" Natalie asked. "What about what we came here for? Does that come into your calculations at all?"

"You still do not tell me what good that will do Honnies," said May. "Another waste of resources, I think."

"I'll tell you what good it could do Honnies, if you're willing," Tommy told her. "Our world is full of humans. If you let us, we can direct you to the ones we don't mind you bringing back here."

"Tommy," said Peter warningly.

"Hammerhearts, obviously," said Tommy quickly, his eyes widening. "I'm just trying to think the way they do. That Honnie Smiley saw may have broken his deal but May looks like she has more honour than that. You do, don't you?" he added.

"Honour?" May repeated, and now her expression changed; she looked like she had suddenly been put on the back foot. Tommy's line of thinking may be heartless and brutal, but that seemed to be the way to reason with Honnies.

"Well, if you made a deal, would you consider breaking it later?" Tommy enquired.

"Only if I intended to break it when I made it," she replied.

"So only if you were bluffing?"

"Yes."

"Is that Honnie convention too?"

"No, but it is not Honnie convention to make deals with humans at all," said May. "We do nothing to give humans leverage over us."

"Okay, fine," said Tommy, nodding, "but just think about this. Our world is packed full of humans—intelligent humans, by your standards. In the current climate, many of them are being killed for pretty much no reason. Is that not also a great waste of resources? Do you think it would be a gain to Honnie society if a Honnie could step in and stop that enormous waste of human lives?"

"*Score*," Peter hissed, his eyes gleaming.

"I am not a collector," May said firmly. "I am a fairly strong Honnie, but I am not qualified to enter your world. Any other Honnie would not listen to you because human affairs are always silly and hardly worth our notice. Tell me how you expect a Honnie to help you."

"I thought we covered that on our first night here," said Natalie. "You just come through with us, take some humans in your mind and muck with them a bit so that they stop causing trouble."

Tommy shook his head. "I get what she's saying, guys. May, you could help us if you became qualified to be a collector. If you're such a strong Honnie, how hard could it be?"

"I do not know," said May. "I have never met a collector, so I do not know how strong they need to be. What exactly do you mean when you say 'muck'?"

"Well it's a nicer way of saying another word that starts with F and rhymes with it," said Peter, but Tommy elbowed him to make him shut up.

"Fit?" May said, confused.

"Forget he said anything," said Tommy quickly. "Look, guys, that's not gonna be enough to convince her. She has to be able to take some humans back with her. It can't be Hammerson, because we need his body as evidence, but perhaps Hall or Cornish—they would deserve nothing better. Their army is big enough that May could have a couple of thousand if that's what it took."

"Is it necessary to kill that many people?" said Rebecca in a small voice.

"Ja'es said it 'ight 'e," (James said it might be,) I reminded them, now understanding where Tommy was coming from. In a way, it was completely heartless, but it couldn't possibly be as bad as how it had ended in 1981. We just had to make sure May took the right people. The trouble through all of this would be keeping her in check; once she got through, May could do whatever she liked, and nothing we could do would stop her.

"I suppose the thing for you, May, will be deciding if we're worth the trouble," said Tommy, "but you said it yourself: No other Honnie would listen to us. Would it be such a good thing for Honnies if the human race practically exterminated itself? The only thing is, in order to fix it, you would need to follow our instructions. Does that sound like something you could consider doing?"

"I do not know," said May firmly, an expression of resolve coming over her face. I swapped a look with Peter, both of us knowing that the subject was now closed. Whether or not Tommy had done anything to convince May to help us, I didn't know, but I knew he'd done enough to make her extremely uncomfortable. I considered my own role to play in all of this, thinking that the final straw to break May's back may have something to do with emotion. If that were so, I was in the best position to push this thing further.

Chapter 25: On the Road

Another two weeks passed without much event, but for me, the main event in and of itself was the ticking I could now constantly hear inside my head. We were quickly running out of time: Every day that passed brought us a day closer to the end, and we still had nothing close to assurance that May would come down on the same side as us. None of the others had pursued the matter any further with her, though, because on the one and only night since Candice's death in which we had slept in a cabin, I had informed them all that I intended to do my darnedest to touch her in the right way—whatever that meant.

That had been on the night of July 31, and it had been the only time I'd been able to talk to the others without the Honnies being present. Granted, May knew everything we were thinking anyway, and also granted, none of the others could understand what we said anyway, but it was still human instinct to discuss them in that way without them being within earshot. We were no longer allowed to wander away from camp; everywhere we went, at least one of the Honnies accompanied us, and when Ingi did whatever it was she did with her brothers that would ultimately lead to her graduation, May kept us all under close guard. It meant that none of us could even have a crap without Honnie supervision (May nearly always seemed to be the one supervising me, I noticed) and on the night we had camped close to a river, they had all watched the five of us as we washed ourselves and all our clothes in it.

This clampdown resulted in us getting much less exercise, which meant that the gradi was beginning to do its work on our bodies. It wasn't too noticeable yet, but the early signs were there. I could feel my own body a little more sluggish than it had been in living memory, and my jeans had become a little tighter than they had been when I'd left. Peter and Tommy looked as though they were going through the same thing. It was even harder to spot with the Fletcher girls, but it was there.

All in all, I thought each of us may have put on three or four kilograms; not much yet, but the whole thing was designed to turn us into big, fat slobs just like the other humans we had seen in this world.

As we were sleeping in drains most of these nights, and as I was still sharing a hole with May, I was using as much time with her as I could to try to get inside her mind. I hadn't forgotten the line Tommy had taken after Candice had died, and I still brought it up from time to time, but it didn't seem to be enough to convince her to go to the trouble of becoming a collector for our benefit. Calling it a favour wouldn't have done any good either because as she had said, Honnies didn't just do favours. None of us were in a hurry to go the same way as Candice, but privately, I thought that if it had to be done, perhaps I had to be the one to do it. Maybe that was the trigger that would be required to set the three momentous steps in motion.... I knew not, but if it came to a situation where we needed to find out, I preferred to take that chance than let any of the others pointlessly sacrifice themselves.

In the meantime, I thought that the one thing I still had on my side was emotion. However different Honnies may be from humans, they were not immune to closeness. May's seeming desire to be close to me was proof of that, and more proof was coming from Ingi, who seemed to be taking more and more to Tommy over the days since Candice's death. I didn't dare ask May what might be going on in Ingi's head, though I was sure she knew, but on the one occasion when Tommy and I were alone but for one of the half-breeds who couldn't understand us anyway, I decided to follow up on what he had told us in the bushes on that fateful day.

"I know. It's strange, huh," he said conversationally from several feet away (both of us had our dacks around our ankles, so we didn't dare look at each other). "I know your opinion of her can't be too high after what she did to you, but I tell you what, she doesn't seem to be quite as robotic as we first thought."

"'Ell 'e know she's not a 'achine," I said, not entirely sure I believed that. (Well we know she's not a machine.)

"I thought she was," he said darkly. "I thought they all were, but since she touched me that day on the path, I guess she does like me more."

"Ha'e you done any'hing 'ith her yet?" I asked. (Have you done anything with her yet?)

"You mean when we've been sleeping together?"

"Yeah."

"More than I thought we would do," he said, and I heard him finishing up. "I sort of wish I could talk to her now because I don't understand why she does what she does. I thought she wanted to kiss me one time, but instead she stuck her tongue down my throat—I mean *right* down it, almost choked me. It should have made me puke on her, but instead it made me horny."

"You don't shay," (You don't say,) I said, believing every word he said and not willing to explain why. "Did you do any'hing a'ter dat?" (Did you do anything after that?)

"Yeah, we did it," he said, and I could hear the mixture of pride, surprise and maybe a touch of shame in his voice. "I'd go back and change that if I could, 'cause I really thought my cheating days were done, you know, but I didn't really think about it—it just happened."

"Dat's 'at dey all shay," (That's what they all say,) I said, feeling my lips twitch in a reluctant grin. "Sho 'ash it good?" (So was it good?)

"Was it good," he said, and it was more of a reflection than a question. "Was it what.... I tell you what, if I'd thought about it, I would have been scared shitless, since she could have killed me a hundred times in there, but that's the whole point—I didn't think about it."

This was more information than I'd ever heard Tommy speak of his sex life. Was it just because it was with a Honnie? I had to assume so, because I couldn't imagine him speaking about Jessica like this.

"But yeah, it was pretty good, in a strange sort of way," he said, and sighed. "It's made her like me a lot more, and she wants it most nights now—or I want it, it's hard to tell. I just don't know if it's all such a good thing. It feels good, but I'm sure it all felt good for Candice before…"

He trailed off, and I felt my stomach lurch horribly. Yes, Candice would have been in a blissful paradise as she hung off the Honnie who would shortly strip the flesh off her bones. This led me to a very unpleasant thought, and I said, "Has Ingi done dat to you?"

"Done what?"

"'At ha'ened to Candice?" (What happened to Candice?)

"No," he said firmly, and now he came over to help me back to my feet, both of us having finished our business. "Do you see me acting like a maniac, trying to kick you guys in the nuts to get to her? No, what I meant is she may have marked me for mating. I don't think I've knocked her up yet, not that I'd know, but if that's what's on her mind, I'll probably have to be the sacrifice for you guys to keep going."

"Cra'," (Crap,) I said bitterly, and he laughed.

"It's not great, I know. Hopefully it doesn't have to be that way, but if it does, I can maybe do my bit. I feel like I've got a bit to make up for; maybe that would do it."

I wondered what he meant by that, but I never got a chance to find out. August 12 was the night that the situation changed again. It was past bedtime and everyone was in the drains—at least, seven out of the nine of us were (Rebecca hadn't wanted to sleep with Gob, and May hadn't forced her to). Whether the others were sleeping or not, I didn't know, but May and I certainly weren't. We were now just four days of travel from Lagalia and our time had become desperately short. It didn't matter that Ingi wouldn't graduate until they reached their home town; once we were past the big city, we wouldn't get a chance to get back home.

For that reason, I decided to have another go at a private assignment I had set myself regarding May. Just the fact that she seemed to like being close to me, this human she found more strange than the others (because I could send thoughts as well as receive them) wasn't enough. Perhaps it was built into Honnie physiology that they should feel attracted to humans sometimes so that creating half-breeds could be possible; that sounded reasonable, in which case it meant that I had to do better. So, what I wanted was for May to be genuinely sorry for what she had allowed Ingi to do to me. I knew that if I could get a heart-felt apology from her, an apology based on the pain I'd been put through rather than her own inconvenience, I would be a long way to getting her to feel for all the people in our world suffering because of the Hammersons. Unfortunately, my first attempt some weeks ago had not gone very well.

"Yes, I was sorry for that," she had told me. "If not for that, we would be on schedule, but that put us several days behind."

"No," I had said firmly. "You know it hurt 'e a lot 'en dat ha'ened, right?" (You know it hurt me a lot when that happened, right?)

She considered this for a moment before shrugging—I felt her do it in the darkness. "Ingi has not had practise yet. If she had been cleaner, you would have felt no pain, but you would also not be here to talk about it. I am not sorry for that."

Not very good—not very good at all. It confirmed that she preferred me to be alive rather than dead, at least for the time being, but it hadn't brought me any closer to touching her emotional side. I hadn't given up, though; I knew I only needed to find the right argument, to present it with the right wording, and maybe a few well-chosen thoughts to go with it. Most of May's actions could be explained with reason (at least, a Honnie version of it) but there was still something different about it. If there were any Honnies in touch with human emotions, it would be those Honnies who understood humans the best. May was in a unique class in that respect. Tommy had been right on the first day: She was perfect for the job, but that still didn't mean she would take it.

So on that night of August 12, I decided to have yet another go at it. May was becoming more and more familiar with how I went about this (no doubt hearing all my thoughts helped) but she still seemed patient enough to listen to me when I spoke. That was another good sign, but yet again, it still didn't help me much.

"Ha'e you eher 'elt pain?" I asked her. (Have you ever felt pain?)

"Everyone feels pain sometimes," she said expressionlessly.

"Yeah, 'ut your own pain," I insisted, "not just 'rom hu'ans' 'inds, 'ut your own 'ody." (Yeah, but your own pain, not just from humans' minds, but your own body.)

I knew it wasn't impossible for Honnies to feel pain—the way the Honnie who'd killed Candice behaved in his final seconds was proof of that—but I needed to know if May had any experiences to help me out. I thought there must be, but if so, May wasn't saying. She must have sensed that this was an area where I could hold leverage over her, which was unacceptable, of course.

"I have nothing to relate to your pain," she finally said. "You can feel that I still have both of my arms. There is not much that could change that."

That would be true, of course—she was such an incredibly strong specimen—but that didn't mean her whole body would be quite as tough as what met the eye. Certainly the human body, male and female alike, had certain spots which could provide enormous pain without much provocation. There were probably certain parts of May's body that would be just as sensitive. Perhaps they would be the same on her as they would on a human female; after all, Honnie bodies were almost the same as humans, once you got past the massive strength and the lethal tongue.

I wouldn't be capable of touching anywhere May didn't want me to, especially with only one arm, but I didn't need to. We were still lying very close, one of her arms around me, my arm resting on her raised shoulder, our bodies almost against each other. She knew exactly where my thoughts were going, and I felt her give an involuntary shudder as those parts of her must have felt imaginary pain, prodded in the right direction by my thoughts. I was satisfied.

"Humans," she muttered condescendingly, but I knew it was only a distraction—she didn't want me to pursue that subject. That was her way of deflecting any situation that I could use to my own advantage. I let her off the hook this time, but I wouldn't forget what had just happened.

The trouble was, I almost did forget it, because little more than two seconds later, giving me an enormous fright, May let out a cry of dismay and bounded up, shattering the panel above us with an explosive crash. Fragments of wood hit the floor all around it, at least one flying over the wall into the sluice, and one striking Peter (I heard him cry out in pain) but none of them hit me. Stunned, I sat up and then pulled myself onto my knees so that I could see what was happening outside the hole. Peter and Rebecca were both sitting up, both fully clothed (thank God) but equally as stunned as me, their mouths open in horror. To either side of them, Dan and Gob had raised their own panels to see what all the fuss was about. Natalie was nestled in there with Dan, not a lot of room for her to move but at least she could lie there without having to cuddle up to him; her face was quite as pale as the rest of ours.

Ingi and Tommy were the centre of attention. May had bounded across the room and ripped up their panel, exposing the two of them together. She hadn't caught them having sex (she must have already known about that) but she did seem to have sprung them in the middle of something. I couldn't see anything particularly alarming though; not at first anyway. Ingi was sitting up against the back of her bed, perhaps having scuttled backward when her mother had burst in on her. She was presently looking up at May like a child caught in wrong-doing—the expression was unmistakable, even on a Honnie face. Tommy was beside her, his arms wrapped around her and his face hidden against her shoulder. He was doing nothing to help her situation; in fact, he wasn't even acknowledging May's presence.

May shouted at Ingi and Ingi burst into tears and shouted something back, looking very much like a human child in that moment. None of us could understand what was being said, of course, except for the half-breeds, who both started when they understood what had happened, exchanging a look across three humans that seemed to be wary. All I could do was swap a horrified look with Peter before turning my attention back to Tommy. What was going on with him?

That question was answered a moment later when May stepped down onto Ingi's bed and, to our collective horror, slapped her daughter across the face. Ingi's head rocked back and hit the wall behind her, causing it to crack (I mean the wall cracked, not Ingi's head). Tommy was jolted from her, hitting the side of the bed but comparatively unhurt. He jerked back toward Ingi, but it was now May he was looking at, and the expression was venomous. 'Don't you dare do that to her again,' it seemed to say, and comprehension hit me with the force of a charging bull. There was no recognition in his face, and now, as far as he was concerned, there was only one object of interest in his world. He may have been in his right mind that day we had spoken of Ingi while dropping our loads, but he wasn't anymore.

"Oh no," I heard Rebecca moan, having understood the same thing.

That had been a very long night indeed. None of us had slept as we sat in a circle around the room, trying to work out what was to happen next. Well, that wasn't quite true; Dan and Gob decided to go back to bed, perhaps on May's orders, having nothing useful to contribute to the discussion. Ingi was the centre of attention and much scrutiny from all corners, and unfortunately Tommy, since he refused to let go of her. After a short interrogation which had been done mentally, May took control of her daughter's mind and quite literally forced her to sit still while she spoke to the rest of us.

"You know what it is," she said, looking at Tommy with an expression that might have been pity. "She was not allowed to do that; no Honnie is allowed to do that until they graduate.

She thought she would try it, because she liked him more than she was supposed to, and she wanted to make sure he liked her back. She didn't know how he felt of her since they could not talk to each other."

"Does this mean she fails?" said Peter bitterly.

May looked confused. "Fails? I do not think so. I did not know she could do that yet. I do not think she knew she could do that. That means she is quite strong, and almost ready. I cannot fail her for that."

"But what about Tommy?" said Natalie shrilly. "What about Tommy?"

May took a moment before answering. "I am sorry, but I cannot fix him," she said, not sounding sorry at all. "This is not recoverable. The most I can do is make sure he is fully utilised."

"What does that mean, exactly?" said Rebecca.

"She must absorb his mind," said May. "There is a bit there for her to get from him, and his body will help her greatly too. It might even be good for her to breed with him."

"So that's it?" said Peter incredulously. "Close the book? Skip the report? No correspondence entered into?"

"What does that mean?" May asked blankly.

"Read my mind and find out," Peter snapped back.

May decided to ignore this provocation. "She does not want to use him. She likes his attention. I think we can keep him at least until we get to Malia, but there is no point in letting him live—he will become an inconvenience to Ingi eventually."

"How could this happen?" Natalie asked softly. "Don't you keep an eye on all our minds? Or is Ingi exempt from that since she's a Honnie?"

"I normally do keep check on Ingi since I have had you humans," she said, looking sharply at me, as though it was my fault that she'd been forced to do that, "but I was distracted when Ingi pulled this on me."

So it really *was* my fault. I couldn't bring myself to take blame for what had happened to Tommy. Ingi could be blamed, since she had done it, but beyond that, the only person who could really be held responsible was Tommy himself. If he hadn't given Ingi that kind of attention, their relationship probably wouldn't have gone any further than whatever was going on between Natalie and Dan—bugger all, in other words. He'd done it without thinking, he had said, and that had been out of loneliness and missing Jessica, he had also said. So basically, he had been betrayed by his penis. Perhaps that was too crude to cover it all properly, but essentially it was true. I supposed he wasn't the first man in history, nor would he be the last, to have his fate decided by that particular organ.

* * *

We continued on our way the next morning but without our usual energy. Dan and Gob were the only ones who were truly awake, but they were forced to pull our cart along at a leisurely stroll compared to their usual bounding steps. There were now only four of us sitting in the cart because Tommy couldn't bear to be out of arms reach of Ingi; she had to literally carry him along in her arms. She was as tired as the rest of us, having not slept either, but she wasn't having any trouble with supporting Tommy; in fact, aside from the bruise on her face where May had hit her, she looked rather content. I couldn't stand to look at either of them, so I switched my gaze to the other side where May was walking. She had changed again since leaving that morning; it may have been nothing more than lack of sleep, but she looked as though some vitality had left her. If anything, it made her look more human. I had to wonder if this whole experience was wearing her down…would that be a good thing for us? If it was causing this reaction, perhaps not. She knew she could solve all her problems by simply killing the whole lot of us; I dearly hoped she didn't decide that would be best.

It was easier to judge distances travelled at this slower speed. We passed through another small town before beginning to climb up a rather large hill whose gradient wasn't steep, but it looked a long way up. I remembered back to one night around the campfire when we had questioned May about

Lagalia, the city where our fate would be decided. She had told us that it sat atop the highest mountain in this land. I didn't think this was it; it was big, but surely not the biggest. Nevertheless, if the terrain was to become more mountainous, we had to be closing in. This morning would slow us down, but the way things were going, it wouldn't be enough. By the time the sun was directly overhead, I estimated we had travelled maybe fifteen kilometres since the start of the day.

We may have proceeded further in the afternoon; May had to be considering it, since the events of the previous night had already screwed up their routine so thoroughly. We didn't get a chance, though, because about half an hour after midday on that day, August 13, we were intercepted by the greatest danger we had faced since entering into this world. This wasn't just trouble for us humans; this was a deadly situation for all nine of us. Another band of Honnies had set up camp to the right side of the road, appearing to be heading in the opposite direction. We only saw five strapping half-breeds on our approach (four male, one female, but she was broad enough for it not to make a difference) but when we drew almost level with them, we were called to a halt by an older male Honnie.

Surprisingly, Dan and Gob were the only ones who immediately gauged the danger of the situation; perhaps they picked up some unknown cues from their fellow half-breeds. Ingi only looked irritated at the interruption and May only looked polite as she stepped forward to address the stranger. Of course, none of us humans had any idea what was going on, but the four of us in the cart seemed to pick up on the danger quicker than May and Ingi; in my case, because I had seen too many ambushes already for my liking. The most obvious sign was the way the half-breeds surreptitiously disbanded, fanning out in separate directions so that they could encircle the cart at what should have appeared a non-threatening distance. At the same time, a group of large, stupid humans replaced them where they had stood and, bringing up the rear from inside the drain they were occupying, a second male Honnie, this one young and bold.

May and the older Honnie were speaking in their language, and now the younger Honnie came over to join them, appraising us all briefly before turning his attention to May. It was impossible to follow the conversation exactly as it developed, not being able to understand the language, but May was able to communicate the general gist of it by planting thoughts in our minds. They had seen us coming, it seemed, and decided that we were worth approaching. The older Honnie had a proposal to make, and after getting a nod of approval from his younger partner—his son, now I came to look more closely at their likenesses…

I guessed what the proposal was at the same time it was spoken just by the reaction of Ingi and the two half-breeds; all three started and, in Ingi's case, growled dangerously. A moment later, May confirmed it. Was this normally how Honnies set their children up with what they deemed a suitable partner? If so, it was very old-fashioned, but somehow I didn't think this was how it normally worked. If this was standard, why the ambush?

"We're in trouble," Peter muttered from behind me.

"No we're not," said Rebecca reasonably. "They'll work it out one way or another and we'll be on our way."

It was as though her words were the catalyst. The two male Honnies seized May and hauled her off the road so quickly that we barely marked their movements. Almost in the same instant, Dan and Gob attempted to make a break for it, perhaps believing they would be next. In fact, they succeeded, but the nearest enemy half-breeds snapped the ropes between them and the cart before they'd gone more than a fraction of a step. The resultant jolt caused the whole cart to flip right over; all four of us screamed as it landed on its front, fortunately coming down the right way up, but the second crash as it landed back on its wheels just about knocked the wind out of all of us.

"*Run!*" Peter wheezed behind me, undoing his belt and hurrying to help Rebecca with hers. I struggled with my own for several moments before Natalie came to my rescue.

By the time we all jumped down from the cart, the situation had already developed. The half-breeds had closed in, not looking on the verge of attacking but looking ready to stop us from trying to escape. The younger enemy Honnie was still on the scene, and he really did look ready to attack, but at some stage while we'd been struggling with our belts, Ingi had put herself between him and us. Tommy was still hanging onto her but now she had shifted him to her back in such a protective stance that I almost felt ready to think good of her. The male Honnie was staring at her as though she were the only thing he cared about, and there was animal lust in his eyes. I couldn't see her face but I hoped she was ready to fight him.

As for May and the older Honnie, they had both disappeared. I didn't know where but I was very worried by what I could feel happening around my mind. I had become so accustomed to that rubber glove feeling around it that I didn't even notice it anymore, but I could feel it now, and the reason why I could feel it was because it was beginning to slip. Whatever that Honnie was doing to May, it was causing her to lose hold of us. Was he penetrating her mind in an attempt to steal Ingi from her? I thought that was most likely, but if that were true, he wouldn't stop there; after all, intelligent humans were valuable resources. If May couldn't fight back, and Ingi couldn't fight this Honnie on her own (I doubted she could), we were hopelessly outnumbered. If they couldn't stand up, our mission would end right here, less than a week from our destination.

"Guysh," I said, "'e ha'e to do so'e'hing." (Guys, we have to do something.)

"What's your plan, John?" Peter asked, appearing at my right shoulder while the Fletchers gathered to my left.

"I dunno—check de 'agsh," (Check the bags,) I told them, because it was all I could think of at the moment.

"We didn't pack any weapons," said Natalie bitterly. "Whoever thought of that, I'm gonna kill them."

"Good thing; how would we go fighting this lot?" said Rebecca.

"'E only le't out 'hings dey could 'hink are 'ea'ons," (We only left out things they could think are weapons,) I pointed out, wishing more than ever we had a few bludginators handy —that would throw them off balance for sure.

"How about this," said Peter, returning to my side and holding something out in his hand.

I stared numbly down at it, simultaneously horrified and enormously relieved. It wasn't a bludginator, or an agonator, or even a stunner; it was better than all three of them. How had someone managed to mix an invisibility toggle in with the clothes, for that was the bag Peter had looked in? How could we have gone more than a month in this world without finding it until now?

"Oh my God," Natalie whispered.

"It was in one of Tommy's pockets," said Peter. "Wonder what other surprises he kept from us? This is for you, Maahoo man."

Quick as a flash, he pointed the device at each of us in turn, then himself, clicking each time. We all vanished from each other's vision and had to hold onto each other to know where we each were. I had a moment to wonder, almost hopelessly, if the magic would firstly work in this world, and if so, would it affect the eyes of Honnies? To my delight, both questions turned out to be affirmative. All the half-breeds around us gasped in surprise and began jabbering at each other rapidly, probably trying to decide what to do. Ingi looked around at us in surprise, and taking advantage of her lapse, the male Honnie before her launched himself forward, knocking her into the cart and shattering it. Tommy, the only human still visible aside from those in the enemy camp, was thrown backwards, landing in bushes on the other side of the road and not emerging. I hoped he had been knocked out and would stay that way until this business was over, one way or the other.

With Ingi and her attacker out of our way, we now had a clear path to the drain in which this party had been camping. The lid was open and I felt sure that May had been taken down there by the older Honnie. I urged Natalie and Peter forward in the direction of the drain, not daring to speak aloud lest one of the half-breeds discover our presence and deduce what was going on. Under cover of the noise Ingi and her assailant were making as he tried to do who-knew-what to her, we hurried forward and, Peter first, slipped into the drain and straight into the sluice. If there had been water in it, the splash probably would have alerted the Honnie to our presence, but he was nevertheless absorbed in what he was doing to pay attention to us.

And what he was doing was utterly terrible. He was crouched on the other side of the room between the two closed panels under which the half-breeds would normally sleep. He had one knee on top of May, holding her down as she struggled for all she was worth. The robe she had left our last campsite with was now ripped almost to shreds, as was her skin beneath it. If this Honnie was anywhere near as strong as her, and he had to be if he could hold her down, he could have killed May easily in the time he'd had. Yet for his own reasons, he had decided that torture by way of a pointy tongue served his purpose better. What was his purpose? To weaken her? To make her give in and surrender Ingi to his son? Something like that, I assumed. He'd done a good job of it; May was still alive and still fighting with everything she had, but she was covered in bright purple blood, as was the floor around her.

Unfortunately, as much as we needed to stop this, being invisible on its own did us no good at all. Meanwhile, the possibility existed that one of the others from upstairs might decide to come down and see if we were here. We had to act quickly. I squeezed Natalie and Peter's hands, hoping they would take that to mean they shouldn't follow, and vaulted the wall one-handed, landing on the other side on my feet. That was the most athletic thing I'd done since—I couldn't even remember when. What I needed was something large and loose that I could strike the Honnie with. One of these panels would be ideal, except that they were all attached to the floor, so that was no good. I instead opened the nearest one, quickly ripped up one of the blankets, arranged it into a makeshift lasso (very difficult one-handed, let me tell you) and threw.

I was never a chance to pull him back, even if I'd had the strength of two arms, but I nevertheless got the best possible result out of it. The blanket fell down on his shoulders, covering his face completely. He yelled in surprise as his eyes were covered, disorientating him. He leapt up, ripping at it and tearing it off, staring wildly around to see who had thrown it and seeing no one. It didn't matter, though, because the room was so bloody small that he had staggered right into me a moment before the blanket had come off. He made to bound back at me, and I probably came within a split second of being strawberry jam against the wall, had it not been for May, who came to save my life for a second time. The Honnie had accidentally released her in his surprise, and now she shot up, not all the way but just enough to take possession of his crotch in one hand. That was enough to throw him back, howling; and a second later, May was upon him, piercing his heart the same way she had dealt with the Honnie who had killed Candice.

The purple blood flew yet again, and this time we were all too close. I was splattered with it, as were the others (I saw it strike their invisible forms in the sluice); it was warm, sticky, smelly and just damn unpleasant. May became drenched in it so that now, in addition to her own blood, she could quite easily have been mistaken for the Flying Purple People Eater. As she had two weeks earlier, she did not stop until the offending Honnie was still and lifeless.

The moment it was all over, two things happened simultaneously. I felt the rubber glove around my mind tighten once again as May regained control over all of us; and at the same time, May herself collapsed, right on top of her attacker turned victim. For a few seconds, nothing whatsoever happened, and I had time to realise that all the sounds from above had also ceased. Then, I felt the command from May push its way into my mind, and although it was weaker than usual, there was no question of disobeying. I vaulted back over the wall into the sluice, not having any trouble with that part of it, but there was no way I could climb the ladder without help; I'd always had May to help me with that before, but she was well past it now.

"Somebody call the cops," Peter muttered from just above me as he and the girls followed May's instructions.

There was nothing any of them could do to help me, and nothing I could do but wait at the bottom of the ladder for something to happen. About a minute later, by which time the others had all reached the surface, it did. Ingi, looking bruised and battered but relatively in one piece compared to her mother, bounded through the drain, landing where I had been standing moments earlier and carrying a human in her arms—one of the enemy camp's humans. It was a middle-aged man, bald and very fat, and he was dead. I didn't need anyone to tell me how it had happened: The moment she had taken control of our minds again, May had also taken control of the minds of all the enemies. The humans who had been with them had been drained immediately, and now she required one of their bodies to make her better. I turned away, wishing I couldn't hear the noises behind me as that man was stripped to the bone.

Chapter 26: Pain

As we had already stepped so far from normal Honnie customs, it hardly mattered what we did next. That afternoon was spent with most of us sleeping under a tent near the death drain, as it would now be called. Nobody discussed what was to happen next; would we sleep under that tent that night as well, or would we continue moving under cover of darkness? The only thing that was for certain was that nobody would be sleeping in the drain that night.

According to May, Honnies didn't have law enforcement because they didn't normally need it; their society was so organised that incidents such as this had to be a once-in-a-blue-moon thing, and nobody had any issue with them sorting out their own fights. There was no danger of anyone being convicted but the fact remained that Honnies would happen along here and would want to use this drain. So while all us humans, May and Ingi rested, the half-breeds (now seven of them) plus the Honnie who had tried to rape Ingi and had been unsuccessful (his name turned out to be Grid, or something that sounded like that) were set to the task of cleaning up the road and more importantly, the interior of the drain.

The only casualties from the incident were the Honnie May had killed, and the humans she had also killed. As I had suspected, she had drained their minds the moment she had control of them, and used their bodies to get her strength back. She was still in a bad way though, badly cut in a lot of places. She was adamant that they would heal on their own, and maybe she was right, but humans wouldn't heal from wounds like that without stitches at the very least. We were able to persuade her to see a doctor in Lagalia if she hadn't healed by the time we got there, but beyond that, she refused to speak of her own health. Ingi looked to be hurt but in fact she had come out stronger and more confident than she had been before. The Honnie who had attacked her looked defeated; he was now in May's control and she was, by way of her thoughts, preventing him from touching Ingi, though he still desired her so.

As for us, nobody had been hurt, though I had been the most exhausted by the physical exertion required to get over that wall. May had been able to help me back out of the drain, after which I could really do nothing but collapse under the tent and rest while the others talked. I was grateful for Natalie, who decided to curl up beside me as I rested, but I was too tired to acknowledge her presence. Peter and Rebecca eventually dozed off in each other's arms a short distance away; and Tommy, who had emerged after the fight with nothing worse than a cut on his forehead, was cuddling up to Ingi as she slept. Only May slept alone, and I hoped that gave her food for thought.

I didn't dream that afternoon, which was definitely a good thing, but in the periods when I was awake, my mind active but my body too tired to work with it, I thought a lot about May. Less than twenty-four hours ago, she had been unwilling to provide me with an example of pain she had experienced. Now, fate had thrown up a situation which almost seemed like destiny. I now felt more confident than ever that we would return to our world, and that May would come with us. I had enormous leverage over her now, not just because I had saved her life (she was still one up on me there) but because I had something to use against her. This time, I would not be deflected.

Grid, the unfortunate man who was mostly held responsible for this series of events in May's eyes, was tasked as the slave for most of that night. It was his responsibility to build a campfire, and to provide us all with food. We all slept under that tent, we humans in our own sleeping bags after Grid kindly retrieved our bags, miraculously unharmed, from the wreckage of our cart. Well, not all of us slept very much; May, Ingi and Tommy slept plenty, as did Grid and all the half-breeds, but Natalie, Rebecca, Peter and I only slept some of the time. Napping in the afternoon is always a good way to make sure you can't sleep much in the evening. I didn't move throughout the night, even though I would have liked to go to the toilet; I was just too weary. Natalie didn't move much either; apart from a brief toilet stop herself, she spent the rest of the time by my side. Our separate sleeping bags made holding each other impossible but nevertheless, I felt closer to Natalie now than I ever had before.

We set out the next morning, moving more quickly than we had the day before, though now we had to go about it differently. With no cart for us humans and no more settlements between ourselves and the outskirts of Lagalia, we had to be carried by the Honnies. Peter, Natalie and Rebecca all rode on the backs of three of the half-breeds, each of them wearing one of the bags from our world, while May and Ingi carried me and Tommy respectively. May couldn't bound at her usual pace; she was still moving rather gingerly, but she had healed a lot more than I would have expected. She was still bruised and wounded in a lot of places, including many I had only seen back in the drain when she had been practically naked, but she had recovered a lot of her strength already. It wasn't inconceivable that she could have been right about healing by the time we reached Lagalia.

Perhaps to make up for lost time, or perhaps to get away from the crime scene as quickly as possible, or perhaps because Ingi had gained a hell of a lot of fighting experience from resisting Grid; whatever the reason, we stopped only for a quick lunch before continuing on the road that afternoon. We crested the mountain about an hour before sunset, and since we were still facing west, we were gifted with a spectacular view of the valley below. It was deep and narrow, and rising on the other side of it, a mountain greater even than this one. The sun would disappear behind it soon, but right now, it was just high enough to reveal the massive city, far away in the distance. There it was; Lagalia, the city where our fate would be decided. Somewhere beyond that mountain, another two or three weeks further on, another city by the name of Malia awaited. If we ended up going that far, we would end up in the same shape as Candice. The stakes were now higher than ever.

Everyone was grateful when May finally called the party to a halt beside another empty drain. I was hungry and need of a toilet break; everyone else had to be all that and a lot more. When Peter slid off the back of the half-breed he'd been riding with, he looked like his arms and legs were full of lead, having held on so tightly for so long. The half-breeds set up another fire, provided us with our dinner and then set up a tent, all communication being done mentally and all of it excluding us. In fact, other than a few words the previous day, May had barely uttered a word since we had saved her life.

This was not a comforting realisation, especially with Lagalia now in sight. If she shut us out now, all would be lost. So, for the first time since I'd tested it that first night, I now tried to send my thoughts outward, projecting them toward May. I needed to talk to her; I needed her to talk to me; I had something I needed to say to her. It was easier this time because I could see her; she was only a quarter of the way around the circle, staring into the fire, apparently lost in her own thoughts. She jerked slightly and looked around at me sharply, all the proof I needed that I could still do it.

I didn't say anything but continued to project the same message, confident that she was getting it and waiting for some kind of response. She stared hard at me for several seconds, perhaps trying to work out what I was getting at so that she wouldn't have to talk to me, but I wouldn't allow it. Once, while speaking to Stella when she had been a Sorcerer, I had made it impossible for her to read my mind by mentally reciting the alphabet. What I did this time was focus so hard on the message that nothing else even entered my mind. Whether or not that would work on a Honnie, I doubted; she could have forced my mind elsewhere if she really wanted to. All she did was stare at me, saying nothing and refusing to meet my mind with any thoughts of her own. Eventually she looked away from me, but I didn't quit. I just kept sending the same thoughts, again and again, with all the concentration I possessed. Remembering what she had said about slamming a sign into her face, I knew I could drive her crazy if I kept it up. I had to do it; it was our only chance.

And it worked. When bed time came around, May surprised just about everyone by letting the humans come down into the drain with her, Ingi, Dan and Gob. The others, including Grid, who should have given rights ahead of us under normal circumstances, had to sleep under the tent. There were no objections, of course—Honnies knew better than to object to someone more powerful—but Grid looked rather disgruntled and sour as he watched Ingi holding Tommy against her. The only other person who looked a little disappointed by this was Natalie, who would have to sleep with Dan again as a consequence. If I had my way, she could have slept alone for one night while I had one last shot at May, but if this worked, it would be worth it.

"What is your deal?" she asked me the moment she had pulled the panel down on top of us. She didn't look at me as she spoke—in fact she hadn't even met my eyes when she had helped me get down here.

"Deal?" I repeated, a little nonplussed as I watched her outline in the darkness. I wished I could see her face—it could be useful during this discussion—but knew better than to expect there to be lighting in here. Honnies didn't seem to need it as much as humans.

"You are such a strange human," she said, still with her back to me as she went through the ritual, rather more slowly than usual, of replacing her old robe with a new one from the panel beside her. "All of you humans are strange, but especially you. Do you not see how things have changed since you came here?"

"No," I said earnestly. "I ne'er saw how it 'as 'e'ore I ca'e here." (I never saw how it was before I came here.)

"Do you really think this is how it always is? Any of this?"

I knew what she was getting at; a lot of what May and Ingi had been put through lately wouldn't have happened if not for us, but I couldn't blame it all on our presence. That ambush would have been there regardless; it was only because of the delay we'd caused that Ingi turned up at the worst possible time. I could have continued the discussion on that line of logic but didn't; it could lead her to decide that she really should kill us all and be done with it.

"Are you 'eeling 'etter today?" I asked her. (Are you feeling better today?)

For a moment she didn't answer. Then she said, "Yes, thank you. Now lie down; we need to sleep so we can make up more ground tomorrow."

"No," I said firmly, though I slid under the blankets anyway; all still going according to plan so far. "'E ha'e to talk now." (We have to talk now.)

"I do not want to talk."

"Too 'ad. I do, so 'e're going to talk." (Too bad. I do, so we're going to talk.)

There was another silence. I knew I was treading on potentially fatal ground here, but the time had come to take that risk. There was no other way to get across the raging river we had set out for. Finally, as I almost expected a blow, I heard May sigh deeply.

"Why?" she said, and she sounded almost sad; it wasn't an emotion I expected, but still not a bad thing—not yet anyway. "You think I do not know what you want? Humans are all the same; you will use anything you can to your own advantage, and now you are going to do that to me."

"Honnies do dat too," I pointed out, preferring not to get into that side of it. "I not gonna use it against you; I just 'anna talk a'out it." (I'm not gonna use it against you; I just wanna talk about it.)

May didn't answer immediately. I heard her put her old robe in the panel in the wall, then felt her pull the blanket back and slide in beside me. She was still on my left, meaning that if I rolled onto my left side (something I nearly always did these days, since it no longer hurt to do so), I could put my arm across her—perhaps even hug her if I really wanted, though I hadn't taken it quite that far yet. That might have to change tonight, depending on how she reacted to what I had planned for her. When she lay beside me, she often did the same thing with her left arm, but when she was lying beside me tonight, she was careful not to touch me.

"Why do you not see how difficult this is for me?" she said in a low voice. "Do you think Honnies always treat humans this way? I cannot even reason with myself anymore. Now I have so much responsibility of more people than ever before, and still you think it is fun to bombard me with your thoughts."

"Not 'un, necessary," I corrected, recognising another deflection; she had a never-ending supply of deflections, it seemed, but I had no intention of allowing her to do that to me tonight. If she wanted to stop me now, she would have to either kill me or force me to sleep by mentally commanding it. I knew I couldn't stop her from doing either of those things, but where she had always tried to avoid me having leverage over her, now I had to do the same thing.

"You know I can hurt you," she said quietly, clearly having read these thoughts out of my head; it cost me every ounce of effort I had not to shudder.

"Yeah," I admitted, "and I 'ould 'e like you 'ere yesterday. You 'ill ha'e 'un 'atching dat, huh?" (Yeah, and I would be like you were yesterday. You will have fun watching that, huh?)

"Pardon?"

"'Hink a'out how it is to 'e in 'ain," I told her. "Re'e'er it, 'ecause it can ha'en to anyone—e'en Honnies." (Think about how it is to be in pain. Remember it, because it can happen to anyone—even Honnies.)

"You are not telling me anything I do not already know."

"You know I sa'ed your li'e, right?" (You know I saved your life, right?)

"I saved yours too," she pointed out, "something a normal human would not deserve. We are even."

"Yeah," I said, "'e are e'en now. 'E both 'elt a lot of 'ain, and 'ine 'as 'ecause o' Ingi." (We are even now. We both felt a lot of pain, and mine is because of Ingi.)

May didn't answer for a moment, during which I took the opportunity to expose the greatest weapon I had in my arsenal, unpleasant as it was even for me. I projected my thoughts again, but rather than sending her a message, I reflected, as clearly as possible, on the explosive pain I'd felt when Ingi had attacked me. I concentrated mainly on the cracking jaw, because that was easier to remember; losing the arm had been reduced to a blur of pain in my memory. It had the desired effect; even though we weren't touching, I felt May pull back slightly, as though wishing she could melt through the wall behind her to get away from me; as though I were coming to symbolise everything she had felt as the Honnie had pierced her with his tongue, all over her body.

I took the step then, the bold but necessary step, of wriggling forward slightly and reaching out for her. She couldn't pull any further away, but she didn't push me away either. I touched her shoulder and then reached around behind her so that we were the closest we'd been to hugging since that very first night when she had tasted me. She didn't respond at first, and I knew it was because the thoughts she'd got out of my head were sinking in very deep. I waited patiently, making sure that she could feel how close I was to her and taking it to mean that I no longer blamed her. Finally, she returned to her senses.

"You are not exaggerating," she said softly, and her voice had changed. At last, I knew I was finally getting through to her.

She touched me then, my shoulder first and then my face, tracing the spot where the break had been. I winced as the pain flared up again, but it was only in my mind; enough time had passed for the bone to be strong enough for this. Her touch was gentle, tender even, and clearly done with great care on her part. I had been right: Something had definitely changed in May, and feeling my pain in conjunction with the horror she had experienced the previous day had done it. I had the advantage; now it was time to push it home.

"Okay, you don't ha'e to talk," I said reasonably enough, "'ut I still 'ant to share so'e'hing 'ith you. Is dat okay?" (You don't have to talk, but I still want to share something with you. Is that okay?)

"What is that?" she said, and now her voice was very weak.

"Just 'atch 'y 'houghts; you'll get de idea." (Just watch my thoughts; you'll get the idea.)

When she didn't respond for a few seconds, I took that for an affirmative. With that done, I focussed my mind once again, but this time I went much further back than the episode with Ingi. I started by showing her the hidden quarters in Marc's old house—innocent enough—and a large group of teenagers sitting around it in a circle. One of them (Lucien) got up, edged his way to the outside of the circle, and opened the entrance, allowing a horde of Hammerhearts to storm us. I visualised the struggle that followed as clearly as I could remember it: Peter, being thrown against the wall and almost being knocked out cold; other nameless faceless teenagers (only because I couldn't remember exactly who did what in that struggle) fighting for their lives, trying to escape; and the torture as several people were placed under the agonator. I focussed on this especially, visualising the way they thrashed and writhed, screaming for all they were worth. Finally, I focussed on Amelia, who was not only tortured, but flung up against the stone and knocked out cold.

I felt May shudder beside me but I didn't stop there; this was only the first scene. Next came the memory, the very clear memory, of Arnold Hammerson, backing me, Peter and Amelia against the back wall of our basement cell. He practically drilled a hole in Amelia's stomach with a bludginator, then flicked salt into it. He raised her into the air and flipped her upside-down when she refused to play along with his little game, and then allowed her to fall on her head back onto the floor. Finally, I focussed on the darkness which followed that scene; the darkness that the three of us were left to stew in.

May was now beginning to twist her body away from me; I tightened my hold on her and continued the story, skipping most of that horrible day and jumping to the evening. I had been tortured then, by way of both the agonator and bludginator, and I focussed as much as I could on what I remembered of that debilitating pain—how weak it had made me. I remembered how I had been placed in that floating cage and Hammerson had attempted to kill me, but for reasons none of us understood at the time, had been unable. Finally, I focussed on Amelia. It didn't matter that I hadn't been present when Hignat and Wilwog had attended to her; I knew what had happened, and I provided May with my best estimation of what it had probably looked like.

"Please stop," I heard May whimper from a long way away, but I was too lost in unpleasant memories to pay attention. This was the first time I had thought so vividly of these terrible events; I had done my best to bury them up until now. Perhaps they had always haunted me ever since; perhaps this retelling would help me get over them for good.

I next imagined, but didn't spend long on, the scene in which Amelia, Harry, Simon, Katie, Sophie, Kylie and Serena had all been tortured for hours by the Hammerhearts, focussing mainly on how Amelia had looked at the end of it and packing as much of the pain they would have felt into my memories. I then jumped straight to the battle two days later, the one that had taken Lisa's life. I showed May the way my classmates had been overcome and, more importantly, how roughly the Hammerhearts had treated the students in the gym that day before Lisa had performed her last great act in order to interrupt proceedings.

The next memory was not one I wanted to relive for even worse reasons, but May needed to see it; and so it was Tulip I thought about next. I showed her how Tulip had been in the last few minutes of her life and, most particularly, how Hall had held her under the power of the agonator for such a long time that it had almost killed her right then and there. Tulip had been barely mobile when I had last seen her, and she had been covered in blood, just as May had been when I'd seen her. I was sure to draw the comparison, and knew it had worked perfectly when May moaned softly beside me.

I had to stop for a moment to think what came next. There had been nothing direct for a while due to the resolution I'd made not to get into any more dangerous situations. Showing her David and Craig's deaths wouldn't help much, ditto Justin and Javelyn, both of whom had been caught spying. I did show her Nicole's death, though, and emphasised the point that it only happened because I'd been there at the time; that she hadn't been the target, and that she had been entirely innocent. To cap the scene, I showed the grief that had followed, not just mine but Mum, Marge, Dad, Charlie and, since May would recognise her, Natalie, who had always been Nicole's best friend outside the Thomases.

Next came the events of April 30; the ambush Peter and I had met on Main Street in Chopville, the fiasco in which we had met Siobhan, and our unsuccessful attempt to find someone else to look after her. All three scenes had resulted in deaths, and none of them had been enemies (I couldn't count the cops who had attacked us as enemies). I focussed more on the carnage than anything else, and to drive the point home firmly, directed it all back to the Hammersons, the people responsible for all the pain and suffering shown so far.

"No more," May moaned, and if I didn't know better, I would have sworn she was close to tears; but my eyes were closed and my mind far away. I had no intention of stopping now because I was building to a very important point that I intended, come hell or high water, for May to understand.

I thought May mostly understood the general point, so instead of drawing it out more than necessary, I gave her a few snapshots: Kylie, beheaded when she had been, for all intents and purposes, sleeping; Stella, tied to a pole and tortured because she was failing an impossible task; my mother, the brutal way she had been executed, and the reason for which it had happened; Smiley, dragged into a compartment on a moving train and tortured by two Hammerhearts with knives (not unlike May, I thought, drawing another comparison); Jane and Serena, locked in a tank where they had no way of escaping the oncoming death; Tommy, bound in a forty-five-degree angle off the floor, tortured again and again so that he wouldn't be allowed to sleep; Peter, tortured on at least two occasions that night in Germany; Natalie, Tankom stamping on her face and demanding she be tortured for at least three minutes while she was carried down the stairs; Rebecca, being tortured for no reason other than the fact that she looked like Natalie.

There was no mistaking it now; May was whimpering. Each snapshot was like a kick in the guts, and the last few the worst of the lot. I'd been sure to include them because they were the people she would recognise; I wanted her to understand that these weren't all just nameless strangers; they were real people in real pain. I had one more thing I needed to show her, and again, I gave it to her in snapshots: The fighting; the bombs; the missiles; the natural disasters which were far from natural; the way all existing authority had been overthrown in favour of a rule that encouraged those within its ranks to steal, torture, rape and kill those who resisted them. Those who fought for right, who fought for freedom, who fought to make sure people didn't have to suffer the sort of thing that May had the day before, had been driven into hiding. Who were those people? Why were they so desperate to save innocent humans from a pain none of them deserved? So desperate that they would step through an inter-dimensional gateway and attempt to get help from a different breed of being?

I yawned and then opened my eyes. That had probably taken no more than five minutes, but it felt like hours. I was utterly exhausted and I allowed myself to sink backward, almost ready for sleep. I had almost forgotten about May, but I remembered in a hurry when her strong arm prevented me from rolling back to my side of the bed. I quickly switched my attention back to her and realised that she was trembling where she lay; I could feel it in her shoulders where my arm was resting, and pretty much all the way down my body—I hadn't realised how close we were pressed against each other. It made me very self-conscious of my own body, and naturally enough, led me to think of what Tommy had already enjoyed with Ingi. I had no idea if May would go the same way her daughter did, or if it would be required for me to get what I needed from her, but I knew I wouldn't jump that way unless I absolutely had to. Well, John, it wouldn't be the first time, I thought, and I too shuddered as I remembered what Lena had required for her cooperation.

"You okay?" I now asked her, not entirely sure what response I wanted.

"John," she said, and I started; that was the first time May had spoken any of our names the whole time we had been here. I assumed that was her way of staying above us, not unlike the way Hall had always referred to his students by their surnames —well, maybe a little better than that.

"Yes?" I said, a little anxiously.

"I…" she broke off, trying to decide what she was going to say, then she said, "I think there is a lot we will never understand about each other. I know how humans think, but I can never understand why, like you can never understand why we Honnies do what we do."

"Okay," I said quietly, "'ut you don't need to undershtand, ash long ash you undershtand dat. 'E need hel', and you can hel' ush." (Okay, but you don't need to understand, as long as you understand that. We need help, and you can help us.)

"I understand that," she said, and sighed. "I never want to feel that again. Please do not make me go through that again."

My stomach fell. If that was how she reacted now, there was no chance of her coming into a world where she would be forced to feel all kinds of pain in the minds of the humans around her.

"Ish dat it?" I said miserably. (Is that it?)

"No," she said quietly, and to my surprise, she tightened her hold on me. For a moment, I thought another tasting was in the offing, and I probably would have allowed it, wire or no wire, but all May wanted was a hug. So May was like her daughter; they both liked being close to certain humans. I allowed her to hug me, and I even hugged her back, but I could feel all the hope I had clung to that day draining out of me.

"Listen," she said, her mouth now very close to my ear, and I had a nightmare image of her sticking her tongue down it, "you were right. You did suffer a lot of pain here, and it was my fault it happened. I am sorry."

That was deliberate; I could tell by the tone in her voice. She was saying it like that because she knew that I was looking for that kind of apology, but I could also tell that this time, it was genuine. Part of it was also in the tone but part of it was in my mind; whether accidentally or on purpose, some of May's emotion seemed to be seeping into my own mind. I wondered if the others were also getting what I was getting; if so, what were they making of it?

"'Hank you," I said, relieved that I had succeeded in that assignment at least. I felt a mixture of pride and affection for May; it must have cost her a lot to say that to a mere human, but even so, I still hadn't achieved my main goal.

"You need to explain to me one thing," she said. "Why do you expect that I would be capable of helping you? What you showed me looks too dangerous, even for a Honnie."

"It 'ouldn't 'e dangeroush i' dey ne'er see you or know you exhisht," I told her. "You 'ould only ushe your 'ind; you 'ouldn't need to 'ight dem at all." (It wouldn't be dangerous if they never see you or know you exist. You would only use your mind; you wouldn't need to fight them at all.)

"I do not believe it could be that simple," she said, a bit of a whine in her voice now, and my heart rose at the sound of it. "I do not like it; I really do not."

"Dere'sh a shaying in our 'orld," I told her, "dat ish, sho'eti'esh you ha'e to chooshe 'et'een 'at ish right and 'at ish eashy, 'ecaushe dey are o'ten not de sha'e 'hing. You re'e'er 'at I told you a'out my dad and hish dad 'en de 'ar shtarted?" (There's a saying in our world, that is, 'sometimes you have to choose between what is right and what is easy, because they are often not the same thing.' You remember what I told you about my dad and his dad when the war started?)

"You said they went to fight," she said quietly, "and they knew they would have nothing to come back home to, but they still went."

"It 'ould ha'e 'een eashy to let oddash 'ight," I said quietly, "'ut dey 'ent any'ay, 'ecaushe it 'ash de right 'hing to do." (It would have been easy to let others fight, but they went anyway, because it was the right thing to do.)

May didn't answer, and this time I didn't prod her. I simply lay there, my mind going blank in the seconds that followed as sleep crept up on me. Now, I really had done all I could. I had no tricks left up my sleeve, no arguments, nothing I could possibly use to explain the desperation of the situation. May simply lay there beside me, still holding me close to her, and we'd been in that position for long enough now that I found it rather more comfortable than I would have liked. All I could do was let her make up her own mind and hope for the best. It took her a few minutes, by which time I had almost dozed off. I jerked back to full alertness when I felt her move so that her lips (no tongue) brushed my ear.

"If it can be done," she said quietly, "then I will try to help you."

* * *

We were up and on the move again the next morning, but once again, the mood in the group seemed to have changed; though I was perhaps the only one who noticed it. None of the others, humans and Honnies alike, showed any signs of having felt anything from May the previous evening, which was a relief. May herself was looking and moving better than she had the previous day, the cuts on her face still visible but already beginning to heal. She wasn't behaving any differently in general, but she was now much more comfortable with me than she had been before; eye contact between us was now a regular occurrence. It was as though deciding to help was the most difficult thing May had contended with, and now the rest was standard.

We had made a lot of ground that day, moving fast down the hill and into the valley. We were already approaching the foot of the mountain atop which Lagalia sat by the time we set up camp that night, and we were still moving the same way we had the day before: May carrying me, Ingi carrying Tommy, and the others riding on the back of half-breeds. Given May's improved health and the fact that we were going downhill for much of the day, we had moved much faster than before. It had been easy for me, but the others (Peter in particular) were looking very strained by the time we stopped for lunch, and even more so come sundown.

There was no opportunity for me to tell any of the others of what I had achieved (none of us got a moment to ourselves these days) but I certainly got plenty of time to communicate with May during the day, only now it was all done mentally while she bounded along with me in her arms. What I learnt that day was that her assistance was still no sure thing; she would have to qualify as a collector, something that was sure to be difficult, and she would be required to find mental strength from somewhere if she wasn't presently strong enough. That would probably mean trading at least two of the half-breeds for fresh humans for her to absorb (a horrible thought, but one I would have to live with). Then there was Ingi to think about; she would keep Tommy, of course, and get all there was to get from him, including at least one half-breed of her own. She would also keep Dan and Gob, since May wouldn't have any use for them in our world, but any more than that and she would probably struggle. Finally, there was Grid and the potential danger he posed if May allowed him to walk free. Would he follow Ingi? Perhaps attack her again? There was a lot to take into account and unfortunately, she couldn't guarantee that one more of us wouldn't be required to provide either her or Ingi with the extra strength required to make everything work.

Chapter 27: The Test

We reached the outskirts of Lagalia on the afternoon of August 16. We probably could have gotten all the way into the city by that evening, but May wanted to spend the night on the outer before heading into the city the next day. This part of town felt a lot like Pralia, and indeed we did spend that night in another Honnie version of a caravan park. During that afternoon, however, May separated me from the others and, leaving Ingi in charge of all the rest, took me to a nearby hospital to have the wires around my jaw removed. It wasn't a pleasant experience, particularly as May was not allowed to come in and the doctor in charge had little regard for human comfort, but was an enormous relief later on when I could finally talk properly again.

It was over dinner that night, the fifteen of us camping around a small fire in a park not far from the cabin, that we finally had an all in discussion about what was to take place in Lagalia. I'd managed to communicate my success to Peter that morning and during the day, he had passed it onto Natalie and Rebecca. All our spirits had risen as a result of this, and even more so by the prospect of possibly returning home within days now. That emotion was strictly human though; May seemed more comfortable than she had before, but none of the other Honnies had any idea how things were to play out until that night. There was little organisation in the discussion; May was forced to translate mentally for both sides when one or the other spoke in their own language, which was all the time since she was the only one who knew both.

Naturally, it was the half-breeds, all seven of them, who were most anxious about what was to play out, because their futures were hinging on whatever May required to make it work. She told her sons that if she were allowed to go through, they would stay with Ingi until she rejoined them in Malia, whenever that would be, but it would be up to Ingi as to what happened to them in the meantime. As for Ingi herself, she was still lugging Tommy around everywhere since he refused to let go of her. It was sad to see, and I knew that sooner or later, I would want her to kill him, to put him out of his obvious misery.

It was Grid who provided the greatest headache. After some interrogation, most of it done mentally, May learnt that his speciality was in management and leadership. Coordination was fairly important in the Honnie world and Grid could be a highly valued member of their society. The trouble was, he still wanted Ingi, and she had no interest in him. Of course, any time they spent together would only be brief enough for them to have two children, as was Honnie custom, but Ingi didn't want even that, and May wasn't about to force the issue. Furthermore, for whatever reason, it was also against Honnie custom for May to just remove Grid's desire for Ingi altogether, something that would have solved everyone's problems. The only good thing was that although he was physically stronger than her, Ingi's mind was stronger than his; it might be possible for her to be his aba, at least temporarily, so that she could decide what his fate would be.

There was plenty of uncertainty about the whole thing but a lot of it would fall into place once May learnt what would be required for her to become a collector. She no longer had any personal qualms about it; her duty to society would be done once Ingi graduated, and all she would have to do after that would be to continue to educate in Malia, as she had always done. Other than this immediate complication, May really wouldn't be losing anything, so long as nothing seriously bad happened to her in our world. The following day, once we had gone into the city and taken a room in a hotel (Lagalia actually had a few hotels as well as these cabins, apparently), we would then go to Lagalia's human collection centre so that May could make enquiries. The end was so close, I felt I could almost touch it.

The ride into the city the next day was pretty incredible. May obtained a new cart, exactly like the last one, and with a band of half-breeds encircling us as we went, Dan and Gob pulling as before, Grid bringing up the rear and May and Ingi on either side of us, we got to see a lot more of the way Honnies lived than we ever had before. It was even better than expected because we were required to move more slowly. The roads were narrow and designed mostly for foot travel. Honnies moved from one place to another at breakneck speed, weaving in and out of each other with no trouble at all, but those with half-breeds and humans, like us, were required to move with more care. All around us, we saw the houses that Honnies lived in when they weren't travelling; they were so very like houses in our world that I felt a huge pang of homesick. The feeling was capped when we passed by a front yard where a small Honnie girl, no more than five or six (if their growth progression was in line with humans), was swinging from a swing hung to the branch of a tree.

The further in we went, the busier it got, and the more grand the buildings around us became. Finally, around lunchtime, we crossed a bridge over a stream of water (no current, so it was probably manufactured by the Honnies) and into the city itself. It was a clear, cold day (very cold, in fact, given the altitude) but even though the sun was out, not much of it reached us here. The tall buildings all around us cast everything into shadows. It was very daunting, especially given that we weren't really city people in our own world, let alone this one.

The Lagalia hotel (it had a name, but I had no hope of pronouncing it properly) was a tall building just like all the others around us. There was nothing really luxurious about it (the Chopville hotel would have beat it for warmth and comfort). May managed to reserve our party an entire floor close to the top of the building—we later found out those were reserved for large groups such as ours. There happened to be one not being used at that moment, but it had taken May a fairly lengthy discussion to get us into it. The sticking point was that none of us knew how long we would need it, but eventually, the receptionist Honnie relented, and we were in.

It was a good spot too. There were enough rooms for all of us to sleep alone and, given that we had that entire floor, we had a magnificent view of the countryside on all sides. There were a few places where other buildings obstructed the view, but not many. We had a great view of the valley we had crossed to get here, the mountain beyond it, and beyond that, the relatively flat country we had spent weeks crossing. To the west, down the other side of the mountain, there was a similar valley and another mountain beyond it. Past that, there were more cities visible in the distance, dotted around the landscape, and May pointed out one in particular, almost on the horizon, as being Malia, the place where she and Ingi lived.

We didn't spend long admiring the view, though. May left Ingi in charge of the main group for the remainder of that afternoon while she took me, Peter, Natalie and Rebecca to the human collection centre. I was surprised she even knew where it was but according to May, she was making enquiries of other Honnies in the area by touching their minds. It was an easy, non-invasive process, apparently. She preferred to walk us all, rather than use the cart (she was above that, I supposed) but the extra time it took made me acutely aware of the looks the four of us humans were getting from those around us (humans and Honnies alike). Whether it was our different attire or our obvious intelligence, we stood out like a beacon in this world.

"Aren't you worried Grid might be up to something back there?" Rebecca asked May as we were entering the building.

"He is sleeping," said May curtly. "I have made sure he will sleep until we return."

There was another receptionist Honnie here and she started when she saw us, her expression eager as she took in the humans. I suddenly wished we hadn't come along for this ride —a place like this where humans were routinely destroyed couldn't possibly be safe, even if we were May's possessions. May quickly engaged her in conversation, and as she had when we had been ambushed, she mentally provided us with a translation of the dialogue. May wanted to know what would be required for her to become a collector. The receptionist wanted to know who we were. May told her we were hers, and repeated the question. The receptionist, after touching May's mind with her own, said that she may not be strong enough, and that she would have to pass a test in order to gain qualification. She also asked what May's current speciality was, and May said it was educating.

The receptionist left us alone for a while after that and the five of us sat in the waiting room for some time before she returned and beckoned us to follow her. So it was through a door we went and down a long corridor. I was utterly horrified when I saw what they kept back here: Humans in jail cells, but these were humans like us, humans who had come from our world and were being kept back here. The distinction was so obvious: They were wearing human clothing, a lot of it dirty but still recognisable; they were of varying shapes, sizes, genders and ethnicities; and they all looked sad and scared. A few of them cried out to us, and I recognised all manner of languages including Chinese, Japanese, Spanish, Arabic, French and, of course, English. It hurt my heart to ignore them but what on earth could I have called in response? They were all marked for death and everyone present knew it.

Eventually, we wound up in a large room at the back of the building, where we were confronted by two more Honnies. They were both tall males; one was quite young, perhaps a few years older than Ingi, while the other was older, around May's age, maybe even more. The receptionist left us alone and another conversation began, May once again translating for us. The older Honnie was a collector, it seemed, and he would test her while the younger Honnie supervised the situation. Exactly what this test involved, none of us knew, and May wasn't saying, but we never saw it—at least not that day. For their own reasons, they all agreed that May was not ready yet, and so it was back to the hotel we went, now in silence, all of us humans anxious to know what went wrong.

"Are we allowed to know what's going on?" Peter asked a little testily as we made our way up the hotel stairs to our floor.

"You will not like it," May said without looking back at him. "I need to decide if it can be done. If it cannot be done, we could all be killed. I will not sacrifice Ingi's life for nothing."

"Ingi's life?" said Natalie, perplexed.

May didn't answer but once we were back on our level and surrounded by the rest of our group, she called us all to a meeting where she explained, mentally, what she would have to do. As it sank in, I began to understand the enormous risk she would be taking. She and the collector we saw earlier would both open their minds and have some sort of arm wrestle to see who was stronger. It would be a strategic match of tug-of-war, where the minds of all those they were each holding would be the rope. May was clearly not confident enough in her own strength to take such a huge risk, and now I understood why. If she had been beaten, as she certainly would have if she'd taken the test today, the five of us humans would have ended up in cells just like the rest of those poor humans down there. May, Ingi, Grid and the half-breeds would all have become living possessions of that collector, and he could have done just about anything with them.

Ingi, Grid and all of us humans had plenty of suggestions for May, but she was hearing none of it—she had her own plan, it seemed. So for the rest of that day, Natalie, Rebecca, Peter and I were confined to a single hotel room with an awesome view where we sat around playing cards. It wasn't that we weren't allowed to roam the rest of that floor, but there was really no point. May had taken one of the strange half-breeds out of the hotel and left Ingi in charge of all the rest of us. Grid was once again sleeping, so there was no danger out there (unless you counted Ingi herself as danger, and from past experience, I didn't take it for granted that she was safe) but none of us had any desire to surround ourselves with those Honnies and half-breeds, especially while Tommy was still clinging desperately to Ingi. If she was sick of him yet, she wasn't showing it, but none of us wanted to see it; the only way we could deal with the loss was to treat Tommy as dead. The only time we saw anyone else all evening was when Ingi came into our room to feed us gradi, something we were all heartily sick of by now, but we still had to eat. Luckily we still had plenty of never-vanishing yummies in the bag.

The following day was just the same as the previous evening, only this time, when May left, she took all the half-breeds with her; at least, all the strange ones. Dan and Gob were so far just as confined as the rest of us and they were getting rather restless. Half-breeds seemed to like physical activity and these two weren't getting enough of it. It was a long day, broken into the periods when Ingi once again placed gradi in front of each of us. We played cards again in the morning, but got so thoroughly bored with each other that we separated for the afternoon. Peter and Rebecca spent it shut in a room together, and I hoped Peter was now giving some thought to how he would handle Siobhan when we got back home, now that it was so close to being a reality. I didn't blame him for becoming attached to Rebecca; she was easy to admire under normal circumstances, let alone the strain of what we had all faced lately. I just hoped he remembered what sort of girl Rebecca really was when she had her choice of boys, and I hoped for his sake, Rebecca did the right thing by him.

When May returned to the hotel floor just after dinner that night, she was alone. All five strange half-breeds that had been forced to join our group over the last few days were now gone, and I preferred not to wonder what she had done with them. Whatever it was, though, it was certainly obvious that May had changed. She looked healthier than I had seen her the whole time I'd known her (you would never know she had been savagely attacked less than a week earlier) and she looked stronger too. To top it off, she now carried an aura that was almost frightening in its power alone. Everyone felt it, humans and Honnies alike, and Grid actually screamed in terror at the sight of her.

The incident that followed was terrifying in its suddenness and everyone got a good view of it. One moment, Grid was staring in horror at May; the next, he had wheeled around and tried to escape into the nearest bedroom (the one Ingi shared with Tommy), perhaps intending to jump out the window; the next moment, he dropped like a stone, not quite dead but almost there. Ingi bounded forward and caught him before he had hit the floor. She straightened up, smiling in a heart-stopping way, carrying his limp body in her arms, and by the time she was fully upright, Grid was all-the-way dead. Ingi had barely flinched, May hadn't moved at all, and none of us humans had time to move; only Dan and Gob had reacted, backing away from their mother as though thinking they might be next, and knowing that they could do nothing to stop her if they were.

"What the hell!" Rebecca gasped, swaying slightly and having to lean on Peter for support.

"Well, much the easiest way to solve that little problem," said Peter, not a little disturbed as Ingi carried Grid's limp body away, perhaps to dispose of wherever it was human bodies normally went. Tommy was still hobbling along in her wake, intent on not letting her go, but she barely felt him.

"It was," May agreed, now coming to join us. "Have you all been okay here?"

None of us knew what to say, and May suddenly realised how much it had startled us. "Sorry," she said, not really sounding sorry but making a better show of it than most of the other times she had tried to apologise, "but it was really the right thing to do. I took half of him and Ingi took the other half, so now we are both stronger."

"You can do that?" I said, a little surprised but now understanding why Grid hadn't been killed instantly.

"Where are the half-breeds?" Natalie asked. "Did you do that to them too?"

"No," said May curtly.

Ingi came back into view then, looking pleased and rather stronger herself as she carried Tommy along on her back. May indicated that she, Dan and Gob should join us and there, she finally told us all what she had done, mentally so that we could all understand. Honnie-bred humans, the ones who were dumb and fat, weren't worth very much when it came to mind power. That was why the Honnie who had killed Candice had received a whole crowd of them in exchange for two half-breeds. In theory, May could have received a crowd two-and-a-half times that size in exchange for five half-breeds, but since she was an educator and possessed a lot of human intelligence that other Honnies didn't bother with, she was able to go one better.

She had reserved a large hall for the previous evening and all day today, something that seemed to come free in this world (I hadn't once seen Honnies exchange anything other than lives). There, she gathered the humans she had managed to acquire, a small crowd yesterday for the one half-breed and a much larger one today. There, she had spent a few minutes with each and every one of them, feeding bits and pieces of her own knowledge into their heads, making sure it was connected appropriately so that by the time she was done, they were up to almost the same standard as us. Humans of that standard were extremely valuable, so by her own labour, May had effectively transformed a bit of granite into solid gold. Finally, she had destroyed them all, a process I preferred not to imagine, but the end result was clear: Her mind was now the biggest and strongest in this part of the city, no small feat, and physically, she was now many, many times stronger than she had been before. Finally, with the booster she had received from Grid, who had been fairly strong himself, she was well and truly ready to take the test.

So after a restless night on my part, excited and terrified in equal measure so that sleep was difficult to come by, the party, now reduced back to nine, set out once again for the human collection centre. When we got there, we found the same receptionist, plus the collector and supervisor, all waiting for us. The receptionist and supervisor both looked scared while the collector wore and expression more difficult to identify, but I thought he was probably impressed.

"How did they know we were coming?" Rebecca asked nervously. "They haven't been keeping an eye on us, have they?"

"They felt a big mind approaching," May told us as we were lead toward the back of the building, passing those same poor, imprisoned humans along the way.

"Are you stronger than him?" Peter asked.

"No," said May, astounding us all, "but I can now compete with him."

That was not a comforting thought at all.

When we reached the large room at the back of the building where we had first clapped eyes on the collector, we came face-to-face with his band of followers. There were two half-breeds, exactly like Dan and Gob; three Honnies (his wife and two children, a boy and girl around the same age as Ingi— at least they looked alike); and, after taking a minute to count them, a staggering twenty-two humans. They, like the ones in the cells, were from our world, and probably recently too. The group presently stood in a line on the opposite side of the room from us, the Honnies and half-breeds looking confident while the humans simply looked blank, as though the collector had placed them all into a temporary trance so that they wouldn't give him any trouble during the test.

May stood to our left, the collector to our right. They faced each other across the room, and the supervisor stood between them. He spoke to them both, his voice official, his language incomprehensible, but May mentally translated for us. It was a test of the mind only; there was to be no physical contact between the combatants. They would both open their minds to each other, and each would try to take possession of all the Honnies, humans and half-breeds possessed by the other, without losing possession of their own. The contest would end when one or the other had possession of everyone on both sides, and (here was the scary bit) they got to keep their winnings. The Honnies on both sides (Ingi and the collector's family) were not allowed to do anything that could interfere with the contest. The only good rules in all of this was that firstly, neither combatant was allowed to hurt anyone, whether it be each other, the supervisor, or the supporters on either side, until the contest was over; and secondly, we humans weren't restricted in any way. They probably assumed that humans could do nothing to make a difference to the contest anyway.

We knew when the battle commenced by the way the supervisor cried something in his language to the two combatants. May and the collector both hunched instantaneously, both going rigid, eyes fixed on each other, faces contorted in what was probably concentration, though this particular facial expression only served to show how alien they both were. I felt the rubber glove around my mind loosen ever so slightly, and then nothing for several seconds as the two Honnies grappled with each other. I still felt like myself but gradually, over the following minute, I saw how May was losing her grip on us.

The most startling thing in all of this was that I began to feel the collector's mind, and knew that I was somewhere in limbo between the two. It felt similar to when the doctor in Pralia had given me back to May, but that had been quick; this process was much more drawn-out, and there was no saying which way it would go. It was as though the two bubbles of their minds had joined, not into one bubble but into something that resembled an open figure eight. Later, I would learn about Venn diagrams, which would turn out to be a much better analogy. I had no idea where I sat in all of it, but I feared that I was close to the centre—too close for comfort.

Be that as it may, I wasn't the first one to fall to the mercy of the collector. He was so confident in his own superiority that he actually demonstrated it. It was probably his way of distracting May so that she would go down even more quickly, but to May's credit, she didn't even flinch as Peter jerked, jittered and then, startling us all, turned and threw himself at Natalie, hugging and kissing her all over her face.

"Hey!" she cried out, trying to throw him off, but Peter was a man possessed—quite literally. He held onto her with all his strength and attempted to hump her leg. Natalie, small and not very strong, lost her balance and toppled to the floor.

"Stop that!" Rebecca shrieked, but a few seconds later, she too fell. A moment later, she joined them on the floor, also trying to hump Natalie, who had no hope of getting away from them both. She stared up at me, a pleading expression in her eyes as Peter and Rebecca had her—not literally, but if this went on too much longer, she would almost certainly have all her clothes torn off her.

May could do nothing to put a stop to it. She was shuddering, all her efforts focussed on the collector, trying to win back what was hers. The collector was still in the position he had begun the battle, still intensely concentrated on May, but not looking as though he were losing his grip on anything. Across the room, his party stood motionless, watching their man do battle and looking confident. On our side, Ingi, Dan and Gob watched their mother in growing terror. None of them looked in danger of succumbing to the collector yet but if this kept on going the way it was, they eventually would.

"Do something, John!" Natalie cried out desperately as her sister and my brother continued to molest her.

I could do nothing to help Natalie, even if I'd had two arms, but did that mean I could do nothing to help May? I thought not, thanks to a major oversight on the Honnies' part. The rules stated that the collector could do nothing to hurt any of us (he hadn't broken that rule yet, in spite of what he was making Peter and Rebecca do to Natalie) but there hadn't been anything in the rules that said I could do nothing to hurt him. I couldn't hurt him, of course (he looked way too strong) but then again, I'd thought the same thing days earlier about the Honnie torturing May. My only hope was to somehow break his concentration, and I thought I knew how I could do it. The question was, what could I use? I only had myself; there were no panels, no compartments, and no bags as we had left all our stuff at the hotel. Using my mind was out; that could easily distract either or both Honnies with unpredictable consequences.

There was nothing else for it. Sighing, trying to ignore the struggle to my right, a struggle that Tommy had now joined (and Ingi could do nothing but stand and watch), I shucked off my shoes and, moving as quickly as I could, undid my jeans and stepped out of them. I dropped them on the floor, picked them up in my one hand by the ankles and, keeping out of the collector's line of sight, moving as quickly as I could in case he took me next, I sidestepped along the wall, past my friends, Ingi, Dan and Gob, and around them till I was behind the collector. I crept forward till I was within arm's reach of him, thankful that May, who could see me, was completely ignoring my presence in her desperate concentration. I took a deep breath and, as I had not so long ago, threw the makeshift lasso around the Honnie's neck. Just as it had before, it came down around his head, covering his eyes and disorientating him completely.

The collector yelled in surprise and turned, probably ready to throw me away from him, and it was only by holding on so tightly that my hand hurt, and by quickly jogging around to the side as he moved, that I was able to evade him. The supervisor shouted something then, and it must have been a reminder of the rules because the collector froze, going rigid. All I could do was stay behind him and hold tight to the ankles of my jeans and hope that he stuck to the rules. If he broke them, May would win, but I wouldn't be around to see it.

But it seemed that the collector was also rather smarter than the Honnie who had attacked May, as well as stronger. Instead of attacking me, he reached up for the jeans and rather than pulling them off, or throwing them, or anything that could cause me to get hurt, he simply tore them in half so that I was holding nothing more than the ends of two pieces of cloth. They fell down on either side of him, pathetic in their complete lack of resistance, and now all I could do was stand there with no pants on. Still, the feat hadn't been completely pointless; I could feel that May had regained some control over us. The rubber glove around my mind felt slightly tighter, although still not as it had been before.

Even better, the situation with my friends began to improve. I had looked in that direction in the moment before it had and what I'd seen had been utterly horrific. The collector had taken Dan, and he had been doing some sort of dance on the spot, shaking his hips and throwing his feet out to either side. For a bloke of his size and stature, it looked so wrong. Gob, who had still been free, had tried desperately to make him stop to no avail. Even worse than that was what my friends had been doing: The collector had all four of them, and was demoralising them completely. All four of them looked a mess, though thankfully none of their clothes were torn; that was one better than me.

May managed to regain a hold of Dan and Natalie in the moment I watched, but as soon as the collector regained his composure, he began to regain the ground he had lost. The pants hadn't been enough; I would have to do more; quickly, before he had a chance to put thoughts in my head too. I thought about using my jumper, and T-shirt if that too failed (that would have stripped me down to my underwear) but I knew there was no point; he would just do to them what he had done to my pants. I had to use something he wouldn't be able to damage, and on that score, I had only one option.

I jumped, throwing my arm around the collector's shoulders and using my legs to latch myself to his back. He was more than a foot taller than me so reaching his eyes was something of a challenge, especially without a second arm to help balance myself. He didn't stagger as my weight hit him but he did growl nastily as I felt blindly for his eyes, meaning only to cover them, not poke them out. I felt his tongue dart out of his mouth as my hand past over it, deadly but in this case, not going in for the kill. It pricked, but I didn't think he had broken the skin—it was more of a warning than anything else. Warning received, I thought, but just try and stop me....

It took a long time but as long as I was there, the collector couldn't concentrate on the battle as much as he needed to. Slowly, May recovered the ground she had lost. Her mind was still open, so none of us were safe yet, but as the minutes past, the commotion by our wall began to settle down. Natalie and Rebecca were themselves again, and they were in tears. When Tommy became himself again, he threw himself away from the fray and bounded at Ingi, who caught him in her arms—she may have been on the verge of tears herself. Peter, pale as a ghost, was the only one who saw what was going on out in the battlefield, and he may have been considering coming to help me, but that was when the fight began to change again.

May was not so arrogant as to humiliate her opponent's humans as she took them, but I could see it happening all the same. One by one, they began to shudder, their absent expressions clearing a little as they became dimly aware of what was happening around them. She may have had six or seven of them in her control, as well as all of us, when the collector decided that it was his turn to do something desperate to change the situation. The rules had been twisted, without being broken, to suit May, and the only way he could turn the situation back in his favour was to twist them himself in the hope that he didn't break them. So of course, it was I who became his target; he didn't dare touch me with his hands, or his tongue, but he began to twist his body to one side, then the other; sharp, jarring twists that almost threw me off with each one.

The only way I could hang on was to cling to his neck, never mind looking for his eyes, and tighten my legs around him. He increased the pressure with every twist, so that it was surely only a matter of time until I was thrown off, but for the time being, I was doing admirably well. My strength was beginning to wane, though, and several joints were beginning to protest loudly at the unrelenting pressure I was putting on them. In our little battle, he was well on top, but in the grand scheme of things, I was winning, because the more he concentrated on me, the easier May's job became. She was no longer shuddering but was standing upright, still strained but no longer feeling his pressure, and she was taking more and more of his possessions into her mind; she now had at least a dozen of his humans, and would soon have them all.

That was when the collector lost control. He let loose a great, bellowing roar that filled the room, bouncing from wall to wall in a terrible litany of echoes. In the same instant, he leaned forward at the waist so sharply that I flew right over his back and over his head. His hands seized me as I fell, swung me around in a dizzying arc so that I had no idea where I was anymore, and then let me loose at such velocity that I flew straight across the room and collided with the opposite wall, breaking my neck and killing me instantly.

At least, that was how it would have happened if not for May. I had been flung straight over her head and she had only to jump up and catch me around the waist, bringing me down and laying me on the ground. I was aware of this only when I was on the cold, hard floor, my head spinning from the sudden movement of the attack. I couldn't feel any physical injuries (whiplash was my greatest fear) but I couldn't take it for granted that I was okay. I could hear a lot of different sounds (yelling and crying from my friends, rage from the collector and some sort of command from the supervisor). I closed my eyes, feeling ready to chuck, my joints still aching from the strain of battling the collector, and just wanting to go to sleep.

"John! John!"

Natalie, Peter and Rebecca surrounded me in short order, helping me sit up, checking me over for injuries and generally making me wish they would all just bugger off. I tried to lie back down but Peter got behind me and supported my weight, making it impossible. Natalie hugged me, still crying, while Rebecca gave me such a look of admiration and gratitude that I felt distinctly uncomfortable. I wished more than ever that they would stop, especially as this distraction would probably help the collector get hold of us all again, but the longer it went on, the more it dawned on me that that wasn't going to happen.

The battle was over. The supervisor had called it off and May had come out victorious by default. The collector was still ranting and raging in Honnie language, probably accusing me of cheating (he was right in the spirit of the game, but I hadn't broken any official rules) but the supervisor wasn't having any of it. I looked over my shoulder to get a look at what was going on: Dan, Gob, Ingi and Tommy remained where they had been before, as did all the collector's humans, but his family of Honnies and half-breeds had all fallen supplicatingly before

May, who stood in the middle of the room, staring down at them.

Then, she dismissed them and, with considerable dignity, I thought, she approached her defeated opponent. He didn't look at her until she touched his shoulder, making him jump, as though he expected her to attack him now that she had defeated him in not-quite fair combat. She spoke quietly to him, and I saw the profound relief on his face at her words. His family, who had heard her, all jumped to their feet and surrounded him; it was a touching scene. May turned away from them and went to join her daughter and two sons; after a brief conversation, probably to make sure they were all okay, she then came to join the four of us, huddled on the floor and all in pieces for a variety of reasons.

"Are you all okay?" she asked.

"No," Rebecca sobbed, looking at May with distinct dislike.

"I am sorry," she said, and for the second time, she looked as though she truly meant it. "I could do nothing to help you. It would have been much worse for you if I had tried."

"She's probably right," said Peter shakily. "Is it all over?"

"Yes," said May, looking back over her shoulder at the collector. "I have right to all of his possessions, but I will let him keep his family. I will only take his humans and split them between Ingi and me."

"Charming," Peter said darkly.

"I'm sorry," Natalie sobbed, still holding onto me, and it took me a moment to realise that it was me she was apologising to, as though she feared I would lose respect for her after what she had done—after what she had no doubt enjoyed doing.

"If you want, I can make you forget it happened," May offered.

That brought us all to our senses. We all straightened up and looked at each other, assessing each other, trying to see the friends we had always had through what we had become in the last ten minutes. Finally, Peter said, "As long as we all swear not to let anyone else find out about this, *ever*."

Natalie and Rebecca looked at each other, both trying to decide if they could live with what had happened. Eventually, they both nodded, and all of us relaxed.

"Thank you," May now said to me, touching my shoulder. "I know you did not do that for me, but I still appreciate you saving me again."

"Sure," I muttered, embarrassed and a little hurt, because I knew she was right; if not for the fact that we all would have died if I hadn't done it, I probably wouldn't have tried so hard to help May.

"We all owe you big-time," said Natalie, turning back to me and hugging me again.

"No you don't," I said, and then looking down and registering what I was seeing, I added, "unless you wanna lend me your pants."

Chapter 28: Homebound

We were lucky because the Honnies in charge of the human collection allowed May to step through to our world later that day. Given that they liked to remain discreet, as Smiley had told us, timing was of the essence. Even more luckily, she was allowed to take the four of us through with her, after convincing them that we were hers, that we would be under extremely close guard so that we couldn't blab about them, and that we would come back through with her when she was done. She was set a requirement of ten humans to bring through, though if we were to survive, that number would have to be bumped up to fourteen. It was better than I dared hope.

Peter, Natalie, Rebecca and I were sent out of the room immediately after the battle while the Honnies sorted out whatever business needed sorting. I was dizzy the moment I was back on my feet and the moment the door closed, I leaned against the wall beside it, trying to persuade my head to stop spinning. Natalie leaned against the wall beside me but seeing how unsteady I was, did me the favour of not leaning on me, despite clearly wanting the comfort. All four of us were considerably traumatised by what we had been forced to do (or in my case, what I had seen) and I wondered if we had made the right decision in keeping the memories. This would take some time to get over but if I had my way, Natalie and I would go through the therapy together.

When the Honnies emerged, the humans who'd been with the collector were nowhere to be seen, and I knew that May and Ingi must have dealt with them already (something I preferred not to think too closely about, given that they had looked fresh out of our world). The supervisor bid May good day and sent us on our way, we humans wondering why we were leaving the building instead of stepping back into our world.

"I have things I need to do first," May told us when I put the question to her. "Ingi will need to go the rest of the way on her own. I think she is strong enough but she needs to know some things, especially since I do not know when I will return to Malia."

"So we're definitely going today?" Peter asked.

"Later, yes," said May. "We will have to do it in there, though, because we are too high. In this space in your world, we would drop a very long way, but they have a tunnel we can use."

Of course we would be too high; if we were somewhere in central Australia, as I estimated we probably were, we would be well above the flatlands of our own world.

"How long do you have on our side?" Peter asked. "Or can you stay as long as you like?"

"As long as it takes me," she said, "although they will get suspicious if I am there for too long. It is procedure that I report to them when I return, and I have to bring my humans with me. I will need fourteen to make up for you four if you do not come back with me."

"I'm not particularly interested in returning here, I have to confess," Rebecca muttered.

"They will not like that," said May, smiling slightly, "but maybe they will not remember your face. I hope they do not, because I will be punished if they learn I left my own humans behind. I would have to convince them that I had killed you."

"I hope you intend to lie about that," said Natalie nervously.

"I think so."

We spent most of that afternoon in the hotel but none of us were in the right spirits to play cards this time. Peter and Rebecca shut themselves away in a room together and I hoped they were patching things up between them after that morning. I couldn't see how either of them could think ill of the other, knowing they had both been driven by a power far beyond their control. May spent the time with Ingi, putting the knowledge she would need to continue her way to Malia in her head, Tommy hanging off Ingi as usual. This was not something I wanted to see (heartless, maybe, but I couldn't wait to get away from Tommy; it would be much easier to grieve for his loss then).

One thing I did want to do was have a word with May, because it only occurred to me when I had time to think about it that she had done us another great favour that day. The collector may have placed the thoughts in their minds to disgrace themselves so, but May taking them back didn't automatically free them from that influence—she had to return them to normal herself. It was a good deed that she certainly hadn't needed to do, given how much strain she was under, and I wanted to know why. After walking around the floor for a while, pleased that I was beginning to feel like myself again, I found May alone in one of the rooms about an hour after we had got back to the hotel, staring out the window at the landscape.

"Are you okay?" she asked me when I drew level with her.

"What are you doing?" I asked her, surprised but pleased that she wasn't too busy to talk to me.

"Nothing," she said, returning her gaze to the window, "but I will not be back here for a while and I will probably get homesick."

"Know the feeling," I said, my spirits rising as I remembered that, very soon, I would be homesick no more. "Listen—"

I put the question to her, and she shrugged indifferently. "You are right, but I did not want to see that any more than you did. Also, he was insulting me by doing that to your friends—I could not have that."

"Thanks anyway," I said, also shrugging, something that felt weird with only one arm to do it. "It just seemed like maybe more trouble than it was worth with everything else going on."

"I do not think so," she said, and then changed the subject. "Are you sure you do not want me to make you forget what happened? I can make you think it went differently."

"Isn't that also more trouble than it's worth?"

"Do you think so?" she said, raising her eyebrows in surprise.

"No, not for us, but for you it must be."

"I would not mind. I can tell that it has devastated your friends."

"I can't decide for them," I said, "but maybe put it on the backburner."

"What does that mean?"

"It means we might ask for that later, if that's okay."

"That is fine," she said. "Whatever you think about me, I do not mind doing that for you."

"And what would we owe you in return?"

"I would expect it anyway, but I would hope you keep me safe when I am in your world."

"Don't worry, there's no reason why the enemy should even know about you," I said, and feeling satisfied, I turned to leave her to her contemplation of the window.

"Wait," she said, reaching out and turning me by my good shoulder back to face her—it was a pressure I had no hope of resisting.

"What?"

For answer, she leaned forward towards me and before I could say or do anything, she tasted me again. It was just as choking and arousing as it had been when she'd done it on our first night together, but with a couple of notable differences: She had leaned down this time instead of lifting me up to her level; and I had only one arm with which to hold onto her. Still, she drew me very close to her in the twenty odd seconds we stood like that, and despite the discomfort of not being able to breathe properly, I had to plead with myself not to have an erection. I was extremely thankful that the room was empty and that there was no one in the corridor who could have seen what was going on.

"A bit of warning might have been nice," I muttered when she let me go, looking more pleased than I could remember. It had been dark the last time we'd done that, and now that we had done it in the light, I could see just how much it meant to her—she was practically glowing with her satisfaction.

"Please," she said dismissively, "I would have done that every night if your mouth had not been shut. You may go now."

I did go, taking a few minutes to circle the floor in the hope of spending the remaining time here with Natalie, the one person whose presence would take my mind off the arousal May had given me. I found Ingi and Tommy, Dan and Gob, and the closed door behind which I knew Peter and Rebecca to be, but no sign of Natalie. Tiring, I settled in the room I'd been sleeping in and lay down, thinking of catching a nap. I may have dozed off too, but at some point during the afternoon, Natalie came to find me, because I registered after some time that she was curled up beside me.

It was four o'clock when May told us it was time to go. She had already said goodbye to her children, who would remain here at the hotel for tonight before setting off for the west side of Lagalia the next morning. She now wanted to be on her way, and none of us protested. It wasn't inconceivable that we could be back in our base, eating dinner off the conveyer belt three hours from now. The thought cheered all of us considerably. Also, there was Tommy; none of us wanted to see him again. It would be much easier to close that chapter once we knew for sure that we would never see him again.

We traced the now familiar route through the city to the human collection centre but this time, when we got there, we were taken through a different door. A minute later, the five of us were in another large, empty room, but this one was rather different from the one we had been in that morning, as was the Honnie who greeted May. A discussion ensued for a few minutes before he turned and left the five of us alone in the room.

"What was that?" I asked.

"He was explaining the process to me," May said, "Since I have never done it before. He also wanted to know why I needed to take humans with me. I told you were mine and

I needed you with me to help me find the best humans to take. He may have been suspicious but he is going to let you come through with me."

"Could we have bypassed that check if we'd done it at the bottom of the mountain?" Natalie asked.

"Probably, but it does not matter now."

"So what's happening now then?" Peter asked.

His question was answered, not by May, but by the room itself, which shuddered and began to descend like an enormous elevator. In fact, that was exactly what it was. I had no idea how fast we were descending, but it didn't feel too uncomfortable. It went on for what seemed like a very long time, and in fact it was a full thirty minutes before it finally came to a stop.

"Come," May said at once, moving quickly to the door through which we had entered and opening it for us. Beyond was another room whose insides were completely black. There may have been power to lower the elevator, but they hadn't bothered to light this room down here.

"What's in there?" Peter asked.

"Nothing, but we must go in there so that they know to raise the floor."

We did, and when May closed the door, everything went completely dark, so dark that waving my hand in front of my face achieved nothing whatsoever. The room seemed to be spacious but it was stone, dark, cold and damp. We must have been right in the middle of the mountain, perhaps lower even than the valley we had crossed to get to it. I reached blindly for the others, any of them would do, and eventually located someone's arm.

"Now what?" Peter asked, his voice echoing around the room and taking a very long time to die.

"Now, I take two of you," said May, "and the other two have to hold onto me."

The following minute or so was spent with the five of us feeling around blindly in the dark, trying to organise and orientate ourselves and achieving nothing except to touch each other inappropriately. It wasn't until May used her minds to keep us still that she was able to take control of the situation. Shortly after, she had Peter and me by the forearms while Natalie and Rebecca stood behind, holding onto each of May's shoulders.

The Honnie moved then, and in a strange way, we all moved with her, even though none of us moved our feet. May herself didn't seem to change position but she definitely moved, and not until several seconds later did I understand that unlike our entry into the Honnie world, she was actually doing what Smiley had done and moving along the fourth dimenssion. That explained why we hadn't seen any of the Honnies' world in the memory of 1981. It also explained why full-blooded Honnies shimmered around the edges in the same way that Smiley had: They were just as four-dimensional as he had been.

Although the room in which we had started was pitch-black, perception itself seemed to fade to nothing as we crossed between the worlds, through a place in which time and space (as we knew it anyway) did not exist. When it came back, it didn't do so all at once but seemed to fade back into being, much brighter than before since we were now outdoors. I recognised where I was before we re-entered our world; not in terms of geographical location, for I was completely clueless there, but that we were in our own shadow, just as Smiley had been in his memories.

The first thing I did when all our feet were firmly back in our own world was look around at my friends, and the first thing I noticed (and it pleased me greatly) was that we had all suddenly become attractive again, at least as attractive as we had always been. Peter and Rebecca were staring at each other as though they'd never seen each other before, and I wondered if the sudden change in light had made them lose interest in each other, but found it not to be the case when they both smiled glowingly at each other. As for Natalie, she was as heart-stoppingly beautiful as ever; perhaps even more so now that she had put on a few kilos. She was still a long way from fat but she now had a little extra curve that served to make her even more titillating.

I'd been prepared for that but I hadn't been prepared for the impact that May had now that she was in our world. Now I knew that it wasn't humans at all: It was the difference between the two worlds that caused that to happen, perhaps some long forgotten piece of magic, who knew. It put everything into perspective for me: The Honnie of 1981 had been dazzlingly beautiful; the Honnie of 2000 whom Smiley had met had been beautiful in the same way the male Honnies we'd seen in their world had been, but nowhere near as beautiful as the one who'd come through to this world. They had been males, however; with May, who was attractive enough in her own world, it was far more pronounced. She was amazing to look at, even in that robe that just wouldn't do in this world, and all four of us goggled at her for several seconds before, with more than a little effort, we regained our composure.

As I came back to my senses, Natalie did something with her fingers, and then exclaimed with delight. "It's all good! I've got my magic back. Quick, everyone stand together."

We all did so, gathering around May, who didn't understand what was going on. She did notice the change in Natalie, however, and stared at her in something that might have been fear. "You have changed," she said.

"No, just got back what I left behind," she said, walking around us and performing the usual invisibility veil, soundproof barrier and untraceable spells. "I tell you, I didn't always have it, but it's a relief to get it back now. We're gonna need it to get back home."

"Yeah," said Peter, staring around at our new surroundings. We had dropped into the middle of nowhere; the landscape was rocky, barren and with no discernible landmark other than a pillar of rock some hundred metres away, jutting up like a defiant finger. "Er, guys, how are we gonna find them, though? If their protection's still good, we won't be able to, not even with magic."

"You doing okay?" I asked May, who looked almost overawed.

"Yes," she said, not very convincingly. "It is just, I know plenty about your world from the humans whose minds I have memorised, but to actually be here? You must understand how it is a bit unreal."

"We know," said Rebecca. "That's how we felt when we first went into your world."

"Yeah, but you get used to it," said Natalie. "You'll probably like it after a while. Human life is a lot more comfortable than what you have to do in your world. To answer your question, Peter, I'm going to contact Amelia telepathically to let her know we're back. I'm looking forward to her pleasant surprise already."

We all went silent then, watching Natalie as she began the telepathy. I agreed with her assessment; after some six-and-a-half weeks gone, knowing Natalie had no magic and we had no way of getting back without a Honnie, they had all probably given up hope that we would return at all. This made me remember the thoughts I'd entertained a few times in my darker moments: What if they no longer required us? What if they'd already won? What if they'd lost? If they were still chipping away at the Hammerhearts, perhaps working on a plan to reacquire the Sien-Leoard Crystal, they would be extremely pleased to have a Honnie to help, but would the plans they'd worked on since allow for it?

Natalie's expression changed several times over the following minute, which meant the telepathy was working and Amelia must still have her magic—a good start. The four of us watched her, all wanting to interrupt but not wanting to break her concentration. May, who probably still had us in her mind, would be getting all of it, but who knew what she would be making of it? Finally Natalie, whose eyes had been closed during the exchange of thoughts, now opened them with a clear expression.

"They knew we were alive," she said, a little stunned. "I don't know how but they knew there were still five of us alive.

They don't know about Tommy yet, though, so that'll hurt telling them that."

"Are they still fighting?" I asked her anxiously.

"What?" she said, confused. "Dunno what you mean by that. They're still in the base and still not far from Chopville; we can teleport straight back into that clearing we left from. We'll need to lift our protection so that they can find us, but once we do, they'll let us back in."

"Did she say anything about how they're going?" Peter asked.

"No. We can ask questions about that later, but I tell you what—she almost had a heart attack when she felt me contacting her. She was over the moon to hear from me, that we're back, and they're all gonna be chuffed we have a Honnie to help us. I don't think any of them expected us to succeed."

"They wouldn't have, after Marc would have told them what happened," said Rebecca. "So what are we waiting for?"

"Waiting for them to be ready for us," said Natalie. "It'll only take a few minutes, but we don't want to get back anywhere near Chopville until we know they're ready. She'll let me know when it's safe to teleport. In the meantime, May, can we do something?"

"Is that really necessary?" May asked, getting whatever it was straight out of Natalie's head.

"Depends. Do you want them to be mildly comfortable in your presence, or would you prefer to be an outcast?"

"Humans," she muttered dispassionately. "I do not think it will make much difference."

"We had to comply with your rules when we were in your world," Natalie pointed out.

"You complied with very little, and what you did, you had no choice."

"Yeah, well you don't have a choice now either."

"I believe I do."

"What are you guys talking about?" Peter asked.

Natalie gestured at May's robe. "You think that's gonna look right when she's with humans?"

"She looks conventional next to Fewul," I said, and Peter laughed at the memory of how the Beast of Magic had been clad before we had left.

"Come on, May," Natalie said, almost pleaded. "Seriously, it's not as bad as you seem to think. Don't you want them to think good of you?"

"It might actually make you stand out less," I added. "Aren't you Honnies all about discretion in this world?"

May sighed. "Okay, fine, but I swear you humans have no idea how much you take for granted."

"You guys go over there," said Natalie, gesturing Peter and I away by some distance. "This is ladies' business now."

"Oh sure, maybe we'll just hide in a bush somewhere," said Peter, staring around at the completely barren landscape.

In response, Natalie magically erected a wall around her, May and Rebecca so that Peter and I could no longer see them. We sat down and leaned against it, looking west at the setting sun. We couldn't hear much from the other side of the wall as the two girls worked on outfitting May, and I wondered if they were communicating mentally. It took them a remarkably short time to do it but it was still long enough for me to realise how hungry I was. I hadn't eaten a thing since breakfast that morning and although some parts of the day had taken away my appetite, it had now returned in full measure.

When one of the Fletchers called that Peter and I were allowed to come around the wall, we found that they had gone to far less trouble with May's appearance than I would have expected. In fact, in jeans and a top rather tighter than anything she had worn prior, it looked deliberate. Good thing too, for I found that my assessment that outfitting would make her stand out less had been horribly off the mark. The clothes she was now wearing showed off her body in a way the robes never had, and although I was fairly familiar with its general shape after the nights we'd spent holding onto each other, it still knocked me for a loop to see it so. It was also the first time she had worn a bra—those robes had made bras unnecessary in their world. To cap the look, they had tied her long black hair back in a style that was supposed to be plain, but instead made her attractiveness even more obvious.

Peter and I almost fell back a step at the sight of her. All we could do was stare, open-mouthed until Natalie and Rebecca slapped each of us to bring us back to our senses.

"Geez, you two," Rebecca huffed, looking mightily pissed.

"Sorry," Peter said, going rather pink, "but what did you expect? I know you went for the plain look but you're really just showing her off even more."

"You humans seem to like things tight," May observed, looking a little uncomfortable.

"Maybe you should have given her a dress," Peter suggested. "That would have been closer to what she's used to."

"Or a skirt," I suggested, visualising it and feeling my mouth go rather dry.

"No thanks," said Natalie coolly. "We'd prefer you boys to keep your eyeballs somewhere in the vicinity of their sockets."

"This will do fine," said Rebecca. "It'll make them admire her appearance and hold her in high regard, but hopefully not enough to drive them crazy."

"You will have to give me different clothes sometime," May told them.

"Perhaps a bikini," Peter suggested, earning another reproving look from Rebecca. That would be even worse, I thought, because May would probably like that. I'd never actually seen her naked, and the robes covered most of their body from the eye, but given that she had changed her robe in front of me without a qualm, it suggested that Honnies didn't particularly mind showing off in front of humans.

"If you guys are done being perverts, we can now teleport," Natalie said sharply.

"Not perving, just imagining," said Peter innocently, and Rebecca hit him again.

"What is this?" May asked nervously.

"Teleporting," Natalie repeated. "We're going to meet the others."

"It doesn't hurt," I promised her, and with some resolve, I took one of May's hands in my own so that she wouldn't fear losing us in what was about to happen.

The teleportation came a moment later, and as it had when we'd teleported into the paddock on that fateful night in late June, it was something of a relief to be doing something so familiar again. It was even more of a relief when we materialised in the paddock a few moments later, right back in the same spot where Marc had initially opened the gateway. It was darker here, perhaps because we had travelled some distance east after all, but it was still a blessed relief to be back on old ground again. May staggered slightly upon landing, squeezing my hand hard enough to hurt, but given that she could have crushed it to mush if she'd really gone for it, I was thankful she held herself in check.

"Everyone okay?" Peter asked into the almost-silence, broken only by crickets.

"Think so," I said, looking around at their faces in the darkness. Other than May, everyone else looked fine.

"Good," said Natalie, walking around us again, lifting the enchantments she had placed there only minutes earlier. "Now we just have to wait for the others to let us in and hope that they do it before the Hammerhearts find us."

"You really think they could?" Peter asked nervously.

"Sure they could, if they're on the ball, but hopefully they won't have thought up any devices that will instantaneously let them know when our positions have been located anywhere on the planet."

"Well don't give them ideas," said Rebecca.

"So, where are they?" I asked after a few seconds of silence.

"Hmm," said Natalie, looking thoughtful. "Should I contact Amelia again?"

That turned out not to be necessary. We didn't so much feel when the cloak of protection around the base was lifted enough to drop over the five of us, but we knew when it had happened all the same. The door into the control room appeared out of nowhere, easy to spot only because of the light that was streaming from it. Nearest to us, clad exactly as he had been before we had left, stood Fewul, evidently the one who had performed the magic. The delay in the magic, it seemed, was due to the shock that had frozen Marc and Amelia in place; both of them stood just outside the doorway, staring at the group in amazement.

It was Natalie who broke their paralysis, hurrying forward and hugging them both. They came to their senses as the rest of us followed. The expression on Marc's face as he stared at the Honnie was much the same as Peter's had been, and how mine had probably been, when we had seen her for the first time in her human attire. Amelia must have spared a glance for her before we had seen them, but now her attention was on me; or more specifically, the place where my left arm should have been.

"Oh my God, John," she said in a small voice, barely audible.

"Er, guys," said Marc slowly, looking troubled as he looked around at us, "did we leave someone behind?"

He was referring to Tommy, of course, and I exchanged a nervous look with Peter. This was telling the girls about Candice all over again. If Natalie was right, they knew that Candice was no longer with us, but since we were here, and there were still five of us alive, they would expect Tommy to be with us.

"He's not coming back, Marc," Natalie said in a small voice.

"Not coming back?" Marc repeated uncomprehendingly. "Why not? You're here, and we know he's alive."

"How do you know he's alive?" Rebecca asked scornfully.

"I tried to follow you guys," he told us, "after you went through. I wanted to see if there was any way of tracing you. I followed your direction across the paddock, re-opening small gateways to look through to see where you were. I only saw you once, but it was enough to trace your life essence. It was the best I could do."

"So that means what exactly?" I asked.

"There's a panel with six lights on it in the lounge room," said Amelia, "one for each of you. We saw Candice's light go out, but the rest of you were always flashing. That's why we knew you might still come back."

"Lucky for you, you were right," said Rebecca, "because more likely we would have stayed alive for a few months while they made us fat so that they could eat us."

"So where is Tommy?" Marc asked.

"Something happened to him," said Natalie. "He's alive, but…he might as well not be. And you had better get rid of that panel because we don't need to know when he dies."

Both of their faces fell as they exchanged a worried look, and Marc sighed. "So, we should treat him as dead?"

"That's what we've been doing," said Peter sadly.

"What about Candice, then?" Amelia asked.

"Can't we explain all that later?" Rebecca said harshly. "Don't you think it might be nice for us to get in the warmth? We've been through a hell of a lot."

"You're right, you're right," Amelia said hastily, gesturing toward the open doorway. "They're all waiting in the yard and they're excited as all hell."

"Hang on," Natalie said quickly. "Guys, what's the date today?"

"Er, August 19th," said Marc. "Why?"

"Good," she said, satisfied, "just making sure time ran the same over there as it did here."

"Yeah, you guys took a while."

"Did you think we would be back in a couple of days?" I retorted, and he went pink.

"Hold on," Marc said quickly as we made to step through the door, and he addressed Fewul. "Will this magic work on a Honnie?"

"Yes, Master," the beast replied monotonously.

There were two more people waiting for us in the control room, watching us all on the display screens: Lucien and James. They saw me first, and both their eyes widened as they registered my cheap amputation. That gave them a shock, but they were totally knocked for a loop when May stepped through the door. It was big enough for James but at least he'd seen Honnies before. Lucien wouldn't have known what to expect, and now that he was seeing one for the first time, he looked as though a few screws in his head, and more than a few in various joints, and been loosened a few turns.

"Guys," said James, clapping Peter on the shoulder and grinning at me, quickly getting over his shock. "My God, it's great to see you, and after a successful mission too."

"Mission is right," said Rebecca blandly.

"We're all very interested in knowing what happened over there," said Lucien, "and why it took so long, but questions can wait. I think you had better get out there before they bang the door down."

He was right. Through the window, I could see that the yard around the control room was crammed with excited chatter. Peter did the honours, opening the door and hurrying into their midst, the rest of us following more slowly. It was hard not to smile at the attention, although I would have preferred it to come without the gasps and exclamations about my missing arm. It reminded me vividly of the time when we had first arrived at the Woodward base after Amelia had got us out of the Hammerheart basement. May, who stayed close to my side as though I were the only person here she felt comfortable with, received plenty of attention herself, but as no one but those of us who knew her knew that she could speak English, it came in the form of respectful, startled, fearful and, in the case of many boys, attracted looks.

Of course, regarding my arm, most of the comments were directed at their friends, rather than me, as though they feared it was a sensitive issue for me and didn't dare ask, despite the fact that they were dying to know how it had happened. There was only one exception to this rule, as anyone could have predicted.

"Hey John, what did the bus driver say to the man with no arms, three heads and one leg?" Harry asked me, and then answered his own question. "'Allo, 'allo, 'allo. You look 'armless, 'op in.'"

"I can still do this," I said, flipping him the bird, and he and Simon roared with laughter.

The only thing I really didn't like was the odd feeling of separation that came with it, and I was no stranger to it. It was the same thing I'd felt in the aftermath of facing Moran for the first time, the mission on Rock Haulter to get the Sien-Leoard Crystal back, and probably a few times since. It was the result of sharing an experience with a small number of people, and then recognising that as much as you may recount it with your friends, they could never understand what it was like for you without having been through it for themselves. No one but the four of us could understand how dangerous it had been over there, or how lucky we were to be back here, no matter how much we tried to impress it upon them. In fact, I doubted that even May would appreciate it, at least if not for her getting it straight out of our heads.

The scene lasted for perhaps five minutes, during which the people who surrounded me didn't quite dare touch me. This was most obvious in Lena and Stella, both of whom looked as though they wished to hug me and yet made an obvious effort to hold themselves back. Stella just looked incredibly grateful and relieved, while Lena looked more thoughtful and more than a bit mischievous, as though she were now remembering what she had told me before I had left. It went on well after that too but for me, it was ended by Marc, who had stood patiently with me throughout and now took me by the remaining arm.

"Come along, Herman from 'The Simpsons'; there's a bit of limb-restoration in order, methinks."

Chapter 29: Catching Up

The reunion had retired to the dining room for dinner by the time I rejoined them, now with two arms again. Marc had taken me into his room to perform the magic, something he felt reasonably confident he could do, in the hope that nobody would have to see it, as much for himself as for me. I was grateful for that because what remained of my left shoulder wasn't pleasant to look at, and nobody else needed to see it. We hadn't been completely alone though; May had followed us into the building without invitation, even a mental one. Marc hadn't said anything about this but he had been rather startled by it. Fortunately for him, May had paid very little attention to what he was doing, most of her attention focused on Fewul, who had followed Marc. I didn't blame her; Fewul almost certainly had no mind she could take hold of. She had looked rather scared of the Beast of Magic.

"How did this happen?" Marc had asked me as he helped me take my jumper and T-shirt off.

"It got ripped off by a hungry Honnie," I had told him. "Er, long story. Tell you later."

"Yeah," he had said. "We're all dying to ask all sorts of questions but I suppose they'll have to wait for some sort of meeting."

"We wanna ask a lot of questions too," I had pointed out. "What's been happening around here while we've been away?"

"With us, not a lot," he had said. "I guess a lot of political stuff's happened, like the Woodwards have made a bit of ground since you left, but with us? We've been mostly spying and working on a plan, waiting to see if you guys would get back. We haven't actually made any moves against Hammerson but we think he knows about us."

"How could he?"

"Because Natalie and Amelia haven't been seen for a long time, and that reminds me of something else," he had said, grinning suddenly. "We couldn't tell them where you'd gone, and they got a little annoyed with us. I think the word a lot of people used to describe your mother's reaction was 'nuclear'."

I had groaned, and he laughed.

"What I'm gonna do here is make everything around your shoulder numb, so you won't feel anything until it's all done. It mightn't be a bad idea to close your eyes while I'm doing it."

I had obliged, deciding not to continue talking to him while he worked. He had never done this kind of magic before, as far as I knew, and I wasn't about to distract him—May's presence was already halfway to doing that. It had only taken about five minutes before he told me to brace, and then had performed the magic to remove the numbness around my shoulder. There it had been, my arm, exactly as it had been the day I had stepped into the Honnie world. He had even somehow recovered my old watch; who knew what had happened to that as everything around it had disappeared into Ingi's mouth. It was an enormous shock when that ghost arm I'd had to put up with for so long was suddenly replaced by a real arm again.

It hadn't been quite usable yet, though; it was very stiff and a little painful to move, as though it hadn't been used for a very long time. That was more or less the truth of the matter. By the time the four of us entered the dining room, though, after much flexing of the muscles and rotating of the various joints, it was beginning to return to normal. Our arrival was greeted with an explosion of clapping as people took in my new arm and much whistling of approval for the man who had performed the magic.

We headed up to the conveyer belt to get our food, something Marc did without any pause but something I took a moment to relish, after having lived on far too much gradi and the food we'd stored in our backpack before starting out. I had just supplied my own dinner and was about to head for a table where Marc had just sat down with Lena (I could put up with her for one evening, as everyone else I would have liked to sit with was on full tables) but before I could, May took me by the shoulder—the right one, as it were.

"What is this?" she asked me quietly, the first words she had spoken since entering the base, and quietly enough so that so far, nobody else yet knew that she could speak English; at least, not unless Peter, Natalie or Rebecca had mentioned it.

"Just visualize what food you want and it'll make it for you," I told her, surprised she hadn't already known that. I could still feel that she had a hold of my mind, and wondered if she'd taken everyone in the base yet.

"It does not work for me," she told me.

"What? Why not?"

"How do I know?"

"Well, what do you want? Maybe I can get it to give you what you wanna eat."

That was the only reason I could think of. Honnie minds were so obviously different from human ones, and at the time Amelia had created this conveyer belt, she hadn't even known of the existence of Honnies. Just as I thought this, however, May came up with her own way of making the conveyer belt work. In the past, when she had ordered us around mentally, she had left some of our awareness so that even though we couldn't resist, we could still think our own thoughts as we did as we were told. Now, though, she took complete control of my mind in such a way that my thoughts were no longer my own. They were thoughts of meat, slivers of it, the stuff that she and Ingi had eaten regularly in their own world. When my head cleared and I could think for myself again, the conveyer belt had done its duty. May was staring at the meat in amazement and, again, a bit of fear.

"There is something very wrong in this world," she whispered, and I was only barely able to hear her.

"That's magic," I told her, "and you're right—it's the cause of all the problems that we're trying to deal with."

* * *

Lucien suggested over dinner, to much fanfare, that an impromptu meeting take place at half past seven, which would be immediately after dinner. It was a very popular idea with everyone except those of us who had just gotten back. Peter, in particular, had to shout that none of us had showered in six weeks and up until a few days ago, we hadn't even gone to the toilet properly. The meeting was instead scheduled for an hour later so that we could spend the intervening time settling in. This presented an immediate problem, however, because for the sake of convenience, most of our rooms had been taken while we had been away. Siobhan was now sleeping in my old room, while Jessica had moved into Rebecca's room and Stella into Natalie's. So at the conclusion of dinner, the four of us, plus Marc, Amelia and 'the Honnie', as most people called her from behind their hands, gathered before one of the elevators to discuss the problem.

"We saved all your stuff though," Amelia told us imploringly. "As long as the possibility existed that you might come back, we've been holding it in six compartments in the storage room. I guess we'll only need to open four of them, though."

"What storage room?" Peter asked.

"It's above the dining room," Marc told us, "a little addition we made while you guys were away. It's mostly for keeping goodies of the Hammerhearts we collect along the way, but your stuff is in there too."

"So where are we gonna sleep if our rooms are gone?" I asked.

"Third floor," said Marc. "Peter, your room is still free, as are Siobhan's, Jessica's and Tommy's old rooms, so I guess you all decide how you're gonna sort it out. Er," he faltered, glancing awkwardly at May, "what about her? Does anyone know if Honnies sleep?"

"They sleep," I told him, "although I doubt it matters what room since she doesn't have any of her own stuff."

"Well, there are free rooms on level three," said Amelia, "and all of level four, of course, or if you guys are okay with giving away Candice's old room…we've been keeping it empty in her honour."

"That should work," said Natalie, but even as she spoke, I felt May pushing thoughts into my mind, and they were in the negative. She didn't want to be surrounded by humans she didn't know, or who were too scared to acknowledge her presence. That confirmed in my mind that she'd taken all of our minds since she'd been so quick to make that observation.

"Why don't we sort her room out later," I said quickly, causing them all to look at me in surprise—or almost all; Natalie looked suspicious as she looked from me to May and back again, and I didn't like it. She was jumping to a completely different conclusion, one I wished I could put a stop to immediately.

"Okay," said Marc slowly. "Well, as long as you can be sure she won't kill anyone in the next hour, I guess she can just go do whatever she likes."

What she wanted to do, it seemed, was follow me wherever I went. My first stop was the storage room, which was accessible on the second floor, directly opposite the elevator on the left side of the building, putting it directly above the dining room. A similar room had been established on the other side of the building, which I would later learn was a computer room. After collecting my possessions, what precious little there were, which had been kept in a bag and locked in a locker, we all went up to the third floor to pick our rooms. It was here, as Peter reclaimed his old room beside James's, that we were all given a good view of the mess Peter would have to clean up over the following few days.

"Drop your things in there and then meet me in my room," Rebecca told him, taking a key to the opposite room, Siobhan's old room, from Amelia as she spoke.

"I was sort of planning to have a shower," Peter said awkwardly, all too aware of the small audience he had. Natalie, in particular, was looking very sceptically at her younger sister.

"So was I," Rebecca said, winking before slipping into her room and out of sight. Marc and Amelia exchanged a look then; it might have been my imagination, but I thought there was relief in it. Peter merely grimaced as he disappeared into his own room. Neither of them bothered to close their doors, which was all the proof I needed of what was about to go down.

The other two spare rooms were right at the other end of the corridor. Natalie took the one beside Sophie, leaving me to take the one next to Simon—Tommy's old room, as it were. After she had provided us with our keys, Amelia went back downstairs. Natalie went to unpack and shower, I assumed, while I went into my own room to make myself as comfortable as I could. A shower would have to wait, though, because Marc and May both followed me in.

"What was that about?" Marc asked me, not needing to explain what he was referring to.

I sighed. "I know it doesn't look good, but you gotta understand how it was over there. We were all pretty sure we'd never get back, right up until about a week ago. When you're under that sort of pressure and you spend a lot of time alone with a person, you can become...attached."

I hesitated for only a moment, because at my own words, my mind flashed back to the hours I'd spent alone with Amelia in a pitch-black basement cell in the Chopville Hammerheart base. Had an attachment been formed then? You bet, and had it been a good thing for either of us? I had no idea.

Marc nodded. "Well, I guess it's a good thing. If Peter had hoped Siobhan would sit around and wait for him, he would have been sorely mistaken."

My stomach fell; Peter's assessment had been right after all. "What happened?" I asked dully.

"Well, since she saw Smiley's memories, she never believed he would get back. She was mighty pissed that he decided to go without even telling her first, and even more pissed that he didn't say a proper goodbye. Her best way of dealing with it was to move on as quickly as possible. She's with Liam now; well, it was he who initiated it, but she went along without any hesitation. It hasn't really reflected too well on either of their reputations around here."

"I bet," I said, thinking of Siobhan, wondering what sort of person she was. I knew there would be good explanations for her behaviour, but it was sad that it didn't take anyone else's feelings into account. Good thing for Peter that he now had someone else, although Rebecca may not be much better in the end. Peter would just have to learn the hard way.

"What about Jessica?" I asked. "Did she wait or move on?"

"Oh," he said, his face falling slightly. "That—er—that was a little more complicated."

"Why? What are you talking about?"

"Well," he sighed. "Let's just say that Tommy not coming back was really not a good thing; we've all been kinda hanging our hopes on him."

"More than the rest of us?" I said incredulously, deciding not to mention that in his last days, Tommy had been having sex with an alien.

"For Jessica's sake, I mean," he said quickly. "See, before he left, Tommy left something with Jessica, and since she found out what it was a couple of weeks ago, she's been spending a fair amount of time in the lounge room, watching his little black light."

"Black light?"

"They're all different colours."

"So—hang on," I said, trying to get my head around what he was saying, "if Tommy left something with her that meant so much, how come she didn't know what it was until two weeks ago?"

"Because he didn't know about it either," Marc said heavily.

This was getting a little annoying now. Why wasn't Marc just saying whatever he was thinking? I glanced at May, whose eyes were only on me, as though Marc wasn't even present. I'd been about to ask her to tell me what was going on when the answer came to me, and it came so suddenly that I thought it was my own reason that came up with it, rather than May's influence. I had to quickly catch my breath, feeling my heartbeat quicken.

"You're not telling me he knocked her up, are you?"

The look on his face was all the confirmation I needed, and my mouth fell open in horror.

"I haven't seen her since you guys got back," Marc said heavily. "She must know Tommy's not coming back by now; I hope Felicity has the decency to make sure she's okay."

"Geez," I breathed, trying to wrap my mind around all the possible consequences of this development. "When did it happen? How did it happen? Weren't they using protection? What's she gonna do about it? Do Marge and Charlie know yet?"

"Slow down, man," said Marc quickly. "Marge and Charlie do know and they're mighty pissed about it, as I'm sure you can imagine. Even Charlie wants her to come back to the adults now so they can look after her. The timing would suggest it probably happened while they were in this base, not the old one, and Jessica says that's probably it because they stopped using protection around then."

"Why the hell did they do that?"

"Because the condoms kept tearing. Apparently, Tommy was too big and too enthusiastic. It would have been smarter to just tell us that at the time; we could have made stronger ones, but they chose to just do without. Stupidity, something everyone is in agreement on."

"Too bloody right," I said darkly, thinking of Tommy and his irresponsibility. I couldn't blame him without also blaming Jessica, but it seemed so typical of Tommy to disregard the potential for trouble, especially after he'd had the nerve to use the Darkness Crystal to seduce Natalie. "So, what are we gonna do about the baby?"

"Well, as you can imagine, it's split the army almost down the middle," said Marc. "Some people, like Felicity, think she should abort it immediately, because we're too busy to have to look after a baby around here—it would be nothing but trouble. Some people, like Amelia, refuse to have anything to do with an abortion, thinking of it as murdering innocence, which is more or less what we're supposed to be fighting against. Then there are some, like James, who think it should be her choice and no one else's."

"And what do you think?" I asked him curiously.

He sighed. "I guess my thinking is closest to James's, but I have to say, if she does have the baby, she really should go back to the adults; none of us have any experience in that sort of thing."

"And what if she chooses to have an abortion?"

"Her choice," he said. "I guess I'll have to be the one to perform it—with the crystal," he added, as though I couldn't work that bit out for myself. "Amelia wouldn't do it, and who knows what Natalie would think. I hope she doesn't, though, because I'd be a lot happier not having that on my conscience."

"And what does Jessica want?"

"So far, she's saying she wants to have the baby," he said heavily. "That may change now that we know Tommy won't be back, but I don't think it will. She doesn't seem to be a pro-lifer, but she wants to keep it—doesn't want the regret."

"I hope you're right," I said. "Tommy put his life on the line; well, we all did, but Tommy was one who didn't come out to see the end result of it. Maybe it's a good thing he got to leave part of himself behind."

I had now finished unpacking all my stuff, and was thinking of telling Marc to leave, and perhaps suggesting to May that she should follow him, when he abruptly said, "So, if I may go back to what you said before, if Peter and Rebecca got to spend a lot of time alone, does that also mean—"

"Not yet," I said, answering the question before he could finish it, and glancing again at May in the process. "I didn't get nearly as much time with her, but maybe something might happen now that we're back."

"Good to hear," he said, getting to his feet—he had been sitting on the bed for most of this time. "Well, I can see you're ready for a shower, and I don't wanna stay to see that."

"Hang on," I said, stopping him before he could turn away. "Can I return the question?"

"In what context?" he asked warily.

"You and Lena?"

"Still on, so if you're still after Natalie, go right ahead."

"So what about Amelia?" I asked. "You two looked more comfortable with each other before than you did when we left."

"Oh yeah," he laughed. "Her doing, not mine. In hindsight, seems like she was only pissed with me because I'd moved on and she hadn't been given a chance to. She's doing a lot better now, though."

"Darcy?"

"How'd you know that?" he said, surprised.

"He asked me about her before I left."

"Well, yeah, they're together now. She resisted at first but he was good to her for a long time. I reckon she made the right decision in the end."

"Good to know," I echoed his words. "Any other blossoming romance within these walls?"

I had only been joking but I became suspicious immediately when I saw the awkward look on his face. "What?" I asked cautiously.

He shrugged. "There is a little something else going on, and it may involve you."

"In what way?"

He shook his head. "It's really more Lucien's business than mine, so I'll let him tell you. He said earlier that he would because he's hoping you'll do the right thing by him."

"And that means what, exactly?"

"It means it's time for you to have a shower, and for me to get out of your hair. Is your Honnie friend going to join you in there?" he added, grinning.

"Doubt it," I laughed, reflecting that May would probably be more comfortable bathing in the outdoor pool than in a shower.

* * *

About half the group were in the lounge room by the time I got down there just before half past eight. I looked around as I entered, saw that Peter wasn't yet present, and that Natalie,

James and the twins were all surrounded by people, and decided to sit in one of the seats closest to the door instead. Before I could, though, Lucien called me over to where he was sitting with Marc, Amelia and Stella. There was one empty seat on that couch but when Lucien offered it to me, I shook my head, glancing sideways at May, who was still following me. She hadn't disturbed me while I'd showered, for which I'd been thankful, but she had still been in my room when I finished.

"I just thought you might as well sit where everyone can see you," Lucien said, looking a little surprised, "since, you know, you're going to get a lot of questions."

"Shouldn't Natalie be sitting there?" I enquired. "I mean, she is the other Sorcerer."

"Let her stay where she is," Lucien said quietly. When I got a chance to look back at Natalie, after I'd seated myself off to the side along with May, I saw why. Natalie was sitting beside Jessica, who looked as though she had been recently crying. Others around her included Felicity, James, Erica and Harry and Simon's sisters, Misty and Michelle. I was glad to see that she had plenty of support.

In the moments before the meeting was due to start, May and I were joined by Peter and Rebecca on our couch. I wasn't sure many had noticed their entrance but I certainly had, mainly because of how they had appeared in the instant before they entered the room. It had looked suspiciously as though they had been holding hands in the corridor outside, and that Peter had quickly let go just as they came in sight of the lounge room. Siobhan, whose presence I had noted before Peter had turned up, looked very awkward as she sat with Liam, something he seemed to be trying to make her forget. I was very interested to know how they would each handle the others' betrayal; hopefully they would both let it go, as they were both guilty. Even more hopefully, they wouldn't make a public scene in the lounge room tonight.

"Okay," Lucien said loudly when everyone was seated, calling the meeting to order. "Firstly, I just want to formally congratulate you for getting back safely," he said, looking directly at the three of us on the couch, and then over at Natalie, "or at least as formally as things ever get around here. Yeah, I know the news isn't perfect, but compared to what could have happened, what we all acknowledged could have happened before you even left, what you've done is an extraordinary achievement. We want to know all about what happened over there, you'll want to know about what's been going on here, and we'll need to bring you into our plans, perhaps even adapt them now that our firepower has increased so drastically. But before we do any of that, I think it would be a good idea for you to properly introduce us to the Honnie, so that we'll all be a little less uncomfortable around her. Er," he faltered, looking a bit embarrassed, "she is a female, right?"

The room erupted into a hysterical sort of laughter. None of us who knew May joined in, nor did anyone who had seen the Honnies in Smiley's memories, but all of us looked quickly at May to gauge her reaction. Her expression was quite bland but she was at least looking at Lucien, conveying without stating directly that she could understand him. Fortunately for him, Lucien hadn't noticed. Through all of this, I exchanged looks each with Peter, Natalie and Rebecca, none of us sure how this should be done. Eventually, when the noise tapered off, it was Natalie who spoke.

"She's definitely female. All the male Honnies we've seen are at least six and a half feet tall, and most of them closer to seven, so you'd definitely notice. You can't over-state the favour she's doing us just by coming over here, or what she had to do just so that the Honnies in charge of gateways would let her come through, so you might as well know who she is. Her name is May and in her world, she's basically a teacher."

"It's a sign, old chap," Harry said promptly.

"Indeed it is, old chap," Simon agreed.

"What the hell are you two talking about?" Peter snapped at them. "You really know how to pick bad times to be silly."

"We'll get to that," said Lucien quickly. "Natalie, is there anything else we should know about May?"

"Like how did you find her?" Marc added. "And why did she agree to come when no one else you met in over a month did?"

"She was one of the first Honnies we met," I told her. "Well, actually, her daughter was, on the very first day over there. She got pissed off when she couldn't break through our thinking caps, so she called May. Stupid things didn't do a damn thing to her—they just shattered all around our heads."

"What?" Marc gaped at me. "But how? Fewul said they would be strong enough against that Honnie in Smiley's memories."

"They may have been," said Lucien, "if they worked against the first Honnie you met, but perhaps May is stronger even than he was. So, you're telling us that you spent over a month with her because she wouldn't let you go?"

"Yes," said Natalie, "but we got really lucky, because according to May, most Honnies would have pretty much eaten us on the first day, and in fact that was her original intention, to feed us to her daughter when she was old enough. Thank God we changed her mind about that before it could happen."

She broke off then, perhaps realising what she was saying. Her eyes darted sideways to Jessica but she didn't elaborate any further. They would want to know what became of Tommy eventually, but now was not the time to tell them.

"Okay," said Lucien again. "With all that in mind, what's the best way for us to deal with her? We need her to be comfortable enough to work with us but not complacent enough to under-estimate the possible danger we may have to face, or arrogant enough to kill a lot of people for the sake of it."

"Why don't you just tell her that?" Rebecca replied, smirking at Peter.

"Ah," Lucien said, realising what she had meant. "So you're saying that we only have to think of what we need her to do and she'll understand?"

"That's not what I meant," said Rebecca, still smirking. "Remember what Natalie said before; she's a teacher. What's the most important thing for a teacher to have?"

"The desire to put us in detention?" Harry suggested.

"I think May's a way better teacher than Hall," Peter told him.

"In every respect," said Simon, and he actually had the nerve to wink at May as he spoke. Whether she understood the sign or was simply gauging his meaning from his thoughts, it got the first reaction out of May since she'd sat down here, but it was me her eyes darted to in that moment—something that gave me no comfort at all.

"What point are you trying to make?" Lucien asked Rebecca. "If you're looking for an answer to your question, I would say communication skills are fairly important to a teacher, but from what I understand about Honnies, they're already pretty good at that."

"The ability to entertain and instruct," said Harry pompously.

"No, no, no," said Rebecca, and she wasn't smirking anymore. "Yeah, sure those things are important, but they don't mean shit if you're stupid. My point is that May is smart; I mean, really smart. She remembers just about everything that's ever passed through her mind by the minds of others, which means she probably knows everything there is to know about everyone in the room if she'd taken us all."

"You can't keep secrets from a Honnie," Peter added.

"Wow, I'd always wanted to meet someone with an eidetic memory," James smiled. "So, she'll know the best way to communicate with each of us then? Is that what you're getting at?"

"Substitute best with easiest and that's pretty much right," said Natalie. "Guys, she can speak English."

A shocked silence followed this as everyone looked quickly at May, perhaps expecting her to suddenly start speaking for herself instead of letting the rest of us do the talking. For her part, May gave no reaction at all to this pronouncement, but now that it was out, it at least answered a question I'd been wondering for several minutes now. If May didn't want anyone else to know that she could speaking English, she could have prevented Natalie from stating it.

"Well," said James heavily after several seconds of nothing, "well, this just about tops it for good luck. May," he said tentatively, looking at her directly, and when she looked at him, he simply said, "hello."

"Hello," May replied blandly, her voice clear in the silence, and it was like an electric shock to everyone in the room. Indeed, several of the boys, the ones who appeared most turned on by May, actually had to close their eyes tight at the sound of it. James looked simultaneously exultant and bashful.

More silence followed this, nobody sure what to say or do, and in it, May's eyes returned to me again, as though somehow I was supposed to integrate her into this world. Finally, Peter said, "Geez, you guys are all acting like you're surprised she could understand what we were saying, or what we were only thinking and not saying, or what we were doing on the evening of March the 22nd in 2003."

"A very good point you make there, Peter," said Simon seriously. "What, pray tell, were you doing on the evening of the 22nd of March in 2003?"

"Trust you to focus on that bit," Sophie muttered.

"You're right," said Lucien quickly. "Guys, let's not talk about her like she's not here and can't speak for herself. It's degrading enough for a human, let alone someone who's doing us an enormous favour. So, how should we proceed? Do you want to tell us about your adventure over there, bearing in mind that you'll be hounded with questions later if you don't speak now, or do you want to catch up on things around here? Shall we take a vote? All those in favour of hearing about the adventures of six teenagers in an alternate dimension?"

"That's not a fair vote," said Peter quickly as around two dozen hands shot into the air.

"All's fair in love and war, Pete," said Harry, "and just between you and me, I'm not sure which of the two this falls under."

"I think that's decided, then," said Lucien, smiling slightly in that way he seemed to do rather often. "I can think of four main questions that need to be answered: What happened to Candice; what happened to Tommy; what happened to your arm, John; and how were you able to convince May to come back and help us. Anyone have anything to add?"

"How many other Honnies did you get to meet over there?" asked Erica. "While you were with May, I mean. You said before that she had a daughter?"

"Yeah," I said, deciding that I might as well get this part out of the way early. "She had a daughter called Ingi, and it was she who did this." I indicated my newly restored shoulder with my right hand. "It was on the very first night and I guess she didn't quite understand why she wasn't being allowed to feast. She must have woke up in the middle of the night and got the munchies, and I was the first person she found. It would have been Peter or Tommy if either of them had been closest to the drain."

"What drain?"

"They sleep in drains," said Peter, smirking again. "Don't ask; we can circle back to that."

"You must have been pretty close to a hospital," said James, "or whatever the Honnie equivalent is, 'cause I imagine losing that much blood would have killed you pretty quickly if it had been allowed to."

"No," I said, "because Ingi took me away from camp before doing it, and I have no idea how far the hospital was because I was unconscious most of the way, but Honnies can run really fast. May stopped her before she could do to the rest of me what she'd already done to my arm."

There was another shocked silence before James finally said, "So she saved your life? Wow, the list of favours is growing."

"Well, I kinda saved hers once too," I admitted, "so that evened it out a bit."

"Really?" said Harry, and he had that silly glint in his eyes again. "Do tell us, young John, what danger can possibly overcome a Honnie that a mere human, with only one arm, was able to rise above? It may be very useful knowledge."

"Are you thinking of trying to get into May's good books, Harry?" Peter asked. "I'm not sure what extra favours you're expecting from her, but just remember that she'll always know what you want."

"We'll get back to that," I said quickly, not liking the way May's eyes kept darting back to me whenever someone's thoughts took that particular turn. "Look, May didn't want me to die any more than she'd wanted Candice or Tommy to because she wanted to get the most out of us. It's all about practicality when it comes to Honnies, and as she pointed out several times, humans who actually have a few brains in their heads are practically walking gold over there. You should see the humans they breed; they're all big and fat and stupid as dog shit."

"If human intelligence is so valuable, why don't they take the time to educate them?" Lucien asked. "It sounds like the sort of thing that May here could do quite easily."

"I don't know," I admitted. "I suppose it's just easier to get good ones from this world. And for the record, I think May normally only teaches other Honnies, not humans. Is that right?" I asked her.

"Yes. Only Honnies are worth that," she said, and there was no hesitation at all when she spoke to me directly. Perhaps that would become the same for everyone else if they put more effort into speaking to May directly, but I supposed that would have to take time.

And indeed, over the following couple of hours (for that was how long the discussion went for), more people did speak to May. They became more comfortable with her the more she proved that she wasn't immediately dangerous, but she didn't seem anymore interested in them than she had at the start of the night. Perhaps, in her mind, nothing about them had changed. The conversation firstly moved around to half-breeds, and there was a lot of curiosity (particularly from the guys) about how they were made. When Liam plucked up the nerve to ask May directly how Honnies mated with humans, all she said on the subject was that it wasn't the same way that Honnies mated with each other, or the way that humans mated. This aroused even more curiosity but nobody was quite brave enough to pursue the matter any further. I wondered if May had forced that lack of courage upon them. If so, I was thankful, because this turn of the conversation was making me very uncomfortable, not just because I knew that somewhere, sometime, Tommy would be going through this procedure, but because I was becoming more and more nervous about the way May kept looking at me.

The tone shifted when the time came to talk about Candice and Tommy. Most of those who had witnessed Smiley's memories had forgotten about the love beam, since it hadn't been demonstrated or played any part in the events of 1981, but they remembered in a hurry when we began haltingly describing what had happened to Candice when that Honnie had looked at her the wrong way. The whole thing seemed to be regarded as an accident in many people's eyes, but they became even more respectful of May when they heard how she first tried to save Candice (what there was left to save anyway, no one added) and then avenged her when the responsible Honnie didn't give her up.

That was good, albeit sad, but there was nothing good about the reaction to the description of what had happened to Tommy, even though he hadn't been killed. Nobody blamed May directly, as we had at the time, but they had certainly gone to town on Ingi. This part of the conversation could have gone just about any way, but it took an unusual twist (or was it a circle back) when I reluctantly mentioned what Tommy had confided in me in the bushes while we'd been dropping our loads.

"He had sex with her?" Peter gaped at me. "You never mentioned that before."

"Sorry," I shrugged. "I figured it was Tommy's business to tell, but it hardly matters now."

"Did you know about that?" Rebecca asked May. "Surely you must have if you can read our minds; even Ingi must have thought about it."

May said, "She was not doing any harm with him until that night, and she was not breaking any rules, so I did not try to stop her."

"Tommy never said anything about how they did it, did he?" Liam asked me now, and I knew where this must be going.

"He didn't," I said, "so maybe—I dunno."

I had to think about that for a moment because I felt sure that whatever May said, Tommy would know if any sex he'd had with Ingi had been unusual. The tasting he'd been aware of, but would he have told me they'd done it if she'd something entirely different to him?

"How did they do it?" Amelia asked May in a hard voice.

May merely looked indifferent as she said, "They did not breed. They only played, so it was the same for them."

"Okay," said Lucien firmly. "Nice to know, now let's move on."

He wasn't the only one to recognise how sensitive to Jessica this topic must be. There were a few people who wanted to continue on how humans and Honnies could have recreational sex, I could tell, but by turning the conversation onto the ambush we'd faced the day after Ingi had taken Tommy, we made them forget about it in a hurry. Beyond that point, though, everyone, Peter, Natalie and Rebecca included, wanted to know exactly what I had done to make May change her mind about coming with us, for it was a story that neither of us had told before.

"Well," I said, having no intention of describing it in detail, "I basically just used my mind to show her what was really going on here, how many people were suffering, and how it could relate to what she'd been through the day before."

"How come she didn't already know that?" asked Felicity. "I thought Honnies knew everything about people if they have their minds."

"Er," I faltered, not entirely sure how to answer, because now that she brought it up, I couldn't believe that none of us had thought of that.

When I looked at May for help, she said, "We only know surface thoughts. I can only learn more about you if I make you think about yourselves."

Which she could do, I thought, as I recalled what had happened to Smiley when he had entered the Honnie world. That Honnie had made him reflect on himself, who he was and where he had come from in considerable detail so that he could learn about him.

Following this, the meeting turned to the others, and what they had been doing all this time. I was glad because it meant that we wouldn't have to relive the events of Lagalia; at least not today. Had all that only happened this morning? They described what had been going on in the war; how the Woodwards had reclaimed small territories but the Hammerhearts had done well to stabilise the much larger territories they had. Hammersonia had now swallowed almost a hundred countries around the world, leaving only a handful of smaller countries remaining before they would begin to conquer the two remaining continents. A military alliance had been formed between most of the countries in South America, which aimed to put up one almighty fight against the Hammerhearts if they made any moves towards them. It was the best they could do, even if it had no chance of succeeding if (when) Hammerson really cared about taking them down.

More importantly for us, we were told of a plan that Marc, Lucien, Amelia, James and Stella had been compiling over the last few weeks, and which they had been planning to put into operation the next week. It would be aimed at Hall, and it was designed to wrest the Villain Crystal from him in, of all places, the school. Hall returned to his old haunt every Monday, Wednesday and Friday, not because he taught there but because it was the base of all on-ground operations in Chopville. That didn't make the underground base obsolete by any means; it was merely the station from which the Hammerhearts, the ones who still worked directly for Hammerson, coordinated with the proper authorities. It would have to be tweaked to include us but it could only be a good thing, now that we had another Sorcerer. Even May would be able to play a part in this plan if she chose, but this was where the discussion got a little thorny.

"Yes," Lucien said unwillingly, "but I was always under the impression that if we did get a Honnie over here, they would work with the adults, not us."

"What good will that do?" Marc asked, surprised.

"Guys, he makes a point," said James seriously. "My initial thoughts when I suggested the idea were that the Honnie could help settle things down after we'd gotten rid of Hammerson, and that would definitely require her to work with the Woodwards, since we wouldn't know the first thing about how to reorganise three quarters of the world. But Lucien, I don't think she needs to go to the Woodwards just yet; she might as well help us deal with the problem directly, since the Woodwards are still not doing a lot about Hammerson himself. I mean, just think, if we can get a fix on exactly how far she can reach out with her mind, we could take Hall down from a pretty good distance."

"And what have the Woodwards been doing lately?" Peter asked.

"They haven't been slacking off, if that's what you're thinking," said Marc. "They've taken a number of countries back from the Hammerhearts, small ones, and have helped prop them up since. Hammerson hasn't bothered to take them back, probably because they're inconsequential to his grand plans, but I'm sure he'll go back for them when he's good and ready. As far as Hammerson and Hall themselves, I'm not aware of them doing anything, although let's face it, they've probably got a whole bunch of plans in the works that we don't know about."

"Very well, then," said Lucien. "I guess May can go to the Woodwards when it seems like the right time for that. Incidentally, we need to decide exactly what to tell them about all of this. Remember, Lillian is the only one who even knows of the existence of Honnies, and we don't really know how much she actually knows about them. A lot less than Smiley did is my guess."

"They need to know as much as we can tell them," said James, "otherwise they won't know how best she can help. The question is when we tell them what we know. On one hand, they need to know that you guys are back because they've been worried sick, and furious with us because we couldn't tell them, but on the other hand, they can't know about May too soon in case they decide that they want her now."

"Let them decide," said Marc fiercely. "They can decide whatever they want; doesn't mean we have to go along with it. Besides, ultimately it's up to May where she wants to go."

"That sounds fair enough," said Lucien, nodding, "but bringing them into the picture is bound to take a while, so we should probably leave that till tomorrow."

Part 4: The Cloak of Steel

Chapter 30: The Project

It was about eight o'clock the following night and there were only two of us occupying the computer room, which had been created directly over the lounge room at some point while we had been away. The single computer that had previously been in the lounge room was now up here, along with about a dozen others (I doubted they had all been in use at the one time at any point as yet). Most of the other people were in the lounge room (the floor dulled most of the noise but some of it still seemed to come through) while I suspected that some (Peter and Rebecca no doubt among them) were spending some quality time with their partners. While I still resolved to finally follow up on my feelings for Natalie, I had found myself distracted by something else that had been going on while we had been away, and now determined to find out exactly what it was.

"It's probably the most important thing I'll ever do in my life," James told me as he leaned behind the computer to unplug the ethernet cable.

"What are you doing that for?" I asked, staring at the loose connector.

"Better to be safe than sorry," he said, returning his attention to the blank desktop on the screen. "While I doubt that these computers are hackable, I keep hearing stories about how rogue countries could set off nuclear weaponry in enemy territory that didn't even belong to them—at least they could, before the Hammerhearts took over. I refuse to put my memory stick in any computer that's connected to the Internet for that reason."

"Because what's on it is far too valuable?"

"Exactly."

"So what is this project you've been working on?"

"Well, it's a bit like what the year tens were working on before school got cancelled," he said, "only much more analytical than anything they would have done, including Lisa.

In fact, it's probably beyond anything anyone at the school would have expected."

"Er—okay," I said blankly. "Why?"

"Well," he said, now looking at me for the first time, "it's kind of hard to describe. I'm basically following up on a feeling I've got about magic in general, and about human nature in general. I'm worried that as long as magic can be claimed by anyone, and as long as people know this, the lure of power will be far too strong to be resisted. How would it be if we put all this work into beating Hammerson and then as soon as we do, someone else steps up and tries to do exactly the same thing all over again?"

"I thought that was the main reason why we got a Honnie to help us."

"Sort of, but this goes beyond just settling down the current conflict. Too many people know that Sorcerers are only normal people whose magic is stored in a separate location, and that the power can be stolen. We kind of advertised it to the world when we made the Fletchers Sorcerers."

"So you're saying that it mightn't even be a Hammerheart thing?"

"Exactly. And obviously, discouraging people wouldn't work; it would mean changing the very basis of human nature, and that's way beyond our capability, even with all the magic we have."

"So what are you trying to achieve with all this research?"

"I'm not exactly sure yet," he said uncomfortably, his eyes shifting slightly in a way that made me think he was lying, "but so far, I'm thinking that the only solution that could possibly work would be to either destroy or neutralise the Magic Crystals altogether. The research I've been doing has been all about Sien and Leoard so far, most particularly how they went about creating the crystals in the first place, and I'm trying to trace the movement of them over the almost-twenty-two centuries they've been around. I tell you, it hasn't been easy."

"How've you been going about it? This sort of information would be really hard to get hold of."

"Well, yeah. Most of the information has never been compiled like this, so far as I know, unless the Hammersons did it years ago. Amelia and Stella have helped me out a fair bit with the concepts of magic in general, but they weren't any wiser about its history. So, it's been the Internet and those discs from the magic display that have helped me out mostly."

I thought that over for a minute while I watched him slide his memory stick into the USB port and begin looking over his work.

"So where did the crystals come from?" I asked curiously, following a train of thought that was, at the moment, completely contrary to what James was working towards. My thoughts were that if we knew where they came from, we could maybe create even more magic crystals. It only took me a few seconds to realise how horrific that would be, and how absolutely right James was to be nervous about this sort of thing.

"I don't have any factual information on that subject yet, but I believe that they came from the cave Lisa mentioned in her diary entries," he said, "the one she said was the very essence of magic."

"I thought that was just a representation of the in-between," I said nervously, shivering as I always did when that cave crossed my mind.

"Well, it might be," he said, just as nervous, "but I'm not sold on that yet. She said in there that the crystals were created in that cave, and if that's true then it must be a real place, since the crystals are physical objects."

"Good point," I said, thinking of something else unpleasant, "but if that's true, how did Sien end up in the cave? She's been dead for over two thousand years."

"I have a theory on that too," he said, looking at me again. "Some of the documents on those discs were compiled by Sien and Leoard themselves—well, those documents were direct translations of their work—and some were translations of work done by Sien's daughter—I have no idea what her name was yet. Anyway, Sien would have lived to a fairly old age and only would have died when her great granddaughter was born. Now, in those days, the descendents would have still been learning the limitations of their power, and the daughter—or perhaps the grandson—thought they could bring her back to life."

"Okay, but then Sien should have stayed in her own time, shouldn't she?"

"Yeah, that's normally how it works, but Sien was different from most other people. She was a Sorcerer, for one thing, and one of the creators of this particular use of magic, for another. Or perhaps one of the existing Sorcerers tried more magic to defy the limitations on magic, trying to keep her around beyond the two-week period, because I imagine Sien would have felt that she only had a limited time herself. This was the best she could do, which probably means nothing to Sien given that there's no time where she is. Anyway, that's mostly speculation; it's only a theory, and so far I have no evidence to back it up. So far it's the best explanation I can come up with that fits all the known facts."

"Well, okay," I said, a little stunned by his imagination, but unable to think of any holes to poke through his theory. "Are any of the others gonna help you with this?"

He shrugged. "Only Amelia and Stella, and possibly Marc, and only them because they can do magic. Nobody wants to help compile the information, or spend hours and hours reading tedious documents. I don't blame them, and I'm not complaining; I enjoy this stuff, and I work fairly well alone."

"What if there's no way to find the information you need?" I asked.

"There will be; I'm confident of that. So far I've avoided using Fewul to help me, because I don't think that Fewul would automatically know the answers to all my questions, but I do think that he could provide me with the means to find the information if there are no existing traces of it."

It was my turn to shrug. Whether or not he was right about that, I didn't know, but I was nervous all the same about the Beast of Magic getting involved. "So," I said, now thinking back to something I had wondered earlier that day, "what on earth were you talking to May about while we were gone?"

As planned during the meeting the night before, we made contact with Frederic Woodward earlier that afternoon, after the eight of us (me, Peter, James, Marc, Lucien, Amelia, Natalie and Stella) had spent the morning ironing out the plan for the following week in greater detail. The communication with Mr. Woodward wasn't just to tell him that we had returned but also to tell him that we had a plan. We didn't go into details with him, partly because we didn't want the adults to get involved and partly because we didn't want to put them in any danger, although they would find out if it succeeded because it would be they who took advantage of whatever aftermath followed. That didn't go over very well but that wasn't the reason why he practically demanded that some of us come and see him in person. Dad and Charlie were out but of course, there were certain other parents who needed to learn of our return, and given how worried they had been, we owed it to them to see them in person for the first time in almost two months.

He and all the others had wanted to know what we had been thinking and why we hadn't made any contact for such a long time. After almost an hour of harassment (it had certainly felt as such), Peter had finally told them where we had gone and what we had been doing. As expected, Lillian understood completely, and even more than she had before when she heard Peter's explanation of it. We hadn't taken May along for the ride because she had been terrified of the Woodwards' base after learning about it from Amelia's mind, the only one who had been inside it since it had been rebuilt. After seeing the adults' reaction to the news, I thought that was probably a good thing; they would have been even more terrified of her.

Not that May was particularly comfortable with life in our base either. She had adjusted very quickly to the way we did things, perhaps due to her prior knowledge of humans; perhaps after having learnt about us before coming here; perhaps because she could read all our minds and was feeding on our own familiarity. Whatever it was, it didn't help her very much when it came to magic, which terrified her in general. She ate from the conveyer belt because she really had no choice, but she always grimaced when the food appeared out of nowhere, and always looked mistrustfully at it, at least until she began to eat. Other than getting my help with the conveyer belt, she hadn't exercised any of her Honnie talents while in our presence, which had made everyone else a little less fearful of her, though not entirely so.

So far, May had spent her time either alone or with those of us who she already knew (me, Peter, Natalie and Rebecca, in other words). The only glaring exception to this was James, who had apparently spent a good deal of time with her while the four of us who'd just returned were catching up with the parents. I had heard about it only when I'd gotten back but all anyone who'd overheard that conversation could say was that it was all well beyond their comprehension, and nobody felt brave enough to join in.

"Oh that," he laughed, "nothing much—just a bit of philosophical discussion. I've always been fairly interested in the way the mind works, and naturally, May is like a professional on that subject. You would be amazed at just how much the mind can create for itself."

"That sounds more like psychology rather than philosophy," I pointed out.

He shrugged again. "I guess you had to be there—it wasn't a particularly normal conversation."

"I don't doubt that," I muttered. "What do you mean, 'the mind creates for itself'?"

"Well just imagine that you're lying in bed, trying to get to sleep and contemplating life in general, when in actual fact your body is in the process of walking across a set of train tracks while a train is thundering towards you. The brain controls everything, you know, including those senses that tell you the angles of your arms and legs. I've known that for sure ever since Moran put the domination charm on me because that eliminated everything. In fact, now I think of it, what May can do is exactly the same as that, only instead of blanking everything out, she can fill your head with false perceptions that are so clear that you don't know it's all made up."

"So you're saying she could make a person commit suicide without realising it?"

"Well yeah, but that on its own isn't much different from the domination charm. Not only would she give you no chance to fight it, she could actually make you enjoy it."

"Geez," I muttered, not entirely sure how I felt about that. I'd always known that May's mind power was even more dangerous than what she could do physically, but this seemed to emphasise the point even further.

"I've had an idea about how we could use that to our advantage," he said, returning his attention to the computer screen once again. "I haven't actually checked it with her but if she's really willing to help, she probably won't mind. It certainly wouldn't be dangerous for her."

"What's that?"

He shrugged. "It's too complicated to explain, but if we do it, it'll be tomorrow or Sunday, so you'll know then."

"What's that?" I asked, now indicating the computer screen. James had opened a fresh document on his memory stick.

"A separate project," he said, "about Honnies this time. May told me a lot of interesting stuff about them earlier and I wanna note it down because there could be some significance in it."

"Like what? You think it relates to your other project?"

"Probably not, but I'm curious about some things, like their history for one. So far as I can tell, their civilisation has developed in line with ours, mainly because every time they drag humans into their world, they learn a bit more about how things are going here. Yet through all that, their politics has never changed from how it began, and so far as I can tell, so far as May knows, it began not very long ago."

"How long is 'not very long'?"

"Maybe a couple of thousand years. Perhaps even less than that, which makes me wonder…"

He trailed off, and I waited, wondering if he would continue. Eventually he said, "I'm thinking that Honnies may have evolved from humans. There has to be a reason why they look so much like us, and we're capable of breeding with them, and I'm thinking that maybe that's it. A Sorcerer may have accidentally opened a gateway into their world at some point in the past and a few humans became trapped on the other side. There were probably already creatures inhabiting that dimension, and when the two met, they tried to fight each other. Anyone would want to defend their own land, and humans are so naturally confrontational, but instead of one triumphing over the other, they merged into a creature stronger than both."

"Did May tell you this?"

"No, this is just my own figuring, and I could possibly back it up with some evidence if May would be willing to donate a bit of hair or skin or something I could take DNA from, but obviously she had no interest in that."

"You know, I think you may be half-right," I said, my mind flicking to something May had told me the previous evening.

"Half-right?"

"Well yeah. I don't know so much about the super physical strength, but I think I might know where the mind power came from, if it's true that humans merged with whatever was over there. I say only half-right because what May told me about came from the next dimension along, not her own, but the two may still have met and merged."

That had been a rather unsettling conversation. The point of it, on my part anyway, had been to persuade May to sleep in Candice's old bedroom because I was increasingly uncomfortable with her continuing to sleep with me now that she didn't have to, but May hadn't made it easy because she was still uncomfortable being alone in this strange place. I had loitered around the bottom floor hallway after the meeting as others around me went off to their bedrooms, but some people

(Amelia, Lena and Stella) all looked like they wanted to talk to me, and probably away from the Honnie. I'd had no desire to get into anything that could be even remotely emotional tonight so I'd taken the stairs before they could take their chance. Peter and Rebecca had gone up to their rooms well before me, and Natalie only a few minutes earlier. They were all beat, and so was I, but this couldn't be put off.

Unfortunately, May still wasn't having any of it. She had known exactly what I was trying to do and although she hadn't forced me to change my mind, as she so easily could have, she had sent strong thoughts back at me that made me certain that she didn't want to sleep in that room. When I had looked at her, she had only looked back, as though daring me to challenge her. I had found myself smiling in spite of myself as I imagined trying to drag her down the corridor.

"Do you have a better idea?" I had asked her, not liking the increasing time we were spending in the hallways.

"It is too strange for me," she had said, and she had looked a little sad as she spoke.

I sighed. "Come on, then."

If I had to let her sleep in my room, I would do so. If I could get her to sleep on the couch, that would be better, but if it had to be the bed, I supposed I could take it for one night. I hadn't liked it, but if that was what May needed for things to be okay, I supposed I had to do it. I could only hope that nothing I was required to do for May would ruin my chances with Natalie down the track. For the time being, though, my only plan had been to talk to her and find out what was going on here.

I had led her up to my room but I hadn't bothered to look around at her until I had ushered her in. This meant that I hadn't seen her expression until then, and when I had, it had frightened me. I had only seen that look on her face once and that had been from a great distance as she had shouted at the Honnie who had killed Candice.

"What?" I had said, taking an involuntary step backward in surprise and apprehension. I couldn't believe that I was about to meet the same end he had, but I had to believe I was in for something unpleasant.

In response, she had gestured for me to shut the door behind the two of us. I had done so, wishing I weren't so tired but feeling even more exhausted than I had only seconds earlier.

"What exactly do you think I am?" she had asked me, taking me by surprise, but not enough to relax me.

"What do you mean?" I had asked.

She had scowled at me, and it was such a human expression that I had been able to pick up her true emotions from it. She had been a little pissed off, but mostly she had been deeply hurt. It hadn't been the same as that day a few weeks earlier after all.

"You treat me like I am an animal," she had said, "like you think you only need to say and do the right things so that I will help you."

"I don't treat you like an animal—"

But she had silenced me, not with her mind but by holding up a hand. She hadn't thought it but I somehow knew that she was making an extra effort to behave like a human so that I would understand her better.

"You do. You just did a moment ago by your thoughts. If this is what I need to do to make her cooperate then I should do it. Is that about right?"

It had been my turn to scowl. Having my own private thoughts so blatantly laid out in front of me like that had been rather offensive. I'd never seen any of the Sorcerers do that, not even the bad ones.

"What do you think I am?" she had repeated the question.

"What exactly do you want from me?" I had retorted, now stung. The beginnings of understanding were there, but I honestly couldn't see how I was supposed to change my own thought processes. Most people couldn't control their own private thoughts to such an extent.

"Why do you not understand that you do not have to treat me this way?" she had asked me. "I have already agreed to help you and I ask for very little in return. I am not going to back out on you."

"I know that," I had said, thinking of the Honnie of 1981 and wondering if I really believed it. Surely May was better than he had been. I had gathered my thoughts to the best of my ability, knowing that it hardly mattered what I chose to say since she had been reading my reactions in my thoughts, but also knowing that there was no way I could get through this if we didn't speak. "At least, I think I know, but you need to understand how it is for us too. We won't feel safe until it's done."

"Yes, and then you will be quite glad to see me go, will you not?"

"Isn't that what you want?"

"Yes, but it still means nothing to you."

I had sighed, feeling a headache coming on. "So what's the problem then?"

"How do you think you would feel if you were me?"

"I have no idea how I would feel, never having been a Honnie at any point in my life."

The sarcasm hadn't been intentional, but I had known, the moment it was out, it was truly how I felt.

"Then imagine it as a human, because it is not much different at all," she had said. She had spent all this time leaning against the wall near the door while I had been sitting on the edge of my bed, but at this point, she had moved across the room to join me on the bed. I had tensed, but she had only sat down on it a few feet away from me; not too close, in other words.

I hadn't answered right away as I tried to get my head around what she was saying. In the end, it hadn't been too difficult to figure it out: May had felt like she was being used and manipulated. I had flashed back to Tommy a few nights before we had left; he had predicted that this could happen, because any human would feel used. If this were true, it meant that Honnie emotions (some of them anyway) weren't much different from human ones. So, what was to be done about it?

There had been no point acting like we really cared if we didn't because May would see right through that. The only good thing about that was, I hadn't thought I needed to fake it.

"Sorry," I had said, feeling the beginnings of shame. "Listen, and stay out of my head for a few minutes if you really respect me," I had added, feeling like this thing would only work if it were mutual. She must have agreed with me because I had felt that glove around my mind, imperceptible most of the time, loosen slightly. What she had said may have been true, but it wasn't the only truth. She had probably known that too but I still had to say it.

"You're wrong if you think I don't like you, or that any of the others don't," I had added, hoping I was right. "I just didn't want to get too close to you."

"Because I am not human?" she had said, and I had shaken my head.

"No. Well, maybe, but you must know what I really want, and how I don't wanna do anything that might ruin that. I would have done the same even if we didn't need your help. You're not the first person I've had to do that to for the same reason."

She had only watched me, hurt still on her face but not as much as earlier. I had wished I knew how to make her feel better. Finally she had said, "I know you all appreciate what I am doing for you, but why can you not appreciate me as a person? I may not be human but I still think and feel and have my own life."

"I know," I had said, "but you know, our initial impression was that Honnies wanted to be thought of differently. Isn't that why in your world, humans are always considered the bottom class of being?"

"We are not in my world anymore," she had pointed out, and I had to admit, she had got me there.

"What do you want me to do?" I had asked, knowing it was about thoughts rather than behaviour, but I had been helpless not to ask. "I've told you how I feel about you. I don't know what more I can do."

It was true; I really hadn't. The worst thing about it had been that at the end of all of it, it had still bummed me out to have to admit it, just as it had bummed me out when I'd had a horribly similar conversation with Amelia months earlier. I hadn't thought May wanted me in that way but I had thought I knew what she was getting at, and I thought I could do it, but it would never be my top priority. Just as I could never make Amelia my top priority around Natalie, May would always be more important to me in the context of the war than—than what, exactly?

"Okay," she had said, attempting a smile which, although not entirely happy, was still stunning in its beauty. "What do you need me to do to help you think of me as a person instead of an alien?"

She had pronounced that last word as though it were one she had never used before.

"I dunno," I had muttered, "just be more like a human, I guess. Why does it matter so much, though?"

She had considered for a moment and then said, "Because it is your world, not mine. If I had only come here to collect, maybe it would be different."

"Okay," I had said, feeling my spirits lift; that would make everyone more comfortable with May if she were serious about what she was saying. "Good to know you can get sick of being top of the tree all the time."

I had been thinking back to when I'd had possession of the Sien-Leoard Crystal; it had been great, but it had also provided me with a responsibility which, at times, had been wearying.

May had looked around herself, as though checking for eavesdroppers, which was ludicrous since there was only the two of us here. Finally she had said, "That is not true. There is always someone above you, wherever you are."

"What?" I had said, completely confused and not realising for a few seconds that she had been speaking not of me, but of anyone. "What does that mean?"

She had looked almost scared then, and I had wondered if she was in fear of something divine. This had sounded more and more like a God job by the second, but when she had spoken again, I understood what she had been alluding to, and it had filled me with awe.

"There are others," she had said, "not in this world or mine, but one above us. We are to them what humans are to us."

"Do you mean," I had said, my mind flashing back to Smiley's description of the fourth dimension, "you know about the next world along?"

She had looked at me for a few seconds, and I had known she was validating what I'd said against what I was talking about by reading my mind. Then she had nodded.

"What do you know about them?" I had asked, intrigued. "Have you ever seen them? Can they come here like Honnies too?"

"I do not know," she had said. "I do not think they would bother; humans would be completely useless to them. They come to us sometimes, like we sometimes come here, but they are no secret in our world because we can feel their presence around our minds if they get close. They are…they do…"

She had broken off, and by then I was sure of it; she had definitely been scared.

"What?" I had prompted. "You might as well speak freely; it's not like they'll hear you from two worlds away."

Not that I could know that for sure, I had thought uncomfortably.

"We call them Satai," she had said, or something that had sounded like that. "They use us the same way we use humans, but they do not have bodies at all. They are just minds, which makes them so much stronger than us. Nobody knows what happens to Honnies who are taken into their world because none have ever returned."

The same way it should be between Honnies and humans, I had thought, but was no longer the case, thanks to Smiley. Now that May had told me this, I had thought I understood better what she was really thinking. Honnies may have their own way of life when it came to humans, but not being at the top of the tree, as I had originally thought, at least gave them some perspective. This had also explained May's initial reaction to us on that very first night when Tommy had thrown up the concept of Honnies being enslaved.

"May I try something?" May had asked me suddenly, taking me by surprise by the change of subject.

"I guess," I had said, my mind then flashing back to what had happened the last time she had spoken those words to me.

And for a moment, it had looked like being the same thing, I thought as she reached out to me, but on that score, I was wrong. There was no tasting this time, no physical discomfort, no feeling of impending suffocation, but pretty much everything else about it was the same. She had put an arm around me, pulled me against her and kissed me firmly on the lips, a soft kiss that seemed to me to be as careful as the touch she had given me the night after the ambush. It had been an utterly amazing moment because, perhaps as May had hoped, it allowed me to think of her in several new ways. It had also made it a hell of a lot easier to just let her sleep in my bed tonight after all, and perhaps without any clothes, but that was where I was able to put the brakes on.

"What do you think?" I had asked her when we broke apart several seconds later.

She had seemed unsure how to answer. Finally, she had said, "it is not as interesting for me, I do not think, but yes, I liked it."

"Are you saying that all you want is for me to treat you like you're just another friend like the others?" I had asked her.

She had smiled then, and it had lit up her whole face, making her almost too beautiful to look at. "I suppose it is, yes."

I had let out a sigh of relief. That really was simpler than I had thought at first, even when you considered the whole mind reading thing, but it still left one matter unresolved.

"May, I'd really appreciate it if you slept in Candice's old room," I had said, now feeling the exhaustion creeping back.

She had watched me for several seconds before saying resignedly, "What should I do in the morning?"

That had been a good outcome because it had cleared my conscience considerably. May had adapted her own morning routine by observing, by reading everyone's minds, how we all went about getting up in the morning. The only thing she didn't do right away was change her clothes, but Natalie was good about taking the time to provide her with a complete wardrobe earlier that day. Not that whatever was going on with May and me had been entirely settled, however. I did my best to treat her the same way I treated everyone else but I couldn't deny two things: that I was attracted to her as much as any guy would be, and that she still kept looking at me suggestively as she had done during the meeting on the first night. Fortunately, though, no more unsettling conversations had taken place between the two of us since then, and with a bit of luck, we could get through this without ever having to address whatever might or might not be going on.

Naturally, I didn't confide all of this in James, but now I told him about the Satai, and he was just as awed as I had been.

"Only, don't go talking about it," I warned him. "We don't know how dangerous they could be to us yet, and they must be pretty bad if even May's scared of them."

"I won't. I don't intend to spread any of this stuff around, but now that you've told me about that, I reckon you could be right. Perhaps the Satai came into their world on one occasion, found humans and sought to make themselves stronger or something. I don't know, and that's probably information I'll never get, even with Fewul's help, but it's a theory at least."

* * *

The plan to infiltrate the school had been entirely settled by early the next morning, and it was then that the rest of us found out what James's idea regarding May was too. With Marc and Lucien's help, they worked out a method that we could use to simulate the plan to get into the school without even needing to leave the base. Marc created twenty-nine boxes in the lounge room, one for every person except for the Honnie, and we would all be locked inside them for the duration. The boxes would enclose us in a space that would allow us enough room to draw breath but not enough to do anything else. May would stay on the outside and conduct the entire simulation in her mind, something she had never done to such an extent before but which she felt sure she could manage.

So far, the plan had the thirty remaining members of the Young Army (including May in that number) divided into several groups. Three groups of five (fifteen in total) would infiltrate the school; a fourth group, this one of four, would be based in Hamster's Stretch Reserve, monitoring developments from a distance, and a fifth group, this one of eight, would be waiting on the other side of Main Street. The remaining three would be in the base, which would be sent away from Chopville for the first time for the occasion, also monitoring developments—but unlike the group in the Stretch, with the ability to contact Mr. Woodward should things get out of hand (a special device had been created for this purpose).

I was part of the second attack party along with Natalie, Peter, James and Rebecca. We would be infiltrating the school via the alleyway on Flint Street at the same time as the other two parties. Marc would lead his group, consisting of Harry, Simon, Katie and Sophie, in through the front entrance on Main Street while Amelia's group, that of Lena, Darcy, Felicity and Erica, would enter from the staff car park on the back intersection of Flint and Corner Streets. The whole thing would be coordinated telepathically between Marc, Natalie and Amelia, and there wouldn't be a need for anyone else to get involved unless something went wrong along the way, as it almost surely would.

If there was trouble, it would be the group on the other side of Main Street who would enter behind us, assuming we had neutralised whatever protection was set around the school. That group would be led by Stella, who considered that she had a score to settle, and consisted of George, Dean, Misty, Michelle, Belinda, Joanne and Della. They would be notified of any trouble telepathically by May, who would (on the day only, not in the simulation) be stationed in the park along with

Lucien, Liam and Siobhan. Jessica was the one left in charge of base ops, a job she had agreed to willingly enough, if a little sadly.

Everyone in the Young Army, including those who weren't even coming out, would be armed for the occasion. The devices that Marc and Fewul had been working on over the last few weeks were really quite incredible. In fact, they were so powerful that we were only allowed to use them on the full understanding that they would all be destroyed when they were no longer needed. They had taken everything that Stella had brought into the base when we had captured her and integrated them all into a single device, which took on the same shape and size as an agonator. Yet it was far more than just an agonator; Marc had pressed Stella for information about every single device her family had ever created, and she had done her best to give him what he wanted. He had also pressed Fewul for any new weapons Arnold Hammerson had created with the Sien-Leoard Crystal since he had acquired it.

Now, we were armed with so much power that many of us, including those who hadn't just got back from the Honnie world, hadn't had enough time to work out how to take full advantage of it. The fact was, I only knew how to use the stunner, agonator, bludginator and the one which shot nets at people, the name of which I'd never known. When I wanted to use any of them, I simply had to think at the device and it would quickly switch to the required mode so that all I had to do was push the button, and I would only have to concentrate long enough to change when I needed to change. I thought I would probably be best sticking to one mode only, and I figured that the solid-outliner was probably the best place to start; that particular weapon was easily the best for putting a great number of people out of action at the same time.

The other great weapon, of course, was Fewul itself. May refused to include the Beast of Magic in the simulation, not understanding its power and unwilling to allow herself to get too close to it, but on the day, Fewul would be instructed not to take on a form but to watch developments from above and be a sort of omniscient presence on the site, capable of coming to Marc's side if necessary. The trouble was, Fewul had no way of identifying untraceable people unless they were out in the open (in a direct line of sight, in other words) which seemed like a strange restriction for the almighty Beast of Magic. Fortunately, though, they had already sorted this part of the plan out weeks earlier.

I had completely forgotten about 3K17 in the events that had passed since we had captured her, but sure enough, Marc and Lucien had eventually found a use for her. After some arguing, some of it heated, they had gone against Lucien's original suggestion that releasing 3K17 and keeping tabs on her was a dangerous idea, both for her and for us. Marc had gone into the prison yard one day, trapped her in a corner (rather like trapping a spider in a jar, he told us, and I knew exactly what he meant), knocked her out and removed her memory of everything that had happened since she had woken up in here. He had then gone about providing her with made-up memories, memories which would be perfectly real to her and therefore authentic to those who would interrogate her about her disappearance later. Fewul had then placed a spell on her mind which would record all of her comprehensive memory in real time and make it available to those in the base, all done from afar so that no traces of it could be found in her mind should any anti-bugging magic be performed on her. She had then been released back into the world, waking up in her own home with the belief that her diarrhoea, the original cause of all her problems, had been so bad that she had been housebound for nearly a week (that was how long she had been held).

The problem with this was that nobody in the school saw her leaving the base, a process that was carefully monitored for obvious reasons. She had been hauled before Commissioner Hall and interrogated as expected, but also as expected, they had been unable to find anything wrong with her story—at least in her mind. They hadn't let it go for a while after that; Hall doing numerous checks on the school boundaries with the Villain Crystal and even once, Arnold Hammerson himself stopping by to speak to 3K17 about it. They understood all too clearly that we knew who she was and that we may target her, but at last, after far too long for Marc's comfort, they had begun to treat her normally again. It was by her knowledge that Amelia, Marc, Lucien, James and Stella had been able to formulate this plan at all, and it would be by this method that the trigger on our attack would be pulled.

The device used to monitor 3K17's movements wasn't exactly like a similar device we had used back on Rock Haulter because this one allowed the person using it to think their own thoughts at the same time; the feature was necessary given that they would be incapable of turning the thing off when they were done with it. In actual fact, it most closely resembled the times I had browsed memories with the Sien-Leoard Crystal, a process I had performed on Serena, Rebecca, Natalie and Sebastian. On this occasion, it would be Robyn who was using the device, waiting for the moment when 3K17 and Hall came into contact.

We knew that Hall would turn up in the school grounds at some point and when 3K17 saw him, Robyn would tell Jessica, who would in turn send a signal to Marc, Natalie and Amelia using similar devices to the one I had used when infiltrating the Hammerheart base on Mr. Woodward's orders. It was a complicated plan but it was the only one we could make use of because, according to both Marc and Fewul, using the Hammerheart's own untraceable technology against Hall wouldn't work; Arnold Hammerson had sought to close that loophole for anyone important as soon as he had worked out how to exploit the initial untraceable spell.

As for the barrier itself, the Hammerhearts had surrounded the school with what seemed to be an invisible dome which stretched more than a kilometre from the ground at its highest point. Actually, it was more like a spherical barrier because the dome circled down below the school as well as above. It let through all of Chopville's atmosphere for the Hammerhearts to enjoy but anyone on the outside would hear nothing from within the grounds, nor would they see anything more than had been there before the base had been set up. It was an unusual spell, which, according to Fewul, caused the outside of the dome to reflect a time nearly three months gone by. This presented only the first of many problems because it meant that we wouldn't know if there was anyone waiting for us beyond the barrier until we broke through it.

The only good thing about the dome was that we seemed to be able to touch it without the Hammerhearts immediately detecting it. This experiment had been performed a week ago by Marc, who had come down to one of the entrances we would soon attempt to break through and bounced a basketball off it. He had then waited for over an hour to see if the Hammerhearts would investigate, but nobody showed up. This didn't necessarily mean that they didn't know it had happened, only that they considered it insignificant. On the downside, though, the dome did a lot more than keep people physically out of the school. It was capable of deflecting anything physical, no matter the strength, weight or velocity of its contact. It also withstood all possible temperatures, from the ludicrously freezing to the deadly heat that they themselves used in their Worship Halls. That would keep all non-magic people out but of course, the Hammerhearts feared nothing of non-magic people. More importantly, the dome kept all Sorcerers out just the same as the Hammerheart bases did, but it was Marc's hope that we would be able to undo that part of the spell when the time came.

The major downside to the simulation was that May had no better idea than us how we could break through the dome, so she was under instructions from Marc and Lucien to make it as difficult as possible; that would give us the best possible chance of covering all bases. Beyond that restriction, however, May had enough to work with just by closely examining all our minds for knowledge of the area, the Hammerhearts and, of course, magic.

"So, everyone's clear on how this is going to work?" Lucien enquired of the room at large. Everyone was standing in their boxes at this point, all our heads poking out of the tops of them, waiting for the simulation to begin. "May, are you clear on what you're doing?"

"Yes," she said, a little dispassionately.

"Good," Lucien went on. "Just so everyone else is also clear, May pushes that button, all our boxes close and we're in the dark until May takes our minds and creates the simulation. Remember, you won't be yourself in there; you'll actually believe it's real, so there's no point trying anything you wouldn't do on Monday. It only ends when May pushes the button to open the boxes again—and releases our minds, of course. Is everyone ready? Let the games begin!"

Chapter 31: Simulations

It was nine o'clock on the morning of August 23, 2010. The day was cool and clear. I was standing with Peter, James, Natalie and Rebecca on the footpath parallel with Flint Street, staring at the school grounds directly ahead of me. There was, of course, an invisible barrier between us and them which, in short order, we would need to penetrate. Nobody talked much; probably we were all too busy thinking about what we would need to do in a few minutes, whenever Natalie received the signal that Hall was in the grounds.

We had been there for about ten minutes before something happened, but it wasn't a signal from Jessica. Without any warning whatsoever, a row of Hammerhearts appeared in front of us, materializing out of nowhere, stepping through the dome as though it weren't there and becoming visible to us. We weren't visible to them, though; we were all under an invisibility veil, all twenty-six of us in fact. At least, we had been, before the attack hit us.

It was very similar to a tactic I had seen used over in England one time, a tactic that had almost cost me, Siobhan and Serena our lives. All of them fired revealers straight ahead to begin with, not knowing our exact location, and unfortunately there was no time for all of us to get out of the way; one of them may have touched the top of one of our heads, which immediately exposed us all.

We barely had time to react before the second wave hit us, this time bludginators. We all yelled as we went down, me scrambling around and pointing my hero device (for lack of a better name, since Marc hadn't bothered to give it one) into the air to get off a shot at one of them. Before I could, however, the third attack hit us, this time solid-outliners. One of those jets hit my right hand, freezing it in place and making it impossible to operate the magic.

"I'm down!" I cried out, clambering to my feet and holding my right arm out from my body, wanting to maximize the time I had left before I would be entirely taken.

I looked around at the others to see how they were doing, looking for a bit of help. A brief glimpse gave me Natalie, who had been targeted more than the rest of us, splayed on the ground, completely white and soaking in a pool of blood; they had really gone for her. She wasn't dead, of course, but they had wanted to put her out of action as quickly as possible. The only good thing about the targeted attack was that other than a few cuts no worse than my own, the other three were so far unhurt, and Peter even had time to free my hand from its white prison before the next wave of attacks hit us.

Unfortunately, this time it was the agonator, and both Peter and Rebecca went down immediately. James and I were able to dodge the jets of light and finally, I was able to straighten up, take aim with my hero device and fire. Nothing whatsoever happened, and it took me a precious moment to work out that it was because I hadn't thought at it to set its mode of magic. I took a moment to think of the solid-outliner, but it was a moment I didn't have. The final attack descended upon James and me, and this time it was guns.

I saw James fly backward in an explosion of blood before something very hard punched me in the chest. I flew backward, the hero device tumbling out of my hand, and saw nothing but the clear sky above me. I hit the ground on my back, tried to get up, but I no longer had the strength. In the end, there was no pain, only an absence of caring about the fundamentals of life. I heard footsteps. A shadow fell over me. A man came across my field of vision. Everything was then blotted out by the barrel of a gun. The deadly eye staring into my own was black and seemed to be telling me that it knew something I didn't. In fact, it knew blackness and nothingness, and it was only too happy to introduce me.

* * *

"Okay, that was a bad start," said Lucien sometime later when the simulation had ended and we were only heads poking out of the tops of our boxes.

The simulation had actually gone on for some time after I had been killed. Amelia and Marc's groups had been attacked at the same time as us, and it had taken the Hammerhearts less than a minute from the start of the attack to kill all of us. Only Natalie and Amelia had survived, and they had been sufficiently disabled for it to come to the same thing. May had then cheated her simulation slightly, as she would have done if she'd been included in it, and told Lucien and Stella's groups what had happened. Both of them had rushed forward and had had a little more success in their attack, but before too long, most of them had been killed too. In the end, Lucien and Stella were the last two remaining, and what the simulation had put them through had been much worse than the rest of us. Lucien had emerged very pale, claiming that he had eventually been killed but refusing to say anymore. Stella had been in hysterics and May had needed to sedate her before we could talk about what had happened. She had filled our heads with most of what had happened after we had been killed but she never told us what the Hammerhearts did to Stella after they caught her. It must have been terrible, judging by how Stella was now.

"Yeah, you could say that," said Marc bitterly. "What on earth went wrong?"

"Well, I'm guessing that's how it would be if the Hammerhearts have some sort of detection device within the school," said Lucien. "Fact is, we weren't ready to attack before the signal came. We assumed that we could just wait for it and relax until it came, and were caught off-guard as a result. Lesson learnt; everyone must concentrate completely on the dome, and be ready to attack at any moment."

"But they don't have detection thingies in there," said Marc, "or they would have picked up on me last week."

"We can't know that," said James. "Just because they didn't investigate you then, doesn't mean they didn't detect you. Also, it might be that something about this was different. Perhaps they could only detect more than one person, or more than one person in more than one position, as if they're surrounded. Or perhaps it goes right down to intent; the dome knew we were going to attack it today, so it warned the Hammerhearts, but you never intended to do anything to it last week, Marc."

Lucien was staring dumfounded at James. Finally he said, "It could be any of that, or none of that. The point is that we weren't ready for it, and we should have been. If that had been real, we wouldn't be here to talk about it. Is everyone ready to try again?"

He was looking most particularly at Stella as he said this. She seemed unwilling as she looked around mistrustfully at May. After all, whatever Stella had been put through had been controlled by the Honnie.

"Maybe we should have a little break first," Peter suggested. "Not much, but we should be fresh going into it, as we will be on Monday. Also, the next one will be just as bad, if not worse, because May is supposed to make them as difficult as possible."

* * *

It was nine o'clock on the morning of August 23, 2010. The day was cool and overcast. I was standing with Peter, James, Natalie and Rebecca on the footpath parallel with Flint Street, staring at the school grounds directly ahead of me. There was, of course, an invisible barrier between us and them which, in short order, we would need to penetrate. Nobody talked much; we were all too busy concentrating on what lay ahead of us, making sure that we were each ready to fight should we receive the same fate in reality that had met us in that one and only simulation. Why Lucien had said we would only need one simulation, that we had learnt our lesson, was a mystery to me; but here we were on the morning of truth, so to speak, and there was no way to go now but forward.

We were there for about fifteen minutes before Natalie started. "Guys, that was the signal; it's time."

As planned, the five of us took off at a dead run, slowing down when we neared the barrier but not quite in time to prevent a collision with it. I didn't fare too badly; I only bumped my shoulder and rebounded, feeling as though I'd dislocated it (though I hadn't) but no worse than that. Natalie, Peter and Rebecca were the lightest of the five of us and they were able to put the brakes on in time, but James was like a big old truck, and he may have still been approaching top speed when he hit. Even worse, he hit dead-on instead of side-on like me. Not only did a loud snap rent the air as his nose broke, but he let out a short, strangled yelp which was almost instantly cut off as he collapsed to the ground at the foot of the dome.

"James!" Natalie cried out, horrified. "Why didn't you slow down? Get up so I can fix—"

She stopped dead. All of us stopped dead, as though time had frozen where it stood. James was not getting up. James was not even moving. Slowly, as though in a trance, I leaned over him, took his shoulder and turned him over so that we could see his face. James did not see me. His eyes were bulging from their sockets but they were not seeing me. The days when James could get back up after a fall seemed to have passed.

I swayed where I stood and for the second time, hit my shoulder on the dome. Once again, I bounced off it and this time fell to the ground beside James.

"John!" Peter cried out, clearly thinking my fate was now the same as James's, but I was able to scramble quickly back to my feet. For some reason, the day seemed brighter than it had a minute earlier.

"What happened?" Rebecca whispered.

"I think," Natalie said softly, "I think it was because he touched the dome."

She considered, staring at the invisible wall just in front of her as though she could see it—as though it was looking back at her. Without looking at any of us, she created a new magical device out of thin air and held it out to her sister.

"What's that?"

"A reanimator," said Natalie, still not looking at any of us. "If there's something that kills anyone who touches the dome, I'm the only one who can test it without being killed, but it might do something to me anyway. This should revive me if it does."

"Nat, are you suicidal or something?" said Peter hoarsely.

"No, I'm not, and that's the whole point," said Natalie. "Look, we need to get through this thing, but we can't risk touching it if it might kill us. But we need to know if it does at all because this thing could have other dangers as well that we don't know about."

"I thought Marc already tested that," I said. "Maybe you should contact him and find out."

"Good point," said Natalie, and she lapsed into silence as she engaged in telepathy. The rest of us waited for her to return to us, but instead, within a few seconds, she said, "I can't reach him."

"What?"

"Amelia's still there," said Natalie, "but Marc's gone, and she can't reach him either."

"You don't reckon," I said, the probable truth starting to come home, "he touched it too?"

"We have to try this," said Natalie, and before any of us could stop her, she stretched out a hand and laid it against the smooth, invisible surface of the dome.

Almost instantaneously, she collapsed to the ground, looking as dead as James did, but of course, she was a Sorcerer. Rebecca quickly pointed the reanimator at her and clicked the one and only button, but nothing happened. We all stared at Natalie's lifeless body in utter horror.

"No," Rebecca moaned, continuing to click the reanimator to no avail, "no...no...no—"

"I suggest we cancel the plan for today," said Peter, his eyes moving between Natalie and James. "Come on, we have to get them back to the base."

"How do we get back to the base?" I asked. "Jessica would have already moved it out of Chopville by now."

"The Stretch then; we can't stay here."

"How are any of us going to carry James?" Rebecca asked dully, her eyes beginning to fill with tears.

"I guess we contact..." Peter began, then realized what he was saying. "Okay, phone time, I guess."

He pulled his mobile out of his pocket and began calling a number out of the phone's memory. While he did, I stared hopelessly at Natalie, hating to see her like this. Clearly that reanimator she had created had been made hastily; she hadn't been concentrating hard enough, and had consequently not created a device that could revive her under any conditions. She couldn't have known what that dome would do to her, so how could she have created counter-magic? That might have been it, but more likely she just hadn't been concentrating on what she was doing hard enough. Who could blame her, after what had just happened to James...

This gave me an idea. I withdrew my hero device, pointed it at Natalie, imagined that she was already dead in the same manner that Stella's killing devices made people look as though they were dead, and clicked the button. I was surprised as everyone else when Natalie groaned and began to sit up.

"Natalie!" Rebecca cried out, and now the tears overspilt her eyes.

"Quiet, you guys," said Peter, holding up a hand and then beginning to speak into his phone. "Harry, you okay? Okay, Katie then; sorry. What's happening out there?"

"Is that safe?" I asked, staring at the phone, remembering what Lucien had said so long ago about cellular signals being too easy to trace.

"What happened?" Natalie asked dully.

"You touched the dome, but you're okay now," Rebecca said, leaning down and helping Natalie to her feet.

"What?" Natalie said blankly, looking around at us, down at James on the ground, and then quickly back up at the dome, as though the sight of James on the ground had brought all the memories rushing back.

"Holy shit," Peter breathed, and then lowering the phone he told us what had happened out by the front entrance of the school. "Guys, Katie and Sophie are the only ones alive out there; Marc and the twins both touched it. Katie says it's because they touched with their skin while she and Sophie only touched through their clothes."

"That explains why I'm still here," I said, feeling almost faint.

"So what now?" Natalie asked. "Do we keep going or do we regroup?"

"I think we keep going," said Peter shakily. "Lucien did say that once we started, we couldn't stop because the Hammerhearts might know and redouble the protection. Katie," he said into the phone, "do you know what's going on with Amelia's group?"

But it was Natalie who answered. "Darcy's down but—but everyone else is okay."

"Darcy?"

"Guys, I really think we should call it off," said Rebecca.

"We can't," said Peter quickly, cancelling the call and stuffing the phone into his pocket. "We have to try to get through the dome without touching it. Come on, Nat; spin a bit of magic."

She never got a chance to, though, because that was when the attack hit us. It was more swift and stealthy than the one in the simulation had been; we didn't even know we were in trouble until our invisibility veil had gone and a jet of black light (yes, it was a bright jet of pure blackness) cut Natalie down right in front of us. It looked as though whatever the dome had done to her had been repeated by someone standing just on the other side of it. Peter and I were both ready enough to launch our own attack but of course, it just bounced off the dome and had no effect on whoever was on the other side of it.

"*Run!*" Peter bellowed, but we never got a chance.

I only felt ropes twist themselves around me in such a way that made it seem as though the ropes themselves were alive and conscious of what they were doing. Out of the corner of my eye, I saw Peter and Rebecca also be seized and wrapped up tightly. My arms were pinned to my sides, my knees were joined together, my ankles were joined together, and I could only move my head a fraction to either side. The only thing it hadn't done was strangle me, but given the tightness around my torso, I would soon be unable to draw enough oxygen anyway.

"Well, well, well," said a silky and most horribly familiar voice behind us, "what do we have here?"

The ropes turned the three of us around so that we were once again facing the dome. The person responsible for the attack had now stepped through it so that we could see him. It was Mr. Hall (that's Commissioner Hall to you, sir) and he was smiling radiantly at Peter and me.

"Come along, boys," he said, gesturing to us to follow him, as though we had a choice. He then stopped, looking back at the two figures on the ground. "I think we may have a use for her, but he can be done away with."

More ropes appeared from his hand, the hand operating the evil magic of the Villain Crystal, and wrapped themselves around Natalie, wrapping her up just like the rest of us. Yet more ropes went for James but instead of wrapping around him, they seized his ankles and levitated him high into the air. My own ropes then tilted my head back painfully so that I had a clear view of what followed: James was being swung violently through the air, exactly as the tentacle on Rock Haulter had swung several of us. The difference was that this time, the ropes let go, sending James's lifeless body flying through the air, over the houses on Flint Street and straight towards the park behind it. It was travelling high and fast enough that the chances were good that it would land in the Jade River.

"You monster!" Rebecca screamed at him, wincing as the ropes made her pay for her insolence.

"Why thank you," said Hall pleasantly, smiling at her. "I'm glad you think so, because other than being the sister of what Arnold Hammerson likes to call 'one of my public enemas', you are just as useless to me as he was."

And to my utter horror, Rebecca was lifted high into the air and put through the same ordeal as James—exactly the same. Her screams were both loud and distant, sounding extremely weird given the terrifying speed at which she was moving through the air. Finally, when I could take no more, she was hurled away towards the park.

"With that settled, it's time for the three of you to come with me," said Hall, turning away from us and leading us into the school grounds. The ropes took us through the dome as though it weren't there; the sight of the new school grounds suddenly replacing the old ones, though there wasn't much difference in what we saw, was a little dizzying.

Hall led the two of us (three if you counted the unconscious Natalie) through the grounds of the primary school and into the grounds of the secondary school. For reasons best known to himself (perhaps he just wanted to use a place that had been fairly good to Hammerhearts over the duration), he decided to take us to the gym. Instead of taking us into the main chamber, however, he decided to use the boys' locker room for his interrogation or whatever he had planned for us.

"First things first," he said, creating some large object in the centre of the room. It looked very similar to the boxes in which we had done that simulation, as if anything in there had helped us here. Once it was done, he released Natalie from her binds, picked her up in his arms and lowered her into the thing, whatever it was, before slamming the lid shut.

"And what's that supposed to do?" I asked coldly.

"I intend for you to see every bit of it, Playman," said Hall dangerously, "and I think it would be good for her to feel it too."

He was right on both counts. The side of the box facing us was clear, and we were able to see Natalie inside it. He had woken her up at some point and now she was on her knees inside, staring at Hall as though wishing death upon him. She was trying to do something magical but whatever she was attempting was failing.

That was all she could do, though, because Hall's intention became clear when the inside of the box suddenly ignited. Peter and I both felt the heat of it from where we sat. The flames shining through the window were dazzling. Natalie's screams of utter agony, though slightly muffled, were nevertheless piercing. What I saw happened to her body over the following minute was something that would give me nightmares for the rest of my life, assuming I lived beyond today.

"Now," Hall began, but before he could go any further, there was a knock on the door, as though Hall and his assistants or minions or whatever they were had already arranged to do the worst of their operation in here. He called to whoever was out there to enter and then stood back as two more familiar Hammerhearts entered the room. They were 3P69 and 3E57, both of whom had been involved in the ambush that cost Tulip her life, and they were carrying something long and white between them—a person in thicky prison, I deduced almost immediately.

"Is it Woodward?" Hall asked, and both men nodded. "What of the kids who were with her?"

"All dead, sir," said 3E57, "as are the two girls who were hanging around with the Seventh Sorcerer."

"Good," said Hall, "but that still leaves H2 and H5 still unaccounted for, not to mention 1H4, so go back and patrol the boundaries."

"What if her folks turn up?" asked 3P69. "Or hers?" he added, glancing at what remained of Natalie's body, still burning merrily in Hall's personal incinerator.

"Solid-outliners, as quickly as you can," said Hall, "and stay on our side of the barrier. Remember, they can't use their own magic to break it, and the only person who could have performed magic that might have worked is now dead."

He was watching Peter and me as he said this, waiting for some sort of reaction. Peter had the cheek to poke his tongue out at our former English teacher but all I could do was continue to stare at Natalie, the love of my life, though I knew she wasn't dead, now being reduced to ashes.

Once 3P69 and 3E57 had left, closing the door behind them, Hall turned his attention to Amelia. "How will it be," he said lazily to us as he firstly knocked Amelia out, then released her from thicky prison, then wrapped her up in the same ropes which still bound Peter and me, "when all of your friends are dead. I'm sure you would be upset, except that of course, you will be just as dead as they are. I suppose Hammerson will probably be spared, but she has a considerable amount of unpleasantness waiting for her when she is caught. She has a duty to fulfil and her father is not prepared to tolerate any objections on her part—he has had enough of that."

"You really don't know what you're dealing with," said Peter boldly.

"On the contrary, Playman, I happen to know that Hammerson has the weakest mind in the world," said Hall, smiling unpleasantly as he opened the incinerator and lowered Amelia into it. From where Peter and I stood, still trussed by one of the walls, we felt a fresh wave of heat roll over us. "Once she is taken by a good bit of magic, she will crumble beneath it, and will give herself over to young Hignat with enthusiasm. I'm sure he will enjoy the experience, and once she's been taken care of, she will too."

He revived Amelia as he spoke, but she had no chance to perform any magic, or even to get her bearings, before she too was engulfed in flames. Watching her burn away to nothing was just as bad as it had been for Natalie.

"Now," said Hall, turning his attention back to Peter and me, now that both Sorcerers were out of commission, "for your cheek, Playman, I think it's necessary to do something to you to ensure that you will never get to experience the pleasures that Hignat will enjoy very soon."

Peter struggled fiercely but he never had a hope of stopping it, because Hall used the ropes to achieve his ends. They snaked their way into Peter's pants and from there, I never saw what they did next. Peter's eyes bulged but he seemed incapable of making a sound. That was quite enough for me. I knew exactly what Hall had in mind and that, on top of knowing that he would soon be doing something just as bad (if not worse) to me, got me moving. My arms were pinned but my right hand was close enough to my right pocket, where I had stored my hero device in the instant before the ropes had taken me. I twisted my hand so that I got a couple of fingers in the pocket, got hold of the device, drew it up into my hand and pointed it in Hall's direction. Thinking that all that mattered right now was that Hall had to pay for what he had done to Natalie and Amelia, what he was doing to Peter, and what he would soon do to Stella, I thought of the Agonator and clicked the button.

Hall, his attention still on Peter as he enjoyed my brother's crippling agony, hadn't seen what I was doing. The result was perfect; he crumpled, yelling and thrashing. One of his feet knocked into the incinerator, knocking it over and causing deadly flames to spread out over the floor. That had not been part of the plan, and given how quickly the flames were spreading, I knew we had to get out of here quickly. Yet Hall had to be dealt with, for if we let him go…but if we left him here, the Villain Crystal…it was no good. There was nothing I could do, for the ropes binding Peter and me would not give, even with the person responsible for them no longer able to keep them in order.

Hall's yells did not change as the fire took him; they were already so bad that burning on the outside was probably nothing compared to what he was already going through. Peter and I screamed plenty though; at least at first. In the end, the pain didn't last long; too long and yet not very long at all. An endless space of darkness was waiting for me just beyond a thin film of light, most of which was dancing as Hall's hellfire burnt up the boys' locker room and all who dwelled within it.

* * *

"You came very close to getting him," said Lucien bitterly sometime later when the simulation had ended and we were only heads poking out of the tops of our boxes.

"I know," I said just as bitterly, my mind still horrified with what I had seen in that simulation. "Those ropes, I had no way to get rid of them."

"Is everyone else okay?" Lucien asked, looking around the room at large.

The simulation had gone on for a bit longer but the end had been horribly similar to the first try. Hall hadn't been involved anymore and the Villain Crystal had remained in the burnt-out gym, but other than that, what had happened to Lucien and Stella's groups (what had happened to Stella) had been horribly similar to the first simulation. The difference was that now, Stella wasn't the only person who was traumatized. James claimed to remember nothing, as did everyone else who had been killed by the dome, but both Natalie and Amelia were in a horrid state, and Rebecca had just about lost her nerve entirely. On that score, I couldn't blame any of them, because Peter and I weren't much better.

"We'll be okay," said Peter bravely. "What time is it?"

"It's after one o'clock, so we can have lunch before we try again," said Lucien, "but before we do, we need to talk about a couple of things from that simulation."

"Yes," said James, "because what May showed us is reasonable; the dome could kill us like that. I suggest we wear gloves on Monday and always put our arms out when we're approaching it, so that we don't touch it with our skin."

"Good thinking," said Lucien. "Also, no mobile phones, because that was how Hall pinpointed your location. It was, wasn't it?" he enquired of May, who had stood impassively near the door all this time, and who now nodded.

"In that case, we need some other method of communication," said Natalie weakly, "in case one of us is taken out again."

"On the day, May will do that for us," said Lucien, "like she did with me and Stella in both simulations. Is there anything else?"

There wasn't, and we all trooped off to the dining room for a well-deserved feed. Those who had been traumatised by the simulations (Amelia, Stella, Natalie and Rebecca the main ones) seemed to be pulling themselves together fairly quickly. I kept an eye on each of them during lunch, ready to talk to any of them should they show signs of needing it, but the Fletchers held up okay, while Darcy and Lucien took pretty good care of

Amelia and Stella respectively. I was particularly glad about the latter because following the meeting the previous day and leading into lunch, Lucien had pulled me aside to add an extra complication to my life.

Neither me nor Stella had shared thoughts during the time I had been in the Honnie world. There was probably a good reason why the connection should have been severed, and probably a good, albeit strange, reason why we should be reattached when I returned, but when I had slept on Thursday night, I entered her mind in the most vivid detail so far— perhaps it had been building all this time, desperate for the two of us to connect. What I had learnt from that dream was something that Lucien would pull me aside to tell me the following day, and a very uncomfortable conversation that had been.

In the time that Stella had been a permanent member of the Young Army, now given to be as trustworthy and dedicated as Lucien was, those two had struck up a special connection. Lucien told me that it was because he understood her in a way that nobody else in the base could, having witnessed so much more of her terrible upbringing than the rest of us. It was essentially true, I knew, for Stella had been reflecting on that very thing, and I could never thank Lucien enough for making Stella feel more welcome and accepted than she ever had before. It was the sort of thing I probably would have given her had she and I been allowed to spend more time together way back when she had first lost her magic, although I probably wouldn't have dated her. I was by no means sure of that because even then, I had been attracted to her, and I could have ended up with her instead of Serena, and for the same reason, had things gone differently.

None of that mattered, though; as Smiley had once said, dwelling on hypothetical scenarios of the past is a complete waste of time. I couldn't stop myself from doing it, though, because I felt exactly as I had when encouraging Darcy to go after Amelia. It was as though part of me was being torn away, a part much closer than Amelia. It hurt to let it go but I knew that if I could, it would make me stronger as a result, and I reflected that this was probably the final test I was required to pass before I could be with Natalie. It wouldn't be an easy test, though, because even though Stella was very happy with Lucien, he was not her first preference. She had made this clear to Lucien in no uncertain terms, told him that she would not give herself over entirely until he became her first preference, and forced him to accept her as she was until things changed. That was why I was very glad that Lucien was comforting her now, because it meant that I wouldn't have to do it. I didn't want Stella to suffer any more than she already had but for the same reason that I didn't want to get too close to May, I didn't want to have to be the one to take care of Stella.

Fortunately, Lucien was man enough to accept Stella the way she was (at least for the time being, although I wondered if he would eventually need more than that), but he still implored me not to take away something that was making him very happy. I agreed, knowing that their relationship would probably remain in limbo until Natalie and I were officially an item, assuming that happened soon. Stella would know from my mind if she had a shot with me and unfortunately, I could never say never until I was utterly content with what I already had. So far, the thing that made me happiest was the fact that I was at least able to resist the temptations that I normally gave into, to control those things which had made it impossible for me to be with Natalie until now—those things which had put it off for nearly six months.

* * *

It was nine o'clock on the morning of August 23, 2010. The day was cold and rain was pelting down upon all our heads. I was standing with Peter, James, Natalie and Rebecca on the footpath parallel with Flint Street, staring at the school grounds directly ahead of me. There was, of course, an invisible barrier between us and them which, in short order, we would need to penetrate. Nobody talked much; we were all too busy concentrating on what lay ahead of us, making sure that we were each ready to fight should we receive the same fate in reality that had met us in the first simulation. I wasn't too worried about what the second simulation had given us; sure it had been rather unenjoyable, but nobody would be touching the dome and in actual fact, the gloves that I was wearing did a good job keeping my hands warm in these most unpleasant conditions.

"Someone should have checked the bloody weather forecast," Peter grumbled beside me.

"Don't get distracted," Rebecca hissed at him. I could barely hear the sound of her voice.

"Guys, that's the signal," said Natalie suddenly. "Let's go."

And so we did, taking off towards the dome with our hands outstretched like blind people, me completing the analogy by slipping over on the wet ground and landing hard on my arse.

"Nice one, John," said Peter, ducking back to help me up.

By the time Peter and I rejoined the others, the five of us were lined up along the dome, all of us with our gloved hands upon its smooth surface, thinking about how we were to break through.

"I've already tried making it vanish," Natalie told us, "but I'm not surprised that didn't work."

"Try making a section of it vanish," said James, "just enough for the five of us to get through—one at a time if necessary."

Natalie obliged, and what we saw happen in front of us was really quite an exceptional view. While most of what we saw was reflective of a school grounds that weren't being pelted with rain (an odd sight in itself given what was happening all around us), a rectangular section of the air directly in front of Natalie showed the grounds in a different light—wet, soggy, and exactly like the conditions we were braving.

"Perfect," said Rebecca, pushing her sister through the opening and following quickly after. James, Peter and I hurried after them, waiting for some sort of indication that the Hammerhearts knew we were here, that they had detected a breech, but none came.

"They may know we're here, so we have to hurry," said James, beginning to pick up speed like a big old truck again. "Never mind what we left behind; we have to get to the admin building. That is where Hall is, isn't it?"

"That's where he was when the signal came, so I assume so," said Natalie—all five of us were running now, skirting the nearest building so that we could cross the open primary school grounds and head for the back of the high school.

"Let Marc and Amelia know how you got through too," Peter told her.

"Already did that."

"Did they both respond?"

"Yeah; nothing bad has happened to their groups yet."

"I like the 'yet' you threw in there."

"Shut up, Peter."

The fence between the primary and secondary schools was in sight now. The gate was open, perhaps because there were no children to separate and the Hammerhearts couldn't be bothered opening it each time they went through. Most of their operations were in the high school but they still used the space in the primary school from time to time, as was our information. The five of us charged through the gate and were once again running through grounds that were all too familiar to us. Unsurprisingly, and perhaps it was a good thing for us, the grounds were completely deserted as all the Hammerhearts would have wanted to stay out of the driving rain, not to mention the fierce wind that had just kicked up.

The only figures moving in sight were heading straight toward the administration building, just as we were, and they were approaching from the direction of the car park. Excellent, I thought, smiling. We didn't join up with Amelia's group, though, because that wasn't part of the plan; at least, not all of her group anyway. Amelia, Lena and Darcy leapt into the air as they approached the building, landing on the balcony over the front of the admin building, while Erica and Felicity joined up with us. If all went to plan, Harry and Simon would soon join us for the next part of the plan.

"Has Marc entered the other building yet?" James asked Natalie.

"Yes, and the twins will be with us shortly. We'll begin as soon as he's ready."

And so we did, with Marc, Natalie and Amelia penetrating the building through the upper, lower and very lower entrances; Darcy and Lena covering the balcony exit and Katie and Sophie covering the tunnels; and the rest of us circling the building, covering the windows as well as the doors, ready to take care of any Hammerhearts who came out. Not just that but, as instructed, Stella's group was also on the move, according to Natalie before she entered the building, and they would soon join us as well. Only Lucien's group was still in position, soaking it up in the Stretch, and they would remain there unless we got in serious trouble.

The plan, at this point, was to knock every Hammerheart unconscious as they left the building, so that we could deal with them later. Lucien, James and Stella had decided against killing them outright because that might make the Hammerhearts fight with greater desperation, not realizing that their fellows weren't really dead but only pretend-dead. As it all had so far, that went exactly according to plan, with Hammerhearts fleeing from something they knew was dangerous but not knowing where or even what it was. They didn't see us, thanks to the invisibility veil, and they had no hope of getting past us.

At some point, however, someone on the inside must have used a revealer, because after a while the Hammerhearts' eyes found us before we knocked them out. Even more unfortunately, the last ones to emerge had a better idea of what was really going on. Most unfortunately, the thing we hadn't planned on, more Hammerhearts came at us from behind. After all, not every person in the school grounds was in the one building, and once they knew the tunnel was blocked, they must have guessed where to go and what to do.

I ducked and weaved, got off two shots (one of which flew wide), ducked, twisted, turned, fired again, spun around and, predictably, slipped on the wet ground and landed on my arse for the second time that morning. Four Hammerhearts were bearing down on me—but then two of them collapsed, out cold as James and Felicity closed in from either side. I was able to take one of the remaining down myself before the last of the quartet fired something at me. I never found out what it was....

* * *

"Now that was much better," said Lucien bracingly, "still not perfect but much better."

"Not that you did anything," Marc pointed out.

"Well yes," Lucien conceded. "Me, Liam and Siobhan would have come if we were needed, but we weren't, so we didn't. Well done, Marc; once again the hero has bested the villain—quite literally," he added, and several people laughed.

It looked as though Marc had been the one to defeat Hall in combat, with Natalie and Amelia taking down every other Hammerheart in the area around the two of them. A few of the others were hurt in the struggle outside the building but none were serious. Only George and Dean had been killed; I had only been knocked unconscious, apparently. Best of all, for her at least, nothing bad whatsoever happened to Stella. I knew that part of the reason we did so well was because May had deliberately given us an easy run, but I was grateful that she had done so. I suspected that someone (perhaps James or Lucien) had asked May to give us an easier go, not because it would necessarily help us on Monday but because it would increase our confidence. We had to have some belief, otherwise we really would go down like a sack of shit.

We decided that was enough simulating for the time being. Having the plan carried out successfully, even if we had been given an easy run, had helped us believe that it could work on the day, assuming we had a bit of luck. If our luck was out, no amount of practise was going to help. Lucien was confident that we had ironed out the key deficiencies in the plan, and told us that between now and Monday, we had to think about our individual roles and make sure that we were mentally prepared for what was to come.

Chapter 32: Exposed

Everyone in the base was awake before six o'clock on the morning of truth, so to speak, and everyone in place by eight o'clock, the base already zooming in a general northwesterly direction. The day was cool and overcast, the conditions closest to those in the second simulation; I hoped that wasn't a bad omen. All thirty of us were untraceable and under a single invisibility veil, not to mention a soundproof veil, or something similar. We waited, watching as people began arriving for the start of another working week in a dream job, helping establish the new regime in a place that may not be heavily populated, but was essentially important to Arnold Hammerson. We didn't see much from where we were on Flint Street because the three main ways of getting into the school for the Hammerhearts were the car park (not much), the front entrance (even less) and the newly installed Hammerheart Highway entrance (easily the most popular).

We had to wait for over an hour for Jessica's signal, which gave us plenty of time to discuss the barrier before us. The simulations were all well and good but then, we had only been facing May's interpretation of the dome, and that had been based on what we ourselves expected to face. This was the real thing, which meant that we were essentially back to square one. It was mainly Natalie, James and Peter discussing the dome while Rebecca and I stood at arms, ready to fire if we came under a surprise attack.

"And you're absolutely sure you can't just create a perfect hole in it?" Peter asked Natalie, just for clarification.

"I don't know," she said exasperatedly, "but I doubt it. Marc seemed to think it would be way more complicated than that."

"But Marc never actually tried it when he came down here," said James. "That said, I think you're probably right, but only because the Hammerhearts surely would have thought of something like that. There may be things they haven't thought of, though. I just can't believe that this thing can withstand all magic that can possibly be performed by any of the Sorcerers —only that which the Hammerhearts know of."

"And Hammerson himself, don't forget that," I pointed out, not looking around at them; because when it came to this sort of thing, Arnold Hammerson, who had surely been the one who'd erected this barrier in the first place, would have closed just about every loophole possible. Just about, I thought, which does not equal all; after all, we had defied Hammerson on more than one occasion before.

"I must admit, I'm more concerned about what we're seeing," said James, staring distrustfully at the dome—or more like, at the school grounds beyond it. "This dome has been in place since the end of May, according to Fewul, but Natalie, you were able to penetrate it with your mind when you caught 3K17. Do you think you can do that now?"

"Probably," she said, "but I wouldn't be able to find Hall with it—"

"I know that," said James quickly. "I only meant, by the time we do get through, the Hammerhearts may have lined up just on the other side of it, and we won't know until it's too late. You remember what Hall did to us in that second simulation—"

"To be fair, they won't know either," said Peter. "I know it's easy to forget while we can stand around like this, but we are invisible and untraceable."

"With their technology, you can hardly claim that much anymore," said James darkly.

"Well let's not worry too much about what we can't control," said Peter quickly. "Okay, maybe making part of the dome disappear is too basic. James is right, they probably would have thought of that. Do you reckon they would have thought of turning a small section of it into a door?"

James looked sharply around at Peter, his face lighting up in a grin. "Pete, that may be just sneaky enough to work."

"What are the other groups up to?" I asked Natalie.

"Nothing yet," she said, not looking at me but continuing to contemplate the invisible wall stretching before us. "You know we're not supposed to bug each other with telepathy unless it's either time or an emergency."

"It's after nine," said Peter, checking his watch. "Surely she's turned up by now."

"She would have," Natalie said, "but Hall probably hasn't. Did Marc happen to mention an approximate time he usually comes?"

"No," said James. "It's probably fairly random, except that we know he definitely comes at some point. We might be waiting here half the day for all we know."

"Should have brought a deck of cards," Peter muttered.

"If you're bored, Pete, you can help us with this," I told him.

But that was when Natalie started. "Guys, it's time! He just walked past her workstation. Let's go!"

We had positioned ourselves a safe distance from the dome so that we would have time to move aside should anyone come through from the other side. Now we hurried forward, covering that distance in a few strides with our gloved hands outstretched like blind people, none of us slipping over as we ran this time. Even so, I hit the thing hard enough to painfully jar both my shoulders; thankfully I didn't go any further than that. I'd observed plenty of invisible barriers before but this was the first which was entirely solid, although I couldn't have said what substance it felt like.

Both Peter and I withdrew our hero devices and began firing various powers at the invisible wall, none of which had any effect and which didn't surprise me. James and Rebecca knew better than to waste their time with such things and instead watched Natalie as she took to it with her own magic, but whatever she was doing was leaving no visible signs of damage on the surface of the dome. Also unsurprisingly, it was not going to be as simple as what May had given us in the third simulation.

"Let me look," said Rebecca, leaning around her sister and feeling the surface of the dome. Finally, she shrugged and withdrew. "No, never mind. I just thought if there was a hole there, you mightn't be able to get through it."

"Make a door," said Peter.

Natalie obliged, but when Rebecca opened it and tried to charge through, she collided painfully with the dome and was forced backwards, crying out in pain but not surprise.

James shrugged, unperturbed. "Try making a door against thin air and make it come out over there, about ten feet in."

"How am I supposed to create the door on the other side?"

"Just look at the spot and make a door appear there. It may not work but it's worth a try."

I thought it was, even if I doubted it would work, and so it didn't. When Rebecca tried to go through it, the result was exactly the same, only less painful since she took it more slowly.

"Well, maybe they expected the Woodwards might try that," I said, and I wasn't altogether surprised.

James, however, was still smiling. "That's because doors are such a standard way of getting into a place. Hammerson would know all about them, given the variety of doors he's set up around all his bases, but you know what I haven't seen him use?"

"A turnstile?" Peter suggested.

James actually laughed. "That's not what I was thinking, but you might as well try it."

For the third time, Natalie obliged with no success whatsoever. Again, I wasn't surprised, because in order to create the turnstile and make it work, she still had to open a hole in the dome.

"Fair enough," said James. "Now, to my original idea. Nat, that spot just there?"

"Yeah?" she said, staring at the spot on the dome James was indicating.

"Turn it into a window, large enough for us to climb through, but don't just create the window; actually imagine that part of the dome turning into a window. You see the difference?"

She did, and she froze in concentration. The rest of us watched her anxiously, waiting to see if she would have any success. When the window appeared, the only visible sign of it was the frame and the latch; the glass appeared to be the same surface as the dome. When Rebecca unlatched it, however, it swung open easily. I still expected that she wouldn't be able to climb through it, but on that score, I was wrong. In fact, given how large the window was, stepping through to the other side was easy, only necessitating stepping over the bottom of the frame and ducking slightly to avoid the top.

She took several steps beyond it, waiting for something to happen, and sure enough, within seconds, something did. With a hole in their security, everything that came through the window was now reflective of the present rather than the past. Other than Rebecca, the visuals through the window didn't look much different, nor did most of the other senses. The visual effect was just as it had been in the third simulation, though with a much smaller discrepancy given the weather conditions, and this time there was a visible frame around the hole. The greatest difference was the loud blatting siren that was sounding, slightly muffled as though, quite accurately, from inside a mostly enclosed room. I looked quickly at Natalie for confirmation of my suspicion, and she nodded, indicating that yes, the siren had only just begun.

"Quickly," said Peter, scrambling through the window after Rebecca and beckoning for the rest of us to follow. James and I were quick to do so but when Natalie tried to follow, her progress was somehow impeded. She couldn't get so much as an inch of her form beyond the point where the dome had been. It looked as though that part of the dome had suddenly been refilled, but when James went back to help her, he was able to reach back to her side quite easily and seize her shoulders. It could have been that the barrier only worked one way, but I thought it more likely that the window had only broken through the physical barrier. The magic preventing the Sorcerers from entering was probably separate from the dome, even if it conformed to the same boundaries. Natalie and James struggled for several seconds, during which he tried to pull her through and she cried out that he was hurting her.

"Give it up, James," I shouted over the siren. "Nat, you'll just have to try to remove that other barrier separately. Come on, we have to get on with—"

I had been turning away from her as I spoke, about to examine the grounds ahead of us, but Natalie's scream caused all of us to look quickly back at her. The scream had been reflexive, there had been no intent in it whatsoever, and yet it had probably saved all our lives. I had only just registered Natalie's pale face and bulging eyes when the attack hit us from behind. I never saw what happened to the others; I only felt something sharp hit me from behind—several somethings. It was so hard and fast that I was lifted off my feet and hurled forwards, smashing into the dome far more painfully than I had earlier. I felt my jaw re-break along the same line as the previous break, and now I had a broken nose to go with it. I collapsed at the foot of the invisible wall, seeing my own blood pool around me on the ground as I tried to move. I was in a world of pain, but not too far gone to notice that even after striking the dome with my bare skin, I was still alive to think about it; that was a relief.

I could hear the others moving nearby, struck down as badly as I had been and trying to regain their feet. Natalie had been thrown right back from the dome but in her case, the attack had hit her squarely in the face, rearranging it into something grotesque. It had also cut her jugular, by the look of the blood flying into the air from her neck. Unlike the rest of us, however, she was in no danger of dying, and apparently still in possession of enough of her faculties to use her magic. She took a moment to fix her neck, and another to clear the blood from her face, but she didn't waste any more time with her own injuries.

She approached the window again but although she still couldn't climb through it, she was able to perform magic from beyond the dome; just as she had done to 3K17, but this time, it was for good. I felt myself being levitated into the air, dangling like a puppet, unable to support my own weight as Natalie directed the four of us into positions where she could see our various injuries. It was an interminably long process for the four of us, although in actual fact it was probably no more than a minute. By the time I felt my feet reconnect with the ground, my face had been fixed up and the places where I had been stabbed or whatever it had been (the back of my head, the back of my neck, the back of my legs and, of course, my back) were no longer stinging.

I turned to the others and quickly assessed them. They all looked as shocked as I felt but like me, they had all been healed. As Natalie turned her attention back to her own remaining injuries, however, I was distracted by distant noises. I didn't have to wonder what else was coming towards us from the direction of the buildings: Whatever had struck us down was nothing more than a wave of devastating magic, designed to deal with any potential danger before the Hammerhearts themselves came to investigate. They were coming now, however, probably a hundred or more, and Natalie still wasn't through the window.

"I've got an idea," James said to us, turning back to Natalie.

"What's that?"

"Just don't panic, okay."

What he did next was so shocking that for a fraction of a second, I wondered if his brain had been damaged in the attack. Before any of us could stop him, he pointed his hero device at Natalie and clicked it. A jet of pure-white thicky prison shot from it and hit Natalie squarely in the belly.

"James! You idiot!" Peter bellowed.

"Remember what I said," James reiterated. "Now Peter, John, if they get here before we're done, you two have to fight them until we're ready. Rebecca, I need you to back me up here. Natalie, lean against the dome and let the thicky prison take you; just trust me on this."

"What do I do?" Rebecca asked nervously, watching her sister in horror.

"When we're through, we'll both be trapped," James told her. "I need you to release us with your solid-outliner. Can you do that?"

"I guess so."

They were coming in earnest now. I still couldn't see them but I could hear the running footsteps, many of them, approaching from the other side of the nearest building. I turned away from James and Natalie, now understanding what James's intention was and hoping against all hope that it worked. If not, there wouldn't be enough time to undo the damage before we were beset upon. The barrier would keep Sorcerers out under all conditions except, of course, if they were assumed to be imprisoned by the Hammerhearts and were being brought in; James was banking everything on that assumption. The barrier was probably designed so that no magic performed by a Sorcerer in possession of a crystal chip could undo it. Marc probably could have undone it if he knew how, but unless the Hammerhearts were also attacking in other directions, I didn't think the other groups had broken through yet. This gave me an idea, and I called to Natalie without looking at her.

"Natalie, tell Marc and Amelia how you got through if you haven't done already. We're gonna need all the help we can get."

That was surely the truth. I hoped that wherever she was in the Stretch, May was picking up on all of this, and that Stella's group were even now sprinting down Flint Street to reach us.

Where we had cut into the school grounds was the northwest corner of the large block shared by the two schools. The division wasn't exactly even (the secondary school was rather larger than the primary one) but in general, the primary school stretched along the northern-most bounds of the block. This meant that between us and the nearest buildings was a basketball court and a play area, upon which I could remember having plenty of fun a good five years ago now before I had outgrown it. I was still a little surprised that the Hammerhearts had left it in place, but only a little; in the time they had occupied the grounds, they seemed to have taken more of the high school's facilities, probably because they were better.

In my peripheral vision, I saw Peter step up beside me, his own hero device at the ready. I was pleased that he had either understood or simply accepted what James was doing and was also getting ready to fight, but I had no more time to think about it because that was when the first Hammerhearts appeared around the side of the building, heading straight for the spot where we were. Three of them were already in plain view when those in the lead slammed on the brakes, skidding to a halt, their eyes widening in surprise as they zeroed in on Peter and me, and if they could see the two of us, that could only mean…

"They see us," Peter muttered as, some fifty feet away, more Hammerhearts hurried around the corner of the building, not seeing the holdup and colliding with those who had stopped at the sight of us. Way to state the bleedin'obvious, Pete, I thought, with no amusement whatsoever.

I could only assume that whatever that first attack had been, it had removed our invisibility veil, and if it had done that, it had probably removed all our other protection as well. Worse, given that the other groups were all under the same veil, including Lucien and Stella's groups, all twenty-seven of us would now be horribly exposed. I thought I also understood the point of the first attack: They knew not what had damaged the dome out here so they had sent ensurance ahead of them so that when the Hammerhearts came to inspect it, they wouldn't have to worry about being lured into an ambush because whoever might be lingering would probably be dead. They had either expected to see a few dead bodies or nothing at all; they hadn't expected to see two teenage boys, standing ready to fight, and three more teenagers beyond them doing whatever it was they were still doing.

The siren cut out at that point but in its place, distant shouts reached us, echoing across the grounds as the Hammerhearts communicated to those behind them that they had a fight on their hands—at least, I assumed that was the gist of it. I knew I was right a moment later when those in the lead, who had now regained their feet, sent jets of varying-coloured light in our direction. Marc had provided us with all the weaponry we could need, but one thing these things didn't do, so far as I knew, was create protective shields around us. Damn, I thought; yet again, we had overlooked something critical. All those simulations should have picked up on this potentially fatal flaw and yet…

I still didn't know enough about fighting on such a large scale to know what to do in a situation like this, and yet what came to both Peter and me was so natural that we could have been subconsciously planning for this fight all our lives. We both shot sideways, me out to the left and he out to the right, exposing Natalie and James and knowing we could do nothing for them. I heard one of the others, probably Rebecca, dodging out of the way as well, but James was too busy to take a moment even for that. Only one jet of light, a golden one I recognised as being from an agonator, came seriously close to hitting either of them, though; the first wave of attacks was rather wild given the distance between. The second wave which immediately followed was a little better, but not by much because aiming while on the run wasn't easy either. This time, Peter was able to deflect one that almost hit James, not with a shield but with a second jet of light from his hero device. I never got a chance to ask him what it had been but I didn't have to; I knew what it meant and how it could be used.

There was time for no more. The distance between us had been halved and was rapidly closing. We would be engulfed within seconds. I took aim with my hero device, thought of the bludginator, and began slashing at the air in a wide, horizontal arc at what would have been chest-height for many of them (perhaps neck-height for the shorter ones). It did exactly what I'd hoped it would do; even with the distance greater than any over which I had used a bludginator in the past, the magical knife found its target, just as it always did. It slowed the leaders of the attack in such a way that they were quite literally trampled by those running behind them.

I repeated the gesture on the new leaders, this time swiping my knife back the other way and stopping just short of catching Peter with it. It was almost as effective but a few of the smarter ones who had seen what I'd done a moment ago had ducked it and were still running. I followed their lead, dropping into a crouch and swiping for a third time, right to left again, now at shin-height. It probably wouldn't have hurt as much as what I'd done the first time, but the end result was even better because it did more than slow them up; it tripped them up and in one case, judging by the loud crack that rent the air, broke someone's leg.

They were the last of the attack party, it seemed, for there were no more Hammerhearts coming behind them. This was a little comforting, but only a little. There were still about a hundred here, even if not all of them could fight anymore, and worse, more would be coming if this lot could notify those in control of this place that the threat was much more serious than a bit of school vandalism. I wished I could take them down as I had in the simulator—by knocking them all out—but that only worked if we could do small numbers at a time; this many all at once would be impossible.

I had a moment before some of them could regain their feet and I used it to look quickly over my shoulder. Natalie was now completely wrapped up in thicky prison and James, who had hold of her, was half-wrapped. Only his legs were still ambulatory as the thicky prison quickly stretched itself downward, and he was using them to haul himself away from the dome. His plan was working perfectly because Natalie was half-in, half-out of the school. Rebecca was standing nearby, her eyes darting rapidly from James to the Hammerhearts and back again, while past her, Peter was watching me, as though waiting for me to lead the attack.

And attack it had to be, for we were still hopelessly outnumbered out here. We may get backup soon, and things would be a lot better when we had Natalie back in action, but for the time being, Peter and I had to distract them. I therefore took aim with my hero device, thought of thicky prison, and pressed the button. Several metres to my right, Peter did the same. Those closest to the two targets had no chance of getting away but the Hammerhearts at the far back of the pack, as well as in the front-centre of it, were able to struggle away and get to their feet.

I moved quickly to my right so that I was once again back in front of James. Seeing what I was doing, Peter came to join me and at the same time, Rebecca moved up behind us, pointing her own hero device between our shoulders as we drew together. What she did next was very creative, but far too slow to be repeated; rather than bludginating or trapping with thicky prison, she stunned the Hammerheart who was first on his feet and then moved her arm sideways so that he, too, was irresistibly shifted. His side connected with the thicky prison and that was pretty much it for his offensive, or at least it would have been, had Rebecca not made the greatest mistake of all by releasing him from her stunner before his arms were trapped. In the moment before any of us could stop him, and before the thicky prison could reach his left hand, he withdrew an agonator from his pocket on that side, took aim and fired.

Rebecca immediately went down under its power, screaming and thrashing. I pointed my own hero device at her, thought of the agonator, and clicked the button twice. It had no effect; apparently she could only be set free by the device which had performed the initial curse. The responsible Hammerheart, however, had no intention of letting her go, and there was no time to think of what else we could do for her. There were at least half a dozen more Hammerhearts on their feet now, and Peter and I had to dive to either side to avoid several jets of golden light from their weapons. I tucked and rolled, spinning myself around a full 360 degrees so that I could get a glimpse of James's progress without exposing myself to the danger any further.

He had succeeded in getting Natalie all the way through the window, but now the two of them were entirely trapped by thicky prison. I quickly switched back to my solid-outliner but before I could fire it, I was roughly seized and hauled to my feet. Some distance away, Peter had also been seized by three men and was struggling fruitlessly against their clutches. I was having no more luck dealing with the three who had got hold of me, even though one of them was a woman, and of course, we were the only two left able to fight.

Clutching tightly to my only hope of getting out of this mess, I switched my hero device back to the bludginator and, knowing they would be caught off-guard by a device which didn't look dangerous on the surface, jerked the wrist holding it sideways so that it slashed horizontally across the waist of the man holding that arm. He yelled in pain but to my dismay, didn't let go. I jerked it again, this time letting the knife cut him vertically up his body, almost all the way to his neck. This time, he had no hope of keeping his grip. He went down, yelling.

The two remaining assailants tried to manoeuvre me into a position by which they could keep a better hold of me, and unwittingly gave me the chance I needed. I spun ninety degrees and brought my knee up; it connected solidly with the man to my right's genitals, and he went down in a gasp of surprise and pain. The woman behind him held on even more tightly—a second mistake on her part. I ducked and hurled myself to the left (only just avoiding the man I had practically gutted) and pulled the woman down with me before she had a chance to let go. In almost the same instant, I twisted my body around so that I came down on top of her. It was far more violent than I had ever imagined I would treat a woman, but I had to remember that this one was just as dangerous as any male Hammerheart.

I scrambled away from her, barely avoiding her hand as she tried to trip me by the ankle, managing to regain my feet with barely a moment to spare. I turned back to the man I'd kneed and slashed at him with my hero device, thinking that I should really try to get him over to the disabled bunch to keep him out of action much longer. I'd expected a slash of blood, given that I hadn't instructed the hero device to switch to a different mode, but what happened next was rather surprising; the man in question was sent flying through the air, no blood in sight, colliding with the group on the ground and immediately becoming trapped by the thicky prison binding them. So, the device responded to my thought and did what I'd wanted it to do. That particular mode must already have been installed, but apparently it could switch between them far more easily than I had originally thought. It would have been nice if Marc had warned me of that....

Never mind, though; still a lot to do. I didn't even have time to assess the rest of the scene, to see where the rest of the ambulatory Hammerhearts were, or what was happening to Peter. I knew that Rebecca had been dealt with because her screams had stopped, but I didn't even have time to see where she had been taken. One thing I did do, though, while I had a second, was (consciously) switch to my solid-outliner and free James and Natalie from the thicky prison binding them. They collapsed on the ground together before leaping to their feet and, Natalie more quickly than James, hurling themselves into the fight.

It was as I was turning back to the woman, who was now on her hands and knees close by, that I got a good look at the rest of the scene. There were at least a dozen Hammerhearts on their feet, many of them surrounding Peter, who was in a bad way but still fighting with everything he had. Rebecca was where she had been left but she had been silenced by thicky prison. The trapped Hammerhearts were still trapped but in the moment I watched, I saw one of the free Hammerhearts turn his solid-outliner on them. Worst of all, however, were the two figures who had not yet joined the fight.

I had thought that all the Hammerhearts who had been sent to investigate the source of the trouble had been flushed out, but I had been misled. Two more Hammerhearts had stepped out from behind the building, and both of them were speaking into mobile phones, no doubt calling for backup now that they knew there was an enemy within the boundaries. I recognised both of them immediately and saw that both of them had already recognised all of us. The taller of the two, the boy with the code 3W41 over his chest, had apparently taken a step back upon recognition; his face suggested that he clearly wanted to run from this confrontation. The shorter of the two, the boy of the code 4H53, had no such compunctions; he was actually smiling as he spoke into his phone.

Not knowing what I had done before, I simply switched back to whatever mode I had been in before and swiped at the woman on the ground—the one who was pointing her own solid-outliner at me. She never got a chance to use it; she was hurled forward, colliding with the pack of Hammerhearts just as her buddy had, only she wasn't trapped—they had all been set free before she reached them. There was still a Hammerheart near me but he seemed unable to fight, so I ignored him and hurried to join James and Natalie, knowing that a shield was pretty much our only hope now. James had set Rebecca free from her thicky prison and Natalie had released her from the hold of the agonator, but before I could get to any of them, before Rebecca could regain her feet or Natalie could turn her attention to Peter, the one who now needed it most, I felt something hit my left leg and begin immobilising it. I knew what it was right away, of course, and turned my hero device on it immediately, clicking the button before it could spread to my knee.

I had forgotten to switch back to the solid-outliner, and the result which followed was extraordinary. I was lifted cleanly off my feet and literally hurled through the air, away from the Hammerhearts (thankfully) and eventually coming down in a skid on the grass. When I got a good look at where I was, I found that I was quite close to the children's playground (the bottom of one of the slides was only ten feet or so to my left). I straightened up and turned back in the direction of the fight, hoping I could get a few good shots off from this distance and deciding that I wouldn't rejoin them unless I had to. There was still one matter unresolved, however, and I dealt with the thicky prison on my leg before doing anything else.

It wasn't good over there. The Hammerhearts who'd been felled earlier were quickly regaining their feet and worse,

Natalie, Peter, James and Rebecca had all been stunned. Natalie was able to break free of her own binds in the moments I watched but before she could help the others, yet another Hammerheart—another woman—shot something else at her. Whatever it was sought the Sorcerer just as those that disabled their magic had done, although I knew this couldn't be the same device since all the Sorcerers were protected from that. Or were they? The adults probably were, and Amelia probably was if she remembered to take care of herself every month, but Natalie hadn't had to perform any magic for over a month.... Had she forgotten?

Probably she had, because in the three seconds I allowed myself to watch, she performed no more magic of her own but began fighting with her hero device just like the rest of us. That was all the confirmation I needed, and my heart sank—the shield was no longer an option, which meant that unless one of the other Sorcerers showed up, or Marc ordered Fewul to help us out, we would have to fight our way out. On the plus side, though, if Hignat and Sebastian really had called for backup, we probably wouldn't have to go and look for Hall—he would find us here.

Our only chance was for me to get the others over here, rather than go over there and get caught up in the struggle. Hoping this would work, I thought of reeling them in as if on the end of a fishing rod, pointed my hero device at Peter, and clicked the button. The result was perfect: Not only did it free him from the effect of the stunner but it sent him flying through the air, straight towards me. I was forced to dodge out of the way as he landed hard on the grass where I had been a moment earlier. He was bleeding in several places and a great big bruise was already blooming on his forehead, but otherwise he was okay.

Before he had even regained his feet, I took a few steps to the left towards the playground, so as not to cause any more collisions, and did the same thing to James. The same thing happened except that the two Hammerhearts who had been holding him were also thrown into the air, the shock of the jolt causing them to let go. He came down right beside me and quickly regained his feet but before he had, both Peter and I were ready to reel in the girls. Peter probably had no idea what I'd done but he seemed to understand how to do the same. The Hammerhearts were ready this time, knowing what (if not necessarily how) we were doing to get away from them. They clung to Natalie and Rebecca with all their might, and two of them continued to cling even as they flew through the air.

Seconds later, the five of us were together again and only with a couple of stray Hammerhearts, who were easily dealt with. Unfortunately, the pursuit was well and truly on now. All of us took aim, Peter and Rebecca with solid-outliners and the rest of us with bludginators, me wishing we had an effective method of dealing with large numbers at a time, and fired. Ahead of us, many Hammerhearts were also firing, and we had to duck and weave and hope we didn't get in each other's way just to avoid them. We couldn't keep this up for too much longer; there were simply too many of them, and soon there would be more. We had two options as I saw it: Get back through the dome and try this another time (hardly an option now that they knew we could get in) or continue with the plan to catch Hall.

"Did you lose your magic?" James asked Natalie as the five of us backed away, me now thinking that we had to try to put the children's playground between ourselves and the Hammerhearts.

"Yes!" she cried out. "I don't think it's the same as before but I can't do anything anymore."

I opened my own mouth now, about to ask if she had communicated our success at breaking the dome to Marc and Amelia, but before I could, the question was answered for me. For the second time, the siren began blatting, causing all five of us to jump and the Hammerhearts to skid to a halt for the second time, looking around wildly to see where the threat was coming from. Past them, Hignat and Sebastian, both of whom had just put their phones away, now took them out again, probably to see if anyone knew where the new danger was. I remembered what had happened to us immediately before the Hammerhearts had shown up and hoped dearly that whichever group had broken through would be as lucky as we had been. In the meantime, though…

"Let's go," said Peter tersely.

It was 9:31 on the morning of August 23, 2010.

Chapter 33: Coldblooded

"Playground," I called as everyone turned, previously intending to try to get around the building. We would have to go that way eventually but I doubted we would get all the way over there before being struck down. To demonstrate my meaning, I cut in front of the Fletchers and jumped over the bottom of the nearest slide, hearing some sort of magic bounce off it less than a second later. Whatever it had been didn't do any damage to the slide, but I was fairly sure it would have done enough to me had it hit.

The others understood; we split up and began cutting through the playground. Jets of red, white and gold light peppered the equipment and did nothing to it—I assumed because it was all fixed to the ground that the solid-outliners had no effect on it. Still, this distraction would only keep them going for a short time—the Hammerhearts were already sprinting towards us, intent on flushing us out and then…who knew what would follow.

I weighed up my options for only a moment before coming to my decision. It would infuriate those who survived, but killing each and every Hammerheart was the only way to prevent them from getting back up again. Of course, they would only be presumed dead if we didn't win the fight, unless of course, Hammerson had discovered the truth of those virtual killing devices Stella had created so long ago. I therefore switched to that mode and, from my vantage point inside a plastic tunnel which led into what kids would use as a cubby house, began taking them down one by one.

I got about ten before they realised what I was doing, and that those I struck down looked dead for all money. I was immediately bombarded with an avalanche of magic, most of it hitting the tunnel (inside and out) and the structure around it. Only one jet was direct enough to get all the way through, and I was able to avoid it easily by simply ducking back into the cubby house. On the plus side, none of the Hammerhearts could get a clear shot at me without me getting an even clearer shot at them first. Further on the plus side, the tunnel was the only way into the cubby house, so I didn't have to worry about being attacked from behind. On the horrifying downside, the surest way to take me down without me having a chance would be to destroy the whole structure. I wasn't sure how they could do that but I wouldn't have put it past them.

"You gonna hide in there all day, boy?" a man jeered at me through a small gap in the woodwork (such gaps were necessary to allow air to filter inside, I supposed). "Come on out, I promise I won't hurt you—kill you perhaps, but never hurt you."

He was pointing something through the hole at me but he never had a hope of hitting his mark. I very carefully pointed my own weapon through the same hole, though higher up so that I wouldn't be briefly in his line of fire, and took him down with a single click. More Hammerhearts tried the same technique, or variations of it, with no success. After a few minutes of this, the attempts ceased, and I could do nothing except listen to the rest of the battle and wonder when would be the best time to emerge. Another siren went off during this time, indicating that the third group had now penetrated the dome, a thought that gave me still further hope. It was impossible to know who was doing what and where, or if any of the others were hurt (worse than before in Peter and Rebecca's cases) but I knew, when I heard alarmed shouts all around me from the Hammerhearts, that the time had probably come.

I scrambled into the tunnel, which felt as though it had shrunk since I'd been a third-grader, and emerged on the other side seconds later. It was clear enough what had caused the distraction, and just as clear that it had thrown the Hammerhearts completely off their game. Several of them were running around nearby, shooting jets of magic in whatever direction as though having no idea who or what to fire at first. A small minority of them hadn't even noticed the distraction and were still trying to get a good shot at James and Peter, who were attacking from atop the monkey bars (how they must have had fun climbing up there). Most of the Hammerhearts, however, had retrained their magic on the opening through which we had entered the school grounds, and I immediately saw why.

Better late than never, the cavalry had arrived. I could clearly see Stella over there with them (she had already climbed through the window and was taking aim at the nearest Hammerhearts, even as they did the same) and just as clearly, on the other side of the dome, waiting his turn to climb through the window, Lucien. It looked as though all twelve of them had arrived—good, we would need them.

And still, I thought, turning and diving behind the tunnel to avoid a stray jet of magic, none of this was what we came here for. We had a plan, part of which had worked but most of which was still yet to be achieved. Having greater numbers would help but the longer we stayed here, the closer the Hammerhearts' reinforcements would get. I had to find a way to get clear of the mob, and the first step towards doing that was to locate the others. Peter and James were fine, but where were the girls?

I scrambled around the outside of the cubby house in which I had just been hiding, putting it between myself and most of the Hammerhearts, and looked around wildly. It only took me a second to locate one of them: Natalie had sheltered in a small gap between the side of another cubby house and a slide which came down from the top of it. I hurried over to her, dodging a jet of white light she sent at me before she recognised me.

"Sorry," she said sheepishly. "What's going on?"

"Lucien and Stella's groups are here," I told her. "Where's Rebecca? We've gotta get on with this thing before it gets too out-of-hand."

"I know, but I can't contact the others anymore without my magic."

I groaned. Our plan had depended on the telepathic communication between the three Sorcerers, but now that one of them was cut off.... It meant that May would have to step in, as Lucien had said after failed simulation number two, but that couldn't happen until we got her over here and were safely out of reach of this lot of Hammerhearts.

"And I think Rebecca hid in there," she said, pointing at a tubular structure connected to the monkey bars where James and Peter were still swinging in and out of a magical assault.

Yes, I thought, that would certainly be a good vantage point in an attack, about as good as mine had been in fact. The thing in which Rebecca was almost certainly sheltered was a hollow metal cylinder which basically led down to nothing at all, and apart from a small hole in its structure near the bottom which could be used to observe the playground outside, had no useful function. I could remember it being condemned by most of the teachers back in the day because it could be dangerous if too many kids tried to get in at the same time. Unfortunately, it had a grave downside: Rebecca wouldn't be able to get out of it without being horribly exposed to the Hammerhearts' attack for several precious seconds.

It was as I was thinking these thoughts that the situation suddenly accelerated. Later, I would barely be able to trace the progression of events that killed at least two dozen Hammerhearts, almost killed us, and almost destroyed this part of the school. The trigger was caused by May, who had a far greater impact on the Hammerhearts who saw her first than any of the others who had preceded her through the window. I had a pretty good view of it from where I stood: The male Hammerhearts were so flabbergasted by the sight of her that they didn't even know they were in trouble until they had already been taken down by Stella and her group of vigilantes.

The female Hammerhearts, though there were far fewer of them on the fighting ground, weren't nearly as susceptible. The first one took to the Honnie with an agonator, which had absolutely no effect whatsoever. She was thrust aside by the woman next to her, who swiped her bludginator in a sideways arc just as I had done some fifteen minutes earlier. This was far more spectacular because not even Honnies were immune to being cut by something as strong as this kind of magic.

The sound of May's scream of pain was agonising in its intensity, so much so that both Natalie and I felt our bodies seize up for a second or two. It was only as it let go that I realised what had caused it; not the sound, but the mind. When May had been attacked in her own world, it had been so swift that she had probably been rendered semi-conscious within seconds. This time, she still had all her wits about her, which was a very bad thing for the two Hammerhearts who had tried to take her down. She was still bleeding profusely even as she bounded forward in a terrifying leap towards the two women, who were already in the process of collapsing to the ground as their minds were sucked out of them.

I looked quickly away from the scene as May fell upon them, already knowing what I was missing and having no desire to see it, but I registered quite a lot in the instant before doing so: Everyone who had seen it, everyone other than me, Natalie and Peter anyway, had frozen in horror as they witnessed a Honnie in full flight, including those who had already been told to expect it. James on the monkey bars, Lucien over by the dome, and all those around him, knew what they were seeing and now understood, if they hadn't already, the potential of the alien who was helping us. I never knew what the Hammerhearts made of May except that nobody wanted to fight her, seeing her as a creature that clearly couldn't be beaten with any weapons they possessed. They all turned and broke for cover, anything to get away from the danger behind them. The trouble was, the way away from May also happened to be straight toward us...and so it happened.

There was no easy path through the centre of the playground, and to go around the entire structure was quite a detour. It meant that most of the Hammerhearts tried to go straight through it, the upside to that being that it slowed them up. The downside was that the ones who got on top had a clear shot at Natalie and me, and quite a few of them weren't too far gone to take advantage of it. We both dodged, fired, dodged again, fired again, and then broke for new cover before we could be overwhelmed. James and Peter had jumped down from the monkey bars and joined us just as we reached the opposite side of the playground.

"Where's Rebecca?" Peter asked.

There was no time for any of us to answer. Jets of light flew at us from the structure behind us, hitting both Natalie and Peter and sending them reeling to the ground. Fortunately, the damage was no worse than that. I turned to see that Hammerhearts were lined up along the top of the structure and many were already beginning to come down the other side. One man had even struggled into one of the tunnels, as though hoping it would provide a shortcut—he hadn't banked on his own size holding him up.

One look at the scene was enough to put the whole thing into perspective for me, and the only possible escape route came to me. I didn't have any time to seriously contemplate the utter horror of what I was about to do; if I had, I probably wouldn't have been able to do it. I thought back to the dark thoughts I had entertained while sheltered inside the cubby house, took aim at the far left of the roof of the structure, and fired my hero device, sweeping it sideways as I went. To everyone's collective horror, allies and Hammerhearts alike, the playground burst into flames, which quickly spread to the adjoining structures. Screams of pain rent the air as the roof quickly melted and collapsed inward, taking those Hammerhearts who'd been standing upon it down with it. A few were able to jump off without getting burnt but most weren't so lucky.

I had known that would be the case. I had known that I was condemning them to a fate that I myself had suffered in the simulator, only for them it would be permanent. However, I also knew that it was the only option. At the end of the day, more lives would be lost if we didn't do whatever it took to weaken Hammerson's army.

"*Rebecca!*" Natalie screamed agonisingly, jumping to her feet, her face twisted in despair as she looked wildly around for her sister. She shot me a look then, one that made my heart freeze in my chest; it was as though she had suddenly realised that I was a monster.

I looked at the cylinder Natalie had indicated earlier. It was impossible to be completely sure, but I was almost sure that someone was in there. Acting instinctively, I switched to my stunner, pointed it at the tiny window in the cylinder, and clicked it, moving it upward as I went. It worked exactly as I'd hoped it would: Seconds before the flames reached it, a stunned Rebecca came flying out of the top of the structure. I carefully levitated her away from the danger and then lowered her to the ground before releasing it. She collapsed for only a moment before jumping to her feet and hurrying over to us.

She wasn't the only one, either; five Hammerhearts were on the move, staring at the five of us with utter murder in their eyes. Also, far to the left, I saw the other group, led by Lucien and Stella, hurrying around the edge of the play area to join us. We had plenty of time before they would get to us, and in the meantime, it was a fair fight—five on five. Or at least it would have been fair, if not for the fact that the other four were still in utter shock from what I had done, and the Hammerhearts now had a personal score to settle.

I ducked the first magical jet of light, dodged to the left to evade the second (which went on to hit James behind me) and then to the right to evade the third (which hit Rebecca). They were both golden jets of light, and neither of them were ready for it; they both went down, screaming and thrashing. Unfortunately, one of James's flailing feet hit one of my ankles, unbalancing me and sending me over, leaving me a sitting duck. I only got off one shot from there, a shot that went well over the Hammerhearts' heads, before the power of the agonator descended upon me in all its glory.

I was gone from the school. I was no longer sprawled on the ground. In fact, for all intents and purposes, I no longer had a body, for I no longer knew the concept of feeling anything other than pain; it was the only thing which existed in my world. I would have been thrashing, of course, just as James and Rebecca had, but such thoughts can only surface after the pain is gone. It was so all-consuming that it quite literally took over all my senses—I saw pain, I heard pain, I smelt pain, I tasted pain. I even thought of pain because it was all I knew, as though it were the only thought I had ever had in my life. This could be the only true existence in life, and it was so unbearably miserable that all I wanted was for it to stop, for the pain to go away, or for me to go away from it.

Sometime later, though time was another concept that had ceased to matter to me, the pain lifted, though not immediately the after-effects of it. It took several seconds for my senses to click into gear and for me to recognise where I was and what had just happened to me. I was on the ground along with the other four (Natalie and Peter must also have been struck down at some point) and they, like me, had all been released. My whole body was aching, particularly my head where I seemed to have hit it on the ground, and my throat felt horribly dry, as though I had only just stopped howling at the top of my lungs.

It was another few seconds before I was able to look up and see what had caused our turn in fortunes. The five offending Hammerhearts were still upright, though now completely immobile as stunners were held upon them from the other group. All their agonators had been wrested by the rest of the group and re-clicked, so that their magic had been turned off. It was a slightly relieving sight but its effect was completely cancelled out by the utter horror taking place behind it. The entire playground was now an inferno, the entire structure burning, melting and collapsing in upon itself. The flames were now taking hold in the bark upon which the structure sat (a pretty good hold too) and would soon spread toward us. If it kept spreading, it would reach the grass, and if that kept it going, the buildings would be in danger. There weren't many Hammerhearts left to be seen, but the few that were still alive made up for all the rest. One man in particular was staring at us, not in hatred but desperation, and his whole body (much of it visible, for his clothing had been mostly burnt away) appeared to be quite literally running.

I knew I had done the only possible thing to give us a chance to escape from them, but seeing this was enough to bring back every moral insecurity I had ever had in my life. That day in the gym when I had felt so terribly guilty about firing on Hammerhearts who might have been innocent; the day upon the not-so-calm waters of the Indian Ocean when I had tried so hard to make sure as few lives would be lost in our efforts to reach the portal; it all felt so close. This was an action I could never get away from, an action I could never live down, for I had stolen quite a lot of lives in one moment of desperate rationale.

Lucien, meanwhile, with the help of George and Belinda, began wrapping the nearby Hammerhearts in thicky prison and binding them together so that they could be released from the stunners of the others. Once this was done, the rest of the group hurried to where the five of us sat in the bark, watching in stunned horror.

"Come on, you guys," said either Misty or Michelle, helping Natalie to her feet. "We have to find Hall."

"Are there anymore Hammerhearts?" James asked, clambering to his feet. I made to copy him but—no—no—no—bad idea. Most of the oxygen in the vicinity had been consumed by the fire and what it was giving us in return, particulate matter consisting of vaporised wood, plastic and (my stomach did a backflip when I realised) human flesh, was almost certainly toxic.

"No," said Lucien, seeing my troubles and helping me get to my feet. I swayed, trying not to inhale the probably poisonous air around me. "A few split but most got caught up in that. That was—er—definitely not part of the plan. Speaking of which, we should get going before reinforcements turn up."

"Shouldn't we try to put that out first?" asked Siobhan.

"I'd agree with that if we had time for it," said Lucien, shrugging and looking pale. Soot was beginning to flake down from the sky now and it stood out starkly on his pale face.

"What are we doing anyway?" Peter gasped as the seventeen of us began to move away from the conflagration.

"Everyone gather around," Lucien said hurriedly when we were out of sight of the destruction we had left behind, shielded from it by a building, "because we have very little time. Is there anything we need to know before we make any decisions?"

"Yes, they took my magic," Natalie told him.

"Took—"

"You know, with those things that makes it impossible to use."

Lucien frowned. "I thought you and the others were immune to that."

Natalie shrugged. "I was, but now I'm not."

"Also, you should know that our invisibility veil is gone," said James. "They did something to us that—well it nearly killed us, but it removed all our protection, so you guys and the other groups will be just as exposed as us."

"That explains a bit," said Stella darkly.

"Okay," said Lucien, looking like he was trying to think at top speed. "Not great, but okay. I tell you what, you five continue with the original plan, but I think it might be a good idea if May goes with you—she won't be so much use to us, and you will need all the help you can get. Natalie, I guess you're one of the common folk now, which means you have to locate one of the other groups before you can get in with the plan. The rest of us will hang back for a bit and then approach the admin building as stealthily as we can and take down any Hammerhearts who try to pass in or out. Guys, that means we stay out of sight at all times and only attack when the group we're dealing with is smaller than our own."

"And how do you intend to stay inconspicuous when they see a whole load of bodies on the ground?" asked Dean.

"So what if they do? They already know we're here; if they try anything, we'll get them first. Everyone ready to go?"

I didn't feel ready at all—delayed reaction to the atrocity I had committed was beginning to set in—but what choice did I have? Lucien was right; there was very little time. The Hammerhearts would be fully on the alert now, and worse, they knew who was here. At least, Hignat and Sebastian had recognised us, and they had been on their phones to someone, presumably in the high school where most of their operations were based. The word would be out, and Hall would be onto it. That was a good thing if it meant he would stay within the grounds; surely he would be too tempted by the thought of bringing the Chopville Quartet into custody (obviously he didn't know about Tommy yet). What was worse was the possibility that, as had happened that night in Germany, Arnold Hammerson would be informed of our presence and take it upon himself to intervene. There was such a thing as too many complications....

And so we split up. Natalie led me, Peter, James, Rebecca and May around the side of the building toward the high school. Now that we were visible, the route we had taken in the simulator would expose us for far too long, especially if the Hammerhearts were sending reinforcements—reinforcements who would, hopefully, do more about the fire than worrying about the person who had caused it. Once again, the guilt and shame for what I had done rolled over me. It was impossible to forget that just two days earlier, I had watched Natalie and Amelia go through exactly what those Hammerhearts had. How that had infuriated me at the time, and how ready I was to put others through the same thing. It was easy to understand why those last five Hammerhearts had attacked us with such passion.

Apparently, something of my emotions must have shown on my face because Peter said, "You gonna be all right, buddy?"

I shrugged. "Maybe, I dunno."

"Too right," said James darkly—he was panting already, and we weren't even running. "What on earth were you thinking, John?"

"It was the only way we could have got away," I said, a little desperately, "but you're right—I shouldn't have done it. I guess I wasn't thinking."

"You should have let me take care of them," said May, surprising me—it was probably the first time she had given us her opinion without being asked since she had stepped into our world. "I could have made them all not interested in you anymore if you had waited a bit longer."

"Guys, come on," said Natalie, suddenly veering sideways into a breezeway, inside which we would be fairly sheltered from the view of Hammerhearts. "Yeah, I know how bad it was, but John was probably right; it may have been the only way. May, you probably could have sorted it out, but after what you'd just been through, it's reasonable to assume you would have struggled to recover so quickly."

It was true. All of us were hurt to some degree, but May was the only one who was still bleeding, and only most of it was her own blood.

"Are you trying to justify what he did?" said Rebecca incredulously. "I almost got toasted in there."

"But you didn't, and it was John who saved you," Natalie pointed out, "and it's like he said once: It's real hard to make the exact right calls under that kind of pressure. Look, we need to let this go for now so we can focus on Hall. John…"

To my surprise, she stepped forward and gave me a hug. It was almost enough to make me break down on the spot, but the sight of James and Rebecca watching on more incredulously than ever kept me in check.

"Thanks," I said, trying to convey my appreciation to her without giving away anything else. I was about to say something else and then suddenly, I forgot what it was. I glanced from one face to the next; Natalie was smiling encouragingly while Peter wore a similar, though perhaps less intimate look, over her shoulder. James and Rebecca were still looking incredulous and, in James's case, impatient, and May appeared to be waiting for us to decide what came next.

On that score, I thought I would be okay. After all, we had a job to do and we couldn't let anything stop us now that we had penetrated the school grounds. True, exactly what we had done to get away from the Hammerhearts had slipped my mind, but it hardly mattered given that there was more fighting up ahead.

"May, we need to know where the other groups are," I told her. "Can you find them?"

May went quiet as she seemed to listen to something inside her own head—at least that was what it looked like, judging by the expression on her face. Finally she said, "They have trapped him inside the administration building with some sort of—"

She broke off, not knowing how to say whatever they had done, so she simply placed it in my head and I spoke the words for her.

"They set up an anti-teleportation ring around the building," I told the rest of the group. "Blimey, that's genius; did anyone think of that beforehand?"

"They thought of it on the spot," said May, "because they do not know what has happened to this group. They have also blocked off the exits like the plan, and the tunnel, but they accidentally set off an alarm when they tried to cut off the—"

"Hammerheart Highway," I said, once again speaking the picture which May had placed in my head. "Marc's standing guard over it now and is fighting anyone who's trying to use it. May, are you serious about Hall being trapped in there?"

"Yes, they are sure that he is in there, but I cannot find his mind anywhere; there is too much disturbance in the air."

"Probably all the protection around the place," said James. "Even if they don't know about Honnies, all the protective measures they've set up may be interfering. May, if you can't get Hall, maybe you can get other Hammerhearts around him."

"That is how I am sure that he is in there," she said. "He left the building when the third alarm went but he went back in there and now he can't get out. He is trying everything with his own *magic*"—she spoke the word very distastefully—"but nothing is working."

"Must be a strong spell, whatever Marc and Amelia did," said Peter admiringly. "So what should we do then? We have to find a way to corner Hall and take the crystal from him, before he gets away and especially before Hammerson gets wind of any of this."

"May, do you know if the anti-teleportation ring works both ways?" James asked.

She stared at James for a few seconds before saying, "Nobody can get in or out. The building is cut off."

"Except for the Hammerheart Highway," Natalie clarified, "and if that's still open, anyone can get in. May, where are Marc and Amelia? Are they actually inside the building?" When May nodded, she went on, "Fine. Let's go find the rest of the group."

"But Natalie, if we're visible, we'll give the rest of them away," James pointed out.

"We don't have to stay visible," she said, raising her hero device. "We'll just have to hang onto each other's shoulders like a train. You ready?"

And so that was what we did, each of us separately invisible, just as we had been on that night in Germany. Hopefully that wasn't another bad omen. The six of us lined up, Natalie in the lead and May at the rear, and began moving forward as quickly as we could, each of us holding the shoulders of the person in front of us (James was in front of me, and May behind). We moved out of the shelter of the breezeway and back into the open, where we got a better idea of what was going on in the grounds.

The Hammerhearts running all over the place clearly knew that something bad was going on (they would have been hard-pressed not to) but they may not have known yet what was going on in the administration building. So far, all the people we saw were running in the opposite direction, heading towards where we had broken through the dome, probably to inspect the damage we had done to it and to make sure the rest of the Hammerhearts down there were okay. Hignat and Sebastian were there, I reminded myself, and I gave myself a moment to wonder what they were doing here—why two teenagers were allowed to work in what was, for all intents and purposes, a military installation.

"Question," Peter said as we walked, but James barked at him immediately.

"Peter, we're not in a soundproof barrier! They'll hear you!"

"They'll hear you if you keep talking like—"

"Shut up, both of you," Natalie hissed.

"Fine," Peter hissed back, and now his voice was barely audible, "but seriously, where's Fewul through all this?"

"Maybe Marc's too busy to call it into action. Let's just get there and see."

We kept walking, moving sideways whenever Hammerhearts came near us but so far managing to stay unnoticed. Soon, however, Hammerhearts came running in the opposite direction, coming at us from behind; we had to quickly get out of the way whenever this happened. What was worse about this was that these particular Hammerhearts were holding their weapons in their hands, ready to attack at the slightest sign that we were in the area.

"Should we attack them?" Peter hissed when they had passed.

"No, but if they do discover us before we get to the admin building," said Natalie, "May, can you take them out before they attack us?"

"I can make them not attack you, yes."

"Good, then do that if we get in trouble; now everyone quiet again."

And so the walk continued, through the gate into the secondary school, which stood open just as it had in the simulations. This corner of the high school was mostly taken up by the oval, which was lined by a narrow band of trees. The oval was what we called it because it was used for playing sport, although its dimensions were more rectangular. It stretched ahead of us as far as the car park; at least that part of it that entered onto the grounds of the secondary school. Some distance to our right, the gym towered over the rest of the school. The main building, the one with most of our classrooms in it, was past the gym; it curved around the majority of the courtyard, across which we would have to walk to get to the administration building.

It was as we turned onto the path that would take us into the courtyard, and as the admin building came into sight for the first time, that noises began to reach our ears. There was a lot of shouting, running, banging noises and, as we actually entered the courtyard, the unmistakable sound of a gunshot.

"Faster," James moaned, pushing against Peter to make him move faster.

It caused a horrible chain reaction in which Peter stumbled, almost fell but managed to keep his balance, but pushed one of the girls over at the same time. Of course, she then knocked into her sister, and so the other one staggered and might have fallen (although it didn't sound as though she hit the ground, so maybe she kept her balance). She and Peter were quickly steady and the other Fletcher took only a moment longer to regain her feet, but now all three of them were unlinked, and several precious seconds were wasted as they tried—and failed —to relocate each other.

"Where is everybody!" Natalie's voice hissed desperately.

"Oh help," I heard Peter moan somewhere to my left; he was moving around, back behind us, probably waving his arms around trying to locate one of us.

"Do we link up again or do we just keep running?" I asked, thinking that we were going to have the same problem when we got to the building anyway.

"We have to stay together, otherwise we'll never know where each other is, and will waste time looking and stuff," said James. "Guys, just come to the sound of my voice."

"This is so stupid," one of the girls muttered.

Someone whacked me across the shoulder. I put my left arm out and managed to find whoever it was and guide them over to James while hanging onto him with my other hand. We might have been able to link up the other two as well, but that was when footsteps sounded behind us as unaware Hammerhearts closed in. May was quick, but not quick enough to prevent another chain reaction. The three Hammerhearts who almost collided with us were standing stock-still on the path, not dead but otherwise unconscious, and they were clearly visible to those coming in behind them.

"Everybody meet up by those doors!" James said, not bothering to whisper this time, and he took off without warning at a run—or at least as fast as James could run from a standstill.

I understood what he was thinking—we had to move and we could worry about relinking later—but his plan failed spectacularly when he collided with either Natalie or Rebecca and sent her flying.

"No! No!" I cried out, deciding that there was absolutely one way only to sort out this mess. "May, take every Hammerheart down who gets near us. Everyone else just stand still."

I withdrew my hero device, pointed it at myself, thought of the invisibility toggle, and clicked the button. I then pointed it at the nearest person and clicked (it turned out to be Peter), then at the spot where James's victim sat and clicked (Natalie) and then at James himself, who was only now turning back to join us. Rebecca, seeing what I was doing, made herself visible too, which meant that only May would remain invisible. That was exactly what I wanted; if any Hammerhearts saw us before May took hold of them, let them think we weren't nearly as dangerous as we really were.

"Is this a good idea?" James asked nervously as another gunshot sounded from the admin building.

"It's the only way," I said firmly. "They already know we're here, and if we need the element of surprise at all, we can let Lucien and Stella's groups take care of it—they'll still be invisible, and probably more organized than us. Come on, we've gotta get over there and find out what's going on."

It was 9:58 on the morning of August 23, 2010.

Chapter 34: Fight the Powers that Be

The administration building was long and rectangular. It was two storeys high at one end and only a single storey the rest of the way along. The one-storey section was separate from the two-storey section; that was to say, there had never been any doorways linking those parts of the building. There may have been tunnels, but I didn't think there were, not from the brief look at the system I'd been granted on that one occasion when we had used it. The single-storey section consisted of three small corridors, each with a couple of classrooms inside, and at the far end of the building, the canteen and toilets behind which we used to hang out. The double-storey section was the actual administration of the school—or at least it had been before it had become the actual administration of the Hammerhearts' operations in Chopville.

The anti-teleportation ring probably surrounded the entire building, but as most of the action would be where the administration was, it was there towards which the six of us ran, no longer caring who saw us. We were all armed, after all, able to defend ourselves against most of what the Hammerhearts could throw at us, and we still had a few extra weapons up our sleeves. They still didn't know exactly who or what May was; they wouldn't know where Lucien and Stella's group was (we had to assume they were still hidden but probably close by) and of course, Marc could call Fewul into the action at any moment. The simulations had taught us a painful lesson in not getting ahead of ourselves, but it looked as though our position was pretty good so far.

The only trouble was, as I had predicted minutes earlier, we had exactly the same problem when we reached the building. Marc and Amelia's groups were undoubtedly around here somewhere but so long as they remained under their invisibility veil, a veil which had been cast since our own had been lost, and so long as everyone with working magic remained in the building, we wouldn't be able to locate them. Looking around, we saw that the main doors were shut but unlocked, but when Peter made to open it, someone pushed him away from the door.

"Better not do that, man," said either Harry or Simon's voice from close by. "I dunno why you lot aren't hiding yourselves but now that you're here, you might as well patrol the perimeter with us."

"Because Nat lost her magic and we kept losing each other when we went invisible," said Peter crossly. "How do we coordinate with you guys when we can't see you?"

The nearby twin swore. "Well it probably doesn't matter. Most of the Hammerhearts seem to be out already; we moved them out of the way so that any more won't be discouraged from trying the same thing."

"What's going on in there?" I asked him.

"Don't know, but if it's anything really bad, we'll find out soon enough."

As though to make a mockery of his words, another gunshot shattered the air. This one was so loud and close that for a moment, I thought it was aimed at us.

"This is really dangerous," said Natalie nervously. "We need to be under your veil."

"Agree, but unless either Marc or Amelia gets out here anytime soon, it's not gonna happen. Maybe you five should just stay out of the way until—"

"Screw that," I said, thinking that we already had the means required to get either Marc or Amelia to come out here and help us. Not wanting to speak it aloud, I thought fiercely at May to take control of one of them and get them to come out, whichever one could do so without disadvantaging the other. She responded with a quick, sharp affirmative which only I caught. I didn't bother asking which one she was working with but instead turned to the others.

"Come on, we probably should get out of the way of the doors."

We made to move around the back of the building, where we found a great pile of unconscious Hammerhearts on the ground, but were brought up short when the twin we had been speaking to (Harry, it turned out) suddenly became visible to us. All our mouths fell open in surprise, and when he saw that we could see him, the colour quickly drained from his face.

"Holy crap. Have we lost another veil?"

"No, I think we're just sharing it now," I told him, understanding what I was seeing, and what May had ordered Marc to do. Instead of interrupting whatever he and Amelia were trying to accomplish on the inside, he had sent Fewul to perform the magic for us. I saw the Beast of Magic appear at the same time as Harry, though from the other side of the door, before just as quickly disappearing. "Don't worry, we're all protected now. Where are the others?"

Part of that question was answered before I could finish it. Lena and Erica came around the corner from the front of the building at that moment; not having been aware of our presence here, they both started and then grinned when they realised.

"Oh thank God," Erica cried out, bounding forward and hugging James (Peter pulled a face at me over James's shoulder).

"Do we have time to ask you guys what happened out there?" Lena asked.

"No, we'll have time to trade stories later," said James, quickly disengaging from his girlfriend and looking around at the landscape. There were quite a lot of Hammerhearts standing around in the courtyard, looking as though they couldn't give a damn if the sky fell down upon their heads, and that number seemed to be growing. None of them were getting any closer to the administration building, however, and still, no more Hammerhearts seemed to be coming out.

"Okay, but just tell us, have Stella's group come in yet?" Lena persisted.

"Yeah, and Lucien's," said Peter. "Don't worry about them; they know what they're doing. Also, so you know, May is here with us but invisible."

"Really?" said Erica, looking around stupidly, as though hoping to catch sight of the invisible Honnie.

"May, what's happening in there?" I said, trying to think fast. Thinking was difficult when so much hung on every small decision we made. So far, I figured that the most important thing was to find Hall and face off with him before any reinforcements could come. There were surely still Hammerhearts in the school grounds who were free of May's influence, Hignat probably among them, and if any of them called for backup...

"He is in there," May said. "They know he is, but they cannot locate him, and neither can I; he is hidden. I do not think he knows exactly where they are, though, because he keeps trying to shoot them."

"Which means he would give his position away each time he fires his gun," said James, frowning. "That's really stupid, and I don't think Hall is naturally that stupid; he must be up to something else."

I opened my mouth, about to ask the all-important question, but before I could get it out, we were joined by two more people: Felicity and Darcy. That made everyone from the two groups except for Simon, Katie and Sophie, the two latter of whom were probably still guarding the tunnels into the admin building. If so, they could become horribly exposed to Hall if he should choose to get out that way. Could they stand up to him, given that both he and they were probably still invisible?

"What's going on?" Felicity was asking. "Whose decision was it to just stop patrolling like this?"

"No one's, it just sorta happened," said Harry, shifting uncomfortably—understandable, given that he was the first to stop patrolling.

"We need a plan," I said, hurriedly pressing on. "I know we're supposed to leave the fighting to those two, but something just feels wrong about this. Should we go in there and see?"

"And what if Hall slips through the door the moment we get out of the way of it?" James retorted.

"What if he just bursts through it right now before any of us can stop him, and then teleports the moment he's out?" Peter fired back. "I think I'm with John on this one, although we probably should put a few people on the doors just in case. Harry, you can do that with Simon, can't you? Where is he anyway?"

"Up on the balcony," said Darcy, jabbing a finger towards it. The balcony was, in fact, directly over all our heads on the second level. There was even a faint possibility that Simon could hear conversation below him, if he was up there and paying attention.

"Are we under a soundproof barrier as well?" Peter asked. When several people nodded, he stepped out from beneath the balcony, looked up and bellowed, "Oi! Simon!"

"Oi yourself," Simon called back. "Get back to work or I'll have to jump down on top of you."

"Maybe we should leave him up there, just in case," I said, urging my brain to move a little faster. "It'll be a poor lookout if we block up this door and leave that one completely unguarded. Maybe we should send Harry up there to help out, now that the stakes are so high."

"I am utterly astounded by your brilliant mind, Sir John," said Harry, bowing to me. "Of course, I will need all of you to create a human ladder for me, because I'm afraid my building-climbing skills are a little below par just at the moment."

"Not necessary," I said, withdrawing my hero device, thinking of the stunner, pointing it at Harry and pressing the button.

Harry went completely still, his face frozen into an expression of shock, his the eyes the only things moving, looking at me as though I had lost my mind. The look was very similar to the one Peter had warn when James had used his solid-outliner on Natalie. I used the stunner to firstly direct Harry out from under the balcony and then, in the same manner I had lifted Rebecca out of the play tube, levitated him into the air and up onto the balcony. As I released him from the hold, I called, "That'll teach you to have a smart mouth on the job."

"Thank you, dear sir. Remind me to bow before you at the church of the great and almighty John next Sunday."

"Is that some kind of toilet?" Peter asked.

"I sincerely hope so," one of the twins responded.

"If those two are up there, who's gonna guard down here?" James asked, swiftly returning our attention to the issue at hand.

On that score, nobody wanted to be the one, so James said, "Perhaps you, Felicity?"

She scowled, but nodded.

"I guess I'll help," Darcy said a little resentfully, "but you guys had better do your darndest to make sure Hall doesn't get anywhere near—"

His words were cut off by a muffled sound that could only be an explosion. It sounded like it had come from inside the building. The sound that accompanied it was much worse: the unmistakable sound of a scream—a female scream—Amelia.

"Let's get in there," said Natalie without preamble.

There was no wasting time. Erica opened the door and slipped through, leaving a narrow gap for the rest of us. One by one, we all slipped through the door, trying to open it as little as possible. The invisible Honnie brought up the rear, closing it behind her and leaving Darcy and Felicity on the outside, watching us anxiously through the window. I waved once at both of them before turning to face the others, all huddled together in the foyer.

"What now?" Rebecca whispered.

"We have to find Amelia," I said, almost certain that it was she who had screamed. If she, Marc and Hall were the only ones left in here, surely it had to be her, because neither of the guys could have made a sound that high-pitched. "May, where's Amelia?"

"On the second floor," May said promptly. What she added only to me, so I thought anyway, was that Marc's current location was on the bottom floor along with us. The entrance to the Hammerheart Highway was located in the same room as the entrance to the tunnels beneath the school, which meant that Katie and Sophie were probably not too far from him. It also meant that if Hall had cornered Amelia, she could be in a lot of trouble, because nobody would be coming to her aid.

Without a word, Erica and James (who had somehow ended up in the lead of this group) took off for the corridor to the right of the main desk. The first door we passed on our left led behind the desk, the second looked upon a kitchen of some sort, and the third opened onto a set of stairs leading upward. We climbed them, now beginning to hear the sounds of magical battle.

I saw James stop Erica at the top of the stairs, looking around cautiously. Both of them were smart enough to know that our best chance of succeeding here was to surprise both Hall and Amelia in battle. Under cover of their contemplation, I reached behind me and, feeling that May was indeed there, said, "Do they see each other?"

"She does not see him," May said, "and she does not know if he sees her."

"And they haven't tried to reveal each other?" Peter asked, surprised.

"They probably have, but haven't been able to," said Lena.

"Can you find his mind, May?" Natalie asked.

"I think I can," said May, but she sounded uneasy. "I can feel that there is a strange mind here, but I cannot take it. I do not know why."

"Probably the magic of the thing," I suggested. "Hall wouldn't know about Honnies, but what he's done has made him so secure that it's had an impact all the same. So, what now? Do we stand on these stairs all day waiting for them to come down?"

"I suggest we flush the place out with revealing magic," said Erica from the top of the stairs.

"But that'll expose us as well."

"Not if we wait outside where they are and only flush inward."

"Erica, Amelia's under the same veil. If we expose her, we'll expose ourselves too, not to mention the guys we left on the outside."

"Bugger."

"It may still be the best option, though," said James seriously. "I know it will expose us, and the guys on the outside, and it may make Hall even more dangerous, but it'll also make it a lot easier to pin him down."

"Let's be practical here," said Lena. "We know that nothing really bad can happen to Amelia because she's a Sorcerer, and we know that Hall is mortal even though he has magic. If we flood the place with magic that disables whoever it hits, it'll do much worse to him than it will to her."

"What magic is that, though?" Peter asked. "We only have these things that Marc gave us. Natalie can't do it because her magic is disabled."

Lena swore under her breath. "Fine, solid-outliners then; that'll make them visible as well as unable to fight."

No one had any objections to that, so at long last, we climbed the rest of the way up the stairs and onto the second level of the administration building. The eight of us huddled together on the landing, looking around and listening for noises. This part of the school was familiar to me from the one and only time I had ever been on the second level of the administration building: We had entered the school via the balcony on which Harry and Simon were guarding, before descending the stairs we had just climbed and then moving around to enter the tunnels to access the rest of the school. So far as I knew, the upper level of this building contained only offices—formerly those of the principal and company, now of those most important Hammerhearts who worked here regularly.

Now that none of us were moving, it was clear from which direction the sounds of magical battle were coming. There was no dialogue but there were a host of other sounds, most of which I couldn't identify. The only one that was clear was the sound of footsteps as Hall and Amelia continually shifted their footing. The battle seemed to be coming from our left, in the direction of the balcony, though not that far down the hallway. The eight of us headed in that direction, now creeping along lest Hall hear something and deduce that he was no longer alone. After that, it was a simple case of following a short trail of destruction. The biggest identifier was the large piece of wall which had been blown outward into the hallway. The result, once you got past the debris, was an expanded doorway, through which we saw everything in vivid detail. Well, not quite everything—everything except the man responsible for most of the damage.

What had formerly been an office of relative grandeur had been utterly trashed. The desk had been overturned, everything on it spilling out over the floor, most of it in many pieces. The window behind it had been blown out and the curtains on either side had been torn off, fragments of cloth strewn around the office. They paled into insignificance, though, in comparison to the amount of shredded paper covering every surface like a thin layer of snow. The computer had been caved in, the screen smashed, leaving broken glass littered on the floor nearby, and the keyboard no longer had any keys in it— they were also strewn around the floor. Then, of course, there was the blood; not really a lot (I'd seen plenty more blood in my time) but it was impossible to do this much damage without spilling a bit of blood in the process.

And in the midst of it all, the battle continued. Amelia, clearly visible to us, though apparently not to Hall, was darting from side to side along the right-hand wall, her feet barely touching the floor as she went, deflecting, reflecting and performing her own magic all the while. It looked as though she were almost levitating; her toes barely disturbed the debris, which meant she wasn't giving her position away. If Hall still hadn't pinned her down after all this time, it was probably working, but I was prepared to bet that he was doing exactly the same thing.

Amelia was so concentrated on what she was doing that she hadn't even noticed the eight of us (seven to her, since she wouldn't have seen May even if she had looked around) standing in the newly expanded doorway. I didn't dare call out to her, though; if she looked around at us, not only would it distract her sufficiently for Hall to take her down (probably) but it would most definitely alert him to our presence before we could initiate a surprise attack on him. I therefore stepped in front of the others and turned to face them so that they would look at me rather than one half of the battle before us.

"Solid-outliners," I whispered to them, not daring to speak aloud, "at the left wall, and try not to hit the same places."

I moved out of their line of fire, withdrew my hero device, and waited for the others to do the same. All seven of them were out, all seven of them were raised, but before we could fire them, something Hall did seemed to force Amelia into the far back corner of the office. She had to turn around to manage it without tripping, and that was when she saw us. Her eyes widened in surprise and what was probably cautious relief before something else came flying across the room and, just as I feared might happen, hit Amelia dead-on, giving her position away to the enemy immediately.

All seven of us fired at the exact moment when Amelia screamed, and someone (who could say whom) actually hit something in the air. It began to spread, showing that whatever it was seemed to be long and round—like a human arm. Not knowing who had been successful, all seven of us fired again, now aiming around the place where we knew Hall to be. It almost worked—we managed to take him down in at least one other place—but either he knew how to remove thicky prison with his magic, or he had a solid-outliner in his pocket, because all of it suddenly vanished.

Before we could launch a third attack, the magic of the Villain Crystal came raining down upon us. More screams shattered the air as we were all thrown backward into the corridor beyond. I hit my head hard on the opposite wall and slid down it, seeing stars and temporarily forgetting where I was. I was grateful a moment later when my thoughts suddenly cleared and I felt much better, thankful because I felt sure that

May had done that for me. The good feeling was immediately dispelled when I saw her standing exactly where we had been before, because I knew what it must mean. If May was visible to us, then all eight of us were now visible to Hall. In fact, make that all of us were now visible to everyone; our protection had been neutralised. Even worse than that, Amelia had sunk to her knees in the corner of the office, her head in her hands, and she seemed not to be moving at all. What had Hall done to her? She didn't look hurt, exactly, but apparently all the fight had been taken out of her.

I scrambled back to my feet as on either side of me, the others did the same. No magic came at us in that time, and I assumed it was probably because Hall was quite as gobsmacked by May's sudden appearance as those Hammerhearts out by the playground had been. She, meanwhile, was rooted to the spot, staring straight ahead and screwing up her face in a way that made her look totally alien. If she was trying again to take hold of his mind, now that she was so close, it still seemed not to be working, but apparently she was picking up enough to know where in the office he was.

She stepped very deliberately over the nearest rubble and to the left, towards where we had initially aimed our hero devices, but that was as far as she got. Her movement seemed to break Hall's paralysis and a moment later, the magic began again. This time, it seemed to be just another Hammerheart device instead of the Villain Crystal though; a jet of pure-white thicky prison came shooting out of nowhere and hit May straight to the chest. Even a Honnie couldn't stand up to this kind of magic, but May still didn't let it slow her down; she threw herself forward in a terrifying bound, hitting something which we couldn't see and driving it against the wall with enough force to cause cracks to spread from the point of impact.

I hoped very much that the battle had been won then and there, but for whatever reason, despite the force of the blow, Hall still seemed to be unhurt, and May couldn't seem to get hold of him, even though she could very well have been on top of him for all we knew. Worse, the thicky prison now wrapping itself smartly around her waist couldn't get hold of him either. The only good thing about all of this was that it gave the rest of us time to gather ourselves and decide what the plan was.

Peter, James and I raised our hero devices, and Erica and Rebecca flanked us as we moved forward. They were probably still thinking of solid-outliners, which was good because we needed to free May from her binds before she became defenceless, but my thoughts were on Hall. It was imperative that we flush him into visibility immediately; there was no way we could win this battle if we couldn't see him. While this was happening, Natalie and Lena scurried down the opposite wall to where Amelia still knelt, oblivious to the commotion around her, and were either trying to assist or protect her.

Before any of us could fire, however, May screamed as for the second time that day, she was taken to with a bludginator. It caused her to fall back and as she scrambled to her feet, she was unable to stop her own momentum in time. She collided with the window frame behind her and before any of us could prevent it, she fell out of the window and disappeared from view.

"Holy crap," said Peter, rather pointlessly I thought, but there was no time for any of us to point that out to him.

Hall was immediately back on his feet and the five of us were forced to duck as a line of what looked like horizontal lightning came shooting across the room toward us. It even felt like lightning too, given that all my hair stood on end as it passed over.

I straightened up, thought of the invisibility toggle, and fired three times in rapid succession, not bothering to reposition the hero device each time, as that had already been proven not to work. Just as I had hoped, as Hall dodged and weaved to avoid being exposed, he unwittingly placed himself directly in the path of the third jet of semi-transparent light. That was all that the others needed; jets of multi-coloured light shot directly at the place where we knew Hall to be. One of them was the unmistakable golden light of the agonator and I had to wonder who was mad enough to use that now.

It mattered not, for all of them other than the thicky prison had absolutely no effect on him. He smiled knowingly at us (he also looked entirely unhurt in the moment I took to look), shot himself with his own solid-outliner, thereby unbinding himself, and then disappeared into invisibility once again. Peter swore at the top of his voice.

"I'm gonna kill him!" he bellowed, raising his hero device and beginning to sweep it sideways just as I had done with mine when we had first entered the grounds. Before he could get all the way across, however, a second jet of golden light came from Hall's direction and hit Peter squarely in the face. He went down immediately, his legs flailing out and tripping Rebecca at the same time.

Once again, I found myself trying to think when there was hardly any time or room for such a thing. Okay, so Hall most definitely had the Villain Crystal, and he was most certainly protected by more than just invisibility. He also seemed to be wearing some sort of invisible shield, for all the magic that should have brought him down had so far failed. It protected him from physical assaults as well as magical ones, since May had been unable to use her great strength against him, and to top it off, though it hardly mattered, he was probably under a soundproof barrier too, as I felt sure he would be taunting us if we could only hear him. And, of course, he was untraceable, which didn't really matter to us, except that if anything, that was probably the thing protecting him from May's mind.

And speaking of May: The Honnie suddenly reappeared in the window, apparently having jumped all the way up from the ground so that she could rejoin the battle. She was no longer bound by thicky prison, but she was bleeding again, I saw, and she also looked mad enough to kill with her bare hands, as she had already done twice today. Before she could get all the way in, however, Hall decided to pull a trick beyond anything he had tried so far. Just about all the light in the room suddenly disappeared as the window vanished, replaced by solid wall. As May began to push against it from the other side, as she could probably have broken right through it if given enough time, a layer of reinforced steel appeared all the way along it, pushing it back into place and, judging by the screaming of anguish from the other side, knocking May off and sending her back to the ground a storey below.

This had to end—this was way out of control. I didn't bother taking aim this time—I just sent jets of revealing light in every direction, trying desperately to think of a way of breaking through Hall's shield. Surely it could be done; for if not, how had I been able to reveal him in the first place? It worked too, and as soon as I saw him, I switched to the killing device and fired without any hesitation at all. Whether or not Hall died in here was beside the point, considering that this thing wouldn't kill him anyway; the most important thing was to disable him long enough to wrest him of the Villain Crystal —that was, after all, the point of this mission.

Unfortunately, he moved too quickly, and the magic that should have rendered him virtually dead missed and struck the newly created steel wall behind him. He wasn't quick enough to get out of the way of yet another jet of thicky prison, though, this time from Erica. The jet hit him straight to the face, but Erica didn't stop there; she kept firing, peppering him with magic, and Rebecca, James and I soon joined her in the attack. Hall was able to remove the thicky prison from his face but this time, he was unable to prevent it from wrapping around his arms and binding them to his sides, thereby making it impossible to point his solid-outliner. It was only then that I understood why the thicky prison was working at all: It was wrapping around the outside of his shield, which seemed to bind itself to his body the same way that thicky prison did, although without immobilising at the same time.

Hall soon lost his balance and toppled over, now almost completely immobilised. James stalked him into the corner as he tried to get out of range, perhaps to hide himself long enough to recover, and shot him one last time so that he became completely immobile. Rebecca and Erica hurried over to the other corner where Natalie and Lena were still huddled around Amelia, leaving me to deal with my brother. Peter was still under the influence of the agonator, although his cries were now horse as his consciousness waned. There was no way to free him without the use of the agonator which had done this to him, and there was no way to get at it without releasing Hall. I had only one option: I pointed my hero device at him, thought of the virtual killing device, and pressed the button. Immediately, Peter went limp as his life was whisked away from his body—for the time being anyway.

"John, what have you done to him?" Rebecca shrieked into the sudden silence which followed.

"I couldn't release him," I told her, approaching where the girls were huddled, "like I couldn't release you either. He'll be okay—we can bring him around once we've sorted Hall out. Amelia, are you okay?"

Amelia didn't answer; she didn't even give any sign that she had heard me.

"I don't think she is," said Lena in barely more than a whisper. "I don't know what's wrong with her but I know that she sees and hears us—she's just not talking or doing anything."

My brain jammed at these words. We needed someone with magic to deal with Hall, to bind him in other ways to prevent him using the Villain Crystal again before we could remove it from his possession. If Amelia couldn't do it, and Natalie couldn't do it, what came next?

"Do we have gloves for handling thicky prison?" James enquired, joining us around Amelia.

We didn't, of course; we had never imagined we would need them.

"Geez," said Erica in a low moan, looking at the prone figure of our former English teacher. "What are we supposed to do with him?"

I opened my mouth, about to bellow at the top of my voice for Marc to come up here, wherever he was now, fairly sure that he would hear me if I yelled loudly enough (and never mind the original plan not to abandon posts) but before I could make a sound, I was distracted by another noise coming from the direction of the stairs. I wheeled around, raising my hero device, ready for another attack, but it was only May returning to the battle area. Thank God, I thought, not that she could help us much with Hall.

"May, we need help with Amelia," Natalie said at once, getting to her feet. "Something's wrong with her. Can you tell what's going on?"

May stopped in front of us, looking down at Amelia with an expression of alien concentration on her face. She was bleeding afresh, I noticed, and the sight of more of that purple blood made me almost retch on the spot. Finally, she said, "Her memory is gone."

"What?" said James, horrified. "What do you mean?"

"She does not remember anything," May said, looking around at the rest of us now. "She does not recognise you, or remember anything about herself. She cannot even remember how to talk."

"So how do we fix that?" asked Natalie, panic beginning to set in. "Surely there must just be something blocking her memory—"

May shook her head. "I do not think so. Her mind is working fine; it is just empty now."

I stared from one horrified face to the next, imagining that my expression was just the same as theirs. I weighed up our options and came to the conclusion that a bit of magic on our side now was our only chance of getting out of this situation. I opened my mouth a second time to call to Marc, but once again, before I could get a sound out, I was interrupted. This time, it was Hall suddenly coming back to life that did the trick. The thicky prison that had been binding him suddenly vanished, and he sprang to his feet without a moment of hesitation.

We all wheeled back around to face him, raising our hero devices in the process, but apparently Hall was done playing games. The expression of livid fury on his face was almost scary to look at, not that I saw it for very long. A few of us managed to get off a shot or two, but none of them connected with him. He simply stepped to the side, then back into his original position, and then sent a positive avalanche of evil magic down upon us.

What came next was difficult to describe, even within my own mind. Something soft and invisible pushed hard against us, pushing all of us hard against the wall behind us. It muffled my sense of sound but not entirely—I was still barely able to hear several of the others crying and choking on whatever it was. It forced my head back so that it hit the wall behind me and made it impossible to see much other than the ceiling. I reached out to either side (an action that took just about every ounce of my strength) and managed to link my right arm with Natalie's left, and take hold of James's right arm with my left hand. Rolling my eyes to either side, I saw that every one of us, including May, incredible as it was, had been forced back against the wall. On Natalie's other side, Lena stood rigid before the wall, trying desperately to raise her hero device to attack again but unable to lift her hand. Amelia was being pushed hard against Lena's legs, but whatever was doing the pushing was also preventing them from falling over. The same was happening on my other side with the unconscious form of Peter being forced against Rebecca, Erica and May's legs.

My hero device was still in my right hand and it was miraculously still pointing outward from whatever force was doing this to us. I thought of the bludginator, thinking that perhaps it could cut a hole in whatever this thing was and release the pressure, but it had no effect at all. Meanwhile, the force continued pushing harder and harder against us, not in a way that could crush but seeming to isolate each of us on the spot. My link with Natalie was still fairly strong but James was being forced further and further away, and my hand was becoming slick with sweat as I tried desperately to resist Hall's power.

It was no good. Hall brought his bludginator down, cutting my left arm and causing my fingers to involuntarily slip away from James. I made one last grab for him, ignoring the flare of pain, but the action had caused him and the four on his other side to be forced further away from me. Then, because I was still forced to look up, and because he was at least half a foot taller than me, Hall's face suddenly filled my field of vision. He no longer looked livid with fury; he was, in fact, smiling gleefully at Natalie and me, the two of us still linked together and, for whatever reason, his chosen targets.

"You are under arrest," he said in a quiet but carrying voice, apparently having dropped his soundproof barrier just for the purpose of delivering this line at the best possible time, "for breaking and entering, trespass, arson, damage to property, attacking an officer of the law, and at least twenty counts of murder."

He raised his hand, a hand that was empty of any Hammerheart devices or the Villain Crystal, and immediately, something much more solid closed around Natalie and me, releasing us from the terrible pressure of whatever had been pushing against the wall but subjecting us to something even worse. The two of us were enclosed in what my poor, tortured brain could only conceive of as some sort of mini dome, similar to the thing that was still surrounding the school grounds. It simultaneously pushed us away from the wall behind us and lifted us from the ground. Then, it contracted horribly, forcing Natalie and I against each other with such brutality that broken bones seemed all but certain. I let go of her arm as quickly as I could and threw it around her body instead, not necessarily to protect her but to hopefully protect both of us—to minimise the risk of either of us breaking an arm. Understanding what I was doing, she did the same to me.

"What are you doing?!" Erica shrieked. Looking around, something much easier to do despite the thing trying to squash me to death, I saw that all the others were still struggling with Hall's original magic. Their faces were contorted by the pressure of the thing. Even May couldn't resist it; I would never forget the sight of her furious face, practically spitting with rage at the man responsible.

"Taking them into custody, as is my duty," said Hall in an icy voice, "and I shall return for the rest of you later. Now—"

And before I could even begin to wonder what came next, the office around us exploded. Everything was suddenly black, white and orange as the building around us ignited. The floor beneath Hall gave way immediately and he allowed himself to go with it, his magic causing Natalie and me to be pulled irresistibly down with him. We sank down to the bottom level where Hall set off another loud *bang*, and through the whirling dust and debris, I clearly saw a horrified-looking Marc go flying across the room, revealing the closed door which he had been dutifully guarding. Hall made for it, but...

"Stop!"

That was James's voice coming from somewhere above where we were now. The explosion had somehow shattered whatever magic Hall had been performing before, and though the others were surely too hurt to fight, they were nevertheless giving chase. Hall gave one contemptuous look over his shoulder before causing a second explosion, and this one was met with accompanying screams from above. Not bothering to see the results of his destruction, and not giving Marc a chance to regroup, he hurried through the door ahead of him, dragging Natalie and me along with him, slamming the door behind him and covering it with a thick layer of stone, thereby eliminating any chance of the others giving further chase. If we hadn't been in enemy territory before, we sure were now, and I felt certain about where Hall intended to take us.

It was 10:16 on the morning of August 23, 2010.

Chapter 35: In the Cell

The station that had been set up for Chopville High was larger than the portals in and out of residences (those were nothing more than a gap in the wall with a button to call the carts, and either a slide or stairs leading up to the home) but was considerably smaller than the great hubs of the Hammerheart bases. The two that I had seen had been enormous, with at least fifty tracks leading in and out of them and a bridge over all of them to give the Hammerhearts access to the ones in the middle. This station had only three tracks leading in and out, but otherwise the setup was much the same.

The door through which Hall had taken us came out on the bridge, and without wasting any time, he hurried down the nearest set of stairs and pounded the button to call a cart as he passed it. He was forced to stop and wait then, his eyes on the door he had just turned into a stone wall, waiting to see if Marc would blast it apart or return it to how it had been before. It probably seemed like a long wait for him, but as far as I was concerned, a cart stopped in front of him all too quickly. He forced Natalie and me inside first, the invisible binds holding us forcing us even more tightly together so that there would be room for the three of us inside the confined space.

Within seconds, we had arrived at our destination, although for whatever reason, I hadn't felt the usual jerk caused by the cart's rapid movement from one location to another. It was a Hammerheart base, of course, and given that we had arrived so quickly, I assumed it was the one I knew all too well. Hall got out of the cart and gave the thing holding us time to follow him out before pushing the button to send the cart on its way. He then turned and, without looking at us, climbed the stairs and hurried towards the entrance to the base. A few Hammerhearts passed him as he made for the stairwell, all unfamiliar to me and all staring curiously at Natalie and me as we floated irresistibly along behind the Police Commissioner.

"Sir, what's happening?" one man asked him as he arrived on the level below the Hammerheart Highway, and my suspicions were confirmed.

"They've attacked the school base, and the bloody bastards made a good show of it. You'd better report to 2C7—in fact, report to 1H3 first; never mind the chain of command."

"But sir—"

"Tell him I have captured H3 and one of the Sorcerers; he'll listen to whatever you say after that."

Hall didn't waste any more time conversing but turned and strode into the Basement, passing the three men standing guard without a word and proceeding into the rows of cells. To my dismay, he didn't just put us in the first cell, but seemed to wind his way in and out of aisles at random, and perhaps it was random for all I knew, but I could think of a very good reason why he would do that—he was beyond taking chances. He stopped, looked at the numbers on the door, then opened it with his magic and directed the two of us inside.

The moment the door slammed shut behind us and the lock clicked home, the thing that had been forcing the two of us together for the last minute (it had probably only been about a minute, though it had felt longer) suddenly disappeared, causing the two of us to fall to the floor in a heap. I quickly staggered upright in the absolute darkness, feeling Natalie doing the same beside me, though more slowly. My body was aching in many places from what it had endured but fortunately, nothing seemed to be seriously damaged. Even more fortunately, I still had my hero device, which had been clenched in my right fist when Hall had attacked and had remained locked in there throughout. Unclenching that fist was exceedingly painful but I eventually managed to get a firmer hold on my hero device.

Which was all well and good, except that I couldn't think of anything I could use to break out of this cell. The others would eventually come for us, I knew, but how long would it take them to get here? Furthermore, how long would it take them to sort out the mess we had left behind at the school? They would have to do something about it because they were all so scattered. Thank God they still had Marc and Fewul, but Amelia...

That thought stopped me cold. Hall had done something very bad to her—very bad indeed. Maybe she could be recovered somehow—maybe—but essentially, the Amelia I had known and loved (in my own way) was gone forever. Everything that had been encapsulated within her brain had been what made her who she was. The fact that she would still have the same body, however attractive that body was, would not make her the same person. Even if her brain could somehow be refilled with knowledge and memories that would allow her to function as a regular human being, she still wouldn't be the same person. She hadn't been killed; she had been deleted, more like an old file on a computer than anything else, and her physical body was nothing but the empty disc space where Amelia Woodward had once lived. The only glimmer of hope was that unless the disc space in question had been smashed to pieces (which in this case, it hadn't), there were ways of recovering deleted files.

I was distracted at this point by a small noise coming from my right. Natalie seemed to be on her feet at last and was getting the sense of where we were. It was her second time in a Basement cell, but I wasn't sure if she remembered too much of the first time, after what she had been put through immediately prior to it. I reached out in the darkness, had to move my hand around a few times, but eventually managed to locate her forearm.

"What happened?" she asked in little more than a squeak. "Where are we?"

"The Basement, in the Chopville Base, I'm pretty sure," I said, picking a direction at random and leading her forward.

In my experiences of this place, it was always best to orientate yourself with a wall, never mind which one, because standing alone in the darkness with nothing within arm's reach was a great way to create panic. It only took me a few seconds to find a wall; I pushed Natalie gently against it and leaned back beside her, thinking that the door was probably along the wall to my left now, although I had no way to know for sure unless I bothered to check. I didn't think it mattered; I would hear footsteps out there if anyone was coming, and I still hadn't thought of any way to use my hero device to engineer an escape, something that I absolutely had to do before either Hall or Hammerson returned. Other Hammerhearts weren't as much of a threat, since I essentially had the same weaponry as them, but the ones with the crystals could easily kill me and, perhaps, kill Natalie too, because what had happened to Amelia was about the same as death when you got right down to it. The body kept on living, but the person was gone for good.

"Oh no," she moaned, beginning to snap her fingers reflexively, as though hoping her magic would somehow return to her on its own. "Oh no—oh no—oh—"

"Don't panic," I said hurriedly, trying desperately to think. It was also essential that we both keep our cool. We needed to think and think fast, and that just wouldn't work if Natalie went into panic mode.

"But they're gonna do awful things to us, and we can't get out, and I can't even see a goddamned thing—"

"Calm down," I said, trying to make my voice as calm and smooth as I possibly could. What came out was an absolutely bloody awful imitation of Barry White (my voice, although broken, wasn't anywhere near deep enough to pass for that). "There may be ways to sort this out, but you have to keep your head."

"Ways? What ways? I can't use my magic, and that's the only way you could get out of here last time."

"We have these things," I said, indicating my hero device and then remembering that she couldn't see it. I switched it to my left hand and put my right arm around her shoulders, hoping that might calm her down a little—and because I'd wanted to do that for a long time.

My mind was too preoccupied to really enjoy the moment, however, as it focussed on the hero device. Now that I had a chance to stop and think about it, I realised that we had all been incredibly stupid about the way we had been using them. It stood to reason that they could do just about anything that all the Hammerhearts had created weapons for, and a bunch of things they hadn't even thought of, because Marc, Lucien and Stella were all pretty creative in their own right. I had thought that these devices were strictly offensive, but if they had the power to make us invisible, didn't they also have the power to put shields around us? I had no idea if such devices had ever been created, but in the heat of the battle, I had assumed those kinds of magic couldn't be done.

So, how to break out of this cell.... The first thing to do was give us a light. I had no idea if this would work, but I imagined a dim light, without a direct source, filling the cell at the click of the button, and pressed it. It didn't work, so I omitted the second part and just imagined the light. That didn't work either, so I imagined a small ball of light springing from the device itself and hovering above our heads, lighting the room. This time it worked, but instead of hovering in the centre of the room, as I had expected, it had remained directly over my head, lighting everything closest to my position but casting a lot of the room into shadows. It was enough to see that I had been right; the door was set into the wall to my left.

That was great, but my mind had already moved several steps ahead. It was important to our chances of survival that should anyone come before either of us had thought of a way to get out, they must not know that Natalie and I were armed. Hall would have told the other Hammerhearts that Natalie wasn't fighting with magic, which probably meant that it had been stripped from her, and the only reason he hadn't taken my device was probably because he thought I'd dropped it in his final attack. All the same, they would proceed with less caution if they thought we were unarmed, and that gave us our best chance. That meant I would have to put the light out before anyone entered, and also meant that we couldn't make ourselves invisible and hope that they would think we were in another cell. Whoever came to see us wouldn't be that stupid; they would flush us out and then remove our weapons for sure.

And then what? Well, what came next would depend on who came to see us. If it was Hall or Hammerson, we would have to launch our attacks immediately and hope that they worked, because they wouldn't give us any chances once they were in the cell with us. If it was anyone else, we could afford to let them in and let down their guard, assuming they entered at all and didn't try to drag us out in the corridor. If it was the latter, we could probably do the same, because these devices might just be powerful enough to let us out of their cages, or at least control them.

For the second time, I was distracted from my train of thought by Natalie. This time it was her letting out a gusty sigh of cautious relief.

"Okay, that's a little better," she said, but there was still an edge of panic in her voice, and the light was only temporarily delaying it, "but we still need a way out."

"I'm trying to think," I told her, "but so far, I think our best chance is to wait for someone to come. I'm gonna have to turn the light out though; is that okay?"

"What? Why?"

I leaned forward and whispered directly into her ear, "Because I don't want them to know that we're armed."

I was probably wasting my effort. If anyone was watching through the security camera, they would have already seen enough to assume that we were carrying something magical. She sighed reluctantly. "Okay, fine, but don't you dare move away from me."

That suited me just fine. I clicked the device again, wondering if I had to think anything else, but the light simply zoomed back to where it came from, leaving us in complete darkness once again.

"Now what?" Natalie asked, and her voice was trembling. After the rollercoaster ride of the last hour and a quarter or however long it had been, her nerves were just about shot. That wasn't good because this day was far from over.

"Don't worry," I told her. "Remember, last time we were in here, we were rescued in short order. There's no reason why

Marc wouldn't send Fewul down here to do that again, assuming he's not too busy up at the school to do it himself. Don't worry about us, and don't worry about the others; things are never as hopeless as what they seem."

And I honestly believed that in many ways. The only exception was Amelia; that really was hopeless, but I couldn't afford to dwell on what had already happened—there was too much at stake. I added, "In the meantime, I'm trying to think of some way we can help ourselves out of this mess."

"I hope you can, because the rest of it sounds like bullshit."

"Well, try to believe it anyway. Trust me, I've been through this before; positivity is the only way to stop yourself going nuts in a place like this."

"Okay," she said, and I felt her shift beside me. I thought then that she might actually be able to do it, and felt a glimmer of hope for both of us, but that was when, with the worst possible timing, a flood of icy water suddenly came down on top of us. It only lasted for a few seconds, and when it was gone, it was as though it had never been (just as I remembered), but it was the first time, I supposed, that Natalie had been subjected to the random magical events the Basement threw up to make the stay as unpleasant as possible for its occupants.

And when it was over, it had taken with it what little had remained of Natalie's calm. She began to scream then, the sound terrifying in the darkness, and before I could stop her, she launched herself away from me into the depths of the cell. The cell wasn't very big, of course, but it was bigger than the cells the Woodwards had had in their prison block back in the day, and no doubt bigger than normal prison cells too. This one seemed even bigger than it really was when you took the complete darkness into account, and being alone in it, as Natalie now was, only made things ever so much worse.

I heard her collide with the opposite wall just as I myself took off after her, my mind now blank of all thoughts except to calm her down before her panic infected me too. Although it was hard to be sure, I thought she was now banging on the opposite wall as though—well, she wasn't hoping for anything in particular. That was the whole point; she had passed out of the realm of rationality. I threw my arms out just as I had approached the dome earlier that morning, waiting for the moment when I came into contact with the opposite wall.

In fact, I found Natalie before I found the wall; my right shoulder bumped her a moment before my outstretched hands slammed into the cool stone. I turned around, feeling for her in the darkness, and eventually got my hand squashed against the wall as she hit it again.

"Natalie," I gasped, barely hearing my own voice over her continuous shrieks to be let out of this cell (I mean *really* continuous; no noticeable pause, even for breath).

I managed to take hold of her shoulders in the darkness, turn her around and pull her into a tight hug. It was the only thing I could think to do, just as I had needed to do the same for Amelia that day in her old bedroom, but this was even more important than that had been for two reasons I could think of. Mostly, I needed her to be calm just for our own chances of getting through this, but also, it had been agonising to hear Natalie fall apart like that, when all this time she had done so admirably well to keep it all together. Anyway, I owed it to her to help her through this now after she had helped me through the aftermath of our entrance into the school earlier.

I was forcefully reminded of Amelia, not without a pang, and the way she had dealt with her crazy in the aftermath of this place. Instead of letting it all out quickly, she had allowed it to fester for over a month until she had unravelled, and had probably not pulled it all the way together again until very recently. This was probably better if it meant that Natalie could deal with our current crisis, and whatever other crazy had built up inside her over the last few months really could be dealt with later—I had every intention of making sure that happened.

And of course, with that thought came the one that would have occurred right away in any less dangerous situation: This was the closest I had probably ever been to Natalie. We had hugged on numerous occasions (especially lately) and she had curled up and dozed off beside me at least twice during our most recent quest, but on none of those occasions could I remember feeling as much of her body against mine as I could right now. My arms were tightly around her and in response, she had thrown hers around me. She had quieted considerably in the twenty-or-so seconds we had stood like this (how it had felt longer to my exquisitely attuned nerves) but she was still making hoarse, sobbing noises every few seconds.

I didn't trust myself to speak, knowing that the only words I could have spoken would have been even more meaningless than the positivity crap I had spouted earlier, as if Natalie wouldn't see right through that. Instead, I just held her, waiting for her to calm down, wanting her to be calm and at the same time not wanting it, knowing it would mean I would have to let go of her.

The rational part of me knew that had to be for the best, because this was an exceedingly inappropriate time to be turned on. Natalie was very vulnerable at the moment, just as Amelia had been on that other inappropriate occasion when I had kissed her, and if I were to give into just one urge right now, whether it be to touch her hair, rub her back or just about anything else, it would only bring on more urges. I had only been with three different girls (not counting Amelia this time) but it was enough for me to understand that urges which were in any way sexual were like train carriages; they were all connected and when you pulled one, the whole train would roll forward, and when you stopped pulling, the weight of the carriages behind would push against the ones in front until all the blockades came tumbling down.

Fortunately, or not, I was interrupted from this train of thought (gotta stop with the train analogies) by Natalie speaking for the first time since her outburst.

"Sorry," she wept, "it's just"—she seemed to choke for a moment—"I don't know if I can do this."

Now that was ridiculous, I thought, but didn't dare say, particularly while I was still this close to her; she was showing no sign of wanting to step back. Instead, I said, "I think you can. I know this probably feels like the most defenceless you've ever been, but remember, even while we're stuck in here, there's plenty going on out there. Even if we can't find a way out ourselves, someone will come."

"What if they come too late?" she said in a small voice, and my insides chilled at the thought. It may only have been an excuse, a rationality perhaps, but it could also have been the truth: She was more worried for me than she was for herself.

"Then, I guess we just have to hang in there as long as we can," I said as confidently as I could, and I actually felt myself smiling. After all, I had practise when it came to 'hanging in there'.

"Ahuh," she said, her voice conveying nothing but resignation so far as I could tell, but then something in her seemed to change. She didn't say anything but she went very still in my arms, as though every part of her—mind and body alike—had been put on pause. I felt myself go just as still in response, my breath stopping in my chest so that the cell became as silent as it was dark.

The moment held for an unknowable period of time (probably no more than ten seconds, although it felt magnified) before, very slowly, Natalie straightened up and moved very slightly back from me. The feeling of loss was so deep that I had to immediately clamp down on my reaction so that I wouldn't give it away, but it wasn't as bad as it could have been; she hadn't let go of me, nor had she moved so far back that I had to let go of her. I had a good reason for keeping my hands on her shoulders: I couldn't allow her to lose her mind again.

"Can you put that light on again?" she asked me, and her voice was strange. I couldn't put my finger on what had changed but it was clear that she had reached a point of—of what, exactly? I'd thought resignation a moment ago, but now it sounded like—resolution? I thought so, but I couldn't go along with it.

"I'd rather not, if that's okay. Here…"

I reached out with my left hand, located the wall we had collided with a minute earlier and tried to orientate her with it, but she refused to move her feet.

"Please? Just for a minute? I wanna—I wanna see your face."

Holy shit! I sure as hell hadn't seen that coming, and my mind had clearly jammed up at the realisation of what could possibly be going on here. I wanted to do it—I wanted to put the light back on so that I could see her face too, because I was dying to know what expression it wore just now—but I couldn't forget our current surroundings, much as I wished I could. I gripped her shoulders and shook my head, predictably forgetting that she couldn't see it.

"Sorry," I said, and now my voice sounded strange too, "but remember what I said earlier? Besides, I dunno if I could make that happen again." I squeezed her shoulder to indicate what would have been a wink in any lighter room.

"Well, okay," she said, not sounding very happy, but otherwise that strange tone was still there, "then just listen."

And so I listened, but for several seconds, I heard nothing but utter silence. These Basement cells sure had a way of making you forget that a world existed outside these walls, I thought, and then my attention returned to Natalie as I heard her take a deep breath.

"Do you remember," she said, seeming to be feeling her way in the darkness, "when all this started four months ago, what I said to you that day?"

It was an important question, I knew, but for several precious seconds, I couldn't, for the life of me, work out what she was talking about. I was about to say so when I recalled that brief conversation the two of us had had in the doorway between the corridor and the living quarters in the old Woodward base.

"Er, you mean the one about not taking things for granted?" I said a little lamely, my heart skipping a beat as the possible implications of what she was saying began to sink in.

She made a small noise in response that might have been laughter. "Yeah, that day. You remember it?"

Of course I remembered it—I'd spent a lot of time recalling it in the immediate aftermath, back when I had still been with Serena and was coming to realise that I was walking the wrong path.

"I think so," I said, hedging for what reason I didn't know.

"Right. Well, it was just after I got back from my first real work as a Sorcerer, and it was basically that everything I'd seen out there had put things into better perspective for me. I wasn't going to take things for granted anymore because I didn't want to regret not being open if something bad happened to me, except—"

She seemed to struggle with herself for a moment, while I contended my own internal struggle. If this was going where I thought it might be going, this was sure not the time or the place I had imagined having this conversation. We were still holding onto each other's shoulders and I had no intention of letting go, regardless of what might be about to go down.

"I'm so stupid," she finally said, and now she sounded close to tears. "I'm always stupid—I never learn."

"What?" I said, sideswiped yet again. "You're not stupid."

"Oh really?" she said, her voice becoming a little breathless now, but that was okay if it meant the tears weren't coming. "We've been through so much since April. You've come within a hair of being killed more times than I can even think of, and we all could have been done in by the Honnies; and after all that, even coming into today, I still haven't learnt my lesson. Well, not anymore."

My heart was pounding so hard in my chest that it was making me feel a little dizzy. If I could see, my vision would probably be swimming. If Natalie were still pressed up against my chest, she would probably be able to feel it. Yes, this had to be what I'd thought it was. For reasons Natalie had just intimated, she had decided that now was the time to take the plunge, and by doing so had taken the matter completely out of my hands. The realization had dawned slowly on me as she spoke, and now it brought with it another realization that made my insides churn sickeningly: This could well be my only chance. Even if we did survive this, if I handled myself poorly now after the courage she had just shown, we may never be able to return to a scenario where I could ask her out and she would say yes.

"Okay," I said lamely, wishing devoutly that I were older and more experienced, desperately hoping that I didn't screw this up. "Well, I dunno how long we have before we're interrupted, and I have no idea what'll happen when we are."

All true, and that didn't help the situation one bit.

"I know," she inhaled deeply, "so here it is. I think—I think I'm in love with you."

My system crashed completely. Even though I'd been fairly sure she liked me, confident enough that she would say yes if I asked her out, I had not expected it to come out like that. Not in any fantasy I'd ever had, not even the ones when she had declared her undying love for me, had I imagined her to be so bold. It was so far out of character for her, which emphasized either the depth of her feeling, or her conviction that she wouldn't get another chance to say it (the second seemed more likely). My whole body had frozen at her words, and after at least two seconds of utter internal mayhem, I willed myself back to life. Please, John, I implored myself, if you can only strap on a pair once in your entire life, make it now.

"You—really?" I finally managed to blurt out, unable to get over her use of the word 'love'. If that had been me, although I felt almost certain that I did indeed love her, I probably wouldn't have plunged so far so quickly. It presented me with a problem which I could afford to spend no more than a fraction of a second grappling with: What was I to say to her in response? The truth, if I were to lay it out completely, would humiliate her and thereby blow my chances of closing this deal. If I said I loved her too, not only would it sound fake, it could cause other problems down the track, though I had no idea what they might be, never having spoken those words to a girl before.

"Yeah, really," she said simply, her voice rather less confident now, her grip on my shoulders seeming to weaken and her own shoulders dipping, as though she wished the floor would open up and swallow her. I couldn't have that. There was only one thing for this situation. I screwed up my courage and prepared to take the plunge.

"I think maybe I love you too," I told her, feeling a goofy grin spreading across my face and was immensely glad that she couldn't see it. I was probably blushing too, but any embarrassment was far outweighed by two emotions I hadn't expected. One was a profound relief that the secret I had kept to myself and those closest around me was now exposed. The other was a kind of helplessness, as though I had given Natalie a great deal of power over me. I supposed it was true: Now that she knew how I felt, she could hurt me like no one else ever could, if she chose to. I felt sure she wouldn't, though, given what she had already confessed, and now that I understood the feeling, I appreciated her courage for speaking out first all the more.

"Really?" she squeaked. "You're not just saying that? You'd better not be because if you are—"

"I'm not just saying it," I told her quickly, needing her to understand now that the cat had been let out of the bag. "I have for a long time—well, maybe more so recently—I just never said anything because it never felt right. I guess I've been taking too much for granted too," I added, hoping that would drive it home.

"Oh," she sighed after several heart-stopping seconds of silence. "Oh."

Now what, I found myself thinking? Whose court was the ball in anyway? Did it even matter? We were, after all, in the Hammerheart Basement, our lives still in grave danger whenever the Hammerhearts found enough spare resources to come down here and deal with us. I didn't want to think about that, though, because something still wasn't quite right here and I didn't know what it was. Regardless of whether we got out of here or not, something else still needed to be said or done.

After a few more seconds where the world seemed to be suspended, I decided that for the first time in Natalie's presence, I would cease rationality and revert to my instincts. Once I had, the answer came to me in about a hundredth of a second. I responded to it immediately, letting go of Natalie's shoulders and once again pulling her into an embrace.

It worked. The tension broke immediately as she responded in kind, throwing her arms around me and pressing herself so close that I almost took a step back out of sheer reaction. I resisted, though, all my senses quickly overwhelmed by the closeness, the intimacy and, above all, that I no longer needed to pretend I didn't feel it. Yet it only took me a second for one thought to pierce through the moment, almost ruining it for me: Remember the train analogy. If we got carried away now, who knew how far we would go right here on the Basement floor; a floor which could append nails to its surface at any moment. We had to keep our cool, at least for now, and yet…

"John," she moaned, her mouth quite close to my ear, and it was just about impossible to resist her, "if you mean what you say, you have to kiss me."

"Is that a challenge?" I asked, that goofy grin resurfacing, although in truth, my heart had recommenced its booming thumps from earlier.

I wasn't too worried about going too far now; it was simply the understanding that in the next minute, I could (would) do something I had spent so many hours fantasizing about. It was impossible to forget, too, that of all the temptations that Returnamy from so long ago had thrown at me, Natalie's kiss had been the only one which had claimed me completely. I had a chance that I may never have again, if I were to believe Natalie's great fears, and I was not about to waste it.

"Maybe," she said, and I thought she was grinning too. "Are you game?"

Absolutely I was, but I had to do it carefully. I still didn't want to put a light on (although I still wished I could see her face) but keeping it off meant that we could possibly miss each other when we went in for the kiss. That would be both embarrassing and just funny enough to ruin the moment, and I could not have that. I therefore gently disengaged from her but instead of letting her go, I trailed my hands over her shoulders and gently took hold of her face. There were so many parts of her I would have liked to touch as I felt the soft, smooth texture of her skin, but I had to resist; that was a thought which, fate permitting, I would revisit at a later time.

Funnily enough, we almost missed anyway. My lips initially found the tip of her nose, and there was a desperate moment when we both nearly laughed, but again, I would not allow it. I tilted her head back very slightly, my lips searching for hers and eventually finding them, and what followed was different from anything I had ever experienced or imagined. I had only ever kissed two girls before (Serena, and Amelia on that one forbidden occasion) and those kisses had been either conservative or pretty damn full-on, with tongues going pretty much everywhere and neither of us having a clue how to make it better, in my case because I hadn't known at that stage that anything could be better. In my fantasies about kissing Natalie, I had always imagined it would be more like that, each of us desperate to explore the mouth of the other, but what she and I experienced there in that cell together was a kind of kiss I hadn't even known was possible until then.

How do I describe it? Well, it was a deep kiss, and there was plenty of tongue, but where the goal had once been to slip it in as far as it could go, now it really was more of an exploration than anything else. Later, much later when I finally had time to reflect, I would think that the two tongues had been united in a mission to be utterly familiar with both mouths. I would never have imagined that tracing my tongue along the tips of Natalie's lower front teeth would be the most sensual experience of my short nearly fifteen years, but at that point, it certainly was. And that wasn't even the full extent of it; now that our mouths were connected, that left my hands free to roam. I slid one arm around her slender waist, pulling her against me for the third time while seeking her hair with my other hand, twirling my fingers through it as I had wanted to do for so very long now. One of her hands was running through my hair too, and the sensation of her fingers on my scalp was so electric that it felt almost orgasmic.

But that was the full extent of it. Who could say how long the kiss went for but eventually, we came up for air. My hand left her hair and settled around her shoulders instead, maintaining the connection while we both tried to get our breath back. I felt more exhilarated than I had in my entire life. I would never forget all that had come before this moment: Tulip as the first, the one with whom I had learnt that when it came down to it, my instincts were all I really needed; Lena, who by sheer virtue of her extraordinarily hot body, as well as the forbidden nature of the occasion, had provided the best sex I had ever had; Serena, whose adventurous streak had made my time with her very exciting, not to mention the feeling of solidarity that came with having a proper girlfriend; Amelia, whose connection had been far more emotional than physical, although I had seen her naked once and learnt, the fun way, that she was an awesome kisser. Sadly for Amelia, her kiss had been thoroughly eclipsed by this experience. I had never been sure until recently that I would ever get to share such a moment with Natalie, but I supposed it had always been inevitable that, if the time came, it would surpass all else. Perhaps on some deep level, those other girls had known it too; girls were generally more perceptive in those matters.

"Wow," I finally managed to say, knowing that it was the most pointless word I had ever spoken in my life. No single word could have done the moment justice anyway.

"Wow," Natalie echoed my sentiment, resting her head on my shoulder and sighing contentedly.

Standing there, wrapped up in the girl I felt almost sure that I loved, I couldn't remember ever being more relaxed in my life. It was probably for that reason that a thought occurred to me then, a thought so simple that I felt like an idiot for not having it earlier. In point of fact, it should already have occurred to several people by now. How could the brilliant minds of Marc, James, Lucien, Amelia and Stella have all failed to foresee the real downfall that would claim us on this day? In hindsight, it was so obvious.

Perhaps we had made a mistake in jumping into action so soon after returning from the Honnie world. Perhaps we hadn't done enough simulations to cover all possible flaws in the plan. Ultimately, though, I didn't think it would have made any difference if we'd done a hundred simulations, not if the simulator (May, in this case) was also blind to the most likely flaw to bring us down. It was the hero devices which were both our greatest weapon and our greatest vulnerability, and the fact that I was still calling it a hero device instead of some properly assigned name illustrated the point fairly well.

We should have spent much more time learning about them. More, we should have been properly trained to use them, not in the simulation but in real life. Marc should have cleared a space somewhere and trained each and every one of us how to get the most out of our hero devices, even if it meant delaying the plan by a month (although May probably wouldn't have liked that). If we had been properly trained, we would have been much more organized when we had first entered the grounds, perhaps not even requiring Lucien and Stella's groups to come to our assistance. Now that I thought about it properly, in no immediate danger, I reckoned that we could have done so many things more effectively if we had only known better.

I had thought that the hero devices were strictly offensive, but that wasn't what Marc had told me, was it? He had said that they contained the power of all the devices the Hammersons created that Stella knew how to encapsulate, plus any extras that occurred to him, her, Amelia or Lucien in the time they were being created. They had the power to produce light, which meant they probably had the power to produce shields. We would definitely have used that one if we'd known about it, but as happens when the brain gets rolling, my mind jumped to the next logical link in the chain. The Hammerhearts had devices capable of disabling a Sorcerer's magic, and that probably meant...

But Natalie suddenly stiffened in my arms before I could properly finish the thought. My senses sharpened immediately and it only took another moment for me to understand why. Footsteps were approaching in the corridor outside. They were coming closer and closer, and there could be no doubt that they were coming for us. I sighed resignedly; it was time to return to the here-and-now.

"Stand against the back wall of the cell," said a familiar voice from just outside the door, and I knew at once who it was. "Do not try anything or we will be forced to hurt you, and we will enjoy every moment of it."

It was 10:37 on the morning of August 23, 2010.

Chapter 36: Interrogation

"Remember, we have no weapons," I said to Natalie, gently pushing her away from me so that we couldn't be taken by a single shot. I had no intention of obeying the instructions from our visitors—they could suck that up. Most of all, though, I hoped that Natalie understood the double meaning behind what I had just said: To anyone listening through the surveillance, I was reminding her that we were unarmed and had better not struggle with them because things would be worse for us if we did. To Natalie herself, I was reminding her to pretend that we were unarmed so that we could take them by surprise when (if) the right time came.

"I know," she said from just out of arm's reach a short distance to my left (further into the cell) and I was impressed by her tone of resignation, hoping that it was only for show and not that she'd actually forgotten about her own hero device (if she still had it, I suddenly thought, and quickly decided not to investigate that line of thinking any further).

We both went still then as a key rattled in the lock outside. We remained still as the door opened a tad and the large figure of a typical Hammerheart security guard stepped inside. We continued to remain still as a second, considerably smaller figure stepped in behind the first figure. We did not move as the door shut softly behind them, plunging the four of us into complete, but only temporary darkness. Only my eyes moved as the room suddenly illuminated, shrinking to slits against the sudden glare, which was rather stronger than the dim light I had produced earlier. This one, unlike mine, lit up the entire cell, rather than just over the head of the person who had created it.

I now saw that I had been wrong a moment ago about the first person being a security guard, unless Ugine Wilwog had become the youngest security guard within the Hammerheart ranks since the last time I had seen him. I had to reflect that it was probably the only suitable role for him within their organisation. His partner in crime, as per usual, was Ather

Hignat, who looked even more cocky than he had earlier when Sebastian had been at his left shoulder. I supposed I understood why; it was exactly how he had looked the last time I had seen him, when he had divested me of the Sien-Leoard Crystal and had me trussed on the floor of someone else's cell. It was also the same look he had given me and those around me when we had been locked in a cage and set on display in the dining hall for the Hammerhearts who frequented this place.

"Perhaps you lost your sense of direction in the darkness," he suggested, his eyes twinkling, "and thought that that wall was, in fact, the back of the cell. I suppose it hardly matters, though."

Hignat was presently unarmed (at least that I could see), although I doubted that he wasn't concealing something in his pockets or around his belt as Stella had when she'd been on the run. Wilwog was a different story; his eyes were continually darting between Natalie and me while he held agonators in both hands, one pointing at each of us. Dull he may be but it hadn't taken anything from his alertness; that must have been how he had looked in the moment before he had king-hit me three months earlier.

"The Police Commissioner has plans for you two," Hignat told us, "and so does Lord Hammerson, of course, but luckily for you, he's not even in the country yet. I'm sure he'll come running as soon as he hears what's happened, but for the time being, your lives will continue to run as they are. While we wait, though, the Commissioner has a few questions he wants answered, and he thought that you would be more likely to open up to me and Ugine, since we used to be old school chums."

In a complete mockery of his words, our current situation and just the whole world in general as I knew it, all four of us simultaneously burst out laughing. Through it all, though, I continued to assess our chances of overcoming these two which, although better than they would have been against Hall or Hammerson, were still not looking that good. It would only take Wilwog a couple of clicks to take us both down, and he could do us both at the same time. Additionally, Hignat could arm himself at any moment and double the trouble. Two on two it may be, but not only was one of theirs so much bigger than any of ours, they had a shitload more weapons, even if ours were more powerful. To top it off, Wilwog had positioned himself so that we would have to step around him to get to the door. Yep, it wasn't looking good.

"And of course, you had better do what we tell you," Hignat continued after the laughter had subsided, "because we have permission to do what we will with you, stopping just short of killing you, of course. That suits me fine since neither of us have actually killed anyone yet, which is more than you can say, Playman."

Ouch! Now that was worth a good hard kick in the guts, not least because it was entirely true. If it was also true that neither Hignat nor Wilwog had committed murder yet, didn't that make me worse, even, than them? I had certainly knocked over a lot of Hammerhearts in my fight for survival (the gym, the Indian Ocean and that night in Germany came back to me in far too vivid detail) and did pointing out that it was either me or them help at all?

"Shut up," Natalie snapped at him then. I looked sideways at her and saw a heart-stopping thing; she was furious, and it was in my defence. I couldn't decide if I was more touched at her loyalty or anguished at what might be about to happen to her in response. She looked amazing in that moment, her eyes wide and intense and her hair slightly messier than usual. I did that, I realized, and the thought almost distracted me—almost.

Hignat's eyebrows rose. "Feisty, Fletcher. I hadn't expected that. All personality reports suggested that you were the softer Sorcerer, that Woodward was more likely to shoot her mouth off. I don't mind; after all, we're here to listen."

Natalie looked like she had at least a dozen things she would like to say in response to that, but her eyes strayed to the agonators in Wilwog's hands. Whatever had been about to come out, she reluctantly bit back. Hignat looked disappointed.

"Okay then," he shrugged, smiling as he turned his attention back to me. "If this were up to me, I would go about this interview differently, but since there's a camera in here, we'll have to stick to the script. Lucky for you," he added, his eyes darting sideways at Natalie again, a horribly familiar expression on his face. It was the same look he'd worn when he had first conceived the idea of raping Amelia, and I knew exactly what he would have liked to do with Natalie, had it been up to him. Maintaining my calm became an intense struggle; if either of them dared to touch her, I would have them, whatever the consequences for myself.

"And what would that script be?" Natalie asked nervously, having either missed or misunderstood Hignat's true desire.

Hignat's grin broadened. "As I said, the Commissioner wants some questions answered. *Your* job"—he jabbed his thumb at me—"will be to answer for both of you. *Your* job"—he jabbed his thumb at Natalie—"well, you'll work out what your job is pretty quickly if we're not satisfied with Playman's answers. Don't even think of trying to fight us; you may not think much of Ugine's intellect, but you would be a fool to challenge his reflexes."

Unfortunately, I agreed with him.

"Why are you two even working for them?" I asked boldly. "Don't you know you should be at school?"

I knew I was in for something unpleasant, but the gob-smacked looks on both their faces made it totally worth it. After a few seconds, Hignat managed to compose himself. "You're right, Playman, and in fact we are enrolled in a school out of town, but if Lord Hammerson or the Commissioner, or even our fathers, have assignments for us, I'm sure you can guess what takes priority. Your smart mouth knows no bounds, Playman. Put him on the floor," he added casually to Wilwog.

There was no time to react. The terrible and all-consuming power of the agonator rolled over me for the second time that day, removing me from all I knew and replacing everything with complete, insatiable pain. It went on and on but eventually, after an immeasurable amount of time (probably no more than fifteen seconds), it abruptly ceased. As per Hignat's instructions, I was well and truly on the floor, my head aching from where it had hit the stone and my throat raw, I supposed, from my yelling, though I couldn't actually remember yelling —it was just what you did when you were in that amount of pain.

It didn't take long to remember my surroundings, particularly with Hignat and Wilwog's laughter ringing around the cell. Not wanting them to enjoy it any more than they already had, I quickly scrambled to my feet, collided with the wall behind me and fell down in a heap again, my legs not yet ready to support me. The laughter became renewed and in that moment, I wanted to kill Ather Hignat. Wilwog was theoretically no better but Hignat was the one I wanted; he was the brains of the operation, which made him the intent behind the operation.

I used the wall that had just floored me to pull myself back up more carefully, looking around to see if the positions had changed. They hadn't; Wilwog stood motionless exactly where he had before, though his laughter was now subsiding; Hignat had moved back a step, perhaps unconsciously; and Natalie was standing stock-still, staring blankly at Hignat. She had been stunned, was still stunned at Hignat's hand by the look of it, and that explained why she hadn't come to help me up.

"Well, that is certainly an excellent way to make a point," Hignat said, releasing Natalie from her stunned state and grinning at both of us. "You stay right where you are, Fletcher, or it'll be your turn. I want five feet of clear space between you two at all times. Understand?"

We both nodded, too incensed to speak. Hignat had become more businesslike now, and as he himself had said earlier, he would enjoy hurting us if we gave him a reason to do so.

"Good," he said, smiling. "So, Playman, I have been told an incredible story of survival, where a skinny teenage boy was trapped beneath hundreds of tons of wreckage and lived to tell the tale. Care to explain how a boy, whose entire magical talent was taken from him by a couple of geniuses—namely us—wormed his way out of that one?"

"Full of yourselves, aren't you?" Natalie said scornfully.

"Just telling it like it is, Fletcher," said Hignat, winking at her, "and you had better not speak when not spoken to again. Anything to say, Playman?"

"Arnold Hammerson already knows the answer to that question," I snapped. "He can't kill me. Setting it up so that something else would kill me doesn't change the fact that it was his work."

"Do not feed me tripe and call it candy, Playman. We both know that kind of magic does not exist, and if it did, Lord Hammerson could have easily over-ridden it with the much greater power of the Sien-Leoard Crystal. Perhaps he would have thought of that himself if he hadn't been so excited by the prospect of killing you; lucky he has people like me to come up with the good ideas. I'll ask you again, Playman: How did you get out of there?"

"Okay, I was rescued by the Seventh Sorcerer. That's not too incredible to believe, I wouldn't have thought."

"That does make sense. Our information was that he was graciously given his power back when the Commissioner—"

"When the glorified high school English teacher, you mean?" I shot back.

Hignat's eyes widened threateningly. "I'm not offended by that slight, Playman, but it was still out of line."

His stunner was back in his hand and once again, it was levelled at Natalie. She was instantly immobilised but this time, no punishment was forthcoming for me. The agonator was still levelled at me, however, so I didn't dare move as Hignat drew another device from his belt (yes, that's where his weapons were, exactly as Stella had carried hers prior to being picked up) and levelled it at Natalie. Ropes flew from its tip and wrapped around her wrists, ankles, hips and torso. Hignat looked positively gleeful as he lazily stowed both devices back on his belt.

"So that's your plan, is it?" I said, feeling my stomach churn horribly as I glanced sideways at Natalie. "Punish her every time I step out of line?"

"Very good, Playman," said Hignat amiably. "Top of the class for you. As I was saying before I was rudely interrupted, his crystal was returned to him when the Commissioner made his presence known…"

I tuned his voice out as I looked sideways at Natalie again, trussed to the wall to my left. She was no longer stunned, which meant that she could move, but given how tightly the ropes were tied, the only part of her body even slightly mobile was her head, and only because Hignat's ropes hadn't touched anything above her shoulders. The fight had gone out of her again; she was very pale, her eyes cast downward, an expression of resignation on her face. She, too, understood that Hignat was going to go to town on her in the next little while, and as it stood, neither of us could stop him…or could we? I remembered the thought I'd had before these two had shown up. If I could only point my hero device at her without either of them seeing…

"When I ask you a question, Playman, I expect an answer," Hignat's voice cut through my musings, now raised in irritation. I looked quickly back at him and saw that his smug smile had disappeared.

"Sorry. What was the question?"

The smile returned. "So you simply weren't paying attention to me? You thought this would be an acceptable time to drift off? To meditate, perhaps?"

"If that was your question, then apparently so."

"You're really not very good at this, are you, Playman?"

"If you think I'm not, then we'll have to agree to disagree."

"And if I disagree to disagree?"

"That's a double negative, which means you agree."

For the second time in minutes, the expression on Wilwog's face was priceless.

Hignat sighed. "I asked you, Playman, where you and your friends went after we flushed you out of the house on the

Morelle Street bridge. Answer my question now and do not give me a reason to make you pay closer attention."

Of course not, I thought angrily, but this time, the anger was directed at myself. Any lapse in my concentration would be taken out on Natalie, and I could not allow her to suffer anymore than I couldn't prevent.

"I don't know where we went," I said, trying to look earnest. "They set up a new base but they never mentioned where it was. Well, not exactly anyway; I think it was in the Northern Territory or something."

"That's a lot of area to cover, Playman; doesn't narrow it down very much, wouldn't you agree? Convenient."

"Maybe that's why they picked there instead of Tasmania."

"Do not waste my time, Playman. I already know that you and your friends, the ones I mentioned in my original question, did not go with the Woodwards and Fletchers that night. You went off on your own, a band of teenagers whose names I'll want you to give me shortly, and I want to know where you went. Answer me."

"Okay," I said, trying to think quickly—I had no intention of providing him with any information that could flush out the base we had worked so hard to keep hidden. "We set up our own base. We had Marc, Natalie and Amelia, and Marc called Fewul, so we had plenty of magic to keep ourselves hidden. The base was always moving but so far as I know, we never went too far from Chopville. Does that answer your question?"

Hignat measured me for several seconds before saying, "What magic did you use to keep yourselves hidden?"

I flushed; he had correctly called my bluff. "I dunno—invisibility, untraceability; you know, the usual stuff."

"Anything else?"

"Probably, but since I don't have magic anymore, thanks to you, I wasn't included in that part of the planning."

"If that is true, then you, Fletcher, must have been right in the thick of it. What other methods were used to protect your base?"

Damn, I thought; he really is good at this stuff. Natalie looked fearful as she gazed at Hignat, clearly struggling to think what she ought to say. Before she could utter anything, Hignat said, "If you have to think that hard, either you're trying to remember or you're trying to think of a credible untruth. Since you've had plenty of time to think about it while Playman's floundered around, trying to deny me the information I want, I believe it must be the latter. Be careful how you answer, Fletcher."

"I don't know," she said in a small voice, and then knowing that wouldn't help her one bit, she added, "There was a soundproof barrier, and the base was shrunken like this place, and I think there was something else as well but I don't know what it was."

"Shrunken, you say?" he repeated, and my stomach fell. That, it seemed, was the important piece of information, and by his own far-too-effective interrogation methods, Hignat had managed to extract it. "Shrunken and untraceable? Well, that explains plenty. Thank you, Fletcher, but unfortunately for you, Playman's responses weren't even close to satisfactory. Stun him, Ugine."

Again, I didn't even have time to react. My body froze in place and all I could do was stare at Hignat as he slowly approached Natalie where she stood, bound and unable to move away from him. I rolled my eyes sideways to keep him in view but I was facing the wrong way—I couldn't see Natalie. That was perhaps a blessing in disguise; perhaps it would torture me less if I only heard her pain, but apparently the same thought had occurred to Wilwog. He must have pressed the larger button on his stunner and twisted his wrist so that my body suddenly pivoted; now my back was to him while Natalie and Hignat were in my direct line of vision.

Hignat was now standing beside Natalie and his bludginator was in his hand. His gaze met mine for a moment so that he knew I was paying attention, much against my will (my eye-lids were immovable), and then he turned to face Natalie again. He reached up with his free hand and gently took hold of her plait; she tried to jerk her head away from him but it was never a possibility. Smiling, Hignat brought the bludginator up and then down again, not making any physical contact with Natalie but allowing its concealed magic to do all the damage. To my horror, so much of Natalie's beautiful hair simply fell away in Hignat's hands, and he tossed it lazily away into a corner of the cell. What was left was a little messy, and now almost as short as my own hair, but I didn't think it detracted too much from her appearance. The expression of devastation on Natalie's face, however, suggested that she strongly disagreed.

"Not painful at all, Fletcher," Hignat said gleefully, "but next time"—he wiggled his bludginator in front of her eyes—"it will be. You can let him go, Ugine."

I felt everything in my body let go at once, but for several seconds, I was unable to move at all. All I could do was stare at Natalie, trying with my eyes to let her know that it wasn't that bad—that Hignat was right, and by comparison, painless. She took no notice of me.

"So, Playman," Hignat drawled, returning my attention to him again, "you created this base of yours almost two months ago. That's quite a long time to be sitting around playing scrabble, wouldn't you say? What else have you and your friends been up to?"

I considered for a moment before deciding that part of the truth would have to suffice. "Well, mostly, we've just been spying on the school, trying to work out how we could get in there. As you saw, it paid off in the end." I considered for another moment and added, "Also, we put a bit of time into tracking Stella down—I'm sure you saw her earlier."

"Yes, I did," he said, grinning for a moment and looking, yet again, like he was thinking dirty thoughts. "I'm rather looking forward to meeting her again, and on that point, Playman, the word around the traps is that you and her are fairly intimate. Is this true?"

"No," I said cagily, but of course, he didn't believe me.

"Be warned, Playman, her father has made me a promise, and I shall hunt you down if you ruin it for me. You don't need to know the details; just know that if she is spoilt when the time comes, you shall be held accountable."

"If you say so, but I believe she and Lucien Moran have been dating for a while now."

I took a moment to thoroughly enjoy the look of horror on Hignat's face. I decided to push my advantage even further. "Also, in case you haven't worked it out, Hammerson intends for Stella to someday become a Sorcerer again, whenever he can get the Sorcerous Crystals back. Do you really think she's gonna take any crap from you once she has her own magic again?"

Hignat's grin resurfaced. "It won't be crap, Playman. On the contrary, she'll want it more than me; I'll probably have to tell her no from time to time, and I'm sure I'll enjoy that. Now, let's talk a bit about your friends, shall we?"

"What about them?" I asked warily.

"Firstly, I want all their names. I already know who some of them are, of course—in fact, between me and the Commissioner, we probably know nearly all of them. Still, I want you to give me their names—all of them. List them off for me, Playman, and exclude nobody."

I sighed. "Why don't you tell me which ones you already know and I'll fill you in on any you've missed?"

"I'll tell you why not, Playman: Because I said so. Can you comprehend, Playman? Do you get what I'm laying down here? We're going to do this my way, and you are going to be dearly sorry for trying to defy me. Now, Playman, the names."

I sighed and began rolling them off. I did not, however, include May in that number; whatever he said, there was no way I was going to inform him about Honnies. He probably wouldn't even believe me if I tried, but once again, he called my bluff.

"Were all of them at the school today?" he asked.

"No; Jessica stayed back with Jason and Robyn."

"Why did they do that?"

"To look after the base."

He didn't need to know about the pregnancy. I hadn't even bothered to tell him that Tommy and Candice were no longer part of the team.

"So, who was the woman who came in with you?"

"Er—who?"

"You know who I'm talking about, Playman," he sneered. "The one who looked like she ate a couple of our people, although I highly doubt it was really what it looked like. Who was she, Playman? I know she was not any of the people you named."

I thought, for a moment, of asking if he knew every single person I'd named, and then didn't bother—that was a path to nowhere. Instead, I told him the only thing he would believe: "That was Fewul."

"The Beast of Magic, you say? I thought that thing could only be controlled by the Seventh Sorcerer—that is what I was told. How do you explain that?"

"Marc ordered him to assist whoever needed him most."

"Why do you call it a 'him', Playman? There was nothing masculine about what I saw in that form. Incidentally, why did he order the Beast to look like that anyway? Was the intention to stun every male in the immediate vicinity into submission? If so, I would say it worked almost perfectly."

"Er—yeah, that was the plan."

"And my original question, Playman?"

"What was that?"

"Why did you call it 'him'?"

"Habit. Most of the times Marc's called it, it's taken the form of Lucien, so I've kind of gotten used to thinking of it as male."

He stared at me for several seconds, measuring me again, before seeming to be satisfied. I breathed an internal sigh of relief—he was far too sharp today. "Fine, Playman. Once again, we got there in the end. Now, Fletcher, open your mouth."

My blood ran cold.

"No," Natalie moaned, barely moving her lips.

Hignat smiled, enjoying the game far too much. He reached out for her—she tried to jerk her head away again, smacking it hard on the stone wall behind her in the process, but was never a chance. He took hold of her jaw in one hand and roughly forced it open while raising his bludginator in his other hand.

"Now, Playman, this one is for trying to avoid naming your friends."

This time, there was blood—plenty of it. There was also physical contact, perhaps because like the time Kylie had been beheaded by this same weapon, it wouldn't have been able to cut through enough if its magic was entirely relied upon. Hignat put the blade in Natalie's open mouth and cut through the soft flesh of her cheek on the right side of her face so that her mouth became elongated by about two inches. She let out a piteous cry of pain but with Hignat still holding her jaw, she could do nothing to escape from it.

"And this, Playman, is for pretending you didn't know which woman I was talking about."

He repeated the process, this time on the other side of her face. There was another small cry from Natalie and a lot more blood—it was pouring from her ruined face, pooling on the floor at her feet. Hignat's hands were coated with it but he didn't seem to mind; he looked flushed and—the thought disturbed me immensely—happier than I'd ever seen him. He was in his element. Out of sight, I heard Wilwog snigger, and it was like a shock to my system. Through it all, I had been paralysed where I stood, unable to do anything more than stare at Natalie.

If cutting her hair hadn't detracted from her appearance, this certainly had. In fact, I strongly suspected that had been Hignat's plan all along, as though he knew that this emotional anguish would be worse than any physical pain he could inflict —or maybe he preferred the more hands-on approach that this method provided. Blood was pounding harder and faster than ever in my veins. My heart beat felt like the thumping of a bass drum in my head. It was a heady rush which was becoming increasingly difficult to control; if I lost it, I would go off like a bomb just like I had right before killing Tankom, and that would probably result in a lot worse trouble for me. Still, I had promised myself that I wouldn't let anything worse be done to Natalie than was absolutely necessary, and I intended to stand by that no matter what.

Hignat smiled at me as he stowed his bludginator away and wiped his bloody hands on his pants. "Do you take me seriously now, Playman?"

"I never didn't," I said through gritted teeth.

His eyes flashed dangerously. "I beg your pardon?"

"I took you seriously all along," I snapped at him.

"Tone, Playman. I feel like I ought to teach you another lesson, but I still have questions for you, so shall we get back down to business?"

I nodded, waiting to see what else he could want.

"In May, you and some of your friends—at least I assume you were one of them—returned to Rock Haulter. Why did you do that, Playman? Trying to relive a few memories, were you?"

My heart seemed to stop altogether for a moment. How on earth could he have known about the memories? After a second, however, it occurred to me that he probably meant reliving memories of the camp from way back in February. Hoping he didn't call attention to that part of his question, I decided to answer the first part with as much truth as I dared. "Have you heard of Rafael Smiley?"

"No, Playman, I have not. Should I have?"

"Well, Arnold Hammerson would have, so if you're gonna report all this back to him, or to Hall, they'll understand. We went there because we'd found out that he was there and we wanted to ask him questions about how the war ended in 1981 so that we could try and make it happen again."

"Indeed, Playman, and he would know the answer to that question because?"

"Because he was there when it happened, and Hammerson probably knows it. Apparently, he's been on their hit list since at least 1996, and they've probably wanted him even longer. Tankom even crashed a plane to try and kill him."

This talking was a lot easier than answering any of the other questions had been; firstly because it was true, secondly because it was useless knowledge that Arnold Hammerson already knew; and thirdly, because I didn't want Hignat, or anyone he might report to, to know any of the important things Smiley had told us. They didn't need to know about the memories, Honnies, the time bomb curse on Lucien, or any of the personal struggles that Marc, Tommy and I had confronted in those few days.

"What did he tell you?"

"Apparently the Woodwards killed about ten thousand Hammerhearts and told the Hammersons they would do it again if they didn't back down. Tankom eventually relented."

Hignat looked disappointed. "I was hoping for something more interesting. Well, never mind; I'm sure Arnold Hammerson will be pleased to know where he's been all this time."

"He'll be even more pleased to know that Smiley's probably dead by now," I told him. "At least, he was dying when we saw him, and enough time's gone by since then."

"I see," he said, looking calculating again. "Which of your friends went?"

"I went," I told him, "Natalie, Peter, James, Marc, Tommy, Serena, Lena, Erica, Siobhan and Underwood."

"Underwood? Who is that? You never mentioned that name earlier, Playman."

He looked dangerous again, and wanting to spare Natalie whatever might come next, I hurried to explain. "He's Smiley's grandson. He was the one who told us where to go in the first place. He stayed on the Rock to nurse Smiley till the end 'cause they'd been apart for most of his life."

"Well, okay then," he said, looking disappointed. "So you haven't seen him since, then?"

"No, and probably never will again."

Hignat considered. "So far as I know, the Atlantic Portal opened a couple of weeks ago, so we missed that chance. We'll have to wait till November, but don't worry, Playman; we'll bring your dear friend Underwood back. I'm sure the Commissioner has plenty of questions for him."

I shrugged. Not that I wanted anything bad to happen to Jacob Underwood, whatever I thought of him as an individual, but that was so far down the track that it was hardly worth worrying about. Besides, if Smiley had passed over, it seemed likely that Underwood would have found a means by which to leave the island and return to the world by now, as Moran had; it would be a lonely place for most of the year, Rock Haulter.

"Anything else?" I asked wearily, deciding that the time had come to pay closer attention to Wilwog. I turned slightly to see what he was doing and was not pleased to see him looking as attentive as ever. Our only chance of getting out of this was for him to become distracted long enough for me to do just one spell with my hero device, but if I tried it now, I would be struck down before I could do anything.

"I ask the questions, Playman, not you. Yes, there is one more thing we need to talk about. We all saw what you and your friends did to the school today, but my question to you is —why? What were you trying to accomplish?"

I considered, my eyes still darting between Hignat and Wilwog, trying to think of an answer to his question and a way out at the same time. Unfortunately, Hignat saw what I was doing.

"Do not even think of it, Playman. You pay attention to me."

Pain lanced across my ribs on the left side of my body. I gasped and tried to cover the wound as blood began oozing out of the cut created by Hignat's bludginator. I looked up at him and saw that his eyes were gleaming with pleasure.

"What do you think we were trying to accomplish? That we wanted to go back to school and resume our education, perhaps? Honestly. My God. We attacked there because it would disrupt the Hammerhearts if we could take it back, since so much of their operations in central Victoria is controlled there."

"It probably would have slowed us down a bit," he conceded, "but I think we both know that attacking this place would have done even more damage. Why didn't you think of that, Playman?"

"We did," I lied, "but we couldn't find a way to get back in here. We used to use the tunnel in Marc's house but that's been cut off for months now. Besides, Sorcerers can't get in here unless they're prisoners."

"I believe the school is protected by that same enchantment, and yet this one got in there without any problem, and the Commissioner tells me that Woodward did too. I think you're hiding something from me, Playman. What might that be?"

"I'm not hiding anything—"

"Playman, I may not be telepathic, but I am a good judge of honesty. You are hiding something from me, and I am becoming displeased by it."

"What if I was telling you the truth and you still didn't believe me? Wouldn't that mean that I'd have to lie to make you happy? Except then you'd find out that I lied, and you still wouldn't be happy. The best thing for you to do at this point is to just believe what I'm saying."

I was in trouble and I knew it, but honestly, I just couldn't stop myself speaking the irritating thoughts that had kept recurring to me throughout this interrogation. I reminded myself of when I had questioned Stella about her father and grandmother's escape from the Woodward base, and she had made much the same point that I was making now. I felt bad for her all over again.

"You have a remarkably poor sense of the occasion, Playman," said Hignat, but he looked pleased. "I understand the point you're making because I've thought similar thoughts when dealing with my own father on a few occasions over the years, but I don't believe that is the case now. You are hiding something from me, and I will not be distracted. Would you allow me to speculate on what it might be?"

"Speculate away," I said boredly.

"The Commissioner said that Woodward and Moran went to great lengths to empty the administration building of Hammerhearts, which on its own would suggest that the building was their target, yet they never made any overt move to chase him from the building. I think, Playman, that you and your friends were trying to capture Commissioner Hall. Would I be onto something here?"

I sighed. "Fine, we were so furious with him after everything he'd put us through that we decided that revenging ourselves against him was far more important than doing anything to stop the war."

"Removing the Commissioner would have done plenty of damage if you had succeeded, Playman," said Hignat, smiling, "but of course, you never stood a chance there. Why didn't you just tell me that from the start?"

"I dunno, maybe I was hoping that 'the Commissioner' would stay a little more complacent so that if we ever get out of this, we can try to get him again?"

This wasn't true, of course, but it sounded true enough even to my own ears.

"I think you were wasting your time, Playman, because you will not be getting out of this. Since you once again tried to defy me the information I wanted, I'm afraid I'm going to have to do something else to your lady friend here."

I groaned inwardly as he turned back to Natalie, whose eyes were huge in her face. Blood was continuing to pour unstaunched from her wrecked face; she had clamped her mouth shut but the gash was still horrendous. Not only had Hignat defiled one girl I cared about and was planning to do the same to another; now he had taken pretty much all of Natalie's physical beauty by his own blade. He'd done more; he had taken her pride. On an emotional level, this experience had probably done her more damage than anything else she had been through so far. Of course, that was Hignat's intention all along, and now he was looking her up and down as he tried to think of more things he could do to her—ways he could punish her even further for my transgression. Finally, he looked back up at what remained of her face and smiled. It was *that* look again.

"You know, Fletcher, while intelligence isn't always reliable, the word on the inside—or what was the inside up until April—was that you were wound tight as a drum. I think the word 'frigid' was used several times in the report. That's rather insulting, don't you think? I certainly found it an unacceptable reference when I read it. What would you say?"

Natalie tried to speak and then just whimpered—it was too painful for her.

"Who on earth told you that?" I snapped at him, and then the answer came to me. "Oh—Sebastian."

My heart sank when I thought of how much else Sebastian had known about Natalie, like the fact that she and I were hot for each other. If he knew, then that meant Hignat must have been well aware of our feelings for each other all along. That spiked my anger all over again.

"Correct, Playman, but I wasn't talking to you. My thoughts, Fletcher, are that maybe we can prove that you're not frigid. What would you say to that?"

She said nothing to that, but she didn't need to. Everyone in the room understood what Hignat was really thinking. I began to see red but before I could do anything, a noise from behind me reminded me of Wilwog. I could do nothing but watch as Hignat's grin broadened.

It was 10:51 on the morning of August 23, 2010.

Chapter 37: Breaking Point

"You just keep yourself still," Hignat crooned at Natalie, trying to look kindly and succeeding only in looking taunting. "I know you're hurting, but that's over now—everything from here on is definitely going to be much more pleasant."

"You're not gonna get away with this," I snarled, wondering how much I could take before I threw caution to the wind.

"Oh shut up, Playman. Just stand still and watch how a real man does his masculine duty. Ugine, don't stun him, but make sure he watches."

Wilwog must have obliged, but I didn't see it and no magic came at me from behind. I could only watch as Hignat, smiling as he held Natalie's petrified gaze, slid his hand up her top.

"Very nice," he grinned. "Not as big as I'd like but still—enough to hang onto at any rate. Hmm…what to do about this bra…"

Whatever he wanted to do required both hands. He slid the other one up there and struggled for a few seconds before his grin resurfaced.

"Now that's much better. I always prefer skin on skin, don't you agree?" he asked her.

Natalie closed her eyes but other than that, she made no response. Hignat didn't seem to mind; he shot me a triumphant look before focussing more closely on what his hands were doing, continuing to taunt her with his words. She was still struggling to try to get away from his touch but with the ropes still binding her, she was no chance to move any part of herself out of his reach. I moved one of my feet at one point, more reflexively than anything else, almost giving into the automatic urge to grab him and thrust him away from Natalie, but that was when the magic came at me from behind—only the stunner, and only for about two seconds, but it was enough to remind me that Wilwog was still watching my every move. I could still do nothing.

"That was nice," Hignat said, removing his hands from Natalie's chest and bringing them back out where I could see them—they were still bloodstained, "but if we are to truly disprove the evidence given in that report, we must go further —much further. Open your eyes, Fletcher; I want you to be seeing me as I do this."

Natalie ignored him completely. Hignat reached up, took hold of her lower lip between two fingers and twisted. The pain must have shot all the way through her face, along the wounds on both sides of it. She screamed, her eyes flying open and rolling wildly around the cell. Hignat grinned at her.

"Don't make me do that again," he told her, "although I must say, I rather enjoyed it. I'll enjoy this even more, though, and given how you just reacted, I imagine you will too."

I had a feeling I knew what the next step would be, and I was right. He slid his right hand into her pants, and she shuddered slightly. My own heartbeat quickened.

"Nice, isn't it?" he asked her, staring into her eyes—she didn't dare look away. Her gaze was tortured, and consequently tortured me to see it. "Yes, I think it is, but it's still not enough."

He withdrew his hand, but only briefly as he used his other hand to firstly pull her pants slightly away from her body, and then to do the same to her underpants, allowing him easy access to the part of her he wanted most. His hand slipped out of sight again and began moving around. I gathered what it was doing every time Natalie winced.

"Not bad," he said, but he no longer sounded all that pleased with proceedings. "It certainly does feel nice, Fletcher, but I'm gathering that you're not enjoying this quite as much as I had intended, and I think I can guess why. I actually find it a little offensive that you are not wet for me; that is unacceptable. You would enjoy it a lot more if you allowed yourself to enjoy it, Fletcher, but since that's a mental problem of yours, I'll have to lubricate it myself."

What on earth was he talking about this time? When he withdrew one hand and took out his bludginator, I thought that he would simply cut her out of her pants; that sounded like the sort of thing he would do. However, I was horribly mistaken.

What came next was utterly horrifying, and as I'd been expecting for several minutes now, it finally caused me to snap. Hignat's hand, bludginator and all, went back between Natalie's legs, and there was a look of intense concentration on his face as he used it to cut, but he wasn't cutting any of her clothing. Her scream was ear-splitting, her mouth opening wide in reflex and causing a fresh wave of blood to pour from her face. I knew what he must have done, and for what purpose. There would certainly be lubrication down there now—plenty of it.

If that action alone didn't galvanise me into action, Wilwog's reaction to the drama certainly did. He chuckled behind me and more because I didn't want to see what else Hignat did to Natalie, I looked over my shoulder to see what was going on. He was still holding his stunner in one hand and his agonator in the other, and while both were still pointing in my direction, his eyes were now on Natalie and there was a hungry look in them. He was having another reaction in his pants, I saw; a mighty big one too. His hands looked a little unsteady, as though they too were having a reaction. I had no doubt that he wanted to be over there doing what Hignat was doing.

His concentration had finally wavered, and that was all I needed. However, I wasn't going to take any chances. I'd considered that he would probably wake up immediately to any sudden movements on my part, which was why I very casually slipped my hand into my pocket, forming the thought in my mind so that I would be ready, withdrawing the hero device and pointing at Natalie. I did all of this as though I didn't care what either of them thought; as though I didn't mind either of them seeing it. It wasn't a case of concentrating on moving casually—I was just too numb to do any more—the adrenalin wouldn't kick in for a few seconds yet. Thinking of a device which could undo the power of those other devices that nullified a Sorcerer's magic (a convoluted thought, but one I felt sure was the best to try), I clicked the button.

I knew immediately that it had worked (to my great relief) by the shudder that rolled through Natalie's body, something entirely different from the pain and disgust (or whatever else) she'd endured at Hignat's hands. Her eyes, which had been wide and horrified, suddenly cleared as she felt whatever it was that Sorcerers felt when their magic, previously missed, was restored. Hignat saw the change in her face and reflexively moved back, but he didn't take his hand out of her pants; nor did he click as to what had happened.

That was the full extent of my plan, and it took a precious moment to work out what to do next. It was enough for me to train my hero device on Wilwog, who still hadn't noticed the change but was probably still the greater threat out of the two of them. I pointed my hero device at him, thinking of a bludginator. He saw my movement and turned, his eyes widening in surprise as he took in my raised weapon. He clicked his agonator at the same moment I began a vertical slash from his chest to his naval, but his turn had thrown his aim and the jet of golden light flew past my right shoulder.

Everything happened very quickly after that. Both Hignat and Wilwog cried out at the same time: Wilwog's shirt tore open and blood began oozing from a shallow but long cut all the way down his front; Hignat was blasted backward across the cell as Natalie put her restored magic into action, his arms waving and his bludginator flying loose. Wilwog took a step back from me but before he could regain his equilibrium, I brought my arm around and slashed sideways left-to-right, straight across his chest. The ropes binding Natalie suddenly vanished and she hobbled a step away from the wall. Wilwog hunched over and with his head lowered, shot blindly at me with his stunner, but missed a second time; I retaliated with a third slash, right-to-left this time at shin level.

"What the hell!" Hignat shouted. "Ugine, what—"

A loud crack cut off his words as my third bludginator swipe broke one of Wilwog's legs. He roared with pain as he collapsed in front of me, and I had to take a step back to avoid his bulk as he went down. It gave me a clear view of Hignat and Natalie, the former straightening up against the far wall, the latter watching him with desperate intent. She still hadn't used her magic to deal with her injuries; I wished she would because it was terrible to watch her like this—and it would make her more able to fight—and it would make her more comfortable.

I needed another moment to decide what to do. Hignat could try to take Natalie's magic again if he had one of those devices that could do that, so I thought of the device I had created months ago to protect the Sorcerous chips, pointed my hero device at Natalie and gave it a click. I didn't wait to see if it had worked because so far as I knew, that magic showed no visible sign anyway; instead I turned my attention back to Wilwog, whose agonised howling was becoming a serious distraction. I thought of a device that would simply knock him unconscious (not the virtual killing ones) and not knowing if such a device even existed, clicked the button again. The boy before me collapsed and went quiet immediately.

His scream was immediately replaced by another, much higher-pitched one. For whatever reason, Natalie hadn't been able to disarm Hignat before he could launch another attack. His agonator was in hand and Natalie was on the floor, writhing and shrieking and sending blood everywhere. His eyes were on her and his smile was gone; he looked furious that his little game, the one that probably would have ended with her rape, had been interrupted.

It was up to me to deal with him, but the sight of Natalie being tortured again, as it had that night in Germany, temporarily drove me out of my mind. If not for that, I would have simply knocked Hignat out as well and the two of us would have been out of there that much quicker. Instead, I vaulted right over Wilwog and flew at Hignat, yelling, *"no—you—don't!"*

His attention had been so exclusively focussed on Natalie that he hadn't noticed the other struggle until my shout. He turned and with lightning reflexes, pointed his agonator at me and clicked it, but due to the magic of the thing, all he succeeded in doing was releasing Natalie from its hold. His eyes widened in dismay as he rapidly clicked it again, pointing the golden light in my direction, but before he could click it a third time to release the jet of evil magic, my closed fist connected squarely with his jaw.

It was very similar to how I had attacked Tankom on that unforgettable occasion, except that Hignat was much younger and much quicker, and after having spent so much time with Wilwog over the years, seemed to know a thing or two about brawling. My blow did knock him down, but his agonator-free hand came rocketing around, collecting me on the side of the head, causing me to stagger. I tried to dive at him but he twisted around and leapt back to his feet with terrifying speed. My momentum carried me forward into a zone of horrible vulnerability, as both of us knew. I threw my arms out to try to push him over as I went but as I made contact with him, he brought his fist down hard on the back of my neck.

The lights didn't go out completely but they did dim considerably. When they returned to something close to functional, there was still plenty of noise happening around me, although I couldn't identify its source. I gathered that Hignat and Natalie were fighting again, that Natalie must have distracted him before he could really go to town on me, but the struggle could have gone either way by now. I struggled desperately to return fully to my senses and only with enormous effort did I achieve it. I got to my knees and then to my feet, using the nearby wall for support as I looked around to see what was going on.

Hignat had been disarmed; his bludginator lay on the floor in the corner along with Natalie's hair, and his agonator lay just a few feet from me, while his belt lay abandoned in the middle of the room a few feet away from the prone Wilwog. He, meanwhile, had been backed into another corner; Natalie was still hobbled by the wound between her legs but she was stalking him like a predator. He looked dazed, as though he couldn't quite believe how this interview had turned out—and as though he had recently received a nasty blow to the head, which might have been mine or something Natalie had done while I'd been out of it.

As I watched, trying to decide if I had the strength to back her up, Hignat seemed to decide the time had come to make his last stand. He straightened up and, not without effort, attempted to charge Natalie. Debilitated in her own right or not, she was ready for him. Just as he was about to reach her, she through all her weight into a sharp kick; it connected solidly with his groin. That was pretty much the end of Hignat's last stand; his breath escaped him in a quiet but high-pitched whine as all the strength seemed to run out of his legs. He toppled over, almost taking Natalie down with him, his hands moving to his sac in an attempt to staunch whatever agony had taken hold and consequently preventing him from breaking his fall. He landed flat on his face and simply lay there, struggling weakly and moaning piteously. Natalie turned around and stepped forward so that if the lighting were different, he would be in her shadow.

"That was for Amelia," she told him fiercely, her words clear enough although the pain they cost showed on her face, "and this is for what you did to me."

She gave him another hard kick, this time in the arse. He let out another gasp of pain and looking a bit like an old turtle, tried to wriggle away from her. She began stalking him again, kicking him in the arse every few seconds, throwing everything she had into it, again ignoring the resultant flaring pain. This was amusing to watch, but after a few seconds of it, clarity reasserted itself in my mind. We had bested these two sufficiently; now it was time to get out of here and get back to the others, wherever they were. I stepped away from the wall and once sure that my balance was reliable, I went after Natalie, catching her by the arm as she was about to go back for her seventh kick.

"That'll do, I think," I told her firmly.

She scowled at me. "No, I wanna—"

I shook my head, firm as ever and pointed at the top right-hand corner (from where we stood anyway) of the cell, where a surveillance camera watched over the scene. "Someone will be watching that, maybe Hall himself, and they'll probably be on their way down here for backup right now. We have to go before they get here."

She struggled with herself for a few seconds before her eyes cleared and sanity reasserted itself. With it came a kind of horror as the events of the last little while began taking their toll. It was probably how she had looked during those moments of insanity that had proceeded our—our admissions. Thinking of that made me flush and, not wanting her to see it, I turned and guided her toward the door.

"Can you use your magic to open that?" I asked. "It'd be quicker than getting the key off Hignat if you can."

"No," a low moan came from behind us. Hignat was still stirring and he seemed to be recovering. Before Natalie could launch into action again, I turned my hero device on him and gave it a single click; he immediately went the same way as Wilwog.

"Come on," I urged her.

She obliged willingly enough. The cell door unlocked with a click and then swung heavily open; we both had to step backward to avoid being hit by it. The corridor beyond was quiet but not completely silent; shouts came to us from a long way off, probably in the direction of the entrance. Had the others got inside the base, or was it because of us? Were reinforcements on their way down here as we stood here like a couple of stunned dear in a spotlight?

I tugged on Natalie's arm and led her out into the corridor, pulling the door shut behind me and hoping that it would lock on its own (it didn't matter that they were both unconscious, I liked the idea of them both being locked up in a Hammerheart cell where just about anything could happen to them). Once outside, I tried to think fast about what we needed to do. Meanwhile, the sound of reinforcements was getting louder.

"Are you up to more magic?" I asked her urgently. When she nodded, I said quickly, "We need a shield around the two of us, one that repels both physical and magical assaults. We also need to be invisible, untraceable and under a soundproof barrier. Can you do all that quickly?"

She nodded again and began casting spells, moving her arms in the air to cover both of us but not bothering to move her feet as she would have if she were fully fit. Although I couldn't see anything as a result of her magic, I felt sure that it was working as it should have—it somehow felt familiar. When she was finished, she looked back at me for instructions.

"Fix yourself up," I said gently, squeezing her arm. There was time for that now that we wouldn't be immediately exposed if Hammerhearts should round the corner while we stood here, although they were still coming, and we would need to move out of the way of this door or they would walk right into us, protection or no protection.

She did her face first, and seeing it returned to its normal state was both enormously relieving and uplifting. Although she was still emotionally scarred from what Hignat had put her through, none of it had detracted from her physical beauty. She followed it up by normalising whatever damage had been done below her waistline, and was then able to straighten up into a normal posture. She took a moment to return her hair to the state it had been in prior to Hignat's assault, and that was everything.

She looked back at me then, again for more instructions, and for the first time since Hignat and Wilwog had burst in on us, all those feelings came flooding back. I saw it in her face and knew mine must have looked the same. I was looking at her in a way that I'd never been able to before; not only was it totally unguarded, unlike most of the time I had known her, but she was meeting my gaze, and hers was just as unguarded. I was lost in her, appreciating everything I had missed in the cell. All my rationality seemed to depart, and I probably would have kissed her right then and there if not for half a dozen Hammerhearts suddenly hurrying around the far corner and approaching us at almost a sprint.

We had to move; I grabbed Natalie and pulled her back away from the door, the wrong way to which we would need to go but the only way to prevent a Hammerheart collision. The leader (3T77 by code) stopped in front of the door, hurriedly unlocked it and threw it open. He charged in and was immediately followed by his fellows (four men and one woman). Someone cried out inside, and the sound was immediately followed by people falling down as someone in front was knocked over by someone in back (Hammerhearts had a habit of doing that to each other).

It left our passage clear and we took it at a run, not bothering to move quietly since they couldn't hear us anyway. We rounded the corner from which they had come and then stopped, me remembering that Hall had zigzagged all over the place to get to this point. Judging by the dismay on her face, Natalie was remembering the same thing.

"Which way do we go?" she asked, beginning to panic. "What are you doing?" she added.

I had raised my hero device and given it a click. Although there was nothing wrong with the lighting in the corridor, a small light flew from the tip and hovered over my head as it had back in the cell. In response, I jabbed my thumb up at it.

"Put a spell on that thing to follow our back trail," I told her. "That might be difficult magic but do you reckon you can do it? The only other alternative I see is waiting for those Hammerhearts to come out and following them back, but this way is quicker and probably safer."

"Okay," she said nervously, screwing up her face in concentration.

For a few seconds, nothing happened, and when it did, the light drifted back along the corridor toward the cell. Natalie groaned, but my spirits rose; of course it would need to go back there first before it could find its way out of here. If I had the magic part right too, the Hammerhearts back there wouldn't even see it. We just had to hope that it reached us before they did.

"How fast is that thing moving?" I asked her.

"Jogging speed," she replied. "Well, that's what I tried to make it do—I guess we'll find out when it—"

That was when it passed back over our heads and took off the way we were facing. We didn't bother speaking anymore but followed it in silence, jogging along side-by-side, winding our way through the twists and turns of the Basement. We eventually reached the entrance, but the Hammerhearts had taken another preventative measure at this point: Not only were there the typical trio of security guards, all looking more alert than usual as they patrolled, but the door which usually stood open had been closed. The light drifted straight through it but Natalie and I came to a halt, me trying to think what would be the best way to tackle this next problem.

Natalie had no such hesitation. Before I quite knew what was happening, the middle guard suddenly dropped like a stone. The other two guards jumped to attention right away but in the moment it took them to focus, the one on the far left also dropped like a stone. That just left the one standing directly in front of Natalie, and although he couldn't see us, he fired one shot of his revealer at us before he too was knocked out. The whole thing had happened in no more than two seconds, and my spirits lifted even higher as it came to me how Natalie had regained a lot of confidence in her spell casting abilities.

"Are we visible now?" I asked her.

"No, I put the invisibility veil and the soundproof barrier inside the shield so that we couldn't be exposed like that."

"What about the untraceability?"

"They would trace the shield if that was on the inside."

"Oh, right."

I was impressed by her quick thinking, but I barely had a moment to dwell on it as Natalie used her magic to open the door in front of us. There were more Hammerhearts waiting beyond, and like the security guards, they sprung into action almost immediately. There were maybe seven or eight here (eight, as it turned out) but one of them went down immediately under Natalie's magic. Two more had dropped by the time the rest were ready to fire, and one of them by my hand (I'd switched my hero device back to whatever had knocked Hignat and Wilwog down). Five jets of light flew at us; two of them were revealers, one was an agonator, one was unrecognisable and the one in the centre was—as I should have expected—from a solid-outliner.

The others had no effect but the thicky prison, once it hit, began spreading over the shield around us. It didn't really do any damage though, apart from obscuring our field of vision and identifying our position to the Hammerhearts. We continued to attack, knocking another two out before the last three could refocus their weapons on the thicky prison. They went with the same weapons as before, except for the bright spark who had initially used the solid-outliner; that one had drawn a gun, perhaps thinking it might get through the shield in a way the magic hadn't. It didn't, of course, and about a second later, all three of them were down and out.

Which left us with the problem of the thicky prison. If I used my hero device as a solid-outliner, I would only cause thicky prison to spread around the inside of the shield and do nothing to the stuff on the outside. If Natalie popped me out of the shield, not only would I be exposing myself to Hammerhearts should they come across us here, but I would probably get caught up in the stuff before I could vanish it. Natalie, meanwhile, probably wouldn't be able to vanish the stuff with her magic due to whatever it was about thicky prison that seemed to allude Sorcerers. So what on earth were we to do?

"I'm gonna get rid of the shield and then create a new one," Natalie told me. "It'll have to go over the top of the untraceable spell but that probably doesn't matter; we can deal with just about anyone like this."

Except Hammerson, I thought, but didn't say; apart from that unlikely but not impossible scenario, she was probably right. She performed her magic then but I didn't focus on it because that was when an external thought pushed its way into my head. I had almost forgotten about May in the commotion that had befallen us after we had been separated from the others, and now that she was getting back in contact, it surprised me that she hadn't tried to help us before now. The thought was that she and the others (whoever constituted the others) were going up to the top level of the base, and that Natalie and I should try to meet them there. By the time I'd processed the thought, the thicky prison was gone and we were re-shielded.

"Top floor," I told Natalie. "The others are going up there."

"What?"

"May just told me telepathically. I dunno what's going on but that's where we need to go."

"You mean where Stella used to live?"

"I assume so."

There were the stairs and there were the lifts. The lifts would be quickest but they would also leave us exposed if anyone found out we were in there—they could send us plummeting down the shaft if they felt like it. The stairs could also be dangerous if we met anyone in there but that still seemed like the best option. I sighed and made in that direction, feeling a great sense of déjà vu; it was that night in Germany all over again.

Before we could get in there, however, footsteps reached our ears. For a fraction of a second, I allowed myself to think that they belonged to our friends, and that they were heading up towards the top floor. Cruel reality set in quickly though; it was only one person, and he or she was thundering down toward this level. The footsteps were urgent and I knew, somehow, as though by premonition, who they belonged to. On this occasion, my premonition was spot-on.

Mr. Hall, English teacher that was Police Commissioner by virtue of being in the right place at the right time with the stupendously wrong intentions, burst through the stairwell doorway and then came skidding to a halt just feet away from Natalie and me, his eyes widening as he took in his fallen fellows. The man looked more dishevelled than he had when he had brought us down here, his clothing messed up and torn in a few places. He was not on his game as he had been back in the school; perhaps he also thought, if he had a chance to think it over, that whoever did this had already fled the scene.

Whatever the reason, he did not flood the room with evil magic as he probably would have done an hour ago.

It was the chance we needed. Before he could react, Natalie and I began our own assault. The spell from my hero device, which should have knocked him unconscious, bounced off his shield and had no effect; in fact it was so ineffective that if not for Natalie's spell, it probably would have gone unnoticed. Somehow, she managed to push her magic right under the shield, and it almost worked, too. Hall staggered and went to his knees, his eyes rolling briefly out of focus before somehow, against all the laws of magic that I knew of (perhaps the Villain Crystal had saved him), he fought it off and jumped back to his feet.

A wave of villainous magic rolled out from Hall in every direction, as I had expected from the first. I didn't know what it had been meant to do but it simply hit and rolled over the top of our shield, leaving Natalie and me unharmed. She and I both stepped forward, our unspoken intention clear: We were going to back him into a corner and render him incapacitated so that we could strip him of the Villain Crystal, thus succeeding in the overall mission and taking something away from this otherwise catastrophic morning.

As Natalie put her magic into action again, however, I was distracted by another external thought forming in my head. I had no idea where May was now or who she was with; all I knew was, 'we're coming'. The thought filled me with enormous relief; Hall wasn't as dangerous now as he had been before and if the cavalry included Marc and Fewul, as it probably would, we would be back in the driver's seat, as we should have been all along if we had only done the thing right from the start.

When I returned my attention to the struggle at hand a couple of seconds later, Hall and Natalie were completely engaged in combat. She was firing spell after spell in a way I had never seen from her, as though whatever understanding was required in order to perform magic masterfully had suddenly hit her. He seemed to know approximately where she was but all his attempts to hit her, including those with his solid-outliner, failed; she was redirecting those spells so that they hit the walls rather than our shield, without missing a beat herself. It was all happening so fast that Hall didn't have a spare moment to make himself invisible. I was pleased to see that his expression had become rather panicky.

I hesitated for a moment, not sure if my involvement in this battle would help or hinder Natalie. The whole thing was on a knife-edge; an outside influence could benefit either party. The last thing I wanted was for Natalie to be distracted as Amelia had been, but it only took that moment for me to decide that this was a different situation. Unlike Amelia, Natalie knew I was here, and although Hall may have suspected that I would still be with Natalie, the thought had probably since slipped his mind.

I switched to my solid-outliner, took aim at Hall's waistline (how immobilising his hips would make life difficult) and fired. The jet of whiteness missed, flying between his legs within an inch of his groin. His expression changed as it passed, shifting from panic to livid fury. Before he could act on it, though, he was blasted backward, Natalie's magic finally getting the better of him. We both hurried forward but before we could take full advantage, footsteps suddenly came at us from behind.

I turned to see the Hammerhearts who had gone to our cell hurrying back down the corridor toward us, their expressions surprised and terrified as they took in Hall's struggle with an invisible force. All six of them were there, and Hignat and Wilwog were bringing up the rear, both lying unconscious in a floating cage that was the Hammerhearts' preferred method of transporting prisoners. Out came the revealers, flying all over the room as they burst through the open Basement doorway, bypassing the three unconscious guards with barely a glance. Two jets of semi-transparent light hit the shield but, as before, had no effect. What *did* have an effect was one of the men in front colliding with me before I had a chance to move out of his way. I staggered and went down and before I could get back up, another Hammerheart collided with me, this one twigging quickly enough to grab me and pull me to the floor as he went down.

The struggle could probably have gone just about anywhere from that point but at that precise moment, distracting me completely from the large man who had hold of me, a bell dinged somewhere over my head. The sound was so unexpected and so out-of-place in this environment that if the danger hadn't been so pronounced, I might have laughed. A moment later, one of the lifts began to open, and I couldn't have been more pleased with who I saw standing inside it.

There were five of them, and they looked more impressive than ever: Marc in the centre, Peter and James on either side of him, and the three of them flanked on either side by May and an ever-eccentric-looking Beast of Magic. Peter, James and May were all armed with hero devices (when had May been given a hero device?) and Marc and Fewul were, of course, armed with their own magic. All five of them were completely visible and, so far as I knew, completely unshielded. It made them all the more impressive in my mind but as gasps of comprehension echoed around the room as the Hammerhearts recognised our company, I dearly hoped that they were shielded: The last thing we could afford to do, now that we'd worked our way into this position, was to become complacent.

"*No!*" Hall roared, and a familiar magical force began pushing hard against us. Hall had started doing that thing that had ultimately defeated us in the school again.

We were all forced backward, Natalie and I together as one due to our shield, unable to resist the pull of whatever it was he was doing. I looked over my shoulder and saw him then; he looked madder than ever but unfortunately, he was regaining his feet and consequently his ability to fight us. A yell echoed from behind me as a couple of Hammerhearts were forced back into the stairwell—they had probably fallen down the stairs. I was being pushed in that direction too but before I got there, the force abruptly ceased.

The Hammerheart still holding onto me let go momentarily in surprise and I took the chance, springing to my feet and jumping away from him. Natalie, too, was regaining her feet; I steadied her and looked back at Hall, trying to decide what to do.

"*Help me!*" Hall roared at those Hammerhearts still left in the room, jabbing his thumb in our general direction.

"Sir, we can't," one of the remaining Hammerhearts said from behind me, and I froze in surprise. "Lord Hammerson has given us orders not to hurt them."

"*What?!*" he bellowed, his jaw dropping slackly and his eyes popping out of their sockets. It was my morning for observing priceless facial expressions, it seemed. I looked around wildly to see what was going on and saw that all the remaining Hammerhearts were backing towards the stairwell, looking nervous. What on earth was going on?

"Well, we tried," one of them muttered, and completing the absurdity, they all turned and hurried into the stairwell, sprinting up the stairs toward the Hammerheart Highway and the way out of this place, the floating cage zooming along in their wake. I looked quickly at Natalie, perplexed, and she nodded at the elevator out of which our friends had just stepped. May was grinning at me, apparently aware of my approximate position (probably from my mind), a look of enjoyment I had never seen on her face before, and I understood what power had taken hold of those Hammerhearts. Now, Hall was alone, and totally disadvantaged.

The battle began in earnest again. Marc and Fewul hurried forward, backing Hall into the corner again, and Natalie doubled around behind them as they passed so that she could join the charge. May moved to block the stairwell in case Hall tried to escape that way (perhaps someone had instructed her mentally that she ought to) while Peter and James covered the elevators. I joined them, tapping each of them on the shoulder so that they would know I was there.

The struggle went on for about thirty seconds that seemed to go on forever. It wasn't quite as intense as the one Marc had contested with Arnold Hammerson that night in Germany but it was pretty damn close. Marc and Natalie were attacking with everything they had while Fewul, for whatever reason, was doing no more than following Marc's lead. Why wasn't he doing more? He was certainly capable of doing more. The Beast of Magic could overpower Hall completely, Villain Crystal and all; why wasn't he?

"Fewul," Marc said through gritted teeth, taking a step back so that Natalie was momentarily doing most of the attacking, "remove his protection."

"No you don't," Hall growled back, his eyes seeming to clear as though he had reached a sobering understanding. "If I can't beat you today, I'll just take you down at a later date."

"*No!*" Marc shouted, but it was too late.

Hall didn't vanish altogether—so far as I knew, there were too many enchantments around the base preventing that kind of escape. Instead, he shrank to a microscopic size. It happened so quickly that it looked almost like he had simply disappeared, but I knew enough about the whole shrinking thing to know what to look for. The wall behind him cracked as magic from either Marc or Natalie flew through the space Hall's head had previously occupied.

"Fewul, where did he go?"

"I do not know, Master; he has made himself invisible, and he is still untraceable."

"He has gone upstairs," May told us. "He passed over my head before I could stop him."

"Couldn't you take him if you knew where he was?" Marc asked, horrified.

"I have been trying. I can get some of his thoughts but I cannot influence them."

"So where is he..." Peter started, and then the comprehension seemed to hit us all at the same time.

There was no time to wait for an elevator. May stepped aside as we all thundered toward the stairwell, Marc accidentally knocking Natalie over as he couldn't see her—I ducked back to help her so that the two of us, along with May, brought up the rear. By the time we burst through the door on the level above and out onto the bridge over the tracks of the Hammerheart Highway, we were again too late. Hall was in a solitary Hammerheart cart in the middle of the spacious room. He was still invisible but one didn't need to be a genius to know he was there; Hammerheart carts never stopped like that. It was only there for a fraction of a second before it disappeared in the same rapid movement that Hall had used a minute earlier. A moment later, he was gone. Marc swore loudly, his voice echoing all over the place.

"Now what?" Peter asked.

"Fewul, where did he go?"

"I do not know, Master; he is still—"

"Untraceable, yeah, I get it. What about the cart he was in? You saw it a moment ago—where is it now?"

"The cart is also untraceable as long as he is in it, Master."

Marc swore again. "Fine. Tell me, what buttons did he push before he took off? Can you trace him by what he did before he left?"

"I'm afraid not, Master. I had no way of looking inside the cart as long as he was there."

"May, did you get any idea before he left?" I asked her.

"Yes," she said, surprising me—I hadn't actually expected that. "He took the cart to a place called B476. Do you know where that is?"

"It's a base, I know that much," I said, remembering how on that occasion I had used a Hammerheart cart to get in here, the letter 'B' had corresponded to bases.

"Fewul, which base is that?" Marc asked.

"That is the base in Toronto, Master."

Marc swore for a record-breaking third time in less than a minute. I couldn't remembering him ever being such a potty mouth. "Of course, he'd go all the way to the other side of the bloody planet. Fine, what should we do? Should we grab a few carts and go after him?"

Everyone looked around at everyone else, waiting for someone to give some sort of instruction. Of course, nobody looked at me or Natalie as we were still invisible. It was James who eventually said, "Maybe we can, but I think we've missed our chance with Hall. We can't just go off now because if Hall's still on his game, he's probably already left Toronto exactly so that we couldn't trace him. We can't go all over the world looking for him now while we've left the others undefended here—we have to rejoin them so that we can plan our next move."

Marc sighed. "You're right, of course, but damn—we were so friggin' close. Fine, let's go up. Oh, and Natalie, make yourself visible, please?"

It was 11:15 on the morning of August 23, 2010.

Chapter 38: Eye of the Storm

The seven of us took one of the elevators to the top floor (well, the second from the top—the elevator didn't go to the top floor). Nobody spoke; each of us was lost in his or her own thoughts. In my case, it was almost all dismay: Now that Hall had escaped, what on earth were we to take from the morning's work? We had certainly disrupted the Hammerhearts today but what did that mean in the scheme of things?

The lift came to a halt and opened on the long corridor which, so far as the eye was concerned, came to a dead end. We piled out and progressed along it, again, in silence. Only when we got close did Marc say, "Everyone stand close so I can put a new shield around us all."

We did as he told (Natalie presumably removing our shield) and Marc did his thing. He then moved on, approaching the wall ahead of us and passing straight through it as though it weren't there, and Fewul was right behind him. He had used magic to pass into the top-security area of the base, the place where only the Hammersons and their most trusted advisors were normally allowed. I had been in there several times but only either as a prisoner or with my own source of magic. What now?

The question hung in the air for several seconds before it was answered by Peter; he walked forward and straight through the wall as Marc had done. James followed with the same result, and then May repeated the process. It was the shield, I supposed, which had been enchanted to pass through, so I led Natalie through into the Hammersons' living quarters. Did Arnold Hammerson still live here? If so, he would be the only one now that Tankom was dead and Stella was with us.

"Oh thank God," a voice echoed from the top of the stairs to my left. Lucien was standing at the top, grinning as he took in the seven of us and the fact that we were all unharmed. "Come on up, you guys; we really need to talk."

The Hammersons' spacious living room was full of people. Some of them were sitting on the couches but there weren't enough to accommodate everyone; plenty of people were standing around the edges of the room, along the walls to either side, on either side of the doorway leading to what had formerly been the Hammersons' bedrooms, and a few were even standing behind the kitchen bench beneath which I had hidden a couple of times. They had been talking amongst themselves before we had arrived but went silent when we joined them. I scanned them all carefully to make sure everyone was present; they all looked rather stunned with the way the morning had turned out but like us, they were physically unharmed. But there was one person missing.

"Where's Amelia?" I asked, watching many faces fall as I uttered her name.

"We sent her back to the base," Lucien said heavily. "She can't help us now, and she could get hurt again. It's just easier this way. Jessica will look after her until we get back.

"Now, people," he called more loudly, addressing the room at large, "we need to work out what to do next. Marc?"

"Hall's left the country," he said. "Is it worth going after him?"

"We're going to have to catch him at some stage, but perhaps today's not the right time for that," said Lucien. "For the time being, though, we've breached their defences and we might as well capitalise on it while we can. We'd better set some lookouts while we discuss it though. Stella, are there any other ways they could get in here other than this door?"

"No, that's the only way in here," she said.

"In that case, maybe two or three volunteers. Anyone?"

A few hands went up and not wanting to waste time, Lucien immediately selected Belinda, George and Dean for the job. A minute later, Dean was hiding in the other corridor while George and Belinda stood guard at the top of the stairs. Lucien also stood guard in the doorway where he could see George's back and listen to our discussion at the same time.

"May, can you do something for us while we talk?" Marc asked her. When she merely looked at him, he went on, "We need to know who is in the base. Can you take everyone's mind in here?"

"I can do that," she said tonelessly.

"Can you also pick up when new people come in?"

"Yes."

"Would you do that for us?" he asked. "We only need them to be monitored; we can worry about control later."

"Okay," she said again. She seemed willing enough to go along with this, although it was impossible to get a good gauge on her emotions.

"Okay," Marc said, and then took a deep breath. "Firstly, we can't spend too long on this, but I think we need to catch everyone up on what's gone down this morning. John, Natalie, are you two okay?"

"Okay enough," I said when Natalie only looked at me. "They put us in the Basement for a while and then Hignat and Wilwog came down to interrogate us about what we've been doing since they took the Woodwards' base. They got a bit out of us—they were really good at it. We overpowered them, though, once I worked out how to make these things restore Natalie's magic. You know that was the big mistake we made in our preparations: Simulations are all good, but we really should have been properly trained to use them. If I'd known I could use it to restore her magic, we would have had a lot less trouble."

Marc was gaping at me as I spoke. When I finished, he managed to compose himself. "That's a good point. I can't believe we didn't think of it like that. They just did all we needed them to do in the simulations."

"How come you guys took so long to come down?" Natalie asked. "We were there for ages before we got our chance. Where were you all that time?"

"Yeah, sorry about that," said Peter sheepishly. "We got pretty badly held up."

"After you guys were taken away," Lucien told us, "Marc tried to re-open the passage he took you through but it didn't work. It was as though Hall had actually removed it instead of just blocking it. So we firstly got Fewul to round up everyone throughout the school and bring them to us, and then Marc made him take Amelia back to the base. After that, he contacted Mr. Woodward telepathically to let him know that we'd taken over the school and the adults ought to come down and secure it for us. Before they got there, though, Hall came back and we all started fighting again and it was a total fiasco. We didn't even have Fewul at that point because Marc had told him to help the Sorcerers get into the grounds in case they couldn't get through the protection on their own. When they finally did get to us, we managed to slip away and leave them to it, but Hall must have known where we were heading because he tried to head us off. Stella showed us where the guest entrance into the base was and by the time we went through it, Hall was already fighting with you guys—Marc came straight down. Did I miss anything?"

"Does Mr. Woodward know what happened to Amelia?" Natalie asked in a small voice.

"No," said Marc flatly. "I didn't want him to know in case it took his mind off the job, but your dad knows, Natalie, so Mr. Woodward will be told soon."

"Can anything be done for her?" I asked a little desperately.

"Not with our magic," said Marc, "but May, tell them what you told us earlier."

"I may be able to restore some of her," May said. "I can give her those memories of hers which I picked up in the time I have known her, and I can take all your memories of her to fill in any gaps. Anyone else who has known her would be able to help me do this. It will not make her the same as how she was before, though."

"That's true," said Lucien sadly. "Most of who we are is determined by our experiences—everything we have ever seen, done and felt throughout our lives—even those things we can't remember. Amelia may retain most of her old qualities, but for all intents and purposes, she won't be the same person we've always known."

A sad silence followed this little speech as everyone digested the implications of Lucien's words. It was exactly as I had feared: Amelia wasn't technically dead, but she might as well have been. Hall had found a way to do in a Sorcerer after all. It wasn't much different from what May could have done if she'd felt like it. I knew that we would all want the Honnie to try to put her back together again, but how would we feel once it was done? I supposed that would depend on how much of Amelia could be recovered. I dearly hoped it was most, and I would spend as long as May needed reminiscing about Amelia —everything I knew and could remember—to help.

"Okay," Marc finally said, looking sad but making a supreme effort to push on. After his own history with Amelia, I respected how much it cost him to do that. "Since the adults are taking care of the school, it seems like the best thing for us to do is stay here in the base and try to secure it for ourselves. If we can, we might be able to start taking over other Hammerheart bases as well. Even down a Sorcerer, we still have a hell of a lot of magic on our side, and we can probably afford to call in another Sorcerer or two if necessary."

"And what good would that do overall?" asked Lena. "Isn't the whole point to try to get their magic back?"

"That was the point of today, yes," James agreed, "and I suppose if we flush all the Hammerhearts out from underground, they'll be forced on-ground, and we don't know what consequences might arise from that. I don't think it'll come to that, though, because they would know that we're here. If they're smart, they'll try to lock the base down until Hall can come back with reinforcements and a better plan, because even after we beat him earlier, he knows that other than Hammerson himself, he's got the best chance of taking us down."

"That's true," said Marc, now looking more enthusiastic. "They'll be prepared for me, Natalie and Fewul—at least as much as it's possible for anyone to be prepared for Fewul—but they still don't know about May. They don't, do they?" he added, suddenly looking nervous as he looked at Natalie and me.

"No. Hignat did ask who she was but I told him she was the form we'd given Fewul. Since nobody saw him at the school, I reckon that story will hold."

"Except that Hall himself would have seen them both in the lift earlier," said James. "Do you think he was attentive enough to notice?"

"Maybe, but even if he did, it still doesn't matter," said Marc, and now he was really getting into the spirit of things, "because even if he suspects something off about her, he can't know exactly what she's capable of. That'll be our advantage if they consider using regular Hammerhearts against the rest of us—May can take care of them real easy. The most important thing is how we handle Hall when he comes back, because I'm sure he will—or Hammerson if he decides to show up. What's likely to happen, do you think?" he asked the room at large.

"Wouldn't that depend how angry Hall is right about now?" Katie asked after several seconds in which no one spoke. "I suppose the normal custom would be for him to tell Hammerson exactly what happened, and then Hammerson would decide what to do about it, but Hall might have been mad enough to make his own plan so he can get his revenge."

"I'm sure Hammerson would come here right away if Hall told him," said Lucien, "and he'd order Hall to come with him, along with backup, like he did that night in Germany."

"Okay, so we need plans for either eventuality," Marc said. "If it's Hall, I guess we just continue the way we did before. We can stay in this part of the base so that when he comes through, George and Belinda will get a clear shot of him before he even knows they're there, and May can let us know when he's about to come through. You can, can't you?" he asked the Honnie, and she nodded silently. "Good, and you can also get the rest of the Hammerhearts to turn against him when the fight starts? Best not to let him get suspicious until it's too late to do anything about it. We can get them to block off the Hammerheart Highway. Or—hey, I just thought of something."

He was pacing around the room now, clenching and unclenching his fists as his brain worked overtime. He looked excited for the fight. "Stella," he said, "how do you activate the security in this place? You know those lines on the floor that can trigger magic if a person tries to cross them stealthily?"

"Yes, we can do that from in here," she said, and now she looked excited too.

"Good. How much of Hall's protection would that remove? Also, would he notice it being removed?"

"He'd notice some things," she said hesitantly, "like if he was shrunken or something—"

"Yeah, that's exactly the kind of escape I'm trying to prevent here. What about his shield? Would it get rid of that without him noticing?"

"It would get rid of it, yeah, but I'm not sure if it'd go unnoticed."

"How many of those lines are there in the base?"

"Heaps," she said. "Probably over a hundred, and they're all over the place. You can choose which ones to turn on. There's a control panel in a room on the other side of this level. If you want to do the fight up here, there's a line that runs parallel with the wall that blocks this part of the base off. Hall would be unprotected the moment he crossed it, and if we're ready to attack him from the top of the stairs, well, I'm sure he'll be expecting something, but he'll assume the shield would protect him."

We were all getting into the spirit of the thing now. Some sort of fight was inevitable as long as we stayed here, and unlike the one we had come prepared for today, we all seemed far more confident that we could pull this off. Why? We were up against the same enemy with fewer weapons than we had started the day with. Even I was excited, no matter how many times I told myself that this was no better than the fight in the school or the fight that night in Germany. Somehow, for whatever reason, this felt different.

"Okay then," said Marc. "When he steps through, he'll be visible, unshielded and, if we're lucky, traceable. That might even make him susceptible to May's talent, we can hope. The only trouble will be that he will still have the Villain Crystal, and that may protect him on its own, but we still might be able to overpower it. May, you need to try to take him the whole time he's here; I know you couldn't before, but things might change if we can break down his protection. The same applies for Hammerson if he shows up. The rest of us will bombard him with magic as soon as he steps through, hopefully not giving him a chance to fight back."

"Maybe we can go one better," James suggested. "We have Fewul with us, remember? There is our greatest weapon of all, but only if we know best how to use it. No amount of magic Hall throws at Fewul will weaken it, but it might wear Hall down after a while. Perhaps if we send Fewul out there disguised as you, Marc, he can fight Hall for us, either winning or sufficiently weakening him so that we can deal with him ourselves."

"Yeah, we will use Fewul," Marc agreed, "but I'm not sure if that's the best way because—hear me out, James—because firstly, Hall might slip away again if we don't get him far enough into the base, and this is about as far from the Hammerheart Highway as he can get. Secondly, we want to get a line or two between him and the exit so that he can't get out without weakening himself even further. Thirdly, and this is most important, once we beat him, we have to take the Villain Crystal from him. Since we know he has it but nobody's seen him use it, that probably means he's swallowed it like my dad did. That means we're gonna have to cut it out of him, and we wanna be somewhere secure when we do that."

Several girls made disgusted sounds at this. It was probably the first they'd heard about this particular use of the Villain Crystal.

"Okay," James said, almost satisfied, "but that still leaves the question of what to do with Fewul. We need to give him a job that would be incredibly difficult for us but easy for him; that'll be the best way to use him. Marc, what are your thoughts?"

"My thoughts are to order him to fight Hall or Hammerson, or both, with absolutely every trick he is capable of," said

Marc, "and that'll probably get around all their protection eventually. As long as I order him to fight before it begins, I won't have to worry about ordering him around during the fight. That's the trouble with Fewul," he added, glowering at the completely impassive Beast of Magic, "he never takes his own initiative."

"Don't complain, Marc," said Felicity quietly. "Wasn't that the whole point of the prophecy? You don't want Fewul to take his own initiative."

Marc shrugged. "I know you're right, Felicity, but that doesn't change the fact that I probably could have stopped Hall in his tracks with Fewul's help if I hadn't been too busy saving my arse to give him an order. Now, that's the plan for Hall; what about Hammerson?"

There was another silence as several of us thought over his question, and others watched us, waiting to see what we would come up with. It was James who spoke first. "First and foremost, if we do confront Hammerson, should we try to kill him here and now?"

That seemed like a no-brainer to me, but Marc took the question seriously. Finally he said, "I don't see why not. I would have preferred to do Hall first, and maybe we'll get a shot at him as well, but the sooner we remove Arnold Hammerson, the quicker we can begin putting the world back to the way it was—or almost," he added reluctantly.

"In that case, the first thing we need to do is the same as Hall: Remove his crystal," said James. "While I suppose it's possible that he's swallowed it like Hall, I'm not sure if it's possible to do that with the Sien-Leoard Crystal—"

"Why wouldn't he, though?" asked Lucien. "I mean, the Sien-Leoard Crystal contains the power of the Villain Crystal, which means it would be just as capable of operating from inside the body. If Hammerson did that, he would be providing the greatest level of protection around it that he has: his own body."

James shook his head. "Maybe, or maybe he would only be able to use the power of the Villain Crystal if he did it that way.

That would make him no more dangerous than Hall. Also, the Sien-Leoard Crystal is larger, which would make it more difficult to swallow—not that that matters," he added. "Still, either way, the first part of the job is much the same as Hall. Get his crystal, and once we have it, then we have to take him down."

"Yes," said Marc, and he stopped pacing and looked around at everyone. "This is the most important part. I think—you think we ought to tell them the big secret?" he asked Lucien.

Lucien considered before saying, "Not at this very moment, but if Hammerson does turn up here, you'll have to bring everyone in before we fight him. I'm just concerned that if Hammerson knows we know his secret, and he manages to slip away from us today, he might think of something new and even more horrible before we face him again."

"What are you guys talking about?" Stella asked curiously, and she wasn't the only one.

"Later, maybe," Marc said. "Actually, we might as well tell you later, Stella, but not here and now. I have to agree with Lucien on this one. For those who do know the secret, though, how do you think we should go about killing him? However we do it, it won't be easy."

"Do these things have the power of the thing John used to kill Tankom?" James asked. "If so, one of us can just do the same thing. Of course, it might be a good idea for one of you to disable Hammerson first; he's bigger and a lot physically stronger than Tankom was."

"That's good thinking," said Marc, "and yeah, they can do that if you think of it. Do you think it would work if we just got May to break his neck or something?"

James shrugged. "It probably would, and if not, it would do enough damage to keep him still long enough for someone else to give it a go."

"I suppose to that end, I don't mind giving it a go," Marc said, staring at his feet and not meeting anyone's eyes. "After what he did to my mother—after what he's done to my whole family—I wouldn't mind getting him back."

I completely understood how he felt, and judging by the expression on his face, Lucien took it pretty personally too.

"May, what's happening around the base at the moment?" I asked.

"Not very much," she said. "There are still a lot of people around, cleaning up the mess from the fight. Some more people have come in and I have taken them all and am making them stay for now. They seem to think you have probably left, but none of them have the authority to come in here, so they cannot check."

"That's pretty good, but we need them to know where we are if we're to set up an ambush for Hammerson or Hall when they turn up," said James. "I guess you could make some of them suggest to them that we are probably up here if we're still around? They'll come prepared but they won't know what to be prepared for."

"I can do that," May agreed.

"In that case, we should set up the line so that we're ready before they are," said Marc. "Stella, you wanna do that? Someone should keep her company, though, in case they're attacked before they get back."

"There's no one else up here—"

"You never know what might happen between now and then," Marc persisted. "Anyone?"

Several people were looking at me, as though they hadn't caught up on the latest news bulletin that I was no longer the number one boy in Stella's life. I didn't want to go with her because I wanted to stay right here with Natalie, but I wasn't about to say that.

"I'll do it," Natalie offered (there you go, John). "It might as well be someone with magic."

"Good thinking," Marc agreed, and Lucien stepped aside so that Natalie and Stella could leave the room.

"What about Hignat and Wilwog?" Peter asked. "Where are they now?"

"They were unconscious in a floating cage the last time I saw them," I told him. "Did you see that?"

"Yeah, I thought those two looked familiar," said Peter, grinning at me. "They look a lot nicer when they're locked up, don't you think?"

"Doubly so when they're unconscious," Harry added.

"I dunno; being unconscious means they can't cry and beg to be let out," Simon mused.

"Where are they, then?" Peter asked.

"May?" I palmed the question to her.

"They are here somewhere," she said. "They are still unconscious, so I cannot take them. I made those other people refuse to work here anymore; they left, but the cage did not go with them."

James's expression broke into a wide grin. "May, that's exactly why we wanted a Honnie to help us. Get used to doing that because that's the sort of stuff we'll need you to do on a much wider scale once this is all over."

"Okay then," she said, and she actually smiled at him—she was rather enjoying this part of the job.

"Marc, while we're waiting for something to happen here, perhaps you should contact one of the other Sorcerers telepathically to see how things are going back at the school," Lucien suggested. "The last thing we would want is for Hall to go back there and give them a hard time after how hard we worked to drive them out of there."

"Good thinking," he said, and closed his eyes as he lapsed into concentration.

"Is everyone still armed?" Lucien then asked the room at large.

There were a lot of muttered yeses, nodding of heads and some people even holding up their hero devices. Nobody had lost theirs so far.

"Good," he said, satisfied. "Now, so far as during the fight goes, there's not much point setting up too many plans because they'll all go out the window once it gets going. I do think we should talk about positioning, though. James, do you have any early ideas?"

"Well, the tough thing about that is there's hardly any space back there," said James, screwing up his face in concentration. "I think that Marc, Natalie and Fewul are obviously the front line of attack; perhaps Marc and Fewul can stand where George and Belinda are now, or perhaps a few steps down, and Natalie can guard the corridor on the other side. Beyond that, I suppose we split the rest of the group up and gather in behind them. Only some of us will get a shot at him—maybe even none of us—so the job for the rest will be only to fight if he somehow gets through the first attack. May should be at the very back, though, because we want her concentrating on her mind rather than the fight. Does anyone have anything to add to that?"

"What's the plan if he goes straight back through the wall and takes off up the corridor to the lifts?" Katie asked.

"He'll have to fight his way through every Hammerheart in the building," said Lucien, grinning. "May, can you do that? Make them all turn against him the moment the fight starts? Not a moment before, because we want him—or them, if it's both of them—to be completely caught off-guard."

"I can do that," May said, "but that means they will have to get into position before the fight starts, otherwise they may not be ready. Is that okay?"

"That shouldn't be a problem if we get them to block the stairwell and hold the lifts on one of the lower levels, like they did to us that night in Germany," said Peter. "We'd better check with Stella to make sure there are no other ways out, though."

"I don't think there are," said Lucien, "but I suppose there are plenty of things about this place that I don't know."

"There's one other thing we need to work out," I spoke up. "What magic should we try to use when the fight starts? I'd suggest knocking them unconscious would be the quickest and easiest way to stop them fighting back, but we tried to do that to Hall earlier; mine bounced off his shield and Natalie got hers in, but it only partially worked, like the Villain Crystal revived him before he could become vulnerable."

"That might be a worry," said James slowly. "Maybe the virtual killing things? The Villain Crystal mightn't be able to undo those."

"I don't think we should use that anymore," said Stella's voice as she and Natalie re-entered the room. "The line's set up," she added in response to James's questioning look.

"Why not?" he asked, surprised. "It's no worse than knocking them out—apart from them not knowing the difference."

"Because they do a bit more than just simulate death," Stella told all of us, "they actually kill. They take a person's life and store it away, leaving the body dead until the life is restored, but it can only be done within a few hours. Once the body goes into rigor mortis, it can't be restored, and that person dies for real. When I did that to you guys," she told James and Peter, "I had to bring you back quickly—before I even had time to get you out of this place."

"That explains why I had to wait in the bottom of a bag all that time," Peter muttered.

"And pretty damn lucky you're here now, after I did that to you earlier," I said, horrified at how close I had come to actually killing my own brother.

"That does make sense," James said slowly. "I should have thought of that, because Erica and I had to wait for hours to get back too, and I never even thought of it until now."

"Okay," Marc said vaguely, opening his eyes as he returned to the here-and-now. "The Woodwards and Fletchers have rounded up all the remaining Hammerhearts and have locked them up. They've been able to shut the dome down altogether, so the school is pretty much defenceless now, but there doesn't seem to be any more danger there. Perhaps the Hammerhearts have conceded defeat there, but that'll make them even more desperate to defend this place."

"May, what's happening outside?" I asked her.

"Nothing yet, but they are trying to secure the base against us in case we get back in; they think we have left. They cannot get to most of the security, though, because it is in here."

"That includes most of the surveillance, too," Stella added, "everything except the screens which monitor the Basement."

"Is there any point in us trying to use the general surveillance system?" Lucien asked.

Stella shrugged. "Why bother, with May here?"

"They are expecting Hammerson or Hall to come back," May went on. "They do not have official word but they believe one or both of them will come back very soon."

"And is there still no one who can get in here?" Marc asked.

May shook her head. "They believe they cannot come through the wall."

Marc looked at Lucien. "You reckon we should get into position now? We may not have a lot of time once they do get here."

Lucien nodded. "Yes, that's good thinking. Everyone out into the corridor in an orderly fashion," he called to the room at large.

"You three," he called back over his shoulder, "into the other corridor so that we can set up."

"Hang on," James said loudly as everyone started to move. "Before we do, we should put up the usual protection first. All this strategy may be pointless if we forget the basic stuff."

Marc's eyes widened in horror. "Geez, you're right. How could we forget that? Everyone gather around so we can do this easily. That includes you three out there," he called, aiming his voice toward the doorway.

We all obliged, forming a large scrum in the space between the doorway and the nearest couch. Marc walked around the edge of the group, performing the usual magic to ensure our protection (including a shield this time) and ordering Fewul to do the same to himself. We then scrambled into action, creating a brief logjam on the stairs as about a dozen people tried to get into the corridor on the other side of the base. Marc, Natalie and Fewul leaned against the wall through which the attack would soon come as some of us (me among them) passed in front of them. In the end, there were ten of us in that corridor:

Natalie in front, then me, Peter, Rebecca, Felicity, Darcy, and the four Maivises bringing up the rear.

"Can everyone hear me from here?" Marc called, and while everyone over here could, we had no chance of hearing the voices at the top of the stairs on the other side. "Okay, I think I can hear everyone. May, has anything changed?"

May spoke for a few seconds, seemed to realise that a lot of us couldn't hear her from wherever she was, and placed the thoughts in all our minds instead. Yes, something had changed: Arnold Hammerson and Commissioner Hall had both arrived in a single Hammerheart cart. Hall had been humiliated by the succession of fights in which he had ultimately been bested and was all the more angry as a result. He was also a little scared, though, because he seemed to sense that we—the teenagers he had once taught—had become stronger since the last time we had fought Hammerson. He, meanwhile, was ready to kick some arse.

"Both of them," said Marc, and there was a steely resolve in his voice. "Okay. In that case, we'll take whichever one of them comes through first. Now, everyone, listen up: We're going to try to kill Arnold Hammerson here and now, today, and that means you all need to know his secret. He has put a spell on himself so that he can't be killed by any magic. He can't be killed by anything, in fact, except the bare hands of another person. Tankom had the same enchantment on her, but John managed to get around it, and we're hoping by doing something similar, we can do the same today. Does everyone understand what we're up against?"

There was a chorus of assent, but it was mixed with a lot of shock and horror at the realisation. I could see it in the faces around me—most of them anyway.

"May, the rest is up to you," Marc called. "Keep us constantly updated telepathically on what's going on out there and when they're about to come through, and remember to get the Hammerhearts on our side once the fight starts. Fewul," he ordered, "I order you to fight them with everything you have the moment they—one or both—come through that wall. Do your best to prevent them getting back through. Is everyone ready?" he called.

A few people answered their assent but most of us remained silent. I, for one, was about as ready as I could be for a fight that had the potential to go spectacularly well or devastatingly badly. The silence continued thereafter as May put herself to work, pushing thoughts into our heads in a different manner than was her custom. They weren't all-consuming, nor were they the simple messages she usually delivered; if anything, this was rather like watching television inside my own head. I was getting audible and visual perceptions from Hammerhearts throughout the base, those closest to where Hall and Hammerson were at the moment. They did not disrupt my own ability to think, and I was able to swap an amazed look with Peter before turning my full attention to what was currently playing out in the small foyer on the level of the Hammerheart Highway.

"Search it again," Hammerson snapped at a Hammerheart by the code 3P71. "This is completely unacceptable and if those kids are not brought to account, you, sir, will be."

"Yes, Sir," the offending Hammerheart responded subserviently, scuttling fearfully into the stairwell and out of sight. There were still a handful of Hammerhearts in the room, watching proceedings and waiting for orders.

Hammerson sighed. "What are we to do about this? Months of nothing out of those kids and now all of a sudden, they take the Chopville surface installation and breach our defences here. Do you think there's any point worrying about the old school now?"

"Not today, sir," said Hall grumpily, "and maybe not anymore either. Its main purpose was to control this area, but now that we know the Woodwards aren't based here anymore, perhaps we can begin moving these operations to a better-resourced location."

"That's a job for another day," Hammerson snapped. "If Frederic and his band of merry dipshits are there now, everything we had there is probably lost. Thank heavens we never store sensitive information on-ground."

"What about now, Sir?" Hall asked. "They probably have run off, but don't we need to be sure?"

"We do," Hammerson agreed, "and for that, I'm going to need you to use the magnifier. Have you ever used it before?"

"No, Sir. Is it difficult?"

"Not particularly. It's through the fourth door on the right in the downstairs corridor. Can you find it?"

"Yes, Sir," said Hall, pressing a button to call one of the lifts.

"Let me know telepathically if there is any trouble," Hammerson told him, "and don't wait for my say-so to lock the base down if they're still in here somewhere. If they are on the inside, we might as well keep them here where we have a chance of controlling them."

"Yes, Sir," said Hall as the doors of one of the elevators began sliding open and he stepped onto it. "I'll be in touch in a couple of minutes."

"Okay, it's just Hall coming up," Marc said loudly, speaking rapidly. "May, now's the time. Bring as many Hammerhearts over to our side as you can, but only the ones who aren't close to where Hammerson is now. Everyone else, be ready for the fight. We'll just focus on Hall for the time being because I don't know if Hammerson will fight or fly once he knows what's going on. Brace yourself now; he just stepped off the lift. Here he comes."

It was 11:37 on the morning of August 23, 2010.

Chapter 39: The Three Momentous Steps

Although he was alone, May was still able to provide us with an indication of exactly where Hall was. He moved with caution along the corridor, approaching the wall behind which we waited in a manner that suggested he was ready for an attack, but May seemed to believe that, although he was prepared, he didn't actually expect any trouble. He believed that we had, most likely, left the base so that we wouldn't get locked up and tortured again. Hammerson probably would have flayed him for his assumption.

He was wearing a police uniform rather than a Hammerheart one, which meant that he had to use his magic to step through the wall. The moment he did, the line Stella had set up kicked into action and he became clearly visible to us. Marc, Natalie and Fewul attacked immediately, taking the man completely by surprise (May had been right, it seemed). He never even got off a shot before he was knocked to the floor by magic cast from whoever but as before, the Villain Crystal wasn't going to give up without a good shot at a fight.

He jumped back to his feet and fired a jet of gold light that could only be the power of the agonator from his hand. He was clearly aiming in the direction from which the attack had come, and his aim was true: The light hit Fewul squarely in the chest, having no effect whatsoever. Nobody was hurt and all of us were still hidden.

In response, Fewul caused thick ropes, which looked a lot like snakes, to wrap themselves smartly around Hall's body, binding his legs together and his arms by his sides. They then drew his ankles off the floor so that they were bound behind his waist. The final touch was for the end of one of the ropes (it had a snake's head, which I didn't want to think too closely about) to slide straight into Hall's gaping mouth and down his throat.

Everyone hung back. Even Marc and Natalie, both of whom had been about to lay into him again, held their fire, watching in amazement as our former English teacher's body contorted and bulged as the snake worked its way through him. He was completely unable to move and couldn't even make a sound due to the amount of snake clogging his throat. All he could do was hang there, his eyes wide and understanding that he'd made a terrible mistake. The moment held for maybe thirty seconds before the snake began to withdraw, and when it's head finally re-appeared, it was clutching the deathly-black Villain Crystal in its mouth.

Two things happened simultaneously then. The moment his mouth became empty, Hall began bellowing at the top of his voice, either calling for help or simply in response to the terrible pain he was probably still in; and May sent an alarmed thought to all of us that moments earlier, Hall had contacted Hammerson telepathically to let him know that there was trouble on the top floor.

It was the end of Hall's fight. Fewul knocked him out with a single wave of magic, took the Villain Crystal from the snake, pocketed it and then made the snake disappear. That had been a big and rather easy win for our side, as it always should have been with Fewul at our disposal. Even with the Villain Crystal fighting for his cause, the Beast of Magic had been able to overpower it easily. That was all well and good, but now what? Hall's body blocked the small space in which Hammerson would soon expose himself; were we even going to use that space?

"Everyone stay in position," Marc called. "We're gonna take the king wanker too—any second now."

Which was true. Hammerson was too pumped to ride leisurely in the elevator; he was pounding up the stairs, a band of Hammerhearts who were now on our side but hadn't revealed as such right behind him. He had already protected himself in the same ways as Hall had but unluckily for him, he wasn't exactly sure where or how the attack had taken place. When he reached the top of the stairs, rather than exposing himself, he decided to try to flush us out first.

Hall's unconscious body was gone; it had been shifted aside by Fewul, sliding along the floor in front of us and into the room to my right—the room where Tulip had met her end six months ago. That meant that when the wall before us was blasted apart, there was no visual indication to Hammerson that the attack had happened there. It did a bit of damage on our side though; Marc and Natalie were able to protect themselves, and those on the stairs were mostly out of harm's way, but we in the corridor copped it pretty bad. Peter took one to the head and went down immediately, not quite knocked out but lucky not to be. I managed to avoid the wreckage although I got a lot of dust in my face.

Hammerson was coming slowly up the corridor, his invisibility removed by Fewul almost as quickly as he'd cast it and seemingly unaware of it. A slow-moving wave of magic was rolling ahead of him; I could see it from where I stood and it was one of the scariest things I'd ever seen in my life. The walls to either side of him were crumbling away at its touch, the rooms behind them vaporising on the spot as he passed them. The floor beneath his feet was turning bright white as he walked over it and the roof over his head seemed to be simply melting away, exposing the corridor above and causing things in it to fall to the floor behind him. The magic was visible, bright but colourless. The fact that I could see Hammerson's face behind it was probably the scariest thing of all. The Hammerhearts who had followed him up were no longer behind him—there was no safe place anywhere near him now.

"Oh no," Rebecca squeaked, and several people around me were making similar noises of dismay.

"Everyone upstairs!" Marc bellowed over his shoulder so that his voice would carry up the stairs, "move around to the other side of the floor! *Now!*"

Holy crap. There were a lot of people up there, and if they were standing in the corridor where the den was located instead of the living room in which we had been planning this battle, they would be subjected to whatever terrible magic Hammerson was currently wielding.

"Fewul," Marc ordered, "fight him. Do everything in your power to strip him of the crystal."

"Yes, Master," said Fewul obediently, wasting a precious second in bothering to speak, and launching himself forward like a javelin.

Unlike Hall, Hammerson really was ready for the attack. Furthermore, he was much more experienced and skilful with magic than Hall (than pretty much anyone alive, probably). To top it off, he had the Sien-Leoard Crystal, a much more powerful weapon than the Villain Crystal. It didn't matter that he couldn't see Fewul—he was up to the fight. The new fight stopped him in his tracks but he did not fold. Even the Beast of Magic fighting with its considerable might, as Marc had ordered, could only break even with Arnold Hammerson.

"Why isn't he winning?" Peter asked, his face deathly pale.

"Natalie, you have to protect everyone," Marc told her as, gripping the Hero Crystal, he stepped forward through the space the wall had previously occupied and out into the corridor.

I knew what the plan must be now: Whether or not Hammerson was expecting Marc to attack him along with the Beast of Magic didn't matter. Even though Fewul couldn't possibly be defeated, the time he was taking to wear Hammerson down—if Hammerson could be worn down— might be enough for the former Sorcerer (still almighty with magic in his possession) to hurt, perhaps even kill, someone up here. With the extra magic, they should be able to overpower Hammerson, but would miscommunication cost them? Probably not, but I never got a chance to see it.

Those who had been hiding up the stairs were now being directed down them by Natalie, who wanted us all together to simplify the task of protecting us. That pushed those of us already in the corridor further back so that I couldn't see the fight as Marc joined it. I heard it, though, and imagined it was like floating in the middle of a thundercloud during a storm. It was so loud that it felt like my eardrums were being pushed deeper into my skull. I could distinguish bangs but just barely, and I had no idea who was doing what. Natalie was still shouting at the others as they hurried down the stairs, May and

Stella now bringing up the rear of the party, but I couldn't hear a word she was saying and I didn't think they could either.

The corridor, even with the walls on either side gone so that it was about five times wider than before, was still no suitable place for a battle of this magnitude. The magical battle between Marc and Hammerson that night in Germany had been less intense than this one, and in a much larger space, and it had still threatened to bring the whole building down. This was much worse and, although I couldn't hear any further effects over the fight itself, I could feel how the floor beneath us was becoming less and less steady, frequently shaking as though we were in the middle of a currently low-magnitude, though constant and ever-increasing earthquake.

Everyone was now in the corridor and had his or her hero device in hand, looking ready to join in if we came under attack. I hope it didn't come to that because we were far more likely to strike each other down in a packed environment like this. Natalie was at the head of the corridor where she could watch the fight, intent on providing a magical barrier between it and us if Hammerson got the upper hand. After everything she had already been through today, it was incredibly brave of her to put herself in that position, but perhaps she understood, as I did, and probably everyone else around, that this was the end. We would quite likely win or lose the war right here and now.

Whatever Hammerson had done to try to flush us out before Fewul had intercepted him had since been neutralised so that, other than the magic he was still casting at a rate of half a dozen spells per second, he was now unprotected. Marc knew this, which meant that May had picked it up from his mind and distributed it to the Hammerhearts at the opposite end of the corridor who had, unbeknownst to their leader, turned against him. They had returned to this level and now, invisible, were creeping back along it, weapons poised, ready to catch Hammerson blindsided whenever they could get a clear shot at him. I thought for a moment of taking a few people out to do the same from the other end and then rejected the idea; we were far more likely to strike Marc or Fewul if we tried it from this side. Even with all the magic that was being performed, none of them had changed their positions, except perhaps that Hammerson had been forced backward a few steps onto a surface that looked more and more like caving in beneath him.

A different idea occurred to me then and rather than try to convey it verbally, something that would have been next to impossible, I sent the thought to May, asking if she could yet take hold of Hammerson's mind. The response came back a few seconds later in the negative, but with a reservation: She couldn't take control of him yet, but whatever was keeping him out of her reach was weakening so that she thought she could slip a few thoughts in, perhaps enough to distract him during the fight. I advised her in the same manner to give it a go and later, when I had time to reflect, I would think that it had been that suggestion, rather than anything I'd done previously, which initiated the three momentous steps.

Seconds later, the floor began to stop shaking and the thunderous noise began to die down. Beneath it, I heard a dismayed cry from someone; and beneath that, a lot of cluttering noises. It was still impossible to tell what had happened, though, and the looks on the faces around me meant that I wasn't the only one clueless. Natalie, however, had seen exactly what had happened, and she shouted to us, "He's getting away!"

Actually, he wasn't—at least not yet. The truth of the matter was pushed into all our minds by May: Hammerson had turned and tried to run for the stairs but had collided with an invisible Hammerheart. They had all revealed themselves then, and instead of wondering what they were doing, Arnold Hammerson, now in a complete panic, had ordered them to stand against the Seventh Sorcerer, who must have been made visible when he stepped over the line (which meant that we all were now). The order had been refused and Hammerson was now being forced to fight his way through them as well.

Somehow, and I would never know how, he managed to put them between himself and the magical enemies behind him, which slowed Marc and Fewul up a great deal. It was enough for him to take off for the stairs before anyone could stop him. We were all running now, storming down the corridor at top-speed behind Marc, Fewul and a small band of former Hammerhearts. By the time I got into the corridor, quite close to the back of the pack, Hammerson had disappeared into the stairwell.

From somewhere up ahead, there was a cry as one of our number slipped, tripped, fell or was trampled. Most people kept on going, their priorities in order, but when I reached Lucien, I stopped to help him up. He was on his knees on the floor, feeling blindly around for something he might have dropped.

"What are you doing?" I asked hysterically. "We have to go!"

"I tripped over—it's here somewhere, I'm sure of it."

"What?"

He got hold of whatever it was and held it up in the empty air between our faces. It was a fistful of thin air, which could only mean one thing. Now I knew why Arnold Hammerson had fled the fight.

"Now we're really in business," he said, grinning and pocketing the crystal. "Let's go, before he gets anywhere near that highway."

But Arnold Hammerson had already reached the Hammerheart Highway, it seemed, only to find three quarters of the remaining Hammerhearts in the base standing in the foyer and out on the bridge. Not only were they stopping any new Hammerhearts coming in but most importantly, they were armed and prepared to fight Hammerson to stop him getting out. He was now a man with no magical power and, so far as I knew, no other weapons on his person either. He had made the same mistake that other Sorcerers before him had made: Once his magic had been stripped, he was defenceless.

He ducked back into the stairwell and thundered down another level to the Basement, the gap between him and his pursuers considerably less. The Basement would have been a great place for him to hide out; its twisting and turning maze of corridors would have kept us looking for hours. It was for that reason that the fourth quarter of the remaining Hammerhearts were guarding it, many of them big and stupid but just as armed and dangerous as anyone on the floor above.

His race was run and he knew it. He could have tried to call an elevator, but we would have caught up with him in the time it took one to come. He couldn't get back to the upper levels where he could have armed himself for the inevitable fight. There was only one thing left for him to do, and it presented him with no chance for survival except for the one layer of protection that still surrounded him: the Cloak of Steel. As long as we didn't know about it, he could use it to protect himself so that one of his faithful followers (Hall, Cornish, Hignat or one of the many others) could assist him in regaining the advantage he had lost today.

Arnold Hammerson turned and fled down the last flight of stairs to the bottom level where a long corridor ended in a heavy door emblazoned with bright, red letters: Execution Chamber. It was a dead end and there were no weapons here because all the power belonged in the hands of the one in control, and Hammerson had no control over those he was leading down here today. Marc and Fewul, meanwhile, were just passing the Hammerheart Highway and from where Lucien and I were, right at the back of the pack at the top of the stairs, I clearly heard him shout to the Hammerhearts ahead of him, his voice echoing all the way up, "Step out there—he's ours." They must have obeyed because I didn't see them again.

The execution chamber wasn't huge but it was comfortably big enough to take everyone who had piled into it by the time Lucien and I reached it and began pushing people aside to get to the front of a pack, exclaiming all the way that along with Marc and Stella (if she wanted), we had more right than most to see what was about to go down. In the end, May was left guarding the doorway (against both Hammerson and outside help) while most people filled the space between her and the front of the group. Marc, Natalie, Stella, Fewul, and now

Lucien and I took the front row where we had a clear view of the cockroach we had backed into this dark, slimy corner.

The configuration of this room was the same as the one in which my mother had been murdered more than thirteen years ago, and the one in which my father had been burnt to a crisp just three months earlier. The key difference between each chamber was the setup: The first time, my family members had been tied to a post in the middle of the room; the second time, such a post had been replaced by some sort of barbecue. Today, since no execution had been planned, the floor was bare, leaving an empty space of maybe fifteen feet between Hammerson and me. He was standing with his back to the wall behind him, facing us, his hands empty, a leer on his face. There was a control panel just by his left hand, the same sort that Tom Hignat had been forced to use once upon a long-ago time.

"It's over," Marc told him, raising his fist so that in the dim light cast by a slightly swinging lantern overhead, the Hero Crystal was clearly visible. "You've got nowhere else to run and no one left to fight for you. If you still want to fight me here and now, you'd better make it a good one because I've ordered Fewul to use everything he's got against you."

"It's hard to take the Beast of Magic seriously when it looks like a girl," Hammerson sneered, but his expression was automatic and defensive; there was no fight left in him and all he could do was stall.

"Oi, we resent that," either Harry or Simon chirped up from somewhere behind me.

Marc actually laughed, but there was nothing humorous in it. "We both know you're not stupid enough to really believe that. Go on, then; if you think you stand a chance against a group of kids and a beast who looks like a girl, take your best shot."

I couldn't tell if Marc knew that Hammerson no longer had the Sien-Leoard Crystal or not. It was pretty obvious that he didn't, though; no way would Arnold Hammerson take this if he had any way of fighting back.

"As if I would even be wasting my time with a pack of adolescents if I didn't know you could be dangerous, assuming you get out of bed on the right side," Hammerson growled. The complete idiocy and pointlessness of his taunts reminded me vividly of when he had been captured and forced to talk to Frederic Woodward in the Woodwards' prison block. On that occasion, he had said something stupid about reasoning with fire, although I had to tell myself that since then, he had stuck pretty closely to his word.

"You killed my mother," Marc said quietly, "and you forced my father to take responsibility for it. The whole time, Lucien and I thought he was a murderer and in the end, the only mistake he made was to get involved with a psychopath like you."

Hammerson sneered. "Sticks and stones, et cetera. You're playing with the big boys now, Seventh Sorcerer. You're gonna fuck yourself up royally if you let your emotions control your actions."

But his words were meaningless because Marc's eyes were flat. Right now, there was no emotion in him at all. Maybe there would be later but for the time being, he was ready to do anything—even commit murder. "You ruined my whole family, perhaps more than you know, and all because a man didn't want to sacrifice his son."

"Are you going to kill me, boy?" Hammerson sneered, the fun going out of his eyes. He had apparently recognised Marc's expression for what it was and understood that distraction wasn't going to work this time.

Marc sighed and smiled. "Yep, I reckon I'm gonna have to. I don't suppose there's any chance of you coming quietly?"

"Why on earth would I do that?" Hammerson asked, and he began to smile again. "That would mean conceding defeat, and while I'm sure you think you've won, you have no idea just how many contingency plans I have put in place in case you have a lucky day."

Marc shrugged. "I suppose there may be some things that I don't know about, like how you're looking for the best chance to push one of those buttons there."

There was a flurry of movement as several people behind me started in alarm. Out of the corner of my eye, I saw a hero device being pointed at Hammerson between Lucien and my shoulders—it was a boy's hand but I couldn't see who owned it. It was pointless, though, because Marc had already cast a spell to bind Hammerson's hands to his sides. He could still move and he could still talk but now, he had no way of reaching the control panel unless he tried to push the buttons with his nose. I supposed Marc gave himself the benefit of the doubt that if Hammerson tried to do something like that, he would have enough time to perform more magic.

"Whatever else you've got around you, I'm sure we can handle," Marc went on. "We have the whole base at our disposal now, plus the rest of your army worldwide if necessary. We have someone with us who can turn every single Hammerheart in the world against you. We have the Beast of Magic, every Sorcerer, and two of the Magic Crystals in our possession."

"Three," Lucien corrected, withdrawing the Sien-Leoard Crystal from his pocket and showing Hammerson that it hadn't been left lying upstairs after all. Hammerson's eyes widened in alarm while behind me, several people cheered triumphantly. Beyond learning about the Sien-Leoard Crystal, though, Arnold Hammerson still didn't look overly concerned.

"Not every Sorcerer," he jeered, his eyes glinting maliciously in the shadows. "I couldn't help noticing that you're down one. No black boy either, I see—where might he be? All the power you think you have but it's come at a cost, wouldn't you say?"

"Yeah, I would," Marc agreed calmly, "and it's a cost you're going to pay, because we have one other thing too. You know what that is?"

"Enlighten me, boy."

"We know your secret, the one only you, Tankom and Cornish were supposed to know. We know how to kill you. We've known since before Tankom died; that's how we were able to do her, and now we're going to take care of you the same way."

That did the trick. Hammerson's expression dissolved as we watched. His cruel calmness evaporated within seconds as the full implications of Marc's words came home to him. There it was, the first momentous step overcome; we had removed his Cloak of Steel. The second step...

But there was something else at play because although Hammerson had been brought close to the point of panic, the point where he might either try to fight with his bare hands or fall to his knees and beg for mercy, he was clinging to some other understanding. What else could he have done to protect himself?

Oh, but I already knew the answer to that question. It wasn't a question of his protection, but the protection of his ideals. We had broken through all his personal protection but killing him wouldn't be the end of the war after all because—because—'to chase him from the soul on which he feeds'....

"You don't understand everything, boy," Hammerson whispered conspiratorially to Marc. "The mark of a true man is the one who can admit that he does not know the entire truth of any matter, including his own."

"Would you like to enlighten me?" Marc asked, raising his eyebrows.

"I don't see why I should," Hammerson responded, but I saw the movement of his eyes in that moment. He didn't need to say any more; I knew exactly what he was referring to.

When he had ordered the death of our mother and forced our father to take responsibility for it, he had also put a powerful spell on Lucien. Smiley had called it the 'time bomb curse' because it would be triggered at some unknown point well into the future. Only Hammerson had known when it would go off and what would happen to Lucien when it did, but I reckoned I could now guess what would trigger it.

Judging by the expression on his face, Marc had seen and understood exactly the same thing. The bottom fell out of my stomach. Was that what this would come down to? In order to finish Hammerson, we would have to doom Lucien at the same time?

"I know about that too," Marc whispered, his face very pale. "I don't know what you've done but if you're saying what I think you're saying——"

He didn't seem able to finish the sentence. I didn't blame him; if I'd been in that position, I wouldn't have been able to say, 'if you're saying what I think you're saying, I don't mind sacrificing my brother.' Hammerson again looked rocked at how much Marc knew but he wasn't about to tell anyone exactly what would happen to Lucien at the point of his (Hammerson's) death. The subject of all this stood beside me, clearly confused by this part of the discussion but otherwise oblivious that Marc and Hammerson were talking about a fate beyond his (Lucien's) control.

"Guys," Marc hissed out of the side of his mouth, conceding defeat, "I don't think I can do this after all."

There were gasps of surprise, alarm and dismay from the group behind us. I didn't dare look behind me to see the reaction; someone had to keep an eye on Hammerson, just in case. The man remained where he had been, watching Marc with a satisfied expression on his face.

"Why not?" asked Lena, horrified. "Marc, he killed your mother—you said so yourself."

I saw Marc shrug and glance at Lucien, who was also keeping his eyes on Hammerson and hadn't noticed. Marc didn't want to speak of the time bomb curse in front of Lucien and I didn't blame him; seeing Lucien's reaction would make it that much harder to do what needed to be done, even if (especially if) Lucien turned out to be willing to sacrifice himself, as Lisa had been.

"You've got no backbone, boy," Hammerson jeered at him. "Some hero you are, don't you think? Perhaps you should kill yourself so that someone else can be the Seventh Sorcerer instead; you are unworthy of the title."

"The title is meaningless," said James suddenly. "It's all the good Marc has done since he acquired the source of his power that matters. He is much more worthy of power than you, who only ever wanted to wield it, never understanding that for the best possible results, the greatest powers in the world must be tamed in order to protect others from them. I suppose you can't be blamed; you were indoctrinated by a crazy mother and an even crazier grandfather, but at some point, even you must have understood that killing people is not the right way to achieve your view of world peace."

"You insolent boy," Hammerson snarled, his eyes burning as they rested on James. "How dare you speak of my family with such a disrespectful tongue."

"Oh, I dare," James said calmly, "because what I'm saying is true. Besides, you don't care very much about your family; does he, Stella?"

"You know, I don't think he does," said Stella, watching her father contemptuously. She also looked rather pale in this light, but not as though she had any intention of jumping to her father's defence.

"I'm disappointed you think that, Stella," he said, "especially seeing as you would have been ruler of the world within eighteen years."

"Yeah, 'cause that's more important to you than me actually enjoying my life," Stella retorted. Unlike Marc, she looked as though emotions could possibly get the better of her. Fortunately, Natalie put an arm around her to stop her in her tracks.

"Enough talking," said Lucien suddenly. "Guys, he'll stall us as long as he can; this has to end now. Marc?"

Marc shook his head. "Lucien, he's made it so that something bad is going to happen when he dies."

There were quite a lot of surprised mutterings at this realisation. One person behind me actually had the audacity to snort with derision. Lucien, however, merely shrugged.

"Whatever it is can't be as bad as what we're going through at the moment."

"He's right, Marc," said James quietly. Unlike Lucien, James understood as much as both Marc and I what was about to happen. "We need to do this. We can use the magic we have to deal with it when it happens, whatever it is. I'm sure we can catch it before it turns into a serious problem."

Marc was struggling with himself. I was struggling, too, because although I didn't think I would be elected to do the dirty deed, a personal part of me (the part that had come to accept Lucien as a brother as well as a good friend) didn't want to go ahead with this. Wasn't there anything else we could do? Perhaps we could find a way to leave Hammerson alive but completely disabled beyond all repair? The trouble with that idea, though, was that even if we did to him what Hall had done to Amelia, something which was probably about as foolproof as we could get, the Hammerhearts might know a way to restore him. As long as that possibility existed, so also existed the possibility of Hammerson returning to power. We had to kill him—it really was the only way—and Marc knew it as well as I did.

"Here," James said quietly, handing his hero device to Marc. "Don't touch that side of it there, okay? I've made it into the thing John used to kill Tankom. Can you do exactly what he did? Bring it down on his head?"

"Think of our mother," Lucien said quietly, "and our father, and everyone else we knew and lost since this all began, because when you get right down to it, this man is responsible for all of it."

"How touching," said Hammerson harshly, his eyes roving the group as though he were looking to see where the weakest point might be, as though he believed he could break through us. With May in the doorway, I knew he had no chance, but given that his legs were still ambulatory, he might try anyway. I kept my hero device on him just to make sure.

"Shut up, you," Peter snapped right behind me. "You've done enough talking. What you're about to get is also for my sister, Nicole, who you tossed aside in your attempt to kill John. I bet you never even knew she existed, did you?"

"Pete," I said quietly, because although we had all lost someone we cared about, letting our emotions get the better of us wasn't the right way to handle this situation. Unless it applied to Marc, of course, because his emotion was exactly what he now needed. He had taken Lucien's words to heart; now he stepped forward, away from the group, with James's hero device in one hand and the hero crystal in the other.

He moved forward to meet Hammerson where he stood, and that was the trigger Hammerson needed to fly into panic. I was unsurprised that he went down the fight-for-his-life path as opposed to falling to his knees and begging—that was never really his style. Given that his arms were stuck to his sides, however, his attempt to fight was extremely pathetic and short-lived. He darted to the left, perhaps to try to get around Marc. Marc stuck out his leg to trip Hammerson; Hammerson tried to trip Marc at the same time and consequently lost his balance and fell on the floor, his head hitting the stone with a hard smack. Not only was he almost knocked out but he would have had a very difficult job getting back to his feet.

Marc stilled the man with a foot to the chest. Hammerson tried to kick for purchase but there was none. All he could do was stare up at Marc, who looked down on him with contempt.

"Any last words?" Marc asked him.

"I will win," Hammerson whispered. "I will win, and when I do, people will praise my name like a god, even though I will be long gone. You, boy, will not be here to see it."

"No, I won't, nor will anyone else."

And with that, Marc bent down so that his knee rested on Hammerson's chest, raised his hero device in his left hand and brought it down on Hammerson's face. My fear that the hero device could not emulate the power of the thing I had used to kill Tankom had been needless; it sank straight through Arnold Hammerson's skull just as it had done to Tankom that night in Germany. Blood, flesh, hair and fragments of brain and bone spread out in a pool of mess around the place, causing several people to cry out in disgust.

To my left, Stella had turned away from the sight in the moment before the kill so that she wouldn't see it. Closer at hand, Lucien had watched on raptly. I kept an eye on him to see what was about to happen but as the seconds lengthened, nothing whatsoever did. A thought occurred to me then, one I should have thought of long ago: How many time bomb curses had Hammerson actually performed in his life? What if he'd stuffed this one up somehow and Lucien was fine after all?

But the answer to that was as simple as before: 'To chase him from the soul on which he feeds.'

Marc stood up and stared down at Hammerson, waiting to see if there would be any sign of life out of him. It was physically impossible; even if Hammerson's prior spell casting could protect him, he couldn't possibly be conscious while his brains were spread out over an area the size of a coffee table. He then looked over his shoulder at Fewul, who stood impassively on Lucien's other side.

"Is he dead?"

"Yes, he is, Master."

It was 11:59 on the morning of August 23, 2010.

Chapter 40: Time Bomb Triggered

It was seven o'clock in the evening. The afternoon had passed in a whirlwind that hadn't allowed me a single moment to eat, and now the usual dinner time was also passing me by and I was bloody starving. I would eat soon—we would all eat soon —but one final matter needed to be resolved before we would be left to our own devices within our base where we could celebrate our victory.

We had fled the Hammerheart base within minutes of Arnold Hammerson's death, leaving his body where it was; nobody wanted to touch it and Stella said that a couple of hours after his death, regardless of where or what shape his body was in, it would be teleported to a hidden and secret graveyard for those of the Hammerson line and, in recent years, their most loyal supporters. The enchantment had existed, so Stella had been told, since just three generations after Sien herself. She also said that sometime today or tomorrow, she would like to go there to say a proper goodbye to her father. Now that he was gone forever, it had finally struck home that she had no family left, and although she had never got on with them, it must have been a sobering realisation.

Marc had contacted Mr. Woodward telepathically to let him know what had happened while Natalie sent a similar message back to the base and whoever was monitoring the technology there (nobody had been, it turned out). Mr. Woodward had ordered us to teleport to the school, which we had done, and then forced us to wait in the gym (what a horrible place it was) while he and the other Sorcerers worked to assess the immediate consequences of the day's events. They would be far-reaching in time but so far, given that the Hammerhearts in the base had already been turned over (and those who hadn't wouldn't regain consciousness until tomorrow), the news didn't seem to have spread. Once Cornish got wind of it, the whole world would, and that would be when the real test began.

It was during this time that May began absorbing as much from our minds about Amelia as she could. She took each of us aside in turn and forced us to roll through every memory we had that involved Amelia, right down to those private details which I hoped she would neglect to put into Amelia's head. When my turn came around, I found it to be one of the weirdest sensations of my life; I lost all awareness of my current surroundings and was so completely lost in memories that it was as though I were travelling in a private time machine. I felt horribly dispirited afterwards when I came to realise that those were the only memories of Amelia I had and now that May had refreshed them for me, even the bad ones, I should hang onto them with everything I had.

Finally, though, we had been allowed to return to our base. Marc had sent Fewul to it so that he could inform Jessica, Robyn and Jason of what had happened, redirect the base back to Chopville and allow us to re-enter. Mr. Woodward and his mother both came in with us so that they could have a final word before closing the book on this chapter. The outside yard, dim and pretty chilly, was full of people; at this stage, the two adult Woodwards facing the rest of us.

"If all goes well from here," Mr. Woodward told us, "you'll all be able to return to something resembling a normal life within a few weeks. It's probably going to be months before things are really normal, though, and there are some things that will never be the same again—I'm sure you all know what I mean. I must say, I like what you've done here, and I think it would be a good idea for all of you to stay in this place until we tell you that it's safe to come out, despite your insatiable desire to not do as you're told. The most important thing for you to do is protect yourselves, make sure nobody can find you, and keep those crystals you have out of trouble. Which ones do you have now, anyway?"

"All of them except the Darkness Crystal," Marc told him, "and John's the only person alive who knows where that is. Incidentally, what should we do with the Villain Crystal? That thing's at its best when nobody's using it."

"Yes, it is," said Mr. Woodward, "which means that it should be hidden along with the Darkness Crystal at some stage. For the time being, though, just hang onto it and keep it out of trouble. Put it in a drawer and lock it with magic or something so that nobody can cause any trouble with it. Now, how are you all doing? Is anyone here hurt in any way?"

I glanced at Natalie and saw that she was watching me—had been for a few minutes, I expected. I didn't think anyone could be more hurt than her, and she was physically fine.

"We're all fine," Marc told him, "except for Amelia, but I already told you about that before. Where is she anyway?"

Everyone's eyes turned to somewhere near the back of the group where Amelia stood, supported by May and looking vacantly at nothing in particular. Although May had absorbed our memories of Amelia, she hadn't yet got around to constructing a working mind for her. That would be a job for a later date, I supposed, after she'd had a chance to put Mr. Woodward, his mother and anyone else who'd ever known Amelia through the same paces.

"Please, bring her forward," Lillian said, directing her voice toward May. While Mr. Woodward had spared an appreciative glance for May, Lillian hadn't been able to take her eyes off the Honnie for long. She was presumably rocked by the clear difference between this Honnie and the one she had met nearly thirty years ago.

"I think she should come with us," Mr. Woodward said sadly as May brought Amelia forward. "We can take care of her, and if you're right, Marc, hopefully she'll be back with us as she was before too long. Now, what's the best way to deal with her?" he asked his mother, nodding at May.

"She can read our thoughts, even though our minds are protected from magical intrusion," Lillian told him, "so she'll understand our meaning without us having to speak it."

"I can speak English too," May said suddenly, taking them both completely by surprise. The look on Lillian's face was particularly priceless.

"Well, that simplifies matters," Mr. Woodward said, smiling at May—he looked incredibly relieved. I wasn't sure how much his mother had told him about Honnies since he had learnt of their existence a few days ago, but he must have been nervous about how the communication would work.

"Can I ask what the Hammerheart death toll was for today?" Lucien asked a little nervously. Those of us who knew about the time bomb curse had kept an eye on Lucien all afternoon but so far, he hadn't showed any signs of being affected by anything that the rest of us weren't. I was beginning to relax now, thinking that either Hammerson had been bluffing for thirteen years, or he had screwed up the curse and now nothing was going to happen. The alternative was that he was only bluffing today and it would be triggered (or had been triggered already) by something else entirely.

"Forty-eight that we know of," Mr. Woodward said curtly, "all in the primary school. It doesn't look like anyone was killed in the high school and we don't know if anyone other than Hammerson himself is lying dead in the Hammerheart base."

"The primary school?" I said quietly so that only those closest (Peter and James) could hear me.

I cast my mind back to the struggle that had ensued immediately after we had entered the school grounds. I had a vague memory of May killing a couple of female Hammerhearts, and I also vaguely remembered killing a few myself with my virtual killing device (I hadn't known at that stage that they would be beyond recovery within a few hours) but that couldn't have accounted for forty-eight deaths. What had the others done that I hadn't seen? I couldn't think, but I was uneasy at the looks Peter and James were giving me.

"The fire?" Peter prompted me, watching my expression closely, but I was completely lost.

"May," James called suddenly, interrupting whatever Mr. Woodward was saying to everyone else, "come over here for a minute."

The greater discussion continued, Amelia now in her grandmother's care, as May came over to join the three of us. "What is the matter?" she asked James.

"Are you responsible for this?" he asked, staring at her and conveying some other message mentally.

"Yes. I made him forget it so that he would not be distracted in the fight," she said, looking sideways at me.

"Made me forget what?" I asked uncomfortably, straining my mind as if I could somehow force the memories to regenerate themselves.

"I think you'd better let him remember," Peter said quietly. "He's gonna hear plenty about it from other people; he might as well know why."

May didn't answer but turned her full attention to me, staring into my eyes. The look made me acutely uncomfortable because there was a great deal of care in her expression, as if she wanted to do this as gently as possible. There was no gentle way to do this, however; the memories, when they came back, were as horrific as ever. The fire—the fire that I had ignited—the fire that had killed plenty, actually melting their bodies as it consumed the children's playground and all who dwelled within it. I shuddered as it all came back.

"Sorry, mate," Peter said quietly, patting me on the back.

"I am sorry too," May told me. "I had planned not to let you remember that, but your friends are right; you should know."

"Thanks," I said bitterly. Now that I knew, I would have preferred she hadn't done that either, but even I knew that they were right. If I hadn't been allowed to remember, the not knowing would have haunted me. Of course, this would probably haunt me too.

"You'd better go," Peter told May, gesturing to the three Woodwards who were about to take their leave. "It was nice knowing you. You'll have to drop by before you go back to your world."

"I will do that," she agreed, sparing me a significant look before turning and heading back to the Woodwards. I thought I understood the meaning in that look; it was loss she was feeling. She knew what had happened between Natalie and me that morning, having picked it out of my head and probably hers at several points throughout the day, and now the time had come when she (May) and I were to part company. It looked as though whatever had been going on between the two of us wouldn't have to be addressed after all. I was profoundly relieved by that, but I couldn't deny that I would miss May too.

Mr. Woodward was telling Marc and Natalie that he would keep in telepathic touch with them to let them know how the process was going. Then, after a few last goodbyes, the three Woodwards and May walked into the control room and out the other side, followed by Fewul, who would release them from the security of this base before they teleported to their own. For about a minute, we all just stood where we were as the truth of the situation slowly came home: It was over. The fighting would stop. The war would soon end and all that remained was the social and political fallout, stuff which was beyond our understanding in general and would consequently be left to the adults. Our job was done; we could relax and get on with our lives.

A minute after they had left, Fewul re-emerged from the control room, having closed it up on the outside and now shutting the door on the inside as well, sealing us inside the base. For several more seconds, nobody moved or spoke. Then, Lucien broke the silence by saying, "So who's up for some dinner?"

The moment broke and everyone began laughing, talking and, in the case of Harry and Simon, cheering. We all went into the dining room where we got our dinners from the conveyer belt and began to eat, but although that part of the process was normal, there was nothing normal about the atmosphere in the room. It had a party feel to it, and I was sure that this party would go well into the night. It would probably also be the first time that any significant amount of alcohol would be consumed since we had created this base. This seemed all but confirmed when Marc stood up at his table, called the room to silence, and held up his glass of Coke.

"I'd like to propose a toast," he said to the room at large, "to victory, freedom, and good friends."

"Victory, freedom, and good friends," the room echoed back jubilantly, and I clinked my own glass of Coke with Peter, James and Darcy, who were sharing my table.

Darcy was a little more subdued than the rest of us after the fate of his girlfriend, but he still managed to smile and not bring the rest of us down with him. We were all feeling the loss of Amelia tonight—it was a bittersweet feeling—but now that it was over, I could put into perspective: At least it was only one person, and that one person could possibly be brought back to something very similar to what she had been before.

The party began to spread out as people finished their dinners, but they all stayed on the bottom floor and nobody went into their bedrooms or the gym. About half past nine found me in the lounge room where nearby, Harry and Simon were laughing and joking around, as was their style.

"What are you guys gonna do with yourselves now that it's all over?" I asked them.

"Well I dunno about you two," said Harry, "but I'm seriously considering opening up a muffin store."

We all laughed and Simon thumped his brother on the back.

"I think the plan at this point is to grab hold of our troublesome sisters and go back to live with our even more troublesome grandparents," said Simon, "and I guess what happens after that will be up to them. I hope we get a say, though, after what we've done—a lot more than them is my guess."

"I would hope so," I agreed. "Looking forward to getting back to school again?"

They both laughed. "You know what, I kind of am," said Harry, grinning slyly, but I thought he meant what he said. "I mean, we'll probably be making trouble within a week—"

"Within an hour, I think you mean," Simon corrected him.

"Yeah, no one can tame us," said Harry, "but it'll be nice to get back to something comfortable. Besides, maybe education will be good for us."

I laughed and went over to talk to Liam, who was on his own. I had asked similar questions of several people already and was getting similar answers to the twins, but I got the impression that a lot of people didn't want to think about the future. I didn't get that because right now, I was looking forward to whatever came next—it had to be better than what we were leaving behind. Liam was particularly morose because apparently, he had asked a similar question of Siobhan earlier in the night and she had told him that she intended to return to England whenever we were allowed out of the base, which would pretty much spell the end of their relationship. Too bad for him, but after all the losses Siobhan had sustained, I couldn't blame her for wanting to go home.

Marc was a different story. When I finally got a chance to catch up with him just before ten o'clock, he shrugged in response to the same question.

"I'm not sure what I'll do," he said, "but at first, it'll be just the usual stuff—you know, school and the like. I guess I could make a little extra money hiring out my Seventh Sorcerer services, though," he added, and laughed. "Lucien suggested earlier that when he turns eighteen in a few months, he could get his own place and Stella and I could go with him—he could be our guardian or something. Until then, though, I don't know."

"I'm sure Mr. Woodward could pull a few strings so that you and Lucien can keep your old place," I suggested.

"He could, but he probably wouldn't," he grimaced. "I'm betting he would rather take the three of us in himself than let us go wandering off into the big, wide nothing, especially while we've got magic of our own. We could look after ourselves easily with what we have, but he'd be worried about us causing trouble—like there hasn't been enough of that. Besides, I don't ever wanna live in that old underground place again."

Incidentally, I had walked past Lucien and Stella on my way to the games room where I was now with Marc. Although

I hadn't stopped to talk to them, for they had been deep in conversation, I had heard some of it as I passed by.

"I think someone should go with you," Lucien had been saying. "I don't mind doing it, but I'll run it by Marc before we go."

"Well, okay, but the control room—"

"I can get in with the crystal."

I had assumed they were referring to the graveyard where Hammerson's body would have been laid to rest, where no mourners other than Stella herself would ever go. Stella was almost as subdued as Darcy this evening. She was obviously excited about what the future had in store for her—what would be a new beginning for her, what would be so much better than the previous sixteen-and-a-half years had been—but it came at a cost. He had been her father and I supposed in her own way, despite all he had put her through, she would miss him. I finally began to understand why James had always had such a hard time trusting Stella: Even though she was a good person, she was still Arnold Hammerson's daughter.

Marc didn't stay in the games room after our conversation but shortly after he had gone, Peter came in, and James was already on the other side of the room talking to George (I doubted those two would ever have stopped to talk to each other in a saner time). When he saw Peter and me together, he excused himself to join the pair of us. This was sane, being with Peter and James, as I had been for most of my life. One of the most relieving things about tonight was the understanding that after everything we had been through, the three of us had come out in one piece and as tight as we had ever been.

"It hasn't really sunk in that it's all over," Peter said, grinning from me to James and back. "How long do you reckon it'll take?"

"A fair while, because the reminders will be everywhere," said James, and sighed. "It'll never be the same for our families, though, not without Nicole, but I guess that part has sunk in."

"Yeah, it has," Peter agreed, "and hopefully the dynamics of our families will have altered as well."

"I know I'll be rather less intimidated by Mum and Marge from now on," I told them, grinning, and they both laughed.

"Will we be allowed to go and live in our old houses, do you think?" James asked. "I still can't decide if that's what I want or not."

"Ditto," said Peter. "I said a while ago that I didn't think I could live in Chopville after this, and maybe that's true, but I guess once things do settle down again, maybe we can."

"No, maybe you're right," James nodded. "This is a time for new beginnings and maybe the best way to do that is to uproot altogether. I just hope our families can stay together because from what I know, my dad and your dad lost touch for a little while after the first war."

"Why don't we make that a condition, then," I suggested. "We can tell them that if they dare move any further from each other than three or four houses, we'll all run away. They'll believe us since we've done it once before."

They both laughed. "Well, if that's how it is, we might as well take it all the way and say that we have to stick close to the Fletchers too," said Peter. "I'd hate to lose touch with Rebecca now, not now that we might have something good going."

"I'll back you up," I told him, and they both grinned. I leaned in towards the others; they followed my lead and I hissed, "Me and Natalie kissed earlier today."

Peter whistled triumphantly and James's grin broadened.

"When did that happen?" Peter asked. "I was with you nearly all afternoon and I don't remember seeing anything happen."

"Yeah, 'cause I totally would have done it in front of the entire group," I muttered, feeling my own smile resurfacing. "It happened in the Basement this morning, right before Hignat and Wilwog turned up."

"Yeah, I totally would have nailed the Basement as the perfect romantic location for a first kiss with the girl of your dreams," Peter laughed.

"Screw you," I muttered, punching him on the arm. "She wasn't sure if we would get out and she didn't want those things to go unsaid. Pretty brave of her because I was too busy trying to work out a plan of action—I never would have thought of doing it then and there. She—"

I hesitated, wondering how much of that episode these two ought to know. Given how much I knew about each of their girlfriends—Erica, Kylie, Siobhan and now Rebecca—I decided that they didn't need to know all the details. The fact that we kissed was enough; the fact that we both confessed feelings of love for each other was unnecessary to speak.

"That's pretty good, man, but what comes next?" James asked. "I only ask because you know, if she was that distressed, the kiss may have been an emotional reaction. It doesn't mean you and her are automatically an item now."

"It was a bit more than an emotional reaction, wanker," I muttered, and I would have punched his arm too except that Peter was sitting between us. "You know how she's felt about me for months now, and you know how I felt about her. I guess it doesn't mean we're automatically dating but now that we've done that, I guess what comes next is me finding out exactly where we stand."

That was only half true. I knew where we both stood regarding our feelings, and I supposed it would only take one more conversation to confirm that we were dating and I could call her my girlfriend (at long last). What I didn't know was how we would proceed into the dating stage of our relationship. How quickly would we move? With Serena, we had engaged in foreplay on the very first night and taken things all the way within a few weeks, but I had a bit of an idea that things mightn't be that quick with Natalie. I supposed I didn't mind waiting if that was what Natalie needed, but I wished I could know for certain that the wait would be worth it. All I knew with absolute certainty was that I wouldn't screw things up the way that Tommy had when he'd been with her.

"Where are the Fletchers anyway?" Peter asked suddenly. "I haven't seen much of Rebecca since just after dinner."

"She was in the lounge room the last time I was in there," I told him, "being tormented by Harry and Simon. I assume Natalie's over there somewhere too since she's nowhere around here."

"Think I might head on over there," said Peter, getting to his feet, and James and I followed. James only went as far as the dining room, though, where he stopped for a little something to eat while Peter and I went out into the hall.

My search for Natalie ended before it could even begin properly. Just after walking down the corridor in which my old bedroom door stood shut against the world, we rounded the corner at the end and Peter collided with her as she was leaving the lounge room.

"Sorry," he muttered sheepishly, passing her and throwing me a wink over his shoulder before disappearing into the lounge room. Of course, I didn't follow, nor did Natalie continue her tread.

"Hey, where were you going?" I asked her, deciding that after everything we had been through, after all the cards had finally been laid out on the table, the time to be proactive had finally come. I had to be careful not to overdo it but I felt confident that I could find the right balance if I paid close attention to her behaviour.

"Well, actually, I was looking for you," she said, smiling tentatively at me. The lighting in here was dimmer than the lounge room, dining room or games room, but it was a whole hell of a lot better than the complete darkness of the Basement. She was great to look at—I could never get enough of it—but I was very conscious of our current location.

"This sure beats being in a cell, huh," I said, grinning at her, and she smiled shyly back at me.

"Yeah, I definitely prefer this," she said, and yawned. My hopes of much more happening tonight dropped—I hadn't even realised until then that I'd gotten them up.

"You had enough of the party?" I asked her, not sure what answer I was hoping for. In truth, I'd had enough of the party too, and also in truth, I was a little tired—it had been a long day and it was now getting on—but I didn't want to be alone. There was only one person I wanted to be with now.

"Yeah, but I'm not going to sleep just yet," she told me, as if she were reading my mind. I supposed it wasn't impossible that she could if she had reached some sort of Sorcerous level beyond the usual, but I highly doubted it. More likely, we were just thinking along the same lines.

I reached out and pushed the button to call the lift, which we happened to be standing right in front of, the doors of which opened immediately. She stepped inside and, before pushing the button to take her to the third floor, looked over her shoulder at me. That was all I needed; I stepped into the lift behind her. In times gone by, I probably would have persuaded myself that she couldn't possibly want me to join her, because that would be very self-centred to think that it all had to be about me, but sometimes, it really was the case.

And it was certainly so that night. The moment the doors had closed us off from the corridor leading down to the lounge room and the gym, Natalie turned around and threw her arms around me. I hadn't expected it so soon (in fact I'd only been a couple of seconds from beating her to it) and the resultant wave of passion which followed almost knocked me off balance. We were very quickly wrapped in each other and kissing again, and it was even better than this morning had been (and not due to the lighting, which had been rendered useless to me since I'd closed my eyes in order to enjoy the feeling more). I supposed that part of it may have been an emotional reaction (different time, different place) but mostly, for me, it was simply knowing that we were in complete control of where we went tonight.

And where we went tonight turned out to be Natalie's bedroom. There was no discussion on the subject; we simply had a choice between the door on the left and the door on the right, and we had gone to the right—perhaps because this was the most right I had ever felt in my life. Once inside, Natalie erected the sound barrier as I would have done in my own room (as though she'd done this many times before), and the two of us had the remainder of the night to ourselves. It was a few hours before we slept and the time between contained just enough talk for me to know exactly where our relationship was at, but not too much talk....

Later, I slept in Natalie's bed with the girl of my dreams (now made reality) beside me, and dreamt that our lives had returned to normal in the aftermath of the war. I was happy with Natalie, Peter was happy with Rebecca, James was happy with Erica, Harry and Simon were as steady as ever with Katie and Sophie respectively, Jessica was happy with the child she had created with Tommy, and our parents were happy that all of us were now allowed to live normal lives in which we could be teenagers again. I would think back to that dream often in the weeks that followed, hanging onto it with something like desperation, thinking that my subconscious had thrown it up in the full knowledge that it was too good to be true.

Harsh reality intervened before I had even awoken in the form of my connection with Stella. The vision first merged with and then smothered the weaker and far more preferable dream. Stella was chilled to the bone, wishing she had thought to bring something warmer than the same clothes she'd been wearing all day. Lucien walked beside her in the darkness; he hadn't bothered with a change of clothes either but the chill didn't seem to bother him. He still had the Sien-Leoard Crystal in his pocket—he had used it to let them out, after letting Marc know that they would be gone a short while and when to expect them back—but she didn't want to ask him to use it, not in a place like this. The thought of magic in use here gave her the creeps—the extra creeps, in fact, because this place was creepy enough the way it was.

They had already passed those graves closest to the entrance—those few had belonged to a number of most faithful servants of the Hammerhearts. Most of them had been killed during the first war, quite a few in the one just passed, and a very small number in between of relatively natural causes (if a car accident could be called natural). Now they were walking through the empty space between in which someday, a long way down the path, future descendents of the Hammersons would lie (assuming the line didn't die out, something which was now possible since they weren't protected by their crystal chips).

The next graves they came to were a row of six, of which only four had been filled: Adele Hammerson (1906–1960), Lester Hammerson (1901–1994), Dorothy Hammerson (1929–2010); and in the fourth, just to the left of the path; Arnold Hammerson (1960–2010). That was the place they needed to go, and they stopped a few feet away from it in the darkness, the only light coming from a magically manufactured moon which shone upon this place every night, regardless of where the real moon was in its orbit of the Earth.

"Don't mind me," Lucien whispered in her ear. "I'll just stand here while you do whatever it is you came here to do. Don't take too long; this place gives me the creeps."

That was something with which Stella agreed wholeheartedly. She took a step forward so that she could look down upon the small tombstone, beneath which her father's remains would rest for eternity. He was gone forever, and the relief definitely outweighed the grief, but Tankom had always told Stella that when a person died, it was important to focus on the qualities that made them special, regardless of how she had felt about them in life. She therefore lapsed into concentration, trying to drag up any positive memories she still harboured of her father.

There were very few, but they were easy to bring forth simply because she had hung onto them all this time. At the age of five, Stella had been standing on the kitchen bench, trying to reach up to take something (something yummy, although she couldn't remember what) from one of the overhead cupboards—this was before she knew how to levitate objects with magic. She had slipped off the bench and hit her head on it on the way down. Her father, who had been over in the den, had heard her cry out and had come running to find her on the floor in tears. He had used his magic to fix her up and then had stayed with her for several minutes while she calmed down. He had eventually told her off for climbing on the bench and then gone back over to the den but for those few minutes, he had acted the way a father was supposed to act.

Ten years later (about a year ago, as it were), Stella defeated Tankom in magical combat for the very first time. Her father, who had been watching hopefully, actually applauded the result before using his own magic to set her grandmother back to rights. It was the proudest moment of her childhood, mainly because it was the one and only time she could remember honestly impressing her father. If anything, that had been the moment when she had passed from being a kid to being an adult in the eyes of her fellow Sorcerers, although due to her weak mind, the weak mind that had been her father's responsibility (he had cursed her so that it could never be repaired, because he wanted to keep a close eye on her thoughts), she had never been considered trustworthy.

There were other moments in between, too, smaller instances when she caught a glimpse of the man Arnold Hammerson could have been if he hadn't been poisoned by the philosophies of his mother and grandfather. They weren't exactly great father-daughter moments but they were all she could think of. The rest of the time, he had been too busy plotting, brooding and bullying to be a good person.

Through all of it, though, despite the fact that she had spent her whole life in the company of her father, grandmother and other like-minded fools, she (Stella) had somehow turned out okay. Part of it was that her father hadn't worked hard enough to poison her the way he had been, but mostly it had been that she was allowed to go outside and be a child like everyone else. She had enjoyed school because it had been an enormous relief to be away from her family, and had thrown herself into her schoolwork so that after a while, she became quite smart (and being able to read the teachers' minds helped a little there). The other kids hadn't liked her much (until recently, anyway) and the teachers had been too scared to treat her badly (she got a lot of unpleasant thoughts from them, though) but she had still enjoyed that more than her father's company.

And she was doing a lousy job at thinking positively about the man who was forever gone from her life, but as she dragged her attention back to the present, she noticed that something had changed. It felt even colder now than it had earlier, and it also seemed to be darker. She looked up into the sky and yes, the moon was still there, but it had been dimmed, as though a filter had been placed between her and it. She began to shiver, not just with cold now but with fear as well, because she and Lucien were not the only souls in this graveyard tonight. Stella knew this as surely as she knew her name, and she took a step backward as the horror began to spread, the alarm bells beginning to signal possible danger. They had to get out of here now.

She turned to find Lucien beside her, staring at her father's tombstone in avid fascination. She opened her mouth, about to tell him that they had to leave, but before she could make a sound, Lucien took a step closer to the grave. He moved slowly, as though he were sleepwalking—or hypnotised. She reached out, intending to grab his shoulder, because the alarm bells were positively clanging now, but before she could touch him, a loud cracking sound broke the silence of the graveyard, making her jump.

She turned back to the tombstone and was paralysed by what she saw. The stone itself had cracked down the middle, and something she couldn't quite see seemed to be issuing from it. She had seen something similar to it once before, and her stupefied brain tried to place it. It was complete and utter blackness, floating in the air before her and Lucien, casting those things around it into shadow. She could only stare while beside her, also seemingly paralysed, Lucien closed his eyes rather than looked at it.

The darkness came forward and enveloped both of them so that, other than the dark shadow of Lucien, Stella could see nothing at all. It was deathly cold and almost impenetrable in its substance. It was the third, Stella knew, and as she came to this realisation, she finally placed where she had seen it before. It wasn't exactly like this, but in that brief period of a few days when she had possessed the Darkness Crystal, it had cast the same sort of shadow as this thing was now. That had been pure evil, and this was almost as bad.

And it had been in her father's grave.

It began to disperse. Relative warmth (still chilly but not as bad as before) began to touch her as the darkness seemed to disappear, allowing her to see the graveyard around her, including the now-cracked-open tombstone at her feet. Lucien also became visible to her; he was shivering with the additional cold but as she watched, he regained control over his body. There was still something wrong, though, because if she knew Lucien like she thought she did, he would now be just as anxious to get out of here as she was. As she thought this, he opened his eyes and turned to face her....

The paralysis broke in a tidal wave of undiluted terror. Lucien stood before her, tall and impressive, smiling down at her in a way that proved he really cared about her. It only added to the thrilling horror, though, because although his eyes were still the same shape and colour, she could see the evil intent of her father behind them. Stella had never known something like this could be possible, but there was no denying what she was seeing: Her father was dead, and yet he continued to live on, his soul now intertwined with Lucien.

She let out a small sob, choked, filled her lungs and began to scream at the top of her voice. It was a pointless but involuntary reaction. She turned and tried to sprint for the exit but before she had even taken one step, Lucien caught her by the arm and turned her slowly back to face him. He was still smiling at her as his free hand entered his pocket where the

Sien-Leoard Crystal lay. She felt him working magic with it and had no idea what it was—she had no idea of anything anymore.

Epilogue

I felt thoroughly unrested the morning after the big day when I had to bring the others into the picture. I had lain awake after my nightmare had woken me up, unable to get back to sleep but not wanting to disturb Natalie's peaceful slumber beside me by getting up. In the end, I had managed to get back to sleep, but my hopes of seeing what was going on with Stella now didn't work out; I only dreamt of Lucien, or more specifically, his soul, which was now being fed on by that of Arnold Hammerson.

Fortunately, before I could tell anyone other than James and Peter at the breakfast table what had happened, Stella herself returned to the base to save me the trouble—I was unsurprised to see that Lucien was no longer with her. Marc had waited up late for her, eventually dozing off in the control room, before she had finally come back into the paddock this morning. Stella was in some state; Marc and Natalie, after trying to make sense of her blubbering, eventually took her into her bedroom to question her more privately. The interrogation had only yielded the truth when Marc used his magic to browse her memories of what had happened. They had then let her sleep while they consulted with me, Peter and James on the subject.

Stella's memories of the event weren't much better than my own in the end. She remembered her father taking possession of Lucien, and then Lucien doing something with the crystal (Marc slapped himself for not thinking to take it off him), but after that, there was a hole in her memory until a few hours before she got back to the base. In that time, she had been lost in a terrible place of darkness, all alone, until she had eventually emerged somewhere within the Hammerheart network. She was physically unhurt and, so far as anyone (including Fewul) could tell, unaffected by any mind-altering magic. Her only problem was considerable distress, but she would recover from that quickly enough—hopefully today, so that we could talk about this some more.

We had all been fools to think that after hours of nothing, the time bomb curse wouldn't eventually kick in. It still made sense that Hammerson could have been bluffing except for one thing: He hadn't meant for us to understand what he was referring to. Marc blamed himself because the trigger, most likely, had been pulled when Lucien came into close proximity to Hammerson's remains—perhaps he hadn't been close enough in the execution chamber, or perhaps we had gotten out of there too quickly for the magic to be activated.

Marc got in touch with Mr. Woodward to let him know what had happened, and to inform him of the possibility that Lucien, with the Sien-Leoard Crystal, may take over as the head of the Hammerheart organisation. Whether or not the Hammerhearts would automatically look to him as their leader remained a mystery, but I thought they probably would if they stayed true to their policy of worshipping anyone with magic if that person intended to use it to enforce their plans. Unfortunately, Mr. Woodward and all the other Sorcerers didn't take the issue nearly as seriously as they should have. Even when he tried to explain about the time bomb curse, none of the Woodwards or Fletchers believed that such magic could exist.

We learned from them, through Marc, that the cleanup was already underway. After a bit of tinkering, they had learnt that all they needed to do was move slowly over an area; May could take every single mind in hers, check it, and turn it against the Hammerhearts if it happened to be pro-Hammerheart, and then release it without them needing to stop. She had proved capable of doing this to thousands at a time, and could reach any minds within a 115-kilometre radius—the exact number was unknown at this point, and it became harder the further out the mind was. They had decided that for the best results, they should clean up the most dangerous countries first, which put Australia fairly low on the list. At present, their base was slowly canvassing the territories that had once made up the United States of America as they tried to neutralise any threat the Hammerhearts over there might cause.

We also found out from them that the effort of putting Amelia back together again hadn't been completed. May was still, whenever she had a spare moment, gathering memories from anyone and everyone that would help her reconstruct a working mind for Amelia, but she hadn't got around to putting these thoughts into Amelia's head yet. Amelia was presently being cared for by some of the Woodwards' many assistants while the Sorcerers focussed their time and energy on the cleanup.

The Hammerhearts, meanwhile, seemed to be continuing with business as usual. It was impossible to know if this was due to Lucien's presence in their midst, assuming Lucien had rejoined them, or because they didn't want mass revolt from the public. Our worst fears had been that their organisation would collapse entirely and every Hammerheart with any sort of power would go for glory; that may yet happen if the Woodwards didn't stop it but so far, they were holding up just fine. What we did know for certain was that those closest to the action in the school were keeping the news of Arnold Hammerson's demise as quiet as possible; Hall and Cornish both knew, but other than that, very few Hammerhearts were allowed to know (not as difficult as it sounded, given that most of them would never have even met the fallen king). As for the general public, they had no idea that the man who had ruled three quarters of the world was dead.

In the base, the celebrations had ended as quickly as they had begun. Part of it was grief and anger at how we had lost Lucien (the anger was split between those who thought of him as a traitor and those who wanted to kill Hammerson all over again), but the greater part was simply not knowing what came next. It had seemed as though we could soon get back to our regular lives but now, the whole future was up in the air. That morning of the 24th, Marc had asked Fewul to locate Lucien for him, but Fewul had said that Lucien had made himself untraceable immediately after removing himself from our existing protection. I tried to send a thought to May to ask her where Lucien was, but got no response, or any indication at all that I was still in May's mind. I could only assume that even if she hadn't deliberately let us go, she was now too far away to interact with us mentally.

One thing we had done (or Marc had done, rather) was take the Villain Crystal and enclose it in a box rather like the one that housed the Darkness Crystal on Rock Haulter. The box had been placed on show in the lounge room for all to see—there was no point hiding it from people, since no one had any chance of breaking it open. The other crystals (Hero and Light) were still in Marc and James's possession respectively, and since we still didn't know if we would need to fight anymore, Marc hadn't bothered to recall the Beast of Magic.

When Stella was finally able to tell us what had happened (almost calmly), she couldn't shed any further light than had been gleaned from her memories. Marc and Natalie both believed that was the best that could be done, and Peter and I agreed, but James looked dubious.

"There's just one thing that makes me nervous about the whole thing," he told Peter and me over dinner on the Thursday night later that week.

"Really? Only one thing?" Peter asked sarcastically. "Honestly, I'm nervous about everything at the moment."

"Yeah, but this isn't so much Lucien I'm thinking of," James said, glancing around to see if anyone was listening. When he saw that nobody was, he leaned in close to the pair of us and said, "Why would Lucien let Stella go? She can't possibly have escaped on her own, and by all logic, if he was really bad, he would want her on his side. How on earth did she manage to get back here at all…?"

The Magic Crystals Series

www.TheMagicCrystals.com

www.ingramcontent.com/pod-product-compliance
Lightning Source LLC
Chambersburg PA
CBHW070341030726
47504CB00001B/23